# PURSUIT OF PARADISE

Thomas N. Smith

Copyright 2014, 2019 @ Thomas N. Smith

Library of Congress Number 201991842

ISBN 978-0-578-56950-5 (e-book)

ISBN 978-0-578-58164-4 (hardback)

ISBN 978-0-548-58666-3 (paperback)

*This book is dedicated to my granddaughters Lily Bell and Lori Bell.*

*Red and Judy Smith loved them dearly.*

*The memories and genetics of their great grandparents live on in them.*

# ACKNOWLEDGMENTS

I couldn't have written this book without the support, encouragement, and editing assistance of my wife, Kathy Smith. She gave me the time to write, and constantly reassured me that this would be an important book. She is, rightfully, the sole reason I was able to complete it with all the other things in life that needed to be done.

I owe a debt of gratitude to my forever friend and Dallas schoolmate, Janie Vogel. From Brentwood, Tennessee, she immersed herself into the editing and proof reading of this book, and gave me the guidance and advice to make it cohesive and readable. She helped me become a better writer as this book progressed. My literary success was fashioned by her input and desire to see this book in final form.

My California friend Margaret Magat helped me with detailed knowledge of Hawaii and the Philippine Islands. I could not have developed the grasp for the Filipino culture, the Hawaiian landscape, or the Hawaiian language without her valuable assistance. She was my connection to her birthplace, the Philippine Islands, and to her later home, Hawaii. She made that part of the book happen.

Every friend, cousin, and associate who cheered me on through the six years of producing this book deserves a personal Thank You from me.

My daughter, Kera Bell, believed in me and looked forward to the story of her dear grandparents being written for all to see, and for all who did not know her Grandma and Popa to become familiar with their sweet and riveting tale. My desire to produce the book for her was a strong element of my undertaking.

I thank my aunt Jean Stacking, who died less than a year before this book was finished. She was my mother's sister-in-law and best friend in the Texas to Arizona days, and gave me a great deal of information about the first few years of my parents' pursuit of paradise.

I especially thank my Uncle Noel for all the stories he told about those early days. He died two years before this book was completed, but I was able to record half-a-dozen conversations with him at his California nursing home. Throughout my life, he was my role-model as the storyteller and comedian of the Smith family.

And, finally, my deepest and most everlasting thanks go to Red and Judy Smith, for giving me the best childhood I could have gotten on God's green Earth, and for giving me their story to tell.

# PREFACE

## A NOTE FROM THE AUTHOR

This is a work of historical fiction. It is also a novel, with character development and dialogue. Although some of the characters in this work were real persons, their conversations are not documented and are mostly fiction. There are some characters who are completely fictional, and any resemblance to persons alive or deceased are coincidental and unintentional.

I have included conversational dialect, phrases, colloquialisms, and vocabularies as accurately as possible, and they are depicted as spoken in the 1940's.

During the Pacific War, there was a vast difference between the Tactical language and the Soldier's language. Therefore, the narrative portions of this book describe the physical Army of Japan as Japanese equipment, Japanese airplanes. Japanese troops, etc. When the GI soldiers spoke, however, the conventional term on the battleground was "Jap mortars, Jap ambush, and Japs" in general. It is not my intention to present an ethnic slur or to offend anyone of Japanese heritage. It is purely to make the dialogue as historically accurate as possible to the time, place, and events that are depicted.

No part of this book may be reproduced, stored in a retrieval system, scanned, or transmitted or distributed in any form without written consent of the author.

# INTRODUCTION

This is the story of an East Texas farm boy, the war in the Pacific, and love.

The boy left his farm, experienced the unspeakable horrors of war, and returned a man, wanting only to go back to work on the farm. His pursuit of paradise, which had taken him through the dark, steamy, enemy-infested, disease-ridden jungles of the South Pacific and the post-war landscape of Japan, now lead him to his dream wife, who, in his absence, had grown from a child to a young lady, and greeted him with open arms and a commitment to share his pursuit forever. Together, they would find Paradise is not a Place, but is a Time. For them, it was the journey they took, the path they walked with each other the rest of their lives.

Their pursuit of paradise was set against the backdrop of the most tumultuous, traumatic, and societally pivotal half-century in American history. The Great Depression. The War to End All Wars. The Petrochemical Industry. The Dust Bowl. The Agricultural Revolution. The Big War. The buildup of the largest war machine in history. The victory of Freedom over fanatical Tyranny in Europe. The Atomic Bomb. The victory of Democracy over Bushido Imperialism in Japan. The massive industrial change-over from War to Peace. The beginning of the Baby Boomers.

In 1900, industrialization was developing in the United States on equal footing with Europe. By 1950, the United States had clearly become the industrial leader of the world. A farming society, scattered throughout the hamlets, villages, and small towns of America, was pulled like an innocent, unsuspecting, blameless lamb to the altar of Change. Society experienced the mechanization of the working man, from the traditional, comfortable world of farms and tools to a new, modern world of cities and shiftwork. Most adapted and survived, and became the very foundation of who we are. Those who did not adapt were lost forever in the ghost towns, ghost jobs, and ghost families that haunted the post-war landscape.

The love story of Horace Garlton "Red" Smith and Clara Juliette "Judy" Smith is not unique. It is shared by those families that now look back to that dynamic half-century in amazement, wonder, and reverence for the incomparable tenacity, resilience, honesty, humility, and simplicity of that generation.

It is the story of my parents.

It is the story for all baby-boomers who had parents like them.

We know what they did, what they survived, what they sacrificed, and, in the end, what they stood for. They did heroic and honorable things that we, in their shoes, would probably not have been able to do.

They were as fragile as us, yet their stoicism rose above their fragility, and their story is the stuff that legends are made of.

May the telling of their story help us follow their example.

# PRELUDE

# BATTLE OF BREAKNECK RIDGE

November 8, 1944.

Highway 2, between Pinamopoan and Limon, Leyte, Philippines.

The night was dark as pitch. Howling winds carried horizontal sheets of blinding, cutting rain. The flashes of howitzers illuminated the landscape where the men were crawling, inch by precious inch, along a section of ridge devoid of all vegetation. There was no soil, just volcanic rock, as sharp as razors, slicing at their elbows and knees as they crawled along Breakneck Ridge. Rivulets of rain drained the rock, collecting in black pools, submerging the razors like shadowy sharks beneath a sinister sea.

"Attack!" the lieutenant shouted.

"Attack! Clear the Japs off this god-dammed ridge!"

In the middle of the worst typhoon the island had seen in decades, the men of the 21st Infantry's 3rd Battalion bore into the defensive lines of a poorly understood and deeply entrenched enemy on a long, tenuous, winding road atop a ridge of rock, hell, and death.

"In the middle of a damn hurricane," a soldier mumbled.

Through the roar of the deafening wind, with the constant booming artillery and hissing in-coming mortars, an officer behind the men barked the order, "Dig in! Hold this line! Get your asses in foxholes!"

The men could feel the solid rock beneath them.

"Dig in? Is he crazy?" a soldier sneered, lying on bare rock along the right flank.

The rain was so heavy that it seemed to be poured onto the men by unimaginably huge buckets, each bucket filling and emptying, filling and emptying, from somewhere up in the pitch-black sky, overflowing every slope and every soul on the saturated ground.

There was a whistle and pop of flares, and the area was suddenly illuminated by an eerie, ghostlike glow. Japanese soldiers were seen scurrying everywhere, frantically moving in uncoordinated directions, darting one way, then another, carrying mounted bayonets.

"Hunker down, men! Bayonets! Here they come!"

Private Horace Smith was laying on flat, solid rock, frantically looking in all directions for a low place, a rock shield, something, anything for protection.

A mortar round hit ten yards to his right, on the downhill slope of the ridge. The soldier on the right flank who had just complained about digging in was decimated, his body thrown upward and outward, reduced to pieces. Smith was pushed five yards upslope by the hot blast, a few pieces of the sharp lava rock striking the thick padding of his chest and legs.

He looked downslope, where the mortar round had blown the complaining soldier to Heaven or Hell, and there was a large section of dark, smoking rock, sideways in the blast crater. A small sliver of an opening, large enough for a skinny man to wedge, lay at the base of the upturned rock. Smith quickly, almost instantly, rolled his body downward toward the crater, up over the lip, and, with his feet, kicked the loose ejecta from under the rock and slid into the cavity, his bayoneted M1 Garand facing outward.

*Come and get me,* he mumbled under his breath.

As if on cue, two Japanese soldiers jumped into the crater, looked around, chattered, and stepped back nervously when they saw Smith. Two quick rounds from his rifle took them down.

His hands were shaking. He was crying tears of fear, tears of joy for being alive, and tears of fear again for what lay ahead. The Japanese were scurrying like rats in big, brown uniforms. Killing, screaming, hellish rats!

Three more of the screaming Japanese rats, alerted by his rifle fire, tumbled into the crater, and aimed their Arisakas at him. Smith pointed his M1 toward the enemy to his right, a snarling, round-faced devil of a man, and squeezed the trigger.

Nothing.

Jammed.

The enemy looked at him, wide-eyed. The others let out a sickening laugh, as all three aimed their rifles at Smith.

There was a sharp, loud hiss from above, and a mortar round hit square between the three men, their bodies disintegrating in an outward force of dirt, rock, and flesh.

Smith lay beneath the upturned rock, completely covered with blood.

A leg lay to his right, twitching at the ankle. A severed head lay to his left, face upward, as if grotesquely admiring the fireworks in the skies above, the mouth in a strange "O" as the mortar and artillery shells made sweeping paths across the wet, tropical sky.

A scream started in his gut and erupted from his mouth, barely audible over the din and death that displayed itself with irreverent clarity.

Then all went softly grey, and became a very quiet, peaceful black.

# PROLOGUE

Christmas Eve
Tuesday, December 24, 1946.

Eleven Mile Corner, near Casa Grande, Arizona.

    As I push the screen door open, I look behind and say "I'm gonna step out here on the porch, Judy, for just a few minutes. I'll be right back."
    A gentle, familiar voice from the kitchen replies "Take your time, Red. I'm just cleaning up in here. Jean's upstairs checking on Linda."
    There is a chill in the air, as the wind sweeps across the yard, down from the Superstition Mountains far to the north. I can smell the dry musk of the desert floor in the wind, the fragrances of the cactus, creosote, and juniper, and the salty dust from the many dried lakes. From behind me, I can smell the left-over aroma of today's supper, drifting through the open window, the curtain playing hide-and-seek behind the screen. Pinto beans, fried potatoes, cornbread and a surprise treat: apple pie. I can still smell the cinnamon through the open window. Judy and Jean managed to turn biscuit dough and two jars of canned cinnamon apples into a really, really good pie.
    The north wind blows across the empty yard, southward, delivering the perfumes of the desert night.
    I stand here every night on the front porch for five or ten minutes and look across the irrigated fields to the lights of Eloy, eleven miles to the south. Eleven miles to my right,

westward toward the Maricopa Mountains, the lights of Casa Grande have begun to shimmer in the twilight that follows the sun as it slips below the horizon. Eleven miles behind me, and toward the northeast, is the town of Coolidge. To my left, a row of new apartments wind around the curved lane, and stop where the creosotes and junipers dot the landscape all the way to the dark night. Nobody could see that far in Hopkins County, not that there was anything to see.

It was much different on Leyte and Mindanao.

Sometimes you couldn't see five feet in front of you, until the enemy was crawling up from his spider hole, in the rainy pitch-black darkness, up to your foxhole. My shoulders tighten as I think back to those days and nights on Leyte and Mindanao. Then I look around me at peaceful Arizona.

The Sonoran Desert is out there, a wilderness hanging on by its fingernails, ready to bite you sometimes, but mostly just giving in to the slow movement west. Farms and small cities are settling in along the rich, fertile valleys of the Basin and Range country. Just like Flora, Sulphur Bluff, and Tira, these desert communities are only fresher, newer, ready to be worked on and waiting to be taken. The fragmented wilderness strikes back every now and then with a drought, a dust storm, or a plague of mice or bugs.

I reach into my chest pocket for a small, tightly wound cigar that I bought at the community store. The **click-snap** of my Zippo and the thick smoke from the first light of the cigar make me think of the war again.

*Sharing a light with Nobel, Pete, and Kenny.*
*And Tim.*
*Breathing in the hot smoke from the mortar tube as we launched round after round after round toward the enemy.*

I inhale, and slowly release a cloud of grey smoke that breaks the dark night, vanishing as the wind carries it upward, to the porch roof, then up and away. I look across the small yard in front of our apartment.

The sun is well below the horizon to my right now, sending pink and orange ribbons into the western sky as a darker blue-black envelope approaches from the east. All is good, here, in Eleven Mile Corner, Arizona.

As I take another draw from the cigar, I hear Judy talking to Jean about the way her tight, bulging tummy feels, and they are both giggling.

I watch the end of the cigar glow red, like a hot, red sun, with each puff.

I recall a similar hot, red sun and the dusty, swirling wind from an East Texas summer a long time ago.

*Baseball. Sweat. And, my first real memory of Judy.*

She was every bit the most remarkable girl I had ever seen in Hopkins County.

*Oh, it was such a hot day!*

*Damn! It was so hot!*

But the summer heat never kept the baseballs from flying during those Texas summers. The baseball diamond was the Great Easel upon which we painted our pleasures, and we could win the world if we were good enough.

*I do believe that was the best day of my life.*

I smile as I remember that day.

There I was, between second base and third base, .......

# CHAPTER 1

# IN THE BEGINNING ...

Mid-August, 1940.

Near Flora, Hopkins County, East Texas.

There was a hot, red sun. It was as hot and red as the end of a cigar on its last puff. And there was a dusty, swirling wind on that East Texas baseball field the summer of '40.
*Baseball. Sweat. And, my first real memory of Judy.*
She was every bit the most remarkable girl I had ever seen in Hopkins County.
*Oh, it was such a hot day! Damn! It was so hot!*
But the summer heat never kept the baseballs from flying during those Texas summers. The baseball diamond was the Great Easel upon which we painted our pleasures, and we could win the world if we were good enough.
*I do believe that was the best day of my life.*
I smile as I remember that day.
There I was, between second base and third base, .......
I believe there was not a time in my life without baseball. As far back as I remember, my Daddy was playing baseball, my uncles were playing baseball, and I was running after any baseball that got away. Baseball was as important to life in Hopkins County as eating, drinking, or having babies. In fact, any of those things could wait until the game was over.
As soon as winter had loosened its hold on the red, sandy soils, and the pastures had taken on the slightest hint of

green, the baseballs would come out and the games would begin. All through the spring, all summer long, and into the last warm days of autumn, the balls would fly, the bats would crack, and the games would be played. Every community with enough men and boys to field a team did so. Sometimes, there were enough boys in one family to field a team, like the Smith family of Sand Hill, Texas. My Daddy was one of the Smith boys on that team. They were known in Hopkins County as the most talented, arrogant, and meanest bunch of boys to ever pick up a bat and a ball. It was all about winning and making the other guy lose.

    Fortunately for me and my two younger brothers, that team was broken up by WW1, and had lost its swagger by the time we approached our teens, about the same time the Depression hit. Baseball was still King in the farm belt, but the Princes and Jacks playing it were far more even-tempered than their fathers had been.

    It was a particularly bright, hot summer day, when the game was tight, and I was playing better than I ever had. I saw Juliette for the first time. I mean, I really "saw" her, in a way that burned into my memory.

    We were playing in a dusty, red clay field that had been covered in thin, short cotton a few years earlier. A quaint, country baseball field had been carved into the landscape at the intersection of two oil-dirt roads. A tall chain-length fence had been erected as a back-catch, and a crowd of perhaps two hundred Texas farmers, workers, businessmen, and ne'er-do-wells had gathered to watch the Saturday afternoon baseball event called, simply, "The Game."

Home plate was a neatly whittled piece of barn-wood; the bases were flour sacks, stitched into squares, stuffed with dry corn shucks, and anchored into the hard clay with railroad spikes. Four-tiered bleachers had been built, two on each baseline, with good knotty pine from a Texarkana mill, courtesy of the Hopkins County Judge.

Two community baseball teams, Birthright and Nelta, were locked in a tie game, elevating their fierce rivalry into a fever-pitched, contentious passion for conquest. I was on the Nelta team that summer.

Earlier that afternoon, the few scattered businesses in Birthright and Nelta had closed early so their employees and customers could attend the game. Some of the businesses had provided flatbed farm trucks to transport the rowdy fans to the Flora community baseball field, where the game was being played. It didn't cost anything, of course, to watch the game, but several hats were passed through the bleachers during the seventh inning to help pay the cost of equipment (balls, bats) and ice for the many jugs and milk cans of water brought by the spectators.

The game had reached a classic, timeless moment, lived and re-lived in every boy's dream: the bottom of the ninth, game tied, two outs. Win it now, or keep playing until hell freezes over. Do or die.

The hot, East Texas sun was burning into my sweaty forehead as I stood, a full one-third of the way between second base and third base, legs spread far apart, arms dangling downward, wrists flicking, fingers twitching nervously, as I was focusing my blue-green eyes straight into the hazel eyes of the pitcher. I was daring the pitcher to throw to the second baseman, who was now inching up slowly, quietly, stealthily behind me from his position on the fringe of center field.

"Just throw the ball, fella, just throw it," I mumbled under my ruddy lips.

"I'll be halfway to third by the time you get it to the second baseman, and I'll be sliding into third before that idiot can throw it to the damn fool at third. Just throw it."

A gust of wind began blowing my red hair, which was hanging in small, sun-bleached ringlets, up from my brow. I was a wiry, five-foot-seven lad, weighing all of one hundred-fifteen pounds. My nineteenth birthday was just two months behind me. The wind, normal for a hot August day in Hopkins County, was drying the sweat on my forehead, giving me some relief from the sweltering heat. I ran my hand up to my brow to tease the hair, then smiled, and winked toward the men, women, and girls in the bleachers along the third base line. My wink coaxed an excited cheer from the teen-aged girls, who were obviously Nelta-fans, and were captivated by my showmanship.

Although the Flora community itself did not have an organized baseball team, most of the families in Flora were quite content to be Nelta fans, since the sons of Flora comprised the core talent and skill of the team from Nelta.

I was a Flora boy, and was, on this day, on home turf, and was rightly enjoying home-field advantage.

"Get 'em, Red," the four girls chanted.

"We're over here, at third. Come on over. They can't stop you."

Their voices, high and thick with Texas drawl, were music to my ears. I knew I was delighting the girls with my performance on the field. Always moving, always daring, my grey light wool shirt, with "NELTA" neatly stenciled across it, was half-opened to expose my sun-burned chest; I was poised for action. Stealing third base was going to be easy. Very, very easy.

"I'll be there. Just gimme a minute," I answered them, with the right side of my mouth, my lips turning upward at the corners to produce a taunting smile.

The wind was kicking up dust now, rearranging my red curly hair and invading the eyes of the excited fans beyond the third base line. Blowing in from the west, the wind had blustered the red soils of the Texas Panhandle the day before, and was gently bathing my chest and forehead.

For the past ten years, the Wind and its father, the Drought, were the one-two punch that had mercilessly desiccated the farmlands in the "Dust Bowl" of the Great Plains. It had meticulously and savagely picked up the rich, promising topsoil, piece by piece, storm by storm, year by year, pushing it, rolling it into sand dunes and dust piles thirty-feet deep, tossing it into the stratosphere and depositing it hundreds of miles downwind. This tandem pair of destruction had almost stripped the life from the precious organic veneer and, likewise, had almost stripped the hopes and dreams from the helpless sharecroppers and tenant farmers who stood, hungry, tired, and thirsty, and watched.

The dust particles that now danced around the Flora baseball field were Children of the Wind and the Drought. The nomadic dust was restlessly looking for crops and rain to end their migration and give them peace. Perhaps here, in this crusty corner of Hopkins County, the wind would cease its endless, ordained duty of dislodging hope from one place and depositing it in another. Perhaps, this day, the wind would build instead of destroy.

The dry wind danced around me, the swirling red dust making a forlorn, whistling sound as it obstructed my view of the third base line and the lively young ladies that beckoned me. For a moment, I thought I could hear the wind whispering to me, saying words that sounded like,

*"Not always this way, not always."*

A chill swept through me, as the wind stopped and the dust floated back onto the baseline, the fans reappearing, as I mumbled to myself,

"I know, I know. There's work to do, there's Life to live. It will not always be this way."

I shook my head, making the red ringlets above my brow jiggle from side to side.

"But it's this way now, and I'm gonna steal that base."

I looked again at the pitcher, could sense the second baseman moving in for the kill, and my eyes moved toward third base.

The girls cheered again. The pitcher stood on the slightly elevated mound, and looked at second, then to third, then back to second, like a pendulum on an antique clock.

Thunder rumbled from a small, white-and-grey cumulus cloud beyond right field, miles away, building upward in Hunt County. A good sound. Several calls of "Yes, Sir!" came from the bleachers, as each person looked hopefully at the sky, wishing, hoping, praying for rain …. after the game, of course. After this daring play.

The pitcher, a tall, self-centered eighteen-year old from Birthright, glared at me, then turned his head to home base, stared at the catcher, and flinched. Yes, he flinched. Ever so slightly, I saw one of his eyes tighten and the crowfeet ripple. He was telegraphing his intentions to the catcher, and I knew what was coming. Inside my gut, I coiled like a panther ready to strike.

"Now he's gonna do it," I muttered, my fingers moving nervously on both hands.

As the pitcher was pulling his hand from his small, wrinkled, tattered glove, his mind and eyes were focused on the second baseman, now leaping toward the bag. The pitcher abruptly spun around, and committed his body to hurl the ball at bullet-speed to second base.

I, on the other hand, had exploded toward third. It felt like I had instantly, almost atomically, changed from my position with legs spread apart, arms dangling downward, wrists flicking nervously, to a seamless blur of running down the third base line. The red Hopkins County dust was floating upward into the now motionless air as all eyes, and the siren trill of the girls, were pulling me toward third base.

The twin bleachers along the third baseline erupted into an immediate cheer, turning the momentary silence into an enthusiastic riot. The second baseman caught the relay from the pitcher with his thin, hand-me-down glove, and threw a blast toward the third baseman, who was leaning slightly down the third base line, watching me - the ruddy, cocky lad from Flora - running toward him, as the dust enveloped both of us. He felt the ball hit his glove as the blur from second base slid under him, my right leg touching the bag and my left leg knocking his ankle free from the bag.

The third baseman gasped as he saw the old, used, brown, crusty ball, ***in slow motion,*** trickle out of his shiny-new glove and drop harmlessly to the ground. Time seemed to stop for the young man, and in front of him lay a pathetic still life, a watercolor canvas of the ball on the ground, me grinning menacingly from on top of the third base bag, the blue coverall-clad umpire with splayed hands, a full-length away from his chest, his lips opened, the word *"SAFE!"* being formed in his vocal chords to be hurled like a dagger into the young man's baseball heart. The loud cheer of the teen-age girls broke the silent nightmare with a sharp, tremendous roar of excitement.

I stood up, brushed the dirt off my open, grey shirt and my grey, worn dungarees, and kicked my thin, brown lace-up boots against the bag. I strutted. I spat once, nodded my head, ran my hand through my hair, and winked at the girls.

"How 'ya doin?" I asked.

There was no need to answer. Anyone with an ounce of East Texas brain could see they adored me.

It was then that I saw her.

A slender, bright-eyed twelve-year old girl, with brown curly hair, was clapping wildly, cheering me, the red-headed Boy Wonder. She screamed with a high-pitched voice, "Way to go, Red!"

I winked, straightened my uniform, and waved. Her voice was lost among the cheers of the other girls, overpowered by their intensity. But, our eyes had met. For a moment, the flash of a second, I had seen more than a twelve-year old girl. I was mesmerized by the broad smile on her face, and the innocence and seduction of her body language. I was captured by her playful, penetrating eyes. I smiled. She winked!

*I thought I was the one that was supposed to wink. Girls don't wink.*

I nodded, my red hair bouncing, and gave an appreciative wave to my young, petite new friend. My army of admirers had just gained a new recruit.

Her name was Juliette Hamilton, from Sulphur Bluff, a few miles north of Flora. The Smiths and the Hamiltons were neighbors, like all families in rural East Texas. These two families, and the matriarchs of each family, Sprague and Herron, with a Thomas and a Posey and a Sandifeer thrown in for good measure, were part of the kaleidoscope of families that comprised this part of Hopkins County.

The wind started to blow again, lifting the nomadic dust into swirls, softening the sweltering air just briefly, drying the sweat on my chest and brow. I could see it was also blowing the brown, curly hair on Juliette's head.

The wind now turned cooler, encouraged by the single, white-and-grey cumulus cloud building high in the East Texas sky, and began dancing around young Juliette, the swirling red dust making a forlorn, dry whistling sound. For a moment, she thought she could hear the wind whispering to her, saying words that sounded like,

*"Enjoy this day. Not always like this."*

She felt a chill, a tremble inside her that quickly passed, as she mumbled to herself,

*"I will know him someday, and he will know me."*

I continued to take quick, inquisitive glances toward her.

I could see there was something different about her. She was no ordinary young girl, not this one.

I caught momentary glances from her as she watched me, The Showman, on third base, barely twenty feet from her.

There I stood, a full one-third of the way between third base and home, legs spread far apart, arms dangling downward, wrists flicking, fingers twitching nervously, as my blue-green eyes stared straight into the hazel eyes of the pitcher.

My brother, Noel, two-years younger than me, was in the batter's box at home plate. He was short lad, and leaned forward toward over the plate. He had a swift, accurate swing and a quick eye. He could place the ball anyplace on the field he wanted, seldom got it out of the infield, but was a master at seeing the weakest place in the infield, and exploiting it like a lumberjack in a virgin forest.

By this late inning, Noel had noticed the pitcher had a follow-through that brought him off the mound with his right foot turned slightly toward first base; if he could just place the ball to the pitcher's right, toward third base, his reaction would be slowed by the cross-over of his feet, and he would not have a good angle to the ball.

I knew that I could out-run this pitcher's slow reaction and could make it all the way home.

*Just do your business, Noel,* I thought. *Show him your business. Let us win this game.*

*For that little girl over there.*

All was quiet at the quaint, country baseball field. It became the Tension Capitol of Hopkins County. All of the spectators, the poor and the not-so-poor, the landowners and the sharecroppers, shared the incredible luxury and the welcomed escape of The Moment.

A scissor-tailed flycatcher darted from a barbed wire fence along one of the narrow, oil-dirt roads, and appeared to stop in midair over first base, wings flapping as if a fierce wind was resisting its movement. Turning abruptly toward right field, it vanished into the rows of brown, dry corn.

"Get outta here, boid," exclaimed a tanned, wrinkled old man behind home plate, his toothless mouth moving like a marionette, his crooked fingers locked into the chain-length fence of the back-catch.

"Ain't no place for you here."

A few men laughed, and the old man smiled at his pronouncement.

The fans, farmers, and ne'er-do-wells along both base lines were on their feet. I knew that this was a "home" crowd, and I knew they would love what was about to happen.

A pair of larger-than-usual great blue skimmer dragonflies crisscrossed the field as if they were dissecting it in mid-air, changing course abruptly three times, and then racing away as quickly and effortlessly as they had appeared.

The wind was still. The powdery, red dust was floating up between the pitches, resembling a diminutive, restless spirit.

The third baseman was playing off the bag, toward shortstop and off the baseline, toward the infield. The short stop was near second base. The second baseman was between second and first, slightly infield. They were of one mind – keep me, the cocky runner, at third, get the batter out, preserve the tie.

Noel watched two balls fly past him in the strike zone, his expression never changing, his baseball mind analyzing the pitcher's every move.

I walked back to touch third base each time, and then resumed my display, occasionally winking at the girls.

"I'll be home d'rectly," I called to them.

"Ya'll be ready."

When young Noel saw the third pitch, he knew in the sweetest part of his baseball heart that it was **the one**. I saw the momentary smile on his face and the flash in his eye, and I exploded toward home.

The ball and bat cracked as they made contact, the ball hit the ground ten feet away, and slowly rolled toward that awful, hideous dead zone between home and third, infield by twenty feet. I raced past the ball on my way home, watching the pitcher stumble embarrassingly as he turned for the ball. He picked it up, stood erect, and threw a bullet to the catcher one second after I slid over home plate.

Noel and I slapped each other's back, the crowd burst into cheers, the girls fell in love, and I stood up, my toothy grin taking the shape of a cocky smile. I rubbed a hand over my forehead, as a cool wind began to dance again across the dusty field.

It was a glorious moment. Me, Horace "Red" Smith, the oldest son of Bud and Altie Smith, stood there, winked at the girls, raised my arms in a victory sign, and trotted back to the bench "dugout" to join my victorious teammates.

Yes, me. The default father and Brother-In-Command of my two brothers and four sisters, and, undoubtedly, the darling of the crowd.

The same sun was shining on young Juliette Hamilton, the youngest daughter of Tom and Nettie Hamilton, and sibling to four sisters and two brothers. She watched intently as I was surrounded and cooed by girls older than she. I didn't know it at the time, but she was, at that moment, making a Princess Promise to herself: that she would, by hook or crook, someday, somehow, win the heart of this Red-Headed Prince and be carried away to Paradise, to live, as they say, happily ever after.

    The uncommonly cool August wind again danced around her, and brushed her cheek. As it blew beneath her brown curls, she heard the dry, whistling sound again, not so forlorn this time. It seemed to be humming, as if it had heard her wish, and was replying,

    *"Maybeee, Juliette. Maybeee you will."*

# CHAPTER 2

# DAY OF INFAMY – RED SMITH

Sunday, December 7, 1941.

Sulphur Springs, Hopkins County, Texas.

I awoke that Sunday morning on a bench in the corner of the Hopkins County Courthouse basement, using my heavy-stitched, cotton jacket for a pillow. Several blankets from a storage room down the arched hallway had been quite useful during the cold night. The basement was a good place to be on a frigid, Texas December night, and it was free. It wasn't the first time I had slept there. I knew the ins and outs, and knew the courthouse security wasn't really secure at all.

    The security at the Mission Theater was lacking, too, especially if you could sneak through the door, slither through it at just the right time, when the "watchers" weren't watching. Once inside, as long as you acted cool and not the least bit suspicious, you could go to the rear of the building, and open the service door for your buddy.

    My buddy, Roy, and I had seen a Gary Cooper movie the previous night, courtesy of the sneaky maneuver. My two brothers and I had perfected the maneuver over many years and many times, getting caught only twice, losing just a little pride and all of twenty cents.

    I stared at Roy, across the room, still asleep.

    *I am twenty years old. I live at home, I come to town on Saturday whenever I can, hang out on the square, drink a couple of beers, catch a movie, sleep in my special guest room at the courthouse, and go back home.*

*I am fond of the routine.*

*I am the oldest son, and the family needs me at home. We have a lot of mouths around the table, and it takes the money that my brothers, Noel and Lester, and I bring home to keep the family fed. One more kid just came along. Mae. I'm twenty years old and I've got a month-old sister. One more reason to work. One more cotton field to chop and pick. One more cord of wood to cut.*

*And, what does Daddy do? He works a little, throws a mean baseball, plays a pretty good guitar, and struts around, full of laughter and laziness.*

*And, what do I do? I keep on being Big Brother. I fill the weekday hours with work. I walk downtown on the weekend with my friend Roy, who's stuck in the same rut and loving every minute of it.*

Roy was well-known for the way he talked in a peculiar way. He was tongue-tied, and had mastered, as much as possible, the art of East Texas conversation. When Roy was a kid, the country doctor had tried to "untie" his tongue three times, using the medical school method of snipping the "tie" underneath the tongue. Roy was a particularly troublesome patient for this procedure, because his tongue healed back all three times to the original condition. Roy was a good-natured boy, and continued to talk as well as possible, and became my best friend early on in life. Because I was his friend, other kids in that part of Hopkins County naturally treated him with respect and Roy was just "one of us." We had some good laughs at some of the things he would say. He would often mispronounce things on purpose, just to lighten things up. He was strong and smart, and we became a pretty swell team roaming the countryside.

Roy was snoring on the bench across the small room. I pushed back my wool blanket, picked up one of my light brown, lace-up, ankle-high leather boots, and gently tossed it at him. The boot bounced off Roy's hip.

Roy snorted, raised his head, and said, "What da hewa, Wed?"

"Time to get up, Roy. Time for coffee and a donut. And another movie, maybe. So, get up and say your prayers, 'cause it's Sunday morning".

"My head hurth," Roy moaned. "What'd we do wath night?"

I shook my head in dismay, my red curly hair bouncing above my eyes. "Well, let me bring you up to snuff on what we did. We walked into town – you remember that, don'cha Roy?"

Roy pursed his lips in disgust, nodded his head, and said, disdainly, "Of courth I do, you moron. I'm athkin you what we did WATH NIGHT, not yetherday."

I pointed at my boot lying on the floor beneath Roy, and motioned for him to toss it my way.

Roy raised up a slight angle, pushed his blanket back, leaned over, and looked down at the single brown boot beneath the bench. He raised one foot, placed it behind the boot, and slid it across the floor to me.

I was proud of those boots. I had picked out the leather myself from the Henderson tannery at Flora, and a retired shoemaker in Mahoney had made them earlier that summer. I paid the old man with a full cord of wood for the winter.

I nodded at Roy.

"We had a hot dog for supper, drank three beers on the square, and went to the movie, just like every other Saturday night. You had a swell time, Roy. You probably drank one too many beers. You almost made a hit on that blonde girl, just before her father came out of the Gus Lilly Cafe and threw you that go-to-hell look."

Roy laughed.

I stood up, stretched my arms and legs, and briskly walked to my right, down a shorter hallway which led to an exterior door. The basement had two doors, one opening up on the east side, at street level, and the other door facing south, below the ground level, near a tall magnolia tree. We had persuaded the night watchman, who was scarcely a watchman at all, to keep the south door unlocked for us, promising to lock it while we slept and to lock it again when we left Sunday morning.

I cracked the door open, and said "Sun's out. It sure is bright. And, it's a wee bit cold. All is clear. Time to move out."

We both visited the restroom at the opposite end of the same narrow, arched hallway that led to the storage room, where we had again stashed the blankets. We splashed our faces with water, combed our hair, and made our way to the south door. We entered the bright, Sunday morning light, and walked north across the shorter end of the town square, hands in pockets, collars turned up to keep our necks warm.

Roy DeBord followed me step for step. It was easy for Roy to follow. It seemed he had been following me most of his life. He told me once there was no better person to follow than me, the oldest Smith boy. Walking across the northern end of Sulphur Springs square, we looked like brothers, the same height, and the same build.

"Oh yeah," Roy remembered.

"We thaw Thergeandt York last night. Good thow. Good thow. Gawy Coopa. Winnin' his medal. Worl Waw One. That wath a heck of a waw, Wed. Heck of a waw."

"Yeah, it was creepy the way the newsreel showed the Germans just pushing everybody around over there again, too," I said.

"And then, there was *Sergeant York*, shooting them like he was in a turkey shoot ..."

I stopped in mid-sentence, pondered the creepiness of it all, and continued.

"It's happening again over there, and here we are looking for coffee on a quiet Sunday morning. Going home tonight, to a good hot meal, chop some more wood tomorrow. Nobody shooting at us here."

Roy looked at me with a somber expression.

"Da Germans are on da looth, and now the Dapaneeth are awe ober da Pathific."

I shrugged my shoulders, an empty look on my face.

"Yep. I don't know what will happen over there, Roy. I feel bad about it, too. And, I feel, I feel ...."

A few seconds passed, as I was deeply in thought.

"Fewa whadt?" Roy urged.

"I feel like some big changes are around the corner. I feel like these days are short. We won't be doing this much longer," as I waved my arm around the town square.

"All these Sunday morning sleep-ins at the courthouse may not happen that many more times. The Army's already drafting folks as soon as they turn 21. They've just built that big training camp the other side of Dallas, out at Mineral Wells. They registered people last year, and again this summer. What was it, June, July?"

"Yeth, id was thith thummer. Thuly 1st, I bewieve," Roy replied.

"They got the Thomas boy, and the Posey boy. Just like that. They got their names, they were 21, then they were gone. Gone to get ready for whatever's coming. They'll get us, too, Roy, next year."

I was quiet. My mind plunged into the magic and the dread of turning 21 in June.

*What am I gonna do? What am I doin' now?* I asked myself.

*I'm farming. Helping the family. Sometimes, being the one thing the family needs. Lord help me, I know I'm old enough to be my baby sister's father. What the hell? Just being Big Brother. Wearing the Big Shoes. Keeping it all together. What would they do without me? What would I do without them? I kinda like what I'm doing, but, still, what the hell?*

*I ain't married, don't even wanna be. Nobody out there worth marrying. No woman out there wants a Big Brother, and I don't want a woman that wants more than me.*

*Doris and I could be married. She knows it. I know it. She'd make a good wife, but a lousy friend. She can satisfy a man at night, and suck him dry the next day. Leave nothing but a shell. All she really wants me to do is sweep her up in my arms and take her to Dallas, get me a job at Sears or at a factory, and live the life she really wants. That scares the hell out of me. I don't want that. I don't want to work a night shift, pay rent, listen to the neighbors quarrel, hear the dogs bark, live with city folks.*

*Everything's okay right here. Things'll change when it comes time.*

*Nothing fits my heart now, except what I've got right here.*

*Besides, Momma and Daddy need me. They made a family too big for the two of them. I've always been the helper they needed, the elder son that was always there. Roberta, Noel, Lester, Dorothy, Hattie, and Alice all look to me for the answers, for the orders, to make things right, before they go to Momma and Daddy. At least Momma nurses Mae now, at least she's not my responsibility – yet.*

I looked across the thick, anxious atmosphere between us, and knew that Roy was thinking the same dreadful thoughts.

I breathed a heavy, suffocating breath from the dark, uneasy corners of my worried mind.

We had made it through the hunger-fear and the dead-end panic of the Great Depression, with a lot of help from the government and Roosevelt's work programs. The WPA. The CCC. We were in the right place. Down on the farm. The farm just belonged to someone else, that's all.

*That's OK,* we were both thinking, simultaneous thoughts in similarly constructed minds. *We're farmers. We're Big Brothers. We can do this thing. Maybe. But then, there's the damn Germans and the crazy Japs. What the hell?*

*Yeah, they'll get us, too. Next year.*

I looked back at Roy, and he was looking back at me, waiting for me to tell him what I was thinking.

"I know the Army pays good, really good. Just like the 3-C's. The money I made there fed all of 'em. I thought they'd have some money saved up when I got through, but, I'll be God-darned, they spent it all, and needed too, I guess."

I looked sarcastically at Roy, "Daddy never missed a baseball game, though. No, Sir. Even got another finger or two broke."

I shook my head slowly.

Roy knew. He was the oldest son, just like me. He knew. These had not been the best of times, but family ties were strong, and he, like me, could not even imagine, much less cause, the family to get by without his work, his efforts, his wages, and his love.

That's what it was all about. We were East Texas farmers, and we were proud of it. We could not, would not, lessen our own stature by demanding to be given what was rightfully ours – our independence, our future, our own road to paradise.

*After all, this IS paradise,* I told myself.

*Right here, in Sulphur Springs, Texas.*

"Freedom." I then said aloud.

Roy's brain broke from the dark questions lurking there, and he was startled.

"Whadt?" he asked.

"Freedom." I answered.

"That's what we have here and that's what the Germans and Japs are taking away over there. We have our whole lives in front of us. Why, we can just get up and walk into town, sleep in the courthouse, and walk home when we want to, and nobody says nothing. And, all the while, those Germans are killing people over there. And the Japs are killing them across the other way. It ain't right, Roy," I shook my head, sending my red hair flapping like a mad man.

"It ain't right, and sooner or later, somethin's got to be done about them."

I looked Roy.

"But, for now, it is time for our coffee and donut!"

We both walked in silence the rest of the way up Church Street, to the First Methodist Church. Marching up the full-story brick stairs to the sanctuary door, we paused to look back at the courthouse, our monumental pink granite and red sandstone boarding room, standing majestically at the northeast corner of the square. The morning sun was highlighting the semi-circle second floor porch and the checkerboard pattern of the brick just below the central tower.

We quietly entered the church vestibule. In a little room, to the left of the front door, the ministry had established an oasis for me and Roy, and any other hungry, tired wretched soul in need of coffee, a donut, and the gospel.

We quietly, respectfully, poured a cup of coffee, one apiece, and picked up a round, brown, glazed donut, like we had done many times before.

The preacher's wife, a petite, gray-haired woman with a pointed, turned-up nose which contrasted a genuinely warm smile, peeked into the oasis and said, "Good morning, gentlemen," just like SHE had many times before.

We lowered our cups, each adopting a slight bow, and replied, "Good mornin', Ma'am," almost in perfect unison.

"Will you be staying for the service?" she asked, her eyes narrowing a bit.

"Pastor Bryant will begin his Christmas Series this morning, and he's been working on it all this week. Why, he'd be very, very disappointed if ya'll didn't pay a listen to it."

"Yes, Ma'am," we said sheepishly, knowing we wouldn't stay long. We would stay, at least, through the first two songs. The first two songs were always stand-up songs. It was so incredibly easy to move swiftly and silently from the back row to the front door while everyone was standing up, belting out "A Mighty Fortress is Our God."

By 10:30, Roy and I were back on the city square, lying beneath a leafless pecan tree, its sinewy branches reaching upward, making a dendritic pattern against the blue East Texas sky. The bitter cold of the night was gone, just a slight breeze, temperature in the forties now. The sun was still low in the December sky.

"Nod muth thade from thith twee. It wohth aw ith weaves wath month," Roy observed.

"Nope, not many leaves left," I replied, watching two squirrels near the top, their fluffy tails flicking nervously.

"It still has a few pecans, though, way up high. Winter is coming fast. Right around the corner."

We both breathed a sigh, and then silence.

Each of us went deeply inward, examining the what-for's, the why-for's, the where-to's of our own unfulfilled destinies.

Roy wondered what his father would do with his bad, swollen knees, and wondered what his mother would do with her headaches, those ghastly, face-changing, tear-jerking headaches. He thought of his brother, his three sisters, the food, the barn, the work.

I thought of my Daddy, not with the bad knees, but with the mean streak that came out, mostly in the dark, in the quiet, when no one knew or expected.

> *Momma, what's that bruise on the back of yer neck, the one yer trying to hide with that scarf?*
> *It's nothin, Red. Must've slept wrong.*
> *It's not nothin', Momma. Daddy had a few too many again last night, didn't he? Why were you so quiet? Why didn't you say somethin', make a noise, anything, just wake somebody up? We'd stop him from...*
> *Aw, hush. Just be quiet. The Time will come, Red.*

My mind, trying to enjoy the day, the town, the moment, rumbled through the memory-pile again, picking up pieces, examining the dark, violent fragments, the sounds, the sights, the suspicions, preventing my daydream escape. My restless thoughts continued their relentlessly unsavory reminiscences, going back to the day when *The Time did come*, indeed. The Day, six months ago, when the bruises were too large to conceal, the leg too painful to walk in a steady gait, one eye a bit too swollen.

> *That's it Momma. It's time we shut this thing down.*

> Noel and I had wrapped Daddy in our four strong arms, me tightly holding his shoulders, his arms pressed and tied against his sides, and Noel at

the feet, holding his knees locked, and tied shins immovable. We loaded him into the back of the wagon like an undertaker would load a stiff, *rigor mortis* neighbor. Lester was up front, holding the reins. He stared ahead, clicked his tongue three times, and swiftly but gently jostled the reins. Ol' Blue, our faithful mule, took off down the road like he had been waiting for this very moment for years and years and years .....

*What the hell do you boys think yer doin?*
*You'll think you've been to hell and back if you make it through what's ahead of you.*
*What ...*
*Shut up, Daddy. Just shut up, dammit! The only way you'll make it back is if you convince us you'll never, ever hit Momma again.*
*What do ya think yer gonna do, kill me?*
*We thought about it. Haven't decided.*
*It's up to you.*
*Anything can happen out here. Anything. A feller could fall and get runned over by a mule wagon, or just hit his head real hard against a rock, or maybe even get himself shot by somebody over a bad debt, or a smart-ass remark.*
*We're all together on this, Daddy. All of us. Nobody changes their mind today except you.*
*Three against one, eh?*
*Naw, it's four. Momma's with us.*
*That's more like four against none, Daddy.*

My thoughts drifted back to the tree, the town square, the coffee, the donut, the sunny day. Thirty minutes passed, both of us gazing through the tree branches as if looking for something against the blue backdrop, each one seeing black behind the blue. Forty minutes. Fifty minutes. An hour. We could feel ourselves drifting, floating (*more like being sucked down*) into that dreamy world *(cesspool of worry)* where sounds become muffled, as sleep *(or death)* silently creeps around you on silky, furry, damp, dank feet, like a cat circling, circling, ready to pounce.

I looked at Roy.

"We can't do this forever, you know."

Roy nodded his approval. His eyes narrowed. He was looking around the square as if trying to memorize it, cherish it, like it was already a lithograph in a New York magazine.

*Yeah, I know, Roy*, I thought to myself.

*I like this town square as much as you do. I wish there was more work around here. I can't go back to the 3-C's, my two stints are done. Colorado and Arizona. And, I helped build that roadside park with the WPA out on Highway 67, near Cumby. Noel and I are still waiting for the next WPA work to come along.*

*Farming is not as good here as it used to be, everything's moving west. Maybe the soil is getting old and tired here. Maybe the soil is just young and ready out west. I guess we'll be moving west, sooner or later. Or, maybe, the Army will get me first. Then what? I love it here; Momma and Daddy look to me to do what Big Brother is supposed to do. Momma looks to me for protection. Daddy looks to me for help. He knowed he was wrong, he kinda turned the daddying over to me. I've got to keep the herd in real tight.*

I smiled at the thought of me riding a big white horse, rope in hand, keeping the other seven Smith kids safe in a circle, Momma in the cabin, cooking, Daddy in the chair, drinking a cup of coffee.

*They need you, Boy, and you need them. You can't live on your own, and they can't live without you. Keep the herd in real tight, now.*

I put one leg under me and stood up, stretched my arms, ran a hand through my red, curly hair, looked at Roy, and said, "Get up. We're going to the Carnation and watch another movie."

Roy pushed himself up with both hands. He looked at me and said, apprehensively, "Thath an ethpenthive pwath. Hard to thneak indo there."

"Yeah, I guess we'll just have to pay, like everybody else. At least one of us," I winked.

We walked back across the square, toward the courthouse again, to the north. Conveniently, the Carnation movie theater was at the corner of Church and Connally, almost next door to our earlier appointment at First Methodist.

The Carnation was the ritzy theater, with uniformed ticket-sellers and snack bar servers. The Mission, where we had performed our sneaky maneuver the night before, was the lesser of the two, no uniforms, just people, working for a living, not all gussied-up.

We stood in front of the theater, reading the marquee.
*The Maltese Falcon.*
*Humphrey Bogart.*

"Thweethardt, I thought you did not wike Bogee," Roy jeered.

"Shut up. I'll go in first. You wait and see what happens."

I shuffled off to the ticket window and stood in the long line of movie-goers. As I whistled, I looked to my left, saw the blue '39 Chevy truck that Mr. Davis, the County Clerk, owned, its front grill smiling like a row of new, shiny teeth. I said to myself, *"Well, Mr. Davis. I'll see you tomorrow. It is wood-chopping time."*

Reaching the ticket window, I straightened one leg as my hand dug into my dungaree pocket, pulled out twenty-five cents, counted it twice, bought a ticket, and vanished though the glass doors.

Roy was probably thinking, *Why do I do this? One day he's not coming out, and he'll be laughing like a clown when I show up inside with my own ticket.*

Once inside, I sauntered to the water fountain, took a long, refreshing drink of unusually cold water.

*Ice cold. Huh. Man, I wish I could do this every day.*

I surveyed the people at the snack bar.

*A few snooty folks,* I said to myself. *Mostly just us, though.*

A portly, middle-aged man was standing by the snack bar, looking frantically though his coverall pockets. A similarly aged woman, nicely dressed in a navy-blue cotton dress with long ruffled sleeves, was standing next to him. I recognized them. They were Mr. and Mrs. Davis. I started to wave, and hesitated; I didn't want to get into whatever it was they were experiencing.

"You can't find them?" Mrs. Davis nervously asked.

"Nope," Mr. Davis sighed, and then glanced at the door, the large glass frame keeping the world outside and the paid customers inside. "I guess I left my glasses in the truck. In the pigeon-hole."

She opened her mouth to say something, then smiled. A second passed, and she said, "I'll wait here, you should go get them."

I stepped forward, and said, "Good mornin', Mr. Davis, Mrs. Davis. Anything I can do for ya?"

Mr. Davis looked up, broadly smiled and replied, "Well, good morning, Mr. Smith. Naw, I kinda left my glasses in the truck pigeon-hole and was fixin' to go out there and get them."

Mrs. Davis nodded, looked at her husband of thirty years, and smiled the same broad infectious smile. "Good morning, Red," she gently greeted.

"Let me go get them for you, I don't mind. I saw yer blue Chevy truck out there. You stay right here," I said with a wave of my hand.

Mr. Davis offered the slightest well-mannered resistance, and watched as I walked toward the door, showed my ticket to the person at the ticket window, motioned back to Mr. Davis, explained my quest for the glasses, and maneuvered through the door. I disappeared to the right and stopped. Out of sight, I motioned for Roy.

Roy briskly approached, held both hands out in a *what's-happening* gesture, and I handed him my movie ticket.

"Go on in, I've got this covered, I think. I'm going to get Mr. Davis's glasses. Don't ask me any questions. I'll see you inside."

I quickly strode to the blue Chevy, opened the passenger-side door, opened the glove box, retrieved the brown-framed spectacles, and returned to the Carnation door.

I caught the eye of the ticket-seller, waved the glasses, opened the door, and stepped in.

Walking straight up to Mr. Davis, I proudly passed the spectacles from my hand to his hand, like a baton being passed from runner to runner.

"Now," I said, "You can see the movie."

The three of us laughed.

"I'll probably see you tomorrow mornin'. Thought I'd come over and chop a little wood for you. Winter's comin' on."

"That would be nice, very nice, indeed," Mr. Davis replied, and nodded his balding head.

I waved a salute with the index finger of my left hand, and immediately stepped away, headed to the snack bar. As I approached, I let my eyes pass over every item, and noticed Roy standing in one of the short lines.

I announced to him, "You owe me a popcorn."

I took another long, welcomed drink of cold water from the fountain. A few minutes later, I met Roy, holding two popcorns, at the middle aisle. We walked down the aisle like Country Club Gentlemen, nodding to the men, saying hello to the women, winking at the girls. We settled into the middle row, middle seats, out of sight, out of mind, melting into the Sunday morning East Texas populace. It was noon.

A few minutes after noon, the show began.

First, a newsreel showing thousands of citizens fleeing Moscow, the Russian capital, after rumors of a German invasion. Then, a preview of *Sergeant York*. We had seen the movie last night, at the Mission. The war in Europe, WW1, the War to End all Wars. York shooting Germans like he was in a turkey shoot.

Next, a much-too-long short flick called *The Gay Peruvian*, with dancing dudes and ballet girls, spectacularly colored dresses, tight pants, make-up on everybody, long-haired orchestra music, dancing, dancing, when-will-they-stop-dancing, guy wants gal, gal wants guy, someone loses, someone wins, everyone dances, please let it stop.

It finally does. Twenty minutes have passed, and most of the popcorn has been eaten. Need another drink.

*Hold this, buddy, and don't eat any of it.*

After that, a color cartoon about a rascally rabbit and mighty Hiawatha, out to catch and eat the rabbit. Something to laugh at now. Cartoon-land. What a wonderful way to make Life anyway and anyhow you want it. The rabbit runs from Hiawatha. Hiawatha chases the rabbit. The audience laughs. The rabbit kisses Hiawatha. More laughs. Hiawatha paddles away, into the sunset.

Another cartoon. Black and white. A pig. Porky Pig. Dressed up like a Doughboy. America preparing for War. Making guns. Planes. Tanks. Funny guns. Funny planes. Funny tanks. America getting ready.

*That's not funny. Germans are killing people over there. We can't get ready with funny guns and funny planes and funny tanks.*

The Statue of Liberty sees enemy planes flying overhead, pulls out a pump can of bugspray, and knocks them out of the sky like flies or mosquitoes.

*Pesky pests.*

Most of the audience laughs. Some don't.

The movie starts.
*Now it gets good, even if it is Bogart.*
*Smart Ass.*
*Gets the women, though.*
It's 12:40. A man is shot. The plot thickens. The private detective tries to find out what the pretty woman wants him to do. Something about a small statue of a bird. A falcon, with diamonds and gemstones crusted on it. Worth a lot of money.
*Wish we had a little money. Wouldn't have to sneak into the movie. Or steal chickens. Or chop wood.*
A fight. More policemen. A little man that talks nice, and dresses fancy. Wears white gloves. A fat man that giggles, and wants the falcon, too. Still, the pretty woman leads the detective on, wants the bird.
The fat man gives Bogie a drink.
*Don't drink that, you stupid detective.*
Bogie passes out.
*We told you not to drink it.*
Bogie wakes up. Keeps looking for clues to the falcon.
I hear a disturbance behind me. Something is going on in the theater, behind us, up in the projector room. I look back, and see shadows moving around back there. Someone raising a ruckus. And voices.
More of the audience hears the distraction. A few men clear their throats. One guy says, "Knock it off."
The lights come on just as the movie screen shows a burning boat, the words "La Paloma" written on it. The boat is sitting at a dock, leaning off to starboard, a fire along the bridge. The movie stops.

A tall man, donned in the theater's familiar dark vest with an embroidered carnation on the left pocket, walked down the middle aisle. He was holding a flashlight, spreading a stream of light down the dark aisle. His face was wrinkled with a peculiar look of confused determination. Everyone's eyes were on him.

*This must be important.*

"Ladies and gentlemen," the man began, his voice wavering a bit, a nervous twitch in his speech, the way his lips quivered after each word, as if a thousand silent words were slipping through, *gotta get out*.

He lowered his arm, turned the flashlight off, and tucked it into his right rear pocket.

"We hate to stop the movie, but we need to announce something." He stopped, looked down, licked his lips, clasped his hands together, his thumbs wrapping around each fist like a vise grip.

He coughed, breathed in deeply, and said, "Japanese planes have attacked us, and bombed our Navy ships at Pearl Harbor, Honolulu, Hawaii."

A woman gasped.

A man said, "What?"

With the exception of those two reactions, collectively, the entire audience took in a deep breath and held it. No sound at all now, just the tall vested man, hands clenched, interlocked fists, quivering lips.

"They attacked us about an hour ago, and damaged most of our ships and killed a lot of our soldiers. Hundreds. We don't know what they're gonna do next. If you want to come out to the lobby, we have the radios on. It's pretty bad."

He shuffled his feet, rocked back on his heels, unclenched his hands. He spread his arms apart, looked up to the ceiling, then back to the audience, and said, "I'm, I'm, uh, sorry that I had to tell you that. I couldn't let you just, just, uh, not know it."

He turned to walk back up the aisle, stopped, turned around, and said "The movie will resume in a few minutes. God bless you, and may God help us all."

A few seconds of silence, then the sound of chatter among the audience. Some cursed in a whispered swear, some cried. Mostly, they just looked at each other, and exchanged a few precious words, and nodded. Slowly, one by one, then two by two, they began to stand up, gathered their coats and purses, and filed up the aisle and out the door like mourners leaving a wake.

I saw Mr. and Mrs. Davis leave the theater from their seats on the left.

Roy and I, without looking at each other, stood up slowly, walked to the front right corner of the theater, opened a small exit door, and left the theater, letting a short, bright burst of sunlight penetrate the dark dungeon that still imprisoned the two dozen or so people that remained, the ones that did not know what to do.

The majority of them, though, had just looked at each other and simply said,

"I reckon we better go home."


Two hours later.

We walked slowly, in near silence, the six-mile journey back toward the small town of Mount Sterling. Our shuffling steps were in near cadence along the crushed rock surface of Highway 19. While the two of us walked, we watched, with hands in pockets, as cars, jalopies, and farm trucks took their quiet, sullen occupants northward, away from the city, toward the shelter and isolation of their homes.

    We ambled northward, out of Sulphur Springs, along the bridges that traversed White Oak Creek first, then Horse Pen Creek. The leafless trees of winter lined the road, but the bottomlands and creek beds were dominated by the yellowing leaves of weeping willows and American beech trees. Summer's life had not given up along the flat, boggy terrain of these saturated kingdoms.

    But, in the territories above these dark bottomlands, Winter had just come very, very early in the hearts of those who had just heard the news of Pearl Harbor. It had taken the soul from their spirit, had ripped it asunder, and had left them worried, anxious, uneasy, and fearful of the inevitable war ahead. They just needed a little time, and they needed to circle the wagons and look into the eyes of their families.

    Roy would nod to folks he knew as they passed. One already-full jalopy slowed, the driver asking the two of us if we wanted a ride, and resumed its exodus after Roy and I shook our heads politely.

    Less than a mile north of Horse Pen Creek, we turned east and continued our solemn journey home along the oil dirt hardpan of Road 1537. Roy peeled off to the left on Farm Road 3236 a quarter mile later, toward his home south of Birthright. We shook hands at the crossroad, an unfamiliar gesture for the both of us.

"See you in a couple of days, I guess," I said.

"Tewa evewyone hi for me, tewa them I'm thtill good-wookin'," Roy grinned.

I nodded, a thin grin across my face.

"Yer the craziest fella I know," I said, as we parted in the late afternoon December sun. Our shadows were long, but our faces were longer. We had met there at the same crossroad the day before, on our way into town.. It felt like it had been a century before. A lifetime ago.

We both sensed it, we both knew it. December 7, 1941 had just been nailed into our souls like the cross beams on the telephone poles along the oil dirt road. The date hung in the sky as if it had been painted by an insane, evil artist, with brushstrokes that filled one's heart with fear, an image far too horrible to look at, with numbers too grotesque to read.

*I need to get home*, I despaired. *I need to get home to my family, and I need this damn sun to go down and come up tomorrow with a better attitude than it did today.*

I walked the next two miles alone, not a car passing or a dog barking.

I saw our white clapboard house up ahead, with curtains blowing behind the open windows. My sisters Roberta, Hattie, and Alice were outside, cooing over Mae, the baby. They looked my way, and waved. Daddy was in a chair on the front porch, a cup of coffee in one hand. He stood up and raised the other hand to wave wearily as his Right-Hand-Man returned from his rest and rehabilitation in town. My mother, brushing the kitchen curtain aside as she, too, looked for the eldest son to return.

*My God, they're glad to see me,* I thought. *The pitiful part is I'm just as glad to see them.*

As I walked up the narrow, sandy trail that led from the road to the house, I heard Hattie and Alice say, "Big Brother is home!" to Mae. Roberta was holding Mae. Her two-year-old son, Darrell, was standing patiently beside her, rubbing Mae's arm, saying "Pretty Mae, pretty Mae." I rubbed my hand through Darrell's black hair. I took little Mae from Roberta, nestled her in my arms, bounced her gently, and said "Yes, he is home, and he is hungry."

I looked up at Daddy.

"Daddy, I guess you heard?"

He nodded his head and said, "Yep. Cap'n is inside, listening to the radio."

My youngest brother, Lester, had been given the nickname "Cap'n" a long time ago, and for reasons no one could quite recall. Perhaps it was the way he issued orders to everyone like a ship's captain. Or, perhaps it was a way of making the smallest, skinniest of the boys feel an ounce of confidence. It had worked.

"Noel worked today, drove the ice truck. He'll be home d'rectly. Yer Mammy's makin' cocoa pies."

I handed Mae back to Roberta. I reached down to ruffle Darrell's hair again, and he gave me a large playful grin. Darrell leaned over and carefully, gently placed his index finger on Mae's lips.

"You two are gonna be like brother and sister instead of nephew and aunt," I observed.

Roberta smiled her infectious, unique smile.

I turned and slowly walked to the porch, opened the screen door, and stepped inside.

Lester looked up from his chair by the radio, nodded, and exhaled a thin, tired breath through his tightly pursed lips.

"God-darned Japs," he blurted.

"Yeah, I heard, at the Carnation. Have they come back again?"

"Nope, not yet. But, the people in California are sure scared."

"Momma, those cocoa pies smell really good," I praised.

She brushed her hands on her apron, walked over and placed a hand on her oldest son's chest.

"You can have as many as you want," she said to me, a slight quiver in her voice. "As soon as Noel gets home."

"Save some for me," Lester retorted. "President Roosevelt is gonna speak to Congress tomorrow. He's got no other choice. He'll ask Congress to declare war on Japan, and they'll do it. Tomorrow, we're at war, Red. Tomorrow, we're at war."

I winced, looked at Momma, slowly nodded my head in agreement, and looked back at Lester.

"Tomorrow, I chop wood for Mr. Davis. You want to help?"

"Wouldn't miss it for the world. He's got some good chickens."

The three of us laughed, a welcomed relief from the tight suffocation of the day.

"I'm not so sure about that," Momma revealed. "Lizzy sent Gene up here a little while ago telling us there'll be no school tomorrow, and I'm sure Mr. Davis is gonna be meeting with the Big Shots over at the courthouse first thing in the morning. I think the less we do tomorrow, the better."

Lester punctuated the statement with a swift nod of his head. "I better stay right here, with the radio, Red."

I looked down, then raised my head to meet Momma's worried glance.

"We'll stay here. Listen to Roosevelt."

"Good," she declared. "Anyway, Mr. Davis ain't providing any chickens tonight. We're having red beans and cocoa pies."

We Smiths had a genuine, culinary affection for cocoa pies. Altie Smith had learned how to make them from her mother-in-law and had become the master chef of these delightful treats. Not just a desert, they were the better half of a main course tandem with pinto beans. By taking biscuit dough, sugar, cocoa powder, butter, and a splash of vanilla, and gently turning and forking them into half-moon pies, then lightly frying them in lard, they became, simply, a heavenly delicacy. Accompanied by pinto beans, they were every Smith's equivalent of dying and going to Heaven.

When she made them, she wouldn't just make a few. She would present a platter stacked with two-to-three dozen cocoa pies, each one as perfect as the other, from crispy top to soggy bottom.

A few minutes passed. Lester turned the drifting radio dial, trying to zero in on WBAP, the NBC radio station in Fort Worth that blasted its clear channel broadcast throughout most of Texas. A few squeaks, a few high-pitched whistles, and he found it again.

I walked over to the window, drew back the curtains with my right hand, and nervously thumped the fingers of my left hand on the sill.

I saw Noel walking up the same road I had walked ten minutes ago.

"Here comes Noel," I announced. "Now we can eat."

I turned and walked back out to the porch, stepping past my mother, gently patting her on her shoulder as I passed.

Bud Smith, born Carl Noel Smith forty-two years earlier, was standing on the front porch, hat on, both feet facing the road, knees slightly bent. He was rolling a cigarette, in his time-perfected manner of holding the open cigarette paper between two twisted, baseball-broken fingers of his left hand while he thumped a tall, thin, rectangular, red can of Prince Albert tobacco into it with his right hand. He then closed the tobacco can and slipped it back inside his right-leg pocket. He raised the paper, now filled with an uneven row of chopped tobacco, to his lips and moistened the top strips of the paper with the pointed tip of his tongue. Rolling and curling the cigarette between his right hand and the twisted fingers of his left, he achieved a lumpy but tight cigarette. Striking a wooden match with a flick of his thumbnail, he raised the match and inhaled as a rather large tongue of flame burned the excess paper at the end of the cigarette. Smoke rolled from his nostrils as he removed the cigarette from his mouth and spat out a few tiny pieces a tobacco that had somehow escaped the confines of the 'quirley.'

Altie Smith, born Altie Herron, stood at the front screen door, looking at her husband of 23 years, and half-smiled at him as he gave her a feisty wink. They were both proud of their large, dispersed family. Their children consisted of three young men, four young women, a baby girl. And a grandson.

Altie, like Bud, was born just before the turn-of-the-century, and had fallen in love with this spirited, devil-may-care man when he was a young, blond, gun-carrying dandy, with a cocky look in his eyes that dared anyone to get in his way. A talker, a tradesman of nothing, a ball player that could throw a knuckle-breaking fast ball (and had obviously caught half a dozen of them from others), and a pretty good guitar player. But mostly, he could talk. And, he was smart. Smart in the back-woodsy way that East Texas men respected, and East Texas women idolized.

He was mean-spirited, gentle, lively, lazy, hateful, loving, a walking contradiction. But he was faithful. A little too faithful, judging by the size of their family.

And she was forgiving, mostly.

Except for that one morning, when he came home drunk just before dawn, too drunk to get sassy, too drunk to do anything but fall into the bed. He was still there after the boys and girls had left for school. Momma had been counseled by the women of the community, in the hushed, secret languages that women spoke to each other about surviving. They protected their own, and their pact was stronger than the vows that bound them to their faulty men.

*We must do some things just to live.*
*You wait, until they're flat-ass drunk, passed completely out, nobody around, then you take control of the situation.*

*You take the bed sheet, carefully wrap it around his drunk ass, sew it very, very firmly, no missed seams now, very, very tightly, you hear me? Very, very tightly. 'Cause he's gonna react like the half-wild ass he is when you take your broom, and ...*

*What did ya think ran over you, Bud? You don't remember me sewing yer lazy drunk ass up in the bed sheet, do ya?*

*Was it thieves beating you up, like you claimed the next morning? Or, was it me, just little ol' fed-up me, banging you with that broom handle?*

*You were pretty messed up the next morning. Confused, you were. Yer three sons had to dress you for a day or two, yer bones were so sore.*

*You have three fine sons, Bud.*

*Those three sons will straighten your ass up one day.*

*One of these days, The Time will come.*

As Noel walked up the narrow, sandy trail that led from the road to the house, my sister Dorothy had joined Alice and Hattie, and all three were standing over Roberta, wooing and cooing baby Mae.

Noel half-raised his right arm in his familiar, trademark gesture, and, slowly lowering it, said, "All hell's going on out there."

Daddy nodded his head and said, "We're all home now. May God help us. We're better off than those boys over there in the Pacific."

I stared straight ahead, past the porch, toward the distant horizon as I let that word roll over in my mind, like a

cannon ball rolling through a pantry with mason jars full of jams and jellies.
> *The Pacific.*
> *The Pacific.*
> *Paradise on Earth.*
> *Lord help us.*

# CHAPTER 3

# DAY OF INFAMY – JULIETTE HAMILTON

Sunday, December 7, 1941.

Near Tahoka, Lynn County, Texas Panhandle, Texas.

Nettie Hamilton pulled the large baking pan out of the black iron woodstove, her hands wrapped by two terry-cloth kitchen towels. Her eyes narrowed in self-defense as heat poured from the oven, giving her chin, nose, and forehead a blast of hotness. The aroma of sage, onion, and celery filled the kitchen as the cornbread dressing was gently placed on a cooling grate, atop the white porcelain drainboard sink.

Not many people had a porcelain drainboard sink in the Texas Panhandle town of Tahoka. Most kitchens had free-standing sinks on porcelain legs. She smiled at the beauty of her fine-looking "workstation," in stark contrast to the weathered wood cabinets, walls, and doorways of the old house. It had a good-sized counter on each side of the sink, and was "built in" to the original cabinets on either side.

Tom Hamilton had surprised her when he bought the drainboard sink in Lubbock two months ago, and proudly presented it to her. He insisted that if she had to live in a four-room "shack," as he and his daughters called it, the least she could have was a first-class kitchen sink. She smiled again as she looked out the window and saw him, the man she affectionately called "my Tom."

He was sitting in a wooden chair beneath a small cottonwood tree that offered only meager shade in the summer, none in the winter. With his legs crossed, he was casually carving a sliver of tobacco from a square plug he kept, neatly wrapped in waxed paper, in his right front pocket. He would slowly slice a narrow, thin piece of tobacco, and place it on his tongue with the blade. He would repeat the process until he had whittled three identically sliced carvings, placing each in his mouth with the same ritual. He patiently closed the pocketknife, stretched his right leg straight until he could get his hand into his coverall pocket, and returned the knife to its safe harbor. His mouth slowly worked the tobacco into a single saturated "chew." He looked up to the sky, as if thanking God for the luxury of sweet tobacco and a few minutes rest.

Nettie had given him the pocketknife on their wedding day, and he treasured it like an endowment from The Almighty.

To Tom Hamilton, Nettie was the closest any human could get to The Almighty. Orphaned at age nine, he professed to have been raised by turn-of-the-century railroad hobos. He had first met Nettie Sprague when he settled down in Sulphur Bluff, a young, sinewy, railroad-scholar, with money saved from a ten-year course in hobo frugality. Nettie was the woman he wanted, and Tom was the man she wanted. On November 19, 1916, their union was bonded on a windy afternoon in Franklin County, just east of Sulphur Bluff, Texas.

The years that followed were both glorious and inglorious, loving and deadly. An infant son died at birth. The war in Europe ended with an armistice. A string of five daughters were born. A great economic depression hit the country, and when the East Texas banks began to collapse in the first ten months of 1930, Tom lost a great deal of money he had set aside for his growing family. Worse than that, foreclosures on older Hamilton holdings locked Tom permanently and hopelessly out of the vast oil income that was beginning to flow from oil production on Hamilton properties in East Texas and Oklahoma.

Today, twenty-five years later, Tom was getting more than just a few minutes rest. It was Sunday, December 7, 1941, and Sunday always meant at least a half-day off for Tom. To make the day even more special, Nettie was cooking cornbread dressing.

"Don't wanna make the Good Lord mad on His day," Tom would say to anyone near him as he spent a few hours doing nothing at all.

"Of course, I can't just do nothin' all day, gotta do somethin' with the family I got," he would say, smiling, winking his left eye, as his open fingers brushed his thin, graying hair up and over his receding hair line.

People knew Tom Hamilton was a hard-working, respectable man, with principles and standards far above most people in his tenant farmer class. He was a 32$^{nd}$ degree Mason, stood a few inches short of six feet tall with a medium frame, and was considered to be a true Gentleman by all those he knew. He had mastered the principles, ethics, and workings of the Freemason fraternity, as well as the moral values needed to be the father of five daughters and two sons. His friends often teased him for having a ridiculous number of daughters in an occupation that sorely needed the help of strong, capable sons. He would smile in his mischievous way, wink, and say "Sons leave you and chase women, just like me and you did. Daughters stay and take care of you when you're old."

Nettie was envied by her four sisters, partly because of her calm nature, and mostly because her cornbread dressing was the best anyone in the Sprague family had ever managed to produce. Her dressing was always the centerpiece of dinner, accompanied by whatever variety of poultry that had been unfortunate enough to die that day. Today, it was duck. Mallard duck. Nine of them, to be exact.

The ducks had been shot by Raymond Wilson and his ten-year-old son the day before. 'Mr. Wilson,' as Nettie and the Hamilton children respectfully called him, had been living with them since his wife had died in '31.

Mr. Wilson and his son had been birding in the reeds and grasses that thrived along on the banks of Lake Guthrie. The natural lake, about three miles southwest of Tahoka, had steep banks surfaced by the sandy Ogallala loam that supported the many tall grasses of the Texas High Plains. The floor of the lake was a shallow bed of limestone, whose origins lay in the time of dinosaurs in warmer, marshier landscapes.

The Panhandle and High Plains were now being invaded by the monsters of another species: the farmers, the speculators, and a host of cast and crew that were picking up the pieces of the farms and families that had been shattered by the decade-long nightmare called "The Dust Bowl." The rains were returning, the farming methods encouraged by the government were being adopted by the few pioneers that remained, and the newcomers renewed the process of changing the ancient grassland into another series of boom towns and boondoggles. Arriving by the thousands, the hungry, eager humans were hastily dispersing in their westward movement along the caprock of the Texas High Plains. These new pioneers, spreading like an invasion of diggers, tillers, and burrowers, had discovered the agricultural potential of the fertile soils that had lain beneath the vast semi-arid grassland prairie for centuries. The flat, treeless plain that Nature had designed in this drought-prone landscape would, once again, turn instantly into a belt of rich, productive farmland with a man, a water well, an irrigation ditch, a tractor, and a plow. With the ditch, the tractor, and the plow came the immediate and urgent need for labor, always more labor, answered quickly by the optimism of the tenants and the desperation of the sharecroppers.

With the industrial advances in farming methods and equipment over the past decade, it was now easier to "strike it rich" along this always westward-moving agricultural front. Better tractors, better plows, and better irrigation methods were luring the Great Depression survivors westward, enticing them to leave their eastern farms and communities and go west, young man, go west, and build your family and win your fortunes in The Promised Land.

Mr. Wilson, taller than Tom with a thin frame, had convinced him the Texas High Plains was a paradise for tenant farmers like themselves. Now that the drought was over, the suffocating, dusty winds had ceased their murderous rampage, and the rich soil was again producing bountiful yields of cotton, wheat, and corn.

Tenant farmers, unlike sharecroppers, usually owned mules and equipment, and lived on the farms they helped maintain. This gave them the ability to work harder and invest in better methods than the sharecropper, who had only labor to devote. Plentiful crops, especially cotton, were there for any and all that came. Pay was good, which meant the tenant's share was high, and living was easy – if you could physically and mentally tolerate the bitter winter wind that often seemed to blow straight down from the North Pole.

"Well, Ray," Tom had said, "I guess we'll just have to go there and try it out. Hopkins County ain't doin' much for us these days."

So, four months ago, on a hot, windless August day, they loaded everything they had onto Mr. Wilson's 1935 Ford truck and left the East Texas home and dried-up farm they had worked on for twenty-five years. They headed west with Mr. Wilson and his son. They found a house with a barn, and negotiated a good share agreement with the landowner, a well-dressed speculator from the East, who happened to be a fellow Freemason and was instantly taken by Tom's infectious trust.

Their new "home" was a few miles east of the Texas Panhandle town of Tahoka. It was a rustic, somewhat under-maintained four-room white clapboard building of questionable construction. Mr. Wilson and his son found the barn to be comfortable and adequate for their means, and Tom squeezed his family of nine into the house, which was immediately christened "The Shack" by his youngest daughter, Juliette.

When Mr. Wilson presented the nine mallard ducks to him the day before, Tom Hamilton instantly knew that cornbread dressing was in his future, and Sunday would be the only day truly worthy of duck and dressing.

*Christmas would be more appropriate*, he mused, *but these mallards are far too small – Canada Geese would be much, much better – but Christmas is still eighteen days away* (he was good at math) *and I am ready for Nettie's cornbread dressing.*

Nettie took the apparently featherless ducks, and inspected them with the scrutiny of a London detective. She grunted a few times when she found a pinfeather, and acknowledged to herself that Mr. Wilson had been without a wife too long. She would try to do something about that when she became more familiar with the Tahoka womenfolk. **HE** must, however, do something about his brazen spitting and unashamed scratching before anything she could do would actually work.

*"Cupid can't do nothin' with stupid,"* she thought, smiling to herself at his expense.

*"And he is so skinny he doesn't have a butt at all, just a flat, straight line that fits a chair perfectly."* She smiled again, shaking her head in mocked disbelief.

*"But, he is a very thoughtful man, and my Tom thinks the world of him, and he is family to us,"* Nettie conceded. *"Besides, he can't help it if these ducks are too small. Times are rough, and this is the best God can do for us this day."*

With the inspection done, she soaked them overnight in saltwater.

That night, she, Tom, and Mr. Wilson had taken the 1935 Ford truck into nearby Lubbock to enjoy a Saturday night outdoor concert, honky-tonk style. A new sound was brewing in the Texas Panhandle and the High Plains, a combination of hill-billy and ballroom music called "Texas Swing." It was being performed by young musicians like Bob Wills, satiating the musical thirst of the hard-working, entertainment-starved depression generation. Tom and Nettie enjoyed a few lively two-step dances as Mr. Wilson politely, visually, and unsuccessfully surveyed the crowd for an unescorted lady. They arrived back home just before midnight, and Nettie checked the soaking ducks one more time. They, like the three tired but well-entertained adults, were tucked in for the night.

Nettie started boiling the ducks Sunday morning in a large dishpan on top of the stove.

The table had been set on the front porch, just narrow enough to allow people to move to and fro around it. The plates and tableware were neatly arranged by Juliette, who enjoyed watching her mother prepare the food, sometimes asking the whys and whats of the process. Nettie would good-naturedly answer her, knowing that being a good cook started long before the need, and that an interest in the food was the foundation of every good cook. Nettie knew that she had that interest, and that her other Sprague sisters did not. Nettie could clearly see that Juliette had more interest than her sisters. She believed that they would all be good cooks – what else could they do? But, they would be good cooks out of necessity. Juliette would be a good cook for the love of cooking.

By noon, all the ducks were cooked, and the cornbread dressing was browned. Green beans and creamed corn had been emptied from canning jars, warmed, and placed into serving bowls. Sourdough bread had been baked, and all was finished. A scrumptious and glorious Sunday afternoon dinner lay before them. (In East Texas lingo, all hot meals served at noon on Sunday were called "dinner.")

The dinner, as usual, began with a prayer of thanks. Tom nodded to Mr. Wilson to do the honor. The Hamilton children preferred that the prayer be offered by their father, who scarcely spoke more than ten words. Mr. Wilson liked to thank the Good Lord for everything, every place, every time, and eventually got around to remembering the reason for the prayer in the first place: the food.

Sitting at the table were Tom and Nettie Hamilton, sons Alfred and Alvis, Juliette, and Mr. Wilson and his son. Juliette's oldest sister, Verna, had been married for a year, and was at home with her husband, Buck Sandifeer. Her other three sisters, Gladys, Maudie, and Arline, were in Dallas, working at Sears & Roebuck.

The Sunday dinner on this partly cloudy, cool December day was flawless. Dessert was a thick, Dutch apple pie, topped with crispy oatmeal, cooked the day before. Much effort had been expended to keep the pie out of sight and out of mind until Sunday's overture. Yet, all could easily see the exact spot where a small, ever-so-neat sliver had been removed, precisely the size and shape of Tom's pocketknife.

When asked about it, Nettie simply smiled.

After dinner, small talk ensued. Mr. Wilson lit a cigar. The boys scurried off to play.

Tom looked at his watch, raised his eyebrows, squinted his eyelids, and nodded his head as if he were confirming an agreement that he and his watch had made. He pushed his chair back, slowly stood up, and brushed some breadcrumbs off his coveralls onto the porch. He raised his left index finger, as if a distinct thought had just entered his mind, and whispered, "Excuse me for just a moment." Turning methodically to his right, and as graciously as a ballet dancer, he opened the screen door and disappeared into the house.

No one wondered where he went. They all knew. If there was one thing Tom did, at least three times a day whenever he was at home, was go into the kitchen, turn on his RCA Victor radio, and listen to the news. If the family was eating inside the house, the rule was strictly enforced: when Tom turned on the radio and the news began, all talking ceased, all unnecessary sounds squelched, and silence reigned.

On this day, even on the porch, the custom was still practiced by the small group of onlookers.

They heard the radio switch go "Pop," and they heard the shrill electric sounds of the wandering dial return to the delicate signal of the NBC affiliate in Lubbock.

What they heard next took the wind from their lungs.

*"From the NBC newsroom in New York: President Roosevelt said in a statement today that the Japanese have attacked Pearl Harbor, Hawaii, from the air. I'll repeat that: President Roosevelt says that the Japanese have attacked Pearl Harbor, in Hawaii, from the air. We will interrupt all programs to give you latest news bulletins. Stay tuned to this station."*

Juliette stared straight into Mr. Wilson's eyes. He quizzically looked toward the door. All was quiet in the kitchen, as well as on the porch. Nettie flinched nervously, and quietly and gracefully pushed her chair away from the cluttered table, stood up, and stepped into the house.

An agonizing minute passed. Mr. Wilson kept his uncertain seat at the table; he set down his cigar, extinguishing it in a small ring of gravy on the edge of his plate. He bent his elbow as if to stand, then relaxed. He looked very, very old. His brown, straight hair had fallen across his brow as he glanced across the dry, caliche yard, saw his son, and grimaced.

*Too young for the Army,* he thought. *Thank God he's too young for the Army. He's all I got. He's all that's left of ... Elizabeth. My God, has it been ten years?*

Juliette stared at the door. Listening. Nothing being said. From the porch she could hear the radio dial being moved by her father's fingers, the noisy static, humming and whizzing, then static again, another whizzing. Then a clear signal.

*"Go ahead, Honolulu."*

*"Several planes have been shot down, and anti-aircraft gunnery is very heavy. All lines of communication seem to be down between the various Army posts. Everyone here in the islands were taken by surprise by the attack, and even yet it's difficult for some people to believe that an air raid on these beautiful islands has actually happened, and that lives have been lost ...... After the attack on Pearl Harbor, several squadrons of Japanese planes came in from the south, dropping incendiary bombs over the city. One bomb dropped in front of the Governor's mansion. Traffic is almost at a standstill. At Pearl Harbor, three ships were attacked. The Oklahoma was set afire. There is great activity there now, in clearing the debris ...... The Governor has proclaimed a state of emergency. The Army has issued orders for all people, the civilian population, to remain off the streets ...... After machine-gunning Ford Island, the first Japanese planes*

*moved to Hickam Field. There were 350 men killed in a direct bomb hit on the barracks at Hickam Field."*

Mr. Wilson pushed his wooden chair back, stood up, and walked toward the barn. Halfway there, he stopped, slowly turned around, and just remained there, hair hanging disheveled across his brow, saying nothing. His right eye twitched, as a December breeze blew across the exposed soil, kicking up curtains of dust. He exhaled a sigh, spat once, drew another breath, and exhaled slowly, much like a whispered whistle. He rubbed his eye. Something in it. Probably some dust. Maybe a tear.

Juliette pushed her chair back, stood up, and moved toward the door, thought again, then turned to her left. She walked in short strides toward the barbed-wire fence that ran down the west side of The Shack. A quick, cool breeze blew her white cotton dress, and she put her arms down to hold it. She reached the fence, extended her right hand, and grasped the fence, avoiding the barbed wire. The cool breeze turned into a gusty, swirling wind. Colder now. She stepped closely against the fence, holding her dress down with one hand, the other still grasping the fence. She stared toward the west, and shook uncontrollably.

"*It's cold*", she said to herself. "*It's cold, and there's a ship on fire out there, way out there, to the west, in the islands. The Hawaiian Islands. They say it's a Tropical Paradise out there. I saw it in a magazine. Paradise? People have died, the radio man said. How many? Did he say three hundred-fifty men? That's like this whole town! The Japanese did it? They're supposed to be harmless – overextended, that's what the radio man said last week.*

*There was a Japanese girl back in Sulphur Bluff, at school. She spoke English. Her father worked at the gas station. How could her people do this? I know she didn't do anything – but what will she do now that They have done this?"*

"What will we do?"

Her troubled, young, innocent, hungry mind continued to question the whys, the whats, and the what ifs.

*"What will ... my friends do, the older ones? Like the Smith boy. No, he's not a boy, he's twenty. What will he do?"*

The wind slowed, sent a shiver through her, and she thought, *"War is sure to come. Men are sure to die. What will we do?"*

She looked west, strained her eyes, saw a sunbeam darting from beneath a cloud, sending a streak across the West Texas sky, highlighting a distant point.

*A farm? A house? A Navy ship on fire?*

*No, just a beautiful sunbeam, a diagonal stream of sunlight, moving from a dark shadowy cloud to the western horizon, down and away, beyond the flat, unbroken horizon.*

Unable to see where the sunbeam actually stopped, she stood there, questioning, wondering, shivering.

"Maybe the sunbeam doesn't stop," she muttered out loud.

"Maybe it goes all the way to Paradise to help those poor, battered men."

"Or, maybe it just goes to some farmer's door, a farmer that has a son, an older son, a ripe, young son-Man, ripe for the Army picking. Maybe the sunbeam is saying it's alright, don't worry. No harm will come to you. You will see him go, and you will see him return."

The wind, warmer now, blew her dress again, and brushed her cheek. She imagined the wind was saying, *"Don't worry, young lady, it isn't the Life that we will take, just the Time. We need to spend a little Time to get things sorted out. Times are ripe for a little misery, a little fear, and a little war. Yes, yes, a little war. That will do it. That will take up some Time. Just a war, another World War."*

She heard the screen door open, and then close with a more-than-usual **clang.**

Her father stood on the porch, her mother behind the door, looking out. Mr. Wilson, standing between the barn and the house, took a step toward Tom, then another. He stopped, spat, looked at Tom, his head to one side, his hair hanging diagonal across his wrinkled brow.

"What're we gonna do, Tom?" he asked, hesitantly, his voice wavering a bit, his knees slightly bent.

Juliette had never heard him talk like that before. Mr. Wilson was always a firm, confident, often cocky man, in control, a Man among Men. Today, right now, he was visibly shaken.

Tom stood there on the porch, pulled out his handkerchief, wiped his face, furrowed his own wrinkled, white brow, and opened his mouth. Nothing came out.

He cleared his throat, and said "President Roosevelt is gonna speak to Congress tomorrow. He's got no other choice. He'll ask Congress to declare war on Japan, and they'll do it. Tomorrow, we're at war, Ray. Tomorrow, we're at war."

They looked at each other.

Juliette approached them, cautiously, watching their every move, their every expression, every sound, and every syllable.

"I guess we better go home, Tom," Mr. Wilson said, sounding a little stronger, pushing his chest slightly outward, and standing straight.

Tom looked to his left, toward the east, toward Sulphur Bluff, 430 miles away.

"Yep. I reckon we better go home."

# CHAPTER 4

# DUTY CALLS

Christmas Eve.
Wednesday, December 24, 1941.

Mount Sterling, Hopkins County, East Texas.

Tom Hamilton, freshly back to Hopkins County from the Texas Panhandle, helped his wife Nettie down from the Ford pickup that Ray Wilson had generously let him use to take his family to the Smith home place. The black truck sported a curved, vertical, oval front grille, skirted fenders, and a laid-back windshield, characteristic of the Ford trucks that dominated the mid-thirties. It had a sleek look that begged for the open road. It was the same truck that had transported Mr. Wilson, his son, the Hamiltons, and all their meager furniture back to East Texas two weeks earlier.

Both sons were in the back of the truck, wrapped in home-sewn quilts to keep out the chilly December air. The quilts were made from patchwork flowers, small circles, butterflies, and random geometric shapes recovered from old faded clothing, and were accentuated with new, brightly colored mill cloth purchased in town. They covered the two Hamilton boys like a holiday wrap. Lying beside them was a stack of freshly cut salt cedar twigs and branches for decoration, a number of them already twisted and tied into several green, aromatic wreaths.

Daddy and Momma were on the porch, with me, my two brothers, my five sisters, and my one nephew, all of us ranging from 22 years old to 8 weeks young.

*"My word,"* Tom Hamilton exhaled through his lips, quietly. *"Bud Smith's family is as big as mine. But, he had one daughter and all his boys first, then the rest of his girls. I had mine bass-ackward. All five girls first, then my two sons, barely able to work. Bud is a lucky bastard."*

"Merry Christmas, Bud, Altie."

"Merry Christmas, Tom, Nettie, kids."

"Sure am glad you made it back here," Daddy exclaimed. "We missed ya this summer. Come on in. Altie baked some tea cakes, and there's a fresh pot of coffee. It's good to see you."

Tom eyed us boys on the porch, exhaled again, and said "It's good to see you young men again, good to see you here at home." He turned and looked at his host.

"Bud, you better keep them here on the farm and outta sight from Uncle Sam."

Daddy looked at me, Noel, and Lester with a proud but somber look and said, "You're right, Tom. Yes, sir, you're right. We're tryin', but time is movin' fast. Ya'll come on in outta the cold. Where are your girls?"

"Verna married one of the Sandifeer boys last year, and is at home. She's about to have our first grandkid. Gladys and Maudie are in Dallas, thinking about their sweethearts. Arline is there with them for a few days in the big city. Those girls sure love the big city."

"Juliette's on her way," Tom said.

"She figured she'd ride in with the Richey boy. He's always riding his horse around the county with somebody. Today it's Juliette."

Tom Hamilton stepped onto the porch and shook hands with Daddy. Nettie, behind her husband, handed Momma two of the cedar wreaths and a jar of preserves. The Hamilton boys, Alfred and Alvis, trailed behind, each carrying an armful of cedar twigs and branches.

"We can make a wreath," young Alfred said.

I opened the door for the group, and smiled broadly as they entered the house. My eyes surveyed each one as they passed, then momentarily locked onto Tom Hamilton's gentle, steel-grey eyes.

"It's good to see you, Horace," Tom acknowledged. "You're still much the Gentleman, and a blessing to your parents."

"It's good to see you, too, Mr. Hamilton. I'm glad you came back from West Texas. It's good to have everyone home again. Especially now."

The front room was soon cozy, filled with fourteen friendly, spirited celebrators exchanging greetings, stories, and Christmas charms, along with the smell of cookies, coffee, and fresh cedar. The couch, two small beds, five wicker chairs, and a deacon's bench were occupied to full capacity. Coats, jackets, and wraps were folded and stacked across a single wooden chair near the door. A five-foot cedar tree stood in the corner, adorned with ornaments made of whittled wood, hammered tin, and a long length of threaded popcorn garland. Two dozen tea cakes, the silver dollar-sized sugar cookies that Momma had baked earlier, had been selectively placed between several large branches of the tree.

The older girls were cooing the baby, Mae, and the Hamilton boys were searching with darting eyes at the dwindling stack of tea cakes on the large table. My two-year old nephew, Darrel, sat on the floor next to Roberta, intently watching everything the Hamilton boys did.

I was leaning back in a wicker chair, legs straight, feet crossed, my arms behind my head, hands interlocked, listening intently as Tom Hamilton was telling the latest war gossip to Daddy. I heard a horse whiney from outside, and stood up as Tom halted his story of Japanese and German misbehavior and announced, "That's prob'ly Juliette. You better go bring her in, Mr. Horace."

I smiled, maneuvered around the many legs between me and the door, and stepped out onto the unpleasantly cold porch.

Jesse Richey, a broad-shouldered lad from the Valley Springs community, had dismounted from his red roan Belgian draft horse gelding, and was helping Juliette down from the double seat saddle that sat atop the muscular horse.

*Son-of-a-bitch bought a double seat saddle, for no other reason than to carry girls around behind him,* I thought as I slowly stepped down the porch steps. *That is one beautiful horse. He has to be at least 17-hands high. Maybe 18-hands. Big for a gelding. You better watch it, Jesse. You may carry the wrong woman behind you someday and find yourself gelded, too.*

"Merry Christmas," I greeted, half of me irritated at the strapping young womanizer and the other half mesmerized by the neatly dressed young girl who now stood beside him.

Juliette had a look of pure joy, an enormous, sparkling smile covering her face, mixed with an intensity of innocence and seduction. She wore a knee-length white dress with small red flowers neatly packed in an almost checkerboard fashion, combined with a dark pink, tightly knit, open front sweater. She was wearing a bright red scarf to keep her neck warm and gently hidden from view. The resulting aura of her presence had driven deeply into my subconscious vigilance, snapping my attention away from the smart-aleck country bumpkin with the single-purpose double seat saddle. My observant male hormones were driven to an unexpected attentive awareness of this newcomer to my world, this visitor that seemed to fall from heaven to stand beside the most obnoxious of mortals, Jesse Richey.

    A few seconds passed. Juliette's young, vibrant, blue eyes met my piercing, captive stare and were held for a moment that seemed to last hours, a warm glow beneath a winter chill, excitement and anticipation wrapped tightly in a red scarf.

    Jesse cleared his throat. "I brought Juliette to the Smith house," the young gladiator in blue denim coveralls declared, his voice breaking the trance, wavering a bit at the conclusion of his brief, unappreciated announcement. He pushed back the wide brim of his brown felt hat and leaned against the roan, right hand on his waist and left hand resting just below his coverall pocket, waiting for some kind of response from the two people locked in what seemed to him to be an eternal stare.

    I kept my eyes on Juliette, stepped toward her slightly, and held out my hand.

    We shook hands briefly.

    "Your Daddy said it would be you," I confessed, an interested smile growing on my face.

"Come on in. You old enough to drink coffee?"

Juliette tossed her head in a baited laugh. "Yes, I am," she teased. "Do you have any?"

I nodded, turned to my side and raised my right arm in a welcome-come-inside gesture, still looking at Juliette.

"Thank you for bringing her, Jesse," I decreed. "Thank you very much. You tell your folks Merry Christmas from the Smiths."

Juliette put her gloved hand on Jesse's left shoulder, lifted her chin, and said, quietly, "Thank you, Jesse, for the beautiful ride. I'll be going inside now, we're having a family gathering this afternoon. Just us and the Smiths. I'll ride home with Momma and Daddy. You have a very Merry Christmas, Jesse."

She patted his shoulder three times, placed a quick kiss on his left cheek, stood motionless for three seconds, then turned abruptly and followed my invitation to go inside.

I followed her motion, could smell her lavender-washed hair as she passed, and gave no further glance to Jesse and the beautiful roan gelding as I escorted Juliette up the porch, toward the door. Opening it, I pushed a few adolescent feet to one side as I made a path into the crowded room for this near apparition called Juliette.

Tom Hamilton stood up, greeted his youngest daughter, and sat back down. He had a remarkable look of contented pride and adoration on his tired, sun-wrinkled face, now saturated by the same enormous, sparkling smile that Juliette had possessed when she had dismounted the red roan.

I pulled out the chair I had abandoned minutes earlier, and offered it to Juliette in a silent nod of concentration and gallantry. She handed me her gloves and sweater, and I gently placed them atop the other winter wraps. She then sat down and draped her scarf elegantly across her knees.

The room was again full of the clatter and happiness of simple, heroic people who shared a common heritage of farming brinkmanship, and now shared a common future of undeterminable events.

As the next two hours passed, another pot of coffee was brewed and then consumed. Time became a fascinating excursion that flurried through the holiday gathering as fast as a stiff wind blowing the dry leaves of winter across a barren field, and as slowly as the studious examination of a newly discovered gemstone in the surprised hand of an exuberant prospector.

When the coffee was almost gone, and the tea cakes had dwindled to a pitiful few, it was time to draw the visit to a close. Pleasantries were exchanged, along with hugs and wishes of Peace on Earth, Good Will Toward Men, This-Night-a-Child-is-Born-Unto-Us, as the Hamiltons boarded the sleek black pickup truck and departed for their home in Sulphur Bluff, seventeen miles to the northeast.

I sat on the couch, slowly twirling my brown ceramic coffee cup in a circle with one finger, as it sat empty on the coffee table that had been given to Momma and Daddy on their wedding day by the large Smith family at Sand Hill. I was deep in thought. I had enjoyed that day with the Hamiltons. This Christmas seemed to be the most important of my life. Things were all mixed up. The war against the Japanese. The war against the Germans. My family. The unexpected reverie induced by the presence of an unexpected new addition to my thoughts.

A memory returned to my befuddled mind, faintly at first, then materialized into cognizance.

*Was it last summer? Naw, it was the summer before. The baseball game at Flora. Yes, yes. The time I won the game by scoring on Noel's hit in the bottom the ninth. She was there, jumping, and cheering, and winking.*

I laughed to myself.

*She winked at me.*

I remembered being mesmerized by the big, broad smile on her face, and the way she stood there, sassy, with body language much older than her years. And I remembered her eyes, those playful, penetrating eyes.

*Who is this young daughter of Tom Hamilton? Why did she just appear from nowhere again? Why is she so young? Why am I so old?*

Momma was cleaning up the cups and dishes in the sink. She walked in from the kitchen and asked me if I wanted the last bit of coffee in the pot. I nodded, mouthed the words *Yes, thank you* on my lips.

As she poured coffee into my cup, she spoke softly, "Juliette sure was pretty today, wasn't she? She's only thirteen, you know. The Panhandle must've brought out the bloom in her."

I sheepishly looked up at her and confided, "Yeah, Momma. She's somethin'. Rode up here on that horse with Jesse Richey."

Momma smiled, and made a quiet, affirmative sound as she walked back into the kitchen with the empty, blue graniteware enamel coffee pot.

"She's somethin'," I repeated, nodding my head, halfway to myself, halfway to God.

*"She's really somethin'."*

Monday, February 16, 1942.

Hopkins County, Texas.

    The sound of the Ol' Blue's hooves striking the crushed rock surface of Highway 19, ***clip-clap-clip-clop, clip-clap-clip-clop***, was the only sound that accompanied the wagon that held me and Daddy as it slowly drifted toward Sulphur Springs. It was early Monday morning, and the shadows of the lone mule, wagon, and two passengers stretched their lengthy pattern across the dry road ditch on the right.
    ***Clip-clap-clip-clop, clip-clap-clip-clop.***
    We sat, heads slightly down, shoulders slightly stooped, as the wagon moved southward down the quiet, East Texas road. We rode past the bottomlands along Horse Pen Creek first, then White Oak Creek, as each one of us looked down the creek beds to see what was stirring in the dark, wet willows. Slowly, as we left the bottomland and the mule carried us to higher ground, the silence began giving way to the usual spatter of Monday morning traffic.
    Daddy and I had left the house a little after sunrise that morning, answering the call that the United States government had issued a month earlier. It was the "Third Registration" of the Selective Training and Service Act, issued to men between the ages of 20 and 45 to appear at their respective Draft Boards to register for possible military service during the three-day period February 14-16, 1942.
    I was 20 years old.

Daddy was 42 years old.

Our pace was slow that morning. Too much to think about. It was almost 9:30 when we finally reached the brick streets of Sulphur Springs. We passed the First Methodist Church on our right, then entered the town square, approaching the Hopkins County Courthouse straight ahead, slightly left. Standing near the northeast corner of the town square, the Romanesque pink granite and red sandstone masterpiece stood as a proud reminder that Sulphur Springs was a bustling city of traders, financiers, farmers, dairymen, and, today, earnest, able-bodied men willing to answer the call of conscription and cast their lot on the good judgment of Local Draft Board Number 1.

I directed Ol' Blue to a shady spot near the Courthouse, beneath a towering magnolia tree, hopped down from the wagon seat, took the reins, and tied them loosely around a hitching rail. Daddy gently stepped down from the wagon seat, a little stiff from the ride, and glanced toward the Courthouse.

A line of perhaps 20 men was positioned at the southwest door, one of the two entrances to the massive building. As we situated ourselves in the rear of the line, I momentary looked to my right, saw the small rectangular service door that led to the basement, and smiled.

*There's the door,* I thought to myself. *There's the door to my private sleeper. That basement has always been good to me, my shelter from the rain, from the cold, my home away from home. I wonder what waits for me on the first floor of this castle?*

Daddy grunted, spat on the new grass that had decided winter was over, and looked at the line of gentlemen working their way up the modest steps to the semi-circle porch. They were moving briskly, no one talking to the other, just merging their unadorned, down-to-earth lives with the unknown, who-knows-where possibilities of Uncle Sam.

I looked at him and said "There's nothing to worry about, Daddy, I told you. It's me they want. You've got a wife and five daughters at home. They want you staying on the farm to feed the Army, or move to town and build airplanes or make bullets."

The thought of Daddy making airplanes or bullets suddenly moved like a wave of sickness through me.

*He better stick to farming. Airplanes have to fly, and bullets have to shoot.*

He looked at me, his oldest son, a wave of pride moving through him.

"Yeah, I know."

There was a glimmer of a tear, the rapid blinking of an eye, and he looked again at the line of men moving up the steps to the porch.

"I hope they have coffee in there."

"We'll go to the donut shop across the street after we leave here. We'll each get a cup of coffee and one of Mr. Phillip's best donuts. It'll make you sick, I know, and you know, but you'll eat it anyway," I told him, my lips a thin smile.

Daddy grunted, spat again, and nodded.

It was a big day for the both of us.

I was putting my name on a list like a juicy bait worm on a hook, twisting and twirling in front of the Big Fish, the one that takes it off the hook and is never seen again.

Daddy was registering as a back-up should things go horribly sour, if the two wars sucked up all the nation's youth in a bitter and not-so-guaranteed struggle for freedom. He knew, deep down in the all-knowing mind of his gut, that the only way he would be called was if the strong young man beside him was already lying in a ditch somewhere far away, the last full measure of heart and soul stripped from him by the devil himself.

As I watched him, I could see a chill run through him as he followed me up the steps up to the makeshift table in the portico.

A broad-shouldered gentleman, seated behind the table, looked up and said, "Good morning, Sir. I am C. A. Hoover, with Hopkins County Local Draft Board Number 1. Could I have your full name, please?"

I leaned forward and answered in a clear, brisk voice, "Horace Garlton Smith."

# CHAPTER 5

# UNCLE SAM WANTS YOU

Wednesday, July 29, 1942.

Mount Sterling, Hopkins County, East Texas.

My Momma fingered the small, legal-sized envelope the postman had personally delivered that afternoon. It was addressed to me, Horace Garlton Smith, RFD 1 Mount Sterling, Sulphur Springs, Texas. The return address was the Local Draft Board Number 1, Sulphur Springs, Texas.

Daddy, Noel, Lester, and I were walking up the narrow, sandy trail that led from the road to the house, coming home after a day of chopping cotton near Mahoney.

Each of us had a hoe propped against our shoulder, like marching infantry at shoulder arms. We were proud of those implements, each with longer handles and heavier, wider blades than the usual garden hoe, and more designed to removing the pigweed that grew between the rows of summer cotton. We were professional laborers, real honest-to-goodness cotton pickers, and our hoes were the tools of our grueling trade. Always hand-sharpened with a large metal file, a good chopping hoe would make the long rows less intimidating as you rounded the edge of a quarter-section and looked down the next half-mile row, like a condemned Texas prisoner looking down the long, haunting, lonely hallway to Ol' Sparky. East Texans had long ago adopted the phrase "another long row to hoe" to describe any dreaded, difficult task or misfortune that fate or Providence had sent your way.

It was hard work, getting the cotton manicured and ready for picking in a month or two. It took concentration, too. You had to know the exact difference between the young, vulnerable cotton plant and the several dozen weeds that Nature had allowed to grow in the newly plowed ground.

We leaned our hoes against the porch rail, looked up at the house, and stumbled up the steps in single file. Daddy opened the door, and we three entered, youngest to oldest, Lester, Noel, and me, in that order. Daddy saw Momma's face, the flat look of nothingness in her eyes, and the envelope. He silently grimaced, with a half-thought, *Me? They want me?*

I had seen it, too. I walked up to her, held out my hand, and took the letter as she released it from her tight grip.

"Well, well," I said, sarcastically. "Fan mail."

I walked to the kitchen table, sat down on one end of the deacon's bench, and, holding the letter in my left hand, slowly ran my right thumb along the seal on the backside of the envelope. I removed the tri-folded letter, spread it out, and stared at the Selective Service System seal at the top center of the very, very official-looking correspondence.

My eyes and lips relayed the message to my family:

**"ORDER TO REPORT FOR INDUCTION**
**The President of the United States**, *To HORACE GARLTON SMITH*
**Greeting:**
*Having submitted yourself to a Local Board composed of your neighbors for the purpose of determining your*

*availability for training and service in the armed forces of the United States, you are hereby notified that you have now been selected for training and service in the ARMY ON AUGUST 7, 1942.*

*You will, therefore, report to the Local Draft Board at Sulphur Springs, Texas at 11:00 a.m. on the 7th day of August, 1942 for instructions."*

The room was quiet. Lester snorted, the dust in his nose forcing a guttural sneeze that interrupted the stillness. Noel's eyes opened wide, he drew in a breath, and slowly exhaled, "Well, I'll be god-darned, Red."

Momma stared at me, her hazel eyes wet, her heart screaming in distress.

Daddy walked over to the table, put his hand on my back, and whispered, "God be with you, son."

I looked up at Daddy, who was now staring out the window, out there, where the wind is free, and the air is clean, where the shade trees grow. I looked at my two brothers.

"I believe this is just the beginning," I said, matter-of-factly.

I stood up, walked over to Momma, put a hand on each of her upper arms, looked calmly into her worried eyes, and whispered "You'll be okay, don't worry," then said, aloud, "What's for supper, Momma?"

The spell was broken. The family was doing what it had always done.

It was time to eat.

Sunday, August 16, 1942.

Sulphur Bluff, Hopkins County, Texas

    I stood on Tom Hamilton's front porch, adjusting the belt on my khaki dungarees, making sure my yellow, broadcloth shirt was neatly tucked. I had ridden the mule-drawn wagon the 17-mile journey from home to Sulphur Bluff, and had barely knocked on the screen door when an angel appeared, a bright, full smile on her face.
    Juliette Hamilton opened the screen door and stepped onto the porch, moving swiftly, more like a cat than a fourteen-year old girl.
    "Why, Red Smith, what are you doing here on a Sunday afternoon?"
    I picked up on her tease, and answered, "I came over to see the Hamiltons. How many of them are here?"
    "Five of us. My sisters are gone to town to see their sweethearts or something. They do that on Sunday. How come you're not with your sweetheart today?"
    *How do you know I'm not?* I thought to myself.
    She smiled, raising her shoulders in an inquisitive gesture. Her smile was infectious, her voice a siren song that could, as far as I was concerned, go on and on forever, that's OK with me.
    "That's not important now. I'm being drafted and was told by the Draft Board to get on the bus to Dallas this Thursday and start basic training, and I wanted to tell you folks bye, and wish you well for the harvest."
    Her smile dampened, a darkness spread over her face, like a September rain. I had never seen a sad angel, except

that one at the cemetery that hovered over a lost love, head bowed, and hands clasped together in an eternal prayer, one marble eye weeping a mineralized tear that seemed to drip onto her sculpted forearm. She, like Juliette, was still the loveliest lady I had ever seen, even in sadness, even in stone.

"I know about that, it's the talk of the town. I was hoping I could say bye, and I'm happy you came over here in person to tell us all bye. I went to the baseball game yesterday, but you weren't there, so I just came back home."

"Yeah, I sat that one out. Couldn't muster up the hankerin' to play ball. Just rode the wagon into town, caught a movie, and went home. You know that mule of ours knows the way home?" I chuckled.

"You just loosen the reins down to where they're a little taut, tie them down, stretch out in the back, and sleep. When you hear the hooves stop clompin', you're home. Unhitch him, put him in the barn with some hay. It's done. Ol' Blue is somethin'."

She watched me tell my story, my enthusiasm in describing the details, my broad smile at the conclusion, followed by a series of rapid laughs. She, too, laughed, raising her shoulders in a little girl giggly way, and then looked at me with her infinitely attentive blue eyes.

"After you've gone, I want to write you. Can I?"

"Swell, I would like that."

A woman's voice from inside the screen door inquired, "Juliette, who's that?"

The angel looked away, toward the door, and answered, "It is Red Smith, Momma. He came to tell us bye."

She looked back, and I saw the promise of a woman behind those eyes, those playful, happy eyes. They penetrated my mind, raising a flag and a hope, and seemed to be saying *I will not always be this young. And you, Sir, will not always be that old.*

*Why are you not with your sweetheart this fine Sunday, this last Sunday before you leave?*

*Maybe I am, little girl. Maybe I am.*

Nettie appeared at the door, her hair pinned up, her apron tight against her not-so-small, not-too-large frame. Her grey eyes looked at me through the screen door.

"Come in off the porch, Red. Come in for a glass of tea."

"Thank you kindly, Mrs. Hamilton. Juliette?" I queried, my arm outstretched toward the open door.

"Thank you kindly, Mr. Smith," she responded, with a slight incline of her head, a nod, and an amusing, tantalizing sparkle in her eye. She danced inside the door. I followed.

We talked for the better part of an hour, about cotton, chickens, families, dust storms, tornadoes, and rain. Tom Hamilton had ventured in ten minutes into the conversation, and gave me his usual firm, friendly handshake, his eyes sparkling like Juliette's, only older, wiser, a world of knowledge swirling behind bushy eyebrows and two-day old stubble. He had piddled around the barn all day – no work, mind you, no work at all. After all, today is Sunday, and you wouldn't want to work on the Lord's Day, no, Sir.

The conversation drifted, and I seemed to float in and out of it, holding my own, keeping my concentration on the here and now, while helplessly watching Juliette tease her hair, rub her itchy ankle, or watch for empty glasses to refill. She seemed to glow, then darken, then glow again, with the intensity of a hot summer sun, then with the soft moon glow of a windless, autumn night.

I looked around the room once, and noticed a nice painting of Jesus praying, leaning against a rock, a light around his head. There was a lot of blue and purple around him, like it must've been late at night.

"I like that picture," I nodded.

"It's peaceful, and friendly to the eyes."

Juliette beamed.

Mr. Hamilton beamed back, a perfect replica of Juliette's smile.

"I got that from one of Juliette's shopping sprees in the Sears catalogue," he laughed.

"It is Jesus at the Garden of Gethsemane, praying for the courage to face what was ahead of him. Much like boys all around us will be doing soon."

He cleared his throat and looked solemnly at me.

"I don't mean to be despondent, Mr. Horace. Forgive me. I know there is a lot on your mind."

I nodded, looked at Juliette while she observed her father with loving affection, and said, "No offense, Mr. Hamilton. I imagine I'll be doing exactly what Jesus is doing up there at Geth-se-man-ee."

We all laughed, as friends and loving families laugh.

I told them about me and Daddy going down to register with the Draft Board on February 16, and Mr. Hamilton nodded his head and said that he had registered on April 27, when the Fourth Registration was ordered.

He calmly smiled, blinked his eyes slowly as he often did while conversing, sighed, and said, "At the ripe old age of forty-seven, I was. I'll be ready to help you boys out if it gets down to that."

We all laughed, as I interestingly compared the way his face lit up with his eyes sparkling just like Juliette's. I felt like I could stay there the rest of my life, wondering how I had missed all of this for all these years.

"I'll tell you," he continued, "I had registered for the Draft back in '17 for the Great War, and I still, to this day, don't know how I got out of that one. I was 22 years old, a young man like you, Horace, and Nettie and I had been married for less than a year. No children. Just a farmer."

He chuckled, "And not a very good farmer. Maybe they thought I would become a good farmer pretty soon, or maybe they thought I was still too fresh from the hobo-jungle and couldn't be trusted."

He laughed heartily at those words, and the rest of us joined in.

"I am glad you made it around that horrible war, and was able to start the wonderful family you have, Mr. Hamilton," I said, as I looked directly at Juliette.

He nodded to me, and smiled.

He and I talked about receiving our questionnaires from the Selective Service System, and filling them out. I told him that shortly after mailing mine back to them, I was ordered to appear for my physical examination. Mr. Hamilton said that was as far as his went.

"A few weeks after mailing my questionnaire back to them, Horace, I got a notice that said I was classified III-B, a farmer with a wife and seven kids depending on him," he said with a gentle, contagious laugh that filled the room.

"Well, Sir," I responded, "Mine picked up the pace at that point and things started happening quickly. I took the physical on July tenth, and a week or two later they told me I was classified I-A, a young man ready for the Army."

We all laughed again, but with a little reserve.

"By the end of July I got my 'Greetings Letter,' telling me to report for duty on August seventh. A few days later, though, another letter came in telling me that I would be sworn in that day, and would have to come back on the twentieth to catch the bus and leave for basic training. That will be this Thursday."

I carefully watched everyone's face. They were all listening to me intently, with feelings of pride and worry, mixed with a quiet sadness, clearly shown on their faces.

Juliette was wearing her sad angel face again, as she leaned forward, looked toward her father, and said, "That's coming up in just a few days. Do you think we should say a prayer, Daddy? Please?"

Mr. Hamilton, nodding his head and wiping his receding hairline with his hand, focused his tired grey eyes on her and gently said, "Of course we can, Juliette."

We held our hands out, grasped each other's to form a tight circle, and I listened to the words of the wisest, gentlest, most compassionate and respectable man I had ever known, as Tom Hamilton said a prayer for my protection, for my blessings, for my peace, courage, and patriotism, and for my safe return back home, in Christ's name we pray, Amen.

A quiet, sweet hush fell over the room. The kind of hush that makes you feel warm and safe, and you wish Life could always be that way.

"Thank you," I said, my voice choked with emotion.

I believe I fell in love with the Hamiltons that day.
I looked up at the small clock on the mantle.
Four-thirty.
Time to head on back.
Sunday night dinner at home.

I stood up. Soft goodbyes were said, warmed by the feel of an angel's hand in mine, a woman's hug by Mrs. Hamilton, and another firm, friendly handshake by Mr. Hamilton. The Hamilton boys, Alfred and Alvis, nodded and waved, impressed by my age and the fact that I was going to be A SOLDIER.

From the road, I looked back. Juliette was on the porch, waving, smiling, sending signals I could not accurately translate, signals that tumbled in my mind and hinted that when I came back *(IF I came back)* things and people might be quite a bit different.

I waved.

She waved back.

I clicked my tongue, and Ol' Blue filled the late shadows with his familiar **clip-clap-clip-clop, clip-clap-clip-clop.**

*There's a good supper waiting at home.*
*Maybe she will write.*


Thursday, August 20, 1942.

Mount Sterling, Hopkins County, East Texas.

It was 5:00 in the morning. Sunrise was still almost two hours away.

Momma stood on the front porch, her hands tucked inside the pockets of her blue apron, her eyes filled with tears that could not stop, would not stop. Beside her stood my four sisters, one of them holding baby Mae, my young nephew Darrell, and my two brothers, wearing long faces and wet eyes. They knew that my departure would leave a hole in the Smith Bridge where the moral compass had been. Noel could be tough, and Lester could be loud, but the real Daddy in this family was going away - going to the Army.

Momma watched. At the end of the narrow, sandy trail that led from the house to the road, Daddy and I sat down in the wagon. Ol' Blue was hitched to the front, pointed toward town, pointed toward infinity.

I removed the knapsack from my left shoulder and placed it in my lap, raised my right arm, and said, with the hint of a lump in my throat, "Ya'll take care. I'll be back."

Daddy clicked his tongue, jostled the reins, and the mule began the familiar **clip-clap-clip-clop, clip-clap-clip-clop** that had accompanied us every trip into town since Time began. I sat in the passenger seat this time, not wanting to be the one to tell Ol' Blue to take me down the road. I took the knapsack from my lap, placed it behind me in the wagon, leaned back, legs straight, feet crossed, arms crossed on my chest, and stared ahead.

I looked at Ol' Blue, trudging along, carrying us into town.

*You always go where we ask, don'tcha'.*

*Where are you taking me today, Ol' Blue? Out there somewhere? To a turkey shoot? To the Germans? To the Japanese?*

*You're the best mule in the world, feller, you have served us well. We have depended on you day in and day out, and you don't even belong to us. Daddy has been borrowing you from Granma Smith for as long as I can remember.*

I looked at Daddy, holding the reins, staring ahead, down the road.

*You don't own anything, Daddy. Not a darn thing. Not a horse, a mule, a house, nothing.*

The only dog we ever had was Sport, and he just wandered up one day, us kids liked him, petted him, fed him, and he decided to stay. I don't know why he stayed around us, we were so poor.

*He was the best dog in the world, just like you, Blue.*

He would follow us kids out to play, and then sit down and watch, all day long, protecting us from anything that might harm us.

I slowly shook my head and chuckled.

Granma had a horse a couple of years ago, a young stallion that could run as fast as the wind, and would go anywhere you wanted him to go. I loved to borrow that horse and ride like a real Hollywood cowboy. I had seen the movies where Tim Holt or Tom Mix would lean in the saddle at full speed and pick something off the ground. One day my hat blew off, and I rode back for it, reached down, and fell flat on by back, tumbling and eating dirt. The good horse stopped and came back to me, and nudged me with his nose. I was in bed several weeks, and still have a sore back that comes and goes.

I watched Ol' Blue make his way in the darkness to the right side of the oil-dirt road, staying on a straight path, black tail flicking with each successive round of hoof-and-hardpan clatter. The buggy seemed to squeak more today than ever before. Perhaps it, too, was bidding farewell to a regular member of the road crew.

I needed small talk - anything - desperately needed something to take away the deafening silence of the pre-dawn cotton patches along the road, to keep the funeral pall of Ol' Blue's ***clip-clap-clip-clop, clip-clap-clip-clop,*** from driving me insane.

"Looks like it'll be another hot summer, Daddy," I said aloud.

"Looks like the hoeing won't be too bad, if it rains a little."

Daddy, aroused from his similar dungeon of thought, looked out at the dark shapes in the landscape as if he had just seen them for the first time.

"Yeah, that's right."

"You make sure Lester drinks enough water, Daddy. He's bad about waitin' til he's almost stroked before he starts drinkin'."

Daddy nodded.

"You, too," I said.

The mule continued down Road 1537 without being coaxed. I smiled at Ol' Blue.

*"He's somethin',"* I admired.

Head down, the mule carried man and son toward Sulphur Springs, one to leave and one to return home. The conversation continued. Cotton. Food. Baseball. Music. Summer. Rain.

War was mentioned, but not much.

I talked about the times I had spent at the CCC camps, about the work, the friends, and the experiences of being well-fed and well-slept. I had spent one year in Colorado and one year in Arizona. Together, they completed my two-year hitch, the maximum you could spend with the Three-Cs. I was paid thirty dollars a month, with twenty-five dollars going back home and five dollars being mine to keep.

In Colorado, we were working at Rocky Mountain National Park, in the Grand Lake area. We did the long-needed maintenance for trails, roads, and buildings, and helped modernize the Park.

In Arizona, I worked at Tucson Mountain Park. We improved roads, built a scenic overlook, and constructed an amphitheater. We made barriers to prevent soil erosion, and built dams, picnic areas, and covered shelters. At Saguaro National Park we built trails and picnic areas.

As I talked, Daddy listened. He would occasionally nod, and grunt a sound of agreement, of understanding, of admiration.

I spoke of the Rockies, the cool nights, the mountain pines, the cold water that came out of the springs and ran down the rivers toward both oceans, the Continental Divide, the tiny, fragile grass of the tundra, and the snow.

I spoke of the desert, the parched air, the dry musk smell of the night, the tall cactus with out-stretched arms, the many colors of the sunsets, the way the thunder would sound between barren mountains, and the sweet rain.

He looked at me, and his eyes narrowed a bit.

I felt like I could hear his thoughts....

*You never saw the jungle, son. There are mountains and pines and snow in Germany, there are deserts and sand dunes and dust storms in North Africa, but there are swamps and vines and rain in the Pacific. Which one are you gonna see?*

….I talked about the money I would be sending home.

"You'll need it, and I'm sure Noel and Lester will be joining up soon. This is a big change, Daddy, but we're all comin' back."

"I swear, we're all comin' back. They'll be more changes after that, but, God-willing, we'll all be here. And, when we're all here again, it'll be alright."

Daddy nodded, looked at me with proud, suddenly old eyes, and mouthed the word *Yes*. No sound, just dry breath.

He reached under his seat, lifted a quart mason jar of water, removed the lid, and drank. Handing it to me, he nodded again. I took the jar, nodded back, and drank the sweet well-water from home. Taking the lid from Daddy's stiff, baseball-broken fingers, I gently closed the jar and returned it to its cubbyhole beneath the driver.

I remembered the hot, dry summer we had seen a few years back, when most of the cattle tanks and streams had dried along with many of the hand-dug wells, including ours.

*What we would have given for a nice cool drink from a mason jar like that,* I said to myself.

I reflected on the hardship we went through the last couple of weeks during that hot, dry summer, when the only reliable water was in an old cotton gin pool near Sulphur Bluff. Every day we would visit the pool and bring back several five-gallon buckets of water. The water level kept falling as two dozen families collected the scarce water, until one day we started seeing tiny squiggly worms swimming in the water as we kept going deeper. We would boil the water at home, then filter it through cheesecloth. A couple of days later, the word spread that someone had seen what appeared to be the body of a dead cow beneath the murky waters of the pool. All water dipping immediately stopped, as the entire community exhaled a collective hiss.

God was merciful to us, though. Before we could even start gagging at the very thought of drinking that water, a monsoon of rain fell across Hopkins County and raised our well water just enough to get us through the drought and into the winter season.

"Remember that dry spell, the gin pool, and the squiggly worms?" I asked Daddy.

A small hiss came out of his throat.

"If I live to be a hundred, I'll never forget that."

A gagging sound came out of his throat.

"Folks hadn't oughtta live like that," he swore.

I smiled.

Daddy never could take anything the least bit sickening. We could always make him gag with sickening stories. It was our way of getting back when his practical jokes got a little out of control.

*Problem is,* I thought, *that squiggly worm story makes me a little sick, too.*

**Clip-clap-clip-clop, clip-clap-clip-clop.**

The next hour was silent. The quarter moon was low in the eastern sky as the horizon behind it was beginning to take on a faint grey glow, reminding us that the August sun would soon rise, on schedule and hot.

I thought about a night back in the mid-thirties, I guess I was about fourteen years old. Uncle Lee Herron, Momma's brother, had the first house in Tira to get electricity, and he had a light bulb in the front room. It was just a single light bulb on the end of a long wire, and a string hanging down to turn it on and off. We all went over there one night, just to sit in the front room and look at the light. It was so modern to have light inside the house when it was dark outside!

When it was time to go home and we all went outside, we could barely see. We learned early you should not stare at it!

Uncle Lee operated the cotton gin in Tira, and had strung the electric line from the gin to his house. I smiled as I remembered Roberta and Noel trying to figure out a way to bring the line all the way to our house.

There was just enough light now to examine the Hopkins County landscape as it flowed past the mule-drawn wagon. The rolling hills, the flat floodplains, the dark bottomlands, the farmlands. The Land of Home. A barn. A farm. A school. A ballpark.

I saw a group of tall pecan trees that surrounded a clearing where a house had once stood. The house was now just a jumbled-up pile of barn wood with a single, lonely brick chimney. It stood like a headstone, keeping a timeless vigil where a family had once laughed and cried, babies had been born, some stillborn, and old people had died. Nature was taking back what the grown children did not want.

Further down the hardpan dirt road, a windmill stood motionless in the early morning coolness, waiting to pump water into a galvanized metal cistern, surrounded by a sleepy half-dozen dairy cattle knowing they would need relief from the not-yet-risen sun. Buzzards would soon sail in circles high overhead, looking for the carcasses of last night's roadkill.

Through the faint light, I saw a single Bois d'arc tree, dripping with green, bumpy horse apples, a dozen lying beneath it, oozing their sticky, bitter, milky juice. A dozen more were being held by the strong, hard wood of its twisted branches. I had never seen a horse actually eat the fruit of what some called the Osage Orange, but had seen squirrels breaking into them for seeds. It mostly served as a hedge plant, and my teacher had told me that the trees were probably from a time long, long, ago, when giant mammoths ate them, spreading the seeds across the lush, ancient plains. I had seen a mammoth tusk in the Denver museum when I was with the CCC, and often wondered what Hopkins County looked like back then.

As we approached Highway 19 in the distance, I looked down the thick, dark bottomland of one of the many creeks that fed into White Oak Creek. The tangled overgrowth that protected the narrow waterway was stifling, thick and ankle-grabbing. It smelled of rotting wood and black, oozing clay, especially now, in the stagnant morning air. Brown, rotten water flowed down hundreds of these soggy water courses between every farm and settlement in Hopkins County. These snake-infested ribbons of darkness intercepted every road and trail that cut across the county.

I smiled, fought back a giggle, as I remembered the many times we had played "Banter," the silly, frightening game that boys would play to prove who was the bravest, and who was the scaredy-cat. It had to be night-time, before the moon would rise, and often the chilly nights of October were the better nights. Windy nights were the best, when the howl of the wind and the moan coming from the trees would make your skin crawl, like the devil himself was out there, down there, in those dark, mushy bottoms. We would all gather along the dirt road, the stars above the narrow lane barely giving enough light to see each other. Several hundred feet away from a bridge that crossed one of these nightmarish gullies, we would determine who would be chosen to experience the terror of Bantering the demons of darkness. The chosen boy would run down the road to the bridge, stop, and gaze directly into the darkness. He would then scream at the top of his lungs,

"Rawhide and Bloody Bones! Come and get me!"

He would then stand there for as long as he could. The rest of us would watch, afraid, jittery, amused, terrified at the slightest sound or rustling from the bottoms below.

True bravery did not require that you stand there very long. Often, just a few moments at the Bridge of Hell were all that was necessary to be baptized by the Fire of Courage. Some of us could not do it. The oldest ones could. I did it once. Maybe twice. Banter was the one game that took us to the edge of sanity, to places where God just might not be at work on that particular night.

We believed, deep in the darkest corners of our hearts, that there was always the smallest chance that ol' Bloody Bones would actually walk out of that muck and snatch the arrogant little bastard that had challenged him to do just that.

*"Gotcha, you loudmouthed bastard!"*

Later on in the night, after the moon had risen and the challenge had been screamed across the bridge several times and no demons had appeared, we would move on down the road. Having bathed our souls and testosterone in enough fear, we could almost smell it on our clothes.

I laughed to myself as I remembered the first time Noel had been chosen to be the Banter-Boy. I had immediately told the others "Not tonight. Choose someone else," I knew that Noel was a little bit more skittish than all the others, and my big-brother responsibility was to protect what was mine. The second time he was picked, which was about a year later, I protested a bit, could see the tremble in Noel's eyes, and then felt the firm *"It's okay, I can do it"* in the way his hand brushed against mine as I reached to touch his shoulder.

I swear, he ran down the two hundred feet to the bridge as fast as I had ever seen him run! Before he got to the bridge, he started screaming, "Rawhide and Bloody Bones...," and then said no more as he immediately began running back, even faster than before, to the safety of the flock.

"I heard something down there!" he whispered between short, desperate breaths.

We laughed and laughed, enough to make it hard to breath. We gave him credit for the try, and teased him a little. We then called the "Banter" finished for the night, turned around, and walked away from the bridge. I believe each one of us looked back over our shoulders at least once as we walked, just in case the "thing" Noel had heard was following us, with wet footsteps being muted by the howl of the wind and moan coming from the trees, our skins crawling with innocent fear.

**Clip-clap-clip-clop, clip-clap-clip-clop.**

My eyes scanned the barbed wire fences along the dirt road, between the cotton fields that stood tall and proud, with round, bulging boles beginning to show an explosion of puffy white fibers. Some of the barbed wire strands were tightly nailed to their short cedar posts, and others were hanging limp in sections where nails had fallen out through the years.

I noticed the fence that ol' Sam Hathaway had strung, a year after the stock market crashed in '29. The fence was a long, tangled web of bailing wire, barbed wire, and small tools. It was almost a solid pattern of disarray, some wire sticking wickedly outward, some wire so densely tightened it looked like dimpled sheet metal. It ran almost a hundred feet along the north side of the road. They said ol' Sam went crazy that year, and could be seen laughing to himself, sitting there along the road, weaving his wiry web of insanity. He would raise his arms into the air at passers-by, sometimes greeting them, sometimes telling them to get the hell off his road. They said he tried to weave a dead cat into it one day, but the Sheriff coaxed him into letting him take it on down the road to bury it.

"Give him a nice Christian burial," ol' Sam told the Sheriff as he was loosening the wire.

He had extended his fence in this crazy way until he died in '35. He just keeled over and died, right there on the roadside. Some say he ate some poison, others say God just gave him a rest from the demons in his troubled mind.

Afterwards, nobody wanted to tear the fence down. They all said don't bother it, the johnson grass and the hackberry elms would cover it someday. But, the johnson grass and the hackberry elms never did grow around it. Nothing would grow along that insane stretch of fence. There it still stood as we drifted by in our early morning wagon, a senseless monument to a broken mind.

Some say they can still hear ol' Sam laughing and cursing as they pass the fence along that stretch of the road on a dark, moonless night.

I never heard anything of the such.

I never walked by there at night.

I never had the nerve to play "Banter" around that fence, either.

*Clip-clap-clip-clop, clip-clap-clip-clop.*

Soon the mule, the wagon, and the two of us made the left turn onto Highway 19, the morning light beginning to rule the sky now. We were near the site of old town Tarrant, where the Hopkins County seat was first located in the 1800s. Floods and the bypassing railroads had shrunk the town to a few houses by the 1900s, and it was now very hard to see where a bustling town had once stood. I remembered the same teacher that told me about the bois d' arc trees had spoken about old town Tarrant, and about the gristmill, the blacksmith shop, the college, the brick oven, the general store, the tannery, and the Hopkins Hotel. I stared across the landscape and could not see anything from old town Tarrant as we approached Horse Pen Creek first, then White Oak Creek. I wondered how Time would treat my own landscape, the one I was leaving behind. I wondered if, someday, somehow (if I survived this war), my own son would ride this same road and stare across the same areas of old Tarrant, and of Mount Sterling, and Mahoney, and Tira, and Dike, and Flora, and Valley Springs, and Sulphur Bluff, and marvel at how hard it is to see where bustling towns once stood. I thought of Time as a moving eraser, wiping out the trace of everything old. Little by little, it would replace the whole kit and caboodle with a fresh, clean slate for a touch of something new.

*Oh, I want to come back here, and find everything the same,* I said to myself.

*The same? Do I want it to be the same? Maybe not.*

*Some things must change, they always do. Daddy will be old. I will be old. My sons can't be born here, if they are born at all. They must be born out there, somewhere, and by who?*

*Everything I leave behind me, all of it, the land and the people, will change. The jobs will move, the towns will die, and Time will change us all.*

*Lord, help me change with Time. Take care of this family, Lord, let them and me change with Time and live through the days that are ahead of us.*

I stared ahead, and felt neither sadness nor pity. Rather, I felt alive and excited. This WAS the change, and the Good Lord would not take it all away without purpose. Time was still on my side, and would be as long as … I… stayed… alive.

A red fox ran across the road. Daddy and I grunted.

*Chicken thief,* I surmised.

*That's OK. So am I. Good luck, little thief. Feed the family. Try Mr. Davis's place. I'll give you my share now.*

An eastern meadowlark whistled its sweet, lazy morning song as it sat atop a cedar fencepost, displaying its bright-yellow belly, a black chevron emblazed across its chest. It continued to sing as we passed, never missing a note as the mule, wagon, and the two of us passed, as if it had been ordered by Nature herself to sing the "Salute to

Soldiers" to all would-be warriors headed down that lonely road.

*The hell with Colorado. I like it here.*

We passed First Methodist Church, with its twin stair-steps leading up to the front door. I nodded as we passed, paying a quiet, respectful tribute to a dear, sweet friend.

Ol' Blue seemed to lose cadence on the brick streets of Sulphur Springs as he crossed Connally Street and rounded the final turn toward the Hopkins County Courthouse. He stopped ten feet short of the hitching rail, in a peculiarly mulish exhibition of stubborn resistance.

"That's OK, Blue, I'll get off here," I said, dryly.

I jumped down, reached back into the wagon for my knapsack, and looked at Daddy.

The sun was rising now, and was reflecting a scissor-beam of light from a tear that was dripping down his cheek.

I jiggled the knapsack and said, "Ya'll will be getting most of this back. Once I get to training they'll give me everything I need." I placed it across my left shoulder.

I stepped around the rear of the wagon to the driver's side, and stood beside Daddy, still seated. I extended my open right hand. Daddy leaned toward me, placed his right hand in my hand, tried to say something. The handshake tightened. I raised my left hand, let the knapsack fall to my left elbow, and then placed the open palm on his left knee.

"You take care of them and yourself, Daddy. I'll be back."

Our eyes met, moist, sad, scared, and locked into place.

"You take good care of Momma, okay?"

My eyes narrowed, and I looked deeply into his soul.

Daddy's eyes, slightly weakened by small, almost unnoticeable cataracts, shifted momentarily, embarrassed, frightened, ashamed, tired.

He nodded.

"I will. You take care of yourself, too, son," his voiced cracked like a cheap fiddle, dry like last year's corn shucks, empty as a shallow desert well.

I patted his knee three times, the handshake lessened, son standing on the ground, father seated in the wagon. We both nodded simultaneously.

"Tell Momma I want cocoa pies when I come home."

My voice cracked as I said the word *home*.

Daddy made a sound, half-laugh, half-cry.

I stepped toward the courthouse, ran my hand along Ol' Blue's neck, and whispered in the mule's left ear, "Take him home, Blue. Take him home."

I patted his neck three times.

The mule turned to the right, stepped forward, and began his slow journey, taking the wagon and man back the same way he had come.

I watched them for a moment, whispered a prayer for my family, and ended it with a clear "Amen, please!" I removed a handkerchief from my right rear pocket, wiped a tear from each eye, took a breath, straightened my posture, and walked up the modest steps to the semi-circle porch.

As I entered the courthouse portico, I was directed to a log-in sheet. My name had already been typed in, and I placed my slow, deliberate, tilted signature in the blank space beside it. I turned, and was welcomed by a middle-aged, smooth-featured, well-dressed, large-breasted woman who wore thick reading glasses on the end of her small nose. She wore her gray hair in a bun with a pencil stuck through it, and looked too much like a schoolteacher to be a government worker. She gave me a paper cup of black coffee, a fried egg and bologna sandwich wrapped in wax paper, and a bus ticket for Tyler, Texas.

"Bus leaves in half-an-hour, …., uh, …" she looked down at the register, "… Private Smith."

"You will be taken to Tyler and then board another bus that will take you to the Dallas Recruiting Main Station. There, you will be put up for the night by your new family, the United States Army. You will then be sent by bus or troop train, whichever is faster, to the Infantry Replacement Training Center at Camp Wolters, your new home."

She smiled.

I tried to smile back, but the coffee and sandwich looked better than she did.

# CHAPTER 6

# EVERMAN PETTY

Wednesday, July 29, 1942.

Clarksville, Red River County, Northeast Texas.

Everman "Pete" Petty was driving the family truck as he drew a puff from his Camel cigarette, leaned toward his younger brother Sam, and said, "These are so much better than those crappy Raleighs I bought yesterday. You're smart, Sam. If you're gonna smoke, smoke a good one. Those things I bought will make you sick and turn your teeth brown, just like Uncle Willie."

Sam, sitting in the passenger seat, looked at Pete and answered with a giggle, "Uncle Willie's teeth are brown because he chews tobacco. He's got a wad in his mouth all day, chewing and spitting," Sam replied, looking up at his big brother with a playful grin.

"Yeah, he does. And when he talks you can see the leaf stems between his teeth and on the tip of his tongue. That's nasty."

They both laughed.

Pete looked at his ruddy brother and wondered if the war would be over soon enough to spare the young man.

*Sixteen. If we can just finish this war in a year or two, he won't have to fight. He's young, he's bright, but he can't think on his feet. He's just a boy, a happy, simple boy with a man's body growing around him like a spider's web, hiding the innocence behind a woven disguise.*

They had gone fishing that day in Hopkins County, down near Sulphur Bluff, at an old gin pool. There were dozens of gin pools in Red River and Hopkins Counties that dated back to turn-of-the-century cotton gins. The gins had been built and operated as cooperative efforts between businessmen and local farmers to process cotton for market. The pools, dug deeply to intercept the ground water, provided a reliable supply of water for the steam engines that ran the cotton gins. In the past decade, the Great Depression, falling prices, and crop damage from the boll weevil infestation had caused many of these local gins to close and be dismantled, leaving only the deep pools as evidence that they had once prospered.

Nature was slowly taking these pools back with vegetation and sedimentation. There was still a good number of big fish that lurked along the bottom of them. Catfish as big as fifty pounds had been pulled out of the black pits through the years.

But none of these big fish were pulled out today, not by the Petty brothers. They caught a turtle, seventeen quarter-pound bluegill perch, and nothing else. The turtle, a yellow-bellied slider, was left behind, his head severed to retrieve the hook. The perch were wrapped in wet burlap, and laid in the bed of the 1935 Dodge truck they had driven the thirty-five miles from their home in Clarksville to Sulphur Bluff. The perch would be for supper. The heads would be removed, and the scales scraped off. They would be gutted and fried to a crispy brown, fins and bones included.

Pete was driving southwest, chewing on a toothpick, having just crossed the Franklin County line, toward the city of Hagansport, Texas. Sam sat to his right, looking at the passing East Texas countryside. Both windows were down, letting the unusually cool July wind blow mercifully through the warm truck cab. They drove through the bottomlands of the Sulphur River. It had cut deeply into the landscape, making the bottomlands appear wild and rugged with thick woods and steep slopes.

"It's like a jungle down there, Pete," Sam declared.

Pete looked out the open window to his left, his black hair blowing crazily in the breeze. He removed the toothpick from between his lips, and flicked it out the window with his middle finger.

His brown eyes narrowed as he gazed across the thick bottomlands along Highway 909.

"Yep," he replied.

*There are worse jungles in the Pacific, with a Jap behind every bush and tree, and sometimes under the ground in a spider-hole,* he thought to himself.

*I hope I go to Europe to fight the Krauts.*

*But, hell, it gets cold over there.*

Pete had visited the Army recruiter in Clarksville the day before, and had joined the Army. He was sworn in, and told he would be infantry. He was given orders to report back to the recruiting station on August 20th to board a bus and begin his trip to basic training at the Camp Wolters Infantry Replacement Training Center, near Mineral Wells, Texas.

He would tell his Dad, Grandma Petty, and brother tonight, after supper. His family knew that he had registered with the draft board earlier in the year, on February 15th. They also knew that he had already been given a physical examination, found to be fit for duty, and had received his "Greetings" letter from Uncle Sam a few days ago, notifying him to report for induction on August 7th.

So, nothing had really changed. He would be going to the Army soon.

His Grandma Petty would be easy to tell. She was in her late seventies now, still spry and witty, with a little arthritis beginning to slow her gait. He could see her in his mind's eye, her black hair mostly gray, looking at him through dark, Cherokee eyes, telling him "you must do as your duty demands, take care of yourself, *'donadagohv i'*, till we meet again."

She was pure Cherokee, and had met Pete's red-headed grandfather when he was on his way to Texas from Indiana. Educated at the Cherokee Female Seminary in Oklahoma, Grandma Petty knew quite a bit about crafts, medicines, arithmetic, and world history. She had been a schoolteacher in Clarksville and nearby Bogata, and some of the older men in town held her in utmost reverence. They would tip their hats with a slight bow and say, "Good morning, Mrs. Petty," or, "Good afternoon, Mrs. Petty," or any number of greetings to express their admiration. She became a widow in '32 when old man Petty died of a heart attack, and the town embraced her like she was everyone's grandmother. She was one of the most admired and important older woman in Red River County, with her fame often spilling over into the adjacent counties.

*I felt like royalty having a Grandma like her,* Pete said to himself.

*Yes, Grandma will be easy to tell.*

Pete's Dad would be much like Grandma. Pete had seen the pride, and the worry, in his Dad's eyes when he saw the Greetings letter. His Dad was an amiable man, had been good at numbers all of his life, and had found a job easily with the Red River County Clerk's office. He had not served in the Great War because one leg had been badly injured in his youth, kicked by a neighbor's horse. His leg had never fully healed, and he walked with a decided limp, too much of a limp for a soldier. So, he had been given a 4-F exemption and missed the war because of an unfortunate encounter with a nervous horse, and had said many times that he wished he could have served his country like his friends.

Pete's Mom had died two years ago from a stubborn heart problem that had been worsening for ten years. His Dad desperately missed her to this day. Pete knew he and his Dad were relieved that she did not have to experience this upcoming war, and would not have to watch her son become a soldier in the combat that lay ahead.

At home, Pete had always taken on the responsibility of doing the hard, physical work around their modest frame house near the Clarksville town square. He was the perfect firstborn, with a deep commitment to his family values and a natural willingness to help keep the home together, and keep little Sam out of harm's way.

Now that his brother was becoming a young man, Pete was confident that Sam would continue in his big brother's steps and conduct the same care-taking duties of home and family.

He looked across the truck cab at Sam, still smiling, red-hair swirling in the wind, watching the landscape change from the bottomlands of the Sulphur River to sandy clay farmland and pasture. The wind was from the east, and a faint whiff of the Talco oilfield drifted through the open windows, bringing with it the smell of sulphur and crude oil.

"Smell that?" Sam asked.

Pete nodded in confirmation, smiled, and asked, "What is it?"

"The smell of money," Sam answered with a laugh.

"Wish our land had some of it."

"What would we do, Sam? Put a derrick in our front yard? Dad might not be able to get a permit for that," Pete said with a smile.

"Besides, we have the money we need. In another year or two I bet the oilmen will let you work down there. This war is gonna need a lot of oil, and you'll be doing your duty helping bring it out of the ground. I'll take you down there next week and introduce you to my boss, and tell him you're just the man he needs. Next year," Pete said, pointing his index finger to emphasize the word "next."

"I've been working there on-and-off for almost four years now, and the money has come in handy for us. It might even help buy another truck in a year or two, with your help, Sam. Maybe you'll be able to keep this one for yourself."

Just south of town, the Talco oil-field began production in the mid-1930's. The living standards in Clarksville took a welcomed good turn. In Room 105 of the Red River County Courthouse, the Clerk's office was kept busy recording new leases. Oil-field roughnecks had brought new families to town, with new money to spend.

The oil boom brought prosperity to Clarksville, helping to soothe the harsh effects of the Great Depression. Public and private construction expanded.

The Petty family had been able to buy the 1939 red truck Pete was driving in the good times that followed. In the very pit of the Great Depression, Dodge had bravely introduced a new style of trucks, and Pete remembered how proud his Dad was to drive it in the boomtown of Red River County.

Pete's mind cherished the memories of the good life his parents had given him in Northeast Texas as he drove into Clarksville. He had a loving Mom during his childhood, a respected Dad, and an absolutely saintly Grandma, perfect examples of decent people, and a heritage to treasure.

But, now, the war was sending its chilly fingers into the hometown tranquility.

The young, ripe men of America were being harvested, plucked from their home hearths for more important work elsewhere.

His Dad had told him last week that it might be better to check with the Army recruiter before Draft Day, just to see if he could get an assignment that wouldn't take him straight to the war front. Pete had listened, nodded, and told his Dad he might do that. What he didn't tell his Dad was the war front was inevitable. He had seen the newsreels at the Avalon and Texan Theatres, and heard the talk around town that soldiers were needed to stop the Krauts in Europe and the Japs in the Pacific. Many of Clarksville's sons had already joined, and he felt it was his time and his duty to serve where he was needed, not where he wanted.

As he turned right onto West Main Street, he looked to his left and saw the clock on top of the yellow-sandstone Red River County Courthouse. The hands of the tower clock stood at perfect attention. It was 6:00 pm.

Four blocks later, as he approached their home at the corner of Main Street and North Lafayette Street, he reached into his left shirt pocket for a fresh toothpick. He gently placed it between his lips, looked at Sam, and said, "Are you ready for supper?"

Sam smiled as they pulled into the short driveway.

Pete's looked at the house, then back at Sam, and his mind raced a mile-a-minute over the past six months, and the last twenty-four hours in particular. After he had signed up with the Army recruiter the day before, he had an urgent desire to tell his best friend, Wanda, about his now-locked-in plans. Unexpectedly, Wanda was about to become the wildest card in the circle of friends that Pete had collected around him.

Wanda Crawford, his friend throughout all the years he had attended school and beyond, had been as close as a sister for all that time. Her parents lived east of town, and had established a successful horse ranch. She had been going to college the past three years at East Texas State Teacher's College in Hunt County. She would visit the Petty family every time she came home. When he told Wanda that he had joined the Army, he asked her to tell no one until he had told his Dad and Grandma. A sadness filled her eyes, then pride in the patriotism of his choice.

"You have to take me to the ice cream parlor right now, this instant, Everman Petty!" she said, emphatically.

As they sat over two soda floats at the Hart Anderson Drug Company, on the north side of the Clarksville town square, she looked directly into his face and told him she had loved him her entire life. She admitted that she was afraid of him being in the war that lay ahead, and prayed that he would think of her, write to her, and remember her when he came back. She would wait for him, and would marry him in a heartbeat if he ever asked. As he watched her talk, he saw her dark, soulful eyes wander the room and then look back at his.

He studied her black hair as it slung back and forth each time she laughed, and saw the woman behind the smile and the saint inside her soul. He fell in love with her right there at the ice cream parlor, and it was as easy as remembering yesterday's sunset. He realized there never was a time in his life when he had not been secretly and silently in love with her.

Wanda was part-Cherokee herself, and was always his grandmother's favorite student. The two women adored each other, and met often for lunch or family events. They had never once spoken to him of their shared desire that Pete would someday find in Wanda the same yearnings and destinies that she had already found in him.

Over the next three weeks, he and Wanda would be practically inseparable, making up for all the "lost time" of simple friendship to find an irresistible affection and intense passion for each other that neither thought would ever come their way. They talked of marriage, and could not decide if it was wise or foolish. They were two grown-up children, basking in the truest of love imaginable. They knew they were consumed with their love, and that war was no respecter of love and marriage. They swore their reverent love over a candle and a Bible one summer afternoon on the muddy bank of the Sulphur River, and placed the rest of their future into God's hands.

They held each other's hands tightly, and prayed to God what they could remember from an old Cherokee ceremony.

*"Dear Lord, we honor Mother Earth, and ask that we grow stronger through the seasons. We honor Fire, so that our love will be warm and glowing deep in our hearts. We honor Wind, and ask that we sail through life safe and calm.*

*We honor Water, so that we may never thirst for love. With all the forces of the Universe You have created, we pray for harmony and true happiness, as we forever grow young together. Amen."*

When Pete left Clarksville for the Army on August 20th, Wanda was with him at the train station to see him off with a kiss, a hug, and a promise to love him the rest of her life.

He told her he would love her forever, and beyond.

Texas & Pacific Railway Engine 610 was throttling its powerful steam engine, rattling the windows of nearby buildings and pouring white, fluffy steam above the rails at the depot. The train cars were loaded with the sons of Texas mothers and fathers, first-born, last-born, and those in-between, headed to wars both east and west. They were the sweethearts, lovers, and husbands of the finest ladies that Texas had ever produced. And some were fathers.

Engine 610 was shipping the youth of Texas, ripened and ready for harvest, far away from the homeland to fight bitterly for the protection of liberty and the preservation of freedom against the hordes of Hitler and Hirohito.

They kissed again, and he stepped onto the train car as it began to move west.

"I will come back to you on this same train."

# CHAPTER 7

# NOBEL HORNER

Wednesday, July 29, 1942.

Sloss Furnaces, Birmingham, Jefferson County, Alabama.

Nobel Lawrence Horner, standing on the floor of the casting shed, was watching the white-hot molten iron running down the network of trenches toward the pig-iron molds, where rows upon rows of the molds lay like piglets suckling at their mother's side.

    He had been working at the Sloss Furnaces since he was fourteen. He had followed in his father's footsteps in the iron foundries of Jefferson County, and remembered his father telling stories at the supper table of the mines, the men, the rock-blasting, and the heat of the furnaces.

    His father was almost deaf from the years of noisy mines and furnaces, and Nobel knew he would have to use his "working voice" when he told his father about the "Greetings" letter he had received from Uncle Sam. Nobel's sister Betty had given him the letter yesterday as she returned from the mailbox. The letter told him to report for induction on August 7, 1942.

    Betty was the oldest of the three Horner children, and had been living there at the Horner residence since her husband had been drafted a year-and-a-half ago, after the First Registration of the new Selective Training and Service Act.

    The Horner's were fourth-generation descendants of English miners, steelworkers, and ironworkers. The ancestors of the Jefferson County Horner family had immigrated from Sheffield, South Yorkshire, England in 1875, leaving the "*Steel City*" of the industrial world to build a new life in the iron-rich mountains of newly formed Birmingham, Alabama. They brought with them the knowledge of mines and metals that would soon make America the world leader in steel-production. Birmingham, Alabama, soon became the southern capital of steelmaking, with a statue of fire-god Vulcan, together with his hammer and anvil, high on the mountain overlooking the city.

By the time Nobel Horner was born on December 30, 1921, Birmingham's major industries were iron and steel production. As an added plus, the city served the railroading industry by manufacturing both rails and railroad cars. Birmingham was second only to Atlanta as one of the two primary railroad hubs in the South.

Nobel was the younger of two Horner sons. His brother, William, had reported to the Jefferson County draft board on July 1, 1941, during the Second Registration, and had been given a 4-F exemption due to blindness in his right eye. He continued to work at the Sloss Furnace as a dock worker, no longer allowed near the casting shed where molten metal had splashed on him two years ago, severely burning the right side of his face. William called it his "once-in-a-million" chance to avoid the draft.

Now it was Nobel's turn to report for duty, as instructed by Uncle Sam.

He turned his gaze from the pig iron molds, and looked up to the big clock at the top of the stairs, above the manager's office.

His green eyes widened in surprise.

"Shit!" he said aloud, as a frown appeared on his round face. "Five o'clock! Katy's waiting for me right now!"

He began removing his thick coveralls as he walked up the stairs, opened the door, punched his timecard, and motioned to the timekeeper that he was leaving.

"Off tomorrow. Gotta get some things done," he told the timekeeper.

He walked quickly back down the stairs, and headed for the double door. Looking toward the parking lot, he saw Katy, standing beside her father's blue '38 Ford sedan, wearing a pink cotton shirt beneath a dark blue dirndl dress.

Katy's brown hair circled the back of her neck, barely touching her shoulders.

*She is so beautiful,* he thought.

Nobel smiled broadly, and waved. She did not wave back. She removed the cigarette from her mouth, dropped it to the parking lot pavement, and crushed it with her left foot.

Nobel muttered to himself, *She's in that pissed off mood again. What the hell?*

He placed his coveralls on a hook just inside the door, in line with a dozen other coveralls, all ready and waiting for the next shift. He walked briskly toward Katy, nervously rubbing the top of his head.

Nobel had known Katy since they were both ten years old. They had developed an interest in each other, and had shared the mysteries and discoveries of puberty together over the ensuing decade. They were still together, if you could call it "together." He was beginning to think she was discovering new mysteries with someone else, somewhere out there, beyond his reach, beyond his limit.

Katy had become impatient, edgy, easily irritated at some of his inabilities to do exactly what she wanted him to do at any given time.

"Hi, Beautiful," he said as he approached her, then gave her a somewhat restrained hug.

She hesitated, then returned his hug, locking her fingers at the small of his back.

"What did you want to tell me?" she inquired, without returning his greeting.

He kissed her forehead, removed his arms from around her, and placed his hands on her shoulders.

"Let's go get us some ice cream at Silver's. I'll tell you there."

Katy nodded, and Nobel opened the driver's door on her Daddy's car. She slid in as he closed it gently, then quickly walked to the passenger side. He had never driven the big blue sedan, and didn't know if it was due to Katy's selfish nature or by her Daddy's command.

*Either way, it don't matter,* he said to himself. *I've been in that big back seat with her a hundred times, and I was The Driver every time.*

*It's been a month or more since I've "driven" in that back seat.*

He glanced over his left shoulder, surveying the back seat, noticing the dark blanket in the floor, awkwardly unfolded and partially jammed beneath the driver's seat.

*By the looks of that blanket, there's been some activity going on back there.*

*Perhaps another Driver.*

*Perhaps a noisy, heated joyride by the new Driver.*

He sighed, shook his head unperceivably, and faced the front.

It was a short trip downtown, travelling on First Avenue from the Sloss Furnaces to Nineteenth Street. Turning right, Katy found a parking space in front of Silver's white brick two-story building, and completed a jerky parallel parking maneuver, almost hitting a Dodge truck that snuggled the curb.

Nobel jumped out of the car, an easy task since Katy had parked a good two feet from the curb. He walked to the driver's side, waited on a delivery truck to pass, and then opened the door for Katy. She twirled to her left, exposing a tantalizing portion of her inner thigh beneath her tightly pleated dress, and held out her left hand for Nobel's gentlemanly assistance.

He walked her to the door and across the spacious floor with the high beaded ceiling to the soda parlour, to their favorite booth, in a corner that they felt was all their own. Nestled next to her, he ordered his usual black walnut ice cream and her favorite chocolate chip mint ice cream.

As she spooned the tall sundae, she looked at him, her green eyes empty of emotion, like small empty green vases, alone and dust-covered on a storekeeper's shelf.

"So," she questioned. "You were saying?"

He stared into his ice cream, twirling his spoon without interest. He felt like he was in front of a door, friendless, everything that was familiar behind him, knowing that he had to reach out, turn the doorknob, and walk into a room full of unknown danger, unexpected desires, unpredicted opportunities, and unforeseen sadness.

He cleared his throat, looked into her empty eyes, and told her everything.

He was in love with her.

He was afraid he was losing her.

He was being drafted on August seventh, just a week away.

He was going to war.

He wanted her to wait for him.

She was his dream, his girl.

He wanted to come home from the war to her.

He wanted to build a home for them, here in Birmingham.

He wanted to raise his sons and daughters in the iron-rich country that ran through his veins.

She looked at him as he spoke, her wide eyes never moving from his face. She blinked several times. A tear appeared, followed by another, and another, until they ran down both cheeks.

"I can't," she whispered.

A deafening silence surrounded him, enclosing the booth, shrouding the light that filtered in from the small single light bulb hanging from the ceiling, an unseen hand pushing on his chest.

He tried to blink.

His eyes were dry, like dead flowers in an empty green vase.

He saw Katy's mouth moving, words forming in a vacuum, his ears dead to their delivery.

He looked at her, his face smeared with disbelief, his mouth trying to form the word *What?*

Katy's voice finally broke the silence.

"What about me? I have a life to live. I can't just stay here and wait!"

"But, but, I…"

"No buts. I just can't! I'm moving to Mobile. Away from here. Away from the mines, the foundries, the smoke, the noise! I'm going to live on the beach. Maybe I'll be there when you get back. Maybe I won't."

"You can't live on the beach, Katy. A hurricane will blow you away! You'll always have sand in your shoes, and in your bed sheets!"

"Yes, I can! You'll see! When you come back, you'll see!"

"Maybe I won't come back," Nobel said in a low, matter-of-fact voice.

"Don't you pull that shit-talk on me, Nobel Lawrence Horner! You'll come back, and we'll see what's waiting for us. We'll see!"

Her voice was beginning to break, a long, lonely cry almost loosening her selfish grip, then stopping as she took a sip of water.

"I can't just sit here and wait, Nobel. I have to live!"

Katy stood up, reached down for another spoonful of chocolate chip mint ice cream, then walked away from "their" corner, and out the door. She opened the door of her Daddy's blue Ford sedan, and drove away, almost hitting a red Chevrolet as she entered the downtown traffic.

Nobel sat at the booth, his head down, wanting to cry, but no tears came.

Just a pain in his throat that felt like hot pig-iron.

*Well, hell. That didn't go well,* he told himself.

*That didn't go well at all.*

*Now I've got to go home and tell Dad, Betty, and Will about the draft letter.*
*Well, hell.*

The next day, Nobel Lawrence Horner convinced himself that he, too, could not "just sit here and wait." He volunteered to serve in the United States Army, and was transported to Camp McClellan near Aniston, Alabama, to await orders. Three weeks later, on August 20th, the Army put him on a train to Camp Wolters Infantry Replacement Training Center in Mineral Wells, Texas.

# CHAPTER 8

# KENNY HERROD

Wednesday, July 29, 1942.

Hampden Sydney, near Farmville, Prince Edward County, Virginia.

Kenneth Robert Lee Herrod, hands in his pockets, was leaning against a chestnut tree in front of Morton Hall, on the campus of Hampden-Sydney College. He was slowly chewing on a tobacco leaf, enjoying its delicate flavor. He had been speaking with his former philosophy advisor about the decision that lay ahead of him.

Kenny, twenty-years old a week ago, was the oldest son of a tobacco-farmer and warehouse merchant. The family had been in Farmville for four generations. His grandfather, Joseph Bell Herrod, had acquired a large brick warehouse on the South Side Railroad line in downtown Farmville, where the family business now stored and distributed products ranging from furniture and tobacco to clothing and medical goods.

His young years had been filled with the quiet dignity of a mother and father fully engaged in family and community. His heritage was rich in perseverance and the promotion of fairness for everyone in that part of the state known as Virginia's Heartland.

Kenny had just finished his second year of study at Hampden-Sydney College. His dream of getting a degree in

Philosophy was at a crossroads. The country was at war in Europe and in the Pacific. His roots to home and family were strong, but his devotion to country and human freedom was stronger.

Now that he had reached his twentieth year, he had decided to enlist in the military rather than wait to be drafted. Yet, he knew that he was sorely needed by his Mom and Dad to help with the family business, especially now with the war effort placing demands on the production and warehousing of clothing, tobacco, and other goods.

His younger brother James, who would celebrate his fifteenth birthday in August, was capable of doing considerable work in the warehouse and at the railroad dock, but had suffered from frequent bouts of asthma and bronchitis throughout his childhood. Kenny knew that the dusty warehouse was not the best place for James, but he could not talk his brother out of working there.

As Kenny looked across the red-brick campus of Hampden-Sydney College, he realized that his role in this war had already been determined by the events of the last six months. Japanese aggression in the Pacific. Nazi aggression in Europe. Imperialism and Fascism against Democracy and Freedom.

*"We are at war,"* he told himself, *"and war is the Natural Order of Things. No matter how deadly, no matter how immoral, it is the Natural Order of Things."*

His philosophy advisor had said those same words last year, last month, and an hour ago.

Kenny had decided that he would go to war, and he would finish up his college degree when the war was over.

The only person he had talked to about his decision was Marie Francis, a classmate in the philosophy program. They had discussed the wars and the effects they might have on their young lives, and Marie knew that it would just be a matter of time before the effects materialized. She was considering her own military service in the Army Signal Corps, since she could read and speak French very well. They were both devoted to their college efforts, and their time together had only been as friends, though they did acknowledge a keen affection for each other. She said she was proud of him, and would write to him often. He said the same of her.

His blue eyes squinted as he looked at the sun's position overhead.

*Must be near 1:00 o'clock. Better head on home.*

He let the wet, crushed tobacco leaf fall from his mouth to the ground, and began to walk down the paved road that ran north, away from the campus.

His six-mile walk back to Farmville was made easier by the timely meeting of a Charlotte County tobacco farmer on his way to town from his tobacco fields near Charlotte Court House. Kenny and the farmer had known each other for the many years the Herrod warehouse had been storing his tobacco.

The farmer had two sons serving in the two wars, one with the Navy in the Pacific and the other with the Army Air Corps in Europe. Their short conversation was less about the war effort and more about the prospects of a good tobacco crop this year. Fortunately, they arrived at the warehouse before too much could be asked or said about Kenny's prospects for the military this year.

His Dad was sitting in a wicker chair just inside the large double door, legs crossed, puffing on a cigar he had just made from last year's tobacco. He waved as they drove up to the railroad tracks. Kenny thanked the farmer for the lift, and was getting out of the truck cab as his dad approached the driver's side.

"Good afternoon, Mr. Lee," he welcomed. "How's the crop this summer?"

"We could use a little more rain, Mr. Herrod, but it's coming along swell. We'll have enough to keep you busy again this year."

"Thank the Lord. I'm happy to hear that. Family doing well?"

"Yes sir, they are."

"And the boys? Have you heard from them lately?"

"Yes, we have. They can't say much, what with the censors and all. But they both say they're well fed and healthy. We just keep praying that it stays that way and the Good Lord brings 'em home to us when the job is done."

"I hear you. They've got our prayers, too."

The farmer nodded his head, looked at Kenny for a moment, then looked back at Mr. Herrod.

"Thank you, Sir. We pray real hard every day for the boys who are there and for the boys who will be joining them. We HAVE to win this war, Mr. Herrod. This country is free, and it must STAY free, Good Lord willing."

Mr. Herrod nodded in agreement, maintaining his eye contact with the farmer.

"We will all do our share, Mr. Lee," he said, as his eyes narrowed slightly.

"One thing is for certain" he continued, "God is with us and WE will win this war. All of us, working together, will win this war."

Both men maintained eye contact for a second. The farmer blinked, inhaled slightly, and shifted his gaze down the railroad tracks, toward the bank.

"I gotta go to the bank, Charlie. Thanks for being a good man and running a good warehouse. I like to think that my boys are getting some of the stuff that you store in there and ship out of these doors. Thank you for what you're doing."

As the farmer drove away, Kenny looked at his Dad.

"He was talking about me, Dad. He's wondering why I'm not over there fighting with his sons."

Charles Herrod stepped toward his son, and put his arm around Kenny's shoulder.

"Well, don't you worry about that old farmer, son. He knows me and he knows you, and he knows that we are doing the best we can with what we've got."

Kenny nodded slowly, and turned his head toward his Dad.

"I've been wanting to talk to you about that," he explained.

Mr. Herrod stepped a few feet away, smiled, and answered, "Yep, I've known it for a while."

"You've been quiet, son, real quiet for the past two weeks. I haven't wanted to bother you with my questions. You're twenty years old now, and they'll come looking for you, surely they will. We don't own our lives or our futures, Kenny. We get what God wants us to get. He gave us these wars, and he expects us to do our duty, both at home and out there."

Kenny's Dad pointed east, up the railroad tracks, saying, "There's a war that way."

He pointed west, down the railroad tracks, and said, "There's a war that way."

He looked down to the ground, at his feet, then raised his head, and spread his arms out wide, palms up, with a solemn look on his face.

"We are right here in the middle. In the best land and with the best people God could give us. We Herrods have been mighty blessed, and it has come time to thank the Blesser for what we have. Whatever you decide to do, son, you'll have my love and my support and my deep respect."

A tear had begun to form in his eye, and he leaned toward Kenny and embraced him with a strong hug. He let it last a few seconds, then stepped back and looked into Kenny's eyes.

Kenny tried to say something, blinking back his own tears.

"You are the best son a father could have," Charles Herrod said.

"I have been truly blessed to have you and Mom," Kenny replied.

They both stood there, outside the warehouse, in the warm Virginia sunshine, each wearing a soft smile that spoke of the trust, honor, and wisdom that had been at the core of their family for generations.

"And we will be blessed upon your return, Mr. Kenneth Robert Lee Herrod."

Three days later, Kenny Herrod proudly walked into the military entrance processing station in Richmond, Virginia and announced to the front desk, "I am here to join the United States Army."

He filled out some paperwork, then raised his hand and took an oath.

He asked the recruiter if he could be given three weeks to help his father prepare the family warehouse for the late summer clothing, tobacco, and other goods being shipped overseas.

The recruiter looked at his calendar.

"Get the hell out of this station and back to the warehouse to help with those shipments, Private Herrod," the recruiter replied with a loud voice and a quiet wink.

"The morning of August 20th, you be here with a pouch of Virginia tobacco. I'll be waiting with your train ticket to Camp Wolters Infantry Replacement Training Center, Mineral Wells, Texas in my hand."

# CHAPTER 9

# YOU'RE IN THE ARMY NOW

Thursday, September 24, 1942.

Camp Wolters, Near Mineral Wells, Palo Pinto County, North Texas.

Camp Wolters, Texas, was the largest and newest Infantry Replacement Training Center (IRTC) in the United States. When I arrived there in mid-August 1942, everything was barely a year-old, carved out of the North Texas landscape in what had been described as "one of the greatest battles against time and the elements" ever attempted in the Free World.

Seventy-five hundred acres of brush and hills were transformed from forests to barracks, becoming Camp Wolters IRTC. Seven-hundred buildings were built in three and one-half months, in the sometimes-bitter cold, in the frequently heavy, violent rain, in the boot-sucking mud, and in the constant, irritating, maddening wind. Eighteen-thousand architects, draftsmen, contractors, and laborers worked around the clock seven days a week during the hundred-day ordeal.

Lumber and building materials arrived on trains and trucks, rolling into Camp Wolters at the rate of up to 50 loads per day. Giant steel machines sheared off full-grown trees, graders and road-rollers worked on the highways, and bulldozers cleared and smoothed every right-of-way. A railroad spur was built from Weatherford, to the south, into the receiving warehouses of the growing, evolving, expanding, teeming metropolis of Camp Wolters.

The work had begun to build Camp Wolters IRTC in mid-November 1940, a full year before the war would begin with the bombing of Pearl Harbor. Three and one-half months from the day the construction started, it was ready for the job ahead – training men for the war that was bound to come. By March 1941, the first troops were moving in, and Camp Wolters began training the would-be-soldiers to kill the enemy, German or Japanese, it made no difference.

Camp Wolters IRTC was divided into six areas. Each area had forty-nine barracks, fifteen mess halls, fourteen storage houses, four administration buildings, three recreational buildings, one guard house, one infirmary, one Post Exchange, and one officer's quarters.

Each two-story barracks building could accommodate sixty men. The buildings were frame inside, with metal siding on the outside. Each barracks had hot and cold water, toilets, sinks, and showers.

I stood outside my barracks in Area 2, the home of Company D, 56th Infantry Training Battalion, 12th Regiment. A delicate September breeze blew across my forehead. The days were still warm, but there was a hint of Fall in the way the sun looked at 1800; the way the wind rattled through the drying leaves; the way the mornings felt a little crisp, a little cool; the way the sun did not explode from the east every morning like a burning ball, ready to suck the life out of you.

I looked to the east, toward Areas 4 and 5, with up to four-thousand infantry recruits in each. I turned my gaze south, across Grant Road, to the trees outlining the obstacle course, down Lee Road toward Area 6, the receiving warehouses, and the front gate. I remembered these names were from another war, not so long ago. My teachers back at Tira and Sand Hill had spoken their names – one from the North, one from the South.

*What were the names going to be for this war?* I wondered.

To the west, my eyes drifted across the barracks and support buildings of the adjacent Area 1, gazing beyond them, surveying the wooded rolling hills and limestone cliffs between Camp Wolters and Mineral Wells. The sun was low enough along the western horizon to slip behind the clouds that wandered the late afternoon skies. Every day about this time the clouds would sneak in from the Panhandle and High Plains, bringing an early end to the sunlit day and offering a cool promise of a better tomorrow.

I thought of home as I pulled a cigarette from the pack of Camels in my breast pocket, dangled it from the right corner of my mouth, and fingered my black Zippo lighter from my right trouser pocket. I opened it, twirled the flint wheel with my thumb, lit the cigarette, and closed the lighter, hearing the familiar and comforting sound of the Zippo "click-snap."

One of Daddy's brothers had given him a Zippo years ago, but he never used it much. He preferred a matchstick, striking it with his thumb nail. His lighter was silver, and I always liked to feel its smoothness and enjoyed the sound of the familiar "click-snap" when I closed it.

Since the war started, Zippo was making lighters from lesser-grade steel because the military industries needed the top-grade steel for the war effort. Chrome and nickel were in short supply, too, so Zippo had to paint their lighters black to keep them from rusting. They added a textured finish, and called it Black Crackle.

Smoke emerged from my lips and nose as I looked across the teeming camp-city, soldiers moving like ants from building to building, jeeps hauling men with manila folders, an occasional salute as a particularly well-adorned officer appeared from a doorway and disappeared into a nearby vehicle. I again fingered the textured black finish of the Zippo, admired it, and smiled as I returned it to my pocket.

I had won the lighter in a poker game, five-card stud, in which I had put a five-dollar bet that my two queens could beat any hand around the table. The two royal paper ladies were good to me that night at the Service Club, earning me twenty-five dollars and the black Zippo. I was not a true gambler, knew the risks of poor judgment and the reality of sparse cash, so I ended my share of the game and walked off to the jeers and complaints of the losers. As I walked away, I noticed a short fellow with an honest, young face, sitting quietly at a nearby table, watching my departure while drinking a tall soda.

The young man, almost a boy, had given me a friendly, approving nod as I passed.

"Good decision," the fellow had said, with a familiar, comforting East Texas accent.

"Thanks," I replied, as I patted my breast pocket full of cash.

"I need the money."

I had been at Camp Wolters for a month, and knew that this was no game; no "busy-work" place like the CCC Camps in Colorado and Arizona. It was near the end of Week Five of the thirteen-week basic training the Army offered at Camp Wolters IRTC. I was deep in the heart of Texas and three miles from Mineral Wells, across the street from Hell, and a million years from Hopkins County.

The food was good, the cots were cozy, but this place was training me to kill-or-be-killed.

The schedule was hectic, yet expertly organized down to the minute. Reveille was at 0600. Breakfast at 0645. Barracks cleanup and inspection commenced at 0700. Drilling and instruction started at 0730 and stopped at 1200 noon, time for chow. The afternoon began at 1300, with more training and more instruction, ending at 1630. The official "army day" usually ended on the Parade Ground, with a Company Formation as the sound of bugles filled the air for "Colors!" at 1715, and the ceremonial retreat of the flag. Supper was served at 1730. I had free time from 1730 to 2130. A lone bugle played Taps and "Lights Out!" at 2200.

Those were the "good" days.

The "bad" days found us out at Hell's Bottom, or Baker Hollow, or Dry Creek, all day and all night, sometimes several days and nights, eating C-Rations, sleeping on the ground, and experiencing the closest thing to war we had ever seen.

We were usually taken to Hell's Bottom at night, where a dozen obstacle courses awaited us. We would stomach-crawl beneath barbed wire with .30-caliber machine guns firing live rounds two feet over our heads. I knew what two feet were, but, on the ground, beneath the bullets, with my chin dragging through the muck and mire from the frequent rains of September, I would feel the panic in every muscle as my pre-soldier mind told me the bullets were racing through my hair, singing and zinging their deadly whine as the heat from them burned my neck, my ears, the top of my head. When we had crawled past the live firing, there was still another fifty-yard infiltration course with barbed wire and brush to maneuver through, beneath, and over before reaching the end, only to find another trainer with another task.

I had almost, but not quite, conquered my fear of heights while inching along a rope bridge that spanned a sour river, with simulated bomb blasts splattering water fifty-feet high on either side. The bridge was made of three ropes – two waist-high, one for each hand, and one at the bottom, for your feet. We would slowly, cautiously walk the bottom rope, one foot at a time - dangling and swaying, smelling the stench of the water as it exploded from below, feeling the realism, watching as a few men fell to the water beneath the rope bridge, concentrating, concentrating, concentrating …. reaching the other side.

I had learned how to hold a grenade tightly, pull the pin, loosen the grip slightly, and throw, with the art of "whatever felt right," as long as I got rid of it and placed it as close to my target and as far away from me as possible. I knew that the grenade would explode within five seconds after I released the safety lever, so I did not take much time to get acquainted with it - *just pull the pin, look downrange, and get rid of that damn thing.*

In Dry Creek, we learned how to fight with a bayonet, learned how to charge and thrust, and especially how to parry, the vital defensive maneuver that turns aside and deflects an incoming bayonet charge. Perfecting the parry could ultimately save our life from a bayonet charge; more importantly, it made us realize the importance of not conducting our own bayonet charges unwisely or too soon, seeing how an effective parry could change the would-be assailant into the mortally assailed.

We learned how to sneak up on an armed sentry and disable him with a sharp knife and some dirty tactics. It was said that if something was worth fighting for, then it was worth fighting dirty for. There were no rules in deadly combat. Whether the bayonet, or the rifle butt, or the hands, or a knife across the throat from behind, all was fair, and all was right. Dirty was definitely popular at Dry Creek and Hell's Bottom and Baker Hollow.

I had learned how to "hightail it" into a foxhole during an enemy attack, to quickly turn and jump headlong into your fox hole, the nearest fox hole, or the lowest ditch in sight.

At one point, out on the other side of Hell's Bottom, I believe, we were marched past a place where mustard gas had been used. We were about a hundred feet from it. The stench was so sharp and pungent, it almost took my breath away a couple of times. The trees and dirt were yellowish, and a lieutenant talked to us about what it would do to you if the enemy ever used it. He held up the gas mask we were going to be issued, and said that we would be dead without it, and it would not be an easy death. I don't think I'll ever forget that smell.

At Baker Hollow, we would be immersed in maneuvers and battle strategies that would last for days. Foxholes and mud holes. Rocks and rills. Run for your life and hit the ground. Planes would fly overhead, closer to the ground than we wanted them to be, and they would drop flour sacks for bombs.

I was hit with one of the "bombs" once, flour flying through the air around the impact barely ten feet from me, and I sat out the rest of the night as a casualty at a makeshift morgue. It was a sobering experience. Just like that – POW! – and you're off the stage. Out of the action. Off of the Earth. Heaven? Hell?

At the morgue, I had plenty of time to think about my last thoughts as I had seen the flour sack tumbling downward. It was odd - I had no thoughts of home or hearth, Momma, or lost loves as I saw the flour "bomb" impact near me, throwing the powdery cloud of death within a fifty-foot circle. I didn't even think about God, or Grace, or Mercy. Just a quick *"Oh, shit!"* and it hit ten feet away from me, taking my fragile, battlefield life with its white veil of death.

Me and the men in my squad laughed, but were quickly silenced when the sergeant said,

"Shut up, you morons! You're dead! You got that? YOU ARE DEAD! Assholes! Now, I got your lousy, stinking bodies to take care of!"

Laughs had turned to controlled snickering, then to smiles, then to somber thoughts of *"Eternity – so soon?"*

We had done – over and over again – amphibious landing operations training – climbing down a rope net on a simulated transport vessel, which we called the "U.S.S. Yardbird." We practiced – over and over again - getting into a large pontoon boat, crossing a small body of water, then establishing a beachhead under the cover of smoke, waiting, waiting, then deploying in an infantry attack.

Tonight, it was time for leisure.

Tonight, a few buddies and I were going to the Service Club. Play some pool. Smoke a pack of Camels. Listen to music. Look at the girlfriends and sisters that would often visit. Don't start any fights.

I would mostly listen as the others talked.

I rubbed my clean-shaven face as I admired the landscape from my "front porch." Since the mornings were pretty hectic, most of us would shave when we took our evening shower after supper, before our free time started. After a hard, sweaty day at training, it was always nice to have the spicy, sweet smell of Skin Bracer or Burma Shave floating through the barracks instead of the filth we had smelled all day.

"Hey, Red!" a voice greeted me from the street. "Are you going down to the Service Club?"

It was a familiar face, a friend from home, from nearby Red River County. Pete was in Company B, 53$^{rd}$ Infantry Training Battalion, 11$^{th}$ Regiment, in Area 1, practically next door.

"Yeah, Pete, as soon as those two Prince Charmings in there finish their grooming. Wait up, it'll just be a minute. Want a cigarette?"

Everman Petty, nicknamed "Pete," hustled over to me, stood on the barracks steps, removed the toothpick from his mouth, and took a Camel from my pack. He leaned toward me as my Zippo clicked and the smoke began to curl.

"These are so much better than those crappy Raleighs I bought yesterday. Maybe we can smoke the Raleighs all up tonight, huh, Red?"

"If they're free, I'll smoke 'em," I grinned.

I had met Pete several times before the war, during the Old Settler's Reunion, held every year on the west side of Sulphur Springs. He would be there a couple of days with his father and grandmother, especially during the cooking contests. Pete's grandmother, Mrs. Petty, was a schoolteacher, and would often visit the schools in Hopkins County and talk to us about the Indians that used to live in East Texas. Pete would be with her when she traveled.

Pete was taller than me by a couple of inches, with a wide forehead that hinted of a receding hairline, even now, a month shy of twenty-one. His hair was dark black, and his eyes were brown, probably from his grandmother, who was pure Cherokee.

He was the most interesting and trustworthy guy I had ever known. If I was ever in harm's way, I wanted Pete to be nearby.

"I'll buy you a coke tonight. I got money from home," Pete said, as he patted his trouser pocket.

"I appreciate it," I nodded.

"Ya'll go to the range today?" Pete inquired.

"Naw," I said in a disgusted snort. "If we had, we'd still be there. Some of those fellers can't shoot worth a flip."

"Can you?"

"I'm not the best, but good enough for Marksman, I think. I never allowed any guns in the house because of Daddy's drinking and mean streak, but we'd borrow one ever-now-and-then to hunt something. Never did like to shoot, but, like it or not, it looks like the shootings about to begin. How about you, Pete?"

"Got one bull's eye last week. I was proud of it. I'll do okay. You said you never allowed a gun in the house at home? Your aunt had a shotgun, though, didn't she?"

"Audrey? Yeah, she had one, or, let's say, her husband Galen Anderson had one. We borrowed it once or twice, until ol' Marvin Chapman borrowed it and shot himself in the head with it back in '33. Son of a bitch! Then nobody wanted to touch it, much less borrow it."

"I remember that," Pete responded, with widening eyes as the memories filled his mind like long-lost words to a forgotten song. "All the men got together and went looking for ol' Mr. Chapman. They looked in the woods, down in the bottoms, in the barns, even tried to make your Daddy look up into the attic of an old house down at Mahoney. Now, that was a story," Pete laughed.

"Yeah, they said they just picked Daddy up by his feet because he was so skinny and lifted him up so he could peek through the little opening into the attic. Every time they would push him toward the opening he would just buckle and fall back like a limp 'tater sack. They never did get him to stick his head up there. I think he was scared."

We both laughed heartily.

"Hell, he really would be scared here."

I laughed again, then grinned, and then just stared forward, into the dwindling sunset, taking in the beauty and silence of the moment.

One man came out of the barracks behind us, followed by another, joining us on the steps.

"Are you purty enough?" I chided, as Nobel Horner ran his fingers across his near-hairless head.

"Purtier than you, Tex," Nobel answered, with a deep southern accent.

Nobel had joined the Army in his hometown of Birmingham, Alabama, and was in Texas for his first time. About my height, his light blond hair was hard to see after it had been shaved off by the Army barbers, and he kept it short so he could rub his head when he talked. He said it made him feel smarter and prettier. His seemingly bald head made his round face look larger-than-life, and made his wise-ass demeanor look authentic. He had a mouth that would sometimes fly without a pilot, and he reminded me of both my brothers. He was talkative and funny like Noel, and was nervously assertive and bossy like Lester. I liked him. He was someone you could always look to for a word of advice, whether it was respectable or off-the-wall, and he never let more than a few minutes pass without saying something.

"I'm not so sure about that, Mr. Horner," Kenny Herrod admitted, in a polite, Virginian manner, his blue eyes sparkling in the evening sun. "And I'm sure Everman would agree with my observation. You are not prettier than Mr. Smith. Red has some eastern blood in him for sure, carrot-top and all, but he will neva', eva' be as ugly as you."

Kenny was our road scholar. He went to college at Farmville, Virginia, and said he would finish up his schooling when this war was over. He showed the manners and dignity of the old Virginians I had read about in schoolbooks and magazines. He was as tall as Pete, with similarly black hair, though not as straight and coal black as Pete's. Kenny had a head of hair that had large, wavy curls, and, if long enough, would probably have looked like the wigs from old Virginia that the big shots used to wear.

He insisted on calling Pete by his given name, Everman. His reason? Because, "It is what it is," he would say.

Kenny was fiercely polite, and eager to accomplish any task set before him as a matter of duty and honor. I figured if

I ever needed a friend when times were in a scrape, I could depend on him. He would do anything for a friend.

Nobel was fast on his feet and quick to the jump, and never at a loss for words.

Pete was as steady as a rock.

They were my new family, and I loved them like brothers.

"Everman," Kenny said, chewing on a few leaves of Virginia tobacco. "If you are ready to accompany Red, his henchman Nobel, and myself to the Service Club, I would be honored," he announced, lowering his arms and head in a display of servitude.

"I will, indeed," Pete responded.

We laughed as we each slipped our garrison caps over our heads, some of us aligning it briskly atop the crown of our head, others putting a slight smart-aleck angle to suit the mood-of-the-moment. We stepped down onto the caliche gravel that lined the streets.

We were a team, like six-thousand other teams on the IRTC, drawn to each other by background, voice, mannerisms, attitude, or by chance acquaintance along the road to war. We had been told that we would soon be assigned to a single Regiment, the 21st Infantry Regiment of the 24th Infantry Division, the "Hawaiian" Division, and that we would, could, and should, be able to maintain our kinship for the duration of the war.

*Or the duration of our lives, whichever comes first,* we each thought to ourselves.

Our camaraderie was the one civil link that held our minds together, keeping the fear and the panic from leading us berserk, sending us over the fence and away, far away, back home, safely back home.

We had only a short distance to go, less than a mile up Grant Road, past Area 3, to the Service Club. The usual chatter was exchanged between us: complaints of chow, mimicry of First Sergeant Matney and Captain Butler, rumors of assignments, ladies-in-waiting back home, things we did before the war, and things we would want to do after the war. It was the after-the-war talk that often took the shine out of our eyes and slowed the click in our step momentarily, as each one of us retreated to that distant corner of our mind where the whisper of death stories and the stench of unfulfilled dreams were laying alongside the sleeping demons of uncertainty.

As we approached the Service Club, the left side of the double door was propped open, and I stood beside it, nodded, raised my right arm in a welcome-come-inside gesture, looked at Pete, and said, "Age before beauty."

As soon as Pete had entered, I looked at Nobel and said, "Beauty next."

Nobel grunted, and entered, with Kenny and me in the rear.

We immediately smelled cigarettes and hamburgers, and heard music and laughter. This was a place to forget Sergeant Matney, forget the .30-caliber machine guns, forget the bayonet, and live the way you would give a million-dollars to live - nothing to do, nobody to please, nowhere to go.

We stood just inside the door for a few seconds, scanning the room, searching for a bench, a pool table, a chair, a woman. You never really stopped looking for a woman, knowing you shouldn't, knowing you couldn't, even if you wanted to, but you looked anyway.

Nobel blurted, "Pool table, left side, Grab it. I'll get some balls."

Kenny looked at him, his face dripping with sarcasm, and countered, "I don't believe you would know what to do with them, my boy."

Nobel looked back as he retreated to the equipment window, his green eyes narrowing as he sneered at Kenny, and raised the middle fingers of both hands, jabbing them in the air several times.

The men laughed, and Pete remarked, "Now, that's a start. He'd prob'ly want to try them out on you, Kenny."

More laughter.

We played pool for the better part of three hours, laughing, joking, swearing, smoking, and observing the room. Pool room sounds were some of the best in this part of the world, this part of life, this side of Heaven. No one was able to "run the table," but each one of us, in our turn, made shots that looked like they were straight out of the sleazy parlors of New York or Chicago.

At one point, with near-motionless lips and a cigarette moving up and down to the rhythm of his words, Nobel uttered, "Shit, Tex, you're purty good. You're really swell with that stick. You been keeping secrets from us?"

More laughter.

I lifted my soda pop in a mock toast, and said, "Thank you, Nobel. No secrets. I am a farmer, with a purty good cue stick."

"There you go, Nobel," Kenny said, lifting his soda pop in similar fashion. "Red has a good cue stick. What do you have, sir?"

Nobel leaned on his cue stick, a broad smile on his face.

"I, Mr. Herrod, have the biggest and best cue stick in Jefferson County, Alabama. Undisputed."

Kenny raised his hand to say something, and Nobel waved him off.

"Undisputed," he repeated.

"I would have no way of knowing," Kenny responded, a grin on his face. "We do not compare our cue sticks in Virginia."

We laughed the laugh of friendship, enjoying our time together, knowing that Fate held perilous cards in her deck for us, when the bonds we were making now would be all that would bind us together if some of her cards were dealt. Bonds that would carry us through whatever Hell lay in front of us.

As 2100 neared, our pace began to slow, knowing it was time to head back to the barracks before Taps was sounded. I looked across the room and saw the same honest, young face I had seen the night I won my Zippo, looking at me, his hand wrapped around a tall soda glass. We exchanged nods, and I leaned my cue stick against the pool table and walked over to the soldier-boy.

As I approached, he nodded and said, "I heard that feller call you Tex," in the same, comforting, reserved, easy, East Texas accent as before. "Some of the fellers call me that, too. I guess we talk the same."

I extended my hand toward the relaxed, seated young man.

"Red Smith, Hopkins County, up around Mount Sterling, north side of Sulphur Springs."

The young man stood up, barely five-foot-five, with a genuinely trusting and confident smile on his face, and grasped my hand in a firm handshake. He replied,

"Murphy, Hunt County, up around Kingston, just north of Greenville. I was working at a gas station in Greenville when I joined up."

"Pleased to meet you, Murphy. I haven't traveled very much, but I know where Greenville is, on the way to Dallas."

"Yes, sir. Can't say as I've been to Sulphur Springs, but I'm sure it is cotton and corn all the way there."

"How long you been here, Murphy?"

"Got here the last day of June, I did. Started training on the ninth of July, supposed to be finished and gone from here in a couple of weeks."

"You're a good month-and-a-half ahead of me. Company D, 56th Battalion, Area 2. You?"

"Company D, 59th, Area 3. You can see my barracks right outside that window there," he said, pointing to the left wall of the Service Club.

"I'm glad we're neighbors. I don't rightly know you, but I'm gonna miss you next month. They say you fellers in Area 2 are going to Europe. Is that right?"

"Yes sir, that's what they say. I'll be going to Fort Mead, Maryland first, for a month or two, then on to North Africa and Europe to join up with the 15th Regiment, 3rd Division. Gonna fight the Germans."

I pulled a chair from the next table, sat in it with both legs straddling, motioned to my friends to finish the game without me. I looked at the still-smiling, friendly Murphy and said,

"We're going to Hawaii, they say. Become part of the 21st Regiment, 24th Division, over at Schofield Barracks. Gonna fight the Japs."

Murphy looked closely at me, put a hand on my knee, and said, "Learn all you can here," the smile lessening on his boyish face, the honesty and sincerity still there. "Don't let the sergeants get to you. They know what they're doing. Learn all you can. Where we're going, we're gonna need it."

I swallowed, and nodded my head. I liked this young man. I could trust him, even though he looked – what? Seventeen?

"I dread the cold, Smith," Murphy said, his eyes staring out the window.

"I heard it gets real cold over there."

"Yeah. I dread the jungle, Murphy. I know what White Oak Bottom looks like, and I don't like it in there. Dark and bushy. Can't see your hand in front of you. I heard the jungle can be two, three times as bad."

"Hey, Tex," Nobel's called from the pool table. "I'm taking the sticks and rack back. We better go. Don't want the Sarge jumping in our shit, do we?"

I looked at Murphy, and said, dryly, "My friend from Alabama has already let the two sergeants get to him. I guess we better go, we got further to walk than you."

The young lad picked up his empty soda glass and responded, "I'll go with you. Let me take this over to the bar and I'll be ready."

We met at the front door, Pete and me from Hopkins County, Kenny from Virginia, Nobel from Alabama, and the easy-going lad from Greenville, Texas.

I introduced him to the make-shift band of brothers, "Boys, this here is Murphy from next door. He's from my neck of the woods. He's finishing up here at Camp Wolters next month and shipping out to fight the Germans."

"Pleased to meet you, Murphy," Kenny said, extending a handshake. "It's an honorable thing you are doing, and I wish you the best."

Murphy, slightly embarrassed by the praise, exchanged Kenny's handshake and said, "Aw, I'm just doing what you fellers are doing."

"Maybe so," said Nobel, "But you're getting there before we do, and I hope you boys do a job on those Krauts while we knock those Nips off their high horse."

"We'll try, sir," answered Murphy, a tired half-laugh behind the words.

"They're just trying to do what they're told, like us, but we've got to stop them because they're wrong. Dead wrong," the young lad vowed, his head moving slowly from side to side to punctuate the negative.

Pete placed his right hand on Murphy's left shoulder, looked him in the eye and said, "We need you back in Texas when this is over, so you just do your job, and the Good Lord will watch over you, protect you, and keep you safe. Don't you go trying to be a hero or somethin'. You do a good job, and I want to see you at the Texas State Fair when this is over."

Murphy nodded, a look of confidence and poise in his hazel eyes.

"Yes, sir," he said.

I could tell my buddies were impressed, as if they were looking at someone who had been to the mountain top - had run the gauntlet - and had lived to tell the story, even though his beard was still peach fuzz.

They began pounding him with questions. How was the chow over in Area 3? When do we get to fire the REAL guns? How many times do we have to go back to Hell's Bottom? How'd you do on the range?

Murphy put his palms out, and said, laughingly, "Hold it, hold it. One at a time. Chow? First, we got the best Mess Hall at the Camp. Private Gray can cook anything just like home. Warren Gray. It's a pity you don't have him. Second, the real guns are waiting for you in Hawaii – that's where you're going, right? Third, Hell's Bottom will haunt you guys at least three more times. You'd better hope it doesn't rain while you're out there. On second thought, I heard it rains a lot in the Pacific. Maybe you need to get used to it. Fourth. How'd I do at the range? I did OK. Marksman. Bottom of the ribbons, but better than a Non-Qual. Like I told Smith, you guys learn all you can. This is the best place to be before shipping out. It starts here. If you don't learn it here, you may not be going home ……..," he hesitated, "….. alive."

My buddies looked down, contemplating the advice coming from an obviously knowledgeable soldier with a somewhat boyish image.

We were already at the row of barracks on the edge of Area 3, and Murphy said, "I'll be peeling off here. You boys take care of yourselves."

Nobel looked up, and told him, "You tell your Momma she's a saint - she raised a fine man, a good soldier. I like your style, Murphy."

The young man's face darkened a moment; he looked down, his smile lessening. He slowly looked up, the smile returning, faintly at first, then broadening proudly.

"I thank you for saying that, Nobel. My Momma was a saint, for sure. She died last year, before Pearl Harbor. I haven't seen my father for longer than that. I'm sending money home to take care of my younger brothers and sisters. My Momma taught me to always do the right thing. Yes, siree, she was a saint."

There was a moment of silence My buddies and I were immersed in swirling pools of thought about our own family, our own home.

"You take care of yourself, Murphy."

"We'll see you back at the Service Club."

"Hang in there."

"God bless you."

We all shook hands, with grips that reflected admiration and respect, and eye-to-eye contact reserved for the most profound of comrades.

I blurted, "Wait. I never got your last name, Murphy."

The lad beamed with a contagious smile that covered his face, and said, "Murphy IS my last name, Smith. My first name is Audie."

"Auggie?"

"Audie."

"Autry?"

Murphy laughed again, this one seeming to consume most of his body, as he leaned toward me and said, "Just call me Murphy, Red. I'm happy with that."

Nobel leaned over to me and feigned a whisper, speaking loudly enough for everyone to hear, "You ain't good at names, Tex. Why don't you just call him Tex?"

We all laughed, as the four of us walked away from the smiling Murphy, waving our wishes of good luck, and walked back to the barracks of Area 2.

The next month, Murphy was on his way to Fort Mead and Europe.

The month after that, my three buddies were on their way to Hawaii and the South Pacific.

I, on the other hand, had no idea where the Army was about to send me, or the misery that lay ahead.

# CHAPTER 10

# ELEVENTH AIRBORNE

Thursday, October 29, 1942.

Camp Wolters, Near Mineral Wells, Palo Pinto County, North Texas.

It was the end of our tenth week of basic training at Camp Wolters. I had been unexpectedly sent to the 56th Battalion Headquarters right after evening chow. It scared the living hell out of me. All I could think was, *Somebody's dead. Momma? Daddy? Who?*

I walked quickly to the Area 2 administration building near the mess hall, saw the large letters that said "56th Battalion," and stepped onto the long, wooden porch. I stood at the entrance, opened the thick, heavy door, and quietly entered a big room with small tables, a few bookcases, and a leather couch. I saw a number of closed doors, one for each Company. A tall, square-faced PFC came from behind one of them, and we passed silently as I moved toward the door that was marked "Delta Company" on the etched glass. I paused in front of it, fidgeted, and extended my right hand. It was shaking. I made a fist, squeezed it twice, and then knocked on the door.

It opened, and a white, pimply face appeared. He looked at me, nervously nodded his head, and said, "Wh-wh-what can we do for you, P-P-P-Private?"

"I was told to report to First Sergeant Matney. I'm Private Horace Smith," I replied.

"Yes, come on in," he said.

"S-sit right over there," he pointed.

"I'll t-t-tell the Top that you're here."

He disappeared around the back wall, down the short, inner hallway that separated his desk from the First Sergeant. As I sat down on the soft, padded chair he had pointed to, I could hear him say, "P-P-Private Horace Smith is here, Sir."

"Goddammit, Corporal Taylor, don't call me Sir," the First Sergeant growled.

"Save that shit for Captain Butler. Tell Private Smith to come in."

The young, nervous clerk came back around the wall, looked at me, blushed, and said, "The T-T-Top will see you now."

I stood up, and walked toward the hallway that led to the growling giant that some called "Top." I preferred to call him by his Army name: First Sergeant Matney.

He sat in his leather high-backed swivel chair, behind a half-lit cigar that rested at an angle in a yellow ash tray, a thin trail of smoke snaking its way up, past the lamp that commanded the right corner of his mahogany desk. There were no pictures on the desk, no smiling faces watching him. Just a foot-long "First Sergeant" chevron-infested emblem carved into a wooden nameplate, a newspaper, three manila folders, and a baseball.

He was a tall man, every bit of six-foot-two, with broad shoulders and a noticeably smaller waist. His face was shaped like a block of wood, with wide jaws, a large pointed nose, and blue eyes that sat in the middle like icy buttons. A smile was not normal to his face; a sneer was more fitting. His voice, on the parade ground, boomed like a cannon. The few times I had heard him talk in a regular way, it sounded like car tires on gravel.

He had done everything he could do to be frightening.

There was something in him, though, that made you feel safe. He carried himself like a man, like a hero waiting to do something heroic. We could tell he was making us ready for what lay ahead.

His head was lowered when I entered his office, and he raised his icicle eyes, head never moving, as I approached his desk.

I stood there, at attention. He reached for the baseball with his left hand, rolled it in his fist, raised his head slowly, looked at me, and said, "Relax, Private Smith. Nothing's happening here, or anywhere. This is the Army, and you're in swell hands. Like this baseball."

He nodded at his left hand, dug the tips of his first three fingers against the back of it, laid his little finger along the seam, and placed his thumb delicately and firmly across the front, his thumbnail digging into the white stitched leather.

"Sometimes the Army throws you a curve, sometimes a knuckleball," he said, rotating his hand from left to right.

"I like fast balls, right down the middle," I replied, lost in a maze of memories.

He grinned like a circus clown, nodded his head, and said, "Me too. Can't throw worth a damn holding the ball like this. I always bluff the sons-of-bitches by making it look like I'm fancy, then I blow them away with heat."

His big chest lifted as he drew in a breath, then fell as he let it out.

The clown face was gone now, and a father's face began to immerge, and then halted.

"Back home, did you play ball, Smith?"

"A million times," I answered.

"Pitch?"

"Yes. And hit, and ran. Winked at the ladies, stared at the men."

He looked at me, his eyes narrowed; a thin smile appeared on his face as he lay the baseball down.

He leaned back in his leather chair, and folded his arms across his chest. "Captain Butler wants you to volunteer for paratrooper school. What do you think about that?"

He cocked his head to one side. His eyes widened. He unfolded his arms, reached for one of the manila folders, picked it up slowly, looked at it, and waved it.

"We've already done the paperwork," he boasted, the grinning clown face returning.

"All you have to do is sign the part that says *I volunteer*."

I just stood there, staring at him, trying to understand what he was saying.

"Captain Butler wants me to do that?" I questioned.

"Yes. I guess he thinks the sun shines out your ass. Maybe it does. Maybe it doesn't. Sit down," he said, nodding his head toward a large, leather, straight-back chair to the left of his desk.

I sat. Leaned back at first, then straightened my posture. *Don't want to look too comfortable.*

I thought about what he had said. *Volunteer for Paratrooper School.*

My mouth opened. I tried to find something to say, something in response to this strange news. I felt confused, like a giant squid was wrapping a tentacle around me. I remembered a con-man at the Hopkins County Fair, holding a small bottle of snake-oil in his wiry hand, telling me it would do anything I wanted it to do.

*Rub yer aching back with it. Rub it on yer sore feet. Rub it on yer pecker.*

I said nothing.

First Sergeant Matney raised his left hand like a magician, waving it as if brushing away an invisible curtain, pointed his index finger at me, and said, in an unusually soft voice, "Let me explain."

His voice was captivating. No gravel road now, just grass beneath his words, palm trees that reached to the sky, and bouquet-clusters of white flowers.

He told me that the Big Brass at Army Headquarters was expanding the Airborne for the war in the Pacific. Things were happening on the paratrooper front. Fort Bragg had begun training the 82$^{nd}$ and 101$^{st}$ Airborne Divisions a month ago. The 24$^{th}$ Division commander, Gen. Frederick Irving, had his eyes on forming a new infantry airborne division, the 11$^{th}$ Airborne, to accompany his division into the Pacific.

Captain Butler had been told to talk his best young men into volunteering for the new schools at Fort Bragg, to be ready when the Eleventh Airborne stood up.

He told me that I had easily passed the physical fitness requirements in pushups, sit ups, and the two-mile run. Twenty-one was the preferred age – not wet-behind-the-ears, just perfect. Captain Butler had recognized a good soldier when he saw one, and he personally drew a bead on me.

"You'll get fifty dollars a month more for being a paratrooper, Private Smith," First Sergeant Matney beamed.

"You'll be part of the Elite," he said with a wink.

I didn't know what "elite" meant, but it must've been really good, the way he said it. He made it sound very, very important.

"I know you're sending a lot of money home to your folks now," he told me. "What if you could send twice as much?"

I listened.

I thought.

"What if I don't make it? Can I be sent back to wherever this bunch goes?"

He leaned a bit forward and said, "We'll do our damnedest to make that happen. Gen. Irving wants you boys to stay together, and stay together you will."

I asked for a day or two to decide.

He grimaced, then grinned with his crazy clown face, stood up, and opened his arms wide, like a preacher calling for lost souls.

"Why not?" he agreed.

"Think on it. I expect you to decide in two days. Captain Butler wants you, and it's my job to make Captain Butler happy. You may go think, Private Smith. Now, get the hell out of my office."

I left with a head full of ideas, a future full of change, a pocket full of more money, less jungle, and a little bit of "elite."

I said nothing to Pete, Kenny, or Nobel.

I said yes to Captain Butler and First Sergeant Matney.


One Month Later.

Saturday, November 28, 1942.

Fort Bragg, North Carolina

    After a two-day train to Fort Bragg and Week 1 of Jump School, I regretted the whole affair. I felt absolutely horrible. My entire body was hurting, and my mind was breaking. My fear of heights got worse every day.
    Week 1 was Ground Week. We spent the whole week learning how to land on the ground safely. They called it "perfecting your parachute landing fall." I called it jumping from too high up and landing without breaking something. They taught us to absorb the energy of our fall with the lower legs and knees, all the way up to our shoulder. The one thing to remember was to land with your feet and knees together.
    We were always jumping from somewhere high to somewhere low, into sand or gravel pits. Each time hurt more, felt harder, and started from higher. Over and over we would do it, with the instructors yelling at us, until our bodies were sore, and our uniforms beaten up. By the end of Week 1, we were jumping from a 34-foot tall tower. They said it felt exactly like an actual jump. I said it felt like hell.
    Ground Week had come to an end. On the weekend pass, I just wandered into Fayetteville with some new buddies, all of them a little too gung-ho for me. We drank, and smoked, and drank some more. I bought a little one-page, white Christmas card of a paratrooper hanging beneath his parachute, with the words "Season's Greetings from a Paratrooper. Merry Christmas and a Happy New Year." I bought two of them; sent one home to Momma and Daddy,

and the other to Juliette Hamilton. I thought it might make everyone back home feel proud.

We had passed all the jump training and another physical fitness test to get ready for Week 2, Tower Week.

That's when I broke.

The week started with the same damn 34-foot tower, then to a suspended harness, and then to the 250-foot tower.

I don't remember very much about what happened after I had been raised to the top of the 250-foot tower. I was hanging there between life and death for a few seconds, and then I was dropped without mercy to my certain death. The world was spinning like crazy. The huge, white chute fully opened with a "Pop!" above me, and carried me at an angle down, down, twisting, rotating, at a much too fast speed, from a much too high elevation. They said I made strange, squeaking, whimpering noises all the way down, kicking at unseen objects, punching at things that were not there. They said when I hit the ground, my kicking was at a lucky angle, because I landed hard in the "right way," rolled to my right side, turned over twice on the ground, and bounded back up to my feet, still squeaking, whimpering like a mad man. I remember someone was yelling at me. I yelled back. I remember someone grabbed me, to calm me down. I remember hitting somebody in the face, his eyes going hollow, and him falling to the ground. I must've been knocked back to the ground, too, because all I remember next was being scooped up and carried away, kicking and screaming, by several tall, strong men in dark green suits.

I stayed in sick bay the rest of the day. Through the afternoon I tried to sleep. They gave me enough pills to sleep, but sleep would not come. I remember shaking, not eating anything they offered me, and shaking some more. By evening chow, I had calmed down a little bit. Some of my class buddies came by to see me after I had eaten a little bit of ground beef and bread.

"Hey, Red," my buddy George from back east told me, "When you floated down from the tower you looked like the devil himself."

Another buddy, Walter, from California, said, "After you landed on the ground you cussed better than anyone I ever heard. You even said some words I can never repeat. I had no idea what they meant, but they sounded like strong piss."

Somebody said that I had hit everybody that approached me at the base of the tower. We laughed and talked almost an hour, and I thanked them for understanding my fear and coming by to see me.

They said they hated to see me go, but they were glad they weren't gonna have to watch anything like that again. I apologized to them, and they wouldn't hear it. They just shook my hand, slapped me on the back, and said they and the 11th Airborne would see me again "over there."

The next morning, after a good sleep, I was sent to the out-processing office at Fort Bragg. I stayed in a transfer barracks for two nights, and the day after that I was standing at the red brick Fayetteville train station, with my barracks bag on my shoulder, holding my orders to Schofield Barracks tightly in my hand.

Thursday, December 3, 1942

Between North Carolina and California

    A four-day ride to San Francisco in a troop train followed. I felt better every day. We would stop somewhere every night, in the middle of nowhere, and pour out of the train for exercises, then get back on it in our wet, smelly uniforms for another day on the rail. Mess facilities had been set up along the railroad. We would stop, get off the train, and eat. Sometimes we had boxed meals and kept moving. There was a coffee station on the train, and I would hit it often. The sound of the rails was music, with every note taking me farther away from Fort Bragg, and closer to Paradise.
    The day we arrived in San Francisco we were taken off the train about noon, boarded an Army ferry, and took a short trip across the bay to Angel Island, a piece of land built up in the bay as a processing station for immigrants during earlier times. It was a processing station for American soldiers now, and was named Fort McDowell. We could see the famous prison island, Alcatraz, nearby.
    "Thank Goodness they didn't take us there," someone said in the ferry. Nervous laughter followed.
    "We haven't stopped, yet, Buddy," someone else said, a gruff in his voice.
    We did not stop at Alcatraz. We were taken to Fort McDowell, and were marched off the ferry. We fell into formation for a roll call, and were then marched in several directions to be placed into troop ships, waiting to sail to Hawaii.
    I got on my assigned ship, barracks bag on my shoulder, still holding my orders to Schofield Barracks

tightly in my hand. We hauled ourselves down three stairways (the sailors called them "ladders") to the third floor down (the sailors called it the "third deck"), and we were assigned our beds (the sailors called them "our berths").

I found my berth down a narrow aisle, to the right side, on the top, against the wall (the sailors called it the "bulkhead"). I was ready for my first ride on a ship. I could already feel a slight motion, a tiny but noticeable rock in the ship. I lay on my bunk, closed my eyes, and it seemed better.

We were called to chow at 1700, and as I looked out one of the portholes, I could see it was already getting dark outside. We walked down the hallway (the sailors called them "passageways"), up a ladder to the second deck, and down another passageway to the mess hall (the sailors called it the "galley").

As I walked, I could feel a tiny, little sway along the deck, and up the bulkheads. The motion made my headache, my eyes blurry, and my feet found it hard to walk in a straight line.

The navy had cooked us a pretty good supper, and most of the guys ate it. Pork, I believe it was. I ate some, it had a good taste to it, but it got a little rough as I continued to feel the ship rocking, ever so slowly, ever so slight, ever so *not right*.

Halfway through the meal, I could not eat another bite.

Back down to the third deck I went, crawled into my berth, and lay there. Sick. Sicker. Sickest. I had never been seasick before, had never been on a boat or a ship, and had never felt so bad, so very, very bad.

I stayed in my bunk the rest of the evening, could hear the guys talking, laughing, playing cards. I lay there the rest of the night, and all the next day, and all the next night. All I could think was *When will this end? When will we get there?*

Sick. Sicker. Sickest.

In the middle of the night I got up twice and staggered down the passageway to the toilet (the sailors called it the "head") and threw up.

As the third day dawned, somebody told me that I'd better go to sick bay or go up topside and get some fresh air.

They practically pulled me down from my berth, put my boots on me, and walked me up the three ladders to the main deck. My eyes squinted at the bright light. I could see the bay, stretched around me, in all directions. Freighters and large troop ships moved slowly around the bay, some pulling out to the open sea, some hovering around Angel Island, waiting to gently slide into an open dock.

I could see Alcatraz Island off to my right, and the busy harbor of Fort McDowell to my left. Soldiers were getting on and getting off the troop ships that lined the docks.

*The bay? The harbor? The docks?*

I took in a deep breath of the morning air, and smiled with disbelief. We were still in San Francisco Bay! I had been down on the third deck dying for two days, wallowing in seasick misery, and we hadn't even left the dock!

As luck and God's mercy would have it, we were given "shore leave" that day, and I walked on "dry land" around Fort McDowell until dark. I found a USO tent and ate the best fried eggs and drank the best coffee that mankind had ever made. I knew I would be seasick again once I got back on the ship, but I had been to Hell and back, and this time I was ready for Hell on my terms.

Thursday, December 10, 1942.

Between California and Hawaii.

    We pulled out the next day on our five-day journey to Hawaii.
    Yes, I was sick. But every day I would go to the mess hall for a late breakfast and early supper. (The Navy served us two meals a day.) At sunset, I would walk slowly up the three ladders to the main deck, get a lung full of fresh salty air, smoke a couple of Camels, and imagine that I could see land all around me. I would smile as I remembered my two days at the dock, sick as hell.
    We saw the Hawaiian Islands on the fifth day. No imagination this time. There they were, just like Paradise.
    Palm trees.
    Flowers.
    Beaches with sand the color of peaches, white as snow, and black as coal.
    Blue-green waves pouring in from offshore, lapping at the beaches with emerald foam.
    As the troop ship carried us toward Honolulu Harbor, we passed Diamond Point, and I saw Diamond Head and Waikiki Beach. I saw a huge, tall pink building on the beach.
    Very pink. Beautifully pink.
    Standing there on the promenade deck, with the wind blowing in my face and the sea birds circling overhead, I remembered having seen that corner of Paradise in books and pictures at school, never knowing that it looked just as beautiful in person as it did on paper.

We got off the troop ship at Honolulu Harbor, and fell into formation along the railroad siding at a train station. Our names were called, and we broke into half-a-dozen groups. Each group was then marched to its designated boxcar for the trip inland. The small train began moving slowly, gaining elevation as it chug-chugged its way up from the harbor, carrying us toward Schofield Barracks. As we rode the rails through Honolulu, I sat in front of an open window, amazed at the beauty of the city, overflowing with flowers, a green landscape touching a blue-green ocean.

Honolulu was a big city, with masses of men, women, soldiers, and children filling the streets, constantly moving. Not moving fast, but moving in a lazy, happy way.

As we approached Pearl Harbor, I saw Hickam Field to the left, then Ford Island, and, finally, the devastation and disaster of the navy wreckage, with death still floating on the bay in Paradise. It was hard to believe, hard to accept as true. I was seeing, with my own eyes, the aftermath of the very attack that had turned a Sunday in early December into the beginning of a war. I remembered the movie that my friend Roy and I had been watching, when the film stopped and a nervous man with a flashlight walked down the aisle and told us the Japanese had just attacked Pearl Harbor, Hawaii.

I saw the boats, men, and equipment of the Salvage Division, working to recover, repair, and restore the battered battleships in dry docks rimming the harbor. Men in rubber boots and one-piece coveralls worked about like bees in a beehive.

Oil was still visible on the water, fuel bubbling up from submerged ships. Cables and winches were strewn across the harbor, retrieving sunken and near-sunken masses of metal from the muddy harbor floor. Divers in breathing suits were being lowered into the water by cranes.

One ship was still upside down in the water, with cables, winches, and cranes to one side, and men scurrying along the ship's exposed hull.

What appeared to be a very large ship was barely visible beneath the water's surface, small boats and men scattered across wooden decks and metal ladders, pumps removing fuel and water from below. Large pools of oil and fuel floated aimlessly around the wooden decks, some men using small siphons to recover the fluid.

*That must be the Arizona,* I said to myself.

*There are still dead men on that ship,* I muttered.

*They'll never get out of there – they'll still be there when this damn war is over, maybe forever.*

I cried on the train as it bounced and swayed in slow rhythm along the rails, thinking of the many men and women who had lost their lives on that December morning. The train made a right-turn near Wilikina Drive, toward the main entrance to Schofield Barracks, and slowed.

The train stopped, and we boarded buses for the short trip into the quads at Schofield Barracks.

*God has put me here,* I told myself, *here, where it all began. He has put me here to help turn it around, to have a hand in making right what the Japanese had made wrong.*

As I stepped down off the bus in front of the new quad, I knew I was in Paradise.

Green grass. Tall palm trees swaying in the trade winds. White flowers.

I proceeded to the in-processing station, barracks bag on my shoulder, and was directed to rejoin Mike Company,

21st Infantry Regiment, 24th Infantry Division, and my three buddies.

As I walked into the squad room, I saw Nobel stand up at the far end, a huge smile appeared instantly on his face, and he announced with his booming Alabama voice, "Well I'll be damned and sent to Tulsa! Tex is back!"

I walked down the middle of the room, past the cement columns, men standing by their bunks, waiting for evening chow. Some looked at me curiously, some smiled, and some just stared blankly.

Nobel was still standing by his bunk, grinning broadly. Pete had stepped forward, and was walking briskly toward me, hand outstretched, showing a familiar, friendly smile like only he could do.

"Doggone you, Red. I thought you were gonna be stuck with those baby-faced paratroopers for the rest of the war. Are you really back?"

We embraced the manly hug of friendship, then kept our hands on each other's shoulders for a long moment. I looked into his dark brown eyes, dark like a deep well dug into brown clay, and nodded an East Texas greeting to my re-found friend from Red River County.

"Yes, Pete, I'm back, and I ain't leaving here unless you guys leave with me."

I turned to see Nobel beside me, his full, round Alabama face beaming like a happy pig, rubbing his hand across his nearly bald head, still covered in stubbles of light blonde hair.

"Hey, Blondie," I said, reaching to shake his extended hand.

"Good to see you, Tex," he interrupted. "It sure is good to see you! I got nobody here that appreciates me the way you do. Are you really back? We're a mortar platoon now, you know. We have the new, and I mean BRAND NEW, M2 Mortar! There's more metal here than I ever saw back at the foundries at home. My God, man, it's good to see you."

Nobel and I shared a hug, slapped each other briskly on the shoulder, and laughed.

"Now, look what we have here," a charming, genteel voice sang from behind me.

"The Prodigal Son has returned."

I turned to see Kenny, just returning from the latrine. He had a towel over his shoulder, a razor and Burma Shave in one hand.

He laid his toiletries down on a nearby bunk, put his hands on my shoulders, and said, "I knew you were Infantry the first time I saw you. No floating down from the sky for you, Red Smith. You are blue-blooded Infantry, and I am honored to serve with you again."

He grinned confidently, and stepped forward for his hug.

"Thank you, my friend," he said. "This war could not be won without you here, right here, with your henchman, Nobel, his trustworthy sidekick, Everman, and me."

With his head next to mine, his lips told me quietly, "I didn't want to fight without you, Red. You're my anchor. It is so very good to see you back. So very, very good."

It was first time Kenny had broken his genteel, confident façade, and I was somewhat surprised that his Virginia courage was, in a way, dependent on me to keep him brave.

We broke our hug, looked at each other in the eye, and, at that moment, we sealed a bond of combat brotherhood that could survive any test to its breaking point.

I turned to face Nobel and Pete.

"I am so glad to be here."

It was the happiest I had been in a long, long time.

We chattered for the next half hour, me asking them about Hawaii, them asking me about Fort Brag.

"Did'ja get sick, Red, on the boat trip?" Nobel asked, his green eyes wide open, as open as a wild, soulless sea.

I could tell by the way he was asking that he had gotten terribly, horribly sick himself.

I almost lied to him, almost told him no, that it was a jolly trip, a damn jolly trip.

I couldn't. There were more boat rides ahead for us, I knew.

"Yeah, I did."

He grinned.

"Nobel, I thought a few times that death would be better than sick, but I thought of you, and I knew that you needed to know that somebody got sicker than you did."

We laughed and laughed, Pete making gagging sounds at Nobel's expense. Kenny just nodded and smiled politely, tapping sympathetically on Nobel's pig-head.

We went to chow, and enjoyed our reunion, dining on beef stew and baked bread.

When we returned to the squad room, the three of them managed to talk a Pennsylvania fellow into moving to another bunk, so I could be in the same corner of the squad room with them. I got fresh sheets and towels from the supply sergeant in the next quad, and settled into my new home. I emptied my barracks bag, placing everything neatly in my footlocker.

The Platoon Sergeant talked to me before taps, and explained to me what was expected and wished me good luck with the mortar training. Before he left, he told me that this was the first time and the last time that he would ever talk nice to me. As he walked away, he told me to get the god-dammed-hell to sleep.

Kenny and Pete smiled as he left. Nobel nervously rubbed his head.

# CHAPTER 11

# HAWAII

Christmas Day.
Friday, December 25, 1942.

Schofield Barracks, Pearl Harbor Naval Base, Oahu, Territory of Hawaii.

I held the Christmas card in both hands, with Momma's smooth, wavy handwriting swirled across the printed "Merry Christmas" greeting, saying "With love from all of us." She had placed the handwritten love-wish just below the picture of a manger holding the baby Jesus, and just above were two more handwritten words "Mom and Dad."

My eyes began to blink, a tear trying to form, as I gently lay the card back on the bunk. I wiped my eyes, forehead, and cheeks with my hands and stood up, flexed my arms, and exhaled.

Standing beside my bunk, I placed my hand on the white metal footboard, took in a deep lungful of air, and released a slow, long breath of relief. The room was almost empty. Yes, it was Christmas Day, and yes, I was thousands of miles from home, being trained for war in the Pacific. Yet, I was so proud to be where I was, in the new quad at Schofield Barracks, Honolulu, Hawaii, with Pete, Kenny, and Nobel.

I could hear the three of them talking their usual jabber in the showers, poking each other with witty insults, each one boasting to be the best at whatever nonsense or sometimes serious chatter going on. I had hit the showers earlier, my mind restless about spending Christmas away from home. I had spent the Christmas of '39 with the CCC in Colorado. Being away from home at Christmas was hard enough back then, even though I was surrounded by majestic mountains, work, and a good amount of play.

Now, in the middle of an ocean I had never seen, and halfway to the Imperial Homeland of an enemy that had attacked the very ground where I now stood, this Christmas was valuable beyond measure, beyond belief.

*"This could be the last Christmas I'll ever see,"* I thought to myself.

I looked around the room, full of empty, well-made bunks. Mosquito nets were rolled up around a metal rod that hovered over each bunk, bracketed to the waist-high headboards and footboards. A footlocker rested at the end of the bunk. Five square cement support columns extended down the center of the room, rifles stacked neatly along its path.

Tall windows extended down the front wall, spaced at every third bunk. My bunk was below the second window.

My gaze stretched out the window, across a green courtyard surrounded by palm trees and tall, rounded bushes with clusters of white bouquets. I had heard a local woman call them "Singapore flowers," and a fellow in our Company told me that he read about the flowers being special in Hawaii as representing everything that is positive.

Among the white bouquets were many short trees with pink flowers that looked like the orchids I had seen at the flower shop back home in Sulphur Springs. The same fellow told me they were called "Hong Kong Orchids."

There were large yellow flowers that were flat and as big as your hand, and blood-red ones that stood tall and straight, with a tiny star-shaped red flower on its tip. There were short trees, the size of a bush, with red berries like clumps of grapes.

I had never seen Paradise until I saw it in Hawaii.

I was so glad to be away from Fort Bragg, where I had felt myself breaking apart on the inside, losing my confidence, trying to be something I was not.

Pete came out of the showers in his skivvies, leaving Kenny and Nobel to their grooming. He walked over to the bunk, a towel hanging over his shoulder, and smiled as he asked, "Red, what do you want Santa to bring you today?"

"Oh, I don't know. Maybe a hot dog," I joked.

He laughed.

"Oh, I think we can do better than that. We can eat a good Christmas Dinner down at the USO."

He looked at me, in his serious, rock-steady way, and said, "I miss my home, Red, I really miss it bad today. Wanda told me in a letter last week," he pointed to his little rubber-banded stack of mail beside his pillow, "to make sure I ate a swell Christmas Dinner today, and spend it with good, decent folks."

"Well," his voice kinda cracked, "I'm doin' just as she said, and I'm gonna make sure she knows it when I write tomorrow."

I looked at him, slowly nodded, and said, "Yep. I wanna be home, too, Pete. Really bad. But, if I can't be there, I guess I'd just as soon be right here, with ya'll."

He returned my nod, and I returned my gaze toward the courtyard, past the lush green grass, the white flowers, and the tall, swaying palm trees.

*I thought Colorado was pretty,* I reflected. *But this takes the cake.*

A few minutes passed, and when I turned around Kenny and Nobel were at their bunks, putting on their brown, gabardine jackets and chuckling. Pete was standing there, fully dressed, staring at me and saying, "Well, are you coming with us?"

I realized that more than just a few minutes had passed, and I reached into my footlocker for my jacket, and admired the newly sewn, round, red patch of the 24th Infantry Division on the left shoulder, with the green taro leaf in the center.

*Hawaiian Division,* I said to myself, as I rubbed the patch with my right hand.

*I'm from Hawaii now,* I smiled.

*And proud of it, too.*

"Well, hell, let's go!" I announced to my buddies.

"Ho, ho, ho!"

We all laughed.

We found an Army bus waiting just down the road, the driver looking at his wristwatch as he read a newspaper. The sign on the front of the bus said Waikiki, with the words Diamond Head underneath. The driver was wearing a red Santa hat, and as we stepped up to the door, he placed the newspaper aside.

"Aloha! Come on in, gentlemen," he beckoned us cheerily, as we exchanged nods.

*"Mele Kalikimaka!* Merry Christmas to 'ya. Headed downtown?"

"Indeed, sir," Kenny replied, as the four of us marched

single file up the small steps into the aisle.

As the driver released the brake and guided the bus onto the roadway, we hand-walked down the aisle, navigating the handrails like monkeys, one hand-at-a-time. On either side, men in gabardine jackets filled the seats, some joking, some giving a smiling nod, some just staring out the window. Nobel wished several of the smiling faces a Merry Christmas, and received suitable replies.

Near the rear of the bus, we found two empty rows and poured ourselves into the bench seats. The bus made several stops along the way, picking men up and letting men off. Two young women in nurse uniforms got on the bus at one of the stops, and several men in the first few rows of the bus stood up, offering them their seats. The nurses were beautiful, and glided gracefully past the men, smiling, saying "No, thank you, sir, stay seated, sir." They continued their walk down the aisle like a white velvet mist, the driver not proceeding on until they had found empty seats several rows behind us. There was no monkey-walk for them. As they walked, *almost danced,* past us, the smell of fresh-washed hair and rose-water hung in the air for a few seconds. Nobel poked his left elbow into my side, as if to say *Would'ja look at them, Tex!*

I leaned over and whispered into Nobel's left ear "They are called ladies. Behave yourself."

He gave me a broad smile. Kenny leaned across the aisle, and rubbed the top of Nobel's head. Pete looked at me and grinned.

"Just like Wanda said, go out with some decent folks for Christmas," he said.

The bus carried us south, toward Pearl City and the

Harbor. Looking out the bus window, I could see fields of sugar cane stretching out from the road for miles, with sugar mills dotting the landscape, in front of the mountains that loomed on either side. Clouds, thick with rain, girdled the slopes. A faint rumble of thunder rolled down the mountain, not with the snap and crack of an East Texas thunderstorm, but with a low and lonely moan, rumbling across the sugar fields like a forlorn traveler, moving slowly, never stopping.

A lake to the left, then Pearl Harbor, still busy on Christmas Day, the salvage operations and ship repair crews pulling the country up by its bootstraps. I saw a man in a red Santa hat, waving at the bus as we passed.

As we approached Honolulu, I could see the city was not as busy as the day I arrived. Some of the storefronts were closed, but most of the restaurants and street vendors were open for business, selling flowers, fruits, and brightly colored shirts.

The bus driver turned his face to his right and announced, "Next up, Hotel Street, Alakea Street, Army and Navy YMCA, Central YMCA, USO Clubs!"

Pete stood up, motioned us forward, and said "We should find something here."

As we filed out the side door, I glanced back at the nurses, raised my finger to my garrison cap in a short salute, smiled, and nodded.

They smiled back.

*My God, they're beautiful,* my brain shouted.

A moment later, I was standing on the sidewalk with Kenny, Pete, and Nobel, looking at the two USO Clubs on either side of us. Pete pointed toward the Army and Navy YMCA, where a large banner was proclaiming that it had

"The Best Christmas Dinner West of Home."

"Merry Christmas, boys," Pete said.

"Will you fellows join me for dinner?"

I could smell turkey. I could smell the sage of the dressing.

We found a short line of soldiers, perhaps ten or twenty men, and joined their journey down the steam line. With mess hall trays and paper plates, we nodded to each server as they piled high the sliced turkey, ham, dressing, corn, something green that I said "No" to, bread, and pumpkin pie. We sat at a long table with folding chairs, exchanging greetings with the strangers who were now our brothers, in a land far away from home, on a mission to do what was necessary and return to those homes when the mission was done. Not much was said, the conversations were inward, between our hearts and our memories. Life was strong here, youth was everywhere. Death lay its solemn head down in Pearl Harbor, but here in the City, Life was strong.

Christmas Day. Hawaii.

*How far is it to Sulphur Springs? Three, four thousand miles? No matter. Christmas Day is happening there as well as it is here. Probably better here, at least more food, and more different kinds of it.*

Damn. I miss home. Momma. Daddy. The family.

And the Hamilton girl.

Hell, I even miss Ol' Blue.

Lord, help me through this. Take me home when it's done.

"Pass me the salt and pepper, would'ja, Pete?"

"Sure 'nuff, Red."

"Man," Nobel said.

"I wish I'd gotten more bread."

Kenny looked at the three of us and exclaimed, "Did I ever tell you about the bread my Mother would bake?"

"Cornbread?" Pete asked.

"Any kind of bread, Everman. All bread. Corn. Wheat. Yeast. You name it."

A thin smile crossed his face.

"Bread was invented in Virginia, you know," he winked.

Nobel turned his face toward Kenny, raised his middle finger, and politely jabbed it toward him.

"Alabama," he grunted.

"You Gentlemen stole it from us," Nobel said.

Pete joined in, "I believe my Mother's family, the Cherokee, was making bread in North Carolina long before any of you Englishmen got there."

A short fellow across from us, his nose bent to one side from one too many fights, his shoulders broader than they needed to be, leaned toward us and said, "I believe the Good Lord invented bread out there in the middle of the desert. Delivered it every day at daybreak. That's what I was taught. Not taking anything away from Virginia, or Alabama. Nor the Cherokee. To God be the glory."

"Thank you, Sir, indeed!" was Kenny's reply.

"To God be the glory for all things, especially this Christmas Dinner. And, for the bread."

Kenny smiled, and Nobel nodded his head.

"It don't matter," Nobel announced.

"I don't believe we caught your name, Sir," Kenny said, as he leaned toward the short fellow, extending his right hand.

"Hawkins. CC Hawkins," the fellow said, grasping Kenny's strong Virginia hand in his, shaking it vigorously.

A moment passed. They both stared into each other's eyes in a mutual sizing-up, a search for trust, hands still clasped in preliminary friendship.

"Pleased to meet you, CC," Kenny said, in an uncommon gesture of informality.

"I'm Kenny Herrod. That's Nobel Horner there, Everman Petty over there, you can call him Pete, he'll answer to that. And this gentleman here is Red Smith."

The customary handshakes ensued, each of us leaning up from our chairs and nodding to our new friend.

"What happened to your nose, CC, if I may ask?" Pete questioned.

"Got into a little misunderstanding with a couple of Oklahoma fellers who thought they owned the world," CC replied.

"They don't own it anymore," he laughed.

I studied CC as he talked, figuring out that he was a fighter, a cocky little dude with manners, and some brains in his head. A good talker, but with a short fuse attached to his temper, not from meanness, but from the sheer love of the fight.

"Well," I said, "Our world started out small, but grew to include Hawaii, and will grow a lot more in the days and months ahead."

"Days and months?" CC snickered. "I believe it will be months and years. There's more Japs out there than all the hairs on yer head."

He looked at Nobel.

'Except for you, Mr. Horner. You'll have a little bit

easier time, since you've lost a few of your Japs."

Nobel rubbed his peach-fuzz head and smiled.

I looked at CC again, noticed that none of the fellows around him were joining our conversation, and that he had not introduced any of them.

*This fellow is alone,* I thought. *Nobody wants to be close to him.*

*Self-defense, I guess. Too many unexpected fights, too much excitement. Maybe we should just.....*

"Walk with us after dinner, CC," Pete invited. "We're gonna walk around a bit, expand our worlds, see some more of Honolulu."

When we had finished eating our Christmas Dinner, we filed out of the YMCA and headed down Alakea Street, turning left onto Ala Moana. Honolulu Harbor was on our right as we sauntered southeast a couple of miles along Ala Moana, passing the Immigration Station and Fort Armstrong, Kewald Basin and Fisherman Wharf, and Moana Park.

There, in front us, lay the most beautiful sight any of us had ever seen. The white sands of Waikiki Beach, yachts, hotels, and blue-green waters lapping, constantly lapping at the foot of massive Diamond Head. I had seen it on my arrival, it seemed like yesterday. This was the one sight I remembered from long back in my childhood, seeing it on travel magazine covers and pictures in shops and stores, even on calendars. We all just stood there, gawking, until CC said, "Come on, boys, yer holding up the tourists."

I looked at him and asked, "Where you from, CC? You sound kinda country."

He looked at me and grinned.

"You've got a good ear for country, Tex. I'm from

Missouri. No place in particular. Just the whole goddamn state. Ever been there?"

"Nope."

"Don't. Too many hillbillies. Too many fights. Problem is, you never know who yer fighting. Could be yer brother, yer cousin. Hell, could be yer sister."

I shook my head and laughed, then turned back to the glorious, almost unreal sight of Waikiki Beach and Diamond Head. I remembered from the CCC that the Rocky Mountains were spectacular. The women in Denver were so beautiful they could've been Hollywood models. But this tropical wonderland was unbelievable.

We walked a bit further, and there it was – Pink! Monstrously, awesomely, gigantamously pink! The Royal Hawaiian Hotel. I had seen it from the boat last month, and wanted to get off the boat and touch it. There it was, now, in front of me.

To my left, Nobel blurted, excitedly, "I'll be damned! That's the Royal Hawaiian Hotel! I saw it in a magazine back in Birmingham! We gotta go in there! There's a beach bar in it with dancing girls and fancy drinks and no-telling what!"

Staring at it with dreamy eyes, Nobel walked toward it, like he was a boy again, approaching a Christmas tree surrounded by ribbon-wrapped gifts, candies, and unbelievable surprises. We all looked at each other, nodded our approval, and followed.

In a moment, we were standing in front of the massive building, looking up at the stunning pink hotel, in all its beauty, bell towers and tall, sinewy palm trees, flowers everywhere – pink, yellow, red, white, orange – big flowers, almost tree-big. Off to the right was an open bar, with flower-print pink awnings, that overlooked a sandy beach with the dancing girls - just as Nobel had predicted. We walked in the front entrance, to the porch, lined with white pillars and a dark grey polished stone floor. Inside, the breathtaking lobby, lined with white arches, the same dark grey polished floors with large colorful rugs, rich pink ceilings, and very big vases of tall, fresh flowers of unimaginable colors.

*How could all this be real?*

Soldiers were everywhere. Navy, Marines, Army. Pete told me the entire Hotel was reserved for the military now. No civilian customers. Just the soldiers, for rest and relaxation.

I followed Nobel and the others to the bar that opened onto the beach. I could see barriers of concertina wire strung down both sides of the Hotel beach, preventing people other than us soldiers from using "our" beach. I smiled at the thought of us having a private beach while Kenny politely asked the lovely, dark-haired Hawaiian hostess for a table near "our part" of the sandy beach. She smiled understandingly, and we trailed behind her to a table with a huge pink umbrella. I heard Kenny whisper to the waitress as he ordered an iced okolehao with pineapple, and I whispered to her *Yes, Ma'am, I'll take one of those too.*

The drink was sweet, strong, and very, very good.

Kenny said it was made from the root of a plant that grew only in Hawaii, and was a very old recipe known in the Islands and nowhere else. He said to be quiet about it, because it was so strong it was almost illegal.

The dancing girls were clothed in flowers that moved when they moved, their hands and hips were hypnotizing, and I swear they were all looking at me.

When Nobel said the same thing, I knew the okolehao was taking me deeply into a Paradise I had never seen, smelled, or tasted before.

The sun was higher in the sky than any December sun I had ever seen in Texas, and it slowly danced from just above me toward the right, following its east-to-west solar road to dusk. In my okolehao mind, I had already married two of the dancers.

I saw Pete stand up, tip his drink glass to a stunning peach-yellow-and-turquoise sunset, and say, "Time to go, dreamers. We have to remain loyal to our futures."

CC looked at him like he was crazy. Kenny nodded and stood up. Nobel said, "I swear, I've never seen such beauty."

I stood, thought of Hopkins County and family, and thanked God for the day and the moment.

We walked back out through the Royal Hawaiian Hotel, and again admired the enormous lobby and the tall vases of fresh cut tropical flowers, and strolled outside to Kalakaua Avenue.

A bus was loading soldiers and families to shuttle them to their destinations, hotels, and barracks. We followed them onto the small, packed bus.

It carried us toward King Street, past City Hall, Palace Square, and more restaurants, bars, and USOs. As it stopped near the Army and Navy YMCA, I saw a photo studio with a pretty lady, standing in the door, smiling, and waving to the bus, waving to homesick soldiers, waving to me.

I nodded to her as I stepped down from the bus, and her wave turned to a welcoming gesture, a beckoning call to *come see, get your portrait here, let's get to know each other.*

The others poured out of the bus behind me, asking "What the hell, Red, what are ya doing? Tex, where are ya going? Who do we have here?"

The lady looked at me and said, "Aloha!"

I gave her a big smile, and said, "Well, hello there! Were you waving at me? What am I gonna get here?"

"A portrait, *'Ula'ula*. You'll get a portrait on Christmas Day that will be better than any Hollywood star in the whole wide world."

I don't remember what we talked about next. All I remember is that this small, olive-skinned, dark-haired beauty with the flirting smile held me in the palm of her hand, and I wanted nothing more than to just stand there and be taken in by her and vanish from this Earth, taken away to a fantasyland of flowers, kisses, and passion.

"You gonna get your picture taken, Tex?" Nobel spoke, interrupting the spell that had been cast on me by the smile of the perfect dream lady.

"Yes, he is," she answered.

"He sure is," I confirmed.

"You have very pretty red hair, Tex," she said as she gently removed my garrison cap.

"What is your name?" I asked.

"Leilani."

"Lay-lah-nee?" I asked, saying it slowly, trying to pronounce it right.

"Yes, Leilani," she answered, saying it a little slower this time.

"Everything about you, including your name, is pretty, Leilani," I responded.

She smiled, bowed slightly (*could she be blushing?*), and said, "Thank you."

"You're welcome."

"Come with me to the camera room," she motioned, as she stepped toward a door at the left side of the room.

"We can handle this, boys," I told the others.

"Ya'll just stay here in the front, I'll be back."

Leilani led me to a room with a couple of chairs, some backdrops with palm trees and beaches, and a camera on a tripod. She pointed to a small stool, and said "Sit here, please."

She disappeared behind the camera.

She told me to look up, look down, back straight, chest out, no, chest in!

Flash!

She stepped out from behind the camera, changed the backdrop.

Disappearing again behind the camera, she told me to put one knee up, look sideways, smile, no, look serious, that's it!

Flash!

Stepping out from the camera, Leilani looked at me and whispered, "Come back after Christmas, in a few days. Your pictures will be ready and maybe I'll take more pictures, '*Ula'ula.*"

"I will, Leilani."

She smiled as I spoke.

She led me back to the store lobby.

"You okay, Red?" Pete asked.

I nodded *yes* as we walked out of the camera shop and back to the bus-stop.

*But I wasn't through talking to her, I thought.*
One bus rolled by, never stopped.
Another bus followed, a sign on the front saying "HALEIWA."

The door opened. A soldier and a slender woman stepped out. Pete leaned into the open door, looked at the driver and asked, "Schofield Barracks?"

The driver shook his bald head, pointed to his left, and said, sympathetically, "No, Sir. 'Sorry. Two streets that way, one street to the left."

The door closed with a squeak and a metallic moan, and continued north.

Pete turned to us and said, "Follow me, gentlemen." He began walking in the direction the bus driver had suggested, then stopped, turned back to us, and said, "CC, we never asked if you were going back to Schofield Barracks."

"I'm going wherever the action is," came his reply.

A simple statement.

But, the ironic honesty of the statement would become quite clear in a few minutes.

Two streets down, one street to the left.

Three visibly drunk soldiers stood at the bus-stop.

Our bus-stop.

A ruckus waiting to happen.

One of them, a square-jawed fellow with a thick forehead that stuck out, looked at CC.

"Looky there, it's a wee little leprechaun," he slurred.

"What did you say, Neanderthal?" CC returned.

"I shaid looky there, it's a wee little tiny man," as he tottered.

"I thought you cave-men died of stupidity a million years ago," CC spat, as we suddenly realized the encounter had grown from mouthy ruckus to certain fisticuffs in a matter of seconds.

I thought I heard CC giggle.

As the other two drunken fools were holding their Neanderthal friend, keeping him from falling down dog-drunk, CC swiftly ran into the fray. His fists tightly clinched, he swung a powerful right and two punching lefts, and the cave man's knees buckled as he slumped gracefully and quietly to the rock-hard street. The two other fools quickly responded, and as one kicked CC in the groin, the other looked at us and snarled.

"I'm gonna knock yer block off," he told me.

I ran toward the snarling idiot, and passed him as he ducked and danced away.

I stumbled and fell to the street.

*What the hell?*

*Where'd he go?*

He covered the space between us in an instant, and raised his right boot to smash me in the face.

Nobel flew at him, knocking him on top of me.

Upon seeing this, the other drunkard ignored CC, jumped into the street, and quickly tackled Nobel. Both began to wrestle, each pushing the other's chin back with one hand and slamming his opponent's chest with the other hand.

Pete and Kenny broke their frozen stance, and joined the chaotic party. Pete pulled the snarler off me, and helped me stand up.

Kenny quickly and effectively dispatched the snarling shithead that had been on top of me by leaning over him and delivering a right blow to his left jaw. The shithead went limp.

Kenny then pulled Nobel and the other drunkard apart, and repeated his Virginia Special to the man's left jaw.

As Pete and I helped lift Nobel to his feet, Kenny rubbed his right fist in a painful wince.

Nobel's beautiful peach-fuzz head had an ugly slash well above his right temple where his flesh and the street had met.

I removed my handkerchief and pressed it firmly over the wound, and told Nobel to be careful with strangers, then glared at CC as he pushed himself up from the street, holding his groin in pain.

He was still giggling.

Pete spoke with a restrained yell, and blasted at CC, "You stupid son-of-a-bitch! We don't think it was so funny!"

"We showed 'em, didn't we!" CC affirmed, with a quick nod of his ruffled head.

"You stupid asshole," Pete yelled back at him.

"You are Ignorance gone to seed!"

He looked back at us.

"Come on, guys," he ordered. "We can't stay here. The MPs will be here soon, we don't want to be part of this."

He looked at CC, pointed his finger, and demanded, "You go the other way. No more of this!"

I grabbed Nobel's belt, held him tight to me, gave him a whispered *"Thank you, buddy,"* and we moved down the street to a quieter area.

Pete put Nobel's garrison cap over the wounded head, and we all marched in cadence to the next bus-stop. I looked back and saw CC kick the Neanderthal again, wave at us, and walk in the opposite direction.

Nobel and I didn't say much, as we adjusted our uniforms, brushed the dirt from our shirt sleeves, and regained our breath. Kenny kept rubbing his right fist, faintly smiling with pride. Pete's eyes flashed with anger and fear, as he surveyed the streets in all four directions, looking for the unwanted MPs and the much-needed bus.

We were a perfect team, as we quietly stood together, 300 hundred feet west of our first battle.

In a few minutes, from out of the evening darkness floated a bus, beaming with a sign on front that said, "Schofield Barracks." As we stumbled up the steps, past the tired, smiling driver, and walked steadily down the aisle, we did not look at the other passengers. We sat silently down near the rear of the bus.

The four of us had won the ruckus, and we had walked away safely.

CC had gone his way, to more adventure and more fights, we were sure.

We rode in silence the entire trip back to Schofield Barracks. I tried to put the pieces of the day together, beginning with the best Christmas Dinner I had ever had, and ending with the street fight. Somewhere, lying in between those two events, I met a short man with a big mouth, saw a gigantic pink hotel, watched hula dancers, drank several glasses of an old Hawaiian spirit, and was touched by a dark-haired, olive-skinned angel.

The bus came to a complete stop at the Barrack's gate, the driver looked over his right shoulder and announced, "Gentlemen, you are home."

We dripped out of the bus and walked, heads high and chins up, into our quad and into our bunks.

*"Merry Christmas to all, and to all a goodnight,"* I sighed to myself.


The Next Day.
Saturday, December 26, 1942.

I awoke to shafts of sunlight dancing along the opposite wall from the window above my bunk. There were only a few soldiers in the room, many choosing to stay off base for Christmas.

Nobel squirmed in his bunk, looked up at me, and said, "Mornin', Tex. My head hurts."

I walked over to his bunk, removed my blooded handkerchief from his head, examined the still-ugly slash near his right temple.

"Mornin', beautiful," I told him. "Looks like we'll be taking you to sick bay after breakfast."

We straggled to breakfast. There would only be two meals in the mess hall that day, a late breakfast and an early dinner. We sat there at a table, drinking our coffee and eating our hot cakes and sausage, with lots of syrup, and Nobel with a big slash across his temple.

I walked him to sick bay, and he explained to the nurse that he had tripped over the street curb, window-shopping.

"I saw this beautiful blue flowery Hawaiian dress that my girlfriend Katy, back home in Birmingham, would just love to have. I thought to myself, she sure would look pretty in that. I guess I was paying so much attention to it that I tripped over my own feet, Ma'am."

I looked at him and thought *Man, you sure are a good storyteller.*

The nurse, an older, stern-faced but sympathetic woman, looked at him with steel-grey eyes and said, "Bless your heart, honey."

She acted like she had seen her share of street curb wounds.


Four Days Later.
Wednesday, December 30, 1942.

There was not much to do between Christmas and New Year's. Each day, we would fall into formation and march around the base several miles. We would then polish up the barracks, and sit through a few classes for first aid, basic infantry tactics, map reading, and close-order drill, *right face, left face, column left, column right, halt.* Duties would end after the noon chow the entire week.

The four of us took a bus tour of northwestern Oahu to celebrate Nobel's 21st birthday. Pete, Kenny, and I pitched in and bought Nobel's ticket to show him how much we appreciated him being born just-in-time to be drafted with us, with one day to spare under the Third Registration of the Selective Training and Service Act, 1940. Pete gave him a pack of C-Ration cigarettes, Kenny gave him a can of Spam, and I gave him a C-Ration chocolate bar.

The bus tour took us west on Military Drive, to the foot of Mt. Kaala, the tallest peak on Oahu. The bus then followed

Military Drive as it snaked south through Kolekole Pass, with thick lush forests on our left, reaching to the mountaintops of the Waianae Range.

A tour guide, an older white-haired gentleman wearing a shirt of wild colors, reds and yellows, greens and blues, palm trees, shacks, and boats, walked through the bus, telling us stories and alerting us to the sights ahead. He wanted to give me a shirt like his, because I was from Texas and I needed something wild and wonderful to "strut my stuff," he said.

He told us stories of the plantations and the hills, about the ancient peoples and their gods, of legends and truths, going on and on with the history and folklore of tragedies and spooks.

Then, down to the beaches of Nanakuli we went, through flatlands of more sugar cane. Turning north onto Farrington Highway, we passed the Battery Nanakuli, with two 5-inch naval guns to protect the Lualualei Naval Ammunition Depot and Radio Station. We then threaded a dozen or so miles up to Kaena Point.

We got out of the bus at the western slope of Kaena Point, had sandwiches and soda from a small market, staffed by locals and a USO fellow from Minnesota. Our tour bus guide was walking with us, so we bought him a sandwich and soda, too.

We could see a dozen or more Army jeeps scattered between the highway and the top of Kaena Point, and soldiers with books, maps, and cameras walking to and fro along the slope, like they were either looking for something or planning something.

"They're looking for us a place to live, Red," Nobel announced, nodding his head twice as I looked at him.

"I reckon. Maybe gonna put a big cannon up there so you can polish it, Nobel," I answered.

"Yes, they are!" our tour guide confirmed. "I've been hearing that you boys are going to be all along this coast soon, putting cannons in big concrete bunkers to keep the Japs from hitting us again."

"Gladly," Kenny said. "That's what we're here for, Sir."

We sat there, outside the market, and ate while our guide told us stories about Kaena Point.

According to ancient Hawaiian folklore, the area was the "jumping off spot" for the spirits of the recently deceased. We looked up to the top of Kaena Point, and thought we could see a flat rock on top, the jumping rock. Nobel was a little spooked with the whole idea of spirits jumping off to go to the Great Beyond, and couldn't keep his eyes off the Point while we ate. The old white-haired guide pointed to the side of Kaena Point and showed us the tracks of the railroad that first connected it to Honolulu in 1898.

He also told us the story about a prophet from long, long ago that lived on Kaena Point. He was considered to be a "reader of omens," and prophesied the future of the ancient Hawaiians. He said that some will rise, and some will diminish, until they completely disappear.

The story of the old prophet sent a chill through me, as I thought about the small towns and farms of Hopkins County, where, just six months ago, Ol' Blue had pulled the wagon, Daddy, and me to the courthouse for my first day in the Army. I remembered the schoolteacher that told me about old town Tarrant, and about the gristmill, the blacksmith shop, the college, the brick kiln, the general store, the tannery, and the Hopkins Hotel. As I had stared across the landscape that day, I could not see anything from old town Tarrant. I wondered how Time would treat my own landscape, the one I was leaving behind. I wondered if, someday, it would be hard to see where bustling towns and farm fields once stood. I thought of Time as a steadily moving eraser across the landscape, wiping out the traces of everybody and everything old, replacing them with new people and new places.

I realized that we were the "new Hawaiians," the soldiers of the 24th Infantry Division, the "Hawaiian Division," standing beside a new bus, looking at the landscape of the ancient Hawaiians. The old prophet who lived on Kaena Point was right. Most of the ancient Hawaiians had already disappeared.

The bus loaded up again and we headed around Kaena Point and drove easterly along Kaukonahua Road. Immediately, through our open windows, we could feel cooler winds begin to blow in from the ocean. The old tour guide said this was historically one of the most beautiful places on Oahu, with the cooling trade winds (he called them the Moae Breeze) bathing the lush vegetation of the fertile valley. On our right, we saw grazing cattle, banana plantations, and more sugar cane.

Rows of tents, looking like small cities, began to appear in the distance. Men and machines were moving about, placing the tent cities between the farms and factories of the north coastline, between the beaches and the highlands. Some of them even extended a small distance up the slopes of the highlands.

*This is where we are headed, I told myself. We'll be living out here soon and working on those cannons.*

We saw fields of taro, the plant whose leaf was on our shoulder patch. The guide told us the ancient Hawaiians considered the taro plant to be an elder brother to the Hawaiian race. According to the folklore, the first child of the Sky Father and the Earth Mother was stillborn, and they buried the dead child near their house. It soon grew out of the ground and became a taro plant. Their second son was considered to be a younger brother to the plant, and was named after the taro.

As we continued east, to our left lay the Pacific Ocean and the old fishing grounds. We saw a sugar mill as we approached the intersection with the road to Waialua Bay and Kahuku Point. Staying to the right, we drove steadily along Kaukonahua Gulch, as it drained the slopes of Mt. Kaala, our first stop earlier in the day.

We were delivered to the Schofield Barracks gate in time to grab a hamburger at the Service Club before it closed.

We didn't know it at the time, but the bus tour that day would prove to be the best day of the war. We all felt young, out of danger, and free as the wind.

We thought to ourselves, *if this is war, then bring it on.*

I slept that night with peaceful scenes of cattle and sugar cane, banana plantations, and shirts with crazy, wild colors.


New Year's Eve.

Thursday, December 31, 1942.

    I took the bus into town early, managing to get away alone while everyone was writing letters and doing laundry. I wanted to go back to the photo studio to pick up my picture and to talk to Leilani, again. As I got off the bus and walked up the sidewalk toward the studio, she was standing in the doorway, wearing a white blouse, smiling, and waving to me.
    "*Aloha.* Happy New Year's Eve, Red. I was hoping you would come back today."
    "Hello to you, Leilani."
    "Your picture is ready. Come in."
    As I stepped toward the doorway, she winked at me, glided into the studio, and said "We have a Special today. Free picture. With me. Just for you."
    "Why just for me?" I inquired, as I entered.
    "Because you are very handsome. *Au makemake e hoomanao.*"
    I looked at her, cocked my head to the left a little, and said "I didn't catch that last part,
Ma'am."
    She shyly looked down, sighed, and looked back up.
    "It means, "*I want to remember.*"
    I looked at her, my brows upward, eyes wide open.
    "Thank you, Leilani. There's not a chance in hell I'll not remember you."
    Our gaze locked, and all was quiet for a moment, a thousand silent words passing between us. She slowly put her right hand behind her, feeling for the studio desk, and turned toward it. She reached for a stack of envelopes, fumbled through them, and pulled one out.

"These are your Christmas pictures. They are both very good."

I opened the envelope, saw two sets of photos, with three wallet-size and six smaller ones on each sheet. I pulled one of the sheets out, and stared at it. There I was, a young khaki-clad soldier, with my left shoulder slightly toward the camera, my head turned enough to face directly forward. I had a thin, tight smile and a comfortable yet confident expression on my face. A beach with a few palm trees lay behind me, in the distance.

"I'm sure I was looking at you when you took this."

"Of course, you were, Red. I was behind the camera."

We both giggled, and I said "No, I mean you. Not the camera. I was looking at You."

She stepped behind me, looked at the picture, and said "*'Ae*. It is a good picture. *Oe i ka pono i loko o kou naau.*"

She smiled at my questioning expression.

"*It means you have good in your heart.*"

A moment passed, another thousand words being passed between her eyes and my eyes. She moved away, breaking the spell.

"We must take our picture. Come with me, to the back."

Leilani led me back to the small camera room. A chair was positioned in front of a backdrop showing a palm tree and beach sand, with a beautiful blue sky. Looking at the chair and backdrop, I could almost feel like I was there, beneath the tree, on the beach, in Paradise.

She positioned another chair beside it, and motioned for me to sit in the chair to the right. She placed a white string of flowers around my neck, which looked pretty good against my dark wool shirt. She then selected a string of small red flowers for her neck, placing it boldly across her white blouse.

Leilani then stepped behind the camera, her busy hands setting the focus and whatever else was needed. She then walked back toward me, and sat in the chair to my right.

"Kalea!" she called.

An older woman walked into the room from behind the backdrop, a slight limp in her step. A broad infectious smile was on her weary, yet attractive face as she said, "Ready?"

Leilani nodded, and replied, "*Ae*."

The older woman looked at me with soft brown eyes, gently gazed into the camera, motioned for me to tilt my head toward Leilani, a little more, smiled again, then nodded and pushed a button on a metallic cord that hung from the camera.

A click, a flash, and she gracefully stepped away from the camera, smiled again, and disappeared behind us, behind the backdrop, out of sight.

"It must be a good picture," Leilani said.

"Kalea only takes good pictures. She taught me. She is the best. It is sad that she is dying."

"What's wrong? Why is she dying?"

"Diabetes. It takes many of the older ones."

I just stared ahead. I knew all of us soldiers would stare death in the eye during the upcoming year, but here was a gracious, charming woman, doing the same. I breathed a long sigh of despair.

"I wish I could do something…."

Leilani looked at me and said, "You just did."

"Did what?"

"You let her take our picture."

"What do you mean?"

"Kalea told me we should have a picture. She saw you Christmas Day."

"I don't remember seeing her that day."

"She has a way of seeing and not being seen."

"Why did she want you to take a picture of us?"

She looked down, took a breath, and looked up, her dark swirling eyes moistening.

"Kalea said there is good in your face, and you should be remembered."

I looked at her, and felt a desire to hold her, to love her.

"She called you *ula keonimana*. The red-haired gentleman."

I touched her hand, squeezing it gently.

"You must go. Return for your picture – our picture – next week. Perhaps we will have more time."

I stood up, nodded, tried to say something.

She nodded back and smiled, and a bell rang as two sailors walked in the front door.

As I left the studio, one of the sailors asked me "Do they take good pictures?"

"Yep." I replied.


New Year's Day.
Friday, January 1, 1943.

On New Year's Day, we had corned beef, cabbage, and black-eyed peas - but no cornbread and no greens. All four of us knew that black-eyed peas always came with cornbread and greens. That's just what people did in Texas and the whole South.

We told a New York fellow sitting next to us about the cornbread and he couldn't understand what we were saying. He said corned beef and cabbage was enough.

"What's with this cornbread shit anyway," he asked.

We didn't have much corned beef in East Texas, though Kenny said he'd had plenty in Virginia. All different times of the year. It didn't have to be New Year's Day.

Nobel said he had an Aunt Kathleen from Scotland that would cook some up once or twice a year. He said he loved that lady, and could sit and listen to her talk and laugh all day and all night, watching her green eyes dance with emerald fire and the dimples in her cheeks move like magic as she tossed her red hair about. I saw a wetness come to his eye as he paused between each sentence, recalling and savoring the memories of his aunt. There was a soft spot in Nobel, just beneath the surface, hiding behind his smart-ass mouth and Alabama brag. The more I was around Nobel the more I loved him like my own brother.

The week after New Year's Day, our full-day schedules returned. We spent all morning drilling and marching, and all afternoon in rifle, artillery, and mortar training, sometimes until after dark.

I would be called aside many days to attend driver training, which I enjoyed more than assembling and disassembling the M2 Mortar. Nobel was a whiz at breaking the mortar down and setting it up. He was fun to watch, eyes seriously focused, hands moving swiftly, knowing every inch of the M2, fingers touching and moving the piece into action with his tongue barely sticking out the right side of his mouth as he concentrated. Kenny would hold the mortar in place as Nobel would finish each step. Pete would feed him the components in correct, hurried sequence as Nobel would inhale and exhale in quick, short bursts of deliberate breath. I was almost useless as the fourth member of this crack team, and would try to look busy having each part ready for Pete to grab at the right time, when Nobel would place his open right hand out like a surgeon, surrounded by assistants, moving his nervous, twitching fingers in anticipation of the next important thingamajig.

They were good, I'll tell you. Nobel was The Natural working with anything metal. Pete was The Solid Rock, holding the mortar together as Nobel worked his art. Kenny was The Thinker, always a step ahead of Nobel's sure fingers.

The free time and passes that we were given during the holidays became less and less, as the Army became more and more serious about keeping us busy.

The months passed.

February into March.

March into April.

I still hadn't made it back downtown to see Leilani and get my second set of portraits. She was on my mind, but not at my fingertips. I wanted to see her again, and tell her I hadn't forgotten about her.

I wanted to find out how Kalea, the older lady, was doing with her diabetes.

I felt Time was slipping away.

Friday, April 23, 1943

Meanwhile, the War was raging on.

In Europe, the Battle of Stalingrad ended with a German surrender. Our boys in North Africa were getting kicked around by Rommel, but the fighting in Tunisia was beginning to weaken his tight hold on the Allies.

In our part of the war, the Pacific War, we took control of Guadalcanal and the Russell Islands. Eight Japanese troop transports were hit and sank in the Bismarck Sea. A group of our POWS broke out of a Japanese prison camp on Mindanao, and they told the horrible story of the Bataan Death March on Luzon in April '42. Almost 80,000 soldiers, who had been taken prisoner on Luzon, were forced to march over 60 miles under brutal conditions to other POW camps on the island. They said almost 20,000 died or were killed on that march. The story hit us hard.

*That's who we're fighting out there,* we realized.
*Murderers.*
*We must live to win this war.*
*If we become prisoners, we die.*
*If we lose, we die.*


Saturday, April 24, 1943.

It was Easter weekend. I could wait no longer. I left Kenny, Pete, and Nobel doing their laundry and writing their letters, and I took the bus downtown to see Leilani at the photo studio.

The bell rang as I walked in the studio door. Leilani was finishing up with a customer, and looked up quickly as I walked in. She was wearing the most beautiful Hawaiian dress I had ever seen, short and tight, with small red flowers against a navy-blue background. Her coal black hair hung full against each side of her neck, shoulder length, and she wore soft red lipstick.

I was falling in love with her, I realized. I hardly knew her. She knew nothing about Texas and farming, I knew nothing about Hawaii and her Pacific ways. I was fire-and-brimstone Baptist, and she was shy, peaceful, hand-gesturing Catholic. My heart, my mind, my body were traveling at break-neck speeds in all directions. I knew I had to slowdown. The War lay ahead. My way of life, my friends back home, my family, they all lay behind me. Uncertainty, fear, combat, and the Great Unknown lay in front of me.

*Get control of yourself. You're not gonna fall in love with anybody. You want her, but she doesn't need you. Not now. Not before any of this hell starts. You're training for war, man. You're going to kill Japs. You don't need to foul her bed with empty promises and cheap words.*

"Aloha, 'ula'ula! I am glad you made it back."

She walked toward me, put both hands on my shoulders, and gave me a gentle hug, being careful not to stand too close for our bodies to touch.

"It's swell to see you, Leilani," I said, as we stepped back from the warm but reserved hug.

"I'm sorry it took so long. The Army is keeping us busy every day. We're off today because tomorrow is Easter. Everyone else is washing clothes and writing letters. I figured all of that could wait, I wanted to see you and get our picture."

I was obviously chattering nervously.

She laid her hand on my shoulder.

"I know. The War is in motion. You will soon be gone. Come back to the camera room and I will find our picture."

We stepped into the room with the chairs and the backdrops. She closed the door behind us, then turned and looked at me with sad, gentle eyes, stepped forward, put her hand against my left cheek, drew near, and placed a soft, wet, inviting kiss on my lips.

She backed away and said, "I will never regret that. It will be the only kiss I ever give to you, *ula keonimana*. I could love you without ever knowing you, we could spend the rest of our years and never really understand each other, but I would love you just the same. It won't happen, Red. I will lose you in this war, not to Death, but to Time. You will be swept away to many islands, you will experience much that you will choose to forget, and when the war is over and my prayers are answered, you will be carried home safely and unharmed on the same boat that brought you here, and you will find your Paradise where you left it. I will cry *lani hoku,* to the stars of the heavens, and I will remain here to fulfill the destiny of my home, my *oiwi kanaka*, my native people, and my Jesus."

My hands trembled. My eyes were wet with admiration.

"I am in love with you, Leilani. But everything you say is true. You are the most honest and gentle woman I have ever known."

We stood there for a long moment. I stepped toward her, and put my arms around her neck. Our foreheads touched. She sighed. I stared into her dark eyes and saw her soft, loving, invincible soul.

She stepped back, blinked, and said, "Our picture! You will be pleased, as I am pleased, and as Kalea is pleased."

"How is Kalea?"

"She is better. She says you made her better. The goodness in your soul gave her life. You have been a gift from Heaven."

"I am humbled."

"She said to tell you *Ke uwe aloha*, she bids farewell."

Leilani opened a drawer, retrieved an envelope, and took out two small photos, and handed one to me.

"This one is for you. The other, I keep."

I felt the room spin and my knees weaken as I looked at the picture. My head lay against her head, with palm leaves dominating the backdrop. A calm, mesmerizing expression on my face, a soft smile on her face, our eyes looking confidently into the camera, a moment stopped in time, an eternity shared by two people, a dream on paper.

"It's... it's... it's perfect," I stammered.

"You will be remembered, '*Ula'ula*."

I put my picture into my chest pocket, over my heart, and just stood there.

The bell rang as the front door opened.

"You must go, Red." Her voice cracked.

"I will be back," I whispered.

"No, you are a warrior with a destiny."

"*Aloha wau ia 'oe.*"


Saturday, May 15, 1943.

The Hawaiian Division was assigned the task of guarding the north coast of Oahu. The three regiments of the 24th Division were being scattered along the beaches and highlands of the north coast, from Kahe Point to Kaneohe Bay.

The 21st Infantry Regiment was sent to a tent city that had been hurriedly constructed at the western foot of Kaena Point. The four of us had no complaints about going to Kaena Point. We already knew the place. We again managed to stay together, and we shared one of the 20-person tents that were reserved for the 3rd Battalion at the foot of Kaena Point near the beach.

We were helping build underground bunkers for heavy artillery all along the north coast. Everything from road building, tunnel digging and blasting, electrical, plumbing, painting, and constant moving of supplies and equipment from here to there and from there to here. We were working a minimum of six days a week, and sometimes a short day on Sunday. If we didn't work that short day, we slept a long day.

Kenny and Pete had been selected to be "crew leaders," which meant each one was in charge of a small 5-man crew engaged in all-the-above. You always needed five bodies to help the road builders, tunnel diggers and blasters, electricians, plumbers, and painters. Kenny and Pete both had the "look" of being authoritative and serious, so it was an easy decision for Platoon Sergeant Malone to select them as crew leaders. Nobel and I had been picked by Battalion Supply Sergeant Wallace to deliver construction materials to the bunker locations. Sergeant Wallace was from Alabama, so he and Nobel had "drifted together" because they spoke the same language. Through the months, Sergeant Wallace and Nobel had many conversations about Alabama football, Alabama politics, and Alabama women. Nobel and I were the perfect pair for the job. I could drive any personnel or equipment vehicle in the Army, and Nobel could remember directions, keep a list of what we had or what we needed, and had the smart-ass voice to appear to be responsible.

One day in mid-June, late-morning, Nobel and I were in a Dodge WC-62 ton-and-a-half truck delivering pallets of cement bags to Battery Arizona, which was being built near Kahe Point, on the west side of the island. A triple fourteen-inch cannon salvaged from the U.S.S Arizona was to be placed in a bunker on top of the solid rock highland, connected to a pair of long tunnels for ammunition and support. Giant generators for lights and ventilation were being installed, and construction had begun on latrines, switchboards, radar, radio, command rooms, water tanks, and storage for a crew of 160 men.

Another triple fourteen-inch cannon from the U.S.S Arizona was being delivered to Kaneohe Bay, on the east side of the island. This bunker was called Battery Pennsylvania, named for her sister ship. The bunker, tunnels, and construction needs for Battery Pennsylvania were the same as for Battery Arizona.

This work was not easy, since the soil on the north coast was hard, black lava-rock. I missed the rich, black clay bottomland soils of Hopkins County, and the brown-red sandy soils along the hard-pan roads between the farms. Little did I know that black lava rock, along with white coral, would be most of what I would see for the next couple of years.

As we were driving to Battery Arizona that morning, I told Nobel that I had been pretty upset when I saw the U. S. S. Arizona at Pearl Harbor the day I arrived in Honolulu.

"The Arizona sitting there beneath the water almost made me cry, Nobel. All those boys still inside, probably forever. I'm glad they're going to use those big guns to stop another attack from the Japs."

"The Japs probably know not to do it again anytime soon," Nobel said.

"There's still a thousand men down there, Tex, down underneath the water in that twisted metal. Maybe these guns can help blow a few thousand Japs to hell."

As we bounced across the rocky road, I looked at Nobel, staring out of the passenger-side windshield, a determined look on his face. I placed my left arm out the driver's side open window, let it lay on the spare tire that was attached to the door, and adjusted my rear-view mirror.

I looked back at Nobel, and said, "We'll need to blow away more than just a thousand of them. Somebody told me there were over five million Jap soldiers out there on all those islands."

Nobel shook his head slowly, and said "We will."

"I swear, Tex, I never thought, growing up in Birmingham, that I'd ever be out here in the middle of the Pacific, with the job we have in front of us. We MUST send those sons-of-bitches back to where they came from, and make sure they never, ever attack anybody again. Shit, what they did to our boys on the march from Bataan was .. was .. was pure sin! Unforgivable! I will make sure, damn sure, that they pay for it!"

He pounded his fist on the dashboard.

For a few minutes, we just bounced along, looking at the scrub brush and low vines with pink and yellow flowers.

Ahead, we saw a jeep facing us, with two soldiers, the passenger-side rear wheel sunk into a wet, muddy ditch.

"How the hell did he do that," I muttered.

"He let the jeep get away from him. Probably driving too fast, not paying attention. Just bounced sideways and into the wrong part of the ditch."

Nobel gave me his familiar giggle, halfway funny, halfway delirious.

"Look, he's carrying big boxes of C-Rations. There's crackers, there's canned peaches, there may even be some chocolate."

I slowed, pulled up in front of him, and stopped.

A tall skinny man with a goofy face stood up and smiled.

"Would'ja help us out?" he asked, with a flat accent, more like no accent at all.

I opened my door, put one foot on the ground, and said "Sure."

To my right, Nobel got out of the truck and announced, "Yeah, but it's gonna cost you, Yank."

"I ain't a Yank, I'm from Pennsylvania. My buddy here is from Wisconsin," he objected, pointing to a lad that looked to be no older than sixteen.

"Well, you ain't from the South like Tex and me, and that makes you Yanks. We're so full of Southern Hospitality that we're gonna put you back on the road for only a few crackers, peaches, and chocolate," Nobel raised his eyebrow when he said the word "chocolate," saying it slowly and deliberately, looking for a reaction to prove that they had chocolate.

"Obviously, you boys didn't get these through the regular channels, or else you wouldn't have been driving so reckless in one of Uncle Sam's best vehicles," I added.

The goofy fellow looked at us, spread his arms wide, took a slight bow, smiled again, and said, "You got yourselves a deal."

We had his jeep winched out of the muddy ditch in a matter of minutes. Nobel completed his duty of getting a lot of saltines, a lot of canned peaches, and a healthy size wrapper of four chocolate bars.

We watched the goofy guy drive his jeep away, down the road we had just traveled. Nobel stashed the "goods" in the truck bed, tightly secured beneath a blanket, directly behind the cab.

It was close to noon when we drove up to the construction gate of Battery Arizona. The guard asked us what we had, pointed toward a line of delivery trucks to our left, said "That-a-way, Private," and waved us through.

An hour later, we were on the road, heading back to the 3rd Battalion motor pool. As we neared the Lualualei Naval Ammunition Depot, I remembered a small side-road that threaded its way across the scrub brush, to a point where it was relatively unseen from the main road. I pulled in, bounced a few hundred feet down the road, and stopped. I looked at Nobel and said, "Break time, Private Horner," as I grabbed our two canteens and stepped out of the truck.

He grinned, opened his door, and got out. Going to the back of the truck, he lowered the tailgate, crawled back into the khaki tarp-covered bed, and grabbed our stash.

We sat on the tailgate. Nobel handed me a box of saltines, a Number 2 can of peaches, and laid the chocolates on his side of the truck bed in the shade. I handed him his canteen. We each opened a box of saltines, removed the lids of the canned peaches with our pocketknives, and sat there like kings looking westward across the scrubby beach to the Pacific Ocean.

Brown birds with long downward-curved beaks prowled the shoreline on tall, spindly legs, using their beaks to dig into the light brown sand. Waves moved shoreward, gently turning to white foam as they hit the beach. Little, dove-like white birds chased the waves as they moved up the beach, looking for clams, fish, anything edible. The water beyond the beach was turquoise blue, touching the horizon where white clouds and indigo blue met.

Overhead, unbelievably large white birds with very long wings, white on bottom and black on top, circled in the soft wind currents.

"What did Kenny call those white birds?" I questioned, biting into a cracker.

"Oh, what did he say?" Nobel replied, with a peach slice impaled on his knife.

"I don't remember, either. Don't tell him we seldom remember everything he says."

"He said something about the pirates. Something about pirates thinking they were the souls of lost sailors. They considered it bad luck to kill them."

"Right. We'll just tell Kenny we saw some of those lost sailor birds."

"Yeah, that's right. We'll tell him that and he'll say its name and we'll just say yeah, yeah, we know," Nobel giggled.

"You know, Nobel, that sure is a pretty sight. I don't like sailing on the ocean, but I like looking at it."

"Yeah. I've been to Mobile, and seen the Gulf of Mexico. It's pretty, Tex, but not this pretty. Katy, my girlfriend back home, wants to move to Mobile and live on the beach. I told her it didn't make a lick of sense, living on the beach. I told her a hurricane would blow her away. I told her she'd always have sand in her shoes and in her bed sheets."

"Maybe she'd be worth moving to the beach. Maybe that's where your paradise might be."

He snorted. It made me think of my brother Lester, back home.

Nobel took a sip from his canteen, then answered, "I don't know. We didn't leave on the best note. I think she was finding someone else to go live on the beach. I just want to go back to the iron foundry, and get my job back after the war."

"That's what we all want to do."

"Have you ever been to a foundry, Tex?"

"No, I haven't."

"Aw, man, the metal gets white hot, and you take a long rod and open the spigot and it bubbles out, sometimes flashing, sometimes burping, as it flows into the molds and makes the little pigs."

I looked at him and joked, "Makes the little pigs, huh?"

We both laughed.

"What if that white-hot metal ever burped on you? Isn't that kinda dangerous?"

"Oh, maybe. Never happened yet. One-in-a-million chance."

"I guess," I said.

"One-in-a-million. Probably better than our chances out there," I continued, pointing to the Pacific.

"Probably so."

We were quiet for a while, watching the birds, the waves, and the ocean, disappearing beyond the horizon.

"Katy wrote me a letter. Says she's going to have a baby. Says it mine, and I need to come back and take care of her."

Nobel was looking at the horizon when he told me that. It was as if he were looking for Truth, for Trust, for Confidence, or just for Hope. I looked at him, my eyes wide open.

"Oh, Nobel, that's a big deal. You can't go home for that. She shouldn't be telling you that stuff."

Nobel nodded, shook his head, and inhaled.

As he exhaled, he said, "Fact is, Tex, it ain't mine. I know it ain't mine. I've been gone nine months now, and we didn't do anything the whole month before I left, just fuss. She's got her another beau, and he doesn't want the baby. I know her."

"Jeez, Nobel. That's too much for you to take on. It might be a year before we get home."

"I know. All I can think about is you, Kenny, and Pete, and staying alive."

"You're right about that!"

Nobel grabbed a chocolate bar, gave half to me, and took a bite of his half.

"I wrote back to her. I said I can't come home until this is over, but I'll think about it and if the baby don't have a Daddy, and if she wants me to be the Daddy, then I'll do it."

I looked at my chocolate bar, bit off a piece, marveled at its smooth sweetness, and nodded to him.

"You did right, Nobel. That's all you can do. Don't reject her. Don't promise her the moon. Just give her a little hope, and let Time and God do the rest. And, stay alive."

Nobel was still staring ahead, at the horizon. Little tears appeared in his eyes. He turned his face away, wiped his eyes with the back of his hand, and then looked directly at me. In a soft voice, he acknowledged, "Thanks, Tex."

I put my hand on his knee and, in a low voice, said, "And help me stay alive, too."

We sat there, on the tailgate, for at least ten minutes. War was a million miles away, and matters of the heart were right there in our hands. There was a familiar world out there, far away, with a home, a family, a future yet lived. Here, looking across the beach, the birds were more concerned with finding food than worrying about Katy and Nobel. The big birds with no name were floating in the sea breeze, looking down at me, asking *What about you, Fellow? You got a home? A girlfriend? A baby?*

"Just lost souls up there, Nobel. Trying to find Home and a Future, just like us. They'll be watching us, helping us find our way back. Home will come soon enough, with the hope that we can pick up where we left off, and live the life that the Good Lord is saving for us."

Nobel grunted his approval.

"But we gotta get this truck back to the Motor Pool first."

It was dusk when we entered the Motor Pool, and refilled the tank with gasoline. Nobel carried the saltines and peaches back to the tent, and stashed them under his bunk. When Kenny and Pete came from chow, they listened to our story, and became quite impatient when they learned about the stash. They were opening the canned peaches with their pocketknives when Nobel and I left to check in with the Platoon Sergeant.

Sergeant Miller told us, out of the corner of his mouth, that we had missed PT and chow.

"I hope you two morons got some exercise today. I don't want to do it again, just for you."

"That's alright, Sarge," Nobel said nervously.

"We carried cement bags all day. We had chow with the boys at Battery Arizona."

He looked at us with surprise, and a little envy.

"You saw the Battery Arizona?"

"Yes, we did. It's really something." I answered.

"Good for you," he replied, with a nod of approval.

"Now get the hell out of my tent."


July, 1943.

Oahu, Hawaii.

We had been in the Army for almost a year, including the past seven months of easy living on the beautiful and dreamy island of Hawaii. Except for the uniforms, the training, and the occasional guard duty, we felt as far away from the war as snow on an East Texas summer day.

Rumors were everywhere about the next move for the 24th Division. Days turned into weeks, and our "vacation" in Hawaii continued.

Some thought we were headed for New Guinea, since the 25th Division, the other "Hawaiian Division," had seen one of its regiments, the 161st Infantry Regiment, locked in a brutally vicious jungle battle on the island of New Georgia, in the Solomon Islands.

We heard stories about the horrible nature of jungle warfare, with some reports of over half the soldiers experiencing combat fatigue, shell shock, malaria, dysentery, diarrhea, and skin fungus.

Other rumors told us we would be heading to Australia, where new training camps were being built for advanced jungle warfare training.

From the shocking stories we had been hearing from New Georgia, it was clear we wanted Australia and advanced training.

If our generals and leaders were learning that the current Army fighting tactics were not good enough for fighting the Japanese in the jungle, we wanted to learn the RIGHT way to win this war before we got in neck deep.

As August arrived and the heat began to rise in the Pacific, we were told to get our asses ready for our next journey.

We were going to Australia for Advanced Jungle Warfare Training.

# CHAPTER 12

# DOWN UNDER

Wednesday, September 8, 1943.

Sydney, Queensland, Australia.

People were lined up along the road, cheering, waving, and tossing flowers at the buses carrying the U.S. Army's 24th Infantry Division, the first major contingent of American soldiers to arrive in the Sydney harbor since the war began.

Our buses were halfway back in the long, single row, riding in green and white double-deckers. Nobel, Pete, Kenny, and I were waving through the open windows of our bus, sitting in the lower level mid-rows. We were laughing and smiling broadly as we passed the noisy, happy people, almost three-to-four deep along the sidewalks.

Kenny looked at me, his eyes more bewildered than I had ever seen, and said, "I have neva, eva, in my life, seen such a jubilant crowd, such a magnificent parade!"

"It's a wonderful thing to see, and, most of all, to be in it!" I responded.

"They sure must be proud, very proud, to see us!"

Nobel looked around, from his seat in front of us, next to Pete.

"We've been in this Army for a year now, and nobody's ever treated us like this! It's like we're kings, or royalty!"

"They've been fighting this war since '39, and they are delirious to have us on their side. We are gonna help push the

Japs out of the Pacific and back to their own damn island," Pete remarked, as he reached around Nobel and took a bouquet of pink snapdragons from the extended hand of a beaming young brunette, running alongside the bus.

"Thank you kindly, Ma'am," he said, appreciatively.

Kenny looked at him with phony astonishment, and said, "That's a mighty big word you just used, Everman. 'Delirious.' You've been hiding a Virginia vocabulary, young man. And you got flowers, too!"

Pete's face was all smiles as he nodded, admiring the pink snapdragons.

"We have swell schools in Texas, smart ass," he proudly said.

"I will show you more fancy words when the action starts, Mr. Herrod."

Kenny grinned in agreement.

"She was a pretty gal, Pete," Nobel said, glassy-eyed.

"She was trying to hand those flowers to me."

"They're half yours, Nobel," Pete answered, as he rubbed Nobel's head with one hand.

"Neither one of us could take her on alone. We'd need support. That's what friends are for."

Nobel grinned.

"Sure, if you say so."

We continued our waving and smiling, marveling at the friendliness of the people of Sydney, and loving every moment of our parade through town.

The weather was very cool, with a little rain, and an occasional stiff wind that made it feel a lot colder. The love and the welcoming cheers made it warm and cozy, like home was just around the corner.

We had left Honolulu ten days ago, and woke up early this morning to a beautiful, breath-taking starboard view of Broken Bay, with its wooded hills, sandy beaches, and rocky cliffs along the Hawkesbury River as it meandered to the Tasman Sea.

A few miles south, Sydney Harbor came into view. Despite the clouds and rain and being surrounded on three sides by the busy city of Sydney, the docks looked like pearly gates beckoning us to enter a new chapter of our Army life, with weather more like an East Texas winter than a South Pacific cruise.

We had traveled from Hawaii on the *SS Lurline*, a Navy troopship that had once been an ocean liner, one of the largest in the world.

The *Lurline* had eight passenger decks. On top were the sun deck, the boat deck, and the promenade deck. Below, there were five passenger decks, Decks A through E.

We had been taken to Deck E, which was a long way down and below the water line. That was OK with me. There was nothing to see, and very little rocking from side to side, which made this trip a lot better than the last one. There were several galleys on Deck E, and plenty of showers and heads. We weren't crammed one against the other down there. We had plenty of room between the berths.

Nobel and I did pretty good. He threw up once, and I almost threw up only two or three times. The Navy sick bay gave us a small, fist-sized box of "Motion Sickness Preventative" large white pills, six to the box, to take 1 pill every 4 hours. Every day we would return to sick bay to be examined and receive another box. I wished I had been given the pills on my five-day trip to Hawaii. But, I guess, that trip to Hell made me half-a-sailor, so this trip was tolerable.

We paid close attention to our habits, eating our two meals slow, avoiding spicy food. There were potatoes every meal (unless there was rice), and we made sure they were our main course.

Nobel and I didn't smoke much, only when we took our daily trip to sick bay and our two trips a day to the promenade deck, letting the wind blow our faces, my hair, and Nobel's peach fuzz.

We saw a whale once, just a couple of hundred feet away from the ship, surfacing on the foamy wake behind us. And we saw dozens of dolphins, playfully jumping in and out of the water, their smooth, broad, elongated waves appearing on the surface of the tranquil ocean.

I liked the dolphins. I would watch them on the port side, then walk across to the starboard side and watch them again. They seemed to be escorting us across an endless sea, from one part of our life to another, chirping like cheerful birds as they guided the ship, and me, onward.

Our days on the *Lurline* were uneventful. None of us had to serve galley duty, and Nobel and I were able to beg off the calisthenics that Pete, Kenny, and most of Mike Company had to do every day at noon. There were about ten of us "non-starters" that stayed behind each day.

Still, ten days at sea took a lot out of us, and we were both as happy as little kids when we saw the coast of Australia, and Broken Bay inviting us to come on in, sit a spell.

When we finally made it down the gangplank, we boarded the buses that took us along the magnificent parade down the streets of Sydney.

Our journey ended at a racetrack on the north side of the city.

Cots were waiting for us at a racetrack, set up along the bench seats, under the cover of the overhanging roof. We laid claim to four cots in the back, far enough away from the overhang to be out of the rain showers which would occasionally break up the slow mist that filled the air.

It was grand, oh so grand, to be on land!

We were given leave the next day to see the city but told to be back to the racetrack by 2200.

The next morning, we were up by 0700 for muster. We grabbed coffee and buttered bread along the concourse, and boarded another green and white double-decker bus, just like the one that had brought us along the parade to the racetrack. Not knowing where to go, we followed the soldiers that did know. Once the bus reached downtown, we watched them. Most of them remained in their seats. When we stopped in front of the Australia Hotel, they started getting off the bus. So did we.

I looked up at the massive ten-story brick building, and heard Nobel ask Pete, "What is this?"

Pete asked a soldier next to him, then turned to Nobel and said, "It's the Australia Hotel. It claims to have the longest bar in the world."

Nobel issued a long "Whoopee!"

The four of us walked through the polished stone entrance and gazed at the white marble stairs and red columns, surrounded by stained glass windows showing brightly colored flowers, tall green trees, and kangaroos.

Pete pointed forward, motioning for us to follow him. Then, we saw it.

It looked like it was one-hundred fifty-feet long, with four single-light chandeliers hanging above it. We saw a couple of soldiers standing beneath one of them, tossing coins at it, trying to make the coins land in the chandelier globe.

The wood along the bar was light oak. It was the longest bar we had ever seen.

Kenny spoke first.

"Follow me, gentlemen. I see some stools on the left."

As we stepped up to the bar, Kenny looked at us and announced, "We're going to have a good Virginia bourbon. On me."

We looked at each other, nodding in agreement. A tall, well-dressed bartender, with a white linen around his forearm, smiled at us.

"Welcome to the Australia Hotel, with the famous Long Bar. What would you gentlemen wish today?"

Kenny motioned with his hand.

"Do you have Virginia Gentleman Bourbon?"

"Yes, sir, we do. Four?"

"Four it is. Neat."

"No ice?"

"No ice."

Yes, sir. Coming up."

When the tall man came back and placed each glass in front of us, Kenny raised his.

We raised ours, lightly touching in a toast.

"To the finest gentlemen I have ever had the honor to meet. To the guidance and protection of our gracious and merciful God. To the friendship we have found and the bond between us. And, to Red, to Nobel, and to Everman."

We each replied, "To Kenny", as we clicked our glasses, and drank our first taste of the smooth, rich, velvet bourbon from Virginia.

My eyes blurred with tears. Nobel wiped both eyes with his fingers and thumb, and Pete looked up to the ceiling, his eyes moist.

"Amen," Pete whispered.

"Thank you, Kenny"

Kenny beamed with pride, as he reached into his coat pocket and pulled out a brown paper wrap filled with a small wad of tobacco leaves. He carefully pulled one leaf out, packed the remaining few back in the brown wrap, and begin to chew the leaf, one small bite at a time.

"I need more tobacco," he whispered to himself, then looked back at us.

We were still looking at him, waiting for the next toast.

He recovered his thoughts, smiled, and said with a quivering voice, "Together, the four of us, until the end of this war. And, to our folks back home."

Our glasses clicked again as we drank another toast.

I sipped my bourbon, looked down the long bar, then across the room, studying the men, both civilian and soldiers. There were a lot more American soldiers than Aussie soldiers. The Aussie civilians, probably about a third of the people in the bar, were well dressed, and sat at tables or stood in small groups alone, not mingling with the soldiers. Their faces were pleasant, but few smiled. The most important thing I noticed was they were all older men, appearing to be in their fifties or beyond. The only young Aussies were soldiers.

As I studied their faces, I noticed a man about Daddy's age sitting at a table by himself, drinking a glass of dark beer. He was neatly dressed in a blue checkered shirt, his brown felt fedora hat was sitting on the table beside him, a racetrack ticket tucked in the hat band. A cigar lay in a metal ash tray at the corner of the table, a thin wisp of smoke rising from the tip. He winked at me, nodded his balding head as a greeting, and held his beer up, a faint smile creasing the wrinkles on his face.

I pushed my chair back, picked up my half-full glass of Virginia's finest, and strolled across the tile floor to his table.

"G'day, mate," he greeted as I approached.

As I reached for the empty chair beside him, I said, "Good day, Sir. May I sit for a moment?"

"Of course. I would like that."

He squinted his blue-grey eyes and looked at me, as if he were trying to put an old memory together.

"You look like my son, mate. You caught my attention. You have the quality of a good man in your demeanor. I see him in you."

His voice cracked near the end, and I placed my hand on his wrist beside his beer.

"He was a soldier, wasn't he?" I said.

"Yes," he nodded.

"I lost him up in New Guinea, more'n a year ago. At Buna."

I didn't know where the hell Buna was, barely knew where New Guinea was. But, I had heard the word going around that as soon as we were trained in one of the new jungle warfare camps here in Australia, New Guinea was likely to be our next stop.

The old man's hand was calloused, but clean and well-manicured. He reached for his cigar, puffed on it three times, and the rich, sweet tobacco smell filled the space between him and me. I inhaled, thanking the Good Lord for smells like that.

He quietly studied me with his tired eyes. Twenty-thousand nights were in those eyes, sad and strong. Twenty-thousand days of hard work, good meals, and staying straight. I figured he was a gentleman, was probably somebody important here in Sydney. He carried Respect on him like an old, comfortable jacket.

And the war had taken his son.

"I am so sorry, Mister. Maybe, maybe I can help win this war, for you and your son."

My eyes moved back to his face, his tired eyes moist now, the faint smile coming back.

"He looked like you, mate. My son. His hair was curly and red, hung down over his brow, his face full of vigor."

He lifted his beer, extended it toward me in a toast.

As our glasses clinked, he said, "God bless you, Son. God bless you and your mates."

We drank a toast to Freedom, Liberty, and to all soldiers who fought on our side.

"Thank you, Sir," I said.

"You can call me William, mate. William Jackson. Can I call you Red?"

I laughed and answered, "Yes, yes you can. That is my name, Mr. Jackson."

"It was my son's name," he answered, his eyes less focused, as if he was looking beyond me, to a better time, an endearing time when his son would drink with him at this very table.

"Thanks for coming back to spend a few precious moments, Red."

I replayed those words in my mind a few seconds, then slowly pushed my chair back, stood up, nodded to the old man, shook his big, strong hand, and told him, "I gotta go now, Pop. You take care of yourself."

He nodded, smiled, and reached for his cigar.

I walked back to the long bar.

"I like that old man," I said, as I nestled back into my chair.

"He lost his son up in New Guinea last year. I think he thought I was him."

Pete looked at me and said, "It's tough losing a son. A lot of old men have lost their sons, here and back home. That's why there's not many young men in here."

He looked at all of us and whispered, "They're still losing them, today. While we're sipping bourbon. God gives, and He takes away."

He glanced at Kenny and said, "No offense, Kenny."

"No offense taken, Everman." Kenny replied.

"We are getting closer and closer to war every day, gentlemen."

He motioned toward the door, and said, "Shall we?"

We all drank the rest of our bourbon and followed our own Virginia Gentleman out the door.

The rest of the afternoon was spent walking around the Harbor, going into shops and watching the ships. Before leaving Sulphur Springs, I had never seen a harbor, smelled the aroma of the sea and wet wood, or heard gulls.

We each bought a cup of corn willy stew from a little kitchen on the dock. It wasn't the best stew I ever had, but it had a good taste to it.

"This is the only time I ever ate something made out of sheep," I said.

Pete winked at me and whispered, "You and Nobel ate it on the boat. We just didn't tell you what it was."

We drank hot tea sitting at a small table on one the docks. I sat there, legs crossed, like Daddy drinking his coffee on the porch, taking it all in, watching all the sights I had never seen, storing each memory away in a little brown box, tucking it carefully into a corner of my mind where priceless things go.

I thought of Juliette.

*I wonder what she's doing? Does she think of me? She's a year older now. What, fifteen?*

"Red, what'cha thinking? You look like you're a thousand miles away," Nobel asked.

"I am," I answered.

"Maybe two thousand. Maybe nine thousand."

Nobel picked up on my thoughts.

"Kenny," he asked, "How many miles home is it?"

Kenny set his cup down, leaned forward, moved his fingers and whispered to himself,

"About nine thousand miles, Nobel."

I quickly looked up and blinked.

Nobel whistled.

"Gentlemen," Kenny leaned back, "We are a very, very long way from home."

Pete took the toothpick out of his mouth and pointed it at us.

"That's why I can never let you morons out of my sight. You don't know the way home and neither do I."

I laughed, knowing he was telling the truth. Lately, I had been finding myself thinking about these three fellas more than I thought about home.

*But, still: there was Juliette. Nine thousand miles, and a couple of years, beyond my reach.*

We sat there on the dock, quietly smoking cigarettes and drinking tea for more than an hour.

Leaving the dock, we found a USO club a short distance away that was serving hamburgers and hotdogs. We ate our share, played some pool, watched a movie with Gary Cooper in a Spanish War, then went back to the Australia Hotel for another bourbon at the Long Bar. We bought Kenny's drink.

We found a tobacco shop for Kenny, too.

We found a variety store, so Pete could buy another pack of toothpicks. He and I bought some picture postcards of Sydney to mail to the folks back home. I bought one with a picture of the Australia Hotel especially for Juliette Hamilton. Pete saw it, nodded in approval, and bought one, too. "For Wanda," he said.

We made it back to the racetrack long before 2200. Local volunteers were giving each returning soldier a boxed meal with a sandwich and some fruit.

The next morning, only a few men hadn't reported back, and their names were carefully noted at muster. Everyone in Mike Company was present.

By noon, we packed up all our gear and boarded a train that took us north through Newcastle, Brisbane, and Bundaberg, skirting the east coast of Australia. With scenic beaches to our right and wooded mountains to our left, we continued as the day became dusk.

By nightfall, we were at our training site, Camp Caves, near the city of Rockhampton.

We were the first soldiers to occupy Area D at Camp Caves, the place for the 21st Infantry Regiment. It had just been finished for a couple of weeks. Just in time for us!

A tent city had been constructed, with all the tents on wooden decks, like our "home" at Kaena Point, Hawaii. The area was wooded, and it sloped eastward to a flat-topped ridge. Construction debris, with stacks of cement, wood, and paint, was scattered around in conveniently placed storage locations.

The four of us claimed our cots in a tent that was on the edge of a clearing, close enough to some trees for shade and cover. We settled in late that night, expecting a short day to follow with orientation and classes.

It was not to be.

The bugle reminded us before dawn that it was time to rise and shine. It was cool, well above freezing, and not raining. After showers and chow, we boarded troop trucks and spent all day at the artillery range.

We fired nearly four-dozen rounds toward the foot of a nearby hill, changing the settings, getting closer, closer, and closer - until finally blowing a barrel of sand to smithereens. All the while disassembling the M2, moving it twenty feet in different directions, reassembling it, trying to catch the stationary barrel, with a range sergeant watching our every move, yelling sometimes, speaking softly other times. We were getting good at the maneuver, with Kenny holding the mortar in place, Nobel assembling it, Pete feeding him the pieces, and me having each part ready for Pete, then Nobel, to grab at the right moment.

    Several times the sergeant turned his back on us and just listened, then grunted with disfavor. At the end of the day, he told us "You boys were good, but you're dead. They found you and they lobbed one in on you."

    Then he just nodded and said, "Get the hell back with the others for chow."


Christmas Day.
Saturday, December 25, 1943

Camp Caves, Rockhampton, Queensland, Australia

    It was a wonderful "summer" day at Camp Caves, almost ninety degrees.

    We had spent the past three and a half months, from early-September to late-December, in tough training, from amphibious landings to jungle infantry tactics to light artillery to personal weaponry. We were out in "the bush" mostly six long days a week, with Sundays usually off.

    We were proud to get a three-day weekend off for Christmas.

    For the four of us, this was our second Christmas together, our second Christmas in the Army.

    On Christmas Eve, we rested. Slept late. Cleaned our personal gear. Wrote letters home. Read letters from home.

That night, we watched two movies.

Two more evening movies were scheduled Christmas Day.

Two more the day after, on Sunday night.

For Christmas Dinner, the mess-halls at Camp Caves were going all out. The Works, they said. Ham. Turkey. Dressing. All the Trimmings. Pumpkin Pie. Pecan Pie. Apple Pie. Ice Cream.

As we sat in the corner of our tent, the flaps rolled up, there was a different smell in the air. Food cooking. Good food cooking.

Even when we straggled to breakfast that morning, it was different. There were more cooks than normal. Some were sent in from other bases, other units. Some were volunteers. Some were family. The smell was different.

Now, back in the tent, Nobel was still talking about it.

"Man! The smell in the air is almost like home!" Nobel remarked, standing outside the tent, moving his head around, sniffing the air with wide-open nostrils.

"Nothin' ever smelled this good that wasn't worth goin' to!" he said in his Alabama drawl, stepping back into the tent.

"My Granma's house always smelled this way," Kenny boasted, sitting on his cot, chewing on a tobacco leaf.

"Everything smells better in Texas," Pete bragged, a toothpick in his mouth as he sat on his footlocker.

A moment passed.

Pete looked at me, spread his arms wide, and inquired, "Well, Red, you got anything to say?"

I looked up, my eyes darted back and forth, and I asked, "About what?"

Kenny came to my aid.

"Everman wants to know if you have anything to say about your family's cooking smells."

I smiled at him, winked at Nobel, and looked innocently at Pete, raising my eyebrows.

"None of my family can cook, Pete. You know that. We just eat stuff raw. There ain't no smells worth talking about."

Nobel burst out laughing, so hard he almost fell back out of the tent.

Pete took his toothpick out of his mouth, sighed, and hung his head, as if crying.

Kenny laughed louder than I had ever heard him laugh before, letting his wet tobacco leaf fall to the deck.

Christmas Dinner was served at 1500. We were standing at the mess hall door when it opened.

A rush of smells came out the door that excited everybody.

"Man!" I remarked.

"That smells just like my Momma's cooking!"

Everybody laughed again.

Nobel looked at me, grinned, and said, "Merry Christmas, Red!"

As we sat down at our table, I bowed my head and said a short, quiet prayer thanking God for the meal, and asking Him to watch after my family and keep them safe.

I looked at my tray. A slice of turkey breast. Two slices of ham, a round bone in each, dressing (not cornbread, but tolerable), yellow corn, a couple of green beans, gravy on the meat and dressing, cranberry sauce, and, tucked into a little corner space away from the serious food, were three stacked slices of pie: pecan, pumpkin, and apple. And three rolls.

It was the best Christmas Dinner I had ever eaten.

After we finished the dinner and all three pieces of pie, we returned to the line for ice cream.

Seated again at the table, Nobel looked at Kenny and said, "Hey Kenny. I prayed that my family would have a good Christmas Day, but I didn't know when to ask the Lord to do it. Is it tomorrow back there, or yesterday? I didn't know if He was gonna do it or had already done it. What time is it back home, anyway?"

Kenny chuckled and replied, "Well, Nobel, let's see. We are eighteen hours ahead of home. Home is eighteen hours behind us. It is four o'clock Christmas Day to us, so," He waved his hands, counted on his fingers, and moved his lips.

He continued, "At home it is ten o'clock last night."

Nobel just looked at Kenny, then at Pete, then at me.

I shrugged my shoulders.

Pete pointed at Kenny, tapped his finger to his temple, and mouthed, *He is smart.*

Kenny smiled.

"Back in Alabama, they are either asleep or still up wrapping presents. Say your prayer tomorrow at breakfast and God can answer it instantly."

"I kinda think God can remember it tomorrow," Nobel said smugly.

We all nodded in approval and continued eating our ice cream.

The next week was back to training.

More amphibious landings.

More jungle.

More ranges.

We learned more things about the jungle than we will ever remember.

Like, combat in the jungle has low visibility, poor communication, and difficult movement. You should use small units only in the jungle. No more than one or two squads can fight on a jungle trail.

And, an old jungle (called High Jungle by Aussies) is not difficult to maneuver through.

But, a new jungle (or Low Jungle) has no tall trees, just bamboo and thorny underbrush, like a mesh. It is very difficult to maneuver without a machete.

And, be ready for Battle Fatigue when you have repeated close combat. Along with skin diseases, sores that refuse to heal, jungle rot of skin and clothing, malaria, chills, followed by intense sweating.

And, when crossing streams, check yourself and your buddy for leeches.

In our training classrooms, there were many posters on Japanese uniforms, badges, and weapons. And drawings of tactics lined the walls.


Friday, January 14, 1944

Nobel was promoted to a Private First Class (PFC). He was the best man with the mortar on our little team, and he was now our leader. PFC Horner, we called him – when we wanted something.

We began to hear rumors that our training was almost over, and we should be prepared to move out to the real world of Japanese soldiers and war.

Would it be New Guinea (where Mr. Jackson's son had died)? The Solomon Islands? The Philippines? Or, all three? Maybe straight to Japan? Maybe straight to Hell?

Elsewhere, as our training heightened, the Marines were invading the Solomon Islands, the Army was landing on shore in the Gilbert Islands, and both the Army and the Marines were attacking the Marshall Islands.

Back at home, my brother Noel had joined the Army Air Corps, and was training to be a bombardier instructor in Nebraska.

Over in Europe, the Germans had taken Italy, and the Allies were trying to take it back. The Russians were rolling through Poland, trying to get to Germany.

Then the word came down: the Hawaiian Division, including the 21st Infantry Regiment (us), were moving to Goodenough Island, to prepare for an amphibious assault on Hollandia in the Dutch part of New Guinea.

We joked among ourselves that it would be good enough.

We left Camp Caves on January 28, 1944, on a dirty, old Dutch Freighter.

# CHAPTER 13

# JULIETTE HAMILTON

Christmas Day.
Saturday, December 25, 1943

Sulphur Bluff, Hopkins County, Texas.

The temperature was as close to freezing at it could get. The red-and-white tin Royal Crown Cola outdoor thermometer said it was 32°F on the front porch. It was windy and frosty in Sulphur Bluff as the day was drawing to a close. The smell of baked goose still lingered, and the aroma of sage and cornbread dressing escaped through the front door as it slowly opened. The tired, smiling face of Tom Hamilton appeared, taking survey of the winter weather, his eyes sparkling as he winked at Juliette. She caught sight of his wink as she sat on the top porch rail, wrapped in a red-and-white patchwork quilt. She had been staring into the slowly approaching twilight, deep in thought. Everyone was inside the house.

"Can you grab one or two more logs of wood for me, Juliette?" he asked embarrassingly.

"I think if I get cold one more time today it will last all night long"

"Sure, Daddy. I'm dressed for it," she smiled.

"All we need is one or two. Three for sure. I'll send the boys out for more later."

"Don't worry about it. I'll come in and enjoy the fire in a few minutes. It smells good here on the porch. There's a clean, crisp chill in the winter wind, the smell of snow is out there, somewhere close. And, there's the smell of Christmas Dinner still comin' out that door every time it opens."

"Yes," Tom sighed.

"I know. I've been opening this door too many times. I want to see it and enjoy it like you do. The older I get the more I want to grab everything there is every day. It's there for the grabbin'. But, I believe it is too cold for the grabbin' tonight."

They both giggled, in that Daddy-daughter way.

Tom disappeared behind the door as it closed.

*I've got the best Daddy in the whole world,* Juliette thought.

*I wish the boys were older, so they could help him more. He's got nobody but Mr. Wilson to help him do the work, since all the girls, except Verna and me, have moved to Dallas.*

*He's the best Daddy in the world.*

Juliette leaned forward, loosened the quilt so she could walk, and disappeared behind the house. A scant minute later, she reappeared with four good-sized logs, neatly stacked in her two arms.

The door opened again, and Tom reappeared, holding a blue-speckled enamelware cup of coffee, which he gently set on the top porch rail by the door.

"Thank you, Juliette. Here's some coffee for you," he acknowledged, as he took each log from her.

"Thank you, Daddy. You tell Mr. Wilson again that his Canada Goose was a little dry, but was perfect in every other detail," Juliette whispered.

Tom burst into a short laugh.

"I don't think I'll say that, but I'll think it. Besides, the goose got dry on its own. Ray is innocent. We sure are blessed to have his friendship."

"Dry goose and all."

He folded himself around the door and slipped back inside the house.

Juliette reached for the coffee, now steaming in the cold Christmas air. She tightened up the quilt and leaned back against the porch rail.

Her thoughts roamed from home to school to church. To the war in Europe. To the war in the Pacific. She crossed her ankles, wiggled the quilt up around her shoulders, looked out to the winter night and saw a few snowflakes being carried in the wind.

She absorbed the natural world like a sponge, taking it all in, the images and the sensations, storing each memory away in a little brown box, tucking it carefully into a corner of her mind where priceless things go.

She thought of Red Smith.

*I wonder what he's doing? Does he think of me? He's a year older now. What, 22?*

Her mother opened the door half-way, letting more dinner smells escape onto the cold winter porch.

"Juliette, what'cha thinking?" she affectionately asked.

"You look like you're a thousand miles away."

"I am," Juliette answered.

"Maybe two thousand. Maybe nine thousand."

Nettie picked up on her thoughts.

"The soldiers are out there," she pointed east, then west.

"It's Christmas out there on the battle front, too. I hope the Good Lord is watching them as well as He watches us."

Juliette set her cup down, leaned a bit forward, and said, "I was thinking about Red Smith, Momma."

Nettie nodded, and looked out into the night.

"I'm sure God's got him wrapped under His wings, covered with His feathers, like it says in Psalm 91."

"I like that chapter, Momma."

Juliette turned her gaze back into night.

"It's not cold and windy in the Pacific, but it is surely dangerous."

"Right smart," her mother answered.

"It's right smart dangerous over there. All we can do is pray and send letters to those poor boys. And, be here for them when they come back."

"Yes." Juliette said, with a note of confidence in her voice. She reached down, picked up her cup, and drank the rest of the cold coffee.

"Let's go back in, Momma. I want some more hot coffee and another piece of that pumpkin pie."


Thursday, December 30, 1943

Juliette pulled the ration coupon books out of her small, dark brown leather handbag. She smiled as she closed the handbag, heard the clear "snap!" of the metal clasp, and caught a whiff of the leather smell. She had gotten the handbag Christmas Eve, a special gift from her father after everyone else had opened their gifts. It was the first leather purse she had ever gotten brand new.

She admired it as she opened the purse again to make sure she had all the coupons. Her fingers probed behind a small bundle of letters and postcards, tied with a rubber band, to find a few single coupons that had fallen out.

Her sister Verna, holding her year-old son, Jerry, leaned over to Juliette and asked, "Are we gonna have enough coupons?"

"Oh, fiddle, yes! We have plenty. With your family's coupons and Mr. Wilson's coupons, we always have just enough. Go out there and see if Buck is waiting for us in the truck."

Verna slipped out the store's front door as Juliette placed the groceries in front of Mr. Barnett, the store clerk.

"Let's see what you have today, Miss Hamilton," he said.

"You have powdered milk, fresh butter, and sorghum syrup. Will you be needing your flour and sugar today, too?"

"Yes, we will. And coffee beans, too. Momma needs the flour and sugar, and Daddy needs the coffee."

They both laughed.

Verna walked back inside and approached the counter. She was wearing the gray-and-blue plaid scarf that Buck had given her Christmas Day and had draped a small yellow quilt over little Jerry's head.

"By darn, it's getting windy out there, and feels colder. Buck is in the truck, and he will be getting five gallons of gas, Mr. Barnett. He also wants you to order him a tire for the right front."

She handed him her gasoline coupon book and a tire coupon. He removed five green bulk gasoline coupons, gave the book back to her, and lay the blue tire coupon by the register.

"OK, Mrs. Sandifeer. I'll go get the flour, sugar, and coffee and bring them out to you. I'll order the tire d'rectly. It should only take a couple of days for it to come in."

"Do you have the flour sacks with the pretty pink roses?" Juliette inquired.

"Yes, Miss Hamilton, I do. Do you want them all in that pattern?"

Yes, sir. Please. It's time Momma made me a new dress. With matching bloomers," Juliette announced, laughing audaciously.

"Oh, Juliette!" Verna teased.

Mr. Barnett blushed, then smiled as he took Juliette's ration book and removed a red coupon for the butter and blue coupons for the other items.

The ladies bundled up their milk, butter, and syrup and placed them in a cotton bag, said their thanks, and returned to the truck. Buck had just finished fueling the truck when Mr. Barnett brought the larger items and began placing them in the truck bed.

The ride back to the Hamilton house, six miles west of Sulphur Bluff along newly built Farm to Market Road 71, was full of chatter about the war. The north wind would occasionally blow across the black-top road enough to make the '38 Dodge truck shake and veer slightly to the left. Buck, with his long, slender legs pressed up against the steering wheel and his sinewy hands in a tightened grip, kept the truck on a straight path.

They talked about how only a few families had been left unaffected by the wars in the Pacific and Europe. At least half-a-dozen boys in the Sulphur Bluff community were already serving in the Army and the Navy, with that many more on the cusp. Two sons of the Bud Smith family, now living near Mount Sterling, were gone, with Red Smith in the Army and his brother Noel in the Air Corps. Other families with distant soldiers included Thomas, Posey, even Sandifeer. Buck, with a wife, a new baby, and a hurt back, remained at home and worked at a ranch to take care of his family and help his new in-laws, the Hamiltons, survive in the ration-and-shortage world of the early-forties.

Juliette thought of Red often and had exchanged a few letters and post cards over the year. She knew that he was training in Australia and knew from the newspapers that the ground war in the Pacific had already spread across the Solomon Islands toward New Guinea. With the Marines engaged in deadly combat on Guadalcanal and Bougainville, and the Army suffering significant casualties at New Georgia and Tarawa, news from the Pacific was grim.

She did not personally know any of the soldiers in Europe. The news from there was frightening, with Hitler showing no mercy on his march to rule the continent.

Later that evening, she went to her "bedroom," which was a single room she had shared with her sister Arline, who, at 18, was already living in Dallas, working at Sears and enjoying the lights of the big city.

Juliette read the letters she had received from Red. A letter from Camp Wolters. A Christmas card from Fort Bragg. A letter from Hawaii. A postcard from Australia, with a picture of the magnificently beautiful Australia Hotel.

The letters were full of news and tales of daily life, and a few pictures. But it was what she was reading *between the lines* that drew her inexorably closer and closer to this lad from her Hopkins County homeland.

Words like *think of you* and *it is lonely here* and *looking forward to coming home*. She was beginning to read the right words and was beginning to *want* and *feel* like there was a direction, a destiny, and a desire to pursue a paradise and share a destiny that had always been deep inside her, waiting to blossom like a floret when the right moment came.

She was beginning to believe the right moment would come when this war was over.

She pulled a pen and paper out of the chest of drawers and began to write:

*Dear Red,*
*Just a note to wish you Happy New Year, and hope all is well. We had a swell Christmas Day here and it snowed that night! It sure was pretty. I guess you don't get much snow down there. Daddy told me a few days ago that it was summer in Australia! Thank you for the postcard, I bet the Australia Hotel was pretty.*
*All of us are trying to get by as well as we can here and are praying that the war will not drag on for you soldiers. We went to Barnett's Store today and got powdered milk, butter, sorghum syrup, flour, sugar, and coffee, and had to use ration coupons for all of them. Buck and Verna took me to the store. Jerry Dell sure is a cute little boy, he is 20 months old.*
*Farm to Market Road 71 is finally finished and is a nice smooth black-top road all the way from Birthright through Sulphur Bluff to Hagansport. I wish you could see it. I'm so glad they didn't have to bother the big tree outside the Masonic Hall.*
*It's getting colder again outside.*
*I do hope the war is over soon and you can return to your family and your friends. Hopkins County will be a much better place when you come back.*

*Take care of yourself.*

*Love,*
*Juliette*

# CHAPTER 14

# GOODENOUGH ISLAND

Monday, January 31, 1944.

Goodenough Island, Solomon Islands, near Province of Papua New Guinea, Solomon Sea, South Pacific.

It took us three full days on a dirty old Dutch freighter to move from our very comfortable quarters at Camp Caves to Goodenough Island. We had joked that it would probably be "good enough," as we walked out of the camp in the beautiful Rockhampton Region of Queensland, Australia. Little did we know that we were beginning the "jungle" part of the war experience, that the appearance of anything "good enough" would not happen again for another year, maybe two, or not at all.

When the 21st Infantry Regiment boarded the freighter at Gladstone, south of the city of Rockhampton, we knew our destination would be Goodenough Island. We knew the British had fought hard for that island and the part of New Guinea next to it, wrestling them from the grip of the Japanese Army. We also knew there was a very important airfield on the island, giving us an advantage over the enemy. And, we knew it was a staging position for us, a jumping off place, a springboard to our advance into the Pacific War.

But that was all we knew.

There were other things in our immediate future that hit us head-on.

Like the Dutch freighter.
Old.
Dirty.

It had an Indonesian crew that kept their curried lamb quarters hanging near the galley, filling the ship with the stench of spices some of us had never encountered.

The freighter had only two saltwater showers and two heads. We had almost three-thousand men in that old Dutch freighter. Needless to say, there were few chances to take a shower or a proper shit.

It took little or no time to notice the smells of the unwashed men, the lack of personal toilet hygiene, and the stench from the galley.

Added to those conditions, the Medical Corps issued atabrine tablets to everyone to help control malaria. The medics would stand at the chow line to give us the big yellow pills and watch while each of us swallowed one.

The side effects of the medicine added to our misery on the freighter. It was not pleasant. There was no reason to fight seasickness. The atabrine gave us the same nausea and headaches as seasickness, with the added "benefit" of diarrhea.

Also, if you took atabrine regularly, it would turn your skin yellow. The "yellowing" wasn't harmful, and it would go away when you stopped taking the atabrine. In the meantime, it was not something you wanted to see in the mirror.

Even worse, the medicine could cause mental problems, like nightmares, anxiety, and, in some cases, full-blown "psychosis," as the doctors called it.

Crazy.

Maniac.

Not something you expected to happen in the Army.

Finally, the big rumor said that taking atabrine for a long time would cause a fellow to become infertile.

There go the family jewels.

Useless.

There go the kids.

All of that terror on a three-day boat ride! Seasickness for many, including me. The foul smells that were coming from everywhere. It was really difficult to eat. But you had to eat because the medicine would make you sick on an empty stomach.

It made many men weak.

Some men were so weak from the short trip they had to be carried off the freighter when they got to Goodenough Island.

Not me and Nobel. We walked off the freighter, with a little help.

Pete helped me, and Kenny helped Nobel. Together, the four of us walked boldly and a bit gimpy down the ramp.

Once off the boat, there was dry land that didn't move beneath my feet and clean air that didn't stink. We were getting our strength back and were able to climb onto trucks that took us a few miles inland to a clearing. The Army had set up a chow line. We were told to stay near the trucks and take a break for a while.

Get some chow.

Get some coffee.

Get some sleep.

Whatever.

Just stay near the trucks.

I got a cup of black coffee and held it up to my nose and it actually smelled good. I brought it slowly and carefully up to my lips and sipped. It tasted good, and it stayed down.

I asked for a piece of bread and meat – it looked like chicken – and walked slowly back to our truck and sat down on the tailgate. I looked up to the sky and whispered *"Thank you, Lord. Thank you."*

A few minutes later, Nobel walked back from the chow line and sat beside me, holding a cup of coffee and a piece of cake.

"This is as good as the peaches and crackers we had in Hawaii, Tex," he mumbled with a grin.

"Yeah, I wish we were back there. It sure was nice, wasn't it?"

A moment passed, and he asked me, "Is the top of my head turning yellow?"

"Naw," I told him. "That is just the natural color of your peach-fuzz, Nobel."

I looked at him again, closely.

"Maybe just a little bit, not much. It makes you cute, Man."

"How come you're not turning yellow, Tex?"

I laughed, and answered, "Cause I'm not taking my atabrine every time, every day. Damn stuff made me sick on that rotten ship. They watch me put it in my mouth, and I spit it out in my hand. See here – my left hand is yellow!"

Nobel shook his yellow head and said, "Shit, Tex, you're gonna get malaria."

I grunted, and said, "Who knows? I can take it. I'm from Texas. I've seen plenty of mosquitos back home."

"Yeah, but not these kind of mosquitos," he told me.

"They will kick your butt and turn you inside out with fever and chills."

I shrugged my shoulders and gazed across the clearing where our truck convoy had stopped. There was some activity going on at the far end of the clearing. A line of supply trucks was headed our way, with officers and soldiers out front, waving and pointing, directing their path toward us. A large group of New Guinea native men followed behind the trucks, looking at all of us and smiling. Their black, stiff hair stuck out around their heads, and their shirtless bodies rippled with the muscles of laborers accustomed to hard work. They wore shorts or cloth wraps around their midsection, and most were shoeless.

"Well, I wonder what they're bringing us," I said.

"I hope they're bringing us our bedrooms," Nobel responded.

I looked around, studying the clearing. All the grass had been cut almost to the ground, with the broad leaves pressed flat.

"Is this the kunai grass they've all been talking about? It looks like the Johnson Grass we have back home, just a lot bigger and tougher."

Pete arrived from the chow line, with more food than I wanted to look at.

"Yep, Red, that's it. Ugly grass, isn't it?"

"It doesn't care if it's ugly," Kenny answered, arriving with an equally unattractive amount of food on his tray.

"This is the jungle, and I don't believe anything is pretty here. But, this is the natural order of things."

I looked at Kenny and Pete and shook my head.

*How can they eat like that with me being as sick as I am?* I sarcastically asked myself.

"If they're bringing us tents," I said, "then we're gonna be living with grass for a floor. It don't matter, just so I have someplace to lay down and sleep. Hell, I would sleep on this grass if that's all I had."

Nobel looked at me with wide-open eyes, holding cake in one hand and coffee in the other, and said, "No, we won't be sleeping on the ground, at least not yet. I heard the servers at the chow-line talking about the last group they brought out here. They had to cut the damn grass themselves, with help from the fuzzy-wuzzies, then were told to sleep on the ground the first night."

"Wait, wait, wait, Nobel," Pete interrupted.

"What the hell is a fuzzy-wuzzy?"

Nobel laughed lightly, then explained to Pete, "I heard the fellers at the chow line talking about them. They call the natives "Fuzzy-Wuzzies." Everyone here loves them. The Army pays them to help us. They help with all the packing, carrying, and setting up equipment. They cut all this grass with machetes. They carry medical supplies, and even carried the sick and wounded for the Aussies and Brits that were in the islands around here before us."

He pointed to the long convoy of trucks and men.

"They're over there getting ready to set our tents up for us."

He took a bite of cake.

"Anyway, let me finish. The folks ahead of us were told to sleep on the ground because the cots hadn't been delivered. The next morning all the top brass was out here, and they raised a big ruckus, saying' that no one, absolutely no one, would be sleeping on the ground here ever again. They said there's a little red bug that lives out in this grass, and, if it bites you, it can really hurt you. Quite a few of the guys got bit and were taken to the hospital. One of them died. Died! In grass just like this! Shit! We can't sleep on the ground out here, Tex!"

    My eyes narrowed as I looked around the clearing, then down to the ground, then over to the trucks that had just arrived. The fuzzy-wuzzies were tossing bundles of canvas tents and folded-up cots.

    "Yep," I said slowly.

    "We won't have to sleep on the ground. That's our bedroom furniture they're unloading over there. We'll be sleeping on cots. No walking around without shoes, though. Not with those little red bugs out here."

    The four of us looked at the kunai grass-covered ground a few minutes, our tired minds full of dread, then turned our attention back to our coffee and food.

    "I think I'll go get some more," I said, as I slid off the tailgate.

    "Bring me some more cake, please," Nobel requested.

    "I sure will. It looks like there's more work yet to do," I answered back, over my shoulder.

    "We've got to pick out where we want to live."


One Month Later.

    As it turned out, none of us were bitten by the little red bug. But I was bitten by at least one malaria-infected mosquito. And that's all it took.

It must have gotten me as soon we arrived at The Island. Pete started calling it "The Island" instead of Goodenough as soon as I started having the shaking chills and high fever in mid-February.

Several days before my chills, I had a headache that just got worse and worse, a little nausea now and then, and my muscles ached. Not just a few muscles. All of them.

The night I awoke, moaning and shaking with the worst chills I had ever had, Pete came over to my cot, lay his hand on me, and said to the others, "We have to get a medic down here. Right now!"

I remember very little of what actually happened that night. Everything around me was wrapped in a fog, and I didn't know where I was. I remember Nobel putting a blanket over me, Kenny putting a pillow under my feet, and Pete just kneeling there, his hand on my chest.

When the horrible shaking chills stopped, my body hurt from head to foot, and I started sweating so much it felt like my entire cot was getting wet. Then I got another chill. Then a man with sleepy eyes and a big pointed chin was looking at me. I kept thinking *'That's not an Angel. She's too ugly.'*

I heard Pete say, "Red, this is the medic."

And then I heard the ugly angel say, "This soldier has malaria. How long has he been like this? Has he been taking his atabrine?"

I heard Kenny say, "Just tonight. We have all been taking our atabrine, as often as we can."

I heard more chatter, and then felt my cot being lifted and carried out of the tent. It seemed like I floated for hours. I drifted in and out of sleep. I heard Nobel talking about turning yellow. I heard Kenny say he looked good in light yellow. Maybe he could start wearing a yellow scarf to accentuate the new look. I didn't know what "accentuate" meant. Then the conversations grew distant and faded to silence. I could see blue. Everywhere blue. I was a red hawk, soaring above Hopkins County. I saw home, Daddy on the front porch, leg crossed, drinking coffee. Momma was in the back yard, hanging clothes out to dry. I tried to say something to them, I wanted them to look up, but they could not hear me. I saw a big, black buzzard above me. He suddenly dropped down, diving toward me. His claws were extended, his beak was open, and I heard him screech, *'You don't belong here. This is my sky. Go away.'* I flapped my wings madly and tried to avoid his attack. I heard a hawkish scream coming from me, *'kee-aah, kee-aah!'*

    Pete, his hand still on my chest, said "Easy there, Red. Easy. Everything is OK. Relax."

    I drifted back to sleep. I was still a red hawk, standing high in a bois d'arc tree, my right claw grasping a mouse. It was bleeding from its nose. I unclenched my claw, and watched the mouse drop through the tree, past the leaves and horse apples, hitting the ground below, bouncing once.

    I woke up in a hospital tent. Two nurses, not ugly at all, were tucking clean, dry blankets around me, and fluffing a pillow beneath my head.

    "Three more tonight," one of them said.
    "When will all this stop?" the other nurse added.
    "Don't stop what you're doing...," I muttered.
    I heard them both giggle.

Mid-March 1944.

It rained every day the first two weeks of March. What a pitiful mood it made at the new 360th Station Hospital. After two-and-a-half weeks of treatment, though, I was feeling better. A lot better. I was ready to rejoin Mike Company.

The doctor stood by my bed, clipboard in his hand, rocking back and forth on his heels. He winked at me and said, "You really should stay a couple more weeks, Private Smith. Malaria is a tough opponent."

"I feel great, Doc. Somebody else can use my bed. I want to go back and be a soldier again," I pleaded.

"Well, you have responded very well to treatment and I'm prepared to say you are ready to be a soldier again, if you think so."

They gave me more atabrine tablets to take every day, twice a day.

With a sigh of relief, I slid into my britches and looked for my shirt.

It wasn't that I wanted to be a soldier again. Instead, I wanted to be back with my buddies. I was afraid that I was going to be left behind. Being left behind was the worst fear I had in this outfit. I didn't want to fight this war with anyone but Kenny, Pete, and Nobel. They had been visiting me almost every day, except when they were out on jungle training or amphibious landings. They kept telling me what they were doing, and the many rumors of us "moving out" in late April. A *real* landing was in the works. With *real* Japanese soldiers and *real* bullets.

The four of us had developed a friendship that went beyond anything we had ever known. For me, I could not even think of a future without them. For them, I believed it was the same. We watched after each other like children in a strange place, always on the alert, knowing that locked inside this eternal-foursome was the only possible hope of survival, the only way to get home.

Things were happening quickly now. Combat gear was being issued, including mess gear and shovels. Jungle tactics were taught constantly, as we stood in chow lines, as we waited for vaccinations, and when forming for assembly. Repetition. Over and over. One soldier in the platoon was chosen to be the "Reader," and whenever we would have a few minutes of time to wait, we would hear the command "Reader Out!" and he would quickly run to the middle of the formation, stand in front, and begin reading his lines to us:

*Combat in the jungle has low visibility, poor communication, and difficult movement.*

*You should only use small units in the jungle.*

*No more than one or two squads can fight on a jungle trail.*

*New jungles have no tall trees, just bamboo and thorny underbrush.*

*New jungles are very difficult to maneuver without a machete.*

*High jungles are not difficult to maneuver through.*

*Be ready for battle fatigue, skin diseases, and sores that do not heal.*

*Be ready for jungle rot of skin and clothing, malaria, chills, and intense sweating.*

*When crossing streams, check yourself and your buddy for leeches.*

The sun, when it shined, was very much brighter on Goodenough Island than in Australia. Kenny said it was because we were a little bit closer to it, higher up in the tropics, nearer to the equator. We all believed him because we didn't know how to disbelieve him.

There were parrots of many colors in the trees, and butterflies were everywhere. Just by looking, you could almost think this little speck of the Army in the South Pacific was Paradise, until the parrots opened their multi-colored beaks to sing. No song came out. Just the clanking of metal, a loud shrill of a scream, and the rat-tat-tat of an old engine. Gentle birdsong was not a requirement for the parrots of Goodenough.

We noticed that one fellow had planted flowers along a tent row. They were tall and pretty, and made you feel that you were somewhere decent, somewhere civilized.


Friday, March 24, 1944


Two large sacks of mail were delivered to the 21st Infantry after noon chow, to the cheers and excitement of everyone. Mike Company was called to fall in at our Headquarters tent, and we waited anxiously as the Company Commander, Captain White, and the Company Clerk, Private Wilson, stepped out of the tent. Private Wilson was holding the mail sacks as Captain White spoke to us.

The Captain explained that the mail sacks had just come in from Camp Caves, where it had been "lost" for several weeks. He said if we thought we had missed some Christmas mail that it would probably be in these bags. He thanked us for everything we had done so far, and wished us a late Merry Christmas. He then motioned to Private Wilson, who began calling out the names of the people getting mail.

    Each of us got packages and letters. We were given the afternoon off to read our mail and catch up on personal things.

    For the next hour it was a delight to hear the camp alive with laughter and conversation, as everyone enjoyed opening their packages and sharing the news from back home. Every few minutes a zippo would click as another cigarette was lit.

    The first thing I opened was a letter from Juliette. It was dated December 30, 1943. She wished me a Happy New Year and talked about the snow they had gotten on Christmas night. She mentioned the new black-top road going from Birthright and Sulphur Bluff to Hagansport, up toward Pete's hometown of Clarksville. She said Hopkins County would be a better place when I came back, and told me to take care of myself. I stared at the bottom of the letter, the ending that said 'Love, Juliette.' I wondered what was ahead – if anything was ahead – or if nothing was ahead.

    "Looky here, I got a whole big box of colored toothpicks," Pete bragged.

    He got a faraway tender look as he half- whispered, "Wanda picked these out herself for me. She knows me better than I know myself."

    "And I got some money from home!"

    Kenny received a Christmas card and a letter from his college friend Marie. He then smiled broadly as he opened a tightly pressed stack of Virginia tobacco leaves, and a deck of cards with "Herrod" written in big fancy letters on the back of each card.

"I don't know what this is, but I think it used to be cupcakes," Nobel announced as he rummaged his hand into an open box.

"I'll still eat them, one crumb at a time," he joked.

I held up a bottle of Old Spice and a really good hair comb, so the others could see.

"I'll be looking swell and smelling good," I declared.

The camp slowly quietened as everyone began to read the letters and cards from home.

"Dammit, just kick him out of the house and never let the sonofabitch come around again!" I heard from a tent to my left.

"Hey! I'm pregnant!" somebody yelled from a tent to my right, followed by laughter.

"Who's the Daddy?"

"What's his last name gonna be?"

I suddenly remembered Nobel and Katy, and the baby that should've already been born. I turned to look at Nobel and saw him staring into space with an open letter in his hand.

"Nobel," I calmly asked.

"Have you heard from Katy?"

He looked toward me, with an empty expression on his face. He was ashen, and his jaw was locked firmly, his lower lip protruding slightly.

"The baby died. It was a little girl. Katy's moving to Mobile, gonna start a 'new life', she says."

All three of us dropped our letters and looked at Nobel.

"Aww. Man, I'm sad to hear that," I said slowly.

Kenny and Pete remained silent. They hadn't even known Katy existed, pregnant or not.

"Thank you, Tex. It wasn't even mine, you know," Nobel acknowledged. He nodded to me, then looked at Kenny and Pete.

"The baby was not mine. But I thought Katy was mine. It hurts me. I hate it that she had to go through that by herself. Hell, I don't even know if she was by herself. But I do know that nobody, I swear nobody, was as good to her as I was. She needed me. I told her I'd give the baby my name when I came back, and be a Daddy to it, and love it with all my heart. God be my witness, I've known her and loved her all my life, and I always will."

Pete walked over and put his hand on Nobel's shoulder.

Kenny told him, "You're a good man, Mr. Horner. You have my utmost respect, and I love you like my own brother. God will help you get through this."

"Yup," Nobel answered, a lump in his throat, tears beginning to swell in his eyes.

He waited a few seconds, took a deep breath, wiped his eyes, swallowed, and looked at Kenny.

"She didn't want to live in Birmingham anymore. She wanted to go to Mobile and live on the beach."

He chuckled, "I told her a hurricane would hit her."

Pete leaned over and spoke quietly.

"After this war, you get your ass down to Mobile and you rescue that girl. You hear me?"

Nobel smiled.

"He hears you, Pete," I said.

"He knows he has some hurricanes in his future, too."

The Next Day

It was a windless day, clouds covering the sky, but no rain in sight. We had been awakened early that morning and marched to chow, then told to get ourselves showered and shaved so we would look good when the Division Commanding Officer, two-star General Frederick Irving, talked to us about the Army's plans for our first taste of battle.

We had been told the night before by Captain White that a big mission was waiting for us. Our part of the Philippines Campaign would begin in a few weeks. We would load up and sail northwest, toward the Philippines, and begin to drive the enemy off every island we attacked. There would be many amphibious landings in our future, island after island, until all the Philippines were liberated, and every Japanese soldier was dead or taken prisoner. As he spoke the word "prisoner," the men would moan, some would laugh. We were all fully aware of the Japanese code, *bushido*, of no surrender, no retreat. Fight to the death. There would be many killed, and few captured.

Captain White said he could not tell us which island we would attack first. We silently looked at each other and nodded, knowing that the rumor running amuck was it would be the closest one, maybe even Dutch New Guinea.

*Mr. Jackson's son was killed in New Guinea,* I thought to myself.

*We'll get justice for the many Aussies that went down. Especially for Red Jackson.*

By mid-morning, we climbed onto troop trucks and took a bumpy 30-minute ride to a large bowl-shaped, grassy field near DIVARTY, the 24th Infantry Division's Artillery Headquarters. The field was large enough to hold, sitting on the ground and standing near trees, all 14,000 soldiers of the 24th Division's three regiments.

A large, elevated, wooden stage was on the edge of the field. A few tall trees stood as a backdrop, with smaller trees along the horizon. A podium and microphone were positioned at the front, facing all the troops.

The four of us sat on the ground with the rest of the 21st Infantry Regiment, halfway up the rim of the bowl-shaped field, just off the left side of the stage.

General Irving walked to the front of the stage, his slender frame moving effortlessly to the microphone. He leaned forward, with both arms on the podium. We could see his sharp features from where we sat, and he spoke with his head moving slowly and methodically across the field of soldiers.

His words were unhurried and casual, as if he were speaking one-on-one to each of us.

He began:

"You're about to embark on your great adventure, probably the greatest adventure that has occurred to you during your lifetime. It is the operation we've been looking forward to for a long time. We're all ready. There are a few miscellaneous things I want to mention tonight. First is, I want to tell you about the confusion of combat. If you keep quiet, the Japs will not know anything about you. As soon as you fire your rifle, it's the same as saying 'Here I am.' At the same time, you have little chance of hitting anyone in the dark. You have a big chance of hitting your own men. So, keep that in mind. Firing at night, spasmodically and so forth, is a mark of untrained troops. I don't expect any of that from this division. In conclusion, I want to wish you the best of luck in this operation. These organizations have a grand reputation. I know that when the story of this war is written you'll have more than your share of decorations and honors. And, there'll be no units, no combat teams, that will equip themselves any better than will this combat team here."

After we were taken back to our camp, we were told to gather up our dress uniforms, mark our names clearly on them, and turn them in for storage. The uniforms had been issued to us at Camp Wolters, and we had worn them in Hawaii and Australia. We wouldn't be needing them on our next "great adventure."


Saturday, April 8, 1944.

All the 21st Infantry Regiment boarded a convoy of ships and made a final practice landing near the small village of Taupoda, New Guinea. We left the Goodenough harbor at 10:20 p.m., and hit the beach at dawn. It was Easter morning, 1944.

The villagers at Taupoda seemed a bit surprised when we all hit the beach in our combat gear, but they did not appear to be the least bit frightened. All went well, all the details accomplished perfectly, and we waited on the beach a few hours. Boarding the ships again, we returned to Goodenough Island.

We were told by all the brass that we were officially ready for our first *real* landing, and everyone expected it to be as perfect as this one.


Monday, April 17, 1944

Eight days later, we left the camp that the fuzzie-wuzzies had made for us, and boarded Landing Ship Tanks (LSTs) for the beginning of our War in the Pacific. The blood pumping through our veins that morning had a different feel, a different chemistry, an electricity that seemed to make us move a little faster, a little more purposeful. Deep, deep inside was the underlying anticipation of conquest, the primitive urge of men to overpower the enemy, to get it over with, to face the challenge, to win.

We hadn't talked very much that week about what lay ahead. But we saw in each other a vast difference in our postures, our bearings, our behaviors, and in our gait as we walked. Our twenty-month stint in the Army was changing dramatically and, perhaps, deadly. The training was done. It was time to use all the teaching and preparation for its intended purpose.

Kill, or be killed.

Without being announced or acknowledged, we began to bring our thoughts and emotions inward. We harnessed our brotherly love for each other in a defensive manner, protecting ourselves from vulnerability should one of us, or all of us, meet our respective rendezvous with death out there, in some disputed jungle.

Each of us had written letters home, to parents, brothers, sisters, and girlfriends. We didn't say anything about what lay ahead, we only recounted our daily habits, our boring duties, and the usual complaints about the weather.

*Don't worry about me.*
*I'm doing fine.*
*I feel like I'm putting on a little weight.*
*Nothing dangerous out here but that little red bug.*
*And the mosquitos.*

I hadn't told my folks about the malaria.

We shuffled up the ramp to the LST, all our combat gear hanging from us, with our thoughts focused on the unknown destiny ahead. Reaching the deck of the LST, we looked around us and were quite impressed. Stretching before us in the harbor were the many ships that were forming off Goodenough Island, and would join up with ships departing Cape Cretin and several other places to become Task Forces 58 and 77. There were destroyers, cruisers, carriers, transport ships, and smaller escorts across the harbor and out to the horizon. We had never seen that many ships before.

We filed down the ladders and passageways to our assigned bunks.

*"Now it begins,"* Nobel and I looked at each other.
*A visit with Mr. Seasick.*
*Again.*

I tried to find a bunk that lay in the same direction as the ship, bow to aft. My theory was the bunk would gently rock side-to-side with the ship, port to starboard, and I would sleep like a baby.

We sailed northwest through the Vitiaz Strait, then north around the Admiralty Islands. Turning south at that point, we sailed toward Dutch New Guinea.

# CHAPTER 15

# WAR BEGINS

Evening, Friday, April 21, 1944.

Off the coast, Hollandia Region, Dutch New Guinea, South Pacific.

As Captain White opened the hatch and walked into the large conference room, we all stood at the command "Attention!" He courteously instructed, "At Ease, gentlemen!" and we sat back down. We all liked Captain White. He was an honest, direct man, and had a friendly face, like a schoolteacher in Ohio or donut shop cashier in Texas.

Two lieutenants were standing at the left side of a table with a good-sized cardboard box, and another lieutenant was on the right side, setting up an easel with a map of New Guinea. Captain White looked around the room at us and announced, "We can finally tell you where and what you will be doing on this trip. And, you will be doing it tomorrow morning."

"We have reached our destination. We are about 20 miles from Tanahmerah Bay in the Hollandia Region of Dutch New Guinea. The Japanese Army occupies all Dutch New Guinea, and we are being sent in to drive them either to the sea or to Hell, and to take three airfields they have built. We are part of Operation Reckless, a pincer movement with the 41$^{st}$ Infantry Division. Our 2$^{nd}$ Battalion will be landing on Red Beach 2, and the 3$^{rd}$ Battalion, with us, will follow them. The 1st Battalion will be landing on Red Beach 1, on the west side of the bay."

He pointed with a lecture stick at each area on the map as he spoke.

"Our three battalions will merge and move east along a native trail and a narrow, muddy, f------up road to an airfield," he pointed again, "here."

We all chuckled at his assessment of the roads.

"We will secure that airfield and occupy the area around it. Any enemy threat encountered will be eliminated."

"Meanwhile, the 41st Infantry Division will be landing east of us at Humboldt Bay, and will be establishing beachheads at White Beach 1 and White Beach 2. They will move west along a similar native trail and the same narrow, muddy, f------up road to secure two other airfields. We will meet in the middle."

He paused, took in a long breath as we chuckled again, and looked around the room slowly.

He leaned against the table, and said, "Get some sleep, gentlemen. We will begin very early tomorrow. No reason to discuss the attack or try to help us with the plans. Just rest. We will be successful in this, and the Good Lord will watch us from on High and keep us safe."

"Now, these two lieutenants," as he pointed to the left side of the table, "Will be issuing you the official timepiece of the US Army, the new A-11 Wristwatch. I pulled a lot of strings to make you, the men of M Company, one of the first in the 21st Regiment to get their watches, so take good care of them. Calibrate them with your Platoon Leaders. After you receive your timepiece, you are dismissed."

He briskly turned to his right and left the room.

Early Morning, Saturday, April 22, 1944.

Offshore, Tanahmerah Bay, Hollandia Region, Dutch New Guinea, South Pacific.

    We were anchored about a thousand yards off Red Beach 2 in Tanahmerah Bay, north of Humboldt Bay. The first light of the morning showed heavy clouds with a light drizzle falling on the assault ships of the Operation Reckless Task Force.
    Each of us was sporting our new, silver wristwatch with a brown leather band. It was the best watch I had ever worn.
    We had been awakened several hours earlier and quickly served a breakfast of steak and eggs, the traditional Navy meal served to troops before a beach attack.
    "I don't care too much for this kind of breakfast so damn early," I said as I moved through the chow line behind Pete.
    "Eat what you can, Red," he replied over his shoulder.
    "This is not my kind of meal, either. They're fattening us up. I know you don't feel too good, but eat what you can, as slow as you can. This is gonna take us to the beach."
    "Nope," I told the sailor as he offered me a thick, juicy, steaming steak.
    I moved on down the line to the next sailor, a tall fellow with a friendly face, who politely gave me a large serving of scrambled eggs. Moving on down, I got potatoes

and toast. We followed Nobel and Kenny to a table against the wall, and sat our metal trays down, slowly.

I really didn't want to sit down with the food, as Nobel nodded his head at his tray.

"This is unbelievable," he said.

"I've heard stories about these breakfasts. I didn't think they were real, but here it is. An 'attack breakfast' in front of me."

"Yep," I sighed as I sat down.

Kenny was quiet as he poked his fork into his steak and sliced off a chunk of fat.

"Our next meal is gonna be C-Rations somewhere out there, and I think I'm looking forward to it," he mumbled.

"Me, too," I told him, as I picked at my eggs and potatoes.

We were given ten minutes to finish eating, then hustled out by Captain White. He just stood in the passageway hatch and announced in a decently firm but low voice, "Mike Company, return for your gear."

By 0530, we and the rest of the 3$^{rd}$ Battalion had climbed down the rope nets into the many landing craft waiting alongside our assault ship. We were busy adjusting and tightening each other's straps and packs. We had done so in training at least a dozen times and had our share of missing a rung on the way down or swinging around. But this time was perfect.

The men of the 2$^{nd}$ Battalion were already in their landing crafts. They were forming in line and moving toward the beach, which lay mostly hidden to us because of the low clouds and drizzle.

I thought to myself, *If we can't see the Japs, then they can't see us, either!*

We moved forward through the waves, bobbing up and down. We stood, shoulder to shoulder and helmet to helmet in the boat, thirty-six men hunkered down, occasionally raising to look over the side, then back to hunkering.

Each one of us was loaded with a cartridge belt, haversack, entrenching tool, first aid pouch, gas mask, poncho, canteen, blanket, jungle hammock, two six-pocket ammunition bandoleers, and four hand grenades.

I leaned against the bulkhead of the landing craft, relieving some of the weight of the mortar base plate I also carried on my back. In addition, I was carrying rations for three days, making the load even heavier. I tried to look up once, and a sudden wave of seasickness ran through me as I saw the beach move up and down with each wave. I hunkered down again and stared at my boot leggings. It helped to relieve the sickness to just stare at something that was attached to me.

Pete lay his hand on my shoulder and asked, "Are you okay, Red?"

He had a blue toothpick in his mouth.

I nodded and answered, "Yes. Are you, Pete?"

He nodded.

Nobel looked our way and said, "Cut the crap."

Kenny lightly thumped Nobel's helmet.

"Leave my Texas buddies alone, PFC Horner," he said, chewing a tobacco leaf.

"They think that's Galveston Beach out there."

A chuckle moved through the soldiers nearby.

The big Navy battleships started firing their guns a minute later. On and on the big guns fired. The shells were arching over us, hitting the beach in thundering explosions that sent sand and water soaring into the air. The bombardment lasted an hour.

A rocket barrage then began from several landing craft ahead of us, the rockets hitting the beach and trees violently. Machine-guns that were mounted on the landing crafts carrying the 2$^{nd}$ Battalion began firing toward the beach. We could hear no fire being returned.

The machine-guns abruptly stopped, and I heard several of the men on our boat announce that the 2$^{nd}$ Battalion had reached the southern half of the beach.

The time was 0709.

"They are on Red Beach 2! No enemy fire!"

"We got the beach!"

"No Japs on the beach! It's ours!"

We continued to move forward.

Minutes later, the Navy coxswain yelled out, "Ramp down!" and the bow ramp dropped open. We saw the northern half of Red Beach 2. It was pocketed with small craters from the bombardment earlier. About thirty yards from the shoreline was a grove of coconut trees. It was a small beach for all of us.

"Let's go! Let's go!" our platoon leader shouted.

We ran down the ramp and into the beach sand, beyond the splash of the waves. It was a good landing.

We ran the short distance to the tree line, and fell into a prone position, our rifles pointed forward.

There was no return fire from the enemy on Red Beach 2. We could hear sporadic gunfire from our far right, toward the landings at Red Beach 1. The 1st Battalion was up there, and it sounded like the enemy was there, too.

Soldiers of the 2nd Battalion, who had landed on the beach shortly ahead of us and to our right, were in the swamp that was beyond the coconut trees. We overheard conversations between officers and sergeants about the swamp not being on any maps, and what the hell were we gonna do about it.

We were told to stay in our position on the beach until ordered otherwise. We stared across at the wide swamp, saw our boys walking through it, water and mud up to their knees, trying to find a way forward. Our bivouacs and supply lines were supposed to be there, instead of that swamp.

The landing continued behind us. Men, vehicles, and supplies were backing up on the beach, with crates stacking up to eight feet tall.

"Where we gonna go when all that stuff gets unloaded?" Nobel asked to no one in particular.

"They will move us before that happens," I replied.

Sure enough, our Battalion Commander, Lieutenant Colonel Ramee, ordered us to move to our left to check the swamp and see if any enemy soldiers were in that area. We formed up and walked along the coconut grove that bordered the swamp, our rifles ready to return any enemy fire that might come our way. Nothing happened. We left our disassembled mortar there at the beach. *No place for light artillery out in that crap. This is rifle country.* We then stepped into the swamp, feeling the mud begin to suck at our boots, with our minds wondering what was down there in that muck. I watched Kenny frown as he pulled his leg and foot up out of the mud's grip.

*No, Kenny, this is not Virginia,* I told myself.

My eyes examined the few trees at the far edge of the swamp. There weren't very many trees, as if the swamp just went on forever. We walked further into it.

An hour seemed to pass.

Step after step into the muddy, oozy swamp.

Sometimes knee deep.

It was hard to keep your balance.

Your body leans forward with each step. Your foot stays where it is, submerged beneath the muck, while the rest of you continues to move forward. You go down. Down into that world beneath the gray, sour water, down where Heaven doesn't even know what is there. Your face goes into the water, and then below it. Your rifle is submerged. You try to use your arms to push you back up, but your hands go deep into the muck. One hand finds your rifle, and you push on it for leverage. The rifle goes deeper. You think you're going to drown, until your buddy grabs you by the belt and pulls you up.

I saw that happen to three men. When they pulled their muddied rifles up, they just started walking back to the beach, one frightening step at a time.

I felt myself lean too much once, and almost went down. I leaned back quickly. *Too much – now I'm falling backwards!* I leaned forward again, slowly. *Whew, now that's it.* I tried to pull my foot out of the muck. It wouldn't move. *Now my foot is even deeper!*

Pete came over to me, held my shoulder, and I held his. As I was pulling my foot out, Pete almost went down.

We looked at each other, eyes dark with rage and panic, and said "Shit!" at the same time. Then we smiled.

"Thanks, Pete."

"At your service, Red."

We continued our slow walk through the swamp.

Another hour seemed to pass.

*"If there are any Japs out there, they are on the other side. And from here, it looks like there is no other side,"* I told myself.

"Fall back, men. There are no Japs here," our squad leader said, breaking the solemn silence.

"Back to the beach."

We sloshed our way out of the swamp and gathered at our previous position.

Lieutenant Colonel Ramee was waiting there.

"Gather 'round," he ordered.

"Good job, men. You proved that there is no enemy resistance in that swamp," he smiled.

"2nd Battalion has been unable to find a trail beyond the swamp and will fall back, regroup at the point of our landing, and wait for orders to proceed to Red Beach 1. Likewise, we are being ordered to regroup. We will leave our current position as soon as practicable and go directly to Red Beach 1 to join up with 1st Battalion. The 2nd Battalion will be to our rear. The 1st Battalion has successfully found the trail that will take all of us to the objective, but they have encountered scattered enemy fire. We will be supporting their advance, on the ready. Grab your gear. Do it!"

"Platoon Leaders, stay with me!"

It was about 1400 when we started our move to Red Beach 1. As we walked along the narrow Red Beach 2, we could see many Navy boats and destroyers in the bay, supporting the landings. A string of supply boats moved between them and the beach. Tanks, trucks, jeeps, cannons, and crates of ammunition were stacked up on Red Beach 2, with much more on its way. Men were scurrying along the beach, arms raised and pointing in all different directions, barking commands to each other, trying to make sense of the delivery and staging of equipment. Officers stood with radios to their ears and frustrated, angry expressions on their faces. I saw a soldier stacking three cages with pigeons.

"Look at that, Red, our communications section," Kenny remarked.

"If I was one of them, I think I'd take my message home," I answered.

"This is gonna be one jammed-up beach," Nobel muttered.

Pete, in the lead, looked back at us and said, "It's that swamp. It's not supposed to be there. The engineers will have to work overtime to put a road in that mess or move THIS mess to another beach."

I nodded.

"If they can."

By dusk, we were near a crest of hills along the trail that 1st Battalion had found. The trail was a red, muddy mess and had been widened by the movement of many soldiers ahead of us. We could hear them, talking loudly, barking orders, and using machetes to improve the trail. There was an occasional exchange of gunfire. After dark, we were about a half-mile behind them, and were ordered to stop for bivouac. We dropped our gear in a small clearing just off the muddy path and set up a secure perimeter. We dug in as much as we could, ate our C-Rations, drank our water, and lay in our foxholes for the night.

Two men shared each foxhole, one to keep his eyes open and guard the area while the other slept beneath his poncho, two hours at a time. I shared a foxhole with Nobel, and Pete was with Kenny, their foxhole just five yards away from ours. We spent our first night of our first invasion with bayoneted rifles close by our sides. This was still a Japanese-held area, and we heard sporadic gunfire all night from up ahead, where 1st Battalion was leading the advance. We had not fired our rifles at all that day. It had been a swell day.

"A merciful God has been with us today, and the same merciful God will be with us tomorrow," Pete said.

A collective "Amen" was uttered by the rest of us.


Sunday Morning, April 23, 1944.

Along the Dépapré-Lake Sentani trail, near Mariboe, Dutch New Guinea, South Pacific

We resumed our advance late that morning, following the 1st Battalion eastward. It had rained several times through the night, and the trail was becoming extremely muddy and difficult to maneuver.

We heard erratic rifle fire from the front, which intensified later in the afternoon. Our pace slowed.

It was raining again.

Shortly after that, we heard airplanes and strafing gunfire, then mortars and heavy machine-gun fire. The unseen battle ahead of us, where 1st Battalion was encountering heavier resistance, was getting a bit more intense. It sounded like our planes had been called in for support.

We were ordered to stop and form defensive positions during this engagement, and the officers huddled around the radio. When the sounds of battle stopped about two hours later, we were ordered to resume our march.

Evidently, the 1st Battalion had walked into an enemy ambush up the road, east of us, near the small town of Sabron, and had fought it back.

Throughout the day, the 1st Battalion had been getting closer and closer to the Hollandia Drome, the first of three airfields along this road. We all expected a lot of resistance from the enemy protecting their string of airfields. They needed the airfields to defend New Guinea and help them attack Australia, and we needed them to attack the Philippines and drive the Japanese to the sea.

At dusk, the sound of mortars and howitzers could be heard from a mile or two ahead. We halted for the night and dug in. Radio activity continued all night at the headquarters tent. Our ears were becoming expertly aware of rifle and artillery fire, and we could tell the difference between our own fire and that of the enemy, and some idea of distance between the two.

Scattered enemy fire toward our bivouac interrupted the late hours of the night. We lay in our foxholes, watching for the direction of fire, and fired back only when we were sure of our targets. Headquarters called in for illumination, and flares began to pop from above, casting an eerie light across the jungle landscape beyond the muddy trail. The trees on our side, leading downslope to a lowland marsh, were creating ghostlike shadows as the glowing flares moved across the sky.

We could see Japanese moving around out there, perhaps half-a-dozen, quickly darting from tree-to-clearing-to-tree-again, like nervous cats. Running, stopping, running again. The reflections from their bayonets added splendor to their dance across the deadly space that surrounded us.

*Stay quiet. Keep your wits. Don't show them where you are.*

Nobel was looking beyond me, to my right. He whispered, almost noiselessly, "Keep your head down, Tex. I'll slice him when he gets here."

I knew by the look in his eyes that he had a Jap locked-in on his visual radar. I slowly, without a sound, lowered my Garand to the lip of the foxhole and lay flat under my poncho.

I felt the impact of the man's boot on my neck as he jumped into the foxhole, then felt it go limp as Nobel let him run full stride into his bayonet. I felt his body move to my left as Nobel slung him out of the foxhole, and I heard Nobel as he removed the bayonet and speared him again, two more times.

Nobel fell back into the foxhole with a tight smile on his face and gave me the thumbs-up sign. I saw him, in the glow from another flare, mouth the words *"My first one!"* and jabbed the air with his fist.

I slithered out from under the poncho and gave him a broad, toothy grin.

"Keep those pearly whites of yours covered, Tex. We're still trying to be invisible here," he whispered, then gave me his own toothy smile.

I turned to get my rifle. As I aimed it outward, another ghostly illumination showed an enemy soldier running directly toward us. I lowered my eye to the sight and squeezed off two rounds. He grunted and fell forward, barely three feet from me.

My first one.

I could smell him.

*Dammit!* I thought.

*I fired. Now they know where I am!*

Nobel put his hand on my back and patted.

"Good shot," he whispered, "I didn't know he was coming!"

Still looking at me, he said "Good God, these shitheads stink, don't they?"

In all that death and disorder, I don't know to this day how I kept from laughing out loud at his expression and his matter-of-fact observation.

Rifles fired around us, and more of the enemy fell.

I heard a soldier scream.

I heard the shouted command, "Get down, asshole!"

More gunfire, and then a slow quietness.

Minutes passed.

"Relax, men. I think we drove them off," the calming voice of Captain White floated across the killing field, barely ten feet behind our foxhole.

"That was some good soldiering you two did," he said, as he glanced at Nobel and me.

"See to your weapons and get some rest."

He walked toward the front of the bivouac.

We looked toward Pete and Kenny. They were giving us their thumbs-up.

"You take the next sleep, Tex," Nobel told me.

"I don't think I can sleep right now."

I disappeared beneath my poncho, knowing that my Birmingham buddy was the most wide-awake man on earth. I was trying not to shake, but everything inside, except my confidence in Nobel, wanted to scream to High Heaven.

I thought I had a slight fever.

*Maybe my shakes aren't fear. Maybe the malaria is coming back.*

I took an extra Atabrine from my haversack and washed it down with water from my canteen.

The canteen was half-full.

"We're gonna need to get more water," I whispered lowly to Nobel.

"Just open your mouth and let it rain in," he answered.

"Smart-ass."

I thought about his comment and folded the edge of my poncho into a tiny funnel and let some rainwater pour into my canteen.

The battle going on east of us lasted all night, right up to dawn.

Whatever sleep we had that night was from the exhaustion of the mud, the rain, the heat, and the slow, difficult walk. The all-night battle, the late-night attack, and the sporadic enemy fire on us robbed us of any real sleep. We were just two days into the Pacific War, and already we were terrified by the jungle, the unending wetness, the stench, and the shadows in the dark.

Monday, April 24, 1944.

Along the Dépapré-Lake Sentani trail, east of Dazai, Dutch New Guinea, South Pacific.

    During the night, jeeps and trucks had noisily delivered stacks of supplies from Red Beach 1. Cases of C-Rations, jugs of water, and crates of ammunition were lined up along the muddy road, at the farthest point the vehicles could maneuver.
    Troops from the 19th Regiment, followed by our own men from the Antitank and Cannon Companies, and a small group of natives were marching along the road toward us. Their purpose was to hand-carry supplies to the men of the leading 1st Battalion.
    "That's a mess down at Red Beach 2, with the swamp that nobody knew was there and this god-awful muddy trail. It is forcing us to hand-carry instead of using our trucks," a soldier said to us as we ate our breakfast C-Rations, curiously watching.
    "They moved the stacked-up equipment and supplies to Red Beach 1, after the SNAFU at Red Beach 2."
    "All that 1st Battalion had when they landed was two days rations. You'll be carrying some of this, too, and we'll need to go back and get you more," he added.
    We were preparing ourselves to resume the advance as we watched them load up for the hand-carry. Some men carried a crate of ammo on their back, others carried crates of bazookas two-by-two. Almost every soldier had a supply pack on his back and one arm carrying another load. The natives had larger loads, most of them carrying jugs of water on their shoulders.

"God bless those fuzzy-wuzzies," Nobel reverently said.

"They are like angels, aren't they?" Kenny responded.

As soon as they had passed us, we gathered our gear and whatever else we could carry.

It started raining again.

A moan ran down the line.

"Dammit!"

"Hello, Rain!"

"God willing that the creeks don't rise!"

Pete tied a case of C-Rations to the base plate on my back, saying "You sure about this, Red?"

"Yep. Everybody needs to eat. Some of this is for us, too. We're all on the same road together."

Pete closed the rain cover on my pack.

"Does it ever rain here?" he asked sarcastically.

"A little bit," I replied.

Down the muddy road we went, each soldier carrying his combat gear and a little extra.

The road became muddier. We could barely carry our own gear plus the extra.

The rain continued throughout the day.

We managed about three miles by nightfall, with frequent rests.

As we set up our bivouac, we knew that sleep would not come easy. We were exhausted by the hand carry of supplies and wet to the bone. But we were unable to rid our minds of the Japanese hiding in the jungle and the alarming urgency to get food and equipment to the men along this tight, thin line of supply.

Tuesday, April 25, 1944.

Along the Dépapré-Lake Sentani trail, between Dazai and Sabron, Dutch New Guinea, South Pacific.

The hand carry personnel left at first light. It was still raining.

We did not advance more than a mile that day. It rained continuously, enough to keep us and the trail wet. We spent the day sending out patrols to find enemy troops and snipers, and to slowly close in on the rear flank of the 1st Battalion.

I was selected to join a Love Company rifle squad, along with two Browning Automatic Rifle (BAR) men to observe the scene of Sunday's ambush near Sabron. As the eight of us approached the ambush area, we found that our artillery and mortar fire had killed a dozen or more of the enemy, and the others had apparently abandoned the position, leaving several weapons behind.

Suddenly, we received fire.

"Three Japs, over there," somebody yelled, pointing to my left.

Two were behind trees and one was on the ground, wounded in the leg, and was firing at us with his Arisaka, leaning on his elbow. I ducked behind a tree and fired three rounds at him. Two other GIs fired at the same time. His body jerked as each of our bullets struck him. The other two were rapidly killed, caught in a BAR crossfire.

It was over as fast as it had begun. We spread out and checked the area, a hundred yards in each direction. All clear. We set up three men as a perimeter, and the rest of us sat down on a huge, fallen tree. I nervously pulled a pack of Lucky Strikes from my chest pocket, pulled one out, and offered the pack to the others. My black Zippo made its comfortable clicking noise as each cigarette was lit. Soon, another pack made the round between us as we smoked several more cigarettes to calm our nerves.

Reporting back to the Platoon Leader, we continued our slow advance forward.

At nightfall, we set up a secure perimeter for our bivouac. We were about five hundred yards to the rear of the 1st Battalion.


0830 Wednesday Morning, April 26, 1944.

Along the Dépapré-Lake Sentani trail, near Julianadorp, Dutch New Guinea, South Pacific.

It was not raining. As we resumed the eastern advance toward the airfields, I looked to my left at the Cyclops Mountain Range, rising sharply up from the river valley we had been following for three days. Small, thick fog banks lay captured between the ridges, with the mountain tops barely visible. To my right, marshes and swamps rested in front of a low rise of hills, and beyond the hills I could see the beginnings of a large lake. A fresh cool breeze was drifting up from the lowlands, much different from the hot, humid breath of the jungle trail. Behind the lake were distant mountains, running east-west along the southern half of the island.

Ahead marched the combined infantrymen of the 1st and 3rd Battalions, with 2nd Battalion behind us.

The view before me was majestic and grand, beyond anything I had ever seen, even in Colorado. The long, winding line of the glorious infantrymen and the artillerymen, the riflemen and the mortarmen, made the scene impressive and unforgettable. A sea of green moved down the muddy road at a cadence as sweet and pleasing as a lullaby. Their bayoneted M-1 Garands sparkled, reflecting the morning sun as they marched. I felt a chill of excitement as we marched along, believing I was part of a great, historic event that would be talked about and written about long after I was gone.

We passed a small village on a hill, a collection of huts with thatch roofs, each on stilts. Many of them were burned and damaged. I saw some pigs and chickens. A few natives were standing on the hill, men, women, and children, waving at us with white cloths.

About a mile further, our advance stopped near a deserted plantation and we took cover as machine-gun fire erupted from a small Japanese bunker. Nobel motioned to me and said, "Base plate."

Pete removed the tripod from his back, then stepped behind me and removed the base plate I was carrying. Kenny helped Nobel take the mortar firing tube from his back. Kenny placed the tripod up into position, and in seconds Nobel had the mortar fully assembled. A courier ran back from the front and handed Nobel a scribbled note from the spotters. The ammo bearers from behind us had opened an ammunition crate and began laying rounds in front of Pete. Nobel adjusted the sights, as recommended by the notes from the courier. Pete dropped the first round into the bore, then another, and another. The mortar rounds began raining down on the machine-gun nest. In a matter of moments, the nest was destroyed, taken out by a direct hit.

A little further down the road, a rifle platoon peeled off from Love Company to eliminate some enemy fire from an old sawmill.

The march paused again, and we could see riflemen firing beyond a white picket fence to our left, toward a thatched-roof building that looked like a barn. Two soldiers walked quickly to the fence and heaved hand grenades at the old barn. The enemy fire was eliminated.

Things were really happening now. We were shooting at them and they were shooting at us. It was thrilling to know that we were part of the action, in control of the war. In that time and place we were seeing with our own eyes the movements and maneuvers that would ultimately win this war. Already, several dozen of the enemy had been killed that day.

By noon, we had reached a hill where we could look down and see the three airfields, stretched out along the north shore of Lake Sentani. The nearest was the Hollandia Drome, the most westerly. It was our objective.

The airfield was covered with what looked to be almost a hundred bombed, burned, and heavily damaged aircraft. Pieces of metal and airplane parts lay scattered across the cratered landing strips. Soldiers were murmuring within the ranks.

*Swell!*

*We showed them yellow bastards what we think of their air force.*

*They got their butts whipped here!*

*Nothing left but twisted useless metal!*

"Hold it down!" yelled the platoon leader.

"Halt!"

We stopped, regrouped, and the order was given by our Regimental Commander, Col Lyman: the 1st Battalion was to clear out a Japanese camp north of the airfield, and the 3rd Battalion was to move across the airfield, secure it, and advance to the southeastern tip of the runway, and hold that position.

By early afternoon the enemy camp had been cleared by the 1st Battalion with little resistance, and we had reached the western edge of the main runway of the Hollandia Drome. We encountered light resistance and eliminated it quickly. Half an hour later, we reached the southeastern end of the runway.

At 1530, Col. Lyman informed Division Headquarters that the entire Hollandia Drome area had been secured.

We felt that we had accomplished the greatest mission of our lives! We had landed on a Japanese beach, walked through a Japanese jungle, and captured a Japanese airport!

There were a few trucks captured at the airfield, and I, along with a handful of other drivers, were told to get the Japanese trucks and drive west from the airfield to meet the hand-carry soldiers. We headed west, met them, loaded our trucks with rations, ammunition, and medicines, and delivered the supplies and the hand carriers to our victory party. That was the best truck-ride I had ever made.

Four days later, we linked up with the 41st Infantry Division, which had landed east of us at Humboldt Bay, on White Beach 1 and White Beach 2. They had moved west along similar native trails and bad roads to secure the other two airfields. When they arrived to complete the pincer movement and trap the enemy in the area, we celebrated another victory party with them.

Early Evening, Wednesday, June 6, 1944.

Overlooking Lake Sentani, near Hollandia Drome, Dutch New Guinea, South Pacific.

Under a bright and beautiful full moon, we were watching a movie, *For Whom the Bell Tolls,* with Gary Cooper. We had seen it at Goodenough Island, but this movie was 'good enough' to watch again. It was about a war not too long ago in Spain. A few minutes into it, the movie was interrupted, and a louey walked down the rows of coconut tree log "pews" to the movie screen and announced that the Allies - us! - had just invaded Normandy, over in France. They called it D-Day. They said one hundred and fifty-six thousand troops were on the beach and headed for Germany. Everyone jumped up and down and cheered.

The war over there, the "other war" as we called it, seemed to be going our way now. It was always on our minds, as if we needed "it" to be over so the country could focus on this war. Our War.

It took a while to get over the celebration. Some of the men went back to write letters, some sat around in groups talking about the invasion, but the four of us stayed and watched the rest of the movie.

Three Weeks Later

After all the battle reports were completed by the Army brass, Nobel was given a promotion to Corporal, and Kenny and Pete were promoted to PFC. Captain White said that Nobel was very good as the mortar gunner, and said Kenny, the college man, was a good thinker. He said that Pete was a hard charger. I was happy to have everyone in my group with higher rank than me. I could've used the extra money that comes with a PFC-promotion, but I was glad to not have extra responsibility. Now, the way it was, all three of my buddies were responsible for me. I told them that. They all snickered.
"We all know the truth," Kenny said.
"You are responsible for all three of us. You're the oldest Texan in the group. You are the rugged desperado."
Since we had taken the Hollandia airfields from the Japanese army two months ago, we had done nothing but rest. Our camping area was set up, with the help of some fuzzie-wuzzies, in a high meadow overlooking Lake Sentani. We had personal tents with hammocks instead of group tents. They were equipped with mosquito nets, and the tents covered us enough to keep the rain out. It did not rain as much there by Lake Sentani as it had on our long walk from the beach. The lake seemed to pour fresh cool breezes through our camp every morning, with the heat not starting until late afternoon. The sun would set quickly behind a high

peak in the Cyclops Mountains, giving only a short time for the day to heat up. At night, the air would turn sharply cool, the sky clear, and the stars brighter than we had ever seen.

Most of our time was spent resting in our tent area. The 21st Infantry was assigned the work of "mopping up" the area, conducting patrols to flush the enemy out of the jungles, caves, and scattered villages. We would go on a four-to-five-day patrol every-other week. The patrols would take us south of Lake Sentani into the Grime Valley or higher into the Cyclops Mountains to search for possible Japanese hideouts.

In the mountains we found the air to be clearer and less humid, but still hot. We carried our weapons at the ready, always on the alert, knowing that there may be an enemy behind the next tree, or a group of them waiting for us to walk into their ambush.

Every patrol netted a handful of enemy soldiers.

We never came back with a prisoner.

On our patrols we would often see small passels of pigs that had gone wild during the occupation of the Japanese and their destruction of villages. These pigs would wander out of the trees into a clearing, grunt at us a few times, and run quickly back into the trees. We would often wish for roast pig for supper, but could not chase and catch these critters, and were told by the officers to not fire our arms at anything other than the enemy.

The same for chickens. We saw a brood of chickens almost every time we were on patrol. They were easier to catch than pigs. Since I was an experienced chicken-grabber (not thief, since I always paid for every borrowed chicken with firewood), I was able to grab an occasional hen and our field cook would gladly fry it for us if he got the pulley bone.

The banana plantations scattered around the island had survived the shelling of Hollandia, and new bananas were beginning to hang from the trees like candy. The bananas were smaller than the ones back home but were the tastiest I had ever eaten. Bananas were in my diet every day. I had dreamed all my life about walking up to a banana tree anytime I took a notion and picking two or three, and I had lived to see that dream come true.

The field kitchen that belonged to our camp could cook up some mighty fine food. By late June, we were getting fresh vegetables and fruits, and the meat was better than ever, better than Camp Caves and Goodenough Island. We guessed the farms of the free world were hard at work this summer trying to keep us soldiers well-fed.

The Army had built a headquarters building for Gen. Douglas MacArthur high up in the mountains, and we began to see a lot of brass traveling the road near our camp. We were always on the lookout for the chance to see MacArthur.


Early-September 1944

Overlooking Lake Sentani, near Hollandia Drome, Dutch New Guinea, South Pacific.

Rumor had it that MacArthur would soon have his chance to return to the Philippines, and the Hawaiian Division's 21st Infantry would be a part of it. Every day more and more brass could be seen going up and down the road. It made us feel that we were now working directly for Gen. MacArthur in the Philippine Campaign. There was a constant buzz in our minds, a thrilling awareness, that we were indeed part of history here on this small island in the South Pacific.

One day, Nobel and I were taking a late afternoon stroll to visit the hilltop village near our camp. We went there often, it was only a few miles down the road and up the hillside. We would give them chocolates and crackers from our C-Rations, and the natives would usually give us a snack of some sort. We normally didn't ask what it was, but the snack was sweet mostly, sometimes a bit spicy.

We saw four or five jeeps coming down the road at a pretty high speed. We stepped a bit farther away from the road, as we had been told to do so by our officers.

"It makes the top brass a little edgy when you boys are too close to them," Captain White had said.

"Besides, if you stay far enough away from them you don't have to salute when they pass."

We were a good thirty yards from the road when they passed.

There he was, sitting in the third jeep.

General Douglas MacArthur.

Supreme Commander, Southwest Pacific Area.

He was holding a corncob pipe as he glanced our way.

We saluted.

He nodded.

# CHAPTER 16

# LANDING ON LEYTE ISLAND

Early October, 1944.

Dutch New Guinea, South Pacific.

Across Europe, the war continued. Hitler began launching the new V-2 rocket bombs into England, with heavy damage and losses. The Allied troops, advancing after D-Day, had liberated Paris and was entering Germany from Italy and France. The Russian Army was pouring down from Poland toward Germany. Nobel had gotten a letter from his sister Betty, telling him her husband had been wounded piloting a bombing mission over Germany, and was coming home.

    On our side of the war, the Marines had invaded the islands of Guam, Tinian, and Peleliu. Casualties were heavy, and the Japanese military was being destroyed, island by island. But there were many more islands yet to be invaded.

    General MacArthur was just weeks away from beginning the Philippine Campaign, and we were going to be the spearhead of his return to the Philippines.

    We kept hearing the rumor that October 20th would be the date. We marked it on our calendars.

    *Maybe that's when we hit the beach again,* ran through our minds.

Pre-Dawn, Tuesday Morning, October 10, 1944.

Offshore, Tanahmerah Bay, Hollandia Region, Dutch New Guinea, South Pacific.

    We had all boarded assault ships and departed from Humboldt Bay for a final practice amphibious landing. The beaches that were Red Beach 1 and Red Beach 2 almost six months ago, in Tanahmerah Bay, were our objective.

    Captain White had told us we were less than a week away from the Philippines, and this would be our last rehearsal before a landing that would most likely be our deadliest yet. Our minds were attentive, and our moods were serious.

    Unlike the first landing at either of the Red Beaches, it was not raining when we climbed down the rope nets into the landing craft. Also, there was no bombardment of the shoreline.

    At 0600, our landing craft rapidly approached the beach, the ramp dropped, and we jumped into water that was knee deep. Our boots dug into the wet sand, and we propelled ourselves forward, out of the water to the crest of the small slope, and up to the line of coconut trees. Falling to the prone position, we each sighted our Garands into the "unknown" beyond the trees.

    The platoon leaders were receiving information from radios, and commanded Mike Company through several maneuvers on the beach. The four of us set up the M2 mortar, ran through the procedure to fire a dozen rounds, setting the desired angle and recalculating for adjustments. This was done three times, each from a different location on the beach.

After an hour of battle simulations, we were dismissed to eat our lunch rations. We then boarded our ships at noon and arrived back in Humboldt Bay at 1600. Many of the officers and staff remained on board the USS Wasatch the next two days, attending conferences and planning sessions around the clock. We spent those two days in our camp, making sure our gear was ready and minds were clear. We had hot chow the first day, then B-Rations the second day.

Friday, October 13, 1944.

Humboldt Bay, Dutch New Guinea, South Pacific.

We had hot coffee from the mess tent that morning, then we were told to gather our gear and prepare to move out. Trucks carried us on a long, dusty ride to the Humboldt Bay beach, where we were transported to our ships by small boats. The bay was choppy from typhoons in the north, toward the Philippines.

As we lumbered up the ramp to our transporter ship, I said to my friend ahead of me, "Hey, Nobel."

He looked back at me.

"Whut?"

"We've got to do it again."

"Got to do what?" he answered, his unfastened helmet bouncing on his near-hairless head.

"Be sick again," I moaned.

"Oh shit, Tex. Don't remind me."

Kenny looked back over his shoulder and remarked, "The Philippines are only thirteen-hundred miles away. It won't even take a week to get there."

Nobel and I moaned.

"Monsoon season, too!" Pete pointed out.

"Shut up!" Nobel and I said at the same time.

Two days later, we departed Humbolt Bay, Hollandia, at 1500.

We joined the many ships that were waiting offshore, and our convoy of 500 combat ships and transport vessels of all types set sail for the Philippines. We could feel the tension and the excitement as we stood in the port corner of our bow, a converted Australian passenger ship. We viewed the fleet of ships in every direction around us.

We did not know it at the time, but we were looking at the beginnings of the largest naval and amphibious fleet ever assembled in the history of the Pacific. The Liberation of the Philippines had begun, and we were going to be in the lead.

For most of the trip, the weather was somewhat clear, with occasional showers. Our 'accommodations' were far better than any trip we had made. Plenty of heads, plenty of galleys, plenty of space.

Nobel and I knew what to do, every day. We took it easy. Everything we did was done slowly.

Eat a little bit.

Slowly.

Take our medicine with some food.

Sleep.

Take a walk in the fresh air every day.

Slowly.

Eat a little bit, again.

We took a couple of showers slowly.

It made us feel a little bit better.

On the morning of the sixth day, we could see the southern Philippines to our west. A few hours later, the Navy destroyers and battleships began shelling Japanese installations along a long strip of the Leyte shoreline between Tacloban and Dulag. The shelling continued mercilessly through the day and into the night.

The shelling stopped at nightfall the next day.


Friday, October 20, 1944.

Leyte Gulf, Philippine Islands.

At 0100, we passed through the entrance to Leyte Gulf. The assault ships carrying the 1st Cavalry and 24th Division (minus us) left the task force and sailed north to their landing locations at Red Beaches 1 and 2. Their job was to seize the Tacloban airfields, secure the San Jaunico Strait, and work their way inland through the Leyte Valley while clearing out enemy resistance along Highway 2.

The assault ships carrying the 96th and 7th Divisions left the task force and sailed to their landing locations at White Beaches 1 and 2, ten miles south of the Red Beaches, near the city of Dulag. Their job was to secure Highway 1 and the bridge while establishing a strong beachhead.

Once well inside Leyte Gulf at 0200, assault ships carrying us and the rest of the 21st Infantry Regiment broke away from Task Force 34 and began sailing toward the Green

Beaches to the south, along the Panaon Strait. Our job was to secure the area and control the entrance to Sogod Bay, preventing Japanese battleships and destroyers from attacking our Navy and Army beachheads on the left flank.

We were already up and preparing for our traditional steak and egg breakfast.

The four of us were already seasoned veterans of this ritual. Kenny and Pete had good-sized trays full of steak, potatoes, and scrambled eggs, but not as much as the first time. Nobel and I had smaller portions of eggs, potatoes, and toast, knowing that the landing boats and the bobbling were still ahead of us. We were quieter this time, after hearing the pounding of Leyte the past two days and being told many times that the Japanese forces were strong and dug-in there.

"Did'ja notice all the shells were going to the north and none of them were going to the south?" Nobel asked us.

Kenny nodded to confirm, and Pete answered, "Yeah, I did notice that," as he placed a fatty piece of steak into his mouth.

"Dammit, Pete, why do have to eat such a fatty piece of meat?" I asked.

He just shrugged his shoulders, looked at me, and answered, "Energy, Red. I'll burn the fat when I get on the beach."

He pointed his fork at me and said, "I saved your ass in that swamp, remember? That took energy."

"Fat like that makes me want to throw up," I answered.

Nobel looked at me and said, "Don't talk like that, Tex. Nobody's gonna throw-up nothing today."

Kenny looked up from his plate and announced, "There are no waves out there, gentlemen. It is a calm sea this morning. It was special-sent for you landlubbers."

"It's about time," I said, with a mouthful of eggs.

By 0300, we had returned to our quarters and helped load each other with combat gear.

Down we descended on the rope nets. We tucked ourselves into the landing craft. We began tightening and adjusting each other's straps and packs. By 0700, there were twenty-five landing crafts full of men circling the ship, ready to be pointed at Green Beach 1.

"Still no shelling of the landing zone," a soldier said to our right.

"Yeah. Shit! What are they waiting for?" another answered.

"Look, look out there. There's people on that beach. Waving stuff!"

"Japs trying to invite us to dinner!"

"I don't know. They don't look like Japs. They look like villagers."

"Well, they better get the hell off my beach 'cause this big boy is coming in!" another soldier said, holding his Thompson submachine-gun, a cigarette dangling from his lips, moving up and down with each word.

"That's why you're in front of me," a soldier said from the rear.

I did not dare get up to look at the beach, knowing it was the horizon going up and down, up and down, that made me seasick. I did as usual: I leaned against the bulkhead and stared at my leggings.

We didn't know it at the time, but two courageous villagers from the tiny little town of Liloan on Panaon Island had noticed the naval fleet approaching the island early in the morning. They knew that the Allies completely bombarded all the beaches they attacked, and they did not want to see their little town blown away, along with the several hundred villagers living there.

They got on a small sailboat and went toward the fleet, hoping to tell the Navy commander that all Japanese soldiers had left the area several days ago. They also wanted to report that all Japanese guns and equipment had been loaded on a submarine and taken away at the same time. The two men were intercepted by the Navy and taken to the war room of the Admiral's flagship, where they spent hours begging the Admiral not to destroy their village.

The Admiral looked through his field glasses, saw people on the beach, and said, "See? There are Japs running around!"

The two men pleaded with the Admiral to go closer. He ordered his ship to within 300 yards of the beach and confirmed that they were villagers. He then issued the orders to proceed with the landing without bombardment.

We knew nothing of the heroic efforts of those two men to save their village. We just knew that we had been bobbing in the water since 0700, and it was approaching 0845.

The Navy coxswain shouted, "We have been ordered to the beach!"

A restrained cheer ran through the boat, each man ready to land but disturbed by the lack of protective bombardment.

Our landing crafts approached the beach at 0855, and the bow ramp fell open.

Nothing was happening on the beach.

To our left, a few villagers – men, women, and children – stood at the back of the beach, in front of a grove of palm trees. To our right, the same thing.

"Let's go! Let's go!" the platoon sergeant commanded.

We splashed into foot-deep water, jumped into the sand, ran forward, and fell to the ground, our rifles pointed inland.

"Remain in position and DO NOT FIRE until ordered to do so."

The villagers huddled together, looking awkward, and giving us a half-wave.

"Listen up!" shouted Captain White, as he walked up the beach from his landing craft.

"There are no Japs on the beach! Just villagers."

He looked left and right, then chuckled.

"At Ease, Mike Company! It is reported that no Japs are anywhere near here. Remain in position until we figure out where we want you to go and what we want you to do."

We began mumbling to each other in disbelief.

"What the hell?"

"Do you believe this?"

"These people are getting a real show!"

"We are the Fighting Army!"

The platoon leader waved his arms.

"Cut the crap!" he yelled.

"Just hold it down! We are a silent Army today," he smiled.

"You can remove some of your gear."

I asked Pete to help me take the mortar base plate off my back.

There we were, reclining on a sandy South Pacific beach, with villagers welcoming us to their little stretch of paradise. A nice-looking young woman with a large basket hanging from her shoulder was giving each of us little round cookies with holes in the middle, like a tiny, flat donut. They tasted swell, like a teacake, only a little sweeter and thicker. We each thanked her as we grabbed several of them, and a Spanish-speaking fellow with us asked her what they were. She said something to him, and he told us she called them "roskeeyas."

We could hear thunderous booms coming from far to the north, where the other two landings were occurring on Leyte, combined with rockets, mortars, and aircraft bombing. It gave us a somber feeling to know we were here, having cookies on the beach, while the rest of the 24th Division was up there, having strong enemy resistance on their beach.

At 0930, the 21st Regiment reported to Division Headquarters that the Panaon Strait had been secured.


One Hour Later.

Near Liloan, Panaon Island, Leyte, Philippine Islands, South Pacific.

After we spent an hour letting the Command Post make all the decisions, we were ordered to pack up what had been delivered to the beachhead and take it a little farther north across an old iron bridge to a suitable location on the Leyte mainland. The Command Post remained on the Liloan side, south of the bridge.

As we crossed the bridge, Nobel pointed down to the water and said, "Look, Tex, look at those whirlpools."

I looked down and saw dozens of little whirlpools spinning around beneath the bridge.

I had never seen water so active before.

Pete looked over the bridge with us and remarked, "Well, I'll be golly. It must be the way the water moves through the strait here. It's kinda magical, ain't it!"

We turned our attention away from the water and gazed back at the little village of Liloan, tucked away behind the beach where we had landed. A tall, gray, stone lighthouse towered above the village.

"Yeah," I said.

"It's all kinda magical."

"I bet that's why we didn't bomb the beach before we took it," Kenny observed.

"Somebody probably told us the village had no Japs and was too damn pretty to destroy."

It was already mid-afternoon when we began setting up our bivouac. We were likely to see enemy resistance at some point in our "stay," so we didn't bother to get comfortable. We easily dug our foxholes, since the soils in the Liloan area were relatively free of rocks. We made sure the foxholes were deep enough for us to stand or sit. We placed a rim of soil around the top of our foxhole to prevent rain from running into the foxhole.

The Army Engineers had begun the work of making roads, digging latrines, and putting up mess tents for the camp. Meanwhile, we set up a secure perimeter, ate our C-Rations for supper, and waited for word from headquarters.

Saturday, October 21, 1944.

Near Liloan, Panaon Island, Leyte, Philippine Islands, South Pacific.

Headquarters decided that the 3rd Battalion would constantly patrol the southern tip of Leyte Island and the Island of Panaon. The Japanese Army had been there, and they would surely try to come back and try to drive us away.

Everyday half of us would go out on patrols north and south of our beachhead. The remaining troops would be busy at the camp on work details or housekeeping, including moving and storing material from the beachhead. Every day we would run into enemy fire, and every day we would drive them back into their hiding places. We would call in the flame-throwers. It was a horrible thing to watch, but we would all breathe a big sigh of relief when we left the area with no live enemy remaining.

Every day, one or two Japanese bombers would fly over the camp and drop half-a-dozen bombs, and a couple of fighter jets would come down low and mess things up with their machine-guns. We would return fire and they would leave, either scared away or out of ammunition. Little damage was done, and only five soldiers were injured by the attacks the twelve days we were there.

Tuesday, October 24, 1944.

Near Liloan, Panaon Island, Leyte, Philippine Islands, South Pacific.

    From south of us, and not very far, we began to hear Navy ships firing the big guns, anti-aircraft guns, and machine-guns about 0930 that morning, and it lasted for hours. Fighter jets could be seen darting through the air from all directions, always turning south to where the fight was happening. We knew something was happening down there beyond the strait. We didn't go very far on patrols, and we set up a strong security perimeter at the camp and around Liloan, where all the villagers were hunkered down in safe places. Our air men and spotters were keeping in touch with the Command Post, telling them that nothing was happening on the ground, it was all a mighty naval battle, and no Japanese troops were seen anywhere close to us on land.
    The battle at sea went on for another two days, with the booming of the Navy guns moving off to our east, and then to our northeast by Thursday. The daily bombing and strafing attack by the enemy aircraft, now down to one bomber and one fighter jet, resumed on Thursday, but was still ineffective.
    On Friday and Saturday, forty-two Japanese prisoners were captured on the beach near us. They had swum from the enemy ships that were sunk in the big battle that took place south of us, off the shore. Someone said that one of the prisoners was a Japanese Lieutenant Commander, and he was immediately sent to the Navy Fleet Headquarters under much protection and observation.

On Saturday afternoon, a monstrous typhoon hit the island, with seventy mph winds. Some of our lighter equipment was blown away, and we had to work very hard at keeping ourselves from being hit by debris and falling trees. Our foxholes filled with water as the rain came down like I had never seen. Nobel and I had to empty our foxhole with our helmets, and build up the dirt rim again to keep more from running in. We saw Kenny and Pete doing the same thing a few feet away. They would look up and we would laugh. Then, minutes later, we would look up and they would laugh.

That night we tried to sleep as much as we could, in water up to our knees, covered by our ponchos. There were no enemy raids that night, and all we heard was thunder, the howling wind, rain pouring from the sky, and trees falling nearby.

The typhoon continued for three days. There were no Jap raids, but the thunder, wind, and rain slowed, until it absolutely stopped on the fifth day. Then, for several days, we watched the water drain away, and the mud dry as much as it could.


Tuesday, October 31, 1944.

Near Liloan, Panaon Island, Leyte, Philippine Islands, South Pacific.

The sun was ablaze in the tropical sky, and it was humid. A few patrols had gone out, but most of the battalion was near the camp, putting it back together after the typhoon and getting our combat gear organized. A rumor was running amuck that we would very soon be returning to the rest of the 24th Division in the northern Leyte combat.

Nobel and I were sitting on a sand dune, overlooking the eastern shore of Panaon Island and Caballan Bay. We had eaten our lunch of C-Rations, taken our atabrine, and were enjoying our box of C-Ration cigarettes. Beyond the bay and across the Surigao Strait, we could see the faint outline of many small islands, against the dim backdrop of a larger beach. Pete sat a few feet to our left, with Kenny beside him. The view, from sand dune to distant shore, was so beautiful it was hard to believe it was real.

Pete removed his cigarettes from his C-Rations box and fumbled for one. I leaned over and handed him my black zippo. He smiled as he took it, lit his cigarette, and clicked it shut.

"I sure do like this lighter, Red. It makes me think of Zorro."

Kenny reached for the zippo. He clicked it twice.

"The music of *The Caballero Negro*," he reflected, chewing on a tobacco leaf.

"Did he ever make it up to East Texas, Mr. Smith?"

"Shur-nuff," I answered.

"I saw him at the Mission Theater a couple of years ago."

He tossed the lighter back to me.

"It's a beauty," he said.

We sat there, musing at the tropical paradise, the blue sky, the dappled sand, the breeze touching our faces as it blew gently inland.

Five minutes.

Ten minutes.

An occasional sigh.

Nobel was not one to let silence continue anywhere, especially in the middle of a paradise.

"There's all those islands out there, guys. And they're probably all just as thick with jungle as what's behind us. Maybe even more darker and thicker. Anything could be out there," Nobel was saying, a blank, faraway look in his eyes, as if he were talking to no one in particular.

I leaned over and looked at Pete, then at Kenny.

"Yep," I said.

"Anything could be out there."

"Probably more Japs than this one," Pete added, a yellow toothpick dangling from his mouth.

Nobel, still staring ahead, uttered slowly, "D'ya think one of them islands might have a King Kong?"

Kenny pulled the wet, chewed tobacco leaf from his mouth, flicked it against the side of a coconut tree, and answered in his slow, deliberate manner, "That's a movie, Nobel. King Kong doesn't exist. They made him for the movie."

Irritated, Nobel looked at Kenny. With a sneer, he retorted, "I know that, Kenny. I saw the movie. But the island was real. They can't just make an island. It's out there. D'ya think there might be some ugly things out there? They don't have to be as big as King Kong. There's stories all over Alabama about a hairy ape-looking man down in the swamps."

I smiled, looked down, remembering the stories from Hopkins County about a "hairy ape-man." I waited for Kenny to answer.

*Here it comes,* I thought.

Kenny sat still a second, then straightened his back, like a judge announcing a verdict.

"Mr. Horner, let me answer that," he stated, matter-of-factly.

He leaned toward Nobel, pointed his left index finger several times for effect, and said, "There's jungle out there so thick that light cannot penetrate it. There will be uglier things than King Kong or the hairy ape-man out there. Hell, there's uglier things than them right here on this island, right now, this very day."

Nobel looked at him, his eyes squinting.

Kenny leaned toward Nobel and whispered, "There's Pete, and there's you."

I tried, but I couldn't stop the laugh from bursting out of me.

Pete stood up, and gently placed a fake slap on the back of Kenny's head.

"I am not that ugly, Kenny. I resent that remark. Nobel resembles that remark. We'll have no more Kong talk. At least, not until we get deeper in the other jungles out there in the wild Pacific."

"And you, Nobel," Pete continued, "You just stay next to Red and me. You are our little blond friend, and no Thing is going to take you away from us."

Nobel just shook his head slowly and smiled.

"You and Kenny need to be protected more than me," he said.

"You're just two smart-asses in the middle of a world war, and I wouldn't have it any other way."

We heard the bugle, calling for Battalion Assembly.

"I believe they are about to tell us what we are going to do," I said, getting a foothold in the sand.

Back in the camp, we all gathered outside the Command Post. Captain White emerged from behind a tent flap, and said, "Alright, men, gather 'round."

He looked around at the men who had gathered. You could tell his eyes were counting, looking for the familiar faces of Mike Company. Satisfied that most of us were there, he spoke.

"Gentlemen, it appears that we are going north to join the 19th Infantry Regiment and the rest of the 24th Division near Pinamopoam, Leyte. The fight is beginning to get a little rough up there, and General Silbert wants his entire Division for the engagement. So, General Krueger has directed General Hodge to tell our Battalion Commander, Lieutenant Colonel Ramee, to move us from here to up there. I guess you can tell there is a lot of high brass telling me what to do."

He smiled at us and we all laughed.

He continued, "Now, the 32nd Infantry has been hit pretty hard up there. One of their battalions, I believe it is the 2nd Battalion, is already on its way here to replace us and get some well-needed rest. Expect to move out tomorrow as soon as we are replaced here. Since we will be the freshest troops available, we can expect to be thrown right into the fight."

Captain White paused, his brow was furrowed down, and he had a stern, yet almost sad, look on his face. He squinted his eyes as they moved across the men in front of him.

"Gentlemen," he continued, "I believe what lies ahead of us will be the most severe and brutal combat we, or any company, have faced during this war. The Japs are dug in, trenched in, and they are hiding in caves, spider holes, and bunkers along a narrow stretch of road up there. I already know the caliber of you men, and I can think of no other men I'd rather lead along that road than you. So, let's get our gear together and wait for the 32$^{nd}$ to show up here to replace us, and let's go send some Japs to Hell. You are dismissed."

We broke up and moved to our camp area. Some men were murmuring, some were excited, most were concentrating on the fight ahead. I turned to look at Pete, and he nodded back at me. Kenny was quite, but serene.

"This will be the real war," he said.

Nobel put his arm around me and boasted, "Tex and I will hold our own."

"I've never seen Captain White so serious," I admitted.

"He knows it's gonna be bad up there, and he wants us to be ready. I'm ready. Are you, Pete?"

Pete grunted.

"Ready and willing."

"Kenny?" I asked.

Kenny looked serious, then opened his eyes wide and smiled.

"War is the natural order of things," he announced, nodding his head.

"Let's go see what we're supposed to see."


6:00 pm, Wednesday, November 1, 1944.

Near Liloan, Panaon Island, Leyte, Philippine Islands, South Pacific.

We were leaving the beachhead at Panaon Island on the USS Anderson and were turning south to join our convoy of cruisers and destroyers when the Japanese fighters and bombers appeared. This time there were a half-dozen of each, and they were ready to strike.

As the Navy was running to the command "Battle Stations," we were running down below. At one point, we were told to remain where we were, no matter where that was, and get the hell out of the way until the Navy had assumed their posts.

We could see the fighters circling and diving and could hear the machine-gun rounds striking the deck of our ship. We pressed ourselves as close as we could to whatever we could. That is a sound I will never forget. Metal against metal.

When we got below, we heard a loud explosion and felt a strong shock. We had been hit by one of the bombers on top, near the bow. We could hear the unexpected noise of sailors yelling commands, and fire alarms sounding. We were looking at each other, not knowing what to do. We all moved from our berths to the hatch, trying to see as much as we could down each passageway. It got kind of crazy down there, with all of us wondering if we were going down. Some of the guys were praying, some were crying, and some were repeating "we gotta get outta here!"

Quickly, a Navy officer appeared at our hatch and told us to relax. He said that damage control had reported no serious danger to the ship, but several "casualties" had been suffered. He told us to remain where we were, we were safe, the fighters and bombers had been destroyed. One fellow asked him if we were the targets, and he said it sure looked like it.

"However, no Army personnel were casualties in this attack," he said as he left.

The four of us just looked at each other with big round eyes.

"They nearly got us," Kenny complained.

"Geez, Red," Pete exclaimed, looking at me.

"Captain White said it was going to be 'severe and brutal,' but I never thought the Japs would chase us onto the damn boat!"

"Well, shit!" I nervously replied.

"I don't think the Navy thought that attack was going to happen. We were all kinda caught with our britches down this time. Let's hope it won't happen again."

I looked at Nobel. He was white as a sheet.

"Are you seasick yet?" I asked him with a grin.

He shook his head slowly, rubbed the top of it with his sweaty hand, and said "No, just scared the hell to death, but still alive. I can't wait to get sick, Tex. Ya gotta be alive to be sick, and I don't think I've ever been this much alive in my life!"

# CHAPTER 17

# BREAKNECK RIDGE

Thursday, November 2, 1944.

North Coast of Leyte Island, the Philippine Islands, South Pacific.

The trip to the north coast of Leyte was a short one. By 0730 of the second day, we landed at Tanauan, in northeastern Leyte. We were moved by truck northwest to near Tunga, a town just south of the coastal city of Carigara. We arrived there at 1300 under heavy rain, and bivouacked for the night, waiting for the rest of the 21st Regiment to arrive from scattered locations.

We awoke very early the next morning, Friday, to a steady rain, and by 0930 we had moved to a new position west of Carigara, near the Carigara River. Our march was halted there, under heavy rain, and we bivouacked again for the rest of the day. We were getting closer to Pinamopoan, the northern gateway to the Ormoc Valley. It was the point selected for us to relieve our sister-regiment, the 34th, who had been fighting the Japanese infantry for fifteen straight days. We could hear the distant rumble of artillery to our west and south, where the battle was occurring in the long area of ridges along Highway 2 beyond Pinamopoan.

On Saturday, we moved westward to a position nearer the city of Copoocan, arriving at 1130. Here, our numbers grew larger as more companies of the 1st and 2nd Battalions joined us, along with several dozen Filipino volunteers to help us carry equipment and be our guides. We moved a couple of miles farther west to the city of Colasion, where we bivouacked for the rest of the day and the night. The rain slowed to a constant drizzle, then stopped.

      The mail caught up with us there, and it was nice to get a few letters from home. Each of us got a couple of letters from our parents. Pete got one from his brother Sam and three from his girlfriend Wanda. Nobel got one from his sister Betty, and Kenny got one from his college friend Marie. And I got a letter from Juliette.

      Both Juliette's letter and the two from Momma and Daddy had a different return address than before - Route 1, Wellington, Texas. It seemed that all the Smiths and all the Hamiltons – except for Buck, Verna, and Jerry – just picked up their belongings and moved back to west Texas where the farms were more productive, and the jobs were many. Juliette said they decided to move because Mr. Wilson, their friend and farm-partner, still had connections there. She said Mr. Wilson told her father there was plenty of work, and convinced him it was worth the effort to move back. My Momma said the same thing, and they were following the Hamiltons. So, they all said good things about the move, and I was glad they were all working steady, but it made me a little sad to think that when this war was finally over, and it was time for me to go back home, it wouldn't be the same home I left, the home I spent 21 years learning every creek, every field, and every hen house. I knew the day I was drafted that everything I left behind me, all of it, the land and the people, would change. The jobs would move, the towns would die, and Time would change us all.

Juliette's letter was short and sweet. She talked about the hot summer, the rain that seldom came, the September showers that ended the drought *(I'd love to see a drought right now, I thought)* and the quiet, lonely nights that everyone in America, including the Hamiltons, had experienced since all of the "Army Men" had gone to war. She ended her letter with a few prayerful words that the Lord would watch over us, in Europe and the South Pacific, and show us the same love that those at home felt for us. Again, she signed it, "Love, Juliette."

I held the unfolded letter in my hand, sitting in the sand on the Colasian beach, for almost an hour.

*I need to write her, but we have no dry paper. I need to tell her how hard it is to write a letter in the rain, and how especially hard it is to get dry paper.*

I looked east toward Colasian Point, the small hill that jutted out into the Carigara Sea, imagining what this Pacific Paradise would be like without the war, this hatred of man against man. As beautiful as it was, I could not visualize myself ever coming back to this place. Even without the war, there had already been too many killings and too much rain to feel fond of it. Texas was where life started for me, and Texas was where I wanted life to end for me.

I was thankful that the rain had stopped so I could smoke a couple of cigarettes and enjoy the letters from home without huddling beneath my poncho. I knew the letters would get wet when the rain resumed, so I read them again, trying to memorize the precious news they delivered.

*Home.*
*Wherever that is.*

Some of the soldiers had gotten newspapers, and the latest updates from the war slowly filtered through the camp. The Russian Army was marching through Prussia, continuing its advance toward Germany. The Allies were marching through Greece, on the way to Germany. Navy carriers were attacking the Japanese forces on the island of Formosa, and American bombers were using the airfield on Tinian Island to conduct bombing raids on Japan. The U.S. presidential election was just days away, with Roosevelt expected to win.

I walked to the regimental headquarters area and found a tent with a little USO table. I saw a small stack of V-mail letter-sheets, and grabbed a couple of them and a pencil. Standing at the table, I hurriedly wrote a short letter to Momma and Daddy, and another one to Juliette. I wrote just enough to tell them I was alright, not a scratch on me, and was staying very busy with the job of infantryman. I told them I was eating good, sleeping well, and would like to send some of the rain back to them. I signed the note back home *I love you and miss you, Red*. I signed the letter to Juliette *With love, and looking forward to seeing you, Red*. I put the new west-Texas addresses on each sheet, folded them, and dropped them into a box that said, "Outgoing Mail." I chuckled as I thought, *"Outgoing? Where else would I want them to go? I wish I could fold myself really tight and crawl into that box with them."*

Later that evening, it started raining again, and we lay on the ground wrapped in our ponchos. All night we heard the sounds of battle from just a few miles up the road, in Pinamopoan. We were told earlier that the 34th was going through the city, clearing it of Japanese soldiers and artillery. They were clearing it for us, as the last killing deed before we would walk through their lines the next day, taking the baton of war.

They were giving the battleground to us, the fresh troops.

Sunday, November 5, 1944.

Day 1 on Breakneck Ridge

A torrential rain was falling. Before dawn we began moving west down Highway 2, as it ribboned its way between the sandy beaches and the swamplands. Made of gravel and crushed rock, the one-lane road ran west out of Pinamopoan, then turned sharply south, weaving its way through a jagged tangle of rocky ridges and barren pinnacles, a dreadfully impenetrable thicket of trees, cogon and kunai grass, and scrub brush. It was along this portion of Highway 2 that the Japanese infantry was expected to be dug-in and well-entrenched, a near-impregnable barrier between victory and death for the GI warriors. Beyond this was the small city Limon.

As we marched west between Colasian and Pinamopoan, the rain began to lessen, and we could see the beaches and coconut trees of Carigara Bay on our right. To our left were swamps that gave way to rice and banana plantations and brushy ridges. In the background were deeply green mountains that pointed to the sky. As we reached the city of Pinamopoan, we saw where heavy fighting had killed perhaps two hundred Japanese soldiers. Their bodies lay scattered around demolished shacks and shattered artillery. After we had established the 21st Regimental Command Post at Pinamopoan, we began our advance to relieve the 34th Infantry Regiment. With our 1st Battalion in the lead, we soldiers of the 3rd Battalion in the middle, and the 2nd Battalion moving up toward the rear of the line, we moved in to relieve them and begin our part of the battle to drive the Japanese forces off of Leyte Island.

As the dawn transformed the dark, wet sky to a grey, dim light, we looked into the eyes of the tired, battle-worn soldiers of the 34th Infantry as they marched through our lines in the traditional infantry ceremony of Relief-in-Place. They were leaving the battleground to us by passing through our open formation. Immediately afterward, we would re-form our columns and march toward the battleground they were leaving.

As we watched them march by, our stomachs tightened, and the shadowy fear of death began to gnaw deep into us. The men marched through our ranks like lost souls on a well-trodden pathway to an unknown place, as slow as cold molasses, putting one deliberate foot in front of the other, with no emotion or sense of destination. The soldiers looked like they were leaving a bad dream yet could not put that dream behind them until many, many steps had been taken. They wore dirty, ragged uniforms, and marched on weary legs, with heavy heads that nodded up and down slowly, and wide-open eyes. Many had wet cigarettes hanging from their lips.

"There they are," Kenny muttered.

"Look at their eyes. That's it! They call it 'the thousand-yard stare.' They're not looking at you, they're looking through you. There goes us in a couple of weeks."

None of us said anything. It chilled me to the bone. Nobel just looked down, not wanting to see them anymore. Pete stared, his red toothpick limp, almost falling out of his mouth.

I saw an officer walking alongside their ranks. His uniform was ragged, with no marking of rank, but I could tell he was an officer by the way he glanced from left to right, with alertness on his tired face.

I started to salute but did not.

The road began to rise as we walked forward, and it took a more southerly course. Ahead of us lay the rough, rocky hills covered in shoulder-high grass, where the Japs would meet us, and we would be at war. A real sustained-combat war, for the first time in our lives.

We halted quickly around noon. Colonel Weber, our new Regimental Commander, ordered us, the 3rd Battalion, to split off from the regiment and proceed forward to help rescue a party of forward observers and a patrol that remained from the 34th Infantry. The men had been directing artillery fire from a hill less than a mile ahead of us but were now surrounded and being attacked by the enemy.

We moved out of the formation as the rest of the 21st Infantry Regiment halted to set up a defensive position. We advanced further south along Highway 2 at a rapid pace. The rain continued. King Company and Item Company were sent to the right and left of the highway. We were sent to provide mortar support for Item Company. Love Company and the rest of Mike Company remained in reserve.

King Company, on the right, secured the northern side of the hill and succeeded in rescuing the stranded party. It quickly encountered heavy machine-gun and rifle fire. We were on the left, and secured a nearby ridge under very heavy enemy fire. We set up our mortar emplacement, moving it every few minutes, to knock out the heavy machine-guns and the scattered Japanese infantry. It did not take long to run short of ammunition. We radioed for more ammunition, and the supply vehicles were sent toward us up the road, only to have their tires punctured by Japanese riflemen.

Since I was the least necessary man on our mortar team, I ran back to the supply line with ten or twelve other riflemen and helped hand carry the ammunition from the disabled jeeps. We ran through sniper fire to get the ammunition where it needed to go. As soon as I had delivered my part of the ammunition to King Company, I stayed with them to help clear out the enemy resistance.

We were receiving enemy fire on both of our flanks. With the aid of two machine-gun squads, we began firing back at them. The Japs could be seen scattering, pulling back beyond a ridge that shielded them. From there they would send mortar rounds and rifle grenades toward us through the rain.

A sergeant directed us to assume defensive positions behind rocks and scrub brush to fire on them as they scurried across the ridge to sight in on us. We were picking them off one-by-one when our own artillery, stationed behind us near the beach, began to drop high explosive rounds on the Japanese positions. We cheered when the artillery support began, and the enemy resistance fizzled. The sergeant ordered a platoon to advance on the ridge the Japs had commanded, and I joined them. Together, we eliminated the rest of the them with our M1's and Browning Automatic Rifle (BAR) machine-guns. A flame-thrower was called up to put the finishing touch to those hiding in their spider-holes and small caves along the ridge.

I returned to Item Company and my mortar team.

"What's it like up there? Nobel nervously asked.

"It sure was nice to see our artillery in action," he continued.

"You can't see much in this rain and through this grass, but the Japs are everywhere, popping out their spider-holes and behind every clump of that grass," I answered, my voice quivering and in a high pitch. Anybody could tell I was nervous, just by listening.

"But we got the Japs who were the closest to us. I was up there on the right, with King Company. I even saw a lot of horses out there hauling wagons and supplies. There must've been twenty or thirty of them!"

"You did good, Red," Pete said.

"Isn't that something," he continued. "We got jeeps and trucks and flame-throwers. They got horses."

Kenny nodded, and smiled at me.

"You're a swell one to be with, Red," he proudly remarked.

I nodded a silent "thank you" to him and remembered what he had told me when I left paratrooper school and reunited with him in Hawaii almost two years ago.

*"I didn't want to fight without you, Red. You're my anchor. It is so very good to see you back. So very, very good."*

I reached over and patted him on the shoulder.

"You're not so bad yourself, Kenny," I told him.

The afternoon continued, and the Japanese defenses maintained their steady resistance against King and Item

Companies. Twice that afternoon we saw American planes fly over us toward the Japanese positions. We heard their machine-guns strafing the area ahead of us and heard their bombs destroying Japanese vehicles, equipment, and men.

We continued to drop dozens of mortar rounds on them throughout the day.

As evening descended on us, we strengthened our defenses and dug in for a busy night. A light rain was falling, and the muddy ground had exposed the rocks just below the surface. Still, we were able to dig in a couple of feet and build a mound of dirt and rocks around us to keep the water out and keep our head from being exposed.

Word spread from foxhole to foxhole like an underground telegraph, reporting that the Japs in front of us were veteran fighting men that had landed in Ormoc a few days ago. They had come from the Japanese occupation force in China and were very good at what they did. Some considered them to be among the best troops Japan could offer.

"It don't matter if they came from Hell. We've got an Army here they have yet to see. We will give them a one-way ticket back to Hell," Nobel proclaimed.

We knew that we were so far in advance of the rest of the 21st Infantry that we would only get limited supplies of ammunition and rations. We ate what we had, settled beneath our ponchos to stay 'dry,' and hunkered down. Nobel was facing south, I was facing north. We didn't stay hunkered down very long.

The enemy began their night attacks.

They hit us four times that night with *banzai* charges, each one with about a hundred men. They would come out of the dark, screaming *"Banzai!"* and *"Yankee, you die!"* With their bayonets mounted on their rifles, they were running in zig-zag patterns, circles, and wide angles, and throwing grenades. Each charge would take a little more out of us, as we fired on them in anger and desperation. As they dashed toward us from all directions, we tried to keep the rain out of our eyes and protect our ammo from the mud. We threw constant fire at the screaming Japs, trying to stop them before they got into grenade range. It was moment after moment of sheer hell each time they charged.

Many of our men were killed or wounded.

All night long we could hear wounded men calling for medics. Some of the wounded men were wounded again in the next *banzai* raid, and some of them would become deathly quiet as the enemy crept from the darkness to slit their throats.

Some of the Japs crawled silently on their bellies through the seven-foot high kunai grass. They had canvas bags around their necks full of hand grenades. They would sneak toward our lines during the *banzai* raids, trying to infiltrate so they could attack us from within.

One of them tossed two grenades between Nobel and me, and we quickly grabbed them and threw them back, then ducked as they landed in front of him, killing him.

In the middle of the night, a call was issued for Mike Company volunteers to go back to Pinamopoan and get a truckload of ammunition. I thought about joining them, but I quickly decided against it.

*These three guys need me here. We're a team, and a team we will stay.*

Six or eight volunteers jumped into a truck and headed back down the road.

On the next raid, a grenade came right toward me, turning over and over in its path. I raised my left arm and, palm outward, batted it off to my left toward two other Japs, then shot the soldier who had tossed it.

Three-in-one.

"Yes!" came the guttural shout from Nobel.

"Three-run hit, Tex!"

Another time, a poorly thrown grenade landed five feet away. I yelled "HEADS DOWN, GRENADE!"

I saw Kenny and Pete duck, then felt Nobel do the same. The grenade exploded, throwing rocks and dirt around us. A second later, I raised my head and waited. As soon as the thrower peeked through the dust to see the damage he had done, I sent two rounds into his peering face.

Their grenades had a button on the bottom that had to be pushed in to start the timer. They would often slap the grenade against their helmet to engage the timer before they threw it. We began to recognize that sound of the grenade against the helmet, and we knew there was a Jap nearby getting ready to throw one at you.

The would often bury their grenades with the button pointed upward, hoping an unsuspecting GI might step on one as he walked between foxholes when the *banzai* raid was over. They were devious soldiers and had many tricks up their sleeves to kill the Americans.

The raid became less intense, then stopped. We heard an exchange of distant gunfire to our rear and thought of the volunteers who had gone back for more ammunition. Captain

White called out for a rifle platoon to form a patrol and check it out. Off they went.

We had just enough ammunition and just enough guts to repel each raid. Afterward, Pete and Kenny would ask if we were alright. We would say 'yes,' and ask them how their ammo was doing.

They would answer back, "Slim, but okay."

During the quiet time, men would report to the next foxhole all up and down the line. Word came back as rumors and runners spread the details of the previous raid.

"Love Company needs more grenades!"

"Medic needed up here!"

Jeeps were coming out of the dripping darkness and maneuvered down the road, filled with wounded. Empty jeeps passed them from the opposite direction, heading up the line for more wounded.

"Hey! King Company made a bayonet charge at the bastards!"

"Medic down!"

"Will those damn Japs stop their f------ screaming? I can't hear myself think!"

"Aw, they're just little men with long bayonets. That's not so bad."

"Sgt. Castro! Where the f--- is Sgt. Castro?"

"He's dead, Mike."

"Jesus Christ!"

"He still lives, Mike."

A small chuckle drifted through a few foxholes.

As the battle zone quietened, Nobel and I lay in our wet foxhole, staring across the corpse-ridden landscape. Slowly, one of us would use his helmet to remove the water that had filled the foxhole while the other kept a vigil outward.

*Outward. Always outward. Death lies out there, and it wants to get in here.*

When we thought the raid was over, one of us would close his eyes and try to grab a precious few minutes of rest. The other would watch.

*Almighty God, please watch over us the next time like you watched us over us this time.*

The rifle platoon that checked on the ammo jeep reported back. All of our soldiers had been killed. I lowered my head and thanked God I had not been one of them.

I thought I had a fever.

One short shiver, and then it would stop.

"Hey, Nobel," I inquired.

He looked up from his rifle sights.

"Yeah?"

"Did'ja notice through all this shit that the rain is warm out here? Back in Texas when it rains the drops are cold. A fella can freeze in July if he gets soaking wet."

"Yeah," he answered.

"Alabama's the same. But this rain is so warm you can feel the jungle rot eating away at your balls, your toes, your ass."

"Yeah," I answered.

"Take care of yourself, Nobel. Put on some dry clothes."

I heard him sigh.

"Swell. I've got smart-asses on my right and a comedian to my left. I love ya' Tex, but get some sleep."

"Yeah."

Each charge would come about two hours apart. Four times they charged, and four times we stopped them as they seemed to almost jump into our foxholes, muddy and slick.

The last one came at 0500. It was frantic, and it was loud, with the light machine-guns we called 'woodpeckers' and mortars and grenades. It was a devil of a dreamscape, and at one dizzying moment it seemed like a Jap was within three feet of me before I brought him down. Then it was over.

It was Nobel's time to sleep. I lay there and tried to pray, but the words did not form.

When the dim gray dawn finally began to appear, the light rain had slowed to become a mist. Nobel opened his eyes and asked me, "What's happening, Tex?"

I looked at him and said, "It's dawn. I'm fixing to go take a shower. Do you want to go, too?"

He shook his head and smiled.

"Boy, what would I give to have a hot shower!"


Monday, November 6, 1944.

Day 2 on Breakneck Ridge

As the dawn spread its light across the landscape, we gazed beyond our foxholes and saw the killing-field around us. Some men were lying beside their foxholes, rifles still pointed outward, their heads face-down in the mud. Medics were moving about, dutifully looking for the wounded, gently stepping over the dead. A prostrate Jap moved his arm, begging for help, and the rifleman escorting the medic bayoneted him. Scattered throughout the nightmarish scene were foxholes filled with muddy water stained with blood, with motionless arms, legs, and heads sticking out of them.

Japanese corpses were strewn across the expanse like they had fallen from the sky. In some places, there were so many you could walk a hundred feet without stepping on the ground, just stroll across their bodies, from one dead Jap to another dead Jap. Some of them seemed to be holding hands, as if in solidarity and kinship.

Suddenly, the area was alive with more Japs running from the grasses and rocks around us, and mortar fire began to rain down on us. We aimed our M1 Garands and tried to meet their charge with our own fire, and the attackers fell as they ran. Grenades were flying toward us, and we began to feel that this charge could not be stopped. We felt like bugs on an empty table, with no place to hide.

Within minutes, the intensity of the attack diminished as more of their number fell to the ground.

One of our flame-throwers stepped in front of our line and sprayed the Japs with liquid fire as he walked toward them. As the dead lay burning and the living ran away, he cut off the flame. Running backward himself, he began to quickly remove his fuel-tanks in retreat.

As if on cue, the command of "Retreat, men! Retreat! Back to the rest of the regiment!" came booming from the road behind us.

We grabbed our mortar and our gear and began backing away from the hellish scene, running a few feet, then slowly backing away, making sure the Japs were not hot on our heels. Pete was helping a stretcher bearer carry a wounded man, and Kenny was carrying Pete's gear. Nobel was loaded down and watched with a clear eye as we retreated. I felt like screaming in fear but held it back as I fired at a couple of Japs running along our right flank, tossing grenades. They fell with their primed grenades, which then blew them skyward when their bags of grenades exploded.

*Legs don't fail me now.*

It was chaos and life, blended together with the focus of retreat and the fear of certain death.

As quickly as it had happened, it began to slow in its panicked pace. Less Japs trailed us, and less enemy fire was directed toward us. There was more support from the rear as the machine-gun squads moved in to halt the advancing Japs with deadly fire.

I will never forget that frenzied retreat for the rest of my life. One moment I was lying in a water-filled foxhole and the next moment I was running for my life.

I felt utterly defenseless and completely exposed to harm's way, like I was carrying my lifeblood and my soul in a paper sack hanging from my belt. During those frightening moments of retreat, I had never in my entire life sensed such vulnerability. Men were falling around me as I backed away from the pursuing Japs. Then the Japs began to fall from our withering fire. Though I couldn't see them, I believe to this day that a whole band of guardian angels were running beside us.

We rejoined the rest of the 3d Battalion on the beach between Pinamopoan and Colasion at 1300. We had C-Rations for lunch, but there was hot chow for the evening meal. I did not get the shower I had told Nobel about earlier, but I did get a good bath on the beach in Carigara Bay and cleaned some of the mud, Japanese blood, and indescribable filth off my clothes.

We were told we were going to attack the ridge again the next morning. We also learned that a battalion from the 19th Regiment would be assigned to the 21st to help with the assault. As the sun settled on the western horizon, the 21st was bivouacked on the beach about a mile east of Pinamopoan. We, the 3rd Battalion, were in the center. The 1st Battalion was on our right, the 2nd Battalion was along the highway, and the 19th Infantry's 3rd Battalion was on our left.

At dusk, we attended a Catholic Church Service up near the road, toward the 2nd Battalion. We had communion. It was the first Catholic Communion I had ever taken. Hell, it didn't matter. God was where He was. I just wanted to be near Him.

At the close of the day, it started raining again, and the enemy still occupied the ridge and the portion of Highway 2 leading to it from the north. The 21st Regimental Command Post was now calling the hellhole we had defended all day and all night by the name "Breakneck Ridge."

Late that night, they launched a *banzai* attack on the 2nd Battalion at their position along the highway. We could hear the rifles, mortars, grenades, and woodpeckers accompanied by the yelling and screaming of both the enemy and our men. We lay in our foxholes on high alert, our weapons pointed in their direction. The attack lasted for what seemed half-an-hour, then ended as fast as it had begun. Runners and rumors drifted across the beach that the Jap raid had been met with superior strength and was repelled. We were all commanded to remain on alert, with bayoneted rifles close by our side.

There were no other raids that night.

Tuesday, November 7, 1944.

Day 3 on Breakneck Ridge

    We moved out at 0800. The assault on Breakneck Ridge, the second assault in three days, was made with the 2nd Battalion in the lead. The first objective was a secondary ridge that extended across the road 400 yards from the front line. Massive artillery fire was aimed immediately in front of us for fifteen minutes before we began, and then moved to the ridge beyond it when we launched our attack.

    The 2nd Battalion reached the first objective in an hour, and immediately came under fire from enemy machine-guns. Well-entrenched Japanese troops then began firing on them at a bend in the road going up to the high ground. Two tanks attempted to move forward and break up the resistance, but an enemy soldier jumped out of the high grass and placed a magnetic mine on one of them. The mine exploded, the tank was disabled, and the other tank retreated.

    Through the afternoon companies were being cut off from the battalion, and as the day ended enemy fire increased. Another torrential rain began. The first objective, the secondary ridge, could not be secured. Defensive perimeters were established on the northern edge of Breakneck Ridge.

    During the afternoon, a flurry of officers and jeeps could be seen around the Command Post, tucked away to our north. Our ammo bearers, returning from the ammunition dump, brought rumors that our Regimental Commander,

Colonel Weber, had just been fired for being too slow with the attacks on Breakneck Ridge. They said Weber was replaced by a new man, Colonel Verbeck. We didn't have the foggiest idea what all this meant to us, though it bothered us a little bit that such a change would happen on the battlefield, under enemy fire, right in front of our eyes. The more we thought about it the more we began to agree that the past three days at Breakneck Ridge hadn't really gone that well at all. Two attacks and one retreat in three days. Of course, we all agreed that the Japs had a lot to do about that. And the rain. But, mostly, the Japs. We decided to just do what we're supposed to do and see what happens.

We watched all of this from the center of the line, all the while being attacked on both sides. We found defensive positions behind rocks and ravines and fought it out all day. The rain slackened, then ended.

We moved from behind the rocks and ravines and set up our mortar emplacement in a small clearing away from trees and brush. The ammo bearers began placing mortar rounds next to Kenny, then ran back to the ammunition dump to get more. Kenny fed the rounds to Nobel. I stayed close to them, allowing no Jap to harm any of them. Several times it got pretty tough, and Pete had to join me with his rifle to defend our position. We changed location several times, as Japanese mortar rounds began to hit nearby. When more rains began, the enemy mortar fire decreased. We covered our mortar with a poncho and set up our night defensives, in preparation for the *banzai* raids again.

The *banzai* raids did not visit us that night, but a typhoon did.

Wednesday, November 8, 1944.

Day 4 on Breakneck Ridge.

The foxholes we had dug were not ready for the weather that hit us in the dark of the night. Torrential rains and extremely high winds raked the area. Some people said the winds were near 100 mph. The typhoon wind and rain prevented the Navy artillery and the Air Corps bombers from supporting us. The jungle slopes became deep, flowing mud.

The typhoon moved in from the west and swept over the entire island. Rain came down in almost horizontal sheets. Palms bent low, and some fell, crashing to the ground. The sound of the wind was frightening as it blew through the high kunai grass, sounding like a mournful howl from the unburied dead.

Much-needed supplies could only trickle in because of the horrific weather. The skies were as black as pitch, with occasional lightening turning the ridge into a freak show.

In the weather that most people watch from safe shelters, the 21st Infantry Regiment, with its new commanding officer, rose from water-filled foxholes and attacked the Japanese lines.

At 0700, the 2nd Battalion launched the assault.

With the typhoon winds at their back and dead Japs at their feet, they overwhelmed the enemy positions, pushing them rearward into their spider-holes, trenches, and caves. Flame-throwers followed the enemy and incinerated them in their retreat. The enemy soldiers caught in the open were shot or bayoneted.

The 2nd Battalion pushed them back so easily that they found themselves cut-off and deep into enemy territory by the afternoon. Under heavy fire, they retreated back to their starting point.

Wounded men lay strewn throughout the expanse of rocks and grass.

The enemy poured barrels of gasoline in the grass along the high ground and set it afire. The tall grass blazed liked an inferno. As the steady rain fell on the burning grass, it turned to steam and hissed like a legion of demons and snakes. As the fire spread, the wounded began to scream and cry for help.

The Japanese infantry was strong on Breakneck Ridge, and it fiercely opposed our assault. Concealed Japanese riflemen fired continuously from the front, flanks, and rear of our positions. Small enemy groups penetrated the lines.

We of the 3rd Battalion moved off the road into protective positions. We were receiving the same persistent counterattacks as the companies of the 2nd Battalion. Pete and Nobel again set up our mortar emplacement, as Kenny received rounds from the ammo bearers and fed them to Nobel. I continued to stay close to them, watching for snipers. As usual, we moved our mortar to a new location several times, as the Japanese spotters found us, and their mortar rounds began to hit nearby to knock us out. Their machine-gunners would find us too, and they would send their 50mm bullets to silence us. It was a battle of find-the-enemy-before-he finds-you.

Throughout the afternoon and into the evening more torrential rains fell.

We were running very low on ammunition. Our ammo bearers had been gone for over an hour gathering ammo. I ran back to the ammo drop-off points in the middle of our line and could not find the ammo-bearers nor any ammunition. I then jumped on the back of a passing jeep that was carrying wounded men and hung on tight as the driver drove frantically back toward the field hospital. As we neared the regimental ammo dump I bounded off. With help of a Filipino volunteer, I grabbed three crates of mortar rounds, including one crate of white phosphorus shells. I flagged down another jeep as it came racing from the rear on its way to pick up more wounded, and the driver and I loaded it with the ammunition. The jeep was splattered with blood and loose combat gear.

We drove madly back through the driving rain to what I thought was our mortar position, unloaded the ammunition, and the driver rushed on toward the fighting to pick up more wounded. I held a crate of mortar rounds and looked for my mortar team.

They were nowhere to be seen.

I looked left. I looked right.

"Nobel! Pete! Kenny!" I screamed.

I felt a sniper's round pass me, taking a piece of the wooden crate with it.

Dropping the crate, I fell to the ground, rolling into a small wet ravine.

*What the hell happened? Did they move?*

Another sniper round hit the corner of the crate.

*The sonofabitch is trying to blow up the ammo boxes!*

I ran to the crates of ammunition. I tossed each one into the ravine, feeling the rounds whistling by, some hitting the ground in front of me, some hitting the ground behind me, kicking up dirt.

I grabbed my rifle and propelled myself into the ravine, splashing water as I rolled further down, away from the ammo crates.

*Where the hell are they?*

I raised my head and looked around.

"Nobel! Pete! Kenny!" I screamed again.

The night was dark as pitch. Howling winds carried sheets of blinding, cutting rain. The flashes of howitzers illuminated the landscape where I could see men crawling, inch by inch, along the top of a ravine. There was no soil, just rock as sharp as razors, slicing at their elbows and knees as they crawled along.

"Attack!" I heard someone shouting.

"Attack! Clear the Japs off this god-dammed ridge!"

"In the middle of a damn hurricane," I heard a soldier mumble.

Through the roar of the deafening wind, with the constant booming artillery and hissing in-coming mortars, an officer behind the men barked the order, "Dig in! Hold this line! Get your asses in foxholes!"

The men could feel the solid rock beneath them.

"Dig in? Is he crazy?" a soldier sneered, lying on bare rock along the right flank.

The rain was so heavy that it seemed to be poured onto us by huge buckets, each bucket filling and emptying, filling and emptying, from somewhere up in the pitch-black sky, overflowing every slope and every soul on the saturated ground.

There was a whistle and pop of flares, and the area was illuminated by an eerie, ghostlike glow. Japanese soldiers were scurrying everywhere, frantically moving in uncoordinated directions, darting one way, then another, carrying mounted bayonets.

"Hunker down, men! Fix Bayonets! Here they come!"

I lay in the wet ravine on flat, solid rock, frantically looking in all directions for a low place, a rock shield, something, anything for protection.

An enemy mortar round hit close, to my right, on the downhill slope of the ravine. The soldier on the right flank who had just complained about digging in was decimated, his body thrown upward and outward, reduced to pieces. I was pushed upslope by the hot blast, a few pieces of the sharp lava rock striking me, leaving rips in the fabric of my pack and my thick cotton shirt.

I looked downslope, where the mortar round had blown the complaining soldier to Heaven or Hell, and there was a large section of black, smoking rock, sideways in the blast crater. It was a small sliver of an opening, large enough for a skinny man to wedge into, and it lay at the base of the upturned rock. I quickly, almost instantly, rolled my body downward toward the crater, up over the lip, and, with my feet, kicked the loose dirt from under the rock, moved into the hole, and stood up with my bayoneted M1 Garand facing outward.

*Come and get me,* I mumbled under my breath.

As if on cue, two Japanese soldiers jumped into the crater, looked around, chattered, and stepped back nervously when they saw me. Two quick rounds from my rifle took them down.

My hands were shaking. I was crying tears of fear, tears of joy for being alive, and tears of fear again for what lay ahead. The Japs were scurrying like rats in big, brown uniforms. Killing, screaming, hellish rats!

Three more of the screaming Japanese rats, alerted by my rifle fire, tumbled into the crater, and aimed their Arisakas at me. I pointed my M1 toward the Jap on my right, a snarling, round-faced man, and squeezed the trigger.

Nothing.

Jammed.

He looked at me, wide-eyed. The other two let out a sickening laugh, and the three of them aimed their rifles at me.

I took in a deep breath and started to scream *"Raw-Hide and Bloody Bones! Come get me!"*

My scream was silenced by a sharp, loud hiss from above, and a mortar round hit square between the three of them, their bodies disintegrating in an outward force of dirt, rock, and flesh.

I lay beneath the upturned rock, completely covered with blood and pieces of flesh.

A leg lay to my right, twitching at the ankle. A severed head lay to my left, face upward, as if it was admiring the fireworks in the skies above, the mouth in a strange "O" as the blazing spectacle of war raged on.

A scream started in my gut and erupted from my mouth, barely audible over the din and death that displayed itself with irreverent clarity.

Then all went softly grey, and everything around me became a very quiet, peaceful black.

Within the serene quiet, I felt like I was floating above the battlefield. I could see my friends down there, with other men, in a circle, rifles pointed outward. Japs began crawling up from their spider-holes, in the rainy pitch-black darkness. I then felt myself descending back down into the deadly fray. I could smell them just seconds before I could see them, snarling lips, teeth shining like rows of tombstones, like apparitions as they appeared with glistening bayonets, screaming like banshees, and thrusting…. my shoulders began to tighten…my closed eyes darting rapidly to my right, my left, then straight ahead, beneath my eyelids. A panic began rising in my chest.

I opened my eyes. I was again in the nightmarishly black night, with a hurricane wind blowing curtains of rain across the barren, shell-torn landscape. The horizontal torrents of hot raindrops were piercing my face like needles. It was a frighteningly fierce devil-of-a storm, with cannons flashing, mortar rounds hissing, M1 Garands pinging, Japanese Arisakas popping, and Thompson submachineguns burping. Japs were running in the dark, sometimes illuminated by the artillery light, fading into black, moving in all directions, their razor-sharp bayonets held firmly in their short rifles, jabbing, piercing, jabbing again, cursing in their damned high-pitched voices.

A scuffle, a wet slashing sound, a GI screamed, and they moved on, closer, closer to my hole behind the rock. A Jap stood ten feet away, staring into my face with a mad clown smile. He moved closer, bayonet tilted up. I jabbed, I missed, he jabbed, I deflected his bayonet, grabbed my knife from my leg scabbard, and forced the blade into his ribcage as we both looked into each other's eyes, reflections of total fear and raging insanity.

Reality began to blur from one frantic scene to another. A Jap would appear, sometimes two. I would shoot one and bayonet the other, or shoot both of them, or bayonet both of them, or toss a grenade if they were far enough away. Once I saw two salesmen in suits with satchels.

I shot them.

Then I saw a smiling cowboy with a broad-brimmed hat, standing two feet from me.

I bayoneted him.

It didn't matter what they were. I would shoot or bayonet everything in front of me.

I saw Momma standing out there, in the rain, with Japs walking toward her, their bayonets mounted on their Arisakas.

I screamed with everyone ounce of scream I had in me, "Momma! Momma!"

I felt myself shaking all inside, like a bomb of energy had just exploded in my body.

Momma vanished as suddenly as she had appeared.

The Japs were still there, walking around, stalking, hunting, thrusting the bayonets at people I did not recognize.

I don't know how many times their thrusted, or how long it was, but it finally stopped.

It could have been five minutes or five hours.

Time played no role in my battle.

The field in front of me became deathly quiet. One of the dead Japs was looking at me.

*"I was a Christian, you know."*

"Shut the f--- up!" I screamed at him.

I screamed again! To High Heaven I screamed, a savage scream from a million years ago.

I fell to my knees into foot-deep water, holding my Garand head-high, and began to shake hysterically. My mind snapped, I screamed again, and again, and again.

"Momma!" I screamed.

And then, from out of nowhere, there stood a man.

Not a Jap, not a GI.

My body began to relax as he looked at me.

In all that death and destruction, he just stood there, barely three feet away from me, shielding me from the overwhelmingly terrible war.

He was a big man.

He was a colored man.

He had a relaxed, friendly smile beneath soft, tender, blue eyes.

Standing there in my wet, bloody rock-hole, he leaned toward me, and helped me stand up.

There was a gentleness in his grip.

His smooth, deep, rich voice began to calmly reassure me:

*"Horace, listen to me. All is fine. Keep your head down, stay quiet, and no harm will come to you this night. Do as I say."*

I was breathing heavily.

"What is happening?" I whispered.

*"I am here to tell you to be still. You will endure this night if you be still."*

I stared at him. He didn't look scared. I sure the hell was. I tried to ask another question, but nothing came out.

*"You WILL survive this war, Horace. There is still much that you must do. But, for tonight, you keep your head down and you stay quiet."*

"Okay," I mumbled weakly.

*"I'll be here with you, in the dark. Think of home, Horace. Think of home."*

I began to cry.

He held his hand out, as if to hold me and protect me.

I leaned backward against the rock.

I closed my eyes, still breathing heavily.

All was quiet.

I heard the smooth sigh of a gentle breeze and felt the delicate touch of soft feathers.

It must have been hours later when my eyes opened to see a grey hint of dawn.

My colored friend was gone.

It was still raining.

I heard heavy artillery shells sailing high overhead, pounding against the Japanese defenses in the high ridges.

I heard American voices, off to my left.

"My God, there was a helluva fight here. There must be fifty dead Japs scattered down this ravine. Is that our ammunition crate down there?"

The voice belonged to Captain White!

I placed a foot forward and stepped out of my rock-hole, holding on tightly to the rock to keep from falling.

The GIs closest to Captain White flinched and turned with their rifles pointed at me. They saw that I was a GI. They stepped toward me, and one of them asked, "Soldier! Are you alright?"

"Smith, is that you?" Captain White asked.

I nodded my head, and leaned forward, falling to the ground.

As they lifted me, Captain White asked if I was hurt.

"Not that I know of," I answered.

"It was really rough out here last night."

Captain White looked around, then back at me, and nodded.

"I can see that," he said convincingly.

"I believe the Lord was with me," I said.

Captain White studied the ravine and the dead Japs, walked up to me, patted me on the chest, and said in his easy-going way, "I believe you, son. I believe you."

He looked at the two soldiers who had helped me off the ground.

"Take this man back and have Doc check him out. He looks okay, but I'd feel better if Doc saw him."

He motioned to the rest of the men with him and said, "Let's go find some more."

Thursday, November 9, 1944.

Day 5 on Breakneck Ridge.

I regained some of my strength and composure while walking down the road in the heavy rain to the Command Post. By the time we got there, I was able to walk without the two soldiers' assistance. My mind was still thinking about my evening visitor and my survival through the night. It was much farther in distance to the Command Post than I expected, which meant I had spent the night well behind the enemy lines. I shook when I thought of that. I beamed with pride when I thought about Captain White and his rescue team this morning coming forward into the Japanese lines to find me and probe the field of battle.

*If my colored friend had not come to calm me down last night, I would've died. That is a fact. The enemy was all around me. I was right there on their front porch!*

We walked past the 2$^{nd}$ Battalion's bivouac on the way, then took a trail to the right and walked a bit longer to reach the medic station. I spent less than ten minutes there. I was sickened by the number of wounded and their condition. Some with no legs, some with no arms, one with no face, some already dead and covered by blankets.

The doc looked at me and asked me if it had been a hard night.

I told him it was pretty rough down there, and he grunted.

He said the boys who brought me in told him they found me very weak this morning when I fell out of a rock-hole.

I told him again it had been a rough night, and he grunted.

He asked me how I felt. I told him I was hungry.

He grunted and said we are all hungry.

He looked into my eyes with his little light and grunted.

He told me to stand on one foot, then another, and he grunted.

He listened to my chest with his scope and grunted.

He asked me what his name was, and I told him his name was Doc.

He grunted.

He asked me my name and I told him.

He grunted.

Then he asked me what day it was, and I said hell I don't know what day it is, Doc.

He grunted, and said this man is okay.

I turned to leave the medic station. As I was walking out, a Filipino nurse told me I wasn't yellow enough and handed me three plastic-wrapped boxes of Atabrine. I grunted and told her thank you, kindly.

Heavy artillery from the beachhead to our north continued to sail overhead and pound the Japanese lines ahead of us. We were going to make another assault, it was plain to see. The Navy was softening the Japanese defenses before we hit them again. The shells were whistling over us and knocking on the enemy door.

The rain was pouring down. In our world, the sound of bombardment and the feel of heavy rain and being wet was becoming normal. There were times when you heard or felt neither one. Then your brain would kick in and you would realize the horror of it all. Discomfort would turn to resentment and then to bitterness, and you hated everything. Killing the enemy was the balm that soothed the hatred.

I walked briskly back up the road and found the 3rd Battalion on the left side, preparing to move out. I looked at the rear of their line and saw three familiar faces, and a hand waving. I heard a welcomed voice, "Tex! Tex! Over here! You're safe!"

*I chuckled inside. Safe? What kind of Safe is this?*

The three of them were standing there, in the rain. Kenny had a broad smile and a bandage around his left forearm. His blood-stained shirtsleeve had been torn below the left elbow. Pete let a yellow toothpick fall from his mouth when he saw me. He was jumping up and down like a little kid. Nobel dropped his wave, smiled, and said "I knew it! I knew you were OK!"

"It looks like you bums are about to move out. Can I join you?" I said.

"I left some ammunition up there at the ravine for us. I spent the night behind the Jap lines, boys. It's quite a story. Not enough time to tell it right now. Do you have enough C-Rations? I'm a bit hungry. Where are we going?"

"Hell, you can have my rations, Red." Pete answered, as he greeted me with a hug.

"My, my, you are a bundle of questions," Kenny declared.

"You are quite the Prodigal Son, Mr. Red Smith. I am so very, very glad to see you, old friend. You will have to carry this base plate I have on my back, though. And don't you worry about this bandage, it's just a small flesh wound. It's not my ticket home, just my first Purple Heart. No one in our little party here has one, just me."

"I told Kenny he could have mine. He can have all of them that wait for me. I do not want a single one," Nobel said with a laugh.

"Same here," Pete agreed.

"Really, gentlemen," Kenny smiled.

"I don't want any more of us to get involved in Purple Hearts. One is enough."

I had already opened a C-Ration and was eating a chocolate bar, a saltine cracker, and a can of peaches. I looked at Nobel and said, "Remember our snack in Hawaii?"

He nodded and smiled.

"For the rest of my life, Tex. The rest of my life."

Minutes after I finished my snack and swallowed two Atabrine tablets, torrential rain began to fall again as the artillery barrage ceased. It was time to attack. We moved south along the road, striking the enemy on our fifth day of battle. The 2nd Battalion proceeded on the right, and we of the 3rd Battalion proceeded along the left.

The rifle companies of both battalions pushed ahead, together with machine-guns, mortars, flame-throwers, and grenades pounding the enemy positions. We set up our mortar emplacement near where I had left the ammo crates the night before, and we sent three dozen rounds up the slope, where the enemy was entrenched along the high ground. Our heavy machine-guns were positioned in front of us, moving left or right as they met return fire. Flame-throwers roamed the advance, eliminating the enemy from their spider-holes and tunnels. Rifle squads were driving the Japs from their fortifications by bayonets and bullets.

In all of this, the driving rain continued to plummet, and the wind continued to blow. Trees that had been felled by the typhoon became obstacles, blocking the riflemen as they lumbered up the wet, slippery slopes in pursuit of the enemy. Litter-bearers clambered up the slopes and down the ravines, trying to extract the precious wounded from the killing ground.

We never retreated that day. It was a continuous advance, using everything we had. We reached and secured the higher ground near the center of Breakneck Ridge and dug in for the night. This time we established our mortar emplacement between our foxholes.

The night *banzai* attacks were weak and served only to rob us of sleep. The rain continued to pour, and the wind still blew, though not as wild as it had the day before. We killed a dozen Japs that night, and not once did we use our mortar.

In the quiet of the night, soaking wet and shivering in my foxhole, I felt a slight smile cross my lips as I recalled the words from the night before:

"*You keep your head down and you stay quiet. I'll be here with you, in the dark.*"

I thought of Juliette.


Friday, November 10, 1944.

Day 6 on Breakneck Ridge.

At 0700, all three battalions of the 21st Infantry attacked the very center of Breakneck Ridge in a classic frontal assault. Battalions from other regiments moved up on the flanks to prevent the enemy's escape and force them to retreat.

Japanese snipers lined the walls of the ravines near the top, hiding beneath the vegetation. They slowed the assault, as rifle squads countered the snipers by rapidly moving toward them and pouring massive firepower on their positions. We set our mortar into action and let it thump white phosphorus shells onto the snipers. Pete and I picked off a few of them as they ran from the fire. Our flame-throwers finished them off. Our lovely, deadly flame-throwers. One by one, the snipers were eliminated.

Some Japanese snipers crawled through our advance and began hitting our support personnel behind our lines, slowing the replenishment of food, water, and ammunition to the battle front. Rations and ammunition had not reached the front line by noon, slowing the assault further.

The rain had diminished. Pools of water lay in every low area, and dribbled down each embankment, turning the soils into slime.

As night fell, we sat squarely on top of Breakneck Ridge. We all felt that the Japanese defensive back had been broken. Their soldiers lay dead in every ravine between us and Pinamopoan, yet the snipers and spider-holes continued to restrict our advance and evade complete elimination.

Again, the weak and poorly executed nightly *banzai* raids served only to cost them their lives and rob us of our sleep.

Less than fifty Japs would attack in each raid, and they would run silently toward us, hoping to catch us by surprise. Their rifles would only be used to mount their bayonets. Less grenades would be tossed.

*They are certainly running out of ammunition,* I thought to myself.

*Yet, they keep coming, again and again. And we kill them, again and again.*

Some of them would only have knives, and would run past a foxhole, then quickly turn and attack from the rear, hoping to drive the knife into the back of a confused GI. A few GIs would be killed or wounded, but no Japanese soldier would survive. Within five minutes, the battlefield would again be quiet.

While Nobel slept, I gazed across the dark, deadly ground and remembered again the words my colored friend had spoken two nights ago during the hellish carnage across the landscape of death:

*"All is fine, keep your head down, stay quiet, no harm will come to you this night."*

I thought of home, and of Juliette.

I thought of my colored friend, wondering where he had come from, still hearing his calming, smooth voice and remembering his unusually soft blue eyes. And the smile that glowed in the night.

*Who was he? Not a combat soldier, certainly. I have seen no colored men in the 21st Regiment. Not a single one. Was he a Filipino? Was he my Guardian Angel? Dear Lord, he had to be. Whoever or whatever he was or is, I will tell no one. They would not believe me. Maybe later, when this war is over, I will tell Juliette.*


Saturday, November 11, 1944.

Day 7 on Breakneck Ridge.

It was raining. Our clothes were still wet from lying in our half-filled foxhole through the rainy night. Several times in the watery foxhole my mind would take me to the cruel realization that what I was doing was exactly like sleeping in a bathtub half-full of water and mud, night after night.

We had a faint odor of urine on us because the only thing you could do in the middle of the night was empty your bladder in your own 'bed.' Sometimes we would use our helmet, then pour it outside and rinse the helmet in the foxhole water. That often turned out to be not worth the effort, as you couldn't really get the smell out of the helmet and the constant rain would wash the urine back toward the lip of the foxhole. You were pissed if you did and pissed if you didn't.

Nobel looked at me and said, "Our clothes should be clean by now. Piss is mostly chlorine, and bleach is all chlorine. They're both the same, aren't they?"

I looked at him and simply said, "Nobel, piss is not chlorine, it is ammonia. It is not the same. Stop saying that."

No one, absolutely no one, dared to leave his foxhole after dark for fear of being mistaken for a creeping, crawling Japanese soldier. If we had to pursue other toilet urges, we would wait until daylight, and make it the last thing we did in our watery shithole.

For more than seven days straight we had been wet. It rained eighty percent of the time. We were seldom dry. Our clothes were beginning to tear at critical junctions, along the crotch, at the knees, and under the armpits. We seldom complained, other than uttering or mumbling a curse word as we found another hole in our cotton armor.

At 0900 we resumed our attack on the enemy from the top of Breakneck Ridge. Our morale was boosted by the realization that perhaps this would be the day when we would begin pushing the Japs downhill, instead of marching uphill into their blistering fire.

The 1st and 3rd Battalions launched the assault side-by-side. We pushed south along the road, and the 1st Battalion pushed westerly, to our right.

We pressed the Japanese soldiers southward, along the crest of the ridge. Japanese resistance stiffened, and we were receiving intense fire from off to our left. An occasional land mine would explode as a soldier or vehicle moved ahead.

Our new Regimental Commander, Colonel Verbeck, was with Love Company, directing the assault. We could see him, walking calmly down the road in front of us, a thin, wiry man with blond hair. He had been in WWI, and we felt he was the best commander to have in a battle like this.

We were caught in a crossfire situation, and sorely needed our tanks to clear the resistance blocking our advance. Believing that the area immediately ahead of us was infested with land mines, Colonel Verbeck ordered a mine-detector squad to clear the area as tanks moved slowly behind them.

It was an interesting and frightening thing to watch. The rain had lessened, and the men in the mine-detector squad would crawl forward on their bellies, probing the soil for mines. The tanks would inch along behind the men, at the same crawling pace. It was a time-consuming process, and quite dangerous. The Colonel confidently walked along with them, between the mine-detectors and the tanks, extending our advance as we moved across the top of Breakneck Ridge. The tanks began firing at the Japs that were entrenched along the crest of the ridge, pouring machine-gun and liquid fire into the enemy ranks.

With the help of the tanks, we made it across the top. Through the broken rain clouds, we could see the green, flat bowl of Leyte Valley spreading across the landscape to the southeast, and the Ormoc Valley to the southwest, as the tanks descended the pinnacles of Breakneck Ridge.

As night fell, we dug in on the downslope side of Breakneck Ridge and set up our security perimeters. Adequate supply runs had ensured we would have our evening rations, and we settled into our newly dug muddy foxholes and hunkered down, waiting to see what the Japs would send us in the dark hours.

As Nobel watched the dimming ridges and ravines, I finished my can of pudding and looked to the other foxhole.

"Hey Kenny."

"Yeah?"

"Are you keeping your bandage dry?"

"Sure. My wet haversack is full of dry bandages."

"You should get the medic to re-do that bandage tomorrow."

"Sure thing. I'll make an appointment."

"Hey Pete?"

"Yeah?"

"Make your bunk-mate do as I say. Okay?"

"Sure. He does everything I say."

"Swell."

Suddenly, the Japs were running and crawling everywhere in the soggy kunai.

Everyone must've been ready, because our return fire began immediately. To our surprise, the battalion had placed machine-guns and mortars around us along higher ridges. They began to batter the Japanese raid with heavy fire, chemical rounds, and high explosive shells.

Distant slopes began to burn when phosphorous rounds were launched toward the rear lines of the charging enemy. Flares began to illuminate the area as they floated down on their paper parachutes, and Japs were seen everywhere and were rapidly eliminated.

I heard Nobel say, "Attaboys! You illuminate, and we will eliminate!"

He laughed.

I looked at him, smiling, and said "Keep your voice down, Nobel. They'll know where we are!"

"Tex, in case you hadn't noticed it, they already know where we are."

"Looks like we were ready for them this time," I observed.

Nobel put a new ammo clip in his M1.

"Bastards!" he said.

"Thinking they could surprise us like that."

Four times they hit us that night. Each time we turned them away.

Just after the third time, I heard someone say from another foxhole, "Damn! How many of them do they have down there?"

Someone else countered, "There's two dozen of them for each one of us. Enjoy the shooting."

A more serious voice rang out, "Hold it down! Stay concentrated! They could come back at us in a hurry. Stay focused!"

During the fourth raid, just before dawn, a mortar up the ridge from us suddenly exploded the instant it was fired. We could hear the painful groans from the other mortarmen and the screams from those wounded.

"F---! A fast fuse!"

"Shit! Some factory worker f----- up!"

"Stay focused, men! Medic!"

"Foxtrot mortar needs a medic!"

The floating flares helped the medics locate the mortar and helped us see the running and crawling Japs.

When the raid ended, we serviced our weapons, replenished our ammunition, and agonized as we listened to the aid being given to the wounded and heard the sounds of the stretcher bearers as they transported the living as well as the dead.

*A fast fuse can be waiting for any of us in all those crates of mortar rounds in the ammo dump. That short deadly second after you drop a round in the barrel can be the last second of your brief, unfulfilled life.*

We tried to sleep, but little came.


Sunday, November 12, 1944.

Day 8 on Breakneck Ridge.

As the dim grey dawn exposed the brutal and ghastly battlefield around us, we knew that we were winning the terrible struggle. Dead Japanese soldiers lay around us like timber in a lumber yard. We felt resuscitated, like we were staring the raging and bleeding bull down in the middle of the ring. Like we were running our hearts out because we could see the finish line in front of us. Like we were sharecroppers in a cotton-field, walking down the last row of the day, on the last day of picking.

We set up our mortar emplacement in the location where the mortar was destroyed the previous night by the fast fuse. We pushed aside the half-used crate of rounds that contained the final round the two mortarmen had fired during their brief but heroic lifetimes, and checked all the remaining crates for the same serial number and manufacture date.

*If a fella or lady can make a very bad assembly-line mistake on a very bad day, they can do it again before the shift buzzer rings. Just look a bad day in the face and push it aside.*

Our mortar thumped flame, fire, and chemicals behind the Japanese lines all day. Our ammo bearers stayed busy, and even changed faces several times during the day. At least a dozen times the spotters would send us messages to change our sights to send our impacts to a different hot spot.

It rained all day.

During the afternoon, I motioned to a medic passing by. I pointed to my arm and then pointed at Kenny. The medic nodded and came back by our mortar after he finished his task at hand.

"Let's see that bandage, soldier," he said to Kenny.

"It's doing alright," Kenny replied as he handed his rifle to Pete.

"Take care of this, Everman," he said, "While I meet with Mr. Smith's personal physician."

He rolled his eyes at me.

I shrugged my shoulders at him.

The corpsman cut the bandage with his mostly clean scissors, then slowly peeled away the bandage. He winced at the stench that briefly filled the air around him as the wound was exposed.

"Criminy," he hissed.

"Is this the shrapnel wound from last week?"

Kenny nodded.

"This wound is infected. You're not keeping it dry and clean," he said as he looked up at Kenny.

Kenny sighed and shook his head in an irritated way.

"Come on, cut me some slack, man. It's not exactly dry and clean out here," he smart-assed back at the corpsman.

"Now, Kenny," I interrupted.

"Mr. Herrod," Pete said.

"Man," Nobel started to say.

"Hold it," the corpsman said, holding up his hand.

"My office," he said, as he waved his hand across the wet battlefield, "is not exactly dry and clean, either. But we still manage to save limbs and lives in it. You're coming with me. You need to stay a few days out of this muck and get this wound – which I must say COULD cost you this arm – properly tended. Let it get some air, let it further disgust everyone who sees it, and just come with me. Your life-saving friends here will watch your gear."

As the corpsman led Kenny to the medic station, we three looked at each other with wide-open eyes and questioning looks on our faces.

"I swear." I said.

"What's he trying to do? Get a trip home at the cost of an arm?" Nobel blurted.

Pete shook his head slowly

"That don't figure. I think he's mad at himself for getting that wound and doesn't know how to take care of it. He's a college boy, you know, and hasn't really done for himself his entire life."

"Maybe the doc can clean that arm out and get him back here," I said.

"Even if he does, Red, I don't think Kenny will take care of it afterward," Pete replied.

"It'll just get infected again."

"You guys tell me," Nobel inquired.

"How's any wound gonna get better in all this shit? It stays wet all the time, we are in mud and God-knows-what all the time, and even our boots rot," he held up his boot and showed us the hole tearing into the leather welt.

"I got fungus between my toes," Pete admitted.

"And I've always been a respectable kind of guy."

"I took my boots off the other day and my socks had melted - just turned to a stringy mush," I told them.

We were quiet for a moment. Each one of us dealt with the jungle-rot as best we could. It would show up as little white bumps, with stinky pus on the inside. The medic would treat the bumps with a liquid that turned our skin a purplish black, and the bumps would be gone. But they came back within a week. The medics called it the "New Guinea Crud."

"We need to get off this island. Kill all those 'things' out there so we can get off this damn island before Kenny comes back," Pete said.

"This crap will kill him."

Nobel and I just looked at each other. I shuffled my boot along the top of the mud I was standing in, and Nobel removed his helmet and rubbed his head.

"Pete," I said slowly.

"You know we're just gonna go to another island when we get through with this one. This is gonna last until the Japs decide to quit."

Pete opened his shirt pocket, pulled out a wet toothpick, frowned at it, and put it in his mouth.

"No telling what little worms I'm putting in my mouth with these," he disclosed.

"You're right, Red," he said as he nodded at me.

He turned to Nobel and said, "You're right, Nobel."

"It's in God's hands now, just like it always has been."

I looked at Nobel, the official leader of our mortar squad.

"Corporal Horner?" I asked politely.

"In the meantime, should I ask for a replacement for PFC Herrod?"

He smiled.

"No, Private Tex. Let's see how it goes. If we need to, we'll grab one of our ammo bearers and show him the ropes. I'll make sure he's another good Southern boy before I do that."

We had three on-time C-Ration meals that day and continued to thump rounds onto the Japanese lines. We had our fair share of all-day rain showers. All around us we could hear the sounds of mortars, machine-guns, and distant shoot-outs.

Army planes continued to fly over us, and the sound of bombardments were heard throughout the day.

War music.

From our side.

Now and again, one of our perimeter guards would see a Jap trying to sneak through our lines and gun him down.

It has never ceased to amaze me how "normal" all that was beginning to feel.

Late in the afternoon, Pete went to the field hospital to check on Kenny. He was gone about an hour and came back just as dusk was settling onto the battleground. He had a serious look on his face as he approached us.

"Kenny's a tough cracker," he said as he stood by us.

"He got a fresh bandage and some antibiotics, and sure did want to come back with me. He doesn't think his wound is all that bad, but the Doc told me it may not heal if he doesn't get some good care on the hospital ship. He'll be transferred there tomorrow. I don't like the way he looks, the way he acts, the way that wound smells."

"What do you mean, the way he acts?" Nobel inquired.

Pete studied a few seconds.

"He is grumpy and distracted. He doesn't want to talk about anything but how crazy it is for them to transfer him. He says if he can't stay with us he doesn't want to stay anywhere. He said they should just take off his arm and send him home. I'd like to think I would act better than that, but it's not me with the infected arm. It hurts me to see him like that. I don't have a good feeling about this."

We looked at him, not knowing what to say.

"We've seen a lot of men die. He's too important. He has to come back."

Nobel nodded.

"Damn," he said.

"Did the Doc say anything about Battle Fatigue?"

Pete nodded his head, and answered, "Yes, I did ask him about that."

He took a toothpick out of his pocket, looked at it intently, and then let it fall to the ground.

"Doc was pretty sure that is not the issue with Kenny. Doc said when he was in New Guinea and the Solomon Islands, he and the other medical staff believed that combat, much like we're seeing here, can give a man what they call Battle Stress in zero-to-ninety-days. Some time off with good food and clean clothes can help a man get over that. But Battle Fatigue can really get a man down if he has seen constant combat for over one-hundred days. Battle Fatigue makes a man psychotic, and he doesn't usually get over it that easily. It can last a lifetime."

I shook my head.

"I don't think that's what Kenny has. Like you said, Pete, I think he does not realize the seriousness of his wound and what this jungle can do to it. He never has faced a problem that he had to solve. He is as sharp as a tack, but his mind floats out there with numbers and.., and.. college stuff."

"Philosophy. He was getting his degree in Philosophy," Pete added.

"Yeah, that's what I was saying," I smiled back at Pete.

There was a lull in the conversation. Nobel looked at Pete for a few seconds, then pointed over to a young man that stood beside me.

"This is Tim Blanchard, Pete. He'll be your foxhole guest until Kenny comes back."

Nobel turned to introduce the dark-headed young man to Pete.

Tim was shorter than Pete. He extended his right hand.

Pete grabbed it and shook hands with the young man.

"Pleased to meet you, Tim. How old are you and where do you come from?"

Tim's smile was shy, and he said with a raspy voice, "I'm nineteen years old, and I'm from Dallas, Texas."

Pete smiled at Nobel.

"A Texas Boy. Thank you, Nobel."

Nobel winked.

"Of course," he answered.

Pete reached into his shirt pocket, fumbled with his bag of toothpicks, retrieved a blue one, stuck it in his mouth, turned toward his foxhole, and then looked back at Tim.

"If I don't talk to you very much tonight, don't let it bother you. It's not about you. Kenny was as close as my own brother to me, and he may not come back. I have a lot to think about, and making a new friend in all this deathly shit is not on my list of things to do right now."

Tim nodded and said, "Yes, sir."

Pete grimaced and replied, "Don't call me "Sir."

"That could get me killed."

"I'm sorry, sir," Tim said, then scowled at himself and looked down.

Pete spat his toothpick out, stared at Nobel and me, and walked to his foxhole.

I put my arm on Tim's shoulder and said, "It's alright. Pete needs a little time. I'll keep him company. You stay with Corporal Horner tonight. He snores, but not very loud. You'll be tired and probably won't even hear him. You should be able to sleep a little bit."

All night long, our artillery behind us pounded the Japanese lines with heavy shelling. We slept as much as we could. We were all worried about Kenny.

There were no *banzai* raids that night, and it did not rain.


Monday, November 13, 1944.

Day 9 on Breakneck Ridge.

Navy gunships at Carigara Bay and heavy artillery along Breakneck Ridge had been pounding the Japanese lines all night long. There was a steady light rain. At dawn, the bombardment ceased and the 1st and 2nd Battalions continued the assault. The artillery had pounded the landscape so brutally that it was scraggy and bare. I had seen scruffy, mangy dogs that looked better than the land.

The rifle platoons of the 3rd Battalion were placed as reserves in the rear of the line. The heavy weapons platoon, including our mortars and machine-guns, were set up along the high ground on the flanks to support the advance.

The Japanese resistance could not keep us from pushing our entire battle line completely off the crest of Breakneck Ridge. All elements of the 21st Regiment were now on the downhill slope, and were a quarter-mile downslope by mid-afternoon.

We moved downhill in support of the assault, changing our mortar position at 100-yard intervals every 2-3 hours. Pete and Nobel would set up our mortar as usual, as Tim would receive the shells from the ammo-bearers and feed them to Nobel. My job was to stay close to them, along with Pete, allowing no Jap to harm them. Tim's confidence in his duty strengthened through the day. When we moved, he would carry the base plate for me while I watched for enemy infiltrators and snipers.

The fighting was intense as the Japanese forces began to reel backwards. We began to see *banzai* raids in broad daylight as the desperate Japanese soldiers would rush down the sides of ravines to surprise our forward line. Each time, just like their nightly counterparts, the raids were repulsed.

The rifle platoons in reserve were ordered to assist the forward lines during the heaviest of the Japanese resistance in late afternoon. All men of the 21$^{st}$ were engaged to eliminate the Japanese resistance. Machine-guns, mortars, flame-throwers, and tanks cleared the path for the infantry to destroy the enemy's presence in caves, spider-holes, and trenches.

When night brought darkness to the southern slopes of Breakneck Ridge, the rain had stopped, and every fighting man held his position, and established security perimeters at the farthest point in the advance.

We moved our mortar closer to our rifle squads to be safer, and dug in as best as we could along a ravine. The ground was very rocky, which prevented us from digging a standing foxhole. Instead, we gathered whatever rocks were available and built a circle around us, so we could at least sit up in a defensive firing position.

Tim and I were eating our C-ration supper when Nobel walked over and joined us. Pete was walking a perimeter around us, keeping his eyes open for any enemy raid.

"You did really good today, Tim," Nobel said.

Tim looked up and smiled.

"Thank you……..." Tim struggled to find the right name to call his Corporal boss.

"You need to call me Nobel. I can't call you Tex because we already have one," Nobel joked as he motioned toward me.

"Thank you, Nobel," Tim answered.

"What did you do in Dallas before the war?" I asked.

"My Daddy operates a streetcar that runs from Dallas to Corsicana, and I mostly just helped keep our house together on Eighth Street," he replied.

"It is always in need of something. Fixing windows, roofing, painting, plumbing, you name it. I had it in real good shape when I shipped out."

"You stay close to us, Tim, and we'll get you back there safely as fast as we can," Nobel told him.

Tim smiled again and said "Swell."

I finished my can of applesauce, gathered my trash together, and stood up.

"I've got to go relieve Pete, so he can eat," I said.

I picked up my rifle and walked over to Pete. I told him it was my turn to be the policeman.

"Thank you, sir!' he replied as he smiled and winked.

"Ooops. I hope that doesn't get you killed," he joked.

"Naw, it won't. Nobody heard you."

Pete was staring out into the darkness, slowly shaking his head.

"You know, Red," he observed, "It sure can get dark out there. You remember that song *Keep on the Sunny Side of Life?*"

I nodded my head.

"Yeah. The Carter Family. We would sing that song when Uncle Clyde would bring his fiddle and we would make music."

Pete smiled.

"That must've been a lot of fun. Anyway, I wanted to ask you how we are gonna stay on the sunny side with all that darkness and death out there?"

I opened my mouth to answer, but he held up his hand, palm outward, to stop me.

"Yes, I know. The Light comes from in here," he said, tapping at his heart, "And from up here," tapping at his temple.

"The Good Lord dwells in both places."

He and I both stared outward and nodded in approval, spending a few seconds reflecting on the Darkness and the Light.

I looked at Pete.

"You know, Pete, Tim is just too nice to be here," I admitted.

"There is no way to not like him."

"I know it," Pete confessed.

"I've been watching him. He carries himself well. He reminds me of my brother Sam."

"Sam should be about eighteen now, right?"

"Yeah. It's taking everything I can say to stop him from joining the Army. But I'm afraid the Draft is hot on his heels. I guess I'll just have to help keep Tim alive and maybe God will do the same for Sam. You think?"

"Yeah, I think. Go eat your supper, Everman."

Pete looked at me. His eyes moistened.

"I sure am worried about him, Red."

"Yep."

"It will be what it will be," Pete said as he walked toward Nobel and Tim.

As I guarded our mortar position, I thought about all of the men who had been killed or wounded the past nine days. With the exception of a few, I had never learned the names or the people behind the faces. Almost fifty men from Mike Company were no longer fighting with us. Like Pete told Tim last night, making a new friend in all this deathly shit was not on my list of things to do right now.

There were two *banzai* raids that night. They never got that close. We were surrounded by the foxholes of our rifle squads, and were safely tucked in.


Tuesday, November 14, 1944.

Day 10 on Breakneck Ridge.

At dawn, we continued our advance down the southern slope of Breakneck Ridge. There was a light rain falling. Japanese resistance was still stiff, but we were no longer walking uphill into it. They would attack us from all directions – both flanks, front, and rear. The machine-gun fire and mortars were clearly coming from our front left, and the city of Limon was in that direction. We fought that day with concentrated fire toward Limon, and put extra riflemen to our rear to stop the Japs who would suddenly appear after we had passed them. Enemy machine-gunners in concealed bunkers would open their peepholes and fire on us, and snipers would open their spider-hole lids and take aim. By this time, we had received a team of war dogs to help us sniff them out of their hiding places.

One of the dogs was walking about ten feet to our right when he broke into a frenzy as he passed an area where we could see nothing. He was jumping around and pressing his nose to the "discovery" he had made. He did not bark. Two riflemen quickly walked to the dog and probed the ground with a metal spade. One rifleman detected the lid and flung it open as the other rifleman sent a burst from his BAR into the below-ground space.

As we passed we could clearly see the crumpled body of a very skinny and sickish-looking Jap at the bottom of a buried steel drum.

"Damn," Pete exclaimed.

"These men have been laying in those drums day and night to shoot us from behind. Did you see how starved and dehydrated that Jap looked?"

"I bet he was sitting in his own shit and piss when he got the burst from the BAR," Nobel answered.

"These guys are willing to do what we would never do," I remarked.

"No wonder it is so hard to stop them. They sure have raised a ruckus from those holes!"

We continued our advance south until we were less than a mile from Limon. We stopped at dusk and set up our defenses. We left our mortar in the ready position in case it was needed, with an open crate of ammo beside it. We dug our foxholes nearby.

As Nobel ate his C-Rations, he looked at Tim and said, "We cleared Breakneck Ridge behind us, all the way back to Pinamopoan."

Tim looked at him and smiled.

"You know, you sure can speak the local language well," he said.

"Pinamerpone. That's hard to say. You got any Filipino in you?"

Nobel flicked a piece of canned meat at him.

"English miners and ironworkers. That's what makes me so good. Where did yer folks come from, Mr. Blanchard?"

"Arkansas and Oklahoma," he said, proudly.

Pete laughed.

"You need to ask somebody to fill in the gaps when you get home, Tim. There's more to you than Arkansas and Oklahoma. With a name like Blanchard, you've got France in your history. One of your great-great-something-great grandmothers had a little Frenchman in her."

We all snickered.

Tim looked at Pete with a boyish grin on his face and said, laughingly, "I'll be asking you to not speak about my grandmothers like that."

Pete laughed and tapped him on the shoulder.

"The French helped this country beat the British," as he pointed directly toward Nobel and me, "and I'll always hold the French dear to me."

"Now how do you know I'm British, Pete?" I challenged him.

"There's a Smith in every British village, Red. Tinsmiths, ironsmiths, goldsmiths, blacksmiths…" he trailed off.

"I don't believe you can call yourself a wordsmith, Red, but I'll hold out hope that maybe one of your children will, after you get home from this war."

"Why, thank you, Pete. Maybe someday a couple of good words might be written about you, good buddy. If I can remember you after all of this," I chuckled.

I turned to Tim and said, while pointing at Pete, "His Grandma is full-blood Cherokee, from her home in Oklahoma."

Pete looked at me and smiled, proud that I had remembered.

Tim grinned in admiration and said, "She must be a swell Grandma, Pete."

Pete nodded.

Tim looked back at me.

"And where are you from, Red?" Tim inquired.

I looked seriously at him.

"I'm from my home in Texas," I answered.

Pete snickered, Nobel sighed, and Tim just stared at me in bewilderment.

"Ain't no home as good as Texas," he declared.

That night, we were hit by five *banzai* raids.

Five times the Japs appeared from nowhere, screaming "*Banzai!*" and "*Yankee, you die!*"

With bayonets mounted and grenades tucked in canvas bags, some of them shirtless, and several of them shirtless and pantless, they ran straight at us. No more zigzagging, no more extra effort. Some of them did not even scream.

I heard a GI moan as an enemy bayonet was thrust into him. I heard his buddy say, "You goddam mother-f-------

!" as he fired a half-dozen rounds into the Jap that had just killed his buddy.

I saw Tim throwing grenades. I saw Pete picking them off like he was turkey-shooting. I saw Nobel meet a jumping Jap with his bayonet, lift his floundering body up and overhead, then fire his M1 to sling the body rearward.

I pulled the pin on a grenade, counted to three, and tossed it into a gang of four Japs running toward me.

I yelled at Pete, "To your right, Petty!"

He saw the crawling soldier preparing to toss a grenade toward him, and put three rounds into him before the deed was done. Seconds later, the grenade exploded in the Jap's dead hand and sent two other Japs flying.

I even saw one carrying a mine strapped to his belly. A ping from an M1 Garand struck him and he fell to the ground, detonating the mine near an unfortunate foxhole.

Each raid would end after fifteen minutes of fury.

The foxholes would ring out with calls.

"Medic!"

"Ammunition!"

"Need more grenades!"

"Shit! Why do they have to keep doing that?"

Nobel just looked at me, breathing heavy.

"I heard a bullet sing right past my ear, Tex. I was almost a goner."

"Almost," I responded.

"Almost, but not. Did'ja ever hear the church song about that?" I asked.

"Almost Persuaded," he answered.

"I've heard it a thousand times. I wanted to go back there and drag that stubborn sonofabitch all the way to the altar and say 'Here he is, Pastor John. You can stop singing Almost Persuaded now.' Birmingham Baptist Church, it was."

We tended to our rifles, loaded more clips, and drank some water.

*Whew! Even though my colored friend told me I would survive this war, those damn raids scare the shit outta me.*

The last one came about an hour before daylight. By the time it ended, some of the GIs were cheering and taunting them to come back. I had to admit I had a slight buzz realizing they wouldn't come again before sunup, that the next time we met them it would be in broad daylight under our terms, not theirs.

Wednesday, November 15, 1944.

Day 11 on Breakneck Ridge.

You could sense the feeling of quiet jubilation running through each foxhole. We had completed the course, from start to finish, on Breakneck Ridge. The Japanese soldiers were frantic, but weakened by the battles fought along the ridge, and the bodies of their fellow soldiers lay blistered and decomposed along Highway 2 and in the caves, spider-holes, and hideouts of the adjacent ridges.

We felt like the end of our hell was very near.
Maybe tomorrow.
We knew the end was coming.
We had broken the back of that ridge.

It did not rain that day. We wore dry clothing on what we hoped was the last day of our Battle of Breakneck Ridge. Almost everyone had a cigarette hanging from his mouth most of the day.

We took the high ground around Limon, dislodging the Japanese Army from the ravines and gullies they had so stubbornly defended.

As we looked across the flatlands from our perch on a ridge, we could see the remnants of the Japanese Army running west, toward the city of Ormoc. We set our mortar emplacement up on high ground and let it rain fire upon them as they fled.

The snipers that hid in the brush and the underground Japs that lurked in their spider-holes were shot out, blown out, or burned out. The smells of gunpowder, liquid gasoline, and burning flesh filled the air as we closed the bloody battle we had been assigned.

Captain White walked through Mike Company's battle position that night, telling each foxhole that we were going to be relieved to get some much-needed and well-deserved rest tomorrow.

"This has been a decisive victory for us, and I am personally proud of everyone in the 3rd Battalion, and Mike Company in particular, for what you did up there on that ridge."

He told us that the 21st Regiment had lost over six-hundred men up there on that bloody ridge, and that he would be eternally beholden to each one of them for the price they had paid. He said the estimated number of Japanese bodies seen and counted on that ridge was two-thousand, and certainly more if you consider the ones trapped in caves, spider holes, and blown to hell. Giving us a reassuring thumbs-up, he turned and walked to the next nest of foxholes.

We thought of Kenny, and put our arms around each other's shoulders, including Tim, and said a prayer that Kenny would heal from his wound and would rejoin us to finish this war the way we had started it – together.


Thursday, November 16, 1944.

Day 12, the Last Day on Breakneck Ridge.

At mid-morning, near Limon, all three battle-weary battalions of the 21st Infantry stood in formation to be relieved by the fresh troops of the 128th Regiment, 32nd Infantry Division. As we stood there in our tattered, filthy uniforms, our collective memory recalled the day, just two weeks earlier *(had it only been two weeks?)* that we had relieved the tired and scruffy men of the 34th Infantry, on the north slopes of Breakneck Ridge. Since then, in the bloody, deadly fray that followed, we, like the 34th, had become the tattered, filthy men with the wide-open eyes. We had become the men who had seen and smelled death in every fashion and had become the instruments that delivered death to the enemy in ways and numbers we had never dreamed we were capable of inflicting.

At the command of "Forward March," we began to silently march through the lines of the fresh troops. Like the tired, weary men of the 34th had done, we moved like cold molasses. We were indeed a ragged group, and I'm sure some of the new replacements saw the same thousand-yard stare in our eyes that we had seen in the eyes of the 34th when we relieved them on our first day at the gory gate to Breakneck Ridge. I felt a sadness in my soul when I looked into some of the faces of the young men replacing us, knowing that they would soon fight the same Japanese Army that we had pushed off the ridge. I knew that many of these young soldiers would die in that struggle, and I sent a silent prayer upward to the Most High on their behalf.

By noon the 128th Infantry Regiment had watched us pass through their lines, and they formed their columns and moved into their first day of battle at the foot of bloody Breakneck Ridge. According to the rumors we had heard, their job was to secure Limon by eliminating the Japanese from the city, and drive them off of the high ground that towered above Limon at a deadly place called Corkscrew Hill.

We began our march toward Carigara. From there, we were told that we would be taken by truck to a bivouac area about 10 miles south, in the vicinity of the city of Jaro. Medical attention, hot chow, jungle hammocks, and clean dry clothing awaited us there.

Our fully loaded M1 Garands still hung on our shoulders. Lit cigarettes dangled from our lips. Filipino volunteers were with each battalion, helping carry equipment, ammunition, and personal gear. We had been through hell, and it would take more than just being replaced by another regiment to clear our minds and calm our nerves. We knew that a significant part of Leyte was still controlled by the Japanese, and danger still prowled the ravines and swamps of the island.

# CHAPTER 18

# INVASION OF MINDORO

Thanksgiving Day.
Thursday, November 23, 1944.

Near Jaro, Leyte, Philippine Islands.

It was still raining, but we were no longer soaking wet. We could stay in our dry, cozy jungle hammocks most of the day, covered with a large poncho to keep the rain out. We had mosquito-nets that we could zip up to keep the bloodsuckers out.

When we arrived in our camp four days after we left Breakneck Ridge, promotion orders were waiting at Jaro. Nobel was promoted to Sergeant, Pete was promoted to Corporal, and I was given my first stripe. I was now a Private First Class.

The Jaro camp was quite comfortable, compared to what we had endured on Breakneck Ridge.

There were steaming cups of hot coffee in the mess-tent where breakfast was served every morning, and a hot dinner each night. C-Rations were always available for a private lunch in our jungle hammock.

Nobel, Pete, Tim, and I were laying in our hammocks, which we had hung from several conveniently spaced trees so we could still be close to each other.

I looked over at Tim, and asked "Have you placed your order for Thanksgiving Dinner yet, Mr. Blanchard?"

He looked up from the Army Manual he was reading with eyes big and his face full of anticipation.

"Yes, I did, Mr. Smith!"

"Well, what did you order?"

"Ham. I did not ask for turkey. I don't believe that any turkeys will make it out to this place except us. But I know there are big cans of ham over in the mess supply tent, I saw them. So, I keep my prayers and requests reasonable."

Nobel gazed up from his letter-writing.

"Cornbread would be swell, but crackers will work."

"My Grandma cooked the best cornbread, ever. Her Grandma would grind the *maize,* they called it, by hand using a mortar and pestle," Pete declared.

"Not our kind of mortar," he chuckled, looking directly at Tim.

"It was a smooth stone with a low place in the middle. She used that until a mill was built with two huge grinding wheels."

"I read about those in school," Tim added.

I sat up straight, and said, "I helped set up a couple of mills in Hopkins County."

Nobel smiled and said, "I'll bet you a dollar that the metal frames of those mills came from Birmingham."

I nodded.

"We need to get you back to Birmingham to make more of that stuff."

"I need to go to Mobile and find Katy first," Nobel responded as he looked toward Pete.

"Amen." Pete said, as he pointed his finger at Nobel.

"You need to rescue that girl. I want to see you do that."

Nobel concurred by slowly nodding his head, looking around the encampment, with a half-smile.

"I'm sure a lot of these fellows will be doing the same, trying to find their old girlfriends."

Nobel calmly raised his arm and pointed beyond us, toward the mess tent.

"Say, do ya'll see that kid over there? He's been hanging around all day, talking to everyone that walks by."

We all looked toward the mess tent and saw the boy, dressed in white trousers and a pullover white shirt, like most Filipino natives. Both trousers and shirt were slightly stained with mud. As he saw us looking at him, he began walking briskly toward us. As he got closer, we could see the friendly, playful smile on his face.

"Hello, little soldier," Pete greeted.

"Hello, *kaibigan*," the boy said in broken English.

"*Kaibigan* means friend," Pete told us, then turned to the boy.

"I am Pete, he is Sergeant Horner, he is Red, and he is Tim."

Nobel blushed and said, "No, you can just call me Nobel. But you can call him Corporal Pete."

We all laughed along with the boy, knowing that he understood every word.

"What's your name?" Tim asked.

"You call me Tony. I am Tony," he answered, patting his chest with his right hand.

"Japs took our home, family scatter. I like to be with GIs."

Nobel studied him a few seconds, furrowed his brow, nodded, and told him, "Well, Tony, we're not going anywhere for a while, so there's no reason you can't stay around here, if you stay out of the way when we do Army things. If you find a better place with better friends, *kaibigans*, you can hang out with them. Deal?"

He extended his hand to Tony, smiled, and nodded for his approval.

The little soldier's face beamed with joy as he shook Nobel's hand, then turned to us to shake our hands.

"Thank you, Nobel. Thank you, Corporal Pete. Thank you, Red. Thank you, Tim!" he bubbled.

"I help you with anything you want. Carry, clean, move, anything!"

"Can you help me eat this extra chocolate?" Pete asked.

We all laughed as Tony answered enthusiastically, "Yes! Tony can do that!"

He walked over to Pete's hammock and collected two bars of chocolate, and began opening one carefully so as to not let it drop onto the muddy ground.

"Did you know that today is Thanksgiving Day for us?" Nobel asked.

Tony nodded yes, holding a piece of chocolate in his mouth.

"Yes, we had a harvest season feast at home, some called it Thanksgiving. A lot of food, sometimes turkey. Will you have turkey today?"

Nobel laughed, and answered, "I don't know, Tony. Maybe there will be turkey. But, whatever we have, we'll see that you get some. I know we will have pie."

Tim added, "I don't expect turkey. Just ham. And pumpkin pie."

Nobel got out of his hammock, rubbed his head, and looked at Tony.

"Walk with me up to supply, and we'll get you a decent hammock, and maybe some other stuff."

Tony and Nobel walked across the gentle ridge where our camp was positioned. I watched as they walked, both keeping the same casual pace, moving their arms and hands as they talked. Tony had some training and teaching back there in his short life, and I wondered what had become of his family. He was definitely not what some would call a "native." There was American in his mix, and I was amazed at how this war and the horrors in it had not broken his spirit, or his faith in the GI way of life.

"Do you think the Japs killed his folks?" Tim asked.

I thought on that a few seconds.

"Naw, I don't think so, Tim. Tony's parents were smart, you can tell by the way he talks to us. I think everybody had to scatter when the war hit their village, and the Japs ran through their area as they were running from our artillery and mortars. Why, we probably had a lot to do with that. We were pounding the area from the sea and from our own firing tubes. I feel bad about that, Tim. Can you imagine that happening in Dallas, or in Clarksville?"

I looked at Pete, chewing on a green toothpick.

"Yes, Red. It would be pitiful to see Red River, Hopkins, or Dallas County being war-torn like that."

I looked at the toothpick in his mouth.

"Is that green from jungle-rot or is it green from the factory?"

He pulled it out of his mouth and smiled broadly.

"Green from the factory. Made in the USA. The box said 'Toothpicks, Wooden, Colored.' They have to be good for you."

"They have Colored water fountains in the big Sears and Roebucks store in Dallas," Tim said, smiling in jest.

Pete answered with a grunt, "Not that kind of Colored, Tim."

He had a distant wishful stare in his eyes, and a slight smile on his face.

"When this war is over, and we all go back home, I think all that separate-stuff is gonna go away. We're all fighting for each other over here. Our freedom. Our way of life. We're gonna be one country, regardless of color. It will happen in your lifetime, Tim, and maybe in what's left of mine."

"I hope so," Tim responded, staring into space also.

"My Momma tells me there's no difference. They drink water and pee same as us. Daddy says every man puts his pants on the same way."

His eyes narrowed, and he looked at me, raising his eyebrows.

"I guess even the Japs can go to Sears and use the same water fountain. Not right away, but sooner or later, they will."

He giggled a bit.

I smiled and told him, "Sooner or later, we will all have the same water fountain."

"After we kill all of these," Pete said, replacing his toothpick with a blue one.

He looked at the toothpick closely. Spinning it between two fingers.

"These blue toothpicks just look better. There's already too much green out here."

Later that day, after Nobel and Tony had positioned a new hammock on the tree adjacent to Pete, we walked to the mess tent. Tony had his own mess kit and canteen, too. Nobel puts his arm around Tony and walked in with him. I realized that it was good to have a Sergeant in our group, because a Sergeant can do anything, especially one with a bald head and a wise-ass mouth. And the southern accent and booming voice boosted his authority to every occasion.

We had ham for Thanksgiving that day. And small turkeys, which meant small portions. Rye-bread dressing, canned green beans, and pumpkin pie. The war seemed a million miles away. We all drank a toast of cranberry juice to our new *kaibigan* Tony, and our old friend Kenny, who was somewhere north of us on the hospital ship *USS Mercy*.

Back in our hammocks, the rain had stopped, and we were telling stories - some true, some lies - and watched as Tony appeared to know the difference. He spoke of his life, of being born in Manila eight years ago to a school-teacher mother and a newspaper-salesman father. They moved to Tacloban, the capitol of Leyte, when the Japanese marched through Luzon. They tried farming with their cousins, and almost made it until a few weeks ago when the GIs started driving the Japanese off the island, westward toward Ormoc. Tony cried a little as he spoke, and made us cry, too. We knew we had a level-headed boy with us, who was all-too-soon being delivered to manhood by this bloody war. Tony and Pete became a team that night, and I smiled at the way Pete treated him like he was his own brother, Sam.

Captain White walked through the camp, wishing everyone in Mike Company a Happy Thanksgiving. As he approached our hammocks, he gestured with his hands in a downward motion for us to stay in our hammocks.

"At ease, stay as you are. Happy Thanksgiving, gentlemen. We have a lot to be thankful for today."

He was glad to see Tony. He told us he had an 8-year old son back in the states, and rubbed his hand through the boy's hair as he reminisced. He then continued his stroll through the camp.

An hour later he returned.

"At ease, stay as you are."

He looked at Tony with a serious expression, and asked, "Son, did you encounter any Japs as you walked from Tacloban over here to Jaro?"

"Yes, Sir, I did," Tony answered.

"Any problems?"

"No, sir, they look and point at me to go away."

Captain White put his left hand under his jaw and rubbed his chin as he studied Tony.

"Do you think you could carry a very important letter to the big general in Tacloban, with no Japs knowing you are carrying it?"

Tony perked up, a big smile on his face.

"Yes, Captain. Tony can do that. Tony wants to do that! Help fool the Japs and help send them to Hell," he said boldly.

Captain White looked at Nobel, and Nobel nodded his approval. He looked at Pete. He nodded his approval. The same with me and Tim.

He then slapped both hands together.

"We will have you do that tomorrow. Have a good night and a good breakfast, son. This Army needs you."

As Captain White walked away, we all patted Tony on the shoulders and told him we were very proud of him.

He cried again, this time with a broad smile on his face.

The Next Day

Half an hour after breakfast, Captain White's runner arrived at our camp. We were all sitting on a makeshift bench made out of a coconut tree log. He told Nobel to accompany Tony to the Battalion Headquarters. Pete, Tim, and I gave Tony a pep-talk. In the short time we had known him, we had grown so fond of the boy that we found it difficult to picture him walking through a Japanese encampment. Yet, he had done just that during his long walk from Tacloban. Pete gave him a bear hug, and saluted him.

Tony had a confident smile on his face when he left with Nobel.

When Nobel came back, he had a tight smile on his face.

"Tony was proud to serve the Army. He'll make it through the Japs and come back in several days, I have no doubt. He said he was going to see if anyone knew anything about his parents in Tacloban. I told him if it looked like the Japs were watching him, to not hang around there. I said he needed to lose himself in the jungle, and to not take the same road back. He needs to take a different way and not run into the same Japs a second time." We nodded in approval, and knew we would be a little antsy the next couple of days concerning his whereabouts.


Two Days Later

Tony showed up late Sunday afternoon, before evening chow, with a huge grin on his face. We had saved him a plate from lunch, just like we had done the day before. Sure enough, he was hungry. He had already reported to Captain White, and had delivered the short note that "the big General" in Tacloban had given him.

As he ate his meal, we asked him all the questions about his journey.

"Did'ja see any Japs?" Nobel asked.

"Few Japs. Mostly moving fast, trying to get to Ormoc, away from your Army," he said, pointing to Nobel.

Nobel smiled and shook his head slowly.

"They're not MY Army, I'm THEIR mortar gunner. And, babysitter for these guys," he explained, pointing to Pete, Tim, and me.

Tony laughed, some food falling from his mouth to the ground.

"They not babies," he joked, defending us.

"How about your parents. Any word from them?" Pete asked.

"They went to Carigara. I need to look for them there."

Nobel leaned forward and said, "I'll take you there on the next convoy, and we'll look for them, maybe tomorrow."

Tony nodded his head *Yes.*

"Thank you, Sergeant," he grinned.

"I need sleep tonight."

The night started right after evening chow, without rain. The ground was actually beginning to dry, and forming a hard, crumpled clay.

After breakfast the next day, Tony borrowed a camera from one of the mess cooks and asked us if he could take our pictures.

"I don't know," I told him.

"Can you?"

He dropped his shoulders, pretending he was frustrated. He looked Pete and asked if he could take our pictures.

"It's up to Sergeant Horner," Pete answered.

"He owns us."

Tony looked directly at Nobel.

Nobel just looked at him.

Several seconds passed.

Tony looked up, then looked back at Nobel.

"So?" he asked.

"So, what?" Nobel answered.

Tony smiled cleverly, and said, "The mess cook told me to take your pictures with this camera. He is a Sergeant First Class, so you need to do as he says."

We all laughed.

Nobel announced, "Tex, Pete, Tim. We need to go stand by the jeep over there and let Tony take our pictures. Mess Sergeant said do it. Let's go!"

We walked over by the jeep and Tony took our pictures, one by one.

"I'll get these developed in Carigara!" Tony said proudly.

"I want the one with me in it!" I told him.

"Yes, sir, Mr. Tex!" he replied with a giggle.

After we walked back to our hammocks, Tony took the film out of the camera and tucked it in his pocket. Pete watched him, a yellow toothpick dangling from his mouth.

"You never cease to amaze me, Tony!" he said.

"You know how to do everything. Maybe you can teach us a thing or two."

Nobel looked at Pete, then at me and Tim.

"We'll all have to take good notes. Tony knows how to survive out there in the jungle, more than any of us. C'mon, Tony, let's get ready and go to Carigara and find your parents."

About five minutes later, he and Tony were leaving with a convoy to Carigara, just ten miles north of us.

"I used to walk that far just to go to a movie," I told them as they left.

Nobel laughed, and said, "We walked that far a couple of weeks ago, Tex, and it was no movie."

"Maybe someday it will be," Tim chimed in.

"The Battle of Breakneck Ridge."

"They don't make movies that bloody," Nobel answered.

"Nobody would want to watch something like that. Maybe they'll just write a book about it, with no pictures."

"Ya'll be careful up there, Nobel," Pete said as he rubbed Tony's head.

"Son, you've got more hair on your head than Nobel can even dream about."

Nobel shot Pete a quick finger and said, "We'll be safe. You morons stay out of trouble."

Tony looked at Nobel and asked, "What's a moron?"

Nobel looked back and smiled.

"Just look at them. They're morons."

Tony smiled and looked at us.

"I love you, Morons."

We all laughed as the convoy drove away.

Pete and I walked over to the medic tent in the afternoon and talked to the staff about the hospital ship *USS Mercy*. We learned that it was supposed to still be docked in San Pedro Bay, near Tacloban. We told them we wanted to visit a close friend on the ship, and asked them how they transported patients, doctors, or supplies back and forth. Several of them had no idea, but Pete was able to talk his way up the chain of command. We finally talked to a 1st Lieutenant who told us we had a good chance of doing so if we get on the Sunday armed medical convoy to Palo, travelling on the Jaro-Palo Road. We would then make a complicated loop of supply boats and ferries to the hospital ship in San Pedro Bay.

Pete wrote down everything we needed to know and thanked the lieutenant. We walked back to our camp and told Tim we were going to see Kenny on Sunday. We explained that he would have to stay at camp and cover for us in case anything happened that needed our attention. He was delighted to help us see our old friend, the person that he had replaced.

Sunday, December 3, 1944

Nobel had returned from his trip to find Tony's parents after only a few days, and reported that Tony had indeed found them on a banana plantation in Dangsalan, between Tunga and Carigara. They were so happy to see each other they all cried, and insisted that Nobel stay two nights with them. Nobel said he was happy to oblige them, since they had a bed in a bamboo hut with real cotton sheets on them.

Tony insisted that the four of us come see him before we shipped out, and Nobel told him we would try our very best to do so. He gave them his address in Birmingham, and told them to write as often as they could after the war.

Pete shook his head and said, wearily, "I sure did like that boy. I wouldn't mind seeing him again."

"He's gonna grow up to be a fine man, Pete. You made a first-class impression on him, and he told me he wanted to grow up to be like his *Tiyuhin* Pete," Nobel responded.

"That means 'Uncle Pete,'" he continued.

Pete's face beamed with a broad smile, and he said "I'm so very glad he found his parents. They are blessed to have him as a son. I can only wish that I could someday have a son like him. I'd name him Tony, that's for sure!"

He smiled again.

I'd never seen Pete smile like that before. He looked so happy.

Nobel reached into his pocket and brought out four cardboard envelopes, each one with our picture in it.

I looked at my picture. Standing there, arms to my side, boots dirty, white rocky ground, jungles hills in the distance, with a serious look on my wartime face.

*John Wayne,* I thought.

We all said we were beautiful, we looked like movie stars, this Army is lucky to have us, we are America's best.

Nobel said that Captain White told him he was pleased to hear that Tony had found his folks because it looked very likely that we would be shipping out in a week or two.

"Where to?" Tim asked.

"Just another damn Jap-infested island," Nobel replied.

"Good!" Pete said, "At least it's not the mainland. Man, do I dread that."

"Me, too," I inserted, "Way too many Japs there."

When Sunday came, Nobel, Pete, and I were awake early to join the medical convoy down the Jaro-Palo Road. We wore clean (which meant 'not so dirty') dungarees and shirts, and had polished our boots for the trip. Nobel had made the necessary arrangements with the Army staff to allow us space on one of the troop trucks, and we watched over three patients being transported to the hospital ship. The medic staff appreciated us so much they gave us a ride all the way across the bay to the *USS Mercy*. It was costing us two days leave to make the journey, and we were beholden to all who helped us along the way.

When we reached the hospital ship, we found Kenny sitting at a table reading a philosophy book. We could see that his left arm had been amputated up to the elbow. We were happy to see him, and sad to see he had lost his arm. We all broke into tears.

We found out that Kenny was being taken to San Diego the next week, and we said a thankful prayer that we had been able to thread the needle of time to visit Kenny a week before he left for San Diego and two weeks before we left for our next landing.

"Where will you be going?" Kenny inquired.

"Hell, we don't know, Kenny. Probably one of those islands that the Japs think they own," Pete answered.

The four of us had never felt as close as we did that day. There was laughter and tears, happiness and sorrow, as we sat together beneath the shade of a potted palm tree that someone had brought onto the boat. We sang songs, said prayers, and played cards with the monogramed deck Kenny had left on Breakneck Ridge. We repeated oaths of friendship and brotherhood.

When darkness fell, Nobel managed to get three racks for us to sleep in several decks down. It sure was good to have a Sergeant with us.

We knew we had to get back to Palo and find a ride to Jaro, so we were up early, hit the chow line, and saw Kenny one more time. Pete and Nobel already had tears in their eyes when we met him at the same table. This time the book was closed. He was looking for us like a lost child in search of his mother.

It got rough when it was time for us to leave, and the tears fell like Leyte rain.

The trip back to Jaro was as easy as the first trip. We were overjoyed that it had been so easy, except for the sorrow of saying *'goodbye, good luck, see you back in the states'* when we left Kenny.

Arriving back at the camp, we each found that Tim had placed a book in each of our hammocks. It was the new copy of the Jungle Warfare field manual, released and issued in late October. I can't say we were all delighted to see it, but we did spend the next couple of days skimming through it, trying to read as much of the tactics as we could. To us, it all seemed too familiar, with the things we did to stay alive appearing in the "new" manual.

Nobel held his book up at one point and said, "At least the new guys have it all laid out. We had to learn this shit as we went along."

All around you could see the men of the 3rd Battalion laying in their hammocks, reading their new Army FM 72-20.


Tuesday, December 12, 1944

Dulag area of Leyte Island, Philippines

We watched the 1st and 2nd Battalions of the 21st Regiment leave our camp to join a Task Force of carriers, destroyers, battleships, support vessels, and LSTs to depart for our next amphibious landing, the location yet to be announced. The 3rd Battalion, us, remained behind in reserve to sail with a resupply convoy later.

The Task Force sailed south through the Surigao Strait. The next day, we heard the distant rumble of a sea battle to our southwest. Later, we learned that a Japanese Kamikaze plane, plunging in from a nearby island, had crashed into the *Nashville,* the flagship of the Task Force. Almost 300 soldiers were killed or wounded.

The men from the 21st Regiment were in LSTs, and were not injured. They were certainly horrified to see the attacks from the air.

Three days later, we were told their amphibious landing had occurred on the southwestern tip of Mindoro Island, to our northwest. The weather was clear, and there was no Japanese resistance on the beach.

Tuesday, December 19, 1944.

Dulag area of Leyte Island, Philippines.

We left our camp at Jaro in the dark morning hours to be taken to docks near Dulag and loaded onto three boats of the resupply convoy headed to Mindoro. The convoy, like the Task Force, sailed south through the Surigao Strait. We had two battleships and a carrier sailing with us.

Once we turned westward at the southern tip of Leyte, we began to see a small formation of Japanese aircraft approaching us. Fighter planes from our carrier immediately met them and drove them away, destroying several of them. These small air attacks continued for the next two days.

We remained in our LST, protected by our warships. We could hear the guns pounding from the nearby ships, and hear the Japanese aircraft strafing us. There was nothing we could do but standby, always wearing life vests.

"Jee-holy, guys! I didn't expect this!" Tim exclaimed, ducking from unseen dangers each time a plane buzzed by.

"Those planes have torpedoes and bombs, right?"

Nobel put his arm on Tim's shoulder.

"Some of them do, most of them don't. They're running out of ammo, Tim. We're on the downhill side of this war. The Japs are losing, in the air, on the sea, and on the ground."

Pete, sitting on his berth beside Tim, said, "He's right, Tim. However, there are more Japs on the ground than in the air or on the sea. That's left up to us. We have to make the Imperial Kingdom run out of Japs."

Tim smiled, gave a boyish giggle, and replied, "Yeah. We'll do that."

"Yeah, I plan on doing that, too, Mr. Blanchard," I affirmed.

I enjoyed calling Tim Mr. Blanchard. It made him feel like one of us, part of the team, older than he was. He always smiled when I said it, showing me that he liked it.

One time he told me, "That's what everyone called my Daddy back in Dallas. It makes me feel grown-up now, when I hear it. Thanks, Mr. Smith."


Thursday, December 21, 1944.

Approaching Mindoro Island, Philippines.

It was the day before we were supposed to reach Mindoro. About 20 kamikazes attacked us. There we were, just like the previous two days, standing around our berths wearing our life vests, when we heard a Japanese plane buzzing, buzzing, then getting louder, LOUDER. Out of nowhere, a ship-shattering BOOM! as flame and pieces of metal blasted through the bulkhead in the far corner of the room. Men were thrown across the room, some were screaming. Everyone hit the deck.

I have often tried to remember what happened in those next few seconds. It is all fuzzy and disjointed. Smoke. Flames on the bulkhead, dripping onto the deck between overturned racks. Soldiers crawling, trying to get away from the fire. A constant exhale of curses, panic, and screams of pain. One second, ten seconds, thirty. Who knows? A body being dragged toward the locked door.

The door suddenly opens, and sailors in yellow suits come running into the room, dragging a fire hose. Some soldiers exit the door with unconscious soldiers draped across their backs. Tim is holding onto me, tightly. I feel his chest rise and fall with each frightened breath. I see Pete and Nobel vanish into the fiery smoke, then re-appear with coughing men, helping them find the doorway. Walking toward the door behind them, Tim is still holding onto me tightly. I see his eyes are forcefully closed.

The fire hoses expel seawater, pushing the fire out of the room and out the narrow hole in the ship's bulkhead that now connects this room with the adjacent room. The sickening smell of burned fuel and hot metal squeezes our throats, refuses our inhalation.

More sailors rush into the room to help us out.

And then it is over, at least the worst part. Bells are ringing, sailors are running, and we are standing, sitting, laying along the passageway.

Uncontrollably, hate enters the mind. Raw, infectious hate fills the passage-way as soldiers' gravelly throats spit the words *"Goddam Jap kamikaze bastard! Damn his soul to Hell, the filthy motherf-----!"*

Two LSTs were hit by suicide bombers that day.

Six men from the 3rd Battalion died. Thirty-two were wounded.

The Navy lost 70 men, killed or wounded.

Two destroyers and a cargo ship were severely damaged.

The two LSTs were so damaged they had to be abandoned, and they sank.

The Japanese lost seven planes and seven men in seven kamikaze attacks that day, and three more planes and men to shipboard antiaircraft fire.

We were transferred to other ships, and our fighting equipment moved with us. Empty LSTs from previous landings raced toward us, and we were re-united with our equipment and platoons on new LSTs the next day.


Saturday, December 23, 1944.

Mindoro Beachhead, Near San Jose, Mindoro Island, Philippines.

We boarded our landing craft in the enormous open mouth of the LST, and were shuttled to the busy beachhead. Crates of ammunition and supplies lay stacked on the beach. Tanks and jeeps were lined up, ready to be dispatched to the interior lines. We walked beyond the beach and formed our platoons in an area that had been cleared of palm trees and short brush, establishing a personnel mobilization field.

Captain White found Mike Company, 3rd Battalion, and approached us to explain the details of our landing.

"Alright men, close up. Gather 'round. Welcome to Mindoro, former home of about one-thousand Japanese soldiers. The Jap population is shrinking every day as we push inward and kill them. There's about seven hundred of them left today. This island is important for the Army's plans to invade the big island, Luzon, just east of us. Every Jap on this island must go!"

He shuffled on his feet for a few seconds. He looked down, as if he was trying to remember what came next in his speech.

"I need to tell you the Japs on this island were completely surprised when our invasion struck them. The Japs in the coastal towns were unable to organize into a striking force. So, they just abandoned the towns and fled to the hills, to become bandits in the jungles and small villages. When we hit them, they had no food, no medicines, and no orders from Japan. The groups broke up into smaller groups, and they plundered, raped, and burned the countryside at will."

He looked around at us. His back was straight. His chin was up. He stood like he was full of piss and vinegar, but his eyes showed a weariness, a slight touch of fatigue, like some of his get-up-and-go had got-up-and-went.

"We survived a kamikaze attack out there," he continued.

"That doesn't happen every day. We lost some good men. Are you soldiers ready to whip some Jap ass?"

A wave of revenge swept the ranks, as we all yelled, "Yeesssss Siirrr!"

"We'll get that chance, later," he added.

"For now, our job is to protect this beachhead in case the Japanese try to take it back. So, we will wait right here, the longshoremen will bring us some C-Rations, we'll have a tropical picnic, and then we will move out when they decide where they want us to go."

Three hours later, we were establishing a bivouac in a small grove of palm trees a hundred yards beyond the beachhead. A field kitchen had been set up at the perimeter of the beachhead, and hot food was being prepared for evening chow.

Before dusk, we tied our hammocks between common trees. It wasn't planned, it just turned out that way. The kamikaze experience, along with Kenny's departure, had left us kinda tied to each other, I guess. It was a good arrangement.

Nobel addressed us, as we lay there beneath our mosquito nets.

"Say, fellows, I heard that President Roosevelt said no soldier in these two wars should spend more than three Christmases away from home. You know what that means? Since the day-after-tomorrow is Christmas, we are closer to going home than we ever have been!"

Pete immediately answered, "All we have to do is survive, and we're going home next year. Ain't that a pleasant thought?"

"This is my second Christmas away from home," Tim said.

"You'll be home before you know it, Mr. Blanchard," I responded.

"Maybe, if this war is over soon, they'll let you go back to Dallas next Christmas, even if you have to take leave. Think on that tonight. You'll sleep like a baby."

"I can't sleep," Tim replied.

"I've been afraid to tell you, but I haven't had the chance to get anything for ya'll for Christmas."

Simultaneously, Pete, Nobel, and I sat up straight in our hammocks and looked at him.

"What?"

"Well, shit, Tim!"

"After all we have done for you?"

Tim blinked, his eyes open wide. Then he started laughing. We all joined in.

It was a relief to be together, alive.

Christmas Day.
Monday, December 25, 1944.

Mindoro Beachhead, Near San Jose, Mindoro Island, Philippines.

It had rained every day since we landed on Mindoro. The daily rains and the high humidity made Mindoro a breeding ground for malaria. I spent Christmas Eve shivering and sweating, as Pete watched after me almost constantly. Somehow, he had gotten me an extra wool blanket to keep me warm during my chills, and to soak up my sweat during my hot flashes.

As we awoke that morning, we could smell the mess tent cooking bacon. Real bacon! Pulling the wet blanket off me, I looked over at Pete and said, "Good morning, Santa. Thank you for getting this wet blanket for me. I wish it was red instead of green."

Pete, getting out of his hammock, replied with a smile, "Good morning and Merry Christmas to you, my little sweaty elf. Want some Atabrine for breakfast?"

"No, no. I want that bacon!" I answered, pointing over to the mess tent.

We looked in that direction and saw Nobel and Tim walking toward our little circle of hammocks. They each had a mess kit full of fried bacon and a mess cup full of hot coffee.

Tim beamed, "Look, Red. See what Sergeant Nobel got us for Christmas!"

We were alive, we were together, and we had bacon for Christmas!

Praise the Lord!

With a broad smile on his face, Nobel pulled five yellow paper boxes from his chest pocket and said, "And more presents! Look! I got each of us another box of Atabrine, and I got two for you, Tex! I don't think any of us took a regular dose on Leyte Island. It's time to get yellow, boys!"

"Are you feeling better, Red?" Tim asked.

"Yep," I answered, holding a piece of bacon.

"I am feeling very much better."

"A couple of us thought we were gonna lose you last night, Tex," Nobel revealed.

"You sweated and shivered most of the night. Once you even talked about attacking a buzzard, and then said you were not gonna eat that mouse."

Several laughed.

"It ain't easy fighting the malarials," I confessed to them.

"Take your Atabrine, Tex," Nobel ordered.

"You look much better with a hint of yellow in your cheeks."

Pete stepped into the center of our hammock circle and started distributing the coffee from the two mess cups. After everyone had coffee and bacon, he raised his cup, looked at Nobel and me, and said, "Merry Christmas to us, Gentlemen, on this our third and last Christmas of the war."

We raised our cups to join his toast.

"May the miracle of the immaculate birth of Christ be with us this day and all the days to follow," Pete continued.

"And may His birth bring Peace to all soldiers up and down this deadly line, and take us down that merciful path to the Glory Train that takes us home."

"To Birmingham, and Katy!" Nobel toasted.

"To home, anywhere in Texas," I added.

"To the blue skies and green grass of Clarksville," Pete closed.

Our mess cups clinked as they touched for the final toast.

"If it be God's will," Pete said.

An "Amen" was repeated by all.

There was hope and a strong bond on that Christmas Day. We had become true friends in the vile dangers and abominable violence of this war, and we looked into each other's eyes with a promise of loyalty and a commitment to see this war to its long-overdue end together, the way we started it.

For our sake and for Kenny's sake.

We knew, with a realization deep in our bones, that we would never, ever share such a tightly woven brotherhood again in our lives. Only in war does this happen, when death stalks in the deadly space across the field of battle, or lies hidden in the next ravine, or crouches silently and maliciously beneath the kunai grass a few feet away.

There would never be another chance, out of necessity or fate, to form a bond anywhere in life the way we had done at Breakneck Ridge. There are no friends on Earth as important to one's soul as a friend on the battleground. We valued each other more than ourselves. We could not see Life without seeing each other, and if destiny had demanded it, we would have willingly died for one another than to have lived apart.

Life itself had become a battlefield, and all the Rules of Life were Rules of Battle.

Later that day, after a respectable holiday dinner of ham and chicken, we were resting in our hammocks when Tim announced, "This is the best Christmas I've had in years!"

I looked at him and said, "Ya know, Mr. Blanchard, this is the second-best Christmas I've ever had in my entire life. No one shot at me, it's not raining, I didn't have to give any presents, and the people sitting around me are my best friends ever!"

"I didn't have to look at Uncle Willie's brown teeth," Pete acknowledged.

"I didn't have to dress up," Nobel declared, then pulled a haversack out of his hammock.

"And," he continued, "Look what I scrounged up over at Supply."

With a toothy grin, he pulled a fifth of Virginia Gentleman Bourbon out of the haversack.

For about three seconds, you could have heard a pin drop.

Pete stared at the bottle, and said, "Kenny's favorite. God bless you, Nobel."

His eyes moistened.

"I don't believe it," Tim said, his mouth hanging open.

I looked at Pete and told him, "It's OK, Pete. Kenny's going home, and he's very much alive."

I then smiled, cocked my head to one side, and looked at Nobel.

"Kenny would be very, very proud of you, Mr. Alabama," I said as I reached for my mess cup.

"And I'm very proud of you, too,"

As our mess cups touched each other in a metallic kiss, Nobel poured three-fingers worth in each.

"Merry Christmas, my friends," Nobel saluted.

"Merry Christmas, Kenny," Pete whispered.

As we sipped the sweet bourbon and savored the caramel after-taste, we looked at each other and nodded. I think we each said "Yep!" a couple of times through the first four sips. Pete looked at me with a wink and asked, "Red, you said this was the second-best Christmas in your life. Did the Best Christmas in Your Life have anything to do with a girl?"

I looked at my cup, then at him, then back at my cup.

"Yes, Pete, it did. Christmas of '41. I watched an angel serve teacakes and coffee at our place. She was too young at the time, but she could already look at a man and make him melt. I imagine she's not that young now, three years later."

Nobel leaned forward with his cup, and said, "Well, let us drink to, to,….. who?"

"Juliette," I answered.

The four mess cups kissed again, and the four of us let the bourbon pour effortlessly into us. The conversation drifted from sports to politics to home. In a St. Louis World Series, the Cardinals had beaten the Browns. President Roosevelt had defeated Tom Dewey to win his fourth term. All four of us were pleased that we didn't change Presidents in the middle of the war. Nobel was still worried about Katy. Pete was still worried about Sam. Tim was worried about his Dad not being able keep the old house maintained. And me, I was worried about Daddy running the family with only one of the sons there. I was worried about Momma being treated well. My biggest worry, which I kept to myself, was Juliette not being bothered by the few young bucks hanging around Wellington, Texas.

Nobel, Pete, and I drank a toast to our last Christmas at war. From Hawaii, to Australia, to this day in the Philippines, we took a sip for each, and topped it off with "bottoms up!"

"Three is enough," Pete declared.

"Kenny's out there on the ocean, between here and San Diego. Let's drink to him!"

Three cups kissed, three shots drank. Tim sat this one out.

As the day became night, and the tropical shadows lengthened beneath each palm tree, we sang Christmas carols. Silent Night. White Christmas. And a few that we obviously did not know. The Virginia Gentleman had muddled our minds.

What we did mostly was laugh.

It was a Christmas I will never forget.

Two days later, on December 27, the San Jose beachhead was bombed and strafed by Japanese aircraft. We all jumped into large foxholes we had dug in case of air attacks. We covered ourselves with crate boxes and wooden pallets collected from the beachhead supplies. Several bombs landed near us. We lay beneath our cover, shooting at the strafing Zeroes.

New Year's Day.
Monday, January 1, 1945

The Town of Bongabong, along the east coast of Mindoro, Philippine Islands

We left the beachhead at San Jose, and sailed east, around the southern tip of Mindoro, then north to the middle of eastern Mindoro. It was raining as we landed on a beach near the town of Bongabong. There was no Japanese resistance at the beach. We advanced northward for the next ten days, marching through swamps and jungle, with heat that was close to unbearable. We received fire from enemy-held villages along the way. Each time, we would respond with mortars, bazookas, and flame throwers. Infantry riflemen would quietly encircle the village while we blasted away at the enemy. The riflemen would then kill every Japanese soldier that had survived our barrage. In each of these actions, Filipino guerrilla forces would help us clear the enemy from our path.

    The guerillas were a rugged band of Filipinos with rifles, hatchets, grenades, and other odd-shaped tools that, when expertly used, would kill every enemy soldier they encountered. From head-wraps to baseball caps, they were all dressed differently, but they gave us the spirited help we needed. They were perfect guides, and unafraid to attack the enemy.

    By January 11, we reached Pinamalayan, the main coastal town on the eastern side of Mindoro. Navy battleships, carriers, destroyers, LSTs, and dozens of other warships gathered in the waters off the beach. Rumor had it that the Navy was trying to deceive the Japanese into thinking we were preparing to board the LSTs and invade the big island of Luzon, about 35 miles to our north.

    Instead of loading onto the LSTs, we continued our slow march north by northwest to drive more enemy soldiers out of their encampments and shelters. We marched toward the hills and mountains of Central Mindoro, following the information that the Filipino guerillas had given us. According to the guerillas, there were half-a-dozen small settlements that the Japanese soldiers had taken from the Filipino natives, just like they had taken Tony's village on Leyte Island. Most of the villagers had fled into the jungle, seeking aid from the guerillas. Some of the displaced villagers joined with the guerillas to help take their homes back, and to deliver vengeance to the enemy for the farmers they had killed and the wives and daughters they had raped.

We could see that the hills were steep, and heavily wooded. Beyond the hills, we glimpsed peaks that rose higher and higher, all covered by jungle. The sky was dark, overcast, and miserably laden with rain. In the distance, the tallest peaks disappeared into the clouds.

Mindoro was vast and wild, with a considerable amount of its interior unexplored. It was much wetter than Leyte, although we had all thought that Leyte was the wettest place on Earth. Gloomy is the best word to describe the forced marches we took on Mindoro to push, by bayonet or bullet, the dozen-or-so enemy plunderers out of each stolen village.

It was terribly hard work to capture and destroy the Japanese troops in this way. We crossed wide areas of volcanic sands, walked over the same type of razorback ridge that we had seen on Leyte Island, and marched through swollen streams that flowed across dense thickets. Good roads were few and far between. Most of our supply lines could only be traveled by Filipino volunteer carriers, and, in some cases, animal pack trains.

Heat exhaustion, jungle rot, tropical infections, and malaria were marching with us, sleeping with us, and eating with us. Diarrhea and nausea were keeping the medics busy. Pete was sick with both a couple of days, and we carried his gear while he just walked. He never stopped chewing his toothpicks, though we told him time and time again that every worm and tiny bug ever created was living on them.

"Awww," he would say, "You morons are wrong. It was something I ate, and you know it. It'll happen to you, too, just you wait and see."

Sure enough, it did.

Tim spent two days throwing up, and the medic gave him some pills.

Nobel had diarrhea for three days, and spent a lot of time in the jungle underbrush. The medic gave him some liquid that Nobel said was gosh-awful, but it worked.

As for me, I sweated a lot and got the chills for three nights and two days. I took my Atabrine like it was candy, and kept my canteen full of clean water. The medic gave me some new pills that would, as he said, "straighten the pecker on a scare-crow." If they did, I didn't ask the scarecrow. The pills really got rid of the pain and agony of malaria, and let you think about other things.

I remember we were fortunate to have all of us sick on different days, so there was always someone to carry the sick-person's gear. Still, every couple of days there would be a serious firefight with the usual dozen-or-so Japanese resistors to keep us focused and aware of the dangers that lay in every ravine and behind every bush.

In mid-January, we stopped our march and bivouacked for three nights. The Battalion Commander said it was a necessary break to help us find our sanity. There was a clear, bubbling spring nearby. It gave us the chance to remove our clothing in the rain, wash them in the clear spring, and put them back on again in the rain.

The mail caught up with us, and a large tent was set up for administrative duties. The tent gave us a place to read and write letters. Nobel wrote a short note to his parents and

Katy, Pete did the same to his parents, his brother Sam, and his girlfriend Wanda. I wrote a short note to Kenny and to my folks, and I wrote a letter to Juliette. Tim wrote a long letter to his parents.

A field mess tent was set up, and we had two hot meals.

Our march through the villages of northeastern Mindoro continued.

At one of the villages, we were met by happy, jubilant Filipinos. A number of them spoke English, and were saying, "Welcome, Yankee soldiers! Welcome to Naujan! You make Japs run to hills. We have village again!"

They must have known we were coming. The native word-of-mouth "telegraph" was often faster than our own communications between these scattered villages. They had already begun preparing a feast for us. Suckling pigs were being roasted over outdoor fires. Chickens that had previously been hidden in caves were brought out to the light of day, killed, and were being cooked in pots. There was fresh fruit, and fish from the many streams.

Our officers huddled in a group, and were smiling when they said we would be honored to stay for the feast. It was the most entertaining and magnificent event in our entire Army life! There were dancing girls in colorful costumes, and a villager dressed as a Japanese soldier being "attacked" by village men with wooden sticks. There was music with drums, flutes, violins, and small guitars, all made of bamboo. The finishing touch was palm wine in bamboo log containers, presented to us by the native families.

Along with the palm wine, the villagers gave the officers a small woven plate of brown eggs. It looked like there were only three on the plate. Pete punched me in the side and said, "Look, Red! They're giving the officers *balut!*"

"What is *balut?* They look like eggs," I asked him.

Pete grinned and said, "Oh, these are not regular eggs, Red. These are fertilized eggs with little, unhatched baby ducks in them. It's very special to their culture and their history. That's powerful stuff. Whoever eats one of those eggs is gonna be pumped up tonight! Most of the officers don't even know what they are. I hope they don't spit it out. That will insult our hosts!"

Sure enough, just as the small plate of eggs were presented, all the officers started telling each other not to take one if they didn't intend to eat it. Three full-bird colonels took one each, and nobody else.

They each cracked their egg and ate whatever "thing" was in it, and nodded their heads.

It was a very good day.


Wednesday, January 31, 1945.

By the end of January, we had advanced toward the coastal town of Calapan, and had a bivouac a short distance west of town. Along the way, from our landing at Bongabong to Pinamalayan to Calapan, we had killed about three-hundred enemy soldiers, and had lost only one man killed and seven men wounded.

We had captured several dozen important-looking Japanese soldiers during our month-long march. Nobel said they were important because of the extra colors on the uniforms.

"Man, it's not the colors on the uniforms that make them important," I told Nobel.

"It's the fact that they are wearing uniforms that still fit or ain't tattered. The poor shirtless or baggy-pant Japs are obviously just like us, unimportant but damn dangerous."

Tim laughed and punched me on the arm in approval.

Pete winked at me and said, "Clothes make the man, Red. We Texans know that."

Nobel looked at us, shaking his head in phony disgust.

"I won't tell you guys any more military secrets."

"But, I will say that HQ Company wants a couple of men to join a guard detail. They are taking all of our captured Japs to Calapan to board a tanker for a POW camp on Leyte Island. Any takers?"

Tim's hand shot immediately into the air.

"I want to!"

I nodded my head.

"I'll go with Tim."

Pete was still thinking it over when Nobel said, "Swell. You two get your rifles, ammo, and report to HQ Company."

Tim's eyes narrowed.

"Is it going to be dangerous?"

Nobel looked at him and smiled, "It's dangerous everywhere. Hell, I'm letting Pete stay here so he can protect me!"

Pete reached toward his rifle.

"Do you want me to shoot him, Sergeant?"

Tim and I had already stood up and were getting our gear together.

"Naw, save your ammo," I answered.

"We'll just get out of your hair."

Pete looked at Nobel and said, "Hell, I'll be the only one left here that has any hair."

Nobel looked up and sighed.

Tim and I walked to the HQ Company tent and fell in with a group of ten other riflemen. A troop truck then carried us to the forward edge of our bivouac, where a roped-off area contained about twenty Japanese prisoners. They were all sitting on a long log, hands tied, with rope leggings around one ankle, connecting them to each other in two groups of ten each.

Two more troop trucks arrived, and the prisoners were ushered into them, one group per truck. The guards motioned for us to ride with them, six GIs per truck.

Most of the prisoners were sitting on the floor of the truck, with the prisoners on each end of the rope legging sitting on the bench seat nearest the driver. We sat on the rest of the bench seat.

The trucks started, and began their journey to the beach area.

There was an awkward silence for half of the journey, with the Japanese prisoners looking down and us GIs trying to not recall the very vivid memories of shooting the enemy point blank, or bayonetting them face-to-face.

There they were, in front of us, subdued. Prisoners. Ashamed and without honor.

Here we were, above them. Yankees. Free. Still alive.

I could hear the voices screaming in my head.

*Yankee, you die!*
*Banzai!*

I noticed the prisoner setting next to me, on the bench, at the end of the rope "chain." His eyes were up, displaying a sense of pride and self-respect the way an eastern meadowlark wears a black chevron on its bright yellow chest. A leather satchel was hanging from his neck, with the corner of a silk cloth visible from its top. The silk cloth had yellow and red images on it, and dark blue Japanese writing. He saw me looking at it and tried to push it back into the satchel, but his tied hands couldn't do it. Two of the GI riflemen got edgy with his efforts, and I motioned for them to calm down, and motioned the prisoner that I was going to help him stuff it back in the satchel. He laid his hands on his lap, and kept his head up as I repositioned the silk cloth. I could see a partially painted picture of a woman's face, some trees, and a mountain. It was all very intricate, and he was quite nervous, as if he had put his heart and soul into the painting.

Having finished, I leaned back and gave him a slight nod of my head. He nodded back, slowly. Something passed between us at that moment, a knowledge or recognition of humanity in a world of hate and violence. I had never held a conversation or exchanged an emotion with a Japanese man beyond the normal cursing and promise to kill. Respect was in that mutual nod, and neither one of us had expected it. No bayonet. No grenade. Just simple respect.

A GI on the other side of the bench seat looked at me and said with a snarl, "Are you a Jap-lover?"

My eyes found his. My muscles tensed. I leaned a bit forward and, with a snarl on my lips, said, "Just shut the f--- up."

Tim, sitting next to me, placed his hand on my arm and gripped firmly.

"Don't worry, Tim," I assured, loud enough so everyone in the truck could hear.

"Nothing's going to happen right now. We have prisoners to guard. When we get out of this truck, anything can happen."

The GI on the other side made a small snorting sound with his nose, then looked away.

Nothing more was said on the remainder of the trip to the beach.

When we arrived, half of the GIs, including Tim and me, got out of the truck and stood below, waiting for the prisoners to step down. As the prisoner with the satchel walked past me, our eyes met again, and the same polite nod was exchanged.

A large group of Military Police were waiting for us, and escorted them to their boarding craft.

We re-joined the rest of the volunteer riflemen and rode a single troop truck back to our HQ tent. Everyone was quiet on the trip back, each one of us privately digesting our first contact with the enemy under a purely professional situation.

When we got back, Tim asked me, "You alright, Red?"

"Sure, Mr. Blanchard." I answered.

"I'm very happy and very fine. How about you?"

Tim moved in front of me and, walking backward while he spoke to me, said, "I am very, very proud of you, Mr. Smith."

I smiled.

We remained at our bivouac near Calapan through February and March, while the Army was preparing plans for our next action.

General Douglas MacArthur had begun the invasion of Luzon, and Manila was liberated in early March. He was ready to invade Mindanao. The Marines were ready to invade Iwo Jima. Both were ready to invade Okinawa.

In April, we were told it was time for us to hit the beach again, but we did not know which beach it would be. The scuttlebutt was Mindanao.

# CHAPTER 19

# KENNY HERROD

Wednesday, March 28, 1945.

Along the Norfolk and Western Railway, fifty miles west of Farmville, Prince Edward County, Virginia.

The full moon had just begun to ascend along the eastern horizon as Kenny Herrod gazed out the train window, seeing his own reflection looking back at him. A slight frown formed on his face.
He reached into his left chest pocket and removed a waxed-paper packet of tobacco leaves, pulled one leaf out, and gently placed it in his mouth. Closing the packet with the same right hand, he placed it back in his pocket and began to chew the leaf, smiling as he enjoyed its pungent sweetness. He looked back in the window, and leaned toward it, turning his head against it to look forward and see the moon dancing around the front of the train, playing catch-me-if-you-can with the engine as the train *clickety-clicked* down the track.

He sat in his sleeper car that he had reserved at the stop-over in Cincinnati, using his own money. He needed help from the porter to prepare his bed, but he was well-rested for his arrival home, just an hour or so away. He looked back at his reflection as the moon disappeared around a bend.

*You've gotten older, leaner, and look wiser,* he told his reflection. His right hand instinctively moved toward his left elbow. His khaki shirt was neatly sewn over the remnant of his left arm, where it had been amputated an inch above his elbow because infection from a forearm wound had gotten out of control.

*Spending Christmas on a hospital ship in the Pacific with a nubbin for an arm is a memory I'll never forget,* he said to himself. He glanced at the letters lying next to him on the little table built into his seat. The letters, from Nobel, Red, and Pete, were written two months ago on an island they could not name.

*God, I miss those men. I'll never have friends as dear to me as them,* he thought, as he picked up the letters.

*They probably spent Christmas in a heavy rain on the jungle floor, with Japs bringing them banzai presents wrapped in grenades. I guess I can live with one good arm and half of another. I pray that they just live, and go home, like me.*

Kenny, twenty-two years old, felt much older every morning since he had been treated at the Navy Hospital in San Diego. He had never known how important two arms were until he tried to get out of his bed every morning and put his cotton robe around himself. He refused to take his meals in his bed, so he would do the necessary work to dress himself rather than lie in bed in a room full of men in much worse conditions than himself.

He had seen his three Army friends in early December, just a week after his arm had been amputated. They had taken all of the weekend leave they were given to make the complicated hop from ferry-to-supply boats out to the hospital ship, the *USS Mercy*. They were able to visit him a week before he left for San Diego and a week before they left for their next landing. They couldn't tell him where they were going because they, themselves, did not know.

The four men had never felt as close as they did those two days. There was laughter and tears, happiness and sorrow, as they sat together beneath the shade of a palm tree. They sang songs, said prayers, played cards, and repeated oaths of friendship and brotherhood. It got rough when it was time for them to leave, and the tears fell like Leyte rain.

There were left-over tears in Kenny's eyes as he remembered the visit and stared out the train window, watching the moon rise higher in the Virginia sky.

**Clickety-click, clickety-click.**

He tucked the letters in his right front pocket.

The train whistle began to sing mournfully as they neared Farmville.

"Farmville coming up, soon, Mr. Herrod," a tall, thin, colored porter announced as he walked down the narrow hallway between the sleeper-rooms, his body moving with the rocking of the car.

"Will you be needing some help with your things, Sir?" he asked.

"No, thank you, Sir. I'm alright," Kenny replied, as he nodded his head in respect.

The porter smiled and continued his dutiful dance down the Pullman corridor.

Kenny could feel the train slowing down, ever so slightly. He started to get up and gather his things together, then looked at his barracks bag, with everything he had in it, lying in the opposite seat, already fully packed and ready to go. He eased himself back into his seat.

He rubbed the end of his left arm with his right hand and felt the smooth bones and sinew that was once an elbow. He nodded his head in approval.

*It took losing this arm, or half of it, to show me how violent and useless war is. The best three individuals I will ever meet walked that rugged and deadly road with me. We saved each other's life so many times it became normal.*

*We saw men, some of them you could literally call 'boys,' drop their life on a sandy road or in a spread-out formation approaching the enemy on the first day of battle. Nothing I have ever done will be as fundamentally important to me as those two years spent in the discovery of what Life stands for, and what the natural order of things really is.*

*My left arm will be the memorial to Life's real meaning to me. For every inch of arm that I lost, I can only estimate that ten Japs lost an entire future. Maybe twenty. For what? A leader? A god? Honor?*

*For our own freedom they lost theirs.*

*For the freedom of the many who were slaughtered in the name of imperialism and conquest, they were slaughtered themselves.*

*I will have to look no farther than my own left arm to see the cost of War. And, I will have to watch nothing other than the wretched ghosts of two-hundred Japs as they float with melancholy faces through my garish dreams to realize the futility of the Freedom-Takers.*

*War is not the natural order of things.*

*Freedom is the natural order of things.*

*And War in the defense of Freedom is the corollary.*

Kenny smiled as the train slowed again and the whistle raised its pitch from a mournful cry to a warm and friendly shout. He knew he would return to Hampden-Sydney College in September and continue his pursuit of paradise in Philosophy.

The Philosophy of Freedom.

He knew his friend, Army Corporal Marie Francis, would be returning to the Hampden-Sydney College when the war was over, and her French-communication skills were less necessary. They would renew their friendship and determine what lay ahead for them.

He could see the white stone walls and the gray slate roof of the Farmville Train Station drawing steadily closer as the train slowed to a near-stop. He stood up, grabbed his barracks bag with his right hand and slung it over his left shoulder, bracing the strap with his strong left upper arm.

He stood behind the porter as the door opened. Following him, Kenny ventured down the doorsteps, pausing briefly at the bottom step, which was higher off the ground than the others. He reached for the kind, smiling porter's hand, and maintained his balance off the last step, finally touching Virginia with his right boot.

"Welcome home, Mr. Herrod." The porter announced.

"Thank you for your service. We owe you a debt of gratitude."

Kenny's Mom, Dad, and 17-year old brother James were standing there in front of him, their faces radiating with love and pride, with smiles like sparkling moonbeams.

James held an enormously large bottle of Virginia Gentleman Bourbon, with a blue checkered bow.

Kenny stepped toward them, grinning through his tears, and began the first day of his new life.

# CHAPTER 20

# INVASION OF MINDANAO

Friday, April 13, 1945.

San Jose Harbor, Mindoro Island, Philippine Islands.

Reveille was sounded at 0400 at the camp, and we rushed through a hot breakfast. We grabbed our gear and were loaded onto a troop ship for our next journey. At 1300, beneath a beautiful blue Pacific sky with scattered white, cotton candy clouds, the naval convoy carrying the 24th Division steamed out of the harbor. We didn't know exactly where we were headed, but our gear and our equipment told us it would be the usual amphibious landing. The 3rd Battalion was on separate LSTs than the rest of the Division, so we took that to mean we might be making an assault on a different beach than the other two battalions.

    Captain White called Company M together for a quick meeting. He looked distracted and little tense when he motioned us to sit down.

    "Men, this meeting is not about our destination. It is on a more somber note. We have just received word from Headquarters that we will be on Alert for a while due to some difficult news from home. President Roosevelt died this morning at 0100 our time, in Warm Springs, Georgia. Harry Truman was sworn in as President a few hours later."

    A wave of moans and gasps ran through the Company.

"As you know, having this happen during a war, especially a World War, can be quite troubling. We will be very quiet on this ship and in this convoy. We are prepared for anything the enemy may throw at us, sensing a vulnerability. You will be restrained to your quarters, except for chow and trips to the head, probably until we get to wherever it is we are going. Remember, there is someone at the helm of the Ship of State, so we will leave it to him like we have all the times before. God bless you, gentlemen, and relax. There is still much work ahead for you. You are dismissed."

We slowly left the briefing room. Some of us looked at the deck, some of us at the overhead. Very few men talked to each other.

Nobel walked in front of us, then turned and said, "We will win this war. Truman will do exactly what Roosevelt was doing. This Army is still The Army."

This was our fourth time to load up and depart for an invasion, and we had become a smooth, well-oiled machine in the beach-landing business. We were directed to our sleeping quarters, and Nobel and I settled in for the personal battle against seasickness. We knew what to do and what not to do. Drink water. Don't eat very much, stick to potatoes and bread. A little coffee in the morning. We had a thick stew one day. No fresh air on the promenade this time because of the Alert. Walk slow always.

Tim did pretty good on the trip. He and Pete were buddies doing all the things Nobel and I couldn't do. Pete kept Tim off galley-duty and other useless details. Both of them were around to help us stay sane in the event of rough seas.

On the second day, Captain White met with M Company in a cramped meeting room. Nobel and I found a comfortable place to sit on the deck in the corner, gently leaning our heads against the bulkhead. It was a day of rough seas, and everybody seemed a little affected by the ship's up-and-down movement.

As a louey was setting up an easel with a map of a large, ragged island, Captain White looked around the room at us and announced, "Alright, listen up."

"Make yourselves comfortable, this is the time when you finally learn where you're headed. We're going to Mindanao, the second largest island in the Philippines."

He looked around the room, a serious and almost-apologetic expression on his face, and said, "I am sorry to tell you this, but Mindanao will be the worst place we have fought during this war. The geography is mean and cruel. The Jap defenses are extensive. There are 50,000 enemy combat troops firmly dug in on that island, mainly over here," he pointed to the lower right corner of the map, at the capitol city of Davao.

"It is the last stronghold of Japs in the Philippines. We will not let them stay there. Some of them are well-fed, like you are," he chuckled and looked around the room. We all laughed with him.

"And some of them are not. They may be hungry, sick, and poorly supported. But they will not surrender, as we have seen, and they will not stop until you kill them, or they kill you."

A wave of quiet moans and agreeing nods moved through the company.

"Like we did on New Guinea, and Leyte, and Mindoro, we will kill them all. Every last one of them."

Captain White looked across the roomful of faces, and saw a determined fire in their eyes, and a somber hatred for the enemy that lay ahead.

"Mindanao is the least explored island in the Philippines. Mountains. Jungles. Crocodile-infested rivers. Lakes. Swamps. Some valleys are full of cogon, a tall grass that is sometimes above a man's head. It is often red, and some call it Japanese bloodgrass. There are vast plantations of abaca, the plant that makes hemp – not the kind you smoke," he paused, raising his finger for effect, as laughter rippled through the company.

"No, men, this abaca is used for paper and rope fiber. It has thick stems, fifteen to twenty feet high, and the plants grow close together, like sugar cane along the Mississippi. A man has to fight with everything he has just to make it into, and through, each foot of that thicket. Visibility is less than ten feet. No breeze ever blows through the abaca, and the Japs will be waiting for us in that hell."

Pete grimaced and looked at me.

"I hate that shit. Sugar cane can go to hell," he uttered with a low snarl.

It surprised me that Pete would speak so disgustedly about anything on the earth.

*The ugliness of this war is getting under Pete's skin,* I said to myself.

Captain White continued, "And, other than the Nips, the people that live in the wild areas include the Mohammedan Moros, an old culture of sword-makers. They are proud, self-confidant fighters, but they are not trustworthy. They can be your friend one day, and lead you into an ambush the next day. There are also other island natives on Mindanao, like the aggressive people that live in trees, and the short, black natives that shoot poisoned darts from blow-tubes. Just like in the Tarzan movies," he chuckled again.

Laughter erupted among the men of M Company. We looked at each other with a smile and a bit of caution.

*That's funny, but not in the same jungle with us.*

"And there are apes, man-sized, that are covered with long hair."

Nobel suddenly turned to me and Pete, eyes wide open, and mouthed the words *I told you there might be a Kong!*

Pete and I half-grinned, and looked down to avoid his accusing glare. When we saw through the corner of our eyes that Nobel was no longer sneering at us, we looked back up to watch Captain White.

"So, stay on the alert," the Captain warned. "This war is about to become weird. On top of all that, some of these island natives are known to be interested in shrunken heads, scalps, and cannibalism."

There was another wave of sound through the men, this time more like a dreaded hiss.

"There are two roads in Mindanao, one that goes up and down from north to south, and another that goes across from west to east," he said as he pointed to the map.

"Neither one of them is good. Movement will not be easy. Again, most of the Jap defenses will be down here," moving the pointer again, "around Davao. We will NOT be landing there," he said emphatically.

"They expect us to land there, and they will be ready. But we will not attack them at their strongest point. Do not be afraid, men. We will sneak up on them like a thief in the night. You are dismissed, and may God bless every one of you."

He nodded, and walked out. The squads started forming and we began leaving the room. Nobel and I stood up slowly, trying not to notice the way the room was spinning in our heads. Around us, the men were shuffling their feet, looking down. Their thoughts, probably like mine, were on all we had been through, all who had died, and all who would surely die.

Pete went ahead of us to lead the way, and Tim walked behind us in case we got needy.

Nobel and I walked from chair to chair, hand over hand, never loosening our grip on something to stop the spinning.


Early morning, Tuesday, April 17, 1945.

Malabang, Mindanao, the Philippines.

On the fourth morning, we awoke early for the traditional steak and eggs breakfast. We did not know it at the time, but this would prove to be the last such ceremonial meal we would be served.

We could smell the steaks cooking from our sleeping area. For Nobel and me, the only thing about the smell that was half-welcoming was the fact that it meant we were leaving the boat soon. Steaks were waiting for us, and there were steaming hot cups of coffee at the end of the serving line.

A little piece of steak, a few eggs, and some bread. That's what Nobel and I ate. Pete was his usual self and started eating a fatty piece of steak as soon as he sat down. I took Pete's advice from an earlier time and put the steak between two pieces of bread, wrapped it in several napkins, and stuffed it in my pocket. Beach food. I said a prayer under my breath that the beach would not be deadly ground.

We gathered our combat gear, and formed up in the big central bay on the LST where the landing craft were positioned. We could hear the distant sounds of artillery. A beach somewhere out there was being prepared for the invasion. We began adjusting and tightening each other's packs and straps.

Through the dim light of dawn, we could see the beach in front of us, from inside the LST. It was a short beach, with what appeared to be small streams draining down from the swamp behind it. There was no activity, No bombardment. We looked at each other, with a simple question on our minds: *Is there no resistance on our beach? Will this be like the Panaon Strait?*

We boarded our landing craft. As we bobbed up and down on our approach to the beach, every soldier in the landing craft was relaxed, a half-smile on each face. *No weapons fire. No explosions. No enemy on the beach?*

Fifty feet from the beach, the bow ramp fell open.

Nothing was happening on the beach.

"Let's go! Let's go!" the platoon sergeant commanded.

We splashed into foot-deep water, jumped into the sand, ran forward, and fell to the ground, our rifles pointed inland.

"At ease! Remain in position and DO NOT FIRE until ordered to do so," the platoon sergeant bellowed.

We pushed our helmets back on our forehead, and looked at each other,

*Piece of cake! We got this beach without a shot being fired!*

"Listen up!" shouted Captain White, as he walked up the beach from his landing craft.

"There are no Japs on this beach! This area has been secured by the Filipino guerillas, just as we were told yesterday. The rest of the Division hit the beach like a thunderbolt twenty miles behind us at Parang. You, however, are no thunderbolt. You are on the quiet beaches of Malabang, just to make sure we understood the Filipinos correctly. Welcome to the safest part of Mindanao that you will see this day."

He looked left and right, then chuckled.

"We do have an island to invade, though, and an enemy to engage. We will move a hundred yards to our left, out of the way, and remain there for a short time while our gear and equipment are off-loaded. Then, we will begin a patrol southward to the Division landing zone and join with them at Parang."

We moved our position north along the beach, and watched as our light artillery, jeeps, combat engineering trucks, tractors, and tanks rolled out of the LSTs and began to resemble a loaded convoy. A group of Filipino volunteers joined the off-loading crews, and helped carry equipment from the staging area to the proper trucks.

I reached inside my knapsack and removed my steak sandwich. Nibbling at it, Pete looked at me and said, "Smart man."

By 0930, most of the 3rd Battalion had begun to move south along a muddy dirt road that led from the beachhead to Polloc Harbor, and the town of Parang. The road had seen better days, and was getting worse as each company moved out. Two M-4 Sherman tanks led each company, with trucks, jeeps, and the infantry following closely behind. Further behind, an engineering squad with a D7 combat bulldozer scraped the road to keep it crossable for the next group. We could smell the mud and stagnant water from the road ahead of us, mixed with the stench of vehicle exhaust and sweat.

Before we started forming up for our place in the convoy, Captain White walked toward us from the makeshift Command Post at the beachhead. He motioned for us to form up in a tight circle.

"Men, I want you to know that we have completely surprised the Japanese today. We are going to attack the city of Davao from the northwest. Like I said earlier, they expect us to attack Davao from the southeast, on more convenient beaches with better roads. However, we know that they have enormous artillery and defenses along those roads that lead from the beaches to the city. Every one of those defensive positions are dug in, with cement and steel. And here's the part that's gonna make you boys feel good, really good. They can't shoot at us while we're attacking from the rear, because all the big guns are facing the WRONG WAY."

He gave a hearty laugh. The rest of us, when we thought about it a few seconds, nodded our heads and smiled broadly. An enthusiastic laugh circulated through the ranks.

"Now, men, since we have surprised them, we can't let them re-form and replace their artillery. We are gonna be traveling that shit-hole road over there," pointing to our left, where the muddy road with the tanks, men, and trucks were moving out, "and we'll be in a forced march for the next two weeks. We must go the 150 miles to Davao as fast as we possibly can, and we will be at quick time, maybe even double-time, as much as possible. The Japs will probably see us staring down their asses, and they will probably high tail it into the jungles and mountains. They will be unorganized and confused, and I suspect the next couple of months we will be tracking the bastards down and killing them handful by handful. Once they're in their jungle hiding places and spider-holes, we'll probably be seeing the *banzai* raids again, over and over again, every night. That's the only fight that's left in them. They'll be raiding villages, killing civilians, raping women, and other despicable things on their way to Hell."

He took a deep breath, surveyed our position on the beach, shook his head, and continued. He was working himself up to his finale.

"This quiet beach is the best it will be until we've stripped this island of every stinking one of them. I pray that we will PUSH them, SHOVE them, BAYONET them, and KILL them until there is NOTHING LEFT OF THEIR DAMN ARMY TO SURRENDER! LET'S MAKE THIS WAR END HERE, M COMPANY, RIGHT HERE ON MINDANAO!" he said loudly.

I couldn't help myself. My mouth opened and a loud, throaty "Yes, Sir!" came roaring out. Tim and Pete looked at me, then jerked their heads to the front and yelled "Yes, Sir!" in perfect cadence. A second later, I believe every soldier in M Company had thrown a "Yes, Sir!" at Captain White at the top of their lungs.

He smiled proudly, raised his fist into the air, pumped it three times up-down-up-down-up-down, and swiftly flattened his fist to a snappy salute, then turned and walked back to the CP. We were more proud of him that day than we had ever been. We would have followed him to Hell and back, never fearing. We loved our Captain White.

We didn't know it, but he WAS leading us straight into Hell, and not all of us were coming back. But we ENDED THAT WAR RIGHT THERE ON MINDANAO, just like he said. There would be a lot of reasons for the end of the war, a lot of Generals would be congratulated for their decisions, and a lot of soldiers would receive awards for their bravery.

I believe to this day that our reason for the end of the war was none of those. It was Captain White.


Three Hours Later.

On the Trail to Parang, Mindanao, Philippines.

The chain of tanks, men, and trucks moved down the jungle road like a lethal snake, armed with 75-mm rounds, .50-cal machine-guns, explosives, flame throwers, .30-cal M1s, grenades, mortars, rockets, and the pent-up testosterone of a thousand embattled men. To the serpent's right lay the undulating blue sea across which it had slithered from beach-to-beach the past twelve months. To the serpent's left, the dark evil jungle lurked, giving way to green deadly mountain ridges in the distance. Death and Triumph lay ahead, as the fortified snake with the bright "V" sequined across its back double-timed along its determined way.

Shortly after the 3rd Battalion began its advance from Malabang, B Company and several rifle squads from C Company peeled off and moved south of the city to secure an airfield.

As we approached the town of Parang, a lone figure stood along the left side of the muddy road, perched on top of a sandy roadcut. It was a dark-skinned, lean, muscular woman, wearing a ragged brown dress, with a matching ragged brown pull-over shirt. Her hair was long, frizzy, and tied into an abundantly shaggy ponytail. She was holding an old American Enfield rifle. As she watched the tanks and trucks passing by with the 24th Division's code letter "V" painted on them, she raised two fingers of her right hand. She smiled broadly, showing her brown teeth and the spaces-in-between, and said with a coarse, gritty voice, "Welcome – Victoree! Welcome - Victoree!"

We smiled at her and raised our two fingers in the same victory symbol.

"Victory, victory," we repeated.

"Heavenly Days! Ain't she something!" I said.

"I bet she can hit you at a hundred yards with that Enfield rifle," Nobel snickered.

Pete grinned and said, "I believe many a Jap has been charmed to death by that Medusa."

Tim laughed, along with several men behind him.

Nobel and I didn't understand what Pete had said, so we just kept grinning.

We waded across three swampy rivers on our way to Parang. When we reached the town, we found it to be deserted and nearly demolished. Every bridge in the town had been destroyed. The cruelty of the Japanese occupation, followed by the bombardment and invasion by the Americans, had driven the town's Filipinos into the mountains.

By the end of that first day, the Division had secured the town of Parang, three airfields, and a 35-mile stretch of coast.

We bivouacked on the south side of town, on the bank of the Simuay River.

No Japanese were encountered that day, and none were seen after dark.

The combat engineers worked all night building new bridges.

Still, even without the Japanese resistance, we managed to suffer two casualties that first night on Mindanao.

A new, combat-virgin replacement crept out of his foxhole to pee. A soldier in an adjacent foxhole saw movement in the dark, raised his rifle, aimed, and shot him dead. Along a dark perimeter, a soldier on guard duty was peering into the blackness and heard, or thought he heard, a noise in some nearby trees. He chucked a grenade into the trees. The grenade hit a palm tree, and bounced back into his foxhole. It exploded, killing him instantly.

These two horrible mistakes in the disorder of war showed all of us the heightened danger that existed even in the most necessary and mundane of actions, from simply taking a pee to throwing a grenade toward a sinister noise. We all took note that the friendliest of fire will kill you just as dead as the fiendish pop from a Japanese Arisaka rifle. One err in judgement, one misstep, one wrong calculation, and a body is dispatched to the grave.


Wednesday, April 18, 1945.

Along the Fort Pikit to Kabacan Road, Mindanao, the Philippines.

  We began our rapid march through the jungle at dawn, in a steady, warm rain. We crossed the Simuay River on foot, in water up to our waists, holding our rifles and our gear well above our heads. As we slowly traversed the muddy, wild river, our eyes darted back and forth, from left to right and then again, remembering what Captain White had said about "crocodile-infested rivers."
  The gentle sound of the rain dripping from the canopy of the forest was accompanied by the splish-splashes of our footsteps on the muddy, worn road. The familiar feel of wet trousers and wet boots fell upon us like a dingy, wet blanket, making our burdens heavier and our gait more uncertain. Men would occasionally slip and fall, with a curse and a splash. Their buddies would help them up, and the men would wipe the mud and decayed vegetation off them with a string of obscenities and disgust.
  At Fort Pikit, we reached the Mindanao River, flowing briskly down from the highlands to our left. The

bridge had been destroyed, and the combat engineers were hard at work constructing a new one. The Fort, undefended, was immediately secured by our troops.

That evening, as we were cleaning our rifles, Tim looked up and said. "Hey, I want to tell you a story I heard today from a fellow in L Company."

We all nodded, put the lid on the rifle cleaner can, and looked at him.

"Sure," Nobel answered.

"I'm ready for a good story."

"Well, this is not to be repeated, you know," Tim replied.

"Although, everybody knows it over there, but still…."

"Yeah, yeah," Nobel assured him, "We'll won't broadcast it. Come on, tell us the story."

"Well, John was telling me, he's a rifleman from Dakota, when we landed on Mindoro a medic came over to his squad and asked if there was anyone there who didn't drink. So, somebody pointed at John and said that he didn't drink. The medic walked over to John and said he was assigning him a jug of whiskey."

Pete raised his head and declared, "That's a good assignment. What for?"

Tim nodded and answered, "The medic said it was to use when someone in the squad was in shock and no medic was around. So, John carried the whiskey. He said he didn't want to carry it, but he didn't have a choice. He said there was a sergeant in the squad who was a drinker, and he did everything he could to get his hands on that whiskey."

"Well, one night the sergeant must've found someone with liquor, and he got drunk as a skunk. So, a lieutenant came up to John and told him to go get the sergeant's rifle. The lieutenant said every time the sergeant got drunk he would try to shoot him."

Tim snickered, and we all joined in a giggle.

"They found the sergeant drunk a couple hundred feet away, and they had to carry him back to their area on a stretcher. John said he remembered the sergeant telling everyone, 'Well this is embarrassing, ain't it.' Then John said as soon as the sergeant got back to his tent he asked him where his rifle was. John asked him how could he know? He told the sergeant it wasn't his job to keep up with his rifle. That's when the sergeant told John he needed his rifle really bad because he was going to shoot the lieutenant!"

We all laughed as Tim said that.

"Your friend John saved that louey's life. And you helped," I said.

"That was a swell story," Nobel said.

"I wonder how many times all over this outfit that story didn't happen, and the louey went down?"

Three Days Later

Building the bridge across the Mindanao River took longer than expected. Rains in the mountains would often cause the water to rise quickly and flow violently down into the wide river, delaying the construction.

Landing craft from an offshore Navy assault ship were sent up the deep river to ferry us across. Afterward, several companies of the 2nd Battalion remained on the landing craft and made an amphibious drive up the Mindanao River to secure the upstream villages and towns. It was an unusual sight, watching the same landing craft that had dumped our huddled soldiers onto the beach now carrying standing soldiers up the river, disappearing into the rainforest at the first bend.

On the other side of the river, we bivouacked. The rain was no longer falling.

Later that evening, members of the 2nd Battalion returned to our bivouac from the amphibious drive and reported that they had seen "no Japs, just crocodiles."

We stayed there for two more days to allow men of the 34th Infantry, which had been the floating reserve, to join us from their landing near Parang.


Tuesday, April 24, 1945.

On the Road to Davao.

It was not raining when we left our bivouac and surged inland toward the Japanese stronghold at Davao. The road across the mountain passes had been unused for quite a while. It twisted with switchbacks through ravines, jungles, cliffs, and streambeds entangled with tall grass, high enough to cover the tanks and trucks. As the sun seemed to burst into flames, the hint of a breeze could not be found.

Through the day, heat exhaustion began to punch holes in our lines in a hundred places.

We met with a group of Filipino guerillas near Matalam, and they told us where to expect Japanese ambushes, and warned us that the enemy had placed mines in the road we were traveling. For a few miles, they walked in front of us, helping our mine detector squad recognize and de-activate them. Throughout our march into Davao, the Filipino guerillas were organized and very strong.

Our march continued all day, from dawn to dusk. We bivouacked at dark, after the forward patrols had cleared the area and confirmed that no enemy was near. We set up booby traps of wires, bells, and small explosives around our perimeter to warn us if any were creeping around.

That night, we were waiting for C-Rations to be delivered. Our supply lines were often spread thin and long, and rations were often delivered late in the day. Soldiers in foxholes all along our perimeter line were alerting the others about giant, whistling man-sized monkeys setting off the booby traps. We could hear the bells and explosives, and didn't want to believe the stories about the giant monkeys.

"I tell you, guys, there's things out there nobody knows about," Nobel announced, his eyes so open they were almost glowing.

Pete reassured him, "Those boys out there on the perimeter are scared half-out of their wits. I think those stupid monkeys are Nips, blowing themselves up by accident and alerting us to their whereabouts."

The whistles and bells and small explosions from the booby traps went on for hours. When the ration delivery personnel finally arrived at the perimeter, they reported to the Sergeant of the Guard, and began apologizing for being so late. They said they had been held up by what appeared to be "Japs all camouflaged with fur coats."

"No, those were not Japs," said the Sergeant.

"Those were apes. They are apes out there, everywhere."

When the word about the real, living apes got to us by foxhole scuttlebutt, we were happy to hear what was causing the ruckus. Nobel continued to be a little skeptical.

He said again, "I tell you, guys, there's things out there nobody knows about."

During the night, a light rain began to fall, lasting only an hour or two.

The next day, we were up at dawn and resumed our march, as the light rain began again. As we marched across the Mindanao River valley, we ran upon many small Japanese detachments. Immediately, they would flee into the jungle as we fired our weapons at them. Most of them would make it back into the jungle, to be safely hidden in the deep, thick underbrush. We soon learned they would sleep all day, then organize into small bands for *banzai* raids after dark.

During the raids, they would wear netting on their upper bodies, fitted with leafy branches and twigs. Creeping slowly up to our perimeter, they could not be recognized from the underbrush. Once they were within ten feet of the Americans, they would jump to their feet, crying *"Banzai! You die!"*

That night, though, the raids did not begin with them yelling *"Banzai!"* Instead, the Japanese attackers were dreadfully quiet, and the raid happened so soundlessly that two of our soldiers were bayoneted before our rifles could begin firing.

It had rained all day and into the night.

Thursday, April 26, 1945.

On the Road to Davao, Mindanao, the Philippines.

    At dawn, we resumed our march to Davao. M Company trudged along the muddy road on the tenth day of the forced march. Our faces were haggard, and our uniforms were dark with rain and sweat. We felt the weight of our packs, heavy with ammunition, food, and an extra canteen. Our rifle muzzles were pointed at the wall of jungle that enclosed us from both sides of the road.
    Our scouts on either side signaled a warning, hearing vegetation being crunched behind the green wall. We all fell to the ground, finding shelter behind tall grass, clumps of bushes, or fallen trees. Tim and I were laying behind a fallen tree, all our senses and both our rifles pointed toward the crunching sound going on in the thickets behind the green wall of jungle.
    Suddenly, out of the forest emerged a skinny, brown, barefooted woman. Circling around her like baby ducklings around their mother were five skinny children. Their legs were all covered with sores. As she walked into the muddy road, the woman looked up and down the empty road, and at the rifle muzzles behind the tall grass, bushes, and fallen trees in the roadside ditches.
    The woman said with a calm, strong-minded voice, "Don't kill. Only medicines I want."
    Every tense soldier along the road relaxed. Tim and I lowered our rifles and smiled.
    "Just a poor mother with a brood of kids, wanting medicine for the damn jungle-rot," I told Tim.
    Tim nodded, "There's prob'ly a thousand more where she came from."

Pete, laying alongside Tim, lamented, "Poor civilians caught up in this war. Forced to retreat into that jungle, that damn killing jungle, where people die of rot, disease, and starvation."

We all rested there as we watched the medic treat the jungle-rot by painting the medicine on the kids, staining their brown, skinny legs to a dark shade of purple. He handed the bottle to the mother, whose broad smile displayed a set of brown teeth. She shuffled her brood of ducklings back into the green wall of jungle.

As we travelled further south, the mountains and jungles gave way to a wide central valley. The rain had stopped. In front of us lay large expanses of kunai grass, palm plantations that had been unkept for years, weedy banana groves, and abaca fields denser than any jungle could be.

Near the village of Lomopog, we were ambushed by what appeared to be fifty-to-a-hundred Japanese soldiers. Our firepower soon overcame their weak resistance, and we killed twenty of them. The rest of them evaporated back into the jungle. Canoe patrols in the estuary of the Mindanao River killed two more.

The Japanese killed two of our soldiers that day, and wounded five.

Advancing further into the central valley, we were overcome with immense swarms of locusts. Marching through the whizzing insect masses, we approached a bridge spanning a river that was not on our map. The bridge seemed intact. For a moment, we were excited to just see a bridge, a darn bridge crossing a small river. A split second later, the enemy blew it up right there in front of us. We saw one laughing Jap disappear into the jungle before we could fire a shot at him.

So, we had to ford the shallow river, carrying our rifles and gear well above our heads. Reaching the other side, we had that familiar wretched feeling of being totally wet again, and many of us left the river crossing with leeches on our arms, legs, and outer clothing. We had a full-scale leech-removal, buddy-by-buddy. The medic circulated through the men daubing medication on each spot where a leech had attached itself to the soldier's body.

We continued on down the road. A detachment of combat engineers remained to reconstruct the bridge.

We began to see the Japanese fortifications that had been placed along the road, each one cunningly hidden along curves in the road or along high points in the road's path. But the fortifications were useless to them. The enemy artillery along the fire lanes all pointed east, toward Davao. It was obvious they expected us to be coming from the east, not the west. We really had caught them by surprise, just like Captain White said!

We could see the Japanese soldiers abandoning their gun emplacements and fleeing into the hills each time we advanced toward them. They left behind burning bridges, barracks, supply dumps, and trucks.

As we maintained our rapid march, we encountered a group of civilians leaving Davao. Among them was a mother with six children. She remained along the side of the road, and by the time we passed her, she begged with a pathetically fearful voice, "Americans, after you kill me, please care of my children."

A supply sergeant standing in an open truck reached down and lifted a case of C-Rations.

He said, "We're not going to kill you, lady. We only kill Japs."

Tossing the crate onto the ground near her, he continued, "Here. You'd better take these rations. Your kids look hungry."

We continued on, and encountered two small rivers, each with impassable bridges. Wading across them, we met bitter Japanese machine-gun and mortar resistance on the other side. Our tanks blasted away at them. We set up our own machine-guns and mortars, and returned their fire with a blistering reprisal. The ambush dissolved back into the green wilderness. Both water crossings were the same. Wade across, receive fire, fight back, enemy disappears.

We bivouacked near a third river. Combat engineers began constructing a bridge. Two rifle squads protected them, inspecting the jungle in all directions. The bridge was completed before midnight. The rain began to fall, heavy at first, then drizzled all night.

All through the late night, *banzai* raids robbed us of sleep. Wave after wave, at least five times, they screamed and ran amuck, brandishing bayonets and tossing grenades. There was no doubt that these were the same men that had ambushed us earlier, at the river crossings. After disappearing into the jungle, they reformed in small groups and hit by dark of night.

The raids were short and fierce, with decreasingly smaller and smaller bands of screaming men, fighting to the death of some, and retreating to reform what was left, and attack again. Toward the end of one raid, I saw a lone

Japanese soldier frantically grab a half-empty C-Rations crate and dash into the darkness.

*You can't blame a guy for grabbing a meal,* I thought to myself.

*Somebody will kill him tomorrow. He's having his death-row meal tonight.*

Nobel and I, hunkered down in our deep, wet foxhole, alternated the watch in one-hour fragments, getting what precious sleep we could as often as possible. We didn't say much, other than the usual "how'ya doing?" and "I sure don't like it here."

Friday, April 27, 1945.

Near Digos Town, Mindanao, the Philippines.

We awoke at dawn near the town of Digos, not far from the Gulf of Davao. The gray light of dawn dimly illuminated the battlefield, where three *banzai* raids had afforded the men of the Victory Division very little sleep. There was no rain.

In a roadside foxhole near Nobel and me, one soldier addressed his buddy.

"Hey, look at that Jap I shot last night, over there, to your left."

His buddy looked over the top of the foxhole.

"Damn," he said. "You shot two."

"No, I only shot one."

"Well, moron, there's two dead Nips lying out there."

Quickly, the first soldier replied, "Then one of them's alive."

He raised his rifle. A very-much-alive Japanese soldier suddenly jumped to his feet and ran toward the foxhole with a grenade.

The soldier pinged two rounds.

"Alright," he announced.

"Like you said, there's two dead Nips lying out there."

Nobel turned to me, smiled sarcastically, and said, "All the more reason to keep an accurate count of the Japs you killed during the night and compare it to how many are on the ground when the sun comes up."

I shrugged my shoulders.

After our C-Ration breakfast, we gathered in a group and Captain White briefed us on the day's expectations.

"At ease, men. As we get closer and closer to Davao, we get closer and closer to the Jap defenders of this nasty island. Keep your eyes open and your ears tuned. They will not leave easy, and they want you to not leave at all. We will plant them in this ground, not the other way around. Watch your buddy and yourself as we reach Digos Town, it will begin to get tough there. I know you will finish the job. You are the toughest men this Army has."

We formed up, and again became part of the fortified snake, armed to the hilt, with the bright "V" sequined across its back, slithering its way at double-time toward Davao.

At noon, we stopped our march for a quick meal and a brief rest. With Tim to my left and Pete to my right, we all leaned against the sandy roadcut, giving our aching backs some relief. Roadside guards and sharpshooters with rifles, loaded and ready-to-fire, paced up and down the roadcut, peering into the jungle, intently studying every tree and bush as we troops on the ground focused on nothing except what was in our own hands. I was tearing my C-Ration box open, Tim was saying something about chocolates, when suddenly a POP! and a ZIP! followed by a BLAST! of soil particles exploded on my left, with a million piercing pricks jabbing the left side of my face, my left ear going completely soundless, with only the echoes of the ZIP! bouncing through my ear canal, leaping around in my brain.

I fell to my right onto Pete, away from the blast. He grabbed me with a strong grip, pulling me closer to him, his own C-Rations box spilling onto the road.

Holding my left hand up to my left ear, I thought of Tim and instantly glanced to my left, toward him.

Tim had fallen to his left onto Nobel, away from the blast. Nobel had covered Tim with his own body, protecting him. Tim's right hand was over his right ear, his eyes were clinched shut.

In an instant, faster than a heartbeat, I knew that a sniper's bullet had missed us both. In that instant of time, I saw one of the most beautiful sights of my life: the silhouette of a sharpshooter, his rifle tight against his shoulder in the classic standing position, aiming and firing a burst at the muzzle-blast he had just seen in a distant tree. The tree branches moved, limbs began to bend, and the body of a Japanese sniper, clad only in trousers, fell with a rope tied to one of his legs. His body jerked as the rope tightened, and his fall ended less than ten feet above the ground.

We were ordered to "Hit the deck!" and I could see many more sharpshooter silhouettes roaming the road.

I looked at Tim, and he was looking me, his face ashen with fear. I nodded my head at him and smiled. He smiled back.

I could hear my colored friend from Leyte, his calm voice talking to me in my soundless left ear.

*"You WILL survive this war, Horace."*

"Okay, thank you," I mumbled weakly.

A medic was at my side, his mouth asking me something that looked like "Are you OK?"

I pointed at my left ear.

"I can't hear nothing from this ear," I said loudly.

On my right, Pete was talking to him, explaining that we had narrowly missed being killed by a sniper.

"That one out there, hanging from that tree," he pointed as he told the medic.

He then pointed at Tim, and told the medic to check him out, too.

Tim and I slept at the medic tent that night, with ear drops and cotton in our ears, and a couple of pills to stop the world from spinning. I think we were there for two days and two nights.

The medic gave us a box of cotton balls and a bottle of ear drops when he sent us back to combat.


Pre-Dawn, Monday, April 30, 1945

Davao City, Mindanao, the Philippines.

We had just broken up a *banzai* attack about 0400, and all was quiet again. Nobel's rifle had jammed toward the end of the attack, so he cleaned it and reloaded. Then he stood up, dipped the muzzle a little bit to the ground, and fired three shots to see if it worked all right. A squeal followed the burst. Nobel had shot a sneaking Japanese soldier by accident! An hour later, he started moaning. So, Nobel gave him another burst to silence him.

Dawn arrived and a light rain began to fall. Soldiers were stirring in every foxhole, gathering their gear together and tearing into C-Rations. Small inconsequential conversations sprinkled across the dimly lit battlefield.

"Look fellows, this one's a dud," said a corporal in the foxhole beyond ours. He held up a Japanese mortar shell that had landed in his foxhole. After a careful inspection he tossed the shell out of his hole. There was an instant explosion. He was stunned and half buried. Slowly he raised himself to his hands and knees.

"Somebody's got to be wrong once in a while," he muttered.

We moved out in the rain. Our job that morning was to seize the two airstrips at Daliao and Talomo. It took a lot of firepower, plus mortars, and howitzers from DIVARTY (Division Artillery) to shake the airstrips loose from the Japanese Army.

All the top brass had told us there were lots of Japanese soldiers in the Davao area, and we could say they were right. They were everywhere, hunkered in houses, in farms, in pits, and in trees. We put withering machine-gun fire on them, some would run north to the mountains, and some would fall limply to the ground. We pried those airfields out of their hands all day and into the night. We did not exactly bivouac, we just dug in where we were, our mortar emplacement a few feet in front of our 4-man foxhole. The ammo bearers dug in behind us, and kept us fully armed through the night.

      The fight slowed after midnight, and reformed as *banzai* raids.

      Tim and I could hear everything from one ear, and little or nothing from the other. We had to put carbon black from our weapons on the cotton in our messed-up ears. Otherwise, the creeping, sneaking attackers that often got to within ten feet of us would see the white cotton in our ears, and the rest would be history.

      The night was long and fierce.

      But the rain had ended.


Tuesday, May 1, 1945

Talomo, North of Davao City, Mindanao, the Philippines

      It was midmorning before the airfields were declared secure. We were replaced by infantrymen of the 41$^{st}$ Division, as we moved further into the hills northwest of Davao to engage the enemy, who was retreating to the high ground to make a final stand.

      I was pulled out of Nobel's mortar squad to help drive a convoy of jeeps going to a beachhead south of the city, along Davao Gulf. Tons of ammo and rations were stacking up on the beach, and were sorely needed at the front lines.

      By this time, though, everyplace a G.I. was fighting was the front line. We were always, at the same time, ahead of the Japanese and behind them. Front Line, rear line, it didn't matter. Disorganized Japanese troops were everywhere, with bayonets and swords. Grenades and mines. Or just knives. It was not uncommon to even find yourself locked in a fist fight with the enemy.

I drove toward the beachhead with a quiet, young soldier in the passenger seat. Our jeep was the last one in the convoy. Unexpectedly, a Jap leapt out of the bushes and tossed a mine under the vehicle, on the passenger side. The mine exploded and the jeep rose into the air. It was wrecked. I was thrown from the jeep. My companion from the 1st Battalion was badly hurt. I was dazed. The Jap that had tossed the mine was now running toward me, with a rifle that was empty, without a clip. I regained my wits in time to shoot the Nip five times with my pistol. Even so, he was still on his feet and kept coming toward me. While still running, he drew a razor from his shirt pocket and slashed his own throat.

For a second I stared in disbelief.

*The crazy fool killed himself rather than be killed by me.*

*What kind of enemy is this?*

I crawled, with every bone in me wailing with pain, around the badly damaged jeep, to my companion. He was dead.

I examined myself for injuries. Nothing. Except for a grass-burn on my elbow, I did not have a scratch.

I looked around.

Small crater in the road.

Wrecked jeep.

Dead passenger.

*"You WILL survive this war, Horace."*

"Yes, thank you, my friend," I said out loud.

"Now, please help me make it back to safety."

I scrutinized the area around me for any landmarks or bearings.

Nothing.

Just the road and the heartless jungle. No other jeeps. I reached down and took the dead man's dog tags from his twisted neck.

*God bless you, young man,* I prayed.
*May you live with Christ forever.*
*I never even asked your name.*
*Forgive me, buddy.*

The other drivers must have left me for dead. I crawled around for a while, my body aching, but nothing broken. I found a thick ragged row of bushes and wiggled inside.

All I could see were Japanese soldiers slithering through the bushes. It was very dark by now.

*Better be still*, I thought.

*If you move around you will be shot for sure, by your buddies or by the Japs.*

I saw tracer-rounds buzzing by. Sometimes one of them would smash into a tree trunk and ignite for a second, looking like a yellow-and-blue flower. Japanese soldiers were yelling to each other, somewhere in the dark. Grenades exploded all around me.

I was in the middle of a battleground, between the good guys and the bad guys.

A thunderstorm came up and the rain came pouring down like a warm, solid cascade. Mortar shells started falling from the sky. They would strike the treetops and burst. The red-hot shrapnel screeched down into the jungle like hellfire.

I could tell by their shriek they were our own mortar shells. No duds. Not one. Our mortars were shelling the Japanese position.

Mortar shells don't know the difference between an American and the enemy, so I crawled out of the thicket and dived between two rocks. My kneecap silently moaned. An explosion threw a bucket-full of mud into my face. I continued to move. I kept creeping and crawling in and out of foxholes that were full of water, lingering for a few moments just to be hidden. I slithered into one, and felt the arms of a dead soldier, as if he were reaching out for me.

*Hello there, please keep me company through the long, dead night.*

The worst of my worstest nightmares erupted in my brain that instant, and I clambered out of the foxhole just as a deafening blast rolled across the ghastly landscape.

Finally, I got out of artillery range.

I crawled into the underbrush for cover, and to rest. Lightning crashed into the jungle. The rain and lightning lasted all night long. I tried very hard to keep my M1 dry and ready to fire. Japanese patrols passed by me in groups of five or six, as silent as death angels.

The night was long, as if dawn would never, ever come. I could feel the malarial fever wrap its cold-hot fingers around me, bringing on the shivers.

I prayed again.

*Lord, don't let this take me.*

*Please, don't let my shivers tell the Japs where I am.*

From across the short killing ground between me and them, I heard my friend again.

*I am here with you, Horace. Be still.*

I started to tell him, *"Quiet, man! The Japs may hear you!"*

Then I smiled.

They can't hear him. Just me.

I drifted off to a quiet sleep.

I awakened to a dim light, just enough to tell me it wouldn't be long til dawn broke. I wriggled out on a trail. I was able to stand. I looked for footprints. The rain had wiped them all away. I staggered through the jungle until I saw a wire.

It was a US wire!

I tracked the wire to the 19th Infantry CP. A corporal saw me stagger out of the green wall of jungle from fifty yards away, and told a guard to go see about that "muddy-looking soldier over there," as he pointed at me.

As soon as the guard approached me, he could tell I was harmless.

"Come with me," he said, reaching out his arm, keeping the other arm firmly attached to his M1.

"Thank you. What is your name?" I asked.

"My name is PFC Strickland. Why do you ask?"

"The last fellow I was with died. I never knew his name. But, it's on his dog tags, here," as I reached to unbutton my shirt pocket.

"It was really rough out there last night," I mumbled.

He took me to the corporal outside the CP tent, who looked at me curiously, then sympathetically,

"Are you with the 21st?" he asked.

"Yes," as I fell weakly to my knees. I kissed the stinking, muddy ground, and tasted the putrid, sweet essence of safety.

They helped me stand back up, and led me into the tent to a chair. The corporal handed me a cup of hot, beautiful coffee.

I took a sip, whispered *"Oh, that's good!"* and looked back up at the corporal.

I put my coffee on the table next to me.

"What's your name?" I asked.

Before he could answer, I passed out.

Wednesday, May 2, 1945

Near Davao, Mindanao, the Philippines.

I woke up sitting in the front seat of an ambulance. There were wounded soldiers in the ambulance and two medics worked over them. The door was open. Outside, I heard some fellows talking. Just then, a young blonde kid came running up. His face was muddy. He was very excited.

"The Old Man got it on the radio," he said. "Hitler is dead! We took Berlin!"

Everybody stopped talking. Nobody asked a question. Nobody said a word. Nobody smiled.

Only one of the wounded fellows tossed around and moaned a little bit. Artillery was busy over Davao, from the Japanese and from us. The flashes covered the mountaintops like a hideous, pulsating veil. The sound of machine-gun fire rolled over the hills like mechanical laughter.

An officer asked me questions about the day before.

"Do you remember where you were?"

"Out there, about a mile or so."

"How many Japs did you see?"

"Too many for me. Two or three dozen, I guess."

"What were they doing?"

"Fighting with you."

"Where were they going?"

"They were going nowhere."

I was driven back to the 3$^{rd}$ Battalion. When I saw Pete, Nobel, and Tim, I don't know who was the happiest to see who, them or me. We all four leaned together, reunited, and all was right again.

I got back just in time to move out.

On the outskirts of Davao, we found a shack. Rather, it looked like something that used to be a shack. We fired a round of bullets into it just to make sure. As we got closer, we saw that it was a machine-gun pillbox. We quickly hit the ground, but not fast enough. Three of our men were hit.

*Crap! That happens fast! One moment you're walking and the next moment you're dead!*

We burned the enemy out of the pillbox with a flamethrower. Five or six came out, running away, flames curling from their backs.

We were glad to see it. But it still made me feel a little sorry for them.

We continued southward, toward the center of the city.


Two Hours Later

We swarmed into Davao over a hastily constructed footbridge, upstream on the wide Davao River. Our battalions flooded into Davao City, surprising the Japanese. There was less opposition than we had anticipated. A good number of them had been destroying the city before they withdrew north to the hills.

It had taken only 15 days, in spite of the severe heat, humidity, and almost-constant rain, for the Division to travel 150 miles and take the last major Philippine city under Japanese control. Here, despite the two-week battle we had just endured, the real battle for Mindanao was beginning.

The 21st Regiment was sent to Mintal, five miles west of Davao, where we fought frantically for an airfield, with help from the Filipino guerillas. I heard the platoon leader tell Nobel it was the Libby Drome, the largest of Davao's airfields. We were hit on three sides by an enemy force larger than us. We were able to repel each attack. We pushed and we pushed, shoving the attackers further and further into the mountains. With each push, the organized resistance buckled, and was broken into small groups. We fought through airfield hangers and found safety in bomb craters. We chased the Japanese soldiers through heavy woods and dense jungle. We ran into thick, stifling abaca fields, where you couldn't see ten feet in front of you.

They moved deeper and deeper into the mountains, and we pursued them into the rough country north of ten thousand-foot Mount Apo as they ran for deep cover.

The shelling from DIVARTY preceded us the entire way, sometimes setting the abaca fields afire. Running through the unburning abaca, we could feel the wind being sucked into the fiery abaca, giving us a generous breeze. The heat, though, did not diminish.

 We fought all night and into the next day.

 We did not bivouac that night.

 We fought where we were, always moving forward.


Thursday, May 3, 1945.

Davao Province, Mindanao, the Philippines.

 The Japanese Army of Davao and the surrounding countryside fought with mindless arrogance, and with an absolute disdain for death. We found ourselves locked in the toughest, angriest, most grueling battle of the four islands we had taken.

 I heard many soldiers, enlisted men and officers, say that the whole of Mindanao was "as bad as Breakneck Ridge. And bigger."

 Davao was a desolate, destroyed city. Few buildings remained intact. Both Japanese and American bombs had rained on the island's largest and most important city for days. The strongest of the Japanese defenses were clustered around the Davao Gulf area, where they believed we would make our landing. There they still waited, and their disbelief that we had attacked them from the rear angered them, intensifying their strict devotion to honor and their utter contempt for death.

 Their belief that they would be attacked from the Davao Gulf convinced them the Americans would ultimately drive them northward from the city. Accordingly, they had constructed a semi-circle of strong defensive bunkers inland, so they could retire and regroup, prolonging the campaign as much as possible.

We bivouacked within the bombed-out ruins of a Spanish church on the outskirts of town, more to regroup and replenish our supplies than to rest.

During the night, the Japanese launched five successive *banzai* charges. It was a crazy, deadly night. They were carrying their light machine-guns, which we called 'woodpeckers,' bayonetted rifles, grenades, knives, and swords. Others had mines strapped to their bellies and some had dynamite fastened to their back, ready to die for their Emperor.

The Next Three Days.

Davao Province, Mindanao, the Philippines.

Day after day an overwhelming heat spilled down from sky and scourged the earth. Heat prostration weakened so many troops that companies sometimes had thirty or more soldiers unable to fight. Heavy rains fell every evening, and some nights up to six *banzai* raids haunted us in the dark.

Fighting progressed slowly, but we were making headway.

After the fall of Leyte and Mindoro, the Japanese soldiers of Mindanao were hopelessly cutoff from their native land. Their air force had been destroyed and their naval ships lay on the ocean floor. The airmen and seamen of Nippon were all fighting as infantrymen.

The most grueling part of the Davao combat was fighting in the abaca fields. The infantrymen battling in the Davao province said the word abaca meant "Hell." An endless number of acres were covered with these plants, and it was just as bad as Captain White had told us. The abaca was so thick that a man would have to fight with his whole body for each foot of progress. Not even the hint of a breeze could be found in the abaca, where the enemy waited in bunkers and lay in spider holes.

Monday, May 7, 1945.

Davao Province, Mindanao, the Philippines.

"Hey, guys! Germany just surrendered!"
Nobel was running back from his platoon meeting at the M Company CP, his arms waving and his high-pitch, anxious voice rolling across the landscape of foxholes.
We all dropped what we were doing – letter writing, weapons cleaning, shaving – and jumped around, laughing, clapping our hands, and congratulating each other.
"It's just the Nips now, and this Army ought to by-god take care of them!" Pete said loudly. Tim and I hugged each other.
"Christmas in Texas!" I said, as Tim nodded in approval.
"And in Alabama, for sure!" Nobel agreed, his eyes wide open in enthusiasm.

Pete pointed his finger at Nobel, and ordered, "And you get your ass down to Mobile and you rescue that girl. You hear me?"

Nobel nodded.

"I will, Pete."

His face slowly took on a more somber expression.

"Though, I do have some bad news."

We all looked at him, growing less happy by the second.

"What?"

"Captain White came down with appendicitis last night, and it's worse this morning. He's on his way to the beach right now. He'll be taken to the hospital ship." he said gloomily.

"He'll be ready for duty again in a month, if all goes right," Pete declared, cautiously.

We looked at each other, then to the ground, across the bivouac, then to Nobel again.

"Who's in charge now?" Tim nervously asked.

"Captain Morgan, from the 19th Regiment. They had too many captains, so we got one of them. Not the best," Nobel raised his finger to pause his sentence, "But he's been through some of the same rough action as us, maybe rougher, and he comes with high praise."

We were silent.

Pete moved the dirt around with his right shoe.

Tim looked at me to say something.

"They don't make them any better than Captain White. And that is the gospel truth. I'll just be assuming that Captain White is coming back and help us win this war, right here on Mindanao, like he said." I announced.

"As God is with us now, He'll be with us the rest of the way," Pete agreed.

"For now, we are an Army fighting one war," Tim added.

Nobel looked at each one of us, nodded his head, and said he could not have been given a better set of buddies than us, and that we would see it all the way through together, to the end.

*To the end of what?* I thought, but smiled anyway.

Nobel told us we would be heading out very early tomorrow, to a town called Talomo, just down the road.

"There is quite the skirmish going on along a railroad and along the Talomo River. They need us to break the stalemate," he said.


Tuesday, May 8, 1945.

On the Road to Talomo, Davao Province, Mindanao, the Philippines.

We formed up at dawn, and again became part of the fortified snake, armed to the hilt, with the bright "V" sequined across its back, slithering its way across the twisting roads of Davao Province toward Talomo.

We could hear the serpent's hiss as we rambled down from the uplands toward the valley of the Talomo River. The cadence of our muddy boots mixed with the spinning tires of the supply trucks and the metallic scraping of the Sherman tanks were composing a menacing symphony, a warning to the mud-covered Japanese at the end of the mucky road that Death was coming, and it was coming for them.

Back on the city squares and farm roads of America, street parties, dancing, and singing was the jamboree of the homeland. President Truman had proclaimed the Eighth of May as Victory in Europe Day. VE Day was a happy holiday for America, but the American soldiers of Mindanao were on the trail, riding the lethal serpent one more time, once more for our country, once more to eliminate the Imperial Army from its Pacific stockpile of stolen land, stolen lives, and stolen dreams.

For the next eight days, we experienced the worst, most deadliest combat we could have ever imagined. We unleashed more bombshells, more artillery blasts, more mortar rounds, more bullets, and more flame from the serpent's mouth than any army on earth could have sustained. Yet, every day, the Japanese soldiers opened their caves, pillboxes, and bunkers to inflict their searing fire on us, and every night they crept into our midst to perform their ghastly raids and invade our dreams with their nightmarish dance of *The Banzai.*

We seized the Talomo Railroad bridgehead, then lost it to the Japanese demolition crew.

We left Talomo to clear the region northeast, near Mintal, of disorganized Japanese looters and murderers.

We moved to the northwest, to counter Japanese attacks along the tracks of the critically important Talomo Railroad.

We made very slow progress clearing the remaining enemy troops along the nearby Talomo Trail.

In due time, The Talomo Railroad, the Talomo River valley, The Talomo Trail, and the town of Talomo were littered with enemy corpses.

And, through it all, there was always the abaca.

We lost more than soldiers in those killing fields.

We lost our friends and the last remnants of our youthful innocence.

Mid-Morning, Wednesday, May 16, 1945.

Near Talomo, Davao Province, Mindanao, the Philippines.

We stood at the edge of an abaca plantation. It had been abandoned for a year, and the plants were entwined and interlocked like a huge basket.

Nobel spat on the ground.

Pete put a toothpick in his mouth.

Tim picked up a small rock and threw it into the twisted, tangled heap of hemp.

I looked across the unwelcomed landscape and thought of home.

*Nothing, absolutely nothing in Texas is this ugly.*

"We believe there's about a dozen Japs in there, living in that shit," Nobel said, disgustingly.

"We've been ordered to leave our mortar gear in the truck and join up with a K Company rifle squad. It is up to us to send those damn Japs to the State of Death. They can't stay in there. Let's do it, here and now," Nobel told us.

"How in the hell did the Japs get in there in the first place?" asked Tim.

Pete looked at him, with a thin smile and a nod of his head. His toothpick moved up and down as he spoke.

"I believe they live there, Tim. That's been their home for a year."

I looked at Pete and shook my head in disbelief.

"If they can't come out, how can we get in?"

Pete shrugged his shoulders, then looked at Nobel.

"I don't have a good feeling about this," he warned.

Nobel looked at all of us, and back to Pete.

"Neither do I, Pete. We are mortarmen. But now, we are riflemen. The rifle team squad leader will tell us. He is Sergeant Willis, and I have watched him for the past year. He is brave, he is smart, and he is alive."

He looked at us.

"And, he is from Texas."

We smiled, and nodded.

"Many of his counterparts are no longer alive. I trust him. This is not his first abaca field."

*"But it may be the first one that looks this ragged,"* he muttered under his breath.

We met with Sergeant Willis and his squad a quarter mile up the road. He and Nobel shook hands, exchanged a few pleasantries, and turned to look at us.

"Sergeant Horner says you guys are the best he has seen. And, he says you're all three from Texas. That's good enough for me," Willis said.

We shook hands with him. We didn't say or ask anything until he was through talking.

"OK," he started. "We have less than a dozen Japs in this field, and they have been picking our guys off all morning. They killed one of us, and that's one too many. We could burn them out, but we think they have women and children from the village in there. We've heard a few voices and what sounded like babies crying in the field. So, we are going to spread out and start moving into the abaca. We think there are paths cut in the field, fifteen-to-twenty feet from the perimeter. Inside, they can run up and down the field as much as they want."

  He looked behind him, to his men.

  "I've got fifteen men, and your four make nineteen. Three of my men have BAR machine-guns. All of my people have twenty grenades each. You will have the same. Before we start, there are men on the other three sides of the field. They will toss four grenades each, as far as they can throw, to make the Japs think they are being approached from those directions. As soon as we hear the grenades, we will press forward, bayonets mounted."

  He nodded to us, we nodded back.

  "When we begin to enter, we will be twenty feet apart. That'll be most of the field. Be on the watch for the pathways. If they fire at you, hit the ground. Conceal yourself. We can tell by the sound of the round if it is them or you. And we will know the direction of fire.

  He clapped his hands together, and formed his men. We crammed more grenades into our pockets, belt, and knapsack.

  We lined up along the field. Our line was almost four-hundred feet long.

  We were to the left of center.

  Tim was on my left.

  Nobel was beyond him.

  Pete was to the left of Nobel.

We waited.

Grenades exploded to our left, ahead of us, and to our right.

We entered the abaca field, slowly.

Sergeant Willis was behind the center man, giving us hand signals.

We disappeared into the thick abaca.

I instantly felt the heat.

It pressed against my chest.

It was hard to breathe.

Stalks were touching me on both sides, and extended above my head.

I used the bayonet to make a thin, quiet path ahead of me to follow.

It was dark, like a green tomb.

Insects were buzzing and whizzing around as I moved on.

I concentrated so hard, I started to grind my teeth. I could hear nothing else but my own jaws grinding my own teeth.

*Stop it!*

*I need to hear what's out there!*

In the seemingly airless and measure-less abaca, time and distance developed unknown values.

*How far have we gone in?*

*Miles.*

*How long has it been?*

*Hours.*

I took another step.

And then another.

I slowly slid my bayonet forward again to push aside the stalks, and – there was no resistance!

I pulled quickly back in, and was motionless.

No sound.

Nothing.

I stepped forward a half-step, and stopped.

Nothing.

I stepped forward another half-step, and – I could see light!

There was a space in front of me, just beyond my reach.

I could hear nothing but the insects buzzing and whizzing.

A large red dragonfly zipped by my head, hovered for a moment, as if to say, *Wait, wait, not yet. Now! Go in!* and then swiftly flew away.

I brushed aside a few stalks.

Ahead was a clearing.

I stepped cautiously out of the abaca, my rifle ready.

Air poured into lungs.

The tomb had been unsealed, and a breeze was blowing down the straight clearing.

I could see nothing ahead of me but several hundred feet of purposely cut abaca, as wide as two men.

I was standing in a narrow path running to my right and my left, around the inner perimeter of the abaca.

I caught a sudden movement to my right and turned in that direction.

Sergeant Willis stood there, his palm outward for *STOP!*

There were more of his rifle squad beyond him, quiet and still as cemetery statues.

I slowly looked to my left as Tim materialized from the green, leafy wall like a magician.

Beyond him was Nobel.

Beyond Nobel was Pete.

Other men were emerging, and stopping with their rifles in forward, assault positions like bronze military heroes on a town square.

Sergeant Willis motioned for everyone to proceed.

I saw infantrymen on my right and on my left creep silently into clearings the same as mine.

Tim walked at my side, Nobel and Pete followed us.

Each step was a lifetime of uncertainty.

All that was in our world now was just the four of us, and several hundred feet of a narrowly cut path through a corridor of unknown demons.

We could hear our counterparts stealthily moving on either side of us.

Tim touched my arm, and pointed ahead, to our right.

There was an indention in the path, a room-like opening.

We stopped and listened.

We heard breathing. Hard breathing. And a moan.

Our pace resumed.

Slowly now, each foot deliberate.

Like cats slowly stalking a mouse.

Closer now.

The bayoneted muzzle of my rifle preceded me into the small opening.

People!

A woman and a small child!

They were each blindfolded and gagged.

The child was a toddler, maybe a year or two old.

Nobel and Pete stood guardedly behind us.

I handed my rifle to Pete.

Squatting beside the woman, I touched her blindfold gently.

She jerked nervously, but made no sound.

I gingerly moved my hands behind her head, and untied the blindfold.

As soon as she saw me, and the three men behind me, her eyes opened wide, and she began nodding her head.

I raised my finger to my lips in a *please-be-quiet* gesture.

She continued nodding her head in approval, her eyes showing anxiety and fear.

I removed the gag from her mouth.

I slipped my hands under her arms, and helped her stand up.

She seemed to weigh nothing, and I could easily feel her skeletal shoulders.

Her hands were tied.

I took my knife from my right legging, and sliced through the hemp rope.

As soon as her arms were free, she instinctively started to reach for the child.

I restrained her, and pointed to Tim to pick up the child.

Tim handed his rifle to Nobel, and reached down to pick up the child.

He lifted it, as a father would take his own toddler from a playground swing.

He held the small, skinny child firmly in his arms.

The child held on to Tim like a wire trap.

I took the frail woman and lifted her, holding her in both my arms, in front of me, like I'd seen John Wayne do a dozen times.

I looked at the others, nodded to Tim, then flicked my head in the direction of the way out.

Pete and Nobel nodded their approval, and I slowly looked out into the pathway, left and then to the right.

JAPS!

A small group of them, four or five, headed toward us!

"Looks like maybe a dozen!"

One of them saw me, and started firing rounds into the abaca as I yanked my head back in!

I know my eyes were wide by the way Pete and Nobel looked at me.

"You guys get back over here!" Nobel ordered.

Pete looked at me calmly and said, "Nobel and I will have to cover you. You and Tim get out of here as soon as we begin firing. Take these people out to safety!"

Nobel approved with a decisive "Yes!"

He and Pete signaled their readiness with a quick nod to each other.

"Start running. Now!" Nobel ordered.

Nobel and Pete coiled and whirled themselves into the clearing, both firing together and yelling a bone chilling howl.

Pete had my rifle under his left arm, and his rifle in the right arm, firing both in a killing barrage of .30-calibre madness.

Nobel did the same with his and Tim's rifle.

Tim and I ran as fast as we ever had, hearing the Japanese Arisakas pop their rounds into the abaca around us.

We never looked back.

We hit the wall of green interlaced fabric, and crashed through it, making it all the way though much faster than humanly possible.

GI's were dashing toward us from the road as the woman slipped out of my arms and stood up.

Tim gently handed her the child, and nodded to me.

Two of the GIs guided the woman and child safely toward the road, where they could get medical attention.

"We have to go back," he said.

We could hear M1's pinging, grenades booming, Arisaka popping, and men shouting from inside the abaca field.

I reached to my hip and removed my pistol from the holster.

A louey was standing there, and he immediately removed his holster and handed it to Tim.

Tim buckled it to his hip, and removed the pistol.

He cocked it, delivering a round into the chamber.

Tim and I turned, and jumped back into hell.

The firing had stopped.

We heard voices inside the abaca field.

*American voices!*

We emerged on the other side, palms outward, letting them know *We are Americans.*

Infantrymen in the clearing twitched as they saw us suddenly appear, then relaxed as they recognized us.

We looked ahead, down the cut pathway.

Two bodies lay on the ground.

Pete.

He was sprawled on his back.

Nobel lay beside him, one leg bleeding badly.

He was holding Pete's head up.

Further beyond them lay a dozen Japanese bodies, like branches beneath a fallen tree, some stacked on top of each other.

None were moving.

Running, Tim and I returned our pistols to our hips.

I reached Pete.

Nobel looked up at me, grimacing.

His eyes were empty, and scared.

"I, I, ….." he tried to speak.

I laid one hand on Pete's right shoulder, and slipped the other one beneath his head.

Nobel removed his hand, and leaned back on an elbow.

He touched his right leg.

A large wound was oozing blood.

A piece of shrapnel was sticking out of it.

An infantryman had begun to tie a tourniquet above it.

"Damn grenade," he said.

Pete looked at me, confused at first, then smiled.

"Hey, Red." he weakly greeted.

"You made it out with them?"

I nodded.

"Safe? Both safe?" he asked.

"Yes, Pete. They are both safe. Thanks to you and Nobel," I answered.

His shirt was soaked with blood, and a piece of shrapnel appeared to have penetrated into the center of his chest.

Pete shook his head, and coughed up a little blood.

"No, no, not just us. We only did the shooting. You and Tim did the saving."

Tim kneeled down, and placed his hand beside mine.

Nobel leaned over to Pete and said, "We shot those bastards up, didn't we!"

Pete tried to laugh, and couldn't. He coughed once more.

With one eye closed, he looked at Nobel.

"Your leg OK?" he asked.

"Yeah, Pete. It's banged up a bit, but it's OK."

"We got ourselves a trip home, Nobel. Now, you get your ass down to Mobile and rescue that girl. You hear me?"

Nobel, a tear in his eye, answered in a cracked voice, "I swear to God I will, Pete."

A medic quickly arrived, and placed himself between me and Pete.

"Let's see what we have here," he said.

He opened Pete's shirt, briefly frowned, and opened a bag of sulfa powder, spreading the white powder on Pete's wound.

He gently covered the wound with a thick bandage of gauze, being careful to not move the shrapnel.

Pete's face relaxed, and he blinked his eyes.

"Tim? Where's Tim?" he asked.

"I'm right here, Pete. Right here," Tim answered, as he patted Pete's shoulder.

Pete looked at him.

"I don't believe I'll be sleeping in your foxhole tonight, Tim. I'll be just over the hill," he said, as his voice trailed off.

The medic yelled, "Where's our stretcher?"

Four Filipino volunteers appeared with a stretcher. They gently placed Pete on it, and stood up, one at each corner.

I politely took the hand of one of them, replacing it with mine.

"I've got it. You see to him," I said, pointing to Nobel.

We walked in unison, carrying Pete to an ambulance that had been summoned.

At the edge of the abaca, our entry port had already been enlarged by a Filipino with a huge machete.

I looked back, and the medic was working on Nobel's wounded leg.

We carried the stretcher up the slight incline out of the abaca to the road, to the waiting ambulance. We gently placed Pete in it.

He was unconscious, but breathing.

On my way back to the abaca, I passed Nobel. He was on a stretcher, four Filipinos carrying him gently across the road.

Just like with Pete, I politely removed the hand of the Filipino at the rear of the stretcher and replaced it with mine. I told the volunteer, "I've got this. He's my *kaibigan*."

Nobel was almost unconscious, but opened an eye when he heard my voice. He tried to say something, but it was all gibberish.

*They gave him his share of morphine. Good. No pain.* I told myself.

I looked down at him.

"Hey, Nobel. We've got you. You're going to see the doctor. The real doctor. They're going to take you to the hospital tent, maybe even the hospital ship."

After we had placed Nobel in an ambulance, I walked back to the abaca, stopped at the road ditch, and sat down.

"I swear." I said.

I cried once, then again.

I saw Tim leaving the abaca, walking toward me.

I was drying my eyes when he sat down beside me on the road ditch.

"I did my crying in there," he said, pointing to our entry hole into the field.

"What happened to the mother and child?" he asked.

I was silent for a second.

Then I remembered.

"Two GIs took them to the medic tent. They'll probably keep them for a day or two, to feed them, get them back in good health, and question them about the Japs."

Tim stared straight ahead.

"That kid will live a long life with his Mom, thanks to the four of us," he said.

I answered, "Yep."

We sat for a long time, saying nothing more.

Tim was staring into space.

I was fingerpicking at a hole in my right boot.

"Mr. Smith?" Tim asked.

*He's never called me Mr. Smith. Why's he doing it now? He must be bothered by something, or wants to talk about something really important or personal. Or both.*

"Yes, Tim?" I responded.

*I normally made it a point to call him Mr. Blanchard. But not now. This is different.*

"I think I became a man today, out there in that hemp field," he said.

I looked at him for a second or two, without expression.

"Why do you think that? Tell me about it," I said to him, as I tied my boot with the hole.

He jabbed at the ground with a little stick, pushing a pebble around.

"Out there, in that hemp. For a couple of minutes there, I wanted to just lay down in that hemp and cry. I didn't want to move any further. I couldn't breathe, and I was afraid to go any farther. I felt like I was gonna scream and scream and scream."

I nodded my head in agreement.

"I kinda felt that way, too, Tim. I wanted to do the same thing."

"You did?" he asked.

"Yes, I did. But, you know what?"

"What?"

"I was out there, with you, Pete, Nobel, and all those other people. And they weren't screaming or crying."

Tim nodded his head.

"I was thinking that very same thing, Red. I told myself, *You can't do that! What will everyone think? I could get us all killed! What would my parents think?* So, I just willed myself to keep walking straight, just like I knew you and Nobel were doing. I was between the both of you, and we were all in it together."

He took in a deep breath.

"A man is like that. He just learns that it is not all about him. He learns he can take all that's being served up to him."

I reached over and touched his boot.

"That's right, Tim. He has to lead himself. And, when you can lead yourself, you can lead others. This war is hell, Tim. But it is teaching everyone what we need to do the rest of our life. Be a man, and stand up to the test."

"Thank you, Mr. Smith," Tim said with a proud grin.

"You're a good man, Mr. Tim Blanchard," I told him.

We just sat there, trying to digest everything that happened to us that horrible day in May. The good and the bad.

At one point, I believe we were both crying again, sitting there on the edge of that abaca field.


Thursday, May 17, 1945.

Near Talomo, Davao Province, Mindanao, the Philippines.

Tim and I had a visitor at dawn, while we were picking at our C-Rations. Neither one of us were hungry. We hadn't heard anything about Pete or Nobel. We had gathered their gear together the night before, and placed it near Pete's foxhole. We both realized their injuries would prevent them from returning.

Our visitor was our new Company Officer, Captain Morgan.

Tim and I tried to put our breakfast down and stand up, but the Captain motioned us to remain as we were. He looked at us both and apologized for not getting back with us earlier about "yesterday's incident."

I looked at Tim and he looked at me. *Captain Morgan is apologizing to us! He has a heart and a soul, this man. We are very lucky to have two good Captains in a row!*

"Gentlemen, both Sergeant Horner and Corporal Petty have been transported to the hospital ship. Petty is in very grave condition, and he may not survive."

These words cut into our hearts like a knife.

I said, "Yes, Sir. We know he was hit pretty bad, Sir."

Tim bowed his head in agreement.

Captain Morgan nodded.

"Sergeant Horner's condition is more positive. He should survive his wound, but he will be sent home. I see you men have collected their gear together. I will be sending an assistant down here to gather it up later this morning. I want to commend you two soldiers for what you did yesterday. Saving that mother and child was a brave deed, and deserving of commendations. I personally promise that each of you will get one. Thank you for doing what you have done, for doing what is honorable, and for helping us try our best to end this war right here on Mindanao."

He turned to leave, then hesitated. He faced us again.

"No need to return this salute, gentlemen. For it is I who salute you."

He clicked his heels together and raised his right hand to a snappy salute, held it for two seconds, then briskly returned it to his side.

"Thank you both," he repeated as he walked away.

Tim and I stared at him as he retreated back to the Company CP.

"Holy Jesus gosh!" Tim muttered.

"He saluted us!"

My mouth was open as I nodded.

"Yep."

I cleared the lump in my throat.

"He was saluting Pete and Nobel, too," I said.

We were silent for several minutes, then picked up our breakfast and picked at it again.

The 3rd Battalion stayed at the bivouac near Talomo for the next four days, to conduct patrols in the area and consolidate the squads and sections of each company. We had suffered many casualties since our arrival in Davao.

Our platoon leader asked us if we wanted to join another mortar squad, and Tim and I both said no. We told him we wanted to be infantrymen. We didn't have to say a word about it to each other. We both knew that neither one of us wanted to see another mortar that wasn't being fired by Nobel Horner, nor see another mortar round that wasn't being handled by Pete Petty.

We told him we wanted to stay with M Company, and he said he would ask Captain Morgan if we could be used in the Headquarters Section on an as-needed-basis as drivers, and do patrols with a rifle squad if necessary. He said that suited him just fine.

So, in the meanwhile, Tim and I joined a patrol with a rifle squad from K Company and the Filipino guerillas each day. The patrol was focused on the nearby town of Tugbok. The enemy troops were numerous in the jungles around Tugbok, and even in the scatterings of houses and huts there.

They weren't hard to find on a patrol. We would just walk down the road in formation and sooner or later we would receive fire. Their rifles weren't shooting effectively, and their aim was poor. After you killed a few of them, the rest would evaporate back into the jungle.

They were giving us the "hit-and-run" opposition in and around the Tugbok area.

This was a different kind of combat that we had seen in Leyte and Mindoro. We weren't fighting organized infantry units. We were fighting smaller and smaller disorganized bands of enemy fighters, hiding along roads and trails, and sometimes from house-to-house.

After four days of such patrolling, the rifle squads of the 3rd Battalion had succeeded in clearing the Tugbok area of this scattered resistance.


Monday, May 21, 1945

Mintal, Davao Province, Mindanao, the Philippines.

Captain Morgan sent a PFC to our foxhole early that morning to tell us the Captain wanted to talk to us. We were a little uneasy about what he might tell us. When we arrived at his tent, the staff asked us to go in. We stepped into the tent, saluted the Captain, and he told us to "have a seat" as he pointed to three wooden crates at the corner of his desk.

He said that he was working on our commendations for rescuing the two civilians in the abaca field, and needed the details. So, Tim and I told him all that we could remember. With the information he wanted, we believed the Captain had the story as complete and factual as possible. We could see that he was really eager to give us the attention he thought we deserved.

He pushed his notes aside, and leaned forward on his elbows.

"These details will also be used in the report we will submit to the Battalion Commander for Corporal Petty. He is still struggling to stay alive, and will be at the Navy Hospital in San Diego by next week. Corporal Petty, along with Sergeant Horner, are both being considered for the Silver Star Medal for bravery and valor in combat. Horner is recovering from the shrapnel wound he suffered, and is on his way to the hospital with Petty. People seldom recover completely from wounds like Horner experienced, so it is likely that he will be going home. We are all still praying for Petty."

He looked at me.

"And you, PFC Smith, will certainly be going home before Christmas, since you have spent three Christmases in this war already."

His face became somber, and leaned forward in his chair.

"In fact, I see that you, Petty, and Horner have spent all three of these Christmases together, and I find it very unfortunate and sad that it took a bloody engagement to break you apart. You have my sympathy, Smith, as we all recognize that war is hell."

"You are dismissed," he said, looking at me and Tim.

"Do me a personal favor, and be very careful out there."

Tim and I stood up at attention, faced the Captain, and saluted.

Captain Morgan returned our salute.

"Thank you, Sir," we said, and we turned and left the tent.

We looked at each other outside, and shook hands. We then held each other in a brief, tight hug.

"Mr. Blanchard, I want to tell you that you are the last buddy I will ever have in this army. Do you remember what Pete told you when you replaced Kenny Herrod along Breakneck Ridge?"

Without hesitating, Tim responded.

"Yes, I do remember. Pete told me, '*I have a lot to think about, and making a new friend in all this deathly shit is not on my list of things to do right now.*' I feel that same way. No more 'hellos' and no more 'goodbyes' for me."

Tim looked straight at me, a sad but proud look in his eyes.

"And I am here to tell you, Mr. Smith, that you are the last buddy I will ever have in this army."

I grinned, and slapped Tim on his shoulder.

"It is up to me to watch after you, and it is up to you to watch after me. Deal?"

"Deal!" he answered.

When we returned to our bivouac, a rifle squad from K Company was moving out to push a group of Japanese soldiers out of Mintal, where we had seized the Libby Drome three weeks ago. We grabbed our gear and jumped on the truck with them.

"You got rations?" I asked.

The reply came.

"We got the best rations in the world. We got C-Rations."

Tim and I found a case of their "best rations" and grabbed our late breakfast.

It wasn't long before we reached Mintal.

We all jumped down from the truck.

I heard the squad leader say to the driver, "Wait here for us. It won't take us very long."

A louey was there, and spoke to the squad leader, pointing down the road. Forming our patrol, we began to walk down the muddy road, the jungle closing in on both sides, downhill toward a deep valley. We crossed a river, and, at the bottom, we received enemy fire. We fought to get up to the other side. From the deep, twisted jungle, three pillboxes and a lot of snipers began pouring murderous fire on us. Several soldiers in front of Tim and me were hit, and lay wounded on the ground. A couple of them were screaming, and the others looked like they were dead. The rest of us, in our frenzy to get out of the line of fire, began to clamor up the slippery slope. Some of our guys lost their footing near the river and rolled downstream with the current.

We were pinned down. Tim and I were in a short ravine, pressed again the ground. Everybody was still and quiet. A wounded man, beyond our grasp, was trying to roll downhill, but couldn't muster the strength. Tim reached up to help him, but a flurry of machine-gun fire put the soldier to rest, and sent Tim back to the ground. The snipers and machine-guns were hammering us, and more of our guys were hit.

Then a sniper near us started throwing grenades. They were exploding so close to us we could feel the shrapnel zapping past, hitting the ground a few feet away. We felt the mud splatter on the back of our necks, and smelled the deadly odor of sulfurous explosive.

At that moment, Tim pushed his rifle behind a tree root so it wouldn't move, and slid down the ravine without a word. The sniper tossed another grenade, and Tim yelled back to us, telling us to stay low. After the sniper threw a third grenade, and before he could reach for another, Tim jumped up and ran across the slope to the sniper, leaped on top of him, and killed him with his knife.

We all raised up, and attacked the three pillboxes, throwing our own grenades, and sending lead into the loopholes. The squad leader called for a flame thrower, and scorched each pillbox to make sure there were no survivors.

We had done our job. We took care of our wounded, and evacuated them. We retrieved our dead. We had seen no enemy soldier escape.

Later that afternoon, a demolitions squad blew up the pillboxes, ensuring that this ambush would never, ever happen again.

That night, back in the foxhole, I looked up at the stars, shining bright and bold through the bombed and blasted holes in the jungle canopy. I wondered if Juliette had seen the same stars the night before.

*I must tell her about all this.*

I looked at Tim, resting his head against his poncho. His eyes were closed.

*Thank you, Lord, for sending us Tim when Kenny was hurt.*

I took a deep breath, and thought of Nobel, and wondered if he would recover enough to find his Katy and rescue her, like Pete had told him a thousand times.

I thought of Pete, and wondered if he were actually alive at this moment, and prayed that he would be.

I thought of Kenny, and wondered if the seeds of his new life in Virginia were taking root.

*Yes, I must tell Juliette all of this.*

*Pete.*

*From Clarksville, just up the road from her home in Sulphur Bluff.*

*Nobel.*

*With fortitude that was forged from the steel of Birmingham.*

*And, Tim.*

*Tim Blanchard, from Dallas.*
*The right young man at the right time.*

I went to sleep that night thinking of my four buddies, the three that left, and the one that stayed.

*Tim Blanchard had become our team member and our buddy when the Regiment was digging Japs from the ravines on Breakneck Ridge, out there in the rain of Leyte. He was with us when our boat was hit by a kamikaze on the way to Mindoro. And, after that, he was with us when we hit Mindanao and hiked a hundred miles over the mountains.*

*When we finally got to the battlefields of Davao, he was still our buddy.*

*All of us were fighting in bloody Mintal, in the hemp hell around Libby Drome, and along the Talomo River where the Japs had heavy machine-guns, woodpeckers, and artillery dug in above the steep banks.*

*He was our buddy on that horrible day, in a hemp field near Mintal, when two of our buddies were dreadfully wounded, and taken out of the war. Then it was down to Tim and me. He was the last buddy I wanted to have.*


Tuesday, May 22, 1945.

Getting Supplies from Davao beachhead, Mindanao, the Philippines..

The HQ Section of M Company told us they needed drivers to pick up map-making materials from the Davao beachhead. We responded as quickly as the message reached us. *Yes! This is a job for us!*

I was driving a Dodge WC-62 ton-and-a-half truck, with Tim riding in the passenger seat. My memories took me back to the day Nobel and I had ridden the same kind of truck through the garden landscapes of Hawaii, delivering bags of cement to the Battery Arizona. He and I had helped some morons remove their jeep from a muddy ditch, confiscating some canned peaches, saltine crackers, and chocolate bars along the way. We enjoyed a scenic "picnic" on the way back to Motor Pool, watching brown birds with long beaks prowling the shoreline on tall legs, digging into the sand with their beaks. We watched waves moving to the shore, turning into white foam as they hit the beach. We saw little white birds chasing the waves as they moved up the beach, looking for things to eat. I remembered the water at the horizon was dark blue, where it met white clouds. The memory that lingered most was the unbelievably large white birds with long wings that circled in the wind currents high above.

*God, I never knew we had it so good that day. Nobel told me about Katy, and the baby. He revealed that he told her, if the baby didn't have a Daddy when he came back from this war, that he would marry her and love that baby like it was his. I saw the gold in Nobel's heart that day.*

That was before Camp Caves, Australia. Before the first landing at New Guinea. Before the time we all grew into men at Breakneck Ridge. Before Mindoro.

*And, I saw the steel in Nobel's nerves when he and Pete stared down a dozen Japs in that abaca field on Mindanao. He was like a brother to me. And Pete. I had known him all my life, it seemed. And Kenny. Now Tim.*

I looked over at Tim, as he was watching the burned out, blasted landscape of Davao in front of us. I became sadly nostalgic, uncertain about the future, impatient to get this war over and go back home.

A voice came back to me, from Leyte. A soothing, familiar, voice that gave me hope.

*"You WILL survive this war, Horace. There is still much that you must do."*

I stiffened my hands on the steering wheel. Took a deep breath. Smiled.

*"Then, let's go do it. Take me back home, my colored friend. Let me do what awaits me. Let me continue my pursuit of paradise there, with whomever and whatever waits for me."*

Between Talomo and the city of Davao, we drove by a wide clearing among the plantations of abaca and bananas. In the clearing was the 24th Division Cemetery. It was a good distance behind the lines. We could easily see that it had grown so large it was beginning to squeeze the plantations around it.

There were rows of little wooden crosses, with each cross bearing an American soldier's name.

Tim and I stopped the truck on the side of the road, and got out for a closer look.

Along with the rows of crosses, there were other rows of open graves with no crosses. Bodies wrapped in olive-drab blankets lay in the open graves. In the sky above the cemetery, artillery shells shrieked as they passed. The thunder of their distant impact explosions wandered over the crosses and the open graves. A lone figure stood poised in front of an open grave, peering down at a blanket-wrapped body.

It was the 24th Division Chaplain, Major Slavik. He was unarmed. Except for the Filipino gravediggers, he was alone.

Tim turned to me and asked, "Do you think one of them might be Pete?"

I was quiet for a few seconds, and answered, "No, I don't. Pete left on the hospital ship. He's going back home..," I hesitated, "dead or alive."

We watched as the Chaplain lowered his head in a silent farewell to the soldier whose body lay in the open grave. He talked to the soldier with the tenderness and love that a man would give his own son.

Tim and I could hear him as he said, *"The Grace of our Lord Jesus Christ, the love of God, and the Communion of the Holy Ghost be with you forevermore, Amen."*

With tears in our eyes, we climbed back into the truck, and continued our drive to the beachhead.


Wednesday, May 23, 1945.

Talomo Bridge, Davao Province, Mindanao, the Philippines.

For the next two days, we were back on patrols with the rifle squad from K Company. More groups of Japanese soldiers had been spotted along the Talomo River valley. We boarded a troop truck with a small group of Filipino volunteers, and were dropped off in a hilly area above a bend in the river.

A lone scout met us, and guided us to the base of a small hill. We had delivered a dynamite bomb in a box that one of the Filipino volunteers was carrying. The scout, who was a sergeant, was eager to proceed with his task.

He was a demolition specialist. As he prepared his bomb, he took a last puff from his cigarette, then spoke to us.

"This is the place," he said. "You can see the cave entrance from here, see?"

He pointed to a small entrance just below a ridge that overlooked the Talomo River.

"I'm going to crawl to that big tree over there with the bomb. When I get there, I will motion to you. At the time, I would appreciate as much fire on the cave entrance as you can deliver, while I get as close as I can. We believe there are Japs in that cave. Many of them. When I raise my hand again, you stop firing. I will then throw that bomb into the cave and high tail it back here."

With that, he tossed his cigarette and crawled up the brush-covered slope.

For him, it was a routine mission: he was going to blow up a cave.

We all hunkered down, and watched as the sergeant crawled through the brush. Our fingers rested on the triggers of our rifles, ready for the sergeant's wave. When we saw the signal, we opened fire on the cave entrance.

The sergeant jumped to his feet and ran. Within twenty feet of the cave mouth, he stopped and waved to us. We stopped firing. He hurled the bomb through the dark entrance. Almost in the same motion, he quickly high tailed it back down the slope, just like he said he would.

A huge explosion followed.

As we watched, there was a second explosion, larger than the first.

Then a third explosion, larger again.

The hill seem to boil. We saw flames bursting from different places along the base of the hill. The ground beneath us moved, and lifted us up, only to have us slammed back down by concussions.

Smoke and dust settled upon us, as rocks and earth rolled down the hillside.

The sergeant staggered back to our position, and sat on the ground.

"I am sorry, men. I thought that was a regular, plain old Jap cave," he said.

Evidently, it had just been one exit of an entire tunnel system full of gasoline and ammunition.


Friday, May 25, 1945.

Talomo River Valley, Davao Province, Mindanao, the Philippines.

We were in an area where Japanese soldiers had been seen moving around in a palm grove. Artillery fire was requested, and the shells came raining down. Tim and I were watching from a safe distance away, smoking our C-Ration cigarettes. When the shells stopped, we were told to accompany a radioman to look around the impact area to confirm that no enemy was still there.

We certainly saw enemy soldiers there, but they were all dead, killed by the artillery blasts, their bodies twisted in ugly, wretched ways. However, there was a clearing in the palm grove that had a couple of untouched palm trees and a small bamboo hut.

We approached the hut slowly, our rifles pointed forward, the radioman looking straight ahead. Tim was guarding in the left direction, I was protecting our right side.

A patch of bright pink flowers shimmered in front of the hut, turning the otherwise shattered landscape into a medley of rich color. We took a closer look, and saw a woman's body lying there, surrounded by pink blossoms. We cautiously walked forward, and the radioman touched her.

"Still warm," he said.

"But dead."

We circled the hut to a back door, and looked inside.

It was very dim, but enough light was coming through to see another woman's body, holding an infant, laying on a pile of colorful blankets in the corner of the little room. In the opposite corner of the hut was a child, a girl, sitting in the corner. She looked to be about three years old, and was staring at us through frightened, dark eyes.

The radioman entered the hut, and we followed. The woman holding the baby looked like she was dead. The infant in her arm was still alive, but was dirty, very skinny, and had some ants crawling on her. The radioman reported what we had found, and called for a medic.

The medic arrived. He examined the woman.

"This woman is dead. She is probably the mother of this child, and possibly that little girl, over there. I think she likely died here a day or two ago, after nursing this child a short while. There may have been no one here, except for that dead woman outside, to give her the proper care she needed after the birth."

He gingerly picked up the infant, examined her top to bottom, checked her eyes, her mouth, her nose, her ears, and brushed the ants and filth off.

"This child needs food. Otherwise, she is breathing clear and all of her parts are moving. She has a way of watching me hold her, a desire to be held, and a will to thrive, in all of this."

Tim watched as the medic laid the baby back down on a cleaner spot, on top of a bright yellow blanket.

"What can we feed her?" he asked.

The medic smiled, and thought about the question.

"We have canned milk with our provisions, and some empty medicine bottles that have droppers."

Tim's face lightened, and he looked at me, excited.

"Can we feed her?"

"Yes, we must," said the medic.

"We need to treat some water with some chlorine, first. I'll do that. We'll clean her up really good. Then we'll mix the milk with some of the chlorinated water."

He looked at the radioman.

"Order canned milk, a gallon of water, and a bottle of chlorine."

The medic then crossed the room to look at the little girl. He reached in his pocket for a chocolate bar, and when she saw it she smiled.

"Hello, Angel." he said, "I need to see how you're doing."

She stood up and moved from the corner. He unwrapped the chocolate and handed it to her. She reached out and took it, slowly but purposely.

"You need some water, too, young lady. You're about three years old, aren't you?"

She looked directly at him, chewing a mouthful of chocolate.

"Is that your sister over there?" he asked.

She continued to listen to him, moving her eyes slowly toward the baby, then back at the medic.

"Did all the bombs scare you?" he inquired, looking at her sympathetically.

When he said the word "bombs" she flinched, then moved closer to him.

She reached one hand to the medic's red cross patch on his arm and slowly said *"doktor."*

The medic smiled, verified *"oo, doktor,"* in Filipino, as his eyes moistened.

He examined her, scanning her arms, her neck, her legs, then turned her around and did the same thing. He then looked at us.

"She probably helped take care of baby sister over there, but was scared away by the Japs, our shelling, and us. The dead woman outside, who knows? A neighbor, an aunt, a stranger? She was alive when the shelling and shooting started, and may have been out here to warn us, to protect them. One thing for sure, these two girls are fighting strongly to stay alive."

He patted the girl on her head, and turned for the door.

"I'll go get some good clean water and some more medical supplies. Wait here and watch…," he hesitated.

"Our children," he finished, smiling when he said 'children.'

After the word spread that we had two children inside, people started coming in to see. Several men gently picked up the body of the mother, and carried her outside. Others were talking to the girls, clicking their tongues at the baby and saying happy things to the little girl.

Outside, six infantrymen dug a double grave for the mother and the other woman. Six other infantrymen stood guard, always watching for movement in the shadows where the small clearing met the dense jungle.

One soldier made two crosses out of bamboo, tying them tightly with Army twine. Twelve infantrymen stood over the graves. One of them opened his Service Prayer Book and read a verse for the two departed women.

I recognized the verse as the same one that Chaplain Slavik had said over the dead soldier at the Division Cemetery.

*"The Grace of our Lord Jesus Christ, the love of God, and the Communion of the Holy Ghost be with you forevermore, Amen.'*

The medic washed the baby with mild soapy water, and made a diaper for her out of first-aid bandages. He then washed the face and hands of her three-year old sister.

Soldiers handed her crackers, peaches, and some of the milk.

The medic was always watching like a father, saying this and saying that.

"Not too much food, she'll throw up," he said.

Tim was eager to feed the baby with the eyedropper once the milk had been mixed with the chlorinated water. He softly touched the baby's mouth with the dropper, and gently squeezed the rubber bulb. The baby started smacking immediately. The medic watched, and told Tim to stop after three eyedroppers full.

"I believe these children will be well cared for," he observed.

We headed back to our bivouac. The children rode in the ambulance, and Tim was one of the many volunteers to ask to ride with them. The medic gave Tim the nod.

"Finders keepers," he laughed quietly.

A tent was already set up for the children when we arrived, with three cots, one for each of the girls, and one for a caretaker.

We were told that we had the girls for the night. The Filipino village had already been alerted and would have local mothers, *"basa-nars"* who had lost their own children but could still nurse, and anyone willing and ready to give the two girls a home.

K Company was ablaze with excitement about the girls. The tent was quiet but crowded the entire night. In the midst of all that war, the baby had given the men a feeling of home and love.

Of softness.

A reminder of daughters, wives, and mothers back home.

Of rebirth.

It took away the horrors of combat and gave them a day with a sense of kindness and an aroma of normality.

The men of K Company, plus Tim and me, agreed to foster the three-year old sister. One-hundred-and fifty-two men became her Foster-Fathers. We named her Grace Irene. Her initials were G. I.

A small but happy group of women from the nearby village came to our bivouac the next morning. One of them was a mother who was still nursing a baby of her own, a real *basa-nars,* and eagerly fed "our" baby a healthy meal. The baby and the little girl were given to the new mother, who was joined by her own smiling parents and several aunts. Our girls had a family.

We were proud, yet sad, to watch them go. For a night and a morning, we had all felt a little closer to our home, and farther away from the dreadful war.

The following day, the patrols continued. They lasted throughout the rest of May, and through the first of June. Every day we went somewhere nearby to root out the disorganized, hungry, sick, and murderous Japanese soldiers that still lurked in the jungle shadows.

The patrols became shorter in mid-June, and continued every-other-day until early July. Sometimes we would go on a patrol and see nothing. We could hear things moving in the jungle and the underbrush, but could see nothing that even resembled a Japanese soldier.

No ambushes.

No *banzai* raids.

An occasional grenade was thrown from an unknown distance, missing us or not even exploding.

# CHAPTER 21

# NOBEL HORNER

Tuesday, July 3, 1945.

Mobile Beach, Mobile, Alabama.

The wind was gusting as the late afternoon approached, picking up the beach sand grains and blowing them around as Nobel walked down Mobile Beach, wearing his Army uniform with the sleeves rolled up. His sunglasses didn't prevent some of the grains from hitting his eyes. He would stop occasionally, place his walking cane under his left arm, pull his handkerchief out of his back pocket, wipe his eyes, remove his garrison cap, wipe the sweat off his head, and return the handkerchief to his back-right pocket. He would then place his walking cane in his right hand, adjust his garrison cap and the small knapsack on his back, and would continue walking, looking from left to right, then ahead.

    A large, red dragonfly followed him occasionally, darting one way, then another, as if similarly searching left and right, staying ahead of Nobel's path down the beach.

    Nobel had walked eleven miles along the beach yesterday, and slept on a thin blanket from his knapsack. He intended to walk eleven more miles this day, to the end of the beach. He was sure the Army would let him sleep somewhere inside Fort Morgan, and maybe get a shower and a bunk. If he hadn't found Katy by then, he would start back again tomorrow. Katy's father had told him two days ago that she spent a lot of time on this beach, sleeping on it at times, and lived in a bungalow cabin near the town of Gulf Shores.

*"After this war, you get your ass down to Mobile and you rescue that girl. You hear me?"*

Pete had said those very words to Nobel a year-and-a-half ago, on Goodenough Island. Before any of the combat. Back when the four of them (Kenny, Red, Pete, and himself) thought they would see the war to its end, and would say their good-byes as they boarded trains for home.

And, Pete had said that many more times, too, right up to the afternoon in May when they both were seriously wounded in a thick hemp field on Mindanao.

*"Now, you get your ass down to Mobile and you rescue that girl. You hear me?"*

Though Nobel had called and written the Army four times, nobody could tell him how Pete was doing. It seemed, with the war still raging, the Army was unable to find any records at all from those dark, killing jungles or from the teeming, gray ships.

*When I find Katy,* he told himself, *I'm driving to Texas and find Pete myself. And he will meet her.*

"Yes, Pete, I will find her. I will do that because I love her, and because you were like a brother to me. I will do it for love, and for you," Nobel said as he walked with his cane down the beach.

His right leg hurt quite a lot. He still had a gauze dressing over the wound, which would occasionally ooze a little blood. There remained a small fragment of shrapnel deep in his right femur, too deep to remove. *"Maybe someday, but not now,"* the Army surgeon told him. *"You go home and regain your strength, then come back when you're stronger."*

He could still walk for hours on that leg, if he had his pills. He could walk as many miles as it took to find Katy. He jiggled the pillbox in his left front pocket.

*My souvenirs from the war,* he said to himself.

*And enough memories to last forever. I will treasure them, because Pete is somewhere in every one of them.*

He could see Fort Morgan ahead, as dusk filled the western sky. Sure enough, a young guard welcomed him, and thanked him for his service in the war. He even took Nobel in his jeep to the enlisted quarters. The guard wanted to talk about the war, but Nobel talked only a little, and that was mostly about Katy. He bade Nobel a good night and wished him the best of luck in finding Katy.


The Next Day.
Independence Day.
Wednesday, July 4, 1945.

Nobel awakened from his deep sleep as daylight filtered into the large windows and was a little alarmed to find he was back in a barracks. After a few nervous moments of not knowing where he was, he remembered where and what he was doing.

He had dreamed of Hawaii, and of Camp Caves in Australia. Pete had been in much of the dream, just talking and chewing on a toothpick, with Kenny and Red. Katy was in the dream, too, but was always beyond, in the distance, looking back at Nobel, occasionally waving for him to join her. There was a little blonde-headed girl with her, a toddler with thin hair and a wide grin. He tried to go to her, but when he looked up again she was gone.

*"After this war, you get your ass down to Mobile and you rescue that girl. You hear me?"*

Pete said that several times in the dream.

Nobel got up, showered, and walked down to the mess hall for coffee and breakfast. As he passed the guard on his way back to the beach, he waved and thanked the young soldier for his service in the States.

The young guard smiled broadly.

The wind was calm as the morning waves moved across the sand. The sun was in front of him as he walked the beach, his Army shirt sleeves rolled up, his gait favoring his right leg a little bit. His sunglasses glinted back to other walkers on the beach, and they would say hi or nod to him as he passed.

He would stop occasionally, place his walking cane under his left arm, pull his handkerchief out of his back pocket, wipe his eyes, remove his garrison cap, wipe the sweat from his head, and return the handkerchief to his back-right pocket. He would then place his walking cane in his right hand, adjust his garrison cap and the small knapsack on his back, and would continue walking, looking from left to right, then ahead.

The lady saw him before he saw her. She looked intently as he approached within thirty yards, a lone walker, limping a little, cane in hand, garrison cap on his head, looking right, then left. She knew it was him, as she gasped and quickly stood up.

Nobel saw the lone lady stand up. He stopped, no breath in his lungs. He inhaled and said simply, "Katy?"

She ran toward him and cried out in a loud voice, "Nobel, Nobel, is that you? Oh, Nobel!"

He leaned forward, and dropped his cane and knapsack. He wanted to meet her at mid-stride, but stayed back, knowing he must have a strong foot hold to meet her rush.

They met in a tight hug.

She was crying, and he was crying.

He held her as close as he ever had.

He smelled her sundried, brown hair.

He touched her cheek.

"Katy, Katy. My precious Katy," he said through his tears.

"Nobel, Nobel," she cried.

He looked at her. They were nose-to-nose.

"I've come back for you, and I want nothing more than to be with you and to love you the rest of my life," he told her as they kept their tight squeeze.

"I thought I had lost you," Katy whispered.

"I thought you would never come see me. I never knew until you left that I loved you as much as I did, and I still do."

Nobel told her, "I kept my love for you through all the war, and I've come back to be with you. Wherever you are, there I want to be."

He looked beyond Katy, back along the beach, and thought he could see Pete, chewing on a toothpick, a broad grin covering his face. A quick glance, a wave, and then he was gone.

*I got my ass back to Mobile and rescued her, my friend,* Nobel thought.

"I have so much to tell you," Katy said.

"I will listen to you with every heartbeat and with every breath left in me," he pledged.

"I want to ask you a million questions, and I want to follow you this time, anywhere you go," she promised.

Nobel and Katy stood there, locked in love's embrace, for five minutes, maybe five hours, maybe forever.

# CHAPTER 22
# EVERMAN PETTY

Tuesday, July 3, 1945.

Clarksville Train Depot, Red River County, Northeast Texas.

The mournful whistle of the Texas & Pacific Railway Engine 610 could be heard in the distance as the townspeople gathered at the Clarksville Train Depot to pay tribute to their hometown hero, Everman "Pete" Petty. Five miles west of Clarksville, Engine 610 was nearing the end of the most melancholy journey it had ever made since it became the workhorse of the T&P in 1927. It was pulling three cars behind it. A mahogany casket, draped by the stars and stripes of a large United States flag, was riding in the funeral car, between the coal car and the caboose. Four uniformed cadets from Texas A&M University stood crisply at Parade Rest, one at each corner, using their rifles to keep them steady during the sometimes-bumpy ride. The cadets had boarded the funeral train when it departed from Fort Worth, bringing the flag with them from the university.

In the closed casket, the body of Pete Petty lay neatly dressed in his Army Class C gabardine jacket, khaki shirt and khaki tie, the same uniform that was issued to him three years earlier at Camp Wolters, Texas. A Distinguished Service Cross Medal lay on top of the casket, fastened to the flag by a thin, black strap. The medal's blue ribbon, bordered by white and red stripes along each side, was lightened by afternoon sunbeams as the funeral car passed from shaded woods to sunny cotton fields along the southeast-bound tracks from Bagwell to Clarksville.

A bronze cross was attached below the ribbon, with an eagle, wings fully spread, resting in the center of the cross. Below the eagle was the inscription "FOR VALOR." On the reverse side, the center of the cross was circled by a wreath with "Everman Pete Petty" engraved along the cross bar. Reflected sunbeams from the eagle and cross moved around the wooden ceiling of the funeral car, dancing with the rhythm of the rails, like guardian angels keeping a symphonic vigil over the returning hero. The funeral car gently rocked while steam from Engine 610 enveloped it in a soft, white veil as the train followed the rails to the awaiting city of Clarksville. The angels had been dancing on the ceiling since the journey began in a bright Fort Worth sunrise, moving north toward Grayson County, then eastward into the morning sun as it neared the Red River.

Engine 610 had pulled the cars that carried thousands of East Texas soldiers to World War II, and tons of East Texas military supplies, arms, and ammunition along the same route it now traveled. This time, however, Engine 610 was returning one single, distinguished hero to his earthly home.

At the Clarksville Train Depot, automobiles, trucks, and horse-drawn wagons were parked in the center of Walnut Street, spilling over onto Cedar Street and along the sides of both. A single wagon, fully draped in black bunting, was positioned in front of the red-brick station. The wagon had been provided by Cliff Adams, owner of the livery stable several blocks south on Walnut Street, across from the Red River County Courthouse.

An exceptionally beautiful Arabian black stallion, owned by the Crawford family, was given the duty of pulling the funeral wagon and casket the short distance to the McKenzie Memorial Methodist Church, where the body of Pete Petty would lie in repose for a public overnight viewing. Pete had ridden the same black horse many times over the past decade, including the half-dozen times he accompanied Wanda Crawford on picnics north of town. Wanda would ride her own Arabian chestnut mare during the three-week courting period they had shared before Pete rode the T&P train to Camp Wolters.

Miss Wanda was waiting at the train station. She was crying ever so humbly and softly beneath her short black veil as the train approached, sending its marshmallow clouds of steam on both sides of the tracks as it eased alongside the crowded depot. The whistle of Engine 610 did not play its sad refrain as it approached Walnut Street and the depot, in quiet respect to the fallen hero and the entire town of Clarksville. Instead, the copper bell atop the engine announced its arrival with a slow ***ding-dong, ding-dong***. All heads were slightly bowed, and all hats were removed.

The black engine rolled past the crowd, then released steam blowouts from each side as it stopped. The copper bell became silent. After a few moments, a small band of local musicians, from high school-age to high-number age, began to play "America the Beautiful."

The funeral car doors were opened by railway attendants. Six sturdy men, all friends and relatives of the Petty family, boarded the car.

One of the men attached a thin elastic strap around the flag, fastening it to the casket so it would remain secured if any wind or breeze was blowing during the funeral march.

The wagon-hearse was pushed to the funeral car door. The County Judge politely handed one of the cadets a flagpole and a United States flag that had flown over the Red River County Courthouse. The cadets attached the flag to the pole and formed a four-man Color Guard, and exited the funeral car with the flag held high. The band started playing the national anthem immediately. Men stiffened their backs, held their heads high, and some saluted. Women tried their best to hold their heads high, but most simply cried as the six Clarksville pallbearers removed the flag-draped casket from the funeral car and placed it gently into the wagon.

Pete Petty had returned to his hometown, on the same train that took him away three years ago.

With the proud black stallion hitched to the black-festooned wagon, the Aggie Color Guard took the lead position and began the march, leading the funeral procession to the church. A team of high-school drummers, with Pete's nineteen-year old brother Sam in front, marched directly behind the wagon. They began their funeral cadence, a simple but melodic rhythm of **tum-tum-tum-trill-tum-tum-tum-trill-tum-tum-tum-trill-tum-tum-tee-tum**, over and over again.

Wanda walked behind the drummers the entire journey from the train depot to the church, alongside Grandma Petty, the full-blood Cherokee schoolteacher and Pete's grandmother. Pete's father was wearing a black suit and top hat, and carried a polished black cane with a silver handle. He walked behind Grandma Petty and Wanda.

The entire town knew that Wanda, being Pete's life-long friend and fiancé, was the comparative widow in this sad war-tale of love and loss. Their life that was to be was now a life that would only live in memories and dreams. She was the center of Clarksville's sympathy, the fallen hero's bride-to-be.

Grandma Petty, now a sprightly 81 years young, was loved and respected by every student she had ever taught. Pete's father, S. E. Petty, Jr., was the only County Clerk these residents had ever known, and was everyone's "best friend." Sam had Pete's shadow to lead him through life, a brother-figure and mentor to always guide him and be his moral-compass.

Wanda had her entire life ahead of her, and was suddenly alone, without the only boy and man she had ever loved.

All of Clarksville would be with her the next two days, and the Petty family would love her forever because Pete had loved her then, now, and forever.

As the funeral procession passed the left side of the Red River County Courthouse, it was three-fifteen in the afternoon. The hands of the clock on the yellow sandstone tower met in a symbolic gesture, pointing at the hometown hero as he slowly passed by. Men standing on the crowded courthouse lawn removed their hats, children waved, and women watched from behind their silk kerchiefs.

The drummers continued their simple, melodic rhythm.

***Tum-tum-tum-trill-tum-tum-tum-trill-tum-tum-tum-trill-tum-tum-tee-tum***, over and over again.

As the black stallion high-stepped in front of the black-festooned wagon, the flag-draped casket was illuminated by the afternoon sunlight. The sun slipped briefly behind a summer cloud, and the shadow placed a soft, grey balm over the procession. The cloud passed, and the East Texas sun shined brilliantly again to pay homage to its home-grown hero.

The procession turned right onto Broadway Street, and slowly marched the three-and-a-half blocks to the front of the red-brick McKenzie Memorial Methodist Church, stopping alongside the sidewalk near the corner of Broadway Street and College Street.

At the corner, another sidewalk ran across the church lawn to a set of steps. The steps led up to a long porch where there were big stained-glass windows. A double door was at the top of the steps, under the tall, white bell tower.

The church pastor, C. D. King, stood at the door.

The same six pallbearers gently lifted the casket from the wagon and proceeded up the sidewalk to the steps. The small band that had played at the train depot now stood on the porch, and began playing "Amazing Grace."

After maneuvering the steps, the pallbearers and casket entered the double door and proceeded down the center aisle of the sanctuary. It took an hour for the casket to be placed in front of the pulpit, opened, the Distinguished Service Cross Medal placed on Pete's gabardine jacket, and the mourners to begin forming a line for viewing.

It was five o'clock. The clock on the courthouse bell tower pealed five times.

Independence Day.
Wednesday, July 4, 1945.

Clarksville, Red River County, Northeast Texas.

    Wanda stayed the night at the Petty house, and was up and dressed before anyone else had even stirred. She had not slept. Her heart was melting in her breast, and she needed at least a few moments completely alone with Pete. She quietly slipped out the front door, and walked the eight blocks to McKenzie Memorial Methodist Church. The dog from next door followed her, gently nudging her hand with his nose occasionally. It was five o'clock in the morning, and she could hear the courthouse clock delivering the five knells.
    Minister Hamilton, an Ordained Elder of the church and old family friend, was holding his night watch at the big double door. No one was inside the sanctuary. Wanda asked him if he could let no one in for a bit while she had a private viewing. She would come back out when she was finished. He said of course, take all the time you need.
    *May the Lord comfort you and give you strength.*
    Though the floor had thick new carpet, it was so quiet in the vacant sanctuary she could hear the soft murmur of her footsteps as she approached the casket.
    She lay her right hand on Pete's chest, and the tears began to flow. Like a river they ran, out of her soul and onto the silk kerchief that Pete had given her almost three years ago. A slow moan poured from her lungs as she tried to call his name, but nothing coherent could be formed.

She remembered the thousands of days she had watched Pete, from grade-school days to high-school days, always trying to be with him at every chance, at every possible moment.

She remembered the holidays she would spend at the Petty house, bonding with Grandma Petty, and admiring her grandson.

She remembered how elated she was every time Pete would talk to her, protect her like she was his sister, and pay attention to her no matter what she said.

She remembered when like turned to love, and when love became a powerful fire that burned in their hearts and bodies the three-weeks before he left for the war.

She remembered the glow that filled her for days after she and Pete had lay in love's embrace, and he had whispered the sweetest and softest words ever spoken. His voice was low and tender, meant for her and her alone.

She cried another river of tears, this one for the love that was presumed to be in her future, the love of a lifetime that belonged to her, and would have belonged to her forever, had it not been for a fateful May afternoon in a land far, far away.

She remembered how she would melt every time a letter would come, and the words would flow, and the ending was always *Wanda, I love you every moment. With love to my sweetheart and future bride. Pete.*

The river of tears flowed.

She remembered what Grandma Petty would say when people would cry.

"Tears from your eyes make rainbows in your soul. Don't be afraid to cry. No tears, no rainbows."

Wanda reached into her pocket for a small cedar cross that she had made, and placed it inside Pete's jacket, along with a photo of the two of them, and an eagle feather. With her left hand, she rubbed his forehead lightly, and said, almost silently, as if he and he alone could hear her, *"I will love you forever, my Sweet, til I am old and gray. You are, and always will be, my only love."*

She took a deep breath, and tried to sing the Cherokee Death Song, a song of tribal pride that she had been taught by her full-Cherokee mother as a child. She could only produce a few lines.

*"The sun sets at night and the stars shun the day, But glory remains when the light fades away.*

*The pleasures of love are too fleeting to last, In a moment of bliss the enjoyment is past.*

*The pleasures of spring and of life fade away, But the laurels of valor will never decay."*

She cried and she moaned for what seemed forever, until her eyes were dry, her lungs were empty, and her soul had been filled with a million rainbows. She placed a kiss on his lips. As she removed her hands from the casket, she pointed at him, and barely had the strength to whisper.

*"I want you to be there waiting for me, Everman Petty. You are the first person I want to see when I get to Heaven. I love you, my Sweet."*

She walked back up the slight incline to the big double doors, the soft murmur of her footsteps echoing throughout the sanctuary.

No one had come to the viewing in the hour she was there. God had graciously granted her the private time she had so desperately needed.

The courthouse clock was delicately tolling six times through the open door as she approached the Elder. He reached his hand out to comfort her and to help her step over the threshold where carpet met marble tile.

"He is in Heaven right now, Miss Wanda. Safe and sound, and waiting for you. I expect he'll be the first one you see when you get there."

She released a breath of laughter, found a smile behind her grief, and said "That's what I just told him, Sir. That's exactly what I told him. Thank you for letting me do what I needed to do. I'm okay now. I will miss him," as her lips began to quiver, "for the rest of my life."

The dog was waiting for her on the church porch. The two of them made the eight-block walk back to the Petty house, at the corner of Main and Lafayette. A few cars were out, and a couple of them offered a hand wave from an open window.

"Thank you for walking with me, Sport," she told the dog and she ascended the porch steps. She immediately smelled coffee, and Grandma Petty met her with a hug in the front room. A small cedar fire was burning in the fireplace.

"We will make it through this day, Wanda."

She handed her a cup of coffee. It was in Pete's cup, the one Wanda had been using for three years.

Wanda smiled, and held it tightly in her hands.

"Thank you, Grandma Petty. I feel like I'm home. I think you'll be seeing a lot of me. Pete is here, in every nook and cranny," her voice cracked. She gracefully cleared her throat and continued, "It's my favorite house on Earth. And you, Mr. Petty, and Sam are my favorite people."

The two women sat and relished the fire, speaking very little. Enough would be said later. They were just two Cherokee women, respectfully and silently remembering their hero, giving their grief the quiet time it needed.

The funeral began at noon, and the church was completely full. People stood in the back, and down the sides of the sanctuary. There were photographers outside the door, covering the sweetly sad story for distant newspapers.

Pastor King read the eulogy, the choir sang "Blessed Assurance" and "Amazing Grace," Pete's favorite. Sam stepped up to the pulpit, said a few sentences, then tearfully handed the rest of his eulogy to the Pastor King, who finished reading it. The Twenty-Third Psalm and The Lord's Prayer were recited, and the closing prayer was offered by Elder Hamilton.

It took almost an hour-and-a-half for everyone to file by the casket, pausing to cry, nod their heads, and place a small token or memento of their affection for Pete.

Wanda was the last one to view the love of her life, lingering only briefly to lay her hand on his chest and leave a folded letter.

The casket was closed and sealed, and the flag was returned to its full coverage. It was again strapped to secure it during the funeral march to the cemetery. The same six pallbearers gently carried the casket up the sanctuary aisle and out the front door. The Aggie Color Guard led the way toward the porch steps. The small band from the previous day had rejoined and was gathered on the church lawn. The melodic, patriotic strains of the national anthem thundered across the churchyard as the flag-draped casket was carried down the steps to the sidewalk and placed into the black-festooned wagon. The black stallion clicked his shoes a few times on the street, then began the journey behind the Color Guard to the Clarksville Cemetery.

Sam lead the small cadre of drummers directly behind the wagon, as the funeral procession moved briefly east down Broadway Street, then took a right turn and moved southerly down Delaware Street.

***Tum-tum-tum-trill-tum-tum-tum-trill-tum-tum-tum-trill-tum-tum-tee-tum***.

Wanda walked behind the drummers the entire journey from the church to the cemetery, with Grandma Petty, limping slightly, at her side, and Pete's father behind them.

Grandma Petty and Wanda began singing a gospel song, in the Cherokee language, to the tune of "Amazing Grace," and Pete's father sang with them.

*U ne la nv I u we tsi*

*I ga go yv he i*

*Hna quo tso sv wi yu lo se*

*I ga gu yv ho nv*

The funeral procession crossed Main Street, which the Red River County Sheriff had closed for the afternoon. County patrol cars were on either side, and the uniformed deputies snapped to attention and saluted as the Aggie Color Guard and the funeral wagon passed in front of them.

Press photographers captured the poignant moment for posterity.

Grandma Petty, Wanda, and Pete's father were still singing the Cherokee "Amazing Grace" as they crossed Main Street. Others were singing with them, some humming, some quietly repeating the English stanzas. A few Cherokee friends sang the old song with them.

Two blocks later, the procession turned right onto Washington Street, and the Clarksville Cemetery could be seen just ahead.

Sam was leading the drummers.

***Tum-tum-tum-trill-tum-tum-tum-trill-tum-tum-tum-trill-tum-tum-tee-tum.***

As they neared the tall cemetery entrance gate, Sam looked forward and, for a fleeting moment, thought he saw Pete, toothpick in his mouth, leaning against the pole that supported the big metal arch that read "Clarksville Cemetery." Sam blinked once, lost a beat on the drum, and looked again. Pete was no longer there.

The Aggie Color Guard and funeral wagon moved through the gate and toward the center of the cemetery, followed by the procession of mourners that numbered in the hundreds.

The cemetery had been there for over a hundred years, with the founders of Clarksville buried inside its gates. The funeral wagon slowly negotiated the gravel drive, threading a path to Pete's grave, passing the graves of soldiers and great men. A veteran of the American Revolution. A signer of the Texas Declaration of Independence. A Texas journalist and a pioneer preacher. A few veterans from the First World War, the "Great War." And confederate soldiers, many of them from the Texas Cavalry.

The somber procession followed the black-festooned wagon, following the drummers to deliver its home-town hero to the shelter of the Texas clay.

The graveside service was simple.

Two rows of folding chairs had been set up along one side of the grave, where the family and relatives were directed to be seated.

The six stout pallbearers gently lifted the flag-draped casket from the wagon, and placed it on the rails above the grave.

The Distinguished Service Cross Medal was unpinned from the flag that covered the casket and presented to Pete's father, who accepted it with tears in his eyes, holding it tightly over his heart. He stood up, looked around at all the people, and spoke in a voice filled with grief and pride.

"Pete was the kind of son every man wants, and the Big Brother that every young feller needs. When he told us he was going to the Army, I knew that he would make a difference, and I knew that his courage and bravery would rise to the occasion. We are very proud of Pete, and will miss him sorely. It's down to Momma, Sam, and me now, and Wanda, dear, sweet, precious Wanda, the love of Pete's life. We thank God for all that we have, and may God bless each and every one of you."

Sam had walked over from his position near the Color Guard when his father stood up, and was beside him when he completed his tribute, holding onto him securely as he sat back down, still holding the medal over his heart.

The flag was unstrapped and removed from its position atop the casket. It was ceremoniously folded by the Aggie cadets into a neat triangle.

The flag was presented to Grandma Petty, who nodded a thank-you gesture and, turning in her seat, gave it to Wanda.

Sam strode fifty feet away from the mourners and fired three rounds from Pete's hunting rifle, one for each Christmas Pete had spent overseas.

A member of the Methodist choir played "Taps" on an old Army bugle.

The poignant melody drifted across the cemetery, stroking the heartstrings of all in attendance, causing many to cry, prompting salutes from men, young and old. Many of those who stayed in town said the bugle could be heard as far away as the Red River County Courthouse.

A short, spirited eulogy was then presented by Pastor King.

Sam said an emotional but uplifting prayer.

As a single drummer played a simple slow rhythm, the Color Guard lowered the flag they had carried, removed it from the flagpole, folded it, and returned it to the County Judge.

And the funeral, at that point, was over.

People stood around and talked.

One by one, they left for home and their Fourth of July evening.

Grandma Petty and Wanda sat on a marble bench near Pete's grave, and waited until long after everyone had left the cemetery. They sang the songs of Pete's, and Wanda's, youth, along with the Cherokee songs they both knew. They each prayed aloud, and watched as the summer wind danced through the trees. A lone dragonfly skittered from tree to tree, and at one point rested on the tombstone marking the grave of Pete's mother. They watched in amazement as the dragonfly took to the air, circled, and placed itself on top of the monolithic tombstone marking

Grandpa Petty's grave. Etched into the base of the marker, the words

> *SAMUEL EVERMAN PETTY*
> *March 4, 1864 Indiana – April 5, 1932 Texas*
> *DEVOUT CHRISTIAN, DEVOTED HUSBAND, LOVING FATHER*
> *AND GRANDFATHER, HONORABLE AND TRUSTED FRIEND*
> *WE WILL MEET IN HEAVEN BENEATH THE TREE OF LIFE*

portrayed the man that Pete had called "Grandpa." He had spent many of his childhood days wandering with Grandpa through the woods of Red River County.

"Pete was like my Sam. Upright and strong. They were both good men," Grandma Petty said, then turned and looked at Wanda.

"You loved a good man, and so did I."

Wanda nodded, and cried another hundred rainbows into her soul.

"Pete told me once," she said, still sniffling, "that he loved his Grandpa so much that he thought he walked on water."

Grandma Petty smiled, and brushed Wanda's black hair with her hand.

They watched the dragonfly, talked to it, and sang an ancient song of Man, Nature, and Earth. They each held a green, leafy cedar bough close to their breasts.

After an hour, they left the cemetery.

"You have been a blessing to me, Wanda," Grandma Petty said proudly.

"God took a dear grandson, and gave me a granddaughter as a token of His love."

Wanda looked at her and replied with a smile, "We are both blessed to have had him for a short period, and to know that he waits for us in Eternity."

"You are like my own Grandma, because Pete was like my own flesh. You are my *Ghigau,* my beloved woman."

Grandma Petty nodded.

"And, you are mine. *The sun sets at night and the stars shun the day, But glory remains when the light fades away.* Pete loved you with all his heart. He told me!" she smiled with pride.

"You were the glory in Pete's eyes."

Back at the cemetery, the gravediggers were patting down the last inch of Clarksville clay on top of Pete's new Earthly home. They spread the multitude of flowers across the mounded grave. As the late-afternoon sun filtered through the cemetery trees, the men talked about the weather, the war, the supper that waited for them at home, and the Fourth-of-July fireworks that were going to light up the sky later that night.

On a Fourth-of-July beach in Mobile, Alabama, Nobel Horner had just found his long-lost love, Katy, and they were bound in a tight embrace that could have lasted forever. Nobel caught a dreamy glimpse of Pete from somewhere deep in the crease of his soul, with a toothpick in his mouth, waving at him in a crowd of beachgoers. He blinked, looked again, and Pete was gone. Nobel did not yet know that a somber train had returned Pete's body to his hometown. He did not know that Pete's countless friends, a grateful nation, and his mournful family had just placed him with great honor in a hero's grave in the Clarksville Cemetery, Red River County, Texas.

On a hastily constructed Fourth-of-July baseball field in Davao City on the island of Mindanao in the Philippines, Horace "Red" Smith was standing at home plate, waiting for the pitch during his first at-bat on a dry, sunny day. He was looking across right field, toward the flagpole, when his war-weary eyes caught a glimpse of his life-long-friend Pete standing there, waving at him, a toothpick in his mouth. Smith stepped away from home plate, blinked both eyes, and looked again. Pete was gone. Smith did not yet know that Pete had died, and that a grateful nation and a mournful family had just buried him with great honor in a hero's grave in the fertile clay of Red River County, Texas.


Later That Evening

Back at the Petty home, Grandma Petty did not go to the fireworks show at the Town Square. She sat on the front porch, holding Pete's Distinguished Service Cross Medal in her lap, occasionally waving at townspeople as they walked or drove by, acknowledging their wishes and condolences. She knew that she had been truly blessed with a grandson like Pete, a man who was true to his values, his country, and his family. She chanted the Cherokee Death Song in a light, melancholy voice, and smiled as she sang,

*"I'll go to the land where my father is gone; His ghost shall rejoice in the fame of his son; Death comes like a friend*

*to relieve me from pain; And thy son, O Alknomook, has scorn'd to complain."*

She softly leaned back in the rocking chair, and closed her eyes. The smile was gentle on her face as she released a sigh.

"Pete, I am so proud of you."

She went back inside and placed Pete's medal on the fireplace mantel. Though it had been a warm July day, she built a small fire of cedar boughs, in Cherokee-fashion. She held her weary hands toward the fire, to feel its soothing heat. She inhaled the pleasant odor of the cedar, and hummed an old Cherokee song of her youth, a morning song in praise of the Great Spirit. Her son, Pete's father, returned from the fireworks show and sat down beside her.

"You alright, Momma?" he asked.

She nodded her head *Yes*.

"We've gone through our share of burying, that's for sure."

He removed his shoes, placing them near the fireplace, let his tired hands absorb the healing warmth of the cedar fire, and they both sang together, patting their stocking feet in unison on the cedar floor.

*We n' de ya ho,*
*We n' de ya ho.*
*We n' de ya ho,*
*We n'de ya.*
*Ho, ho ho ho*
*He ya ho he ya,*
*Ya ya ya.*

Wanda had accompanied Sam to the fireworks show, and saw the wonderment of a boy's eyes in Sam as he watched the fountains, rockets, and dense clusters of glittering stars, and heard the whistles and pops of the missiles as they screamed skyward. She had seen the same wonderment in Pete's eyes long ago as they maneuvered their way between childhood, puberty, and adulthood. She cried a few times when Sam could not see her.

      She knew that Pete would not have enjoyed the fireworks show as much as Sam, as he had often remarked in his letters about how the deadly skies of the jungle nights would light-up with mortar illumination rounds and cannon fire. Though God had given Pete the knowledge of Wanda's love and the hope of a long and fruitful life, He had also delivered the sacred and eternal gifts of Heroism and the Last Full Measure to the young man of Wanda's dreams.

      She had loved him her entire life, and would love him forever.

      Wanda would become a schoolteacher like Grandma Petty. She would be loved by every student to her dying day, just like Grandma Petty.

      She stayed in Clarksville, and never married.

# CHAPTER 23

# END OF WAR

Independence Day.
Wednesday, July 4, 1945.

Talomo River valley, Davao Province, Mindanao, the Philippines.

There were no patrols that day. We were allowed to stay at bivouac and celebrate the Fourth of July. Hot dogs were delivered from a nearby mess hall, along with chili and crackers.

It did not rain.

The engineers had set up a baseball field, made to exact measurement. The Army had unbelievably found a bat and four baseballs, and we wrapped our hands in pieces of wool blankets for gloves. We played baseball all afternoon.

All the platoons played down to two winners, and the championship game was played before evening chow. It was Headquarters Platoon against Charlie Platoon. There were some big fellows in Charlie Platoon, a couple of them from the minor league. They won the game, of course. Tim and I played on the Headquarters team, and we all did pretty good, making it all the way to the Big Game.

The first time it came my turn to bat, I remember looking across right field, toward the flagpole by the CP tent, and I swear to this day I saw Pete standing there, his weight shifted toward his left leg, with his right hand fingering a toothpick in his mouth. He waved with his left hand. I stepped away from home plate, blinked both eyes, and looked again. He was gone.

I rubbed my eyes, acted like something had blown into them, then stepped back in. I got a hit, although my teary eyes never saw the ball.

My mind was on Nobel and Pete the rest of the day. I got kinda choked up again a couple of times, knowing how much fun they would've had. It reminded me how much those two were in the fabric of my Army, and in the depths of my heart. I wondered what they were both doing on this National Holiday of 1945.

I laughed when I thought of Kenny, knowing he would have spent the whole day discussing the philosophy of baseball, from the father figure on the pitcher's mound to the children at each base. All the way down to the ninety feet between each base, stretching the human limits of each player to outrun a pitch to first base, or the impracticable possibility of stealing home. I knew this, because he had said all that before during a game at Camp Wolters.

Immediately, I told him that I had stolen home one summer afternoon back in 1940 during a game at Flora. It won the game.

He look at me with a question mark in both eyes.
"What is a Flora?"
I just rolled my eyes and looked the other way.


Thursday, July 26, 1945.

Talomo Beach, Davao Province, Mindanao, the Philippines.

By late July, our bivouac was relocated to the south, and established near the Talomo beach on the Davao Gulf. It was a regular Army camp, with real tents, wooden floors, and real cots. And, there was a mess tent with hot chow.

And, occasionally, a lone Japanese soldier would still throw a grenade at someone.

American soldiers were still dying, and we were still killing Japs, one at a time.

By the first of August, one thing remained completely undone and unreconciled: Tim and I had never heard a single word about Pete, or Nobel, or Captain White.

We would often say to one another, "I wonder about them..." or, "I wish we knew..."

But we never asked. We were so tired of that bloody war, so numbed by the ever-present dead and the empty foxholes, that we just stopped asking. We did not want to be told they were dead. That's what we didn't want to hear.

*If they are dead, don't let us know it.*
*Dear God, let us not think about it.*

We thought of home. We knew that if we didn't die we would all go home. The one certainty I had was what my colored friend had told me during that hellish night on Leyte. I believed I would actually survive this war, without even a scratch, and live to do many things.

I thought of Juliette.

Tim and I didn't write many letters. It was too hard to say the same things every time. Plus, the censors would remove every line we wrote about the cruelty of the enemy or the horror of death.

Besides, it was too hard to write a letter on wet paper. Even though we were sleeping and living in tents, the humidity made everything damp. Our shirts were never dry, our socks were never dry, nothing was ever dry.

We accepted the vagueness of war. When a soldier died, he was gone. Another soldier took his place. Your best friend was your rifle. We had lived that kind of life for months. For the long time that Pete, Nobel, and Kenny were at my side, I was insulated against that vagueness. Then Kenny was taken away. Tim took his place. When Pete and Nobel left, there was no one to take their place. It all changed that May day in the abaca field.

In a single minute of time, it had all changed.

Tim and I had steadfastly reached that moment in a soldier's life when the desire to make a new friend was choked, and conversations about the future were strangled. We loved each other dearly, and we knew we were desperately important to each other. The only thing we could do was look after each other like brothers in a deranged game of Banter, with real demons and real monsters reaching for us from beyond. The smell of death wafted from beneath every bridge we crossed.

Tim told me once, "We are on a remote island, with danger everywhere around us. But when we hunker down and eat our C-Rations, it feels like we are safe."

When Tim told me that, I just looked at him. Then I looked at my C-Rations spread in front of me like a buffet, and then back at him.

I gave a light laugh. It felt good to laugh.

"Tim," I answered, "That is a sad thing. But I completely agree with you. When I eat this…," I counted the cans in front of me, "This five-course meal with you, I feel like a King."

We both laughed for five or ten minutes.

Without Tim, I don't know how I would have made it through that final part of the war.

Monday, August 6, 1945.

Talomo Beach, Davao Province, Mindanao, the Philippines.

We were waiting for evening chow, sitting in our tent trying to finish letters that had no intention of even being started. My paper was empty, except for "Dear...." I couldn't figure out who I was writing it to. At least Tim's letter had "Dear Mom" written on it. He knew who he was writing to, but could not figure out what he was going to say to her.

Suddenly, there came an order from outside, "M Company, form up on the main road!"

It was the company First Sergeant, who we had seldom heard bark his own commands.

"Damn!" announced Tim.

"This must be something important! I was almost finished with my letter, too."

I looked at his blank "Dear Mom" letter and threw him a smirk.

"Me. too." I said.

We quickly lay our incomplete letters aside, grabbed our helmets, and ran toward the dirt road that ran down the center of out tent "neighborhood."

The Company had formed into the platoons and squads in proper sequence pretty swiftly, and all ears were open for something important.

First Sergeant Haney stepped out of the Company CP tent, Captain Morgan behind him.

"Atten-HUT!" the First Sergeant barked.

Captain Morgan stepped up beside him and said, "At ease, men."

He was keenly aware of our curiosity, as we tried to figure out where we were going or what was happening at such an odd hour, so late in the day. He was holding a small piece of paper, glancing at the information written on it.

"Gentlemen, something historic has happened today that may very well end this war quickly."

A buzz ran through the Company.

"Listen up!" barked First Sergeant Haney.

"We have just learned that an American aircraft dropped an Atomic Bomb on the Japanese city of Hiroshima earlier today, causing vast destruction over the area. We believe that as many as a hundred-thousand people may have been killed in the blast. The bomb was equal to fifteen-thousand tons of TNT, and it flattened three square miles of the city. Now, gentlemen, this is the first time in human history that one of these bombs has been created and used. As long as you live, you will remember that you were right on the lip of Japan when it happened."

We looked at each other, as a mumble of approval moved through the ranks.

"We will be on high alert this weekend. All of you will be combat-ready at all times. And, pray that this will be the first day of the end of this war!"

He turned and walked back to the CP tent.

First Sergeant Haney held his arms up, and moved them down and up several times as he said, "Keep the chatter down, combat-ready means quiet and orderly. When you're through with chow, go straight back to your area and settle in for the night. You are dismissed."

Tim looked at me and I looked at him.

"That's a big bomb," he said.

I nodded.


Thursday, August 9, 1945.

Talomo Beach, Davao Province, Mindanao, the Philippines.

We had been back from evening chow about a half-hour when First Sergeant Haney barked again.

"M Company, form up on the main road!"

A minute later, we were all there, eager to hear what was so important that it made Haney howl once more.

All was the same again. First Sergeant Haney walked out of the CP tent, with the Captain behind him. He told us to "Listen up!" and Captain Morgan, with another piece of paper to read, stepped forward.

I wondered, *Why didn't Haney yell 'Atten-HUT!' like he always does? Is he slipping, thinking too hard on the bomb stuff? The Captain looks a little distracted, too.*

"Gentlemen," Captain Morgan began, "A second Atomic Bomb has been dropped on the mainland of Japan. This time, the city of Nagasaki was hit, with the same effects as the bomb that destroyed Hiroshima. The wires are hot with messages going back and forth. As soon as we hear something, you will know. Right now, all we can do is be combat-ready, and sit and wait. And, pray some more. Good night, men of M Company."

First Sergeant Haney just stood there and watched us, making sure we all went back to our tents and behaved ourselves.

"Well," I said to Tim, "are they gonna fight or give up?"

"If they fight," Tim replied, "who are they gonna use to do the fighting?"

"And what are they gonna use to fight with?" I said, more with my arms than with my mouth.

"Rocks? Dirt?"

"I'm tired of killing Japs," Tim uttered.

"I'm ready for this to stop."


Wednesday, August 15, 1945.

Talomo Beach, Davao Province, Mindanao, the Philippines.

We were watching a movie on the black sands of Talomo Beach, sitting on a small set of bleachers under a little grove of palm trees. It was drizzling rain, and the projector and speaker were beneath rain covers. The screen, barely ten-feet by ten-feet, was wet, and we were gathered together under ponchos. I cannot remember what particular movie we were watching, but I believe it was a western.

Off to my right, I could see a Navy ship in the gulf begin to turn its deck lights on and off, rapidly.

*That's strange*, I thought.
*I've never seen that before.*

The movie was suddenly interrupted by an officer, holding a flashlight. He walked quickly to the bleachers and stood in front of the first row. An enlisted man ran to the projector and turned it off.

Soldiers in the bleachers began to complain.

The officer waved the complaints off.

"We just received a radio message that the Japanese have surrendered!"

We all leaped up, as an enormous cheer erupted and swept over the dark jungles. All of the Navy ships in the Davao Gulf began flashing their beacon lights.

Their foghorns began to bellow with a rich, thick, low resonance. For four minutes, one for each year since 1941, the fighting ships were croaking the deep powerful, booming news that the Pacific War had ended!

We slapped each other on our backs, and continued the cheer for what seemed an hour.

The "thing" that had become a heavy burden in all our hearts, the feeling that our lives would be eternally spent in this muddy, wet, jungle, had suddenly been lifted from us. From out of nowhere, in the middle of a movie, on a dark half-moon-lit beach, WE HAD ENDED THIS WAR RIGHT HERE ON MINDANAO!

I sat back down on the bleacher, put my poncho around my shoulders, and let the warm rain bathe my face. I imagined that I was washing off the bloodiness of this horrific war.

I thought of a Sunday afternoon in December a very, very long time ago in Sulphur Springs when this nightmare had begun with a movie being interrupted by a man with a flashlight.

Now, it had had ended the same way.

A movie had just been interrupted by a man with a flashlight.

Carbines and Garands pounded like rolling thunder. As the news spread to the outer perimeters, machine-guns rattled toward the sky, beyond Mount Apo, and across Davao Gulf. Men howled like wolves and crowed like roosters.

Parachute flares illuminated the rain-shrouded sky, cheerily floating between the clouds like glowing white doves holding olive branches in their tiny claws. Whistles could be heard from deep in the swamps. Tracer rounds arched like moonbeams from the Davao abaca fields.

And, all the while, as jubilation poured over the island of Mindanao, the rain continued to fall.

The Japanese Army of Mindanao, oblivious of the empire's downfall, thought a night attack was underway and sent storms of lead into the drenched darkness.

In a little palm grove, on the black sands of the Talomo beach, the enemy soldiers who were secretly watching our movie decided to toss grenades into the happy crowd. Tim and I saw the explosions to our left, and plunged beneath the bleachers to the wet, puddled ground.

The Japs who had thrown the grenades were pursued into the black jungle, and were beaten to death by angry men of the 21st Regiment.

Back in the bleachers, two soldiers had been killed by the Japanese grenades.

Such was our new-found peace.

The Japanese who remained in the jungle were in no hurry to stop being heroic martyrs. They had not yet been given the order to surrender.

For both Japanese and Americans, obedience to the order to cease firing was very, very tough. The reversal of an old habit is almost impossible. Killing Japanese on sight had become a matter of human reflex and instinct. The sudden requirement to control the urge to kill caused confusion, emotional turmoil, and psychologic mayhem in some soldiers.

For sixteen days the assaults, ambushes, raids, and battles continued. There were thousands of poorly armed Japanese still occupying the mountains of Davao Province in loose, disorganized bands. They were not in contact with each other. Most had no radios, and no direct commanding officer. They stole their food from villagers and Army supply lines.

To make it even more confusing, there were thousands of well-armed Moros and Filipino guerillas roaming the forests, disobeying any orders to cease firing.

Back at camp, we set up an even- stronger defensive perimeter, and waited for orders to do otherwise.

Army planes dropped leaflets in every forest and every village, informing the people of Mindanao, in their native languages, that the war was over on their island.

Two weeks passed, and we were told that the highest Japanese brass remaining on Mindanao had informed the United States Army that all personnel had been told of the surrender, and all hostilities were ceased.

Late August 1945.

Talomo Beach, Davao Province, Mindanao, the Philippines.

      We were told that the 24th Division had been ordered to occupy Japan. Deployment would be soon.
      Over Davao Gulf, the sky was a cloudless blue, and the peak of Mount Apo rose majestically above the cobalt horizon. A hot sun flamed on the calm, turquois sea.
      Across the black sands of Talomo Beach, men of the Hawaiian Division lay on the beach and swam in the blue-green waters. Offshore, a convoy of gray Navy transports lined the coast. Soldiers thronged the decks of the ships – young, crisp, clean soldiers, battle-virgins fresh-picked from the training camps.
      The skinny, yellow veterans on Talomo Beach watched as the newcomers came ashore.
      The newcomers were grinning bravely as the tropical sunlight reflected from their new, clean helmets.
      We of the 21st Regiment were very happy to see them.
      One fellow, standing beside Tim and me on the beach, looked across the troopships coming in and said, "Christ, I sure am proud to see this day!"
      "I never thought I'd leave this god-damned island so alive and so soon. Back home the houses will be more drab than we pictured them in our dreams, and the women won't be as glamourous as our pinups, but they'll be wonderful and sweet all the same. People will wear shoes and have soap to make them smell clean and everything will be whole instead of wrecked and ruined as we had to wreck and ruin these

islands against our own will. Look at Mount Apo! Hell, they'll be killing Jap stragglers up there ten years from now."

Sunday Morning, September 2, 1945

Talomo Beach, Davao Province, Mindanao, the Philippines.

At 8:00 am that morning, we were all sitting outside our tents on palm tree logs, beneath a cloudy sky, listening quietly as loudspeakers spat the buzzing, static-filled radio broadcast of the Japanese surrender ceremony throughout the camp. The radio signal from Tokyo Bay was a bit fuzzy, but we could hear the narrator describing the moment the Japanese officials appeared on the deck of the *USS Missouri*.

It gave me goosebumps when Gen. MacArthur, who I had seen in person in New Guinea, began to speak:

*"We are gathered here, representatives of the major warring powers, to conclude a solemn agreement whereby peace may be restored.*

*The issues involving divergent ideals and ideologies have been determined on the battlefields of the world, and hence are not for our discussion or debate.*

*Nor is it for us here to meet, representing as we do a majority of the peoples of the earth, in a spirit of distrust, malice, or hatred.*

*But rather it is for us, both victors and vanquished, to rise to that higher dignity which alone befits the sacred purposes we are about to serve, committing all of our peoples unreservedly to faithful compliance with the undertakings they are here formally to assume."*

Tim and I listened as the radio broadcaster described the Japanese officials, one of them in "top-hat and tails," signing each copy of the surrender, followed by the Americans, dressed in open-neck khaki with no ties, as they signed each copy. We all laughed when the reporter said that MacArthur had told him earlier, "We fought them in our khaki uniforms, and we'll accept their surrender in our khaki uniforms."

The ceremony lasted less than an hour, and at the close Gen. MacArthur spoke again. That last speech of the morning gave me more than goosebumps. It brought some tears to my eyes as *'The Old Man'* talked about all the guns being silent:

*"My Fellow Countrymen:*
*Today the guns are silent. A great tragedy has ended. A great victory has been won. The skies no longer rain death - the seas bear only commerce. Men everywhere walk upright in the sunlight. The entire world lies quietly at peace. The holy mission has been completed. And in reporting this to you, the people, I speak for the thousands of silent lips, forever stilled among the jungles and the beaches and in the deep waters of the Pacific which marked the way."*

When he spoke of the silent lips, forever stilled among the jungles, I wondered about Pete and Nobel, and prayed that I could hear them speak again, somewhere, sometime, beyond tomorrow.

On that cloudy Sunday morning on Mindanao, the war that had started on a sunny Sunday morning at Pearl Harbor was finally over. I was going home, to see Momma and Daddy, my brothers and sisters, and Juliette.

Going home to Texas.

Peace was more than just a word. I felt it in the fabric of my clothes, I smelled it in the air, I tasted it on every piece of Army chow I ate, and I dreamed of it in the dark, steamy, stagnant tropical night.

I no longer feared the malarial shivers and sweats that came in the night, when I least expected them.

I was alive, and going home.

From the time of my birth to that very Sunday, I had never felt better in my life.

My Paradise was in front of me, nine-thousand miles away.

I knew I was going home.


Tuesday, September 25, 1945

Davao Province, Mindanao, the Philippines.

The ships continued to bring fresh troops to occupy Mindanao, and to prepare to accompany us to Japan. The ships also brought bags and bags of mail. One of the bags had two letters for me. One from Momma and one from Nobel.

I read the letter from Momma first. All was well in West Texas. All said Hi. My youngest brother Lester had joined the Army, and he was a guard at a prisoner-of-war camp. She said that he mentioned something about going to a camp in the Philippines.

I then reached for the letter from Nobel. It was postmarked August 15, 1945, and I smiled as I saw the return address, in Birmingham, Alabama. Tim and I were alone in our tent, as I opened the letter with half-dread, not knowing what it would say.

He had found Katy, and they were together, husband and wife.

He was working at the foundry.

They would go to Mobile every other weekend, so Katy could sit on the beach.

Kenny was back in college.

He had plans to get a PhD in Philosophy.

Nobel said he had seen a story and pictures in the Birmingham newspaper about an Army soldier from Texas who had been awarded the Distinguished Service Cross for bravery. He was returning to his hometown of Clarksville, Texas, for a somber and beautiful hero's burial on the Fourth of July. He said the soldier was Pete, and that the Distinguished Service Cross is the second-highest medal a soldier can receive.

He said he had gotten one, too.

*Pete ... hero ... burial ... hometown.*

I had read that part of the letter with pure ignorance, not knowing that Pete had died.

As the long-delayed news of Pete's death sank into me, it slid like a ton of glass shards down my throat, into my heart, piercing my chest, filling my stomach, cutting my groin, going all the way to my feet, and then spreading across the ground like a dark, sticky liquid until it was everywhere around me.

The letter fell onto my lap.

Instantly, I burst into crying.

I had never in my life cried like that.

I tried to stop, but couldn't.

I cried and I cried.

When Tim saw me, he dropped what he was doing and sat by me, putting an arm around my shoulder. He must've glanced down and read the letter from Nobel, because he started crying, too.

It felt like we sat there for hours, days, even years, crying and crying. It slowed down and stopped rushing like a wild, remorseful river. It slowed even more, becoming a sluggish, heavy, heart-breaking grief.

The war had touched us, with a mighty blow to the gut.

A sharp, merciless knife to the heart.

It had killed a friend.

A dear friend.

Pete was Tim's foxhole buddy. He was the best friend Tim could've ever had during his taste of war.

I had known Pete a good deal of my life. It seemed as if his blood was my blood, his bones were my bones. He was as much a part of me as my own flesh, my own future.

There was a hole in my heart where my home used to be.

Everman "Pete" Petty.

From Clarksville, Texas.

Just down the highway from Sulphur Bluff, where Juliette was born.

It had suddenly become as far away as Mars.
As far away as Eternity.
As close as Death.

# CHAPTER 24

# OCCUPATION OF JAPAN

Wednesday Morning, October 10, 1945.

Talomo Beach, Davao Province, Mindanao, Philippines

Over Davao Gulf, the sky was a cloudless blue. A hot sun scorched the calm, turquois sea.
A convoy of Navy ships lined the coast, stretching almost to the horizon. We had been watching the ships gather for weeks, setting their anchors as they waited to become the Task Force that would take us to Japan.

The day before, we gathered at the Company M Headquarters tent. As they called out our names, each one of us would step up and receive our dress uniforms, the ones that the Army had taken from us last year on Goodenough Island and put into storage. They smelled a little bit like mothballs, but getting them back was another reminder that the awful war was over, and we needed more than combat fatigues to wear in "Today's Army."

At 0800 in the morning, we sat in formation at the beach for over an hour, after the standard "hurry up and wait" tradition they had maintained for almost three years. It had not rained for days. The sea breeze was blowing in, toward us. The wind propelled black sand from the beach toward our formation.

The 3rd Battalion had been selected to be the "Shore Battalion." The Navy called it the Shore Party, those troops chosen to make sure all supplies, equipment, and vehicles were distributed from the shore to the right individuals or units of the regiment. As such, we were to be on the first ship and the first wave arriving at our destination point, Hiro Wan seaport in Okayama, Japan.

Our rifles were packed away in lockers. As the Shore Party, we would not be carrying them.

The war was over, and the combat troops, over-laden with battle gear, were supposed to be a thing of the past. It was assumed that we had clambered down the last rope ladder, and eaten the last steak and egg sacrificial breakfast.

Yet, there was a remaining uncertainty about the landings on the Japanese mainland. The 2$^{nd}$ Battalion was selected to be prepared for an assault landing, if required. If there was unexpected hostile resistance by Japanese military die-hards or renegade locals, the Army would be ready to secure the beachhead by force.

That did not prove to be necessary.

By 1000, we were loaded onto landing craft, just like all the other times, and taken out to our ship, the *USS Mifflin*. We could see the huge numbers '207' stenciled in white across the ship's bow.

I heard a fellow behind us say, "This is same ship that carried fifteen-thousand of the Marines to Iwo Jima and Okinawa."

"It probably has its share of ghosts," another fellow said.

We continued up the ramp, silently thinking about the pieces of history we had touched between New Guinea, Leyte, Mindoro, and Mindanao.

Aboard the *Mifflin*, we appreciated the "new feel" of this trip to sea.

No combat gear.

No tight fist in the middle of our gut.

No deathly dreams, or prayers of redemption.

All we were gonna do was land on Japan, and walk around.

Help them recover from all the hell they put themselves and us through.

It sounded easy, friendly, and the right thing to do.

We didn't know what to expect.

I saw men on their knees begging the Lord to help them act right.

Tim and I found a small area of berths deep down in the ship that weren't stacked, and picked two in the corner. We put our duffel bags beneath them.

"We found some good racks this time," I told Tim.

We stood there, looking around the room. Men were quiet, distracted.

*Close to going-home time, guys. Don't know what waits for you.*

"Hey, Red," Tim asked me as we settled into our berths.

"Have you ever seen that painting of Jesus where he is leaning on a rock, his hands crossed like this," he put his hands together in a prayerful display, "And his head upward in prayer?"

"Yeah, I do. There was one at Juliette's house," I answered, remembering one summer day back in '42 when I paid my one and only visit to the Hamilton place.

"I've seen men all over this outfit doing that, like they are afraid of what to do in Japan. I guess sometimes being friendly is harder than being mean."

He smiled tightly and shook his head slowly.

"You're not afraid are you, Red?"

I smiled back.

"No, Mr. Blanchard, I am not afraid in the least. I never did like killing Japs. I just turned on and off every time they came at us. I never put a name to them or a man in them. Except when we met that prisoner on the truck. The one with the silk pictures. He had a soul, a heart. God knows they all do."

"Yeah," Tim replied.

"I'll always remember that. You were very honorable to him, and him to you."

"I'd like to meet him again, and shake his hand." I acknowledged.

We sat there a few moments, our minds on the new "normal" around us.

We laid back on our berths.

A long time had passed when Tim looked over at me.

"You know that I know that I gotta take care of you and your seasickness, and I'm proud to do it. Nobel had it the worst, bless his heart. God, I miss him. I'm glad he found his girl just like Pete told him to do."

When he said 'Pete' his voice cracked like the yellowed page of a very old book.

I just looked over at him and said, "I know."

We just stared at the overhead.

10:00 am, Monday, October 15, 1945

Onboard the USS Mifflin, Gulf of Davao, Pacific Ocean.

  The *USS Mifflin* left the Gulf of Davao and set a course for Japan. As the sailors would say, the weather was good, the sky was clear, the wind was negligible, and the seas were moderate. As I would tell you, it was only rough enough to make me a little bit seasick. I spent a lot of time standing near the hatch, topside, feeling the wind in my face. A cigarette every couple of hours, and all was as good as it could be.
  Our destination was the seaport at Hiro Wan, Okayama, Japan. Other troop ships in the Task Force were going to Matsuyama, Japan.
  Mindanao was behind us, as we sailed in a four-column formation. The *Mifflin* was the second ship in the first column. The entire Hawaiian Division was sailing that beautiful day, leaving the Philippine Islands and World War 2 behind them. Mighty, gray-black ships surged onward, cutting the sea into slivers of white and blue, leaving wide wakes of foam as other vessels followed their course, one after another, crossing the dark blue northern Pacific Ocean.
  A series of "V's" spread across the seascape.
  It was such a grand sight to see!
  I enjoyed my frequent walks to topside, to take in the ocean breeze and gaze across the waves at the Navy ships carrying us farther and farther from the dark memories and ghosts of the thick, deadly jungles. I met Captain Morgan in the passageway one afternoon. Holding a small stack of manila folders under his arm, he nodded to me, and I stopped.

"Captain Morgan, Sir. I was wondering, do you know anything new about Captain White?"

He looked at me, and he sighed sadly.

"Ah, yes, Smith. He made it home. It breaks my heart to tell you, though, he died a little while back. He saw his wife and kids, they said his health improved, then he took a dive. They called it 'stump appendicitis.' Very rare. It was like it came back. He led you men through hell, and it took something rare to take him down. But, remember that he made it home, my friend. Back to Memphis, where he was born. He was buried with honors in his hometown. I swear, he was the best officer I have ever known. I walk in his shoes, but I don't fill them. I am not deserving of that honor. I am sorry."

I stared at the deck, then looked back up.

"You're a good man, Captain Morgan, Sir. Don't feel bad. There's not an officer in this here Army that could've filled his shoes. We have been honored to serve under both of you, Sir."

His face relaxed.

"Thank you, Smith. Have you heard anything about your friend, Mr. Petty?"

My eyes moistened. My heart stopped for a moment. I felt the hole in it.

"Sir, he died. He was a hometown hero, too, and was buried with honors where he was born. Just like Captain White."

He nodded his head.

"We are just a month or two away from going home, both of us. God bless you, Smith."

"And God bless you, Sir."

Six Days Later

Mid-Afternoon, Sunday, October 21, 1945

    We were in the Iyo-nada Sea, which cuts through the central heartland of Japan. The Navy Task Force was realigned, as half of the troop ships split off on an easterly course to Matsuyama, Japan, and we continued northeasterly to Okayama. This time, we sailed in a two-column formation, as the seventh ship in the first column.
    We sailed through the day, slowing as the maritime traffic near Japan increased, and mine-sweeping ships explored the once-hostile waters. We passed small islands to our left and right.
    Ahead, we could see the buildings, sea walls, docks, concrete ramps, and beaches of the Hiro Wan seaport.
    By nightfall, we were anchored in Berth 38, outer anchorage, Hiro Wan.


5:00 am, Monday, October 22, 1945

Hiro Wan Seaport, Okayama, Japan

    The Navy "Beach Party," the official masters of the unloading of materials and equipment, landed at the concrete sea plane ramp at Hiro Wan. They surveyed the facilities on the beach and organized it so the unloading of troops and equipment could be conducted in the best possible manner. We came ashore an hour later, and gathered alongside the sea wall at the right side of the beach. We quickly and easily left the boats, like a professional staff of expert movers. No jumping into the water, screaming and running up to the top of the beach like so many amphibious landings in the past.

We brought beach markers, which were immediately set up by the Beach Party to organize and direct the placement of men, materials, and equipment.

Two hours later, the remainder of the troops on board the *Mifflin* walked ashore on double-floats that were attached to the docks along the sea plane ramps.

Then, an hour after that, the Navy began delivering our cargo.

Everything moved along smoothly. Vehicles were swiftly and easily unloaded. The conditions at the beach were ideal. They could drive directly from the boats onto the concrete sea plane ramp. However, there was a moment when a boat loaded with trailers had no jeeps or trucks to haul them off. Tim and I hustled around and found a jeep with no driver, and drove it from ship to shore the rest of the day, towing trailers full of gear.

Three cranes were available, with two Japanese operators in each, at the ramp for cargo unloading, two on the right and one on the left. More than enough trucks were available at all times, and more boats could easily unload the gear directly into the trucks.

The beach was kept clear and without confusion by the speedy removal of all vehicles and cargo. Tim and I, and the rest of the Army Shore Party, did a good job. As the day progressed, plenty of vehicles were available and immediately put to the task at hand. Working parties were formed to manhandle cargo, and no time was lost in unloading any boat.

By noon the next day, all men and equipment had been unloaded from the *Mifflin* and delivered to the mainland of Japan.

The 21st Infantry Regiment had just been delivered successfully to the last field duty of the war. We had been withdrawn from combat after sixty-three continuous days of deadly action on Mindanao, inflicting almost 2,000 Japanese casualties.

We were now officially assigned to the Okayama Occupation Force. Our mission – to put into action the stand-down of the Japanese military forces in the city of Okayama.


Thursday, October 25, 1945.

Okayama, Honshu Island, Occupied Japan.

We moved by train to our camp at Okayama City and established our headquarters in the CP of the Task Force at the former post of the 48th Japanese Infantry. Our quarters were barracks that had been used by Japanese soldiers during the first years of the pre-war build-up.

Tim and I were up and running every morning at first chow, eager to take our jeep to Regimental Headquarters and wait for someone to need transportation.

I can say one thing for sure, Tim and I finding that jeep our first day at Hiro Wan Seaport and taking it like it was ours was the best thing that could have happened. We immediately began acting like it really did belong to us and, sooner or later, some supply sergeant was bound to say,

"Here, you need an authorization for that jeep. Take this Form."

We had a jeep and no one to tell us what to do with it. So, we just parked outside of the Battalion Command Building every day and waited for some officer or high-class Army civilian to tell us where they wanted to go or what they wanted to get or who they wanted to see.

We took an American reporter-photographer with a Second Lieutenant escort to Hiroshima, a two-hour drive, and saw the awful devastation of that once-thriving city. We witnessed charred buildings standing in barren landscapes that had no trees, some buildings with no floors, rising like twisted, hollow, brick skeletons. We didn't say much, as the U.S. military guards waved us along every time we slowed for the reporter's camera.

On the way back, beyond the ghastly ground zero, we drove through a small Japanese village with a central, open park. The dusty residues of the atomic bomb blast had been cleaned away to show green grass pushing its leaves upward. It wasn't the kunai or the cogan or the abaca of our recent memories, but green grass like the town squares of home. We parked and got out of the jeep, grateful for the chance to breathe cleaner air and walk on ground that had not been baked in Hell's oven.

There were Japanese civilians sitting in the grass, some surrounded by trinkets, bags, and pitiful items, wishing to trade them for food or drink. I didn't want to walk through their misery and misfortune, but a Japanese man sitting beside easels of painted silk cloths caught my eye, forcing a gasp of astonishment.

*It was the prisoner with the sketched silk cloths! There, right in front of me!*

I walked toward him on unsure feet, peering to get a glimpse of his face.

He looked my way, his eyebrows raised, and he abruptly stood up.

As I approached, a sudden look of recognition swept across his face, and a thin smile crossed his lips.

He gently bowed toward me, remained a second, and straightened his back.

I slowed, nearly stopping, and bowed.

I resumed my walk toward him and, at ten feet, began extending my right hand in a gesture of acquaintance.

He offered his right hand to me, and our hands met in a firm grip.

The handshake had little motion, but was ten seconds of familiar recognition and mutual respect.

He looked into my eyes and winked.

I smiled broadly and winked back.

He waved his hand across the easels of silk paintings and sketches, and raised his eyebrows to see if I wanted any.

I said slowly, "They are pretty, and belong in a museum."

I waved my arms, like I was describing a very large building.

He smiled, bowing his head in appreciation.

I then pointed to a small, well-made, shiny wooden box in front of him, with a brass tag on the top with Japanese engraving. I raised my eyebrows, showing interest in it.

He smiled from ear to ear, emptied some paintbrushes and coins from it, and handed it to me.

I took the box, opened and closed it easily, and wanted it dearly.

I nodded my head approvingly, and reached into my pocket for what little money I had.

He raised in hands, palms out, and shook his head.

"No pay," he said, in very broken English.

"*Watashi no yujin*," he said.

He then pointed at me and said, "My Friend," in pretty good English.

I pointed at him and said, "My Friend."

We nodded, bowed again, and shook hands. He took his left hand and placed it over our clasped hands. I placed the box on the grass and did the same.

Retrieving my box, I turned back toward the jeep, thanking God for the chance to close the loop, to acknowledge the man I had befriended in the most unlikely of places, under the most unexpected of circumstances.

When I got to the jeep, I looked back toward him.

He waved.

I waved back.


Sunday, November 11, 1945.

Okayama, Honshu, Japan.

At noon, the 21$^{st}$ Regiment performed a parade of foot troops and motorized units on the city streets of Okayama. This was in commemoration of Armistice Day of World War I and also a demonstration of Allied Military Power to the Japanese people.

There was Tim and I, in the middle of the parade, driving our beloved jeep with a full-bird Colonel we did not know. Several Army Bands were spread along the parade, and they played upbeat military marching tunes and a few popular songs we had heard on the radio. The Japanese civilians lined the streets that day, offering reserved but genuine cheers as we passed.

I had gotten word a week before that my go-home papers were being prepared, and the feeling was setting in me more and more that Japan would soon, very soon, be a memory. I tried to get the most out of every day, to learn and appreciate as much as I could about the restrained courtesy and honorable behavior of the Japanese people.

Tim and I would listen to the conversations of the officers and diplomats we would drive to meeting after meeting in all parts of town. Our passengers would constantly remark that the attitude of the Japanese civilian, military, and governmental agencies had been good. They would say that all the civilian agencies had been highly cooperative in delivering accurate reports, and in disposing of Japanese military material and supplies.

We took Army brass to inspect the schools, and heard them talk about the textbooks becoming more like America's textbooks. They talked a lot about the elimination of Military Training in the public schools.

They were impressed that no works of art had been looted from any of the nations the Japanese had invaded.

We were part of a convoy of officers and specialists that were granting permission for factories and industries that had produced war equipment to begin making civilian goods, like clothing, furniture, and other dry goods.

Another convoy was inspecting Japanese Army lands and turning them over to local farmers for food production.

Though Tim and I never took them up on it, overnight passes for US soldiers, no more than 400 at a time, were approved for Saturday nights only.

On November 12, Tim was told by Sergeant Haney that his go-home papers were being drawn up, and he would be leaving in less than a week. Tim was delighted, and smiled like I had never seen him smile before when he said he might be home for Christmas.

The next day, the good sergeant told me it would be my last day in Japan.

Tim and I had a lot of whiskey that night, and cried some tears at our parting. But we laughed more while we drank at the pure joy of going back to Texas.

# CHAPTER 25

# OPERATION: MAGIC CARPET

September, 1945.

The Army, Navy, Merchant Marines, and the War Shipping Administration gathered all their ships together and formed *Operation Magic Carpet,* with the goal to quickly send the almost two-million troops in the Pacific back to their homes. The War Department promised they would all be home by June 1946.

In late 1945, *Operation Santa Claus* was added to the Pacific Magic Carpet rides, and almost seven-hundred thousand soldiers were loaded onto whatever ships were available and were returned home before Christmas.

December 1945 was the busiest month.

Wednesday, November 14, 1945

Okayama, Honshu, Japan.

My Magic Carpet ride started on November 14, 1945.

The first group of Army replacements had just arrived in Okayama that day. There was a hundred of them. All were wide-eyed, green enlisted men. I chuckled at the thought of how all of us looked to the fresh new troops. We were thin, lean men, hardened by combat, tempered by war, and yellowed by Atabrine.

Tim was told his Magic Carpet ride would start on Sunday.

As he walked me down to the docks, we swore to each other that we would meet in Dallas soon.

"Home alive in '45," could be heard everywhere a group of men were gathered, packed and ready to board.

When we reached the boarding area for my ship, we looked up and realized it was a huge aircraft carrier.

"Man, that is one big ship, Red."

All I could say was, "Yep. Never been on something that big."

We looked at each other, knowing it was time to part. When we took our farewell handshake and hug, both of us had tears in our eyes and a broad smile on our face.

He looked at me and proudly announced, "Red, we made it! Without a scratch!"

I nodded to him whole-heartedly and agreed, "We did, Mr. Blanchard, we sure did. It took the Good Lord's help to get us here, too."

"Through all of that, Red, did you think it would happen?"

"Yes, Tim, I did. I knew that death and danger walked with us every day, but I felt I would make it all the way to the end. I just had a feeling that God and His angels would fight alongside us. Like little sparrows in a storm, we made it through."

*More than just little sparrows, Tim,* I thought to myself.

*I had a guardian angel tell me face-to-face.*

*"All is fine, keep your head down, stay quiet, no harm will come to you this night."*

We stood there, looking at my ship, feeling the presence of thousands of happy men going home, sensing our own almost-uncontrollable urge to get on those magic carpets and sail as quickly away as we could, up, up, and away.

At times the war memories were just a finger-touch below our consciousness, waiting to suddenly appear as a jolt, or an unexpected chill as the frightening memories slashed through our minds.

A mortar blast. A Jap soldier screams as he hauntingly runs toward me, bayonet pointed straight at my chest. Pete and Nobel lying on the ground. A high-pitched bullet whistles by, the *thump* as it hits bone and flesh, and someone beside me sinks lifeless into the kunai grass.

Then, the reality of the moment returns, and the hallucination vanishes as suddenly as it had appeared.

All is well.

I'm going home!

I looked up the gangplank that disappeared into a large opening on the side of the gigantic ship.

"I'm gonna get really sick on that crowded boat."

We both laughed, and Tim said, "You know what? I bet you won't. Those ships will be so crowded that you'll be in big, humongous rooms with cots everywhere. Big rooms are better to ride in those waves, better than those tiny rooms jammed with racks five or six high. Besides, you'll be going home and maybe you can find a bunch of seasick guys and ya'll can suffer together" as he laughed loudly.

A tall, lanky fellow beside us, his barracks bag thrown across his shoulder, looked at me as Tim laughed

"I'm one of them, that's for sure!" he announced in a slow drawl.

"I get sicker than a dawg every time. Let's stay together, start us a Sick Man's Club. My name's Pete. Pete Clemens. From Oklahoma."

Tim and I looked at each other in a flash. A thousand images ran through our brains at the same time.

*Dammit to hell! Why does his name have to be Pete?*
Tim spoke up first.

"Pleased to meet you Mr. Clemens," as he reached to shake his hand.

"You're from our neck of the woods. I'm Tim Blanchard, and this here is Red Smith. He's going back to East Texas. I want you to watch him really close, and he'll watch you. I expect you'll both be pretty good at being seasick, so you can do it together."

A huge smile filled Clemens' sunbaked face. He knew he had just found a way to make it across the ocean without being alone.

"Clemens, I'll be sick with you," I told him.
"Guaranteed to be true,
I have never failed to be sick on the ocean blue.
That's what I do.
I'm going as far as Texas with you.
Tim's gonna follow us in a day or two."

"By damn, Red, you're a poet. All of your sentences rhyme. I hope you can do that rhyming when we're sick. It'll make the days pass quicker," Clemens exclaimed.

We laughed, and Tim explained, "Red don't talk too much when he's sick."

We laughed again.

Providence had found a way for Tim and me to split up that day without bawling our eyes out. Clemens, a tall drink of water from Oklahoma, was put in our midst to distract us from our sorrow.

"See you in Texas, Tim."

"See you in Texas, Red."

Pete Clemens and I walked up the gangplank together, each carrying our barracks bag slung across our shoulders, hanging from our backs. All of our worldly possessions were in those bags, and they were going home with us.

We approached the large opening below the top deck, and realized our magic carpet, an aircraft carrier, had no aircraft. We could see the wide, expansive hanger bay, normally packed with planes, was now full of cots, some already claimed by men spreading the contents of their barracks bag on and below the cot.

Clemens and I gazed inside, letting our eyes get accustomed to the much darker landscape within.

"Let's look for something in the corner," I said.

"Someplace away from people who will be moving around, smoking, joking, playing cards, and making us even more sicker."

Clemens nodded in approval, and we walked further into the huge room.

"Look, there's a place over there to the left, along the bulkhead. I see some empty cots, and they are close enough to this big-ass door that we can get some fresh air and puke in a bucket anytime we want to," he said as he chuckled.

"Swell. That sounds like a lot of fun. Let's get those two cots over there," I said, pointing in the direction of what appeared to be two cots by themselves, between a small partition and the big-ass door.

We were set. This would be our home for the next sixteen days.

The ship started moving away from the docks just before dusk, and sailed into the Pacific and away from Japan as darkness fell over the calm sea. The lights along the shore, growing ever smaller and smaller, was our joyous evidence that our magic carpet ride home had begun.


November 15-30, 1945.

The Pacific Ocean.

From the beginning of our journey home on the big carrier, Clemens and I noticed that we were not as seasick as we expected. The big ship was not tossed about on the waves, and the layout in the hanger bay was better than the crammed quarters of our earlier rides, just as Tim had predicted.

Clemens turned out to be a good buddy, and told some funny Oklahoma stories. He was a decent, honest fellow who was fair in everything he said and did, and treated everybody we met on that magic carpet with the same big smile and down-home manner. He never told a joke that made fun of anyone or anyplace. Clemens was the perfect friend on my journey home.

Every day we would have a late breakfast and an early supper. We spent a lot of time up on the flight deck, sitting and smoking cigarettes, my Zippo lighter making its click-music in the tropical winds.

The ship went back to Leyte Island after it left Japan and picked up a couple hundred soldiers headed for home, then back to Goodenough Island to do the same. We did not get off the ship either time. Clemens and I had no desire to touch soil until it was American soil. We were told Seattle, Washington was to be our arrival point after three years in the islands of the Pacific Ocean.

*Was it only three years?*
*So much life and death crammed into those three years.*

It was great to just sit on the flight deck, watching the clouds, feeling the wind, carrying on slow, treasured conversations about home and friends and family and history.

We had lived and performed a lot of history those three years. We had seen hundreds of warships, like the magic carpet we were riding, pounding the beaches in front of us with tons of bombs and rockets. We had watched the flashes in the distant night skies as battles raged on the seas around the islands, smelling the stench of death and knowing that victory did not come without a terrible price of death, mutilation, and broken minds. Even on the flight deck we could see the men on crutches and the ones walking slow, being helped around by a buddy. The most pitiful were the ones who would stare forward with that "thousand-yard stare" we had seen on Leyte, emotionless, until they would react defensively to a boom or a blast that was silent to all except them.

So we sat on that flight deck, Clemens and I, every day, on our folded-up wool blankets, even when it rained. We smoked and talked and smoked some more. We saw whales once, rolling up to the surface and blowing their sprays of water high into fountains of reflected colors. We saw hundreds of dolphins, playfully jumping in and out of the water in groups of ten or twenty, following the ship for miles. I pictured them being our happy guides, showing us the way back to the lives we had left behind.

Clemens had been in the 34th Infantry Regiment, our sister-regiment of the 24th Division. So, he was part of the Hawaiian Division, too, and wore the Taro Leaf on his jacket like me. In fact, it was the 34th that we replaced on Day 1 of Breakneck Ridge, after they had cleared Pinamopoan of Japanese resistance.

I told him I could still see the image in my mind's eye of that grey, dim dawn, when we looked into their eyes as they marched through our lines in the beautifully sad and gloomy ceremony of Relief-in-Place. I recalled how they wore dirty, ragged uniforms, and marched on weary legs, with heavy heads that bobbed up and down slowly, and wide-open eyes. staring blankly ahead as they placed each foot in front of the other, walking steadily forward, away from the horrors that lay behind them.

Clemens listened carefully as I described them. He nodded slowly.

"Those were some bad times, Red," he confessed.

"Yep," I answered.

"I don't remember seeing you. All y'all looked the same. I reckon we looked the same two weeks later, after we cleared Breakneck Ridge."

Clemens told me about Kilay Ridge on Leyte. For three weeks they held the ridge against uncountable attacks by the enemy. Low on rations and short on ammunition, the 34th held its position.

But the worst was yet to come, on Mindanao.

Clemens and I talked about the three-straight-months of fighting while we cleared the Japanese Army off on Mindanao. Sometimes one of us would be talking about a particular day and place, as much as we could remember, and be describing a battle or an ambush - when we would just stop, look around, fidget with the blanket we were sitting on, and mutter something like, "I'm through with that story. That was all I wanted to say about it, anyway." Our memories had just replayed a horrifying and nightmarish incident that did not want to come out into the light of day. We knew exactly when one of us would reach that point. We just touched the other's knee and said, "No more. I know. I saw it. That's enough."

One afternoon I heard a voice from the crowded deck say loudly, "Hey, Red Smith! I'll be damned! Hey!"

I quickly looked in the direction of the voice and saw my buddies George and Walter, from the Eleventh Airborne school!

We talked the rest of the day, through the afternoon, during evening chow, and right on up to Lights Off about absolutely everything. They had been on Leyte, and had landed a week after the horrible typhoon that tore us up on Breakneck Ridge. They said it tore them up as they lay seasick in their racks offshore. They spent three months fighting to clear a mountain pass along Ormoc Road, to drive the Japanese defenders from it and the surrounding heights. They had fought on Luzon, and helped liberate Manila.

We talked about my crazy experience at paratrooper school, when I came screaming out of the sky at the 250-foot tower, fighting everyone within fist-range. They all came to visit me at sick bay that night, before I shipped out the next day, saying they were glad that they would never have to watch something like that again. Clemens laughed more than I had seen him laugh since we met.

    We would all gather, almost every day on the flight deck, and enjoy our magic carpet ride. When Thanksgiving Day reached us on November 22, the cooks in the Navy galley did all they could to provide us with a fitting and proper Thanksgiving Dinner. They cooked turkey, a little ham, sweet potatoes, dressing (not cornbread), green beans, brussel sprouts (not for me), pumpkin pie, ice cream, and the best yeast rolls I had ever eaten!

    Watching the others, I could see that each person was carrying a deep memory of past Thanksgivings by the way they would momentarily stop and stare at their plate, not necessarily examining the plate, but looking at it as if it had been transported to an earlier time, a different place, where far-away family was gathered around the table or friends, now lost, were within a smile's-reach. They would hold their knife and fork motionless for a few seconds, or just close their eyes. I know this, because I watched them do it, and I did it myself.

    I missed Pete, and Nobel. I missed Kenny and Tim. I missed them more than my own family that day. I knew I would see my family in just a handful of days, but I knew I would probably never see my friends again. Maybe I would see Tim in Dallas. Maybe not.

    I remembered the Thanksgiving on Leyte last year, after we had beaten Breakneck Ridge. We met the little Filipino boy Tony that day, and took him in like he was family.

I tried to remember the Thanksgiving at Camp Caves in Australia the year before Leyte, in '43. The more I tried, the farther away it slipped. It must not have been much, maybe mutton and dressing. But the clearest memory was the four of us – Nobel, Pete, Kenny, and me – going to the Australia Hotel and enjoying Kenny's favorite bourbon, Virginia Gentleman, at the Long Bar. I met Mr. William Jackson that day, as he sat alone drinking a toast to his son, Red Jackson, who had been killed on New Guinea. The old man took me into his heart that day and showed me how even a perfect gentleman struggles with the loss of a son in war. Mr. Jackson told me that I looked like his son, and wished me the blessings of God when I left his table. I could still hear him saying, "Thanks for coming back to spend a few precious moments, Red."

    I could not remember a single thing about the Thanksgiving of '42, when I was spending my first week of paratrooper training at Fort Bragg, Georgia. I felt myself shiver as I thought about it, then tried to cram the memory of paratrooper training back into a dusty corner of my mind, far away from the little brown box where priceless memories go.

    I thought of Juliette, and of all the missed Thanksgivings of this war with all the families we had known. The Hamiltons and Thomases. The Sandifeers and Poseys.

    I thought of Juliette and smiled.

    *"Are you ready for me to come home?"* I pondered.


Friday, November 30, 1945.

Seattle, Washington.

We could see the many villages and towns along the islands and inlets of Puget Sound early that morning, and the entire ship was buzzing with excitement. It was chilly on the flight deck, probably about forty degrees. In the distance was the mountain they called Rainier, disappearing in and out of the rain clouds. As we slowly moved into the narrows of the Sound we could suddenly see the buildings and streets of downtown Seattle, then the hundreds of docks and Navy ships clustered around the Puget Sound Naval Shipyard. We saw dozens of battleships, carriers, and destroyers sitting in the docks, with men, like ants, scurrying across them as they worked.

Each of us had received a short note from the many "headquarters" that had been organized on the ship to tell us where we were headed, along with our formal orders and vouchers to travel home.

Clemens and I had vouchers in our pockets telling us to board Bus 10 as soon as we left the carrier. It would take us to the rail station nearby, where we and our barracks bags would get on the 5:00 pm east-bound train.

When our feet touched the ground, there was no American soil to kiss, just concrete. So, we both reached down and softly touched the cement dock of Bremerton, Washington, with our palms, and whispered to ourselves, *"It is over. I am back in America."*

Bus 10 was waiting for us in the middle of a long row of buses, and we climbed onto it like children boarding a school bus, giggling and laughing, goosing each other up the steps. An hour-long drive and a tall bridge later, we arrived at the train depot, a huge brown-brick building with a tall clock tower.

    A small crowd of USO volunteers, some in Santa caps, were waiting for us, asking us which train we needed and handing out half-pint cartons of milk and bologna sandwiches. I stared at the two cartons of milk in my hands and couldn't believe it. Pure, fresh milk! After months - years – of powdered milk, here was the real stuff!

    Clemens and I drank both cartons, then asked for two more. Then I asked for two more, relishing each mouthful. Then, two more. I drank eight half-pints of milk there on the steps of the Seattle train depot that day. I would remember that milk the rest of my life.

    We were directed to our 5:00 pm train. We sat on the benches along the track, anxious to board the iron-horse that would carry us back east, through the beautiful western states, galloping across the Rocky Mountains, to a more beautiful place called Home.

# CHAPTER 26

# JULIETTE HAMILTON

Wednesday Morning, November 14, 1945.

Wellington High School, Wellington, Collingsworth County, Texas Panhandle, Texas.

Juliette was slowly walking up the front steps of Wellington High School when she hesitated on the last step. She watched the other students walking through the open door, playfully chatting with each other, a few books under their arms. No one had talked to her on the school bus this day. Her friend Dorothy Smith, her ONLY friend, had not been on the bus that morning, and there was no person friendly enough to even say "Good Morning" to her. That's the way the other girls in the senior class acted. You were either a City Girl or a Farm Girl, and they had already decided that Juliette Hamilton was a Farm Girl. And you didn't have to talk to the Farm Girls.

It was in the clothing. You either bought your dresses at Franklin's in Amarillo or they were made at home.

*Look closely at the pattern and you could always see material from a Martha White flower sack on the Farm Girls, not to mention the obvious homemade quality.*

But seventeen-year-old Juliette was not wearing a flour sack dress this day. She was wearing her pretty grey tight knit dress with the light blue stitching and two dark blue bows embroidered above each breast. It was her best dress, and she always felt good in it. But not at this moment.

She was tired of the prissy-ass girls and the way they made her feel inferior. This would be the last day she would put up with it. She had already made an "A" in every class, and her English teacher told her a few days ago that she could easily graduate without going to another class.

Juliette had given that possibility a great deal of thought the past few days.

*It would be so nice to never have to deal with these snoots again,* she thought to herself.

However, the letter that she had gotten from Red Smith a few days ago had been the biggest thing on her mind this week, far more important than the high-minded girls in the senior class. Red had written that he was just a few days away from boarding a ship and coming home. She liked the way he had said it. He called it his "magic carpet ride to Texas."

*"I'll be coming to Dodson, and I don't even know where it is,"* he had written.

*"But I've been a lot of places the last three years and I didn't know where they were, either, so this trip should be easy. I hope to see you by Christmas, Juliette. Love, Red."*

She wanted to be there at the Smith place when he came home. She wanted that with all her heart and soul. Nobody knew when the date and time would be, but she had already put the things in motion to make it happen.

Juliette was already spending a lot of time with the Smiths. Her other sisters had already left the nest, flown the coop, and either had jobs in Dallas or a husband and son in Sulphur Bluff. Her brothers, Alfred and Alvis, were fifteen-years old and thirteen-years old, and were helping Mr. Hamilton in the fields and at home. So, she would walk the short two miles from the Hamilton place near the Collingsworth County Line, a stone's throw from Oklahoma, to the Smith house near Dodson almost every day, spending time with Bud and Altie Smith, talking to the younger Smith sisters, including little Mae, now four-years old. She wanted to know every detail of Red's homecoming, and had already read all the letters he had sent home.

    Her plan was for Red to see her first, and see none of the other snobby girls in the county. She felt like she knew him more than any other man, though she had spent so little time with him.

    *Knowing his family is like knowing him,* she thought.

    *He will fall in love with me, and I will fall in love with him. That part will be so easy because I already love him, and have for as long as I remember,* she assured her heart.

    *It will happen.*

    She opened the big double door of Wellington High School, and walked between the two Gothic pinnacles that adorned the front entrance. Inside, she strolled into the auditorium for one more look at what she believed was one of the prettiest sights in the world. It was quiet inside, exactly what she needed. She gazed down the sloping aisles, past the wooden-backed seats with armrests. The stage curtains were partially open, revealing what appeared to be a stage set. Soft light was entering through the windows along the left wall, and, at the end of the aisle, a set of steps led from the auditorium floor to the left side of the stage.

    She sauntered down the aisle and up the steps, wanting to feel what it was like to stand at center-stage, looking out across the seats. Light fixtures were suspended from the ceiling throughout the auditorium room. It was a breathtaking experience, and set a hundred dreams into motion in her Cinderella-spirit as her heartbeat raced in her chest.

The Stage.

The Broadway of West Texas.

*"I stood there!"* she bragged to herself, as she walked back to the steps and up the left aisle, toward the auditorium door.

She opened the door and noiselessly ascended the stairs to the second-floor corridor.

Lockers were mounted on both sides of the hallway, and the classrooms doors were closed. She ran her fingers along the decorative brick that covered the lower portion of the hallway walls, beneath the lockers.

Juliette found her locker, and reached into her dress pocket for the key. Opening the locker quietly, she took her personal things out and replaced them with the geography book she had taken home the night before.

All things done now, she silently closed it and walked farther down the hallway to the Sewing Room, where her favorite teacher was bound to be.

Sure enough, Mrs. Balinger was there, preparing for her second period class. She sat at one of the three long tables, spreading out some white fabric with tiny pink flowers on it. Her gray hair was neatly brushed back and tied into a long ponytail with a dark green band. One wall was full of little storage shelves with small doors, each shelf holding some of her many sewing supplies neatly and securely packed inside. She looked up and smiled.

"Well, Juliette, are you roaming the halls?"

"Yes, I am, Mrs. Balinger. I'm getting all my things together before I slip on down to the office and tell them I'm gonna be gone for a while. We got family coming in and I'll be busy helping my folks, now that all my sisters are chasing their dreams in Dallas. You remember them, don'tcha?"

"I sure do, Juliette. They were always looking out that window there," as she pointed to her left.

"They always liked what was out there more than what was in here."

Juliette giggled, and agreed.

"Since they're all gone to Dallas, I can tell you now that you are one of the best students I have here in Wellington. I know you can go, there's nothing keeping you here. Your good grades will attest to that."

Juliette nodded her head with a smile.

"Thank you, Mrs. Balinger."

"I don't suppose the family that's coming in might be including that Smith boy I've been hearing about? You know, Dorothy Smith's brother, Red?"

The teacher looked at Juliette with a sparkle in her eye.

"I don't blame you, Juliette. Dorothy showed me his picture. I would do it, too, if I were your age. Come to think of it, I did it, when I was your age."

She chuckled, and blushed slightly.

"My Daniel was coming home from the War to End All Wars," as she shook her head back and forth when she said those words. The ponytail rushed to catch up each time.

"I was five years younger than him. I absolutely stopped what I was doing and waited a month for him at his parents' house up in Texarkana, then waited two more months until I had convinced him that we were made for each other. And we have been sailing these seas together for twenty-seven years now."

They both laughed together, and Juliette let out a long sigh.

"That's a very romantic story, Mrs. Balinger," she admired.

"Maybe, perhaps...."

"Oh, you can bet your life on that, Juliette. I feel you have that power. You know, I married into the Balingers and never had a doubt that it wouldn't work. The last name Balinger is what they called old ships back in the 1200's, and we've never hit a rough spot yet. Dan's been a good Captain. You know, a Smith can do anything, from stone to metal to wood to words. I believe your Mr. Smith will do anything to make you happy, Juliette."

They both hugged for a minute, and Mrs. Balinger looked at her intently.

"You will find your Paradise out there, Lady Hamilton. You get along now, and don't forget to come visit me often."

Juliette bowed gently, and walked out, heading for the stairs. She danced down them like a Princess headed for the Gala Ball.

She entered the office and told them she was sorry to go, but had to help her family. She lay her locker key on the office table, and didn't wait for any response.

The bell was ringing for the second hour to begin, and was surprised to see Dorothy Smith coming in the front door. Late again.

She was a year older than Dorothy, but Dorothy was more than a just a year ahead of Juliette in zeal and knowledge of Life.

Including men.

And smoking.

And drinking.

Above all, Dorothy was fun to be with. A redhead with no limits, no match.

Juliette told her what she had just done, and they both started laughing and jumping up and down in the hallway.

"Let's go!" Dorothy proclaimed.

"I know someone who can take us home, eventually," she laughed.

When they both walked out of the school, Juliette felt better than she had ever felt. She was confident that all was going to be perfect.

Paradise lay ahead.

# CHAPTER 27

# RETURN HOME

Friday, November 30 – Friday, December 7, 1945.

Fort Sam Houston, San Antonio, Bexar County, Texas.

I took the train from Seattle on Friday evening, under cloudy skies and the temperature in the mid-forties, and for the next seven-and-a-half days I saw some of the most beautiful country I had ever seen. No more jungles. Just majestic peaks topped with marshmallow clouds under a big blue sky. At the foot of the mountains lay vast plains stretching from horizon to horizon, with grass rippling like waves on a beach as the north-wind breathed across the landscape.
    Mile after mile.
    Forests.
    Rivers, some mighty, some just a trickle.
    There were times when a landform would bring a jerk to my senses, reviving a deeply buried memory of a bitter battle in a distant land, where the trees would explode with machine gun fire, and Arisakas would pop as men fell. I would move my face from the window, close my eyes, and let the moment pass.
    Night after day, day after night, and then five more times again. Sometimes Clemens and I ate in the dining car, sometimes we ate from a box. A big Army coffee urn was always ready and waiting in the club car.

The train would stop at almost every city along the way, letting soldiers off. Family would often be waiting for them at the station. Mothers, fathers, brothers, sisters, wives, and sweethearts would cheer and grab the soldier, covering him with hugs and kisses. Most stations would have red, white, and blue banners with "Welcome Home Soldiers" stretched between the pillars of the passenger arrival area. As the train would approach and the steam would waft past them, the banners would ripple like the many red-white-blue flags we had planted in the jungle villages and hilltops we had taken from the Japanese.

The most memorable were the many scenes of a single, worried lady, waiting, watching intently as each soldier stepped from the train, a brief apprehension in her eyes, a look of near desperation, then a glorious smile erupting across her face as her soldier, her man, her lover, her husband, set his foot on the homeland of their future. It would make us shiver on the inside, often cry, as we watched that wonderful moment play out in front of us, as the end of that couple's long nightmare of separation turned instantly into the beginning of their new paradise.

Sometimes the layover would be as much as an hour, and we would get off to buy cigarettes or something we needed that wasn't available on the train. Lighter fluid. Socks. Toothpaste. Even gloves for the cold nights, something we hadn't needed for three years. I saw some colored toothpicks at the store once and I thought of Pete.

*I'll never see another colored toothpick again without thinking of Pete, smiling at me with one of them hanging from the corner of his mouth.*

We never stayed off the train very long. Clemens and I did not want the iron horse to leave without us and gallop away with our hopes and dreams.

Our world took on a fairy-tale charm as the rail-song of **clickety-clack, clickety-clack** was always in the background. The whistle would announce each road crossing with a **woooh-wooooh** to tell us we were getting farther and farther away from the terrifying sounds of war and the gut-wrenching smells of death.

On the fourth day I asked the porter if there was any way to get my dress uniform cleaned and pressed, and he said, "We sure can, Sir, yes indeed we can." I put on my combat pants and shirt, and he kindly took my dress uniform back to his work area near the dining car and had it back, fresh-smelling and neatly pressed, the next day.

*I'll go home in a clean suit, after two weeks at sea and a week on the train,* I told myself.

My combat fatigues were comfortable, and I would occasionally touch the torn places and run my fingers along each stain, trying to let the good memories outweigh the bad.

As we followed the rails deeper into Texas, I could see the landscapes were becoming more and more familiar. We passed though Mineral Wells, and all the memories of Camp Wolters came back to me as gently as the smell of woodsmoke on a winter jacket.

It felt like Texas, too, with the daytime temperatures in the mid-seventies and a blue-and-white partly cloudy sky. This was not the Pacific, nor was it Seattle.

Saturday, December 8, 1945.

Fort Sam Houston, San Antonio, Bexar County, Texas.

    The processing center at Fort Sam Houston in San Antonio was our destination, and we arrived there late Saturday afternoon, more than a week after we had left Seattle. The two barracks buildings at the processing center were over-crowded, but we found a place for two cots in a corner on the second floor, overlooking the Fort Sam Houston cemetery across the street and to our right. It was a somber sight, and Clemens and I thought it was fitting that we would spend our last few days in the Army close to the honored soldiers and heroes that were now "at home" in the green field of honor.

    Sergeants and Lieutenants were working the next day, Sunday, to manage the newly arrived men like us and get our paperwork started for discharge.

    When Monday morning came, Clemens and I, with our barracks bags across our shoulders, were processed and sent to many different offices to talk to many different people. Some of the lines were pretty long, but the Army was doing a good job getting the soldiers in and out as fast as possible.

    I met with a Major Mays, who signed my Honorable Discharge and presented it to me with a handshake. I saluted him briskly, did a very sharp about-face, and left his office feeling like a Knight. I believe that was the last time I ever saluted an officer.

    Things were happening so fast I was whirring on the inside.

I walked across the big, crowded room to the paymaster office. I saw Clemens standing in a line, grinning like a possum eating a sweet potato. He looked at me and gave me the thumbs up.

I entered the paymaster office, and sat in front of a desk. I watched as a Chief Warrant Officer looked through my records. My eyes got wide as he ciphered with his pencil a moment, then removed a stack of twenty-dollar bills and some small change from the cash drawer. My eyes got even wider as he counted out three-hundred and eighty-six dollars and sixty-five cents, and placed the money in a dark brown envelop with a string and button closing in the middle. He shook my hand and said, "Thank you for your service, Mr. Smith."

I was Mr. Smith now!

I opened my mouth and tried to say something, but nothing came out.

He smiled, nodded his head, and said, "Now don't spend that all in one place. Go home first, and buy you some snappy clothes."

I managed to nod my head and say, "Thank you, very much."

"No," he replied.

"Thank you."

I walked out of the paymaster's office and saw Clemens in line, second from the front. I opened my money folder slightly, showed him what was in it, and he whistled.

Rainbows filled my mind, and I thought I was the richest man on Earth.

I went into another office and they stamped my discharge orders.

I went into another office and they gave me my service record.

I went into another office and they gave me a train ticket.

I went into another office and they said what are you doing here.

I said I don't know! Somebody said come in here.

They said whoever told you that was wrong, get out.

I smiled and thought, *They wouldn't talk to me like that if they knew how rich I was.*

I went into another office and they asked if I was waiting for a train.

I said yes.

They said go outside and get on the bus.

I went outside, gazed across the stone wall that surrounded the cemetery, and nodded goodbye to all the marble headstones. I got on the bus with the sign "Train Station."

A few minutes later Clemens got on the bus and we laughed, and we laughed, and we laughed.

As soon as the bus got full of soldiers and bags (and it didn't take long), it carried us the short distance to the big pink train depot near downtown San Antonio. It was very busy inside, full of soldiers in many different uniforms going home. Clemens and I just stood there a few seconds, looking at the raised ceiling with stained glass windows, dark wooden rails along the balcony, and beautiful mosaics. We stepped up to the ticket window, found out we were both on the same train, and were directed to the gate.

The train was waiting, steam rolling out from beneath the engine in a white mist.

.

A conductor was standing in the train door, wearing a Santa cap.

"Going north, gentlemen?" he asked politely.

"Yes, we are, Sir," I answered.

"This fellow is going to Oklahoma, and I am going to Dodson, Texas."

The conductor reached for our tickets, and said, "I know Oklahoma is north, and wherever Dodson is, we can find it. We can always find Home."

The train followed the tracks south of San Antonio, then turned north and carried us slowly through a number of cities and stopovers. All day and well into the night it chugged along, getting closer and closer to home with every blast of steam and every **clickety-clack, clickety-clack** of the rail song.


Tuesday, December 11, 1945

Wichita Falls, Wichita County, Northwest Texas

It was a little after dawn when we pulled into Wichita Falls. This was the first changeover in my trip to Dodson, my home of record since all of the Smiths, Hamiltons, and Thomases had moved there. Clemens was headed on north into Oklahoma, so we parted with a lot of smiles and a couple of wet eyes. We had been exactly what each other had needed for the past month, and wished each other well as we continued to drift toward home.

I went into the train station and handed my ticket to the agent.

"Well, let's see, young man. Do you know where you're going?"

"No. I do not," I replied.

"I have never been here, and I have never been to Dodson, Texas, either."

We both laughed.

"Well, you're going from here to Childress, then on to Wellington and to Dodson, Texas. I don't know where that is, either," he said with a smile.

"But, there is a slight wrinkle here. The next train to Childress is in a month," he said with a serious, troubled look on his face.

*A month!*

He looked at me.

"You don't want to wait, I'm sure. What I think you should do is get on that highway out there," he pointed to the north, "over there, about four blocks. You can hitch a ride to Childress, west of us, right away. Everybody stops for servicemen in uniform. Once at Childress, about a hundred miles, you'll need to get off and take another ride, to the right, to Wellington, about thirty miles. Then, Dodson is," he looked closely at his map, "a little ways to the east, maybe ten miles. You'll be home for lunch."

"If I can find it," I answered, as we both laughed again.

Sure enough, as soon as I started thumbing, a car pulled over.

"Where 'ya going, soldier?"

"Childress, then to Wellington," I told the middle-aged driver.

"I'm going to Amarillo, hop in, I'll drop you off in Childress," he answered.

A hundred miles later, I was on the road to Wellington. The first car that came my way stopped, and let me ride. I got to Wellington about forty-five minutes later.

The town square was two or three blocks off the highway. I figured if I walked around the square, I might see or meet my cousins, who had moved to Wellington, or find someone who knew them. I asked several people if they knew Uncle John Thomas, or his sons John Lavern and Bill. I couldn't find anybody, so I asked someone if they knew the way to Dodson.

I was pointed in the right direction, and began walking. My barracks bag was very full, and was slung over my shoulder.

The sun was overhead. It was noon. It was cool and comfortable, must've been about fifty degrees.

For eleven miles, I walked to Dodson.

Past houses and farms.

Past mustard greens, some cabbage, and last year's corn.

Past acres and acres and acres of fields.

Some had been plowed and were just weeks away from the planting of spring cotton.

Others still had the stalks from last summer's cotton standing in a broken and ragged jumble, waiting for next summer.

There was not a dog, a car, or a horse that passed me.

I figured once I got to Dodson I could find somebody who knew where my home was.

Up the road, at a distance, I could see a few houses and a row of brick buildings running down the left side of the main highway. A small road sign said Dodson Texas Population 357. It was just the usual small town. Off to my right, there was a house and a guy sitting under a tree. He waved at me.

"Hey, come over here."

I walked his way.

"Where are you going?"

"I'm trying to get home."

"Do you live here?"

"Naw, I don't know where my Momma and Daddy live. I've been writing them about a year now, and they get their mail at Route 1, Dodson, Texas."

He told me, "I don't have any idea where they live, but I know the man that delivers their mail."

So, we got in his car and we went to the home of the post office carrier. He was gone, but his wife came to the door.

I told her, "I'm trying to get home, but I don't know the way there, just that it is Carl N. Smith, Route 1, Dodson, Texas."

"I know right where they live," she answered.

So, we jumped in her car and she drove me right to it.

The only people there were my sister Roberta, her son Darrell, and Grandma Herron. When Roberta heard the car drive up she ran out the door screaming, "My brother! My brother!"

After a big hug, I asked her, "Where is everybody?"

"Well, Dorothy's gone into town to pick up some things at the drug store, and Momma and Daddy are at the

Childress bus station right now waiting to bring you home! They found out some way that you were being discharged and on your way home, and that you would change buses at Childress. So, they got in the truck and they went there."

I said, "Oh, no."

The postal carrier's wife looked at me and said, "Don't worry. When I get back to the post office I'll call the Childress bus station and have them announce over the loudspeaker, telling Altie and Bud Smith that their son, Red Smith, is at home."

Roberta and I stood out in the front yard to wait for them. We would hear a car coming, and it wasn't them. Then we heard another car, and it wasn't them.

Then, after about an hour, we heard another car. It was about a half-mile down the road, but we could see kids standing up in the back of the truck with their hands waving.

The truck pulled into the front yard, and they all ran to me.

They let Momma get to me first, and Daddy stood back as my younger sisters Hattie, Alice, and Mae ran to me and hugged me.

Hattie was thirteen years old now, and Alice was nine. Mae was four years old, and surprised me the most. She was only six months old when I left for the Army, just a baby, and now she was waist high.

Daddy was still standing back, waiting for everybody to get through hugging and kissing me. He didn't say welcome home or glad to see you, he just stood there and said, "Thank God you made it."

There was a very pretty lady standing off to my left, wearing a white dress and a dark pink sweater. She grabbed me and hugged and kissed me, just like all the others had done.

Momma was beside me, and I whispered to her, "Momma, is that Tom Hamilton's girl, Juliette?"

Momma whispered back to me, "Yes, and she's here to see YOU."

I walked over to her, held my arms out again, and she fell into them as easy as a dancer on a sawdust floor.

I said, "It's good to see you again, Juliette. You've gotten older."

She smiled.

I felt the Earth beneath my feet move.

"Perhaps it is you that has gotten younger, Red Smith."

"Maybe so," I replied.

I looked into her eyes and I said, "There are many things for us to talk about."

"Yes, there are, Red," she agreed.

"May I call you Judy?"

She nodded her head approvingly, and answered, "I would like that very much."

# CHAPTER 28

# COURTSHIP

December 12-25, 1945.

Dodson, Near Wellington, Texas, Collingsworth County, Northwest Texas.

Since my arrival home, Judy and I had seen each other every day. Either she came over to the Smith house or I walked the two miles over to the Hamilton house. I did not expect to become so instantly infatuated with her, but I was, from the first hug and kiss in front of the house to the every-day hug and kiss since then. She had the ability to take all the horrors and anxieties I carried inside me from Breakneck Ridge and Mindanao and cover them with a blanket of sweetness and charm. Tim Blanchard and I had dealt with our distresses in shared sadness and few words. Pete Clemens and I had shared the dismay and sense of loss on a magic carpet with a backdrop of blue ocean. Judy Hamilton never asked me anything. She just folded her arms around me and brought me home.

Sad to say, I couldn't just talk to Judy as much as I wanted to, which was all the time. There was everybody else in the family that wanted some of my long-delayed attention. My brothers, Noel and Lester, were still in the Army, but everyone else was home. Roberta, the oldest, had married Joe Racadio, a Filipino cook who was still in the Army, and was living with us. Her son, Darrell, was now six years old. My younger sisters Dorothy, Hattie, and Alice were still in school, and, of course, Mae was at home. Momma had a thousand things to talk about, but Daddy was a little distant.

Judy and Dorothy were good friends, just one year apart in age. My Momma and Daddy called her Dorothy Jack, and had ever since she was a toddler. I guess it was the way she was so fun-loving and belligerent, and the boyish middle name fit her. I just called her Dorothy to make it simpler. Like changing Juliette to Judy.

Dorothy told me that Judy had walked out of school a month ago, ready to rid herself of all the snooty girls at Wellington High School. Besides, she had taken almost all of the classes for high school and her grades were perfect. That was okay with me, because it gave me more time to see her each day!

On my third day at home, Friday, I walked over to the Hamilton house to see Judy and eat some of her mother's delicious cabbage soup. It had started snowing late that afternoon, and it continued to snow into the evening. Judy and I sat on the front porch, wrapped in blankets to stay warm, and watched the snow drift down from the Texas dusk. We talked about the Hopkins County past, the West Texas present, and the unknown future. Paradises lost, paradises happening, and paradises yet to be pursued. The snow was beautiful, wandering down from the sky like white, fluffy refugees from the dark, cold, windless night. I can still close my eyes and see that vision of the white snow, reflecting the beam from the porch light, falling ever so gently, seeking the quiet solitude of the winter ground, with Judy snuggled beside me.

I slept on a pallet in the front room that night, and we all awoke to a hot cup of Hamilton coffee and fourteen crystalline inches of snow. They said it was the first moisture that had fallen from the Collingsworth County sky since October.

Judy and I went to Wellington on Monday of the next week and I bought some new civilian clothes at Dodgin's Men's Store. Afterward, we had a sandwich and an ice cream float at Goat's Cafe. They sold Taylor's Ice Cream there, and the float was sure good.

A few days later, Dorothy and Judy asked if we could go to a skating rink in Hollis, Oklahoma.

"I don't know how to skate," I told them.

"That's alright, we'll teach you," they both told me.

So, we went.

I wore my Army gabardine jacket just in case the skating rink wanted to give me a discount.

They did.

And, when we got there, I found out that neither Judy nor Dorothy knew how to skate.

Each one of us fell five or six times, but we finally got the hang of it and had a lot of fun. It didn't take Dorothy long to find a boyfriend there, so it kinda turned into a double date after that. The fellow she met had his own money, too, so it was easier on me.

The skating rink had a snack shop and a photo-booth. After a hot dog and soda pop, Judy and I got our picture taken in the booth. The picture turned out pretty good, though she said I looked a little wild.

And, wild I was. Wildly in love.

By the end of the week, Dorothy and Judy decided it would be a good idea to have a slumber party at the Smith house. Of course, Roberta, Darrell, Hattie, Alice, and Mae all joined in and said yes, yes, yes, yes, and yes. So, we made sure we had lots of popcorn and coffee and tea and we made it happen. We talked, we sang, we talked, we joked, we told stories, we whistled, we talked, and the young ones started dropping off after midnight. And we talked some more, a little slower as each hour crawled by at a sleepy snail's pace. At the end, it was me and Dorothy, sitting outside and smoking cigarettes, with me clicking my black zippo. As the sun came up, and people started stirring, we found two empty beds and caught a few hours of sleep, even with Momma and Daddy beginning to talk in the kitchen.

  As soon as everyone was awake and moving, I took Daddy's truck, Judy, Hattie, Alice, and Mae on a drive north along the county line to the thickets that grew beside the Salt Fork of the Red River. We all managed to pack ourselves in the truck, with Alice and Mae riding in the space behind the seats. We found two good-sized cedar trees for Christmas, and chopped them down. We dropped one of the trees and Judy off at the Hamilton house and took the other tree to the Smith home. I helped the sisters cut and trim the tree, then left the decorating to them and walked the two miles over to the Hamilton house to see Judy again.

  I stayed there that evening and helped Judy decorate their tree. Tom and Nettie Hamilton were expecting their older daughters, Arline, Gladys, and Maudie to come home for Christmas that day from Dallas, where they were working at Sears & Roebuck.

Sure enough, they showed up at dusk in time for supper. With them, in Gladys' big sedan, were my cousins John Lavern and Bill, the Thomases that had brought us all to Wellington in the first place. It looked like John Lavern and Judy's sister Maudie were holding hands a lot. Judy and I exchanged winks as we watched them.

The two cousins went on home to Uncle John and Aunt Lizzie, my Momma's sister. Judy and I snickered as we talked alone about how it was looking like the Thomases might be kin to the Hamiltons pretty soon, and that would make the Hamiltons kin to the Smiths in a round-about way. We laughed as we kept trying to figure out the family tree if Maudie became a Thomas. We kept getting confused.

*Was that gonna make us some kind of distant cousin?*

Judy and I tried to finish decorating the Christmas tree as the Dallas group got settled in. After supper, Judy and I placed the final garland around the tree, as well as a few new ornaments that Gladys and Arline had brought with them. It was already late at night, and Gladys offered to take me home in her car. I could tell the sisters were eager to talk most of the night, so I took her up on the offer. Deep inside, though, I wanted to stay with Judy and talk to her.

I hadn't even been home from the Army two weeks yet, and I realized that my attraction to Judy was far too strong to deny. I enjoyed watching her and listening to her, and I could tell that she liked me.

When I got home, Momma was still up, crumbling biscuits and cornbread for the Christmas dressing. I sat at the table with her, stirring the big ceramic bowl of crumbled bread, and we talked about the things we hadn't been able to talk about for almost three and a half years.

"You and Juliette are becoming a couple of lovebirds, aren't you?"

I snickered a bit, looked down into the bowl of bread, blushed slightly, then looked back up at her.

"Yes, Momma, I think you're right. I wrote her a time or two over there in the Pacific, it made me feel good to exchange nice, pleasant letters with a girl back home. But when I came back and saw her, I realized the girl in the letters was a real person, and very, very pretty at that. She doesn't demand anything of me, she just likes me, and I liked her right from the start. Being with her makes me feel that the war is far away, and sometimes I swear I feel like it never happened, except in the dreams and in the fear that comes from out of nowhere and quickly leaves when I touch her. I want to be with her all the time."

Momma smiled and touched my hand.

"I felt that way about Bud long ago, and still do, mostly."

I thought on that word she used, *"mostly."*

I looked at her eyes, her face, her arms.

No bruises, no discolorations.

Her arm had a suspicious spot.

"Ran into a door frame," she said matter-of-factly.

"Do I need to talk to him? He's been distant from me since I came back."

"He's afraid of you. You're the soldier he never was. He has been on his best behavior since you returned. I'm glad you're back."

She was still tearing the cornbread into small pieces, but slower.

"All of us love him more than he deserves, and he loves us. He likes his large family. He likes to act like the rooster that he thinks he is. He's very, very glad you came back. There were days here that he looked frail and sad, then your letter would come, and he would get better."

I watched her as she set the cornbread down.

"He's been mean to the girls," she confessed.

"Not rough, just mean. He tries to take their money, especially Dorothy Jack. Hattie just gives him some, and keeps the rest. She just says, *"This part is mine, and mine only."* She shares it with Alice. That's the only way they get good clothes. But Dorothy Jack fights him tooth and nail, she's just like him. Stubborn and mean-spirited. I think she will move out soon, out to California with some friends she knows. One man in particular. He rides his motorcycle down from Seattle every month. Talk to her, Red, tell her that you're here and she's safe. All the girls look up to you. You're the Man around here, not Bud."

She picked up a pastry cloth, and cleaned the crumbs off her hands, then placed her hand on my cheek. She kissed my forehead, looked in my eyes, and said, "I never told you this, but the day you were born I knew, deep down in my heart I knew, that you were gonna be this family's leader. You had a gentle nature, and a strong hand. You knew what was fair and what was right. You showed it when you began to walk and talk. You watched everything, and could see in somebody's face if they were happy or sad, content or troubled. We didn't have to teach you any of that. You just KNEW it."

She smiled with a faraway look in her eyes, like she was observing me from a score of years past, peering through the lens of time, reliving an earlier, simpler life, before the hard work and the disappointments began. When life was rich with promise, and Paradise was out there, within reach of her young, nimble fingers.

"Bud is a decent man, and I will love him until we are both dead, but you are the true Daddy of this family. The Lord kept you unharmed in this war because this family would be lost without you. Absolutely lost. Those years you were gone were the worst years of my life. I worried that you would not come back, and I dreaded the very thought of it."

"There is much that you must do. You keep Bud on a short, tight leash. You marry your Judy. She will be good to you, and I know that you love her. You do all these things, and all my grandkids will be the happiest bunch of cousins this Earth has ever seen. You wait and see."

I thought of my colored friend.

*There is still much that you must do.*

Goosebumps ran up my neck.

I kissed Momma's forehead, and said, "Thanks, Momma. The day will come when I will have to tell him harshly and roughly to leave the girls and their money alone. Mostly, they will all just leave one by one. In the meantime, I'll get a job and put some more money in your cookie-jar."

We stood there a few moments, and Momma looked at me intently and said, "While you were at war, I remember one afternoon hearing your voice, as loud in my mind like you were as close to me as you are right now. You said *Momma! Momma!* just like that. And then a few minutes later you said *Momma!* again, and then no more. I was frightened. You sounded frightened. I sank to my knees right there and prayed that God would send an angel to protect you, and I felt better."

My body trembled on the inside. I took a deep breath, and let it out slowly. I knew right then that she had heard me that horrible night on Leyte, when I was surrounded by the enemy, and panicked. I realized that somehow we had connected from nine-thousand miles away, and I remembered my colored friend, my angel that appeared from out of nowhere to calm me and promise me that nothing would happen to me if I would just be quiet and be still. I wanted to tell her about my friend with the soft blue eyes and the smooth, relaxing voice.

I decided that was a story for Judy, and for no one else.

"Yes, Momma, there was a night that was very, very rough. I was losing it, and I thought I saw you and I called out for you. A fellow came over to me, from out of nowhere, and told me to be quiet and keep my head down and I would be okay. He made me feel better by telling me that. I guess you really heard me call for you, and he was the angel you beckoned. It was so bad I cannot talk about it."

We both looked at each other for a minute.

I touched her cheek, and I continued, "I came out of that war without a scratch. There are things in this family that I must do, and it may take the next few years. I will know when it is done. This family is very important to me. God has watched over me, He kept me alive when I thought I was a goner, and He has given me the most beautiful and exciting woman I have ever seen to enrich my life. If I hadn't spent those three years in the Army, I prob'ly would've married Mary Campbell or Doris DeBord, and I don't think I would ever be as happy as I am right now. The war tightened me, made me appreciate freedom, and inspired me that nothing is too hard to do if it is the Right Thing to do. I had to spend three years in the worst type of combat, things you'll never hear me talk about, but in those three years Judy ripened, and I was brought back to be The Picker. Ain't that something! I am The Picker! I think it will be a very Merry Christmas this year!"

As I looked at the big bowl of bread for the dressing, I declared, "And this will be the first cornbread dressing I have had in three years."

As I drifted off to sleep that night at home, I had gentle dreams of Judy holding sugar plums and peppermint sticks, and wearing a ring.

When I awoke the next morning, I realized I had bought no one, especially Judy, any kind of Christmas gift. It was Sunday, and, because of the Texas Blue Law, very few stores would be open. As soon as I had a couple of biscuits and ribbon-cane syrup for breakfast, I hopped into Daddy's old truck and drove into Wellington to see what was happening at the stores.

It was mostly quiet, but the Palace Dug Store was open. I wandered inside, and I found everything I needed. Candy for Mae. Pretty silk handkerchiefs for Bert, Alice, and Hattie. English lavender hand lotion for Momma, and a can of Virginia tobacco for Daddy. (I fondly thought of Kenny when I bought that.) A sparkling cigarette case, with tiny slim cigarettes, for Dorothy. And, a silver manicure set in a black leather pouch for Judy.

Monday was Christmas Eve, and I brought Judy to my home for Christmas Eve Dinner and the usual tea cakes and coffee. We had ham and Momma's cornbread dressing. The family made a pretty good choir as we sang all the Christmas songs we knew, and some we made up. Everyone liked their presents, especially Judy and Mae. Daddy had somehow gotten a bottle of moonshine from his brother Clyde, and he, Judy, Dorothy, and I enjoyed a small glass or two on the front porch for a short while. It was beginning to get a bit chilly, with the temperature dropping to near thirty degrees. I thought of Nobel, Pete, Kenny, and Tim, and shared a toast with everyone on their behalf. I almost cried when I did so, and Judy held my hand tightly and made it better.

Uncle Clyde and Rosie came over that night, with more moonshine, and Clyde played his fiddle while Daddy and I took turns playing the guitar. It was a beautiful moment in time, watching Clyde cradle the fiddle in his arm, elbow resting above his knee, the bow sliding smoothly up and down over the strings, releasing the melodies to pour over us like sweet honey. Daddy was sitting in a chair, leaning forward, strumming the old guitar with his thumb, his face smiling at Clyde as he sang *Wabash Cannonball.* At just the right moment, I would make the sound of a train whistle, and the girls would laugh. Daddy handed me the guitar after a half-hour, and I sang a few Jimmie Rodgers songs. The girls would dance while Judy, with a smile on her face and enchantment in her eyes, sat and listened to me sing and play the guitar.

Judy stayed with us that night and slept with Dorothy and the girls.

On Christmas Day, I walked Judy back to the Hamilton house and had the best cornbread dressing I had ever eaten, with roasted Canada Goose.

*I didn't tell Momma that Mrs. Hamilton's dressing was better than hers.*

Mr. Wilson, their farming partner, said Grace, and thanked the Good Lord for everything and more, and said a good word for the soldiers coming home, and thanked God for sparing his son from the war. Nettie Hamilton had made her famous apple pie, and Tom Hamilton, Mr. Wilson, and I had hard apple cider and a Virginia cigar on the porch after dinner.

Collingsworth County and Wellington City had passed an ordinance to prohibit the sale and use of fireworks on Christmas and New Year's, in respect to the returning WWII veterans. I was very pleased they did. I believe the booming of firecrackers and the sight of missiles flying through the air that night would not have settled well in the dark frightened corners of my fragile subconscious peace.

We just watched the passive December stars fill the sky as we drank our cider and smoked our cigars, with only the occasional falling star to brighten the heavens and convince lovers that their wishes might very well come true.

Judy came out to sit with us on the front porch, and we sat close together, took advantage of each falling star to make a silent wish for a mutual Paradise.

Gladys drove me home again later that night.

The Hamilton sisters stayed a couple more days, and left Friday for their return to Dallas. They had been telling me and Judy for several days that Sears was hiring, and needed people to help them put Christmas behind them and prepare for the Spring and Summer season. They told me it would be a good idea if I tried to get on at Sears. They said Sears was paying well and needed good help. I said I would think about it.

Judy decided to go with them and work for a few months at Sears, before the Hamilton spring cotton crop that her father and brothers had planted needed to be picked.

Tom Hamilton had decided to plant cotton early for an April harvest, and then corn for a late-summer harvest. He had an idea that he might plant cabbage for the fall and winter crop. One thing I had learned from talking to him, he didn't like to see the farmland empty.

"Soil was made for growing, and nothing's gonna grow unless you plant it," he would say.

As Judy, her sisters, and the Thomas boys pulled out on Friday, I told her I would be in Dallas sometime the next week.

I told Tom Hamilton not to worry. I told him I would be back by cotton-picking time, no later than March. I also told him my brother Noel would be home from the Army in late-February, and he would help us, too. I said I would make sure Judy was home by then, so she could do the bookkeeping for the cotton crop.

Wednesday, January 2, 1946.

Dallas, Dallas County, Texas.

I spent the entire weekend before New Year's Day at home, enjoying my sisters and Momma's cooking. Even Daddy and I had a few conversations about farming and the days ahead. The way he talked, it looked like there was a pretty good chance that the Smiths would be talked into moving to Arizona where a big boom in farming was happening. Water wells were being drilled and the flatland deserts west of Phoenix began to bloom like the Garden of Eden.

Three of Uncle Clyde's boys were already there in Arizona, and Aunt Lola Smith's daughter and son were there. They were talking up the sweet promises of Eloy, Arizona.

I was missing Judy more than I could stand. She had just been gone for five days and it felt like it had been forever. So, I packed a pile of clothes in my barracks bag and hit the road. I walked into Wellington and thumbed a ride to Childress and then another ride to Wichita Falls, where I caught a bus to Dallas.

The bus took me to the Dallas airport area, where I got on a city bus for Oak Cliff, south of downtown, where the Hamilton girls and the Thomas boys were staying. The bus fare was ten cents, and the transfers were free. I took two transfers, finally getting on the bus that crossed Eighth Street. The driver drove a short distance, then turned to me and said, "Eighth Street, up ahead."

He motioned me to walk east.

So I walked and walked. The addresses got smaller and smaller, then started over again, getting bigger and bigger.

Finally, after what felt like about three miles, I stood at the door of the boarding house where they lived. It was late, and I could see Gladys's car in the driveway, so I knew they were at home, and, most of all, I was at the right place.

I knocked, and to my delight, Judy opened the door. Her face blossomed into a huge smile. We hugged and kissed once or twice, and went inside and I found a supper of bologna sandwiches and iced tea.

Arline asked me what my plans were for the rest of the week, and I told her I was thinking about going to Sulphur Springs the next day and try to look up a few friends.

"Some old girlfriends?" she asked sarcastically.

I smiled, shook my head, and answered sheepishly, "Well, I don't know. It just depends on who's there."

A laugh went around the table, and Judy tightened her grip on my hand and looked at me suspiciously.

Arline looked at Judy and then at me.

"I tell you what, Red," she continued.

"Why don't you leave with us in the morning, and go into the office at Sears and sign up for a job? Then, when you come back from Sulphur Springs, you'll have a good job waiting for you."

I answered her immediately.

"Swell, I'll do that."

The next morning, after coffee and scrambled eggs, we piled into Gladys's car and drove the short distance to Sears, on Lamar Street. They went to their work areas and I went to the hiring office.

I filled out an application. It took a couple of hours. I handed all the sheets of paper I had filled out to a fellow in a suit sitting at a desk.

The fellow said they look pretty swell. Now, take this small stack of paper and go to our doctor for an examination.

The Doc is two blocks that way, a lady said. Make sure you're ready to pee in a bottle.

I said I've been ready for an hour or more. They might need two bottles.

She smiled.

When I got to the doctor's office, I peed in a bottle, and Doc looked me over and over.

Say Ahhh. Cough. What word is on the card I'm holding?

I said what card?

We laughed.

I told him the word on the card was Today.

What color are those two sticks?

I said red and blue.

Bend your wrist. Bend your back. Forward, right, backward, left, now straight. Touch your toes. Why are your toes so yellow?

I said jungle-rot and Atabrine.

The Doc said hmmmm. Here's some salve. Rub this in and it should help. Got any diseases you didn't tell me?

I said nope.

Ever had venereal disease?

Not me, Doc. Several of the men did. Is it catching?

Doc smiled and said, no, not from them.

He signed my papers and told me to take them back to the hiring office.

On the way back to the hiring office I bought a hotdog and a soda for lunch.

I handed the examination papers to another fellow in a suit sitting at a desk.

He looked at them, and walked back to a file cabinet to get my application. He looked at both and said you're fine. Come back tomorrow morning at 7:00 and start to work.

Tomorrow?

*There went my planned trip to Sulphur Springs!*

I told him okay, see you tomorrow.

It didn't bother me. I was glad to know I didn't have to go there the next morning. There was nothing in Sulphur Springs for me. Nothing but old memories that seemed a bit stale now. If anybody I used to know was still there, they certainly weren't the same as they were. Or, maybe I wasn't the way I used to be.

The past was pale, like an old photo in a museum, a scratched and torn image of a nameless man with a beard and a smaller, frowning woman in a dress with a lace collar. All had changed. The cars were different. The roads were different. Sometimes it seemed the sun was brighter as it escaped the horizon every morning, and the moon was more enchanting as it danced across the evening sky.

Judy was there, right there in Dallas, and I couldn't get her off my mind. I wanted to be with her all the time.

Everybody was glad to hear about my job.

"What will you be doing?" they asked.

"I don't know. I'll prob'ly be in an office. They'll change their name tomorrow to Sears & Roebuck & Smith," I teased.

"I'll need to buy a couple of suits."


Thursday, January 3, 1946.

Dallas, Dallas County, Texas.

My job turned out to be pretty decent. Ninety-six cents an hour to do whatever they needed me to do. Move boxes around in the warehouse. Fix a leaky pipe. Paint a wall. Drive a truck to Union Station and pick up materials shipped by train. Move more boxes around.

I had breakfast with Judy every morning. I had lunch with Judy every afternoon. We had supper every night. I was falling deeper and deeper in love with her as each sunrise and sunset passed between the two horizons.

The first weekend we went to a John Wayne movie, rode the bus out to White Rock Lake, rented a canoe for a couple of hours, and went to a hamburger joint for supper.

The second weekend I found Tim Blanchard's house, and we surprised him and his parents with a big can of ham.

When Tim answered the door he almost screamed for joy.

"Red! Red!" he was yelling as he jumped up and down. We both grabbed each other and hugged like we were long-lost brothers.

Of course, his parents insisted that Judy and I stay for supper that day.

When Tim and I talked about Pete, we both cried. So did Judy, and so did Tim's Mom and Dad. When Tim got up to get us another iced tea, his Mom leaned over to me and said "Thank you so much, Mr. Smith, for being his friend and for coming over here. Tim is a good son, and he was so happy to get back and help keep this old house running. He never talked about anyone but you, Nobel, and Pete, and that was not very often. And now, to hear him talk to you and laugh and cry and fill in some of the details, we are so thankful to meet you, and to meet your beautiful Lady Judy!"

Judy blushed, and thanked Mrs. Blanchard.

Tim came back with our teas and said, "Red, Red! I am so glad to see you, and so happy to see us both back in Texas where we belong. Tell my folks about those two little girls we found in that shack. You remember them, don't you?"

I stretched my legs out.

"Of course I do, Tim. They were sweet little girls. I like to think the oldest one is gonna remember us the rest of her life."

I looked at Judy, took a long breath, and began the story.

"It was on Mindanao. We called artillery fire on a place where Japanese soldiers had been seen. When the shells stopped, Tim and I were sent with a radioman to look around.

We saw dead enemy soldiers, and a small bamboo hut.

There were bright pink flowers in front of the hut, and a woman's body in the flowers.

The radioman said she was dead.

We looked in the back door of the hut.

It was very dark. We saw another woman, laying in a bed, holding a little baby.

In the corner of the hut was a little girl, sitting on the floor. She was about three years old, and was just staring at us.

The radioman said the woman was dead, but the baby was alive. He called for a medic.

The medic arrived. He said the woman had been dead a day or two, and was probably the mother of the baby.

He said the baby was alert, dirty, and hungry.

Tim asked if there was anything we could feed her.

The medic said yes, we have canned milk and chlorinated water.

He walked over to the little girl in the corner. She stood up and met him, and he gave her some chocolate.

She touched the medic's red cross patch on his arm and said *"doktor."*

We were all crying with joy by then.

After the medic got the girl and baby cleaned up and mixed the milk with the clean water, he let Tim feed the baby."

Tim leaned forward in his chair, and said, excitedly, "Yes, Red. That little baby drank three big droppers full of that milk!"

I continued the story.

"Our boys buried the two women, said some Bible verses over them, and left two crosses over their grave.

We took the girls back to the camp, and the Filipinos had set up a tent for them.

We stayed all night long watching those two girls, and the next day a Filipino woman who was still nursing her own baby fed our little baby.

The woman and her husband took the two girls and they became a family.

Every soldier in our company voted to be the girls' Godfather, and we named the three-year old girl Grace Irene. G.I.

I hope she remembers us. I hope she remembers Tim feeding her little sister."

When I finished the story, everyone in the room had tears in their eyes. Tim's Mom walked over to Tim and hugged him, Tim's Dad walked over to me and shook my hand, and Judy leaned over and hugged me.

She kissed me on the cheek and said, "That is a sad, beautiful story. Thank you, Red."

Telling that story made me feel better, like I was already pushing some of the horrible war behind me, putting it into an empty black box, and keeping only the purest and wholesome memories for me and the little brown box in my heart, where precious things are stored.

Tim wiped his eyes with his handkerchief, and looked at me the way he had looked at me at the abaca field near Mental, when he told me he became a man that day.

"I want you to know, and I know I've told you this before, but you are the best thing that ever happened to me over there, and I came back a Man just like I told you. And you are the reason I came out of it both alive and sane."

He had a pack of Camel cigarettes in his hand.

"I brought this back with me, and I swore to myself I would never light one until Red Smith lit it with his black Zippo! Let's go out on the front porch!"

Judy and I thanked the Blanchard's for the great supper, and we sat with Tim for another two hours on the porch, until all the Camels were gone. Tim was the same Tim I had grown to love like a brother, and he told me he was going to school next Spring to be a carpenter's apprentice. When he asked me what I was going to do, I just looked at Judy. Tim laughed.

"Right now," I said, "Farming is still the best thing I do, and we have a cotton crop to bring in for Judy's Daddy. After that, I don't know. My brothers Noel and Lester will be coming home from the Army soon, and our sisters are all still in school, except for Roberta. We'll just have to see what this year brings, Tim. There are quite a few things left for me to do back home."

Tim looked at me and grinned.

"When I grow up, I wanna be just like you, Red Smith!"

He laughed a genuine, Tim Blanchard laugh, and we laughed with him.

"Let me tell you, Tim," I said.

"You are already grown up, and there are plenty of things for you to do here."

Mr. Blanchard came out the front door, and looked at me and Judy.

"You two need to be my guests on one of the Bluebonnet Specials, the electric railway cars that go to Corsicana and back. You can catch one at any of the Texas Electric Railway stops between Eighth Street and downtown, and spend a couple of hours in Corsicana. I work for the Railway, and here are two roundtrip tickets on the Corsicana run. You can shop, have a sandwich, or find an ice cream parlor on your layover. There's a fruitcake bakery there, too! You'll have a wonderful time. On us!"

"Oh, thank you, Mr. Blanchard. Judy and I will do that next weekend, for sure," I told him, as I reached for the tickets.

It was beginning to get cold on the front porch, so Judy and I bundled ourselves in our jackets and gloves. We said our good-byes and left Tim on the front porch a short while later. There were tears in mine and Tim's eyes as we parted and wished each other the best that Life can offer. He was standing there at the top of the porch steps, his gloved right hand fully extended, waving at us. From a block away, I turned around to look back, and he was still there. He waved again. I returned his wave. Judy held me tight around my waist as we walked, and I told her, through more tears, that he was the best friend I ever had.

As Life would have it, he would remain the best friend I ever had, though I never saw Tim Blanchard again.

Monday, January 14, 1946.

Dallas, Dallas County, Texas.

By the beginning of the second week in Dallas, I was growing tired of the Sears job and the city. I wanted the sunshine, the dirt, and the wind. I had spent the past three years in the war-torn Pacific, and the only things I remembered as being familiar were the sunshine, the dirt, and the wind. I wanted to be a farmer again.

I received a letter from Momma that said Noel would be home from the Army Air Corps the middle of next month, and that Uncle Clyde was still bugging them about moving to Arizona.

*"There's money in Arizona and in California to be made,"* he said.

*"There's rich land, plenty of water, and plenty of jobs."*

In Dallas, there was plenty of people, plenty of cars, and plenty of noise.

Judy and I talked about it often. She knew she had to go back and help her Daddy keep the books when the cotton was ready to pick. She knew she had to go back to do some paperwork to get her Degree from Wellington High School. My hands were itching to pick cotton and work the soil.

On our third weekend in Dallas, we took the Texas Electric Railway car to Corsicana. It was as much fun as Mr. Blanchard said it would be. We boarded our dark blue and cream-colored Bluebonnet Special on Eighth Street, with leather seats, two on each side of the aisle, for the hour-long trip. The railcar even had a restroom!

We walked around downtown Corsicana on a sunny, cool January day. Judy enjoyed the shopping, and I bought a cigar and sat outside, soaking up the small-town sounds of farm trucks and train whistles. I bought Judy a dark blue head scarf from a leather store. We had lunch at a drug store soda fountain, and an ice cream to top it off.

Judy and I walked a pretty good number of blocks down to a fruitcake bakery, and I bought a good-sized fruitcake in a pretty, round Deluxe tin for all the Hamilton sisters, and the Thomas boys.

Catching the next Bluebonnet Special, we rode home as the late afternoon January sun was sinking in the western sky. I wished this simple life could go on forever, with Judy and me shopping, eating ice cream, and riding electric railway cars somewhere new every day. But my life of farming told me, *Not so, Mr. Smith.*

*Paradise is a day's work for a day's pay, a good supper, and woman like Judy to spend it with. Love and Work. Work and Love. You can't live without Work, and you can't be happy without Love. Enjoy these days when they happen. There are still things that you must do.*


Saturday, January 26, 1946

Eagle Ford, West Dallas, Dallas County, Texas

On our fourth weekend in Dallas, I called my old friend from Sulphur Springs, Roy DeBord, and learned that he had moved to the small town of Eagle Ford, just west of us. I wanted to see him, and introduce him to Judy, so we caught a bus on a cold and cloudy Sunday and made the transfers to get to his aunt's house, where he lived.

Judy was a friend of one of the DeBord girls, and knew that Roy was tongue-tied, and could be hard to understand at times. He and I had spent many weekends together roaming the streets of Sulphur Springs and the Hopkins County countryside. I was with him the day Pearl Harbor was bombed, watching a movie at the Carnation Theater in Sulphur Springs.

I was anxious to see how he had made it through the war years, knowing that he had not joined the military and was not drafted because of his speech problem.

When the bus let us off in the Eagle Ford community, we were amazed at the number of new houses being built. There were many people, most of them soldiers and their families, living in temporary shelters and tents, waiting for the new houses to be finished. We could see roads lined up between orange engineering-stakes, stretching across the black-dirt landscape. Several big construction sites for factories and office buildings were scattered throughout the patchwork quilt of roads and property lines. Not much construction was happening on Sunday, and the people in the shelters were generally sitting inside, their doors open, bundled up in quilted jackets and furry hats, on folding chairs around picnic tables.

We found Roy's address to be one of the older houses near the center of town, and we stepped up to the front porch.

When we knocked on the door, Roy opened it quickly, smiled, and greeted, "Hey, Wed Thmith!"

Judy and I entered his front room.

Roy and I had not seen each other since the summer of '42, three and-a-half years ago.

"Well, Wed, ith good to thee you!" he said happily.

Our handshake turned quickly to a hug, and I asked, "How'ya doing, Roy! Are they treating you right up here?"

"Oh yeth, dey are."

He looked at Judy and smiled, reaching out his hand to shake hers.

"So, dith ith Thnootnie! Pweased to meet ya, Thnootnie!"

Judy smiled and shook his hand.

I smiled, too. I did not know if "Thnootnie" was his best try at the word "Judy," or if he just chose that name because it sounded better than what naturally came out. He was very good at doing that, making do with one thing over another.

"Pleased to meet you, too, Roy. Red has said a lot about you. I'm one of the Hamilton girls from Sulphur Bluff. I knew your little sister."

"Yeth, I wememba."

I patted him on the shoulder, pointed outside at all the construction, and asked, "So, Roy, what have you been doing out here? How come you're not building these houses?"

He laughed with a half-snort.

"Ith my day off, Wed. Ith Thunday, man. I do a wot of cawpentwy and a widda bid of pwumbing for the home-buildath. I dell ya, there are a wod of soldars movin' oud here tho dey can work in Dawwath and riv oud in da coundry!"

"Well. that's good, Roy. I remember you being pretty good with a hammer and nails and with a pipe wrench."

We walked through the neatly furnished house, a four-room wooden home about the same size all of Smiths lived in before the war. In fact, the house in Dodson was not much bigger than Roy's house.

"This is a nice house, Roy."

"Thank you, Wed. Thith bewonged do yer Aunt Thallie Wushin, on yer Mommath thide, with the Herronth."

"Tell me, how are you kin to the Herrons, Roy?" I asked.

"I don'th know. They thaid I wath, and thad I could have thith houth. Tho, I haventh twied do figure id oud."

We laughed.

"Aunt Sallie Rushing died quite a while back, didn't she?" I inquired.

"Yeth, I think in '38."

"I remember her a little bit. She was a nice lady, really nice." I revealed.

"You live here by yourself, Roy?" I asked.

"Yeth, duth me. I do okay. They pay preddy good for cawpenteth. Do ya wand a beer, Wed? Wouldt you wike do have a wine, Thnootnie?

Judy snickered a bit, and answered, "Just a very small glass, Roy, thank you."

"Good! Have a theet ad the dable," he said, motioning toward the dining table.

We removed our jackets and made ourselves comfortable at the small, wooden table with four chairs.

With the beer and wine, and some potato chips Roy served us, the next two hours rolled by. We talked about old things and new things, who left Hopkins County and who stayed, who married who, and, sadly enough, who did not come back from the war.

It was time well spent, and as Judy and I left to find our bus stop, Roy and I promised to stay in touch.

I did see Roy several more times.

He stayed in the Dallas area, and found his Paradise.

Judy and I took the long way, going as far west as we could go to pursue ours.

# CHAPTER 29

# MARRIAGE

Friday, February 8, 1946.

Dallas, Dallas County, Texas.

Judy and I talked about quitting our jobs at Sears all week, and decided to turn in our resignation papers at Sears by the end of the first week of February and go back to Wellington. I knew my brother Noel was getting out of the Army sometime before mid-February, and that he and his family would come to Wellington. I was anxious to meet his wife Jean and little Linda, who was seven months old.

Tom Hamilton's spring cotton crop would be ready to pick in about two more months, and Judy always did the bookkeeping when it came time to pay the pickers and weigh the cotton. She also had to get some things finished at Wellington High School so she could get her High School Degree.

On Saturday, we loaded our things, what little they were, and Gladys took us to the bus station in downtown Dallas for our trip back. It took all day. Daddy picked us up in Childress, Texas, and we arrived home by supper time. Judy slept with my sisters that night and I took her home in Daddy's truck on Sunday. Noel sent a telegram the next day saying that he had been discharged from the Army on Sunday, the tenth of February. He said he would bring Jean and Linda to Dotson in another week or so.

For the next week, I saw Judy every day. Either I was over at the Hamilton house or I would bring her over to the Smith house. Two times that week we went on a double date with Dorothy, and her boyfriend provided the car. We went to a downtown movie and to a cafe on the town square, and later that week we went to a gin pool north of Wellington and fished. We caught a good number of sun perch and two pretty-good sized catfish, about five pounds each. I helped Momma fix a terrific fish fry the next day.

On the weekend, I drove Daddy's pick-up to Palo Duro Canyon, north of Lubbock. I managed to squeeze all my sisters into the truck except Roberta and Mae. We had a good time driving through the magnificent canyon, took a couple of short hikes, and ate a picnic lunch. I was proud to see the signs that said the CCC had built the park roads and buildings, and bragged a bit about myself helping build Rocky Mountain National Park with the CCC up in Colorado. It was beautiful on the canyon floor, but there were a few parts of the canyon that looked too much like the bombed and blasted ravines of Breakneck Ridge. All I had to do was say, "I'm not fond of this part, it looks too much like someplace I've been," and the girls would turn around like a marching band and retreat back to the truck, no questions asked.

Judy told me that all the color was gone from my face in one of those desolate places, and she held me tight as we walked back to the truck. She said I muttered something about "grabbing our gear and retreating, running a few feet, then slowly backing away, making sure the Japs were not close behind us."

She said I told her, "Pete was helping a stretcher bearer carry a wounded man, and Kenny was carrying Pete's gear. Nobel was loaded down and watched with a clear eye as we backed away. I felt like screaming in fear but held it back. I fired at a couple of Japs running along our right. They were tossing grenades at us."

She said I then stopped talking, and just walked back toward the truck with her still pressed against my side. She said my face was blank and my eyes were open wide, as if I was seeing it all happening in front of me again.

We got back to the truck and it all seemed to disappear back into the dark, bloody corners of my mind as the girls collected pretty rocks and we all got a cool drink of water from our Mason jars.

Judy looked in my eyes and told me calmly "those memories will last a while, but will soon fade. I'll help you push them aside."

I felt so safe and protected with her, falling more and more in love every day.

Later that day, I told her I wanted to marry her. Her eyes opened wide. A huge Hamilton smile materialized on her face.

"That would be swell," she simply replied.


4:00 pm, Monday, February 18, 1946.

Dotson, Collingsworth County, Texas Panhandle.

Noel came driving up in a '38 Dodge truck with Jean and Linda. The back of the truck was loaded with suitcases, a mattress, boxes of clothes, dishes, and a dining table with four chairs.

    We let Momma greet him first, then we all welcomed our brother home and met Vernice Lorraine Smith, his slender brunette wife from Nebraska. She introduced herself as Jean. She was holding seven-month old Linda, and handed her to Momma first, who passed her around to all my sisters. Jean watched intently as Linda was cooed, bounced, and hugged by each. I saw the look of relief on Jean's face when the baby was given back to her, and could tell that she was not prepared for so large a family of touchy-feely people.

    After a supper of cornbread and pinto beans, I helped Noel bring in his suitcases and mattress and lay it on the floor in the front room, next to the kitchen. We talked for a couple of hours, and everyone began the nighttime ritual of finding their beds in the small four-room house.

    I took Noel, Jean, and Linda to the Hamilton place the next day, and spent a wonderful time, completely the opposite from the previous night. Judy and Jean were instant friends, and spent most of the day talking between themselves outside, under a leafless sycamore tree behind the house. Noel and I talked inside the house, and on the front porch, with Tom and Nettie Hamilton.

    It was easy to see that Jean did not want to go back to the Smiths, so we waited until long after supper to do so. She did not like the small house, lack of privacy, the outhouse instead of an indoor toilet, and the way Momma kept telling her how to take care of Linda.

    "Let her do this … don't let her do that … here's the way I did it … it would be better if you did it this way," on and on.

Jean asked me if I could get Momma to stop doing that. She said Noel was afraid to tell his Momma to stop doing it.

"He won't take up for me, Red. He never has. Somebody has too, or Linda and I are going back to Nebraska. I can live with Noel, but I can't live with the whole damn family like this."

I nodded my head, and agreed with her that she needed some help with this situation.

"My brother is not comfortable making decisions," I said.

"Boy, you can say that again," Jean replied.

"I'll do it."

Once or twice I told Momma that Jean wasn't used to such a large family, and that she wanted to raise Linda her way. But, like Noel, I felt uncomfortable saying that to her. I could tell Daddy to straighten up or we could make him disappear, but I could not talk to Momma like that.

I had been protecting her all my life.

So, when things would get a little out of control, I would just look at Jean and say, "Come on, let's go outside."

I knew it wouldn't, couldn't last much longer.

Sure enough, Noel and I came back from the government assistance office a few days later, and Jean had gotten help from Dorothy to get a ride into Wellington. She and Linda were on a bus back to Nebraska.

Noel was embarrassed about it, and didn't know what to do.

"Vern told me she was gonna do it," Noel explained.

"But I didn't believe her. I told her I thought we were all supposed to live here."

"Vern?" I asked.

"Oh, that's what her folks and I call her. All her friends call her Jean."

I nodded that I understood.

I thought quietly for a few seconds, then asked him if there was anything in Nebraska that he would rather do than stay here in Texas and farm like we had always done. He shook his head.

"I don't know, Red, there's plenty of farming in Nebraska. Bigger and better machines to get corn into the ground and then off the stalks. But it just doesn't feel right there. The winters are cold and the people there are expecting too much from me. I asked about staying in the Army, but the Army said No, we're shutting down. We don't need any more bombardiers."

"Well," I replied, "Let's get Jean and Linda back down here and we can go off on our own and find good farming jobs west of here, where's it's really booming. At least you and I will be together, but not like this. Besides, this part of Texas is drying up. I always thought that, after the war, I would be going home to Hopkins County. But I guess farming has already petered out there, too."

Knowing that Big Brother had to do something about it, I told Noel we had to find a place for him and his family to stay, and to bring Jean and Linda back. I told him the family had to at least try to stay together for now, that us being in Texas and him being in Nebraska didn't feel right to me this soon after the war.

I knew deep inside that I could, maybe, help keep things running smoothly until Judy and I got married and had a chance to start our own life, too.

I figured the time was close, very close, that Momma and Daddy would just pick up and move west. Uncle Clyde and his boys, along with Aunt Lola, were making pretty good money there as farmers in Eloy, Arizona.

A week later, Noel and I found a small house to rent for him and his family, a couple of miles away from the Hamiltons. It had two bedrooms, an indoor toilet, and the kitchen had a kerosene stove. The next day, we took Daddy's old truck, two-hundred dollars of our own money, and traded it in for a bigger and better '38 Chevrolet truck. Noel and I were slowly getting our plans together to head west and find good jobs.

Noel sent a telegram to Jean at her parent's house in Nebraska, telling her that he and I were driving up there, and that he would be asking her and Linda to come back to Texas with us.


Monday, March 4, 1946.

Dotson, Collingsworth County, Texas Panhandle.

Noel and I drove his Dodge truck to Jansen, Nebraska. I met Jean's parents, Carl and Hilda Brockmeyer, and spent the better part of two hours talking to them while Noel talked to Jean in the back bedroom.

I think it's funny now when I think about the Brockmeyers having a *back bedroom*. Every house Noel and I ever lived in had two, maybe three rooms and a kitchen. We never had a *back bedroom* like the Brockmeyers, and it was easy to see why Jean was having a hard time living with the Smiths.

When Noel and I left Nebraska that day, Jean and Linda were with us. In the back of the truck was an icebox that the Brockmeyers had given us because they had gotten a new electric refrigerator.

By the next day, Noel and his family were in the house we had rented. It was, of course, still much smaller than what Jean was used to in Nebraska, but all was calmed down with the privacy of the new, peaceful setting.

For the next two weeks, things ran smoothly. Noel and Jean were in their own place with their baby Linda. I was staying at home, and went to the Hamilton place every day. There was always fresh milk there, since they owned a cow. I would get a large Mason jar full of milk, wrapped in a linen towel and placed in a crock, and take it to Jean. I would sometimes take extra food that Nettie Hamilton had cooked to Noel's, and eat supper with them. Then, back home to the Smiths I would go, looking forward to another day of courting Judy and delivering milk for Linda.

Tom Hamilton's cotton crop, in a forty-acre plot five miles east of Wellington, was looking better every day. The cotton bolls were beginning to split, and we expected it to be a sea of fluffy white by the first of April. Noel and I would take a couple of days every week and chop the weeds, wandering down each row from morning to night. Judy would bring a lunch to us, and sometimes Jean would bring Linda out for a few minutes of sunshine.

Judy would do her bookkeeping and give us decent pay for what we did. Combined with that, the federal government was giving Noel and me twenty dollars apiece for a year, as part of the "52-20 Club," to help us until we found permanent jobs. We spent what we needed, but we saved for what we knew would be needed later, on our journey west.

Monday, March 25, 1946.

Wellington, Collingsworth County, Texas Panhandle.

      Judy and I decided that we would get married in March, but told no one except Noel and Jean at the time.
      I told my sister Dorothy about it a day later, and she went to downtown Wellington with me to pick out an engagement ring. Parsons Drug Store had a lot of jewelry, and we found one with a pretty diamond top, with smaller diamonds running down each side.
      "Judy will love this ring," Dorothy said.
      "I know she will, because I love it!" she winked as she twirled it around on her finger.
      She put it back in the little box and handed it to me.
      "Now, when is the big day?"
      "Aw, we don't know yet," I answered.
      "Any day now, but we're not quite sure. It'll happen when it happens."
      Two days later, on Thursday, I drove myself into town. I walked up the Collingsworth County Courthouse west entrance, opened the right-side door, and found my way to the Office of Margaret Shields, the County Clerk.
      Within a half-hour, I had applied for a marriage license and had the paperwork in my hand. All I needed was

a preacher or a Justice of the Peace to sign it and it was done. To that moment in my life, I had not experienced anything as truly momentous as holding that marriage license. The thought of marriage had bounced around in my brain many times as a kid, but meant nothing to me because no face or name was attached to it, and my life was surrounded by the offspring of Bud and Altie Smith's marriage. By the time I was fifteen, there were two brothers and four sisters gathered around me, all looking to me for guidance. By the time I was twenty, there was another sister. Then the war happened. There was no way whatsoever to add a wife into my world. There was no girl or woman in my tiny corner of the world that was unselfish enough to share this inherited family, and no room for me to love anyone as much as I now loved Judy.

Judy came into my life like sunshine through a closed curtain.

My steps out of the Collingsworth County Courthouse were less focused and single-minded as the steps going in. They now seemed to float on air, filled with dreamy glimpses of the paradise that awaited me.

Any day now.

It'll happen when it happens.


Friday, March 29, 1946.

Wellington, Collingsworth County, Northwest Texas.

Judy told her parents that she was going with me, Noel, and Jean to Mangum, Oklahoma for a rodeo. I told Momma and Daddy the same thing.

Just the four of us knew we were getting married tonight.

Dorothy stayed with Linda at Noel's house.

We started out a little before dark, not to Oklahoma, but near the state line to a Collingsworth County Justice of the Peace, Mr. W. G. Nite. He and his wife were sitting down for dinner when we showed up at his door. He was a very polite and generous man, and said, "Sure, that's my job. It'll just take a minute. Do you have your Marriage License? I will need to fill it out and take it to Margaret at the County Clerk's office."

I fumbled in my coat jacket and pulled out the license.

"Yes, I have it, right here, Sir."

I handed it to him, my hand shaking nervously.

"Thank you, let's see…Horace. Calm down, don't be nervous. I have done a hundred of these. Nobody gets hurt," he chuckled.

I blushed, and looked down at my shoes.

*I should've polished my boots.*

"Now, do you want to get married in here or outside?"

"Outside, please," we replied.

The JP and his wife lived just off the road in the middle of a cotton field, and his wife suggested we stand close to it, with the cotton crop as a backdrop.

We giggled our way over to the cotton field like little kids and Mr. Nite began. I spoke the vows to Judy:

*"I, Horace Garlton Smith, take thee, Clara Juliette Hamilton, to be my wedded wife, to have and to hold, from this day forward, for better, for worse, for richer, for poorer,*

*in sickness and in health, to love and to cherish, till death do us part, according to God's holy ordinance; and thereto I pledge myself to you."*

As Judy repeated the vows to me, my eyes became wet, and she tightened her hand over mine. She was so beautiful, standing there in the edge of the spring cotton field, in the white cotton dress with pink flowers she had borrowed from Jean. It was the last light of dusk when I placed the ring on her finger. Her eyes were wet with tears.

It was over as soon as it had begun.
It had happened when it happened.
We kissed.
Noel and Jean whistled and clapped their hands.
The JP said, "May God bless you now and always."
We kissed again.
I looked at my watch.
It was eight o'clock, and the sky was dark.
We were Man and Wife.
We thanked the JP, and I gave him a ten-dollar bill.
He thanked us.
Noel drove us to the Wellington town square.
I thought I was in Heaven.
We had supper at a corner café.
We all four had hot dogs.
Jean and Noel did most of the talking.
Judy and I were kinda lost for words.
We walked across the street to the O'Neil Hotel.
We checked in as Mr. and Mrs. Horace G. Smith.
Noel and Jean checked in as Mr. and Mrs. Carl N. Smith, Jr.
My hand trembled a bit as I signed the hotel ledger.

We carried our little bit of luggage up the two floors to our room.

Judy and I got the corner room.

Noel and Jean got a room down the hallway.

The honeymoon in the over-sized double bed did not exactly turn out in the dreamy way I had expected. Of course, I had never had a honeymoon to compare it to, so who was I to say or judge? We spent a considerable time kissing and holding each other tight, trying to grapple with the absolute truth of being married, being husband and wife, and pledging to be each other's everything for the rest of our lives on Earth.

To pursue our mutual paradise side by side, from this day forward, for better, for worse, for richer, for poorer, in sickness and in health, to love and to cherish, till death do us part.

I knew I wanted to be with her all the time, but could I do all of that? I believed I could.

*You'd better believe you can! God was watching and listening when you promised to do it!*

We explored each other's body like two children in a fairy-tale, talking quietly as each enchanting moment gave way to mesmerizing flashes of delightful pleasures.

When the stimulations had reached their peak and the riveting instance of consummation occurred, Judy began to tremble and whimper in pain and discomfort. Mutual sensualities had quickly turned to singular distress. I quickly became embarrassed at the thought of causing discomfort to my wife of only a few hours, and an awkwardness filled the room.

"Are you okay, Judy?"

"Yes, Red. It just hurt bad. It felt good, but then burned like fire. I'm bleeding, too."

"I did not know. I'm sorry."

She hushed me, and patted my cheek with her soft, gentle hand.

"I was told it might do this. I guess you have to do it to find out."

"What should I do, Judy?"

"Nothing. Let me clean myself up and lay here with you some more. I was told this only happens once; it won't be like this the next time."

"Ohh, I'm so sorry, my love."

"Shhh, just lay here with me, Red. I'm so happy."

"Ohh, I am happy, too. So very, very happy."

Long moments passed.

Bliss entered our souls as little baby-like sounds of contentment filled the room.

Sighs were exchanged, and long, wet kisses sealed our conclusion of lovemaking.

The hot, raging fires of desire had delicately changed to the soft, glowing embers of undemanding love.

After another hour, Judy looked at me and said, "I want to go home, Red. Can you take me home? It will look better if I come home in the middle of the night instead of in the morning. I want to see to myself and clean myself up in my own room, at home."

"Sure, Judy. I'll tell Noel we're leaving."

"Does he need to know?"

I smiled and said, "I need his truck."

She smiled.

I quickly showered and dressed. Quietly opening the door, I tiptoed down the wood-floor hallway and gently knocked on Noel's door.

Nothing.

I knocked again, and heard water splash and footsteps walking toward the door. From the inside, Noel said, "Who is it?"

"It's me," I answered.

"Judy wants to go home. I need the truck."

"Well, I'll be god-darned, Red," I heard Noel mutter as he unlocked and opened his door slightly. I saw he had a big white towel wrapped around him, and soapy water was dripping on the floor.

I made a small chuckle.

"What the hell, are you taking a bath?"

He blushed, and said in an embarrassed voice, "Vern and I are taking a bubble bath," then snickered like a little boy.

He reached toward the chair by the door, took his ignition key out of his folded-up pants, and handed it to me.

"Come back and get us in a little bit," he said.

"We'll be ready to go home, too."

Judy was still in the bathroom, getting ready to go. I saw that she had tried to get some blood stains off of the bedsheet, and had done a good job. I felt horribly sorry, and apologized to her through the door. She opened it slightly, stuck her head out, smiled, and said, "You stop it. Everything is okay. I'm very glad to be a Smith." Then, with an even-brighter smile, disappeared behind the closed door.

I took her home, and walked her to the door, just like we were coming in late from the rodeo. As I walked back to the truck, I heard Mrs. Hamilton say "I'm glad you're back safe. Did'ja have a good time?"

I drove slowly back to the hotel, to give Noel and Jean time to get their things together. When I knocked on their door, it quickly opened, and they were ready to go. Jean had a smirky smile, and asked if Judy was okay. I smiled back, winked, and said she told me she was okay, and happy to be a Smith. Jean smiled back and said that's swell.

We went straight to Noel's house, and he made a pot of coffee. It was 3am. Dorothy was in the bedroom, sleeping with Linda. Jean laid down with them. Noel and I stayed up until dawn and talked about everything from the pre-war years to the post war year, and all that lay ahead. The fact is, after we talked about it, we realized we didn't know a darn thing about what lay ahead. All we knew was that we wanted to do what we knew best, which was farming. Bombardiers and riflemen weren't in strong demand anymore, not that we would want to do it again. We wanted to be happy, to find our own paradise out there.

Holding our coffee cups and looking down at our shoes, then up at each other, we promised we would do it. Stay here a while, then push west, where the farms were new, and the money was better.


Friday, April 5, 1946

Wellington, Collingsworth County, Northwest Texas.

Judy kept the marriage a secret from her parents for a week. I understood why she did not tell them. It was because she was as important to her family as I had been to mine before the war. I was the leader of the domestic pack, and the protector of Momma. Not that she was in danger, but Daddy needed an *authority* in the vicinity to keep his ne'er do well character in tow.

All four of Judy's sisters had left the nest, and were pursuing those things that a tenant farmer's life could not give them. The industrial years of the war had arrived just in time to lure them away from the farm and into the big city. Tom and Nettie Hamilton were left with two boys in their young teens, Alfred and Alvis, and a very bright girl in her late teens, Juliette. She was as important to them as the Smith's adult male child had been four years earlier. She was as devoted to them as I was to my parents.

The Army had lessened the grip of my family on me, just enough to answer the urge to take the perfect lovemate and begin a separate life, although not totally apart. Judy and I both knew that our parents still had a grip on us, but the years were getting short. *How long would it last?*

*Probably as long as two or three years, or as short as a childbirth.*

I mentioned to Momma that Judy and I had gotten married, and the rest of the family just played along. Judy had privately told her mother after the first week that she was married, but her father did not yet know.


Friday, April 12, 1946

Wellington, Collingsworth County, Northwest Texas.

Judy kept the marriage a secret from her father for another week, making it two weeks. We saw each other every night during those two weeks. Noel and I would work the Hamilton cotton patch or do other farmer chores during the day, and I would be at Judy's house or she would be at mine every evening.

The cotton crop was coming along, and the time was getting closer and closer for Judy and me to move out to our own *place* when the picking started.

According to Judy, when her mother finally told her father that the marriage had already happened, he just stared ahead a few seconds, shrugged his shoulders, and said, "Well, they may as well be married, she's over there all the time anyway."

# CHAPTER 30

# PURSUIT OF PARADISE

Christmas Eve.
Tuesday, December 24, 1946.

Eleven Mile Corner, near Casa Grande, Arizona.

As I push the screen door open, I look behind and say "I'm gonna step out here on the porch, Judy, for just a few minutes. I'll be right back."

A gentle, familiar voice from the kitchen replies "Take your time, Red. I'm just cleaning up in here. Jean's upstairs checking on Linda."

There is a chill in the air, as the wind sweeps across the yard, down from the Superstition Mountains far to the north. The temperature will be in the thirties again tonight. I can smell the dry musk of the desert floor in the wind, the fragrances of the cactus, creosote, and juniper, and the salty dust from the many dried lakes. From behind me, I can smell the left-over aroma of today's supper, drifting through the open window, the curtain playing hide-and-seek behind the screen. Pinto beans, fried potatoes, cornbread and a surprise treat: apple pie. I can still smell the cinnamon through the open window. Judy and Jean managed to turn biscuit dough and two jars of canned cinnamon apples into a really, really good pie.

The north wind blows across the empty yard, southward, delivering the perfumes of the desert night.

There is never a time here in the Arizona desert when my senses aren't being teased and pleased by the sights, sounds, and smells of the southwest.

This ain't Texas, and it sure as hell ain't the Pacific.

I stand here every night on the front porch for five or ten minutes and look across the irrigated fields to the lights of Eloy, eleven miles to the south. Eleven miles to my right, westward toward the Maricopa Mountains, the lights of Casa Grande have begun to shimmer in the twilight that follows the sun as it slips below the horizon. Eleven miles behind me, and toward the northeast, is the town of Coolidge. To my left, a row of new apartments wind around the curved lane, and stop where the creosotes and junipers dot the landscape all the way to the dark night. Nobody can see that far in Hopkins County, not that there is anything to see.

It was much different on Leyte and Mindanao.

Sometimes you couldn't see five feet in front of you, until the enemy was crawling up from his spider hole, in the rainy pitch-black darkness, up to your foxhole.

My shoulders tighten as I think back to those days and nights on Leyte and Mindanao. Then I look around me at peaceful Arizona.

The Sonoran Desert is out there, a wilderness hanging on by its fingernails, ready to bite you sometimes, but mostly just giving in to the slow movement west. Farms and small cities are settling in along the rich, fertile valleys of the Basin and Range country. Just like Flora, Sulphur Bluff, and Tira, these desert communities are only fresher, newer, ready to be worked on and waiting to be taken. The fragmented wilderness strikes back every now and then with a drought, a dust storm, or a plague of mice or bugs.

I reach into my pocket for my Zippo, and feel the textured, black finish. I hold it like an old, precious, lucky charm from a time of death averted and victory won, with Life wrenched from the grip of everyday Death.

*You brought me through some tough times, my little friend. A worker at the post office last week called you "mi zippolitta negro," my little black zippo. The music of your **click-snap** is still one of the best melodies a man can hear.*

I light a cigarette.

**Click-Snap.**

I've been home a year now, and so much has happened it is hard to believe it has only been one year.

After getting married in March, Judy and I moved into a large rent house in Wellington. I swear, it only took a week before everybody lived in that house. Momma and Daddy, my sisters, my three Thomas cousins. Noel and Jean stayed in their house, and Judy visited with Jean almost every day.

We helped Mr. Hamilton pick cotton through April and May. Judy kept the books for the workers' wages and the weighing. It was good cotton, really good cotton, "fair-to-middlin" as the cotton market graded it. Mr. Hamilton made some good money on that crop.

I laugh now as I remember the day Judy came out to bring me lunch, and then hung around for a while as she talked to some of the workers. She had known these people a long time, some of them even from the Sulphur Bluff days, as they followed the crops westward during and after the war. The war needed good cotton and good food production, and East Texas could no longer offer the best.

But Arizona could offer the best, so here we all were. Some of us were picking cotton, and some of us were listening to Judy talk. I enjoyed it for a short while, then I realized we were losing time and money on chatter. I looked up at Judy and said, "You better go on back to the house, now."

She looked at me and asked, "Why?"

I answered, "Because you're keeping us from working. You better go along now."

She smiled and said, "These are my friends. They're working. See?"

She looked around and half-a-dozen people were standing there, cotton sacks limp along the ground, looking at her and listening to her.

I reached down, and pulled a cotton plant from the rich ground. The root was hanging firm and long, from my hand down to the plowed dirt.

I started spinning it by holding the green end, the root whipping in the air like a bullwhip.

I said again, "You better go on home now, Judy," and I made a few steps toward her.

She instantly stood up and walked briskly toward the house, saying "Good-bye" to her friends as they said, "Good-bye, Juliette," to her.

I smiled and looked at the workers. They all smiled back, some laughing. Leaning forward, they began picking cotton again.

"Miss Juliette sure is somethin', ain't she!" I heard one say.

"She's a humdinger," I heard another.

I laugh again as I remember that day.

I light another cigarette.

**Click-Snap.**

I look back in the house and see Judy and Jean at the kitchen sink, washing dishes. I smile as I watch them, knowing that for a long time neither of them had a sink with running water on our journey west.

In May, after the cotton was picked, we moved to Levelland, Texas, near the New Mexico border.

My eyes look again toward the lights of Eloy as I stand on the front porch and remember the four-room house we shared in Levelland with Noel, Jean, and Linda. Noel's job was to irrigate the newly planted summer cotton at night, and I did odd jobs around the farm during the day.

Two months later, I believe it was in July, we got word that Momma and Daddy were leaving Wellington and were coming to Levelland. Another farmer had convinced them to work on his farm for more money than they were getting in Wellington. So, Noel and I drove our two trucks back to Wellington to get them.

They got a farmhouse to live in, so they didn't have to stay with us. I smile and nod my head as I remember Jean telling Noel as we left, "Don't bring them back here to live with us. I'll go back to Nebraska, guaranteed."

As soon as they got moved in, my brother-in-law Joe Racadio was released from the Army. He came to Levelland to get Roberta and Darrel, along with the money that Roberta had saved from his Army allotment. That was a good week, seeing Joe and visiting with him. A short man, Joe was always smiling. He told some good stories of his childhood in the Philippines, and the stories made me feel better about those islands from which I had brought back so many dark, deadly memories. We all laughed as he told and re-told the story of him meeting Roberta in a washeteria in Arizona back in '43, and getting married in Nogales. Each time he would tell it, he would change it from Nogales, Arizona to Nogales, Mexico, then back again.

We all watched Joe drive away with his family, Roberta and Darrel, as he followed his own pursuit of paradise into California. He was a cook in the Army, and his dream was to open his own café and serve the thousands and thousands of people streaming west through southern California, then north along the San Joaquin Valley.

To this day, I still don't know which city Joe and Roberta were married in, and I doubt if he knows, either.

About a month later, Uncle Clyde's son, Bubber Smith, came to Levelland and talked Momma and Daddy into moving to Eloy, Arizona.

"More money for less work," he told them, which was right down Daddy's alley.

So, in August, Daddy decided that he, Momma, and the remaining girls, minus Roberta and Darrel, would move to Arizona.

The day Noel and I loaded them and everything they had in our two trucks was the day things finally came to blows between Daddy and me.

Noel was in his truck, with Daddy and Momma. I was in mine, with the girls, waiting for Dorothy to come home from her job in town. A man, one of Dorothy's friends, pulled his car up near us, let her out, they said their good-byes, and he drove off. She was walking toward my truck, putting money in her purse when Daddy jumped out of Noel's truck and ran to her, trying to take her money from her. She was crying out, "Stop it! Dammit! Leave my money alone!"

I jumped out of my truck and walked briskly toward them, yelling at Daddy, "Stop it, leave her alone!"

Daddy turned toward me, and said with a wild look in his eyes, "This ain't none of your goddam business."

I quickly advanced toward him. I tightened my first, brought it low behind me, then lifted it on a high path through the air and slugged Daddy right in his face, knocking him down. I still remember Noel's jaw-dropping expression, his mouth formed into an "O," and Momma's half-smile.

I dragged him back to Noel's truck, and told him, "What you do to these girls IS my goddam business. Don't you EVER do ANYTHING to these girls again. Or to Momma, either! Nothing!" I crammed him into the cab, slammed the truck door, and quickly walked back to my truck. Hattie, Dorothy, Alice, and Mae were waiting.

"Did you hurt him?" Mae asked me.

"Hush," Hattie told her.

Dorothy looked at Mae and said, "You should ask Brother if he hurt HIS hand."

Mae looked back at me, and with a half-smile, innocently asked, "Did you hurt your hand?"

"No, I did not," I answered, looking at her.

"But I'll tell you something, I think I need some ice cream as soon as we get down the road."

She smiled that cute, priceless smile, and said, "Me, too."

In our two trucks, loaded with people and all their belongings, we began the 650-mile journey from Levelland to Eloy.

I have never seen Jean smile so broadly as that day, when we pulled out, hauling her in-laws to Arizona.

Noel and I dropped them off with Uncle Clyde in Eloy, then drove back to work the farm in Levelland.

But things were beginning to go wrong in Levelland. The rain did not come when it should have. The temperatures were above one hundred degrees for long periods of time. Bugs began to appear. The plants looked stunted, and brownish green. The soil was dry and crusty. White crystals were scattered around, like someone had sprinkled salt all over it. The owner came to us and said his banker was beginning to talk down the prospect of success, and suggested we think about moving further west before his farm went belly-up. He said he thought an oil well used to be where his cotton crop was planted. He was muttering, "Damn oil men!" as he walked away.

I snuff out my second cigarette, and light up a third one with my Zippo.

**Click-Snap.**

Judy opens the door behind me, hands me a cup of coffee, and says, "Here. This is the last cup. We'll make some fresh for Noel when he comes in from work."

"Thank you, Judy. It sure is nice out here. I'm just trying to remember all that we've gone through this year, and it's not easy. There's been a lot."

She smiles.

"It sure has. But I'd have it no other way."

I set my cup on the porch railing, reach for her, and hold her as tight as her big, pregnant tummy will allow.

"I'd have it no other way, either," I replied.

After a minute of holding each other, rocking in perfect motion to unheard music, she steps back inside.

"I hear Linda waking up," she says.

I stay out on the porch, and look toward the lights of Eloy. I remember the first week of September, when Noel and I decided that the farm in Levelland really was about to go under. It was then that we packed up our two families and moved west, to Arizona, where "more money for less work" was the name of the game. Neither Noel nor I believed that in the least. "More money for more work" was more like it. We were ready for that.

We stayed with Aunt Lola and my cousins Nellie and Buck Foote, and Buck's wife Frances, in Eloy for the first night, then looked for our own place the next day.

We found a government settlement in a town called Eleven Mile Corner, and moved into the only apartment available. It was the best place we had ever lived. There was a living room, dining room, and kitchen downstairs, and two bedrooms and a bathroom upstairs. The kitchen had a gas stove. We had our own icebox, the one the Brockmeyers had given us in Nebraska. All of that for sixteen dollars a month.

*Pretty close to Paradise,* I tell myself.

And it was very good for Noel and Jean, since Momma and Daddy lived eleven miles away, in Eloy. In fact, a month later, Momma and Daddy moved with Uncle Clyde to California, where they worked on a large lemon ranch near Riverside. The old family was breaking up now, but all of us seemed to be going in the same direction. West.

My coffee cup is empty as I step back inside the house.

"Man," I say to anyone who can hear.

"I sure could use another cup of coffee."

"Ladies, that pie was swell. Is there enough left for another slice?"

"Coming right up," Judy replies, as she reaches up to get a freshly washed cup and saucer.

I walk over to the couch we got from Aunt Lola, when we first arrived in Eloy in September. I look at Jean and say, "This sure is a good couch. Lola and George Foote were really nice to us when we got to Eloy, weren't they?"

She walks over from the kitchen, holding Linda, and hisses with a big smile.

"Yes, and I will never forgive you for what you did to us that night, Red Smith!"

I spread my arms with innocent disbelief.

"What did I do?"

"You saw that green Army blanket Lola handed me for Linda. You saw the bedbugs crawling on it. Even your cousins Buck and Francis Foote saw them. And Nellie did, too."

"Yeah, My cousins are nice looking, aren't they? Buck Foote is a loud, happy man, and his wife Francis has pretty dark hair. And Nellie Foote is tall and skinny, with dark hair, too. Like you."

Jean points her finger at me.

"Don't you try to change the subject, Red. Everything in George and Lola's house was dirty. When Lola said ya'll can stay here tonight you answered really quick and said no, Judy and I will stay with Buck and Francis. Noel, Jean, and Linda can stay here with you."

I laugh. I can hear Judy laughing in the kitchen. Jean is laughing, too.

"Noel and I slept on the floor, with Linda between us. We were up before the sun came up, ready to leave."

"Airing this couch out and spraying it with that new bugspray DDT was the best thing we ever did. We just turned this on its side and the dead bugs came pouring out of it."

I slap my open palm on the cushion.

"See? No bugs anymore. All gone."

Jean just nods her head, and says, "This apartment is the best place I've ever lived in as a Smith."

Judy brings me my apple pie, and a fresh cup of coffee.

"When are we gonna get more of those big potatoes?" she asks.

"Those darn things were the size of a football."

We all laugh, knowing they were big, but not that big. Noel and I had first seen them when we were laying them on the abandoned runway at Coolidge Army Airfield. Schenley Liquor Company was paying us to crush them and dry them out for their whiskey distillery. I would keep them spread out on the runway while Noel would drive a big steamroller over them. After a day of drying in the Arizona sun, we would shovel them into a truck trailer and Schenley would pick them up. It was good money, and quite a few of the big potatoes made their way home with us.

"It took all four of us to eat just one of them," Jean adds.

"We'll check the store tomorrow. Maybe he's got some in," I say, forking a piece of the pie into my mouth.

We hear Noel's truck pull in, and a thin smile appears on Jean's face.

She stands up, hands Linda to Judy, and goes into the kitchen to get his supper plate ready. As we wait for him to come inside, I remember back to the time a few weeks ago when he and I both got a bad case of the pink eye.

I laugh under my breath when I remember the night Noel sat at the table, with his knife and fork in each hand next to his plate. The knife and fork were pointing up toward the ceiling. He had just finished mashing pinto beans and potatoes together into a mush, because he had a bad toothache, too. His eyes were red and wet, just like mine. And itchy like crazy.

"You know, Red," he confessed, in a whiney voice.

He was staring at his upright knife and fork.

"I feel like I just wanna slam my face on these to stop my eyes from itching like they do."

We all laughed, and he did, too.

"Judy, where did Noel and I get the pink eye a week or so back?" I ask as Noel opens the door.

"From those cows you were working with," she answers, as she clicks her tongue at Linda.

"Did'ja work with any cows today, Noel?" I ask.

Noel slips his shoes off, and places them against the wall, beside a coat rack. He takes his brown jacket off and hangs it on the coat rack. He looks at me, half-raises his right arm in his familiar, trademark gesture, and lowers it as he says, "God-darn no. I don't even want to get close to those cows. I'll drive out of the way to not pass them."

I laugh at Noel, then look at Judy and ask, "What did we take to get rid of the pink eye?"

"Boric acid. We rinsed your eyes with boric acid."

"Gee, that was a hard time," Noel says.

"Let's not even talk about it."

Noel washes his hands and face at the sink. He and Jean exchange a quick kiss. He sits at the table and Jean hands him a plate of beans, potatoes, and cornbread.

I sit at the table with him.

"There's apple pie, too," I tell him.

"And Christmas presents," Judy says, pointing toward the decorated cedar tree in the corner of the front room.

I feel good, satisfied, and blessed sitting at the table with Noel. We exchange small talk as he eats. People. Work. Trucks. Irrigation ditches. Fences that need mending. Cows that we need to stay away from.

I tell Noel, "It's too bad we can't have meat more often. They sell ground meat at the store down the street. Didn't we buy some last month?"

I know right where I am going with this question, and I don't have to wait very long until Jean says, "Good God yes, we did! And it was made from a lizard!"

Judy joins in, "It was a Gila Monster, Jean. We found his claw in it!"

"God-darned, Red," Noels whines.

"I was trying to forget that."

Jean walks over to the table, and declares, "While we were breaking it apart to make patties, it felt all greasy and stringy. And then Judy found that claw in it, with four little fingers with pointed nails."

I laugh.

"Well, the store owner was sure sorry about it. He said he was never buying meat from that fellow again. He gave us some hot dogs, so we at least had some meat that day."

Noel snickers and says, "We looked them over really good to make sure they didn't have claws in them, too. Remember what the package said, Red? It said Meat Weenies. It didn't say anything about beef or pork. It just said Meat."

We all laugh a few minutes over that.

Noel finishes his supper, enjoys the slice of apple pie, drinks his second cup of coffee, and goes upstairs to bathe.

I get up from the table and walk toward the front door. I grab my jacket from the row of hooks on the wall that hold four jackets. Opening the screen door, I tell Judy and Jean, "I'm gonna smoke a cigar out here, don't want to bother you with the smoke."

As I stand on the porch, my mind drifts back again to Leyte, and I reach into my chest pocket for a small, tightly wound cigar that I bought at the community store. The **click-snap** of my Zippo and the thick smoke from the first light of the cigar make me think of the war again.

*Sharing a light with Nobel, Pete, and Kenny.*
*And Tim.*

*Breathing in the hot smoke from the mortar tube as we launched round after round after round toward the enemy.*

I remember a nightmarishly black night. A hurricane wind was blowing, with cutting curtains of rain, piercing my face like needles. Cannons were flashing and mortar rounds were hissing. The enemy was running in the dark, sometimes illuminated by the artillery light, fading into black, moving from foxhole-to-foxhole, their bayonets held firmly in their short rifles, jabbing, piercing, jabbing again, cursing in their damned high-pitched voices.

I remember standing in knee-deep water, holding my rifle head-high, and beginning to shake uncontrollably. I remember screaming, again, and again, and again.

And then, from out of nowhere, there was my friend, my big, smiling, colored friend with the soft, tender, blue eyes, standing there in the wet, bloody mud. He leaned toward me, and his smooth, deep, rich voice began to calmly reassure me:

*"Horace, listen to me. All is fine. Keep your head down, stay quiet, and no harm will come to you this night. Do as I say. I am here to tell you to be still. You will endure this night if you be still. You WILL survive this war, Horace. There is still much that you must do. But, for tonight, you keep your head down and you stay quiet. I'll be here with you, in the dark. Think of home, Horace. Think of home."*

My fingers are calm as I think of my colored friend, my dark angel on that horrible, killing night, saving me from my lunatic fear. I raise the cigar to my lips and light it again with my Zippo. The flame-light illuminates and dances off my fingers, bringing back a thousand memories of familiar faces, sharp noses, half-closed eyes, when the singular moment of "sharing a light" became the code signal for *You are my Friend, and We are safe right now.*

I close my eyes, inhale, and slowly release a cloud of grey smoke that breaks the dark night, vanishing as the wind carries it upward, to the porch roof, then up and away. I look across the small yard in front of our apartment.

It is desert land, yes. But, it is rich and friendly. It's not mine; I don't know if I will ever own the land I stand on. Don't know if I even need to. I fought for this land, one of my buddies died for this land, two were wounded for it, and it's as much mine as my own breath, my own wife, and my own child.

I stand here every night and take it all in, the peace and the quiet. The freedom. The life.

The Journey. The path that Judy and I are following on our pursuit of paradise.

The sun is well below the horizon to my right now, sending pink and orange ribbons into the western sky as a darker blue-black envelope approaches from the east. All is good, here, in Eleven Mile Corner, Arizona.

Christmas. What a year this has been!

Last Christmas, just back from the war, Judy was waiting for me there at Momma's. Waiting to take my heart, soothe the demons of war that danced in my head, and give me my life again. From the Texas farms of Wellington, to the city jobs in Dallas, back to the farms of Wellington, to a Justice of the Peace in a cotton field, to another farm in Levelland, and then to Arizona. Along the way, between Wellington and Levelland, a baby was conceived to start the family of my dreams, the Paradise that I've been chasing all my life.

I realize that my Paradise is not a place, it is each day waking up with Judy and living life with the freedom that I fought for.

Here we are, still raking and scraping for a place to call home, working the fields, picking the crops, learning how to operate the new machinery that keeps coming from the factories. Paradise is simple on the farm. It's good enough for me and mine.

There are a few presents under the cedar tree that Noel and I found at the Coolidge Army Airfield. Growing among the cobbles and pebbles of the arroyo that ran beside the flight line, it had the perfect shape for the perfect Christmas tree.

Judy has two presents under that tree - a hand mirror and a pair of white, cotton, lacey gloves. I bought them for her in Eloy last week. I've got a couple of presents under it, too, from her. It sure looks like Christmas in there!

Even little seventeen-month old Linda has a present under the tree. I bought a doll for her last week, when Noel and I went into Eloy for a new truck tire. It was the right size for her, with a soft, squeezy body and a cute, smiling face. Noel and Jean weren't gonna get her a present, and I couldn't stand the thought of her not getting anything. When I gave it to Jean to wrap, she asked me, "Oh, Red, why did you go and do that?"

I told her, "Every little girl needs a doll for Christmas."

Jean was very happy about that, and she thanked me with a smile and two wet eyes.

*Thank you, Lord, for the road you lay before me, from Hopkins County to Hell to here. I made the trip all in one piece. Thank you for putting me right here, in this Arizona apartment, with a wife and a baby coming any day now. Judy is a lovely person to live with, helping me in so many ways. She has helped me adjust to civilian life. It has not always been easy for her, and I will be forever thankful for her loving care and patience. I cannot make it without her. I cannot experience my everyday Paradise without her. May it go on and on and on, til my final breath.*
*Amen.*

As I take another draw from the cigar, I hear Judy talking to Jean about the way her tight, bulging tummy feels, and they are both giggling.

"It's getting harder and harder to go up those stairs to the bathroom," Judy tells Jean.

"Yeah, but that's good for you. It'll make the birth easier," Jean advises.

"Well. if that's true, I ought to go climb some rocks at Superstition Mountain in two or three weeks," Judy declares.

I smile.

*Maybe we will.*

Noel will be running the irrigation ditches again tomorrow, opening the valves at precisely the right time for the water of life to flood the neatly plowed crops. Again, there will be plenty of supper waiting for him when he's through, and we'll sit at the table once more and talk and laugh.

I watch the end of the cigar glow red, like a hot, red sun, with each puff.

I recall a similar hot, red sun and the dusty, swirling wind from an East Texas summer a long time ago.

*Baseball. Sweat. And, my first real memory of Judy.*

She was every bit the most remarkable girl I had ever seen in Hopkins County.

*Oh, it was such a hot day!*

*Damn! It was so hot!*

But the summer heat never kept the baseballs from flying during those Texas summers. The baseball diamond was the Great Easel upon which we painted our pleasures, and we could win the world if we were good enough.

*I do believe that was the best day of my life.*

I smile as I remember that day.

There I was, between second base and third base, ……..

# EPILOGUE – RED

December, 2012.

San Antonio, Bexar County, Texas.

In the busy, quiet dining room of a newly opened rehabilitation clinic, thirty elderly patients were shuffled, wheeled, and directed to their allotted spaces around a dozen tables. Some smiled, most just looked down in a somewhat melancholy posture, positioning their pleated, plaid bibs with tactile fingers attached to stiff, tired hands. A few spoke genuinely friendly greetings to familiar faces, and were acknowledged by nods and a slow, arthritic wave of a hand.

The attendants hustled about, delivering plates of nutritious, dietary-restrictive, sometimes-tasteless food to those seated. The usual sounds of mealtime were there, accompanied by the ancient smell of a school cafeteria.

One man sat next to his wife, and tended to her needs lovingly and patiently. She was strapped into a rather elaborate wheelchair, her head leaning constantly to her left, her eyes bright with perception, a multicolored silk scarf tightly wrapped around her palms, providing a resting place for her Parkinson hands. She was neatly dressed, as was he.

A Christmas tree stood at the left-most wall, mostly decorated in white lights and silver garland, punctuated with modestly sized sparkling dragonflies. Hand-written notes and crayoned pictures were pinned to the tree, balancing the tree with sincerity. A woman in a white apron pushed a light blue metal cart with brown plastic coffee cups half-filled with weak, hot coffee. Stopping at each table, she would give a cup to those that nodded, and would smile as they embraced the cup with both hands, raising the cup to their nose and then shakily to their pursed lips as if they had waited all their lives for that one, luxurious cup of caffeinated nectar.

    Ninety-one-year-old Red Smith was wheeled to his table, near the Christmas tree, and his wheelchair was strategically placed so he could see the entire dining room. He watched as patients were delivered through the door to their tables. He spoke very little to the others, did not know any of them by name, but would smile broadly, nod his head, and raise his hand in a weak wave if the staff addressed him as they hustled around the dining room.

    He had been in the clinic for three weeks, after a late-night fall in the bathroom of the apartment-cottage he and Judy shared at a senior-citizen complex in Leon Valley, Texas. The fall had given his tired, aching body a jolt from which he could not recover. His mind knew it, and he had knowingly and respectfully begun the closure process of his full, rich life in a dignified manner, patiently watching as each day followed another, the numbers counting down to a certain destination and confident reunion with those he had outlived.

    He felt the resilience draining from him like water from a rusty, cracked tin. It hurt to stand; it hurt to move from bed to chair, then from chair to bed. It hurt to relieve his bladder, to empty his bowels. It hurt to chew, and it was becoming increasingly difficult and painful to swallow. Food often had no taste, and was becoming more nuisance than delight.

    He was easily chilled. A cold, chilling wind would come from nowhere, and would bend his bones.

Bed was a good place to be, and sleep was a kind, good, reliable friend. With sleep came visions of a quiet, bright countryside with a warm, gentle breeze that revived the colors of spring, restored the familiar baseball fields of summer, and brought the fragrant memories of times past, encouraging his return to the camaraderie and renewed conversations with long-departed family and friends, his Momma and Daddy, his brothers and sisters, and a beloved granddaughter.

The warm, gentle breeze was always there, just a sleepy hand away, reaching out to brush his red, curly hair from his brow, and bring back the smell of lavender-washed hair, brown and soft, and the angel-smile on his Judy's face as she looked deeply into his eyes, sharing the warm breeze and the promise of love.

Sometimes, when he would be awakened from a nap, he would ask if he could sleep a little longer, if he could wait a few more minutes before he got up.

"Is it time to go to work?" He would ask, to a memory-face in a memory-time.

"Can I sleep just a few minutes longer?"

He could feel the dread of another hot day in the cotton field, another terrifying, typhonic night on Leyte, one more tall tree to fell and turn into cordwood, another assault through the deadly, machine gun-infested abaca fields of Mindanao, one more long wall to paint, one more wobbly step to take along the dizzy, rocky path to find Paradise, to find Home.

He could feel the wind now, and looked down at his hand grasping the brown plastic coffee cup. The vision of summer disintegrated slowly, as he raised the cup to his lips.

He shivered slightly, and then sighed. The wind eased, warmed, and he felt better.

*"The coffee is good,"* he said to himself.

*"Is it raining? The wind ..... I hear it. Sometimes, when it's cold, the wind hurts. We better close that door. Put some towels under it, keep the wind out."*

*"All is okay. The Lord has given me and Judy a good life. We've always had enough. Ooo-whee, I need to go back and lay down."*

He dangled now, his mind halfway in the dining room, halfway to Heaven. He raised his eyes, watching the woman walking toward him, with eyes not as clear as in his youth, and asked,

"Is that you?"

The woman said, "Yes, it's me."

He said, "I'm glad you're here. Have you had your supper yet?"

She said, "No, not yet."

She sat down beside him, keeping him company, while he slowly, ever so slowly, ate his meal.

"This has a good taste to it," he said.

"How's Judy doing?"

The woman said, "She's doing just fine. She wanted to come with me, but it is getting cold and she was tired."

He could see that it was getting dark outside, so he said, "I guess I better go back to my room and lay down now."

The woman took off his bib, put her hands on the back of his wheelchair, maneuvered him away from the table, and pushed him gently down the long hallway into his room, and to his bed by the window. She tucked him into his bed, and pinned the nurse's call button on his sheet next to him. She adjusted his pillow and his blankets.

"Now that feels right," he said.

"You better get on home now, it's dark. You be careful driving home."

The woman smiled and hugged him, and said,

"Good night. I'll see you tomorrow."

"Thank you, Kathy," he said.

She looked at him, knowing she was blessed to be his daughter-in-law, thankful for the private time with him, storing it away as one of a thousand precious memories. She didn't know what the future held at that time, but she knew and sensed that the time she had just spent was special and unique. She admired his quiet dignity, his polite manness, and was always impressed with the "Thank you" he gave for all the things that were done for him. She observed the manner in which he seemed to accept his situation with such poise and graciousness.

She turned to leave the room, her thoughts remaining on the farm boy, Red Smith, who returned home from "War II," wanting to continue to live the simple life he had always lived.

Later that night, she told her husband, Tom, Red's youngest son, "He is an example of how to live life to the fullest without much money, power, or any other trappings of life that other people yearn for most of their lives. The things in his life that matter most are his Lord and Savior, his beloved wife and children, his large extended family, and love of a country he would have died for."

Later that night, Red Smith, tucked and snug in his bed, continued his slow, gentle walk down the path to the Good

Land, aided by the warm wind of summers-past and the confident bond of a Forever-Love. As his remaining days became the number of fingers on two hands, he ate less, slept more, and surely felt that warm wind lift him gently and carry him forward to the better days of his life, to Completion.

He was taken to the hospital emergency room when his remaining days were on one hand, and he spent New Year's Eve on a respirator, as the world watched the Old Man 2012 be shuffled off, replaced by the New Infant 2013. He was in and out of awareness, but was very much awake two days later when Judy came to see him one last time.

He could say very little, the oxygen mask and the diminishing strength reducing the few minutes to a hand squeeze, a word or two, mumbled through tubing on both their faces, accentuated by a remarkably soft hand brushing his cheek, lovingly ruffling what was left of his red hair on his brow. A precious wind blew gently across them, through them, and danced around them, whispering in their ears, *"All is well. I have made your days, your life together, sweet. You have done well."*

Her hand was still gently brushing his cheek when their eyes met. A powerful love passed between them, a million thoughts, a billion conversations about dreams, desires, aging; remembering quiet moments when a word barely passed, yet thoughts were exchanged instantaneously by a nod or a smile, or a thin exhaled sigh. This was his child bride, the young girl behind third base, the woman who had met him when he returned from war, his smiling Angel Judy who had shared his life for almost sixty seven years, the girl and woman who had danced in his dreams for much longer than that, the mother of his two sons, the soul mate of his full, rich life. She was, undoubtedly, the most important thing to him that remained in this world. He knew the time was near for him to leave this world, and he knew that she would have to stay, that he would take this trip without her. His thin, dry lips smiled, tried to say something through the tubing, did not have the strength to do so, and they both acknowledged with their personal, private, familiar nod.

Her hand slowly fell from his cheek, and she gripped her walker. The moment had passed, the good-byes had been said, and she turned and pushed her walker from the intensive care room. She looked straight ahead as the warm wind followed her, down the hallway, down the elevator, out of the hospital, into her son's car, out of the multi-storied parking lot, and back to her apartment-cottage, their castle, the Kingdom of Red and Judy.

Later, in the privacy of that castle, she cried.

Later, in the intensive care room, Red Smith slipped back into his sleep, watching the years replay themselves in the misty Memory-Gardens … the laughter … the joys … the pleasures … the Totality.

He walked through the misty gardens, savoring the memories, the sounds, the smells of his youth. He saw a railroad, weaving a circuitous course around mounds of yellow roses and beneath trees adorned with ripe, round peaches.

A train, full of years, ran along the rails through the Memory-Gardens, occasionally sounding its melancholy whistle. He could see the passengers in each car, some looked familiar, all looked peacefully tucked into their seats, passing through the years, the laughter, the joys, the pleasures, the pains that weren't so bad. He felt a soft wind from the train as it moved slowly by him, the rhythmic engine delivering a pulsating cloud of rich steam that enveloped him, soothing his face, dampening his yellow shirt.

Through the mist, he heard Kathy say, loudly,
"Popa, open your eyes!"

His eyes fluttered open, and they looked at the real world, the bright world of tubes and monitors, and he spent a few fleeting seconds hearing his family laugh and say,

"Hi, Popa! There you are! Hi!"

His lips tried to move, his eyes blinked a few weary times, and he then closed them, and drifted back to his stroll through the Memory Gardens, along the railroad track that weaved its way through the mist.

He saw the train again. It slowed, whistled, and stopped.

He felt himself being helped onto the train, saw other passengers smile at him as he boarded, and was taken to a seat with his name on it. He quietly and proudly eased himself into the seat. The train whistled once more, the steam began pouring from the engine, and it returned to its journey through the years.

He settled comfortably into his reserved seat on the Last Train to Heaven. The seat was soft. The ride was smooth. He thought he could hear Hank Williams singing *I Saw the Light.*

He looked out the partially open window, felt more steam bathe his face, and saw a pristine river, glowing like a reflective glass ribbon, meandering across an ancient, serpentine valley.

He heard his Judy talking in his left ear.

"I love you, Red. We have had a good life together. I'll see you at the East Gate, by the tree of Life. I love you…….you go on now…….we've talked about this…..they're waiting for you……..I love you……..I will see you…….."

His earthly heart slowed, his breathing stopped. For a full thirty minutes, his heart methodically continued its nine-decade chore of *pump-pump, pump-pump, pump-pump*. Its rhythm slowly weakened, as Judy's comforting voice accompanied his thoughts as they transitioned from flesh to spirit. His brain was alive with timeless thoughts of Judy and all the things they had done, all the sights they had seen, all the laughter they had shared, and the time – the simple tick of a clock – that they had spent with each other, the familiarity, the dependence, the love. It was a True Love, a Forever Love, which they together had perfected. The Greatest Love anyone could have possibly accomplished, they did.

Those thoughts remained; her voice reverberated in his ear, along the dulling synapses of the physical house where his soul had called home for ninety-one years. His soul was packing up now, taking the bundles of memories, the recollections, the songs and Bible verses he had memorized, and he was beckoned by a Higher Power to strike the tent.

He felt arms, soft and delicately strong, lift him up from his seat on the train, as a gentle wind was blowing across his face.

*"It's time to get off, and go home,"* a reassuring, familiar voice whispered in his ear, with a resonance as clear and brisk as the sounds of his youth.

A tall, black man, lightly bearded with salt-and-pepper stubble, his voice still resonating in Red's ear, appeared at his side, and extended his hand in a gesture of friendship. His face, as familiar as a well-remembered dream, full of compassion and steadfastness, was highlighted by soft blue eyes and an unforgettable smile. When Red took the man's hand firmly in his own, his soul was inundated with memories of peace and comfort, of hope and protection, no matter how bright the artillery flashes, how shrill the scream of riflery, nor how loud the booming of cannon. His memories marched back, past decades of home and hearth, to a garish night, a deadly, frightful night, in a wet foxhole full of death, long, long, ago, when he had been delivered from terror by the same calming handshake.

"I have seen you before," Red spoke quietly.

"Yes, yes, you have, Horace. It's good to see you again," the man whispered back.

"You ... it was you ... on Leyte ... you told me I would live."

He looked up at the man, whose face was shining with a saintly light, detailing a smile that seemed more angelic than human. The man looked at him, nodded his head, and spoke with a low, tranquil voice,

"Yes, Horace, it was me. And I'm proud to welcome you Home this time."

The man handed Red a note card and a pencil.

"You might want to leave a note for your wife," he said.

Reaching out confidently with steady hands, Red took the note card and pencil, held them for a moment in his flexible fingers.

"Thank you, sir."

With ease, he wrote a short message, neatly placed it an envelope, penciled 'Judy' on the front with the same graceful fingers that had once strummed melodic notes on a guitar in a time long ago, amongst aged and brittle reminiscences. He turned, more like *floated*, and placed the note on the seat of the train.

"*Let's go, I'm ready.*"

The man pointed toward the front of the train, and Red could feel a gentle, warm wind lifting him further, giving him the sensation of being carried away, far away, across a vast ocean, taking him from his earthly home to a heavenly home, as if he were flying.

He could hear a woman melodiously singing, "*I'll fly away, oh glory, I'll fly away.*"

A calm series of smooth, elongated waves appeared on the oscilloscope monitor his son, daughter-in-law, and granddaughter were watching. The waves traveled across the monitor as though a gentle wind was blowing them across a vast ocean, bringing him back from a jungle far away, from battles and victories and pleasures created just for him. A team of dreamy dolphins were protecting his journey, playfully jumping in and out of the water, their smooth, broad, elongated waves appearing on the monitor against a backdrop of total tranquility. He, the myriad of dolphins, and the harmonic, serene waves were all being helped along by that gentle warm wind, the wind that had guided and accompanied him all the moments of his life, bringing the heroic pilgrim home.

The uncommonly warm January wind gently left the Earth and touched the Heavens.

The gentle wind returned to Earth, as quickly and effortlessly as it had left, and brushed the cheek and caressed the graying hair of his wife, now a widow, as if to say,
*"He waits for you in Paradise, Judy."*

# EPILOGUE – JUDY

December, 2014.

San Antonio, Bexar County, Texas.

Judy Smith had spent almost two years living alone, in the same apartment that she and Red had shared, enduring the constant battles of health and loneliness that widows often do. However, she had also found the "personal time" that widows often find when the house-of-two becomes a house-of-one. Do what you want. Sleep as late as you want. Eat what you want.
    From the outside, looking in, her daily life seemed much similar, if not indistinguishable, from what it had been during their life together
    From the inside, looking out, she said she felt like Red was still there, just down the hallway, taking a nap in his bed, as he would frequently do several times a day. She said she was not lonely, that she did not feel alone.
    "I'm okay," she would say. "I feel that Red is still here."
    The loneliness that could-have-been was diminished by her daily telephone calls to her dear friends, the Breedloves, in Dallas, and to her former daughter-in-law, Cindy, in Austin; her regular visits by her neighbor, Ruby; and her visits each day either by her youngest son, Tom, or by his wife, Kathy.
    During the first year of widowhood, she had filled her "personal time" with audio books that were provided free of charge through the State of Texas' Talking Book Program. Her eyes, dimmed and nearly blinded with macular

degeneration, had reduced her life-long love affair with books and magazines to a few precious note cards and leaflets placed beneath a telesensory video magnifier. Her audio books of choice were western novels, crammed full of heroes and heroines with the Louis L'Amour, Max Brand, and Zane Grey signature brands. She had listened to over 400 books, day and night, by the end of the first year.

The second year was a not-so-pleasant experience of three falls, each resulting in extended visits to the hospital and rehabilitation facility, all spread over a span of six months, from April through December.

Through it all, she maintained her characteristic zeal for life and social grace that was so endeared by her family. Her enthusiasm for life, in spite of her failing health and near blindness, were testimonials of stoicism, character, and dignity tempered by the steel and fire of her generation.

It was the Sunday fall in early November that heralded the beginning of the end for Judy Smith.

The day and evening had been delightful - a good, sloppy, old-fashioned hamburger dinner, complete with onion rings, a victorious Dallas Cowboys game, and a shower. It was after the shower, in the bathroom, where the final destinies of Red and Judy Smith converged. Like Red, who fell in the bathroom late one evening two years earlier, Judy would fall this particular evening, from the bathtub onto the bathroom floor, and would be taken out of the apartment on a gurney, just like Red, never to return home again.

The first week in the hospital was dramatized by a rapid drop in vitals, and a heroic rise from the ashes by the Phoenix that was Judy Smith. She impressed all those who watched: family, friends, and healthcare givers. An open-reduction-

and-internal-fixation procedure was performed on her broken right femur. The surgeons, staff, other patients, and family were again encouraged by her persistence and tenacity. She was ready for the next phase.

By mid-November, she was no longer "hospital material," as they say in the business, and she was discharged and transferred to an active, results-oriented rehabilitation clinic, the same one that her visiting sister Arline had gone to with a fractured hip during a vacation trip from Kentucky several years earlier.

Her hopes were high at first, but they soon began a constant downward slope as each goal was abandoned, and life became a series of wheelchair sitting, bedpans, hoisting, inactivity, and disappointment. She maintained her humor, but inside her heart, during the long, seemingly endless days, Tom, Kathy, and she would discuss the needs and desires of an ending life.

She had made the decision long before Tom had reached it, and had begun discussing it with Kathy in late November, after Thanksgiving, during the second week of her rehabilitation tenure.

*"No more treatment,"* she was deciding.

The thin, broken osteoporotic femur would never again hold her weight. The other, unbroken, but equally osteoporotic leg would never be able to absorb the increased workload demanded of it.

The tired, diseased heart, with decades-long congestive-heart-failure, was not able to effectively circulate the necessary blood to the vital organs.

The lungs, with their increasing chronic-obstructive-pulmonary-disease, could no longer provide the necessary oxygen to those vital organs.

And, the kidneys, deathly close to failure, could not regulate the blood chemistry and provide the necessary waste disposal to keep the heart and lungs functioning.

There would be no rehabilitation from this fall. The broken femur was repaired, but unusable. She had grown tired of the healthcare workers coaxing her into restoration when she knew in her bones that this was the Closing Act.

On Judy's third Thursday morning at the rehabilitation clinic, and her last Thursday morning on Earth, Kathy walked through the door and approached her bed by the west-facing window. She knew, as soon as she had walked through the door, that something was different. Judy was different. There was no smile, no light in her eyes. She had made her decision.

The truth was, they had both known from the beginning that she would not recover from this traumatic injury.

The day had come, on the morning of December 11, 2014.

As Kathy stood by her bed, she took Judy's hand and gently said,

"What can I do for you?"

An unpretentious yet firm reply came from Judy's very dry lips, accompanied by a nod of her head.

"You can get me out of here."

Her face was controlled, but had a mild strain, waiting for Kathy to answer.

Kathy asked if she was ready to go to hospice, and without a blink, she said, nodding her head again,

"Yes."

As soon as Kathy had assured her that she would indeed go, the strain relaxed in her very worn and tired face.

She then appeared to have a thought that disturbed her. She looked at Kathy and spoke with a troubled voice,

"Tom will take this hard."

"Yes, he will take it hard, but he has me, and, besides, Popa is waiting for you," she answered.

Judy nodded in approval, and agreed,

"That's right!"

Kathy sat by her side the rest of the day. She was very aware of each hour, and treasured all the details of the passing of precious time with the brave, aging warrior.

Judy was very quiet that day, but extremely alert. She would ask Kathy throughout the day if she was still there, being unable to see across the room. Stoically, she would ask her to read aloud the *23$^{rd}$ Psalm*, and sing *Amazing Grace*.

The nephrologist came into the room at 8 o'clock that night, on his appointed rounds. Both Judy and Kathy were ready for him, and said hello to him as he entered. The well-dressed, compassionate, olive-skinned physician extended a very cheerful hello, quickly followed by an honest, trusting smile that was directed at Kathy, with a look that conveyed the knowledge that he knew how special and extraordinary Judy was.

As he began the usual business of relating the blood work data and the results from her daily kidney tests, Kathy stopped him. He gave her a puzzled look. She told him that Judy had something to tell him. He drew closer to Judy, and she reached for his hand. As calmly as saying 'it is raining outside,' she made her wishes known. She looked toward him, with eyes that could barely see him, and announced:

"I am ready to go."

He continued to hold the 86-year old hand, and, with a face that went through a half-dozen expressions, slowly said,

"I think you have made a good decision."

He understood. The tight-wire-performance between kidneys, heart, and lungs had been all too clear. His relief was obvious; he was impressed at her courage, humbled by her dignity, and proud of the fight she had endured. He, like most other physicians, agreed that it takes far more bravery to submit to the Will of the Most High than to place upon their medical shoulders the burden and emotional cost of a losing battle.

Goodbyes were said, and, as Kathy watched, she could see the deep respect and personal care the young physician from India had for Judy shining in his face.

After he had left, Judy turned to Kathy and, with a lovely, child-like sparkle dancing around in her worn and weary eyes, asked her to sing *I'm Going Home,* by Mary Fahl.

She leaned back against her pillow, knowing that this would be her last night at the rehabilitation center, that she would leave the hustle-and-bustle, hard-at-it world of tomorrow-grabbing, and she smiled.

As Kathy sang about going home, she looked at Judy with pride and awe. Judy had always been the last to quit, the first to press on. Now, as she looked at Judy's smiling face resting upon the pillow, she realized that this lady-warrior was pressing on once again, with a peaceful and confident air; this time, she was pressing onward, to higher ground.

By mid-afternoon the next day, Friday, Judy was transferred to a hospice facility.

She settled herself in, pleased with the simple relaxation that awaited her. Her lunch and supper arrived, acceptable to hospital standards, but she only ate sparingly. Her appetite had been left behind a week ago. It was hard to chew, hard to swallow, hard to manipulate the once-automatic mechanics of mastication and voluntary muscular action.

She was given morphine later that night, when the Friday midnight crew made their nocturnal drug-dispensing mercenary rounds.

By Saturday morning, the sedative effects of the pain-killing narcotic were challenging her cognitive-state, reducing her to slow, syllabic speech, and evasive attentiveness.

Her sons, daughters-in-law, granddaughters, and great-granddaughters began converging at her bedside throughout that day, her last day on Earth. Some came in the morning, some at noon, and the remainder at nightfall.

Judy's mental state improved, as she rallied to enjoy the company of her sons and daughters-in-law in the morning. By noon, her next-to-youngest granddaughter and the two great-granddaughters that accompanied her arrived, and Judy perked up again to share hugs, kisses, and abbreviated conversations with each one.

She rested the afternoon, anticipating the arrival of her remaining two granddaughters and great-granddaughter after nightfall.

It was not easy. She was given more morphine.

She struggled in and out of the misty fog that accompanies the closing of life, when Time and Space become indeterminable, comingling with Present and Past with no regard to continuity or discernment. She would slip in and out of sleep, watching the years replay themselves in the misty Memory-Gardens … the laughter … the joys … the pleasures … the pains that weren't so bad … the Totality.

She would respond, slowly at first, when her hand was squeezed, and she was told,

"We are here. You're doing a good job. The kids will be here in a little bit."

She would nod, try to say something, weakly squeeze the hand in her own, and then become silent again, returning to the misty regions.

Once, through the mist, she heard Kathy say, loudly,

"Judy, can you open your eyes for me?"

Her eyes fluttered open, and they looked at the real world, the bright world of oxygen masks and monitors. She spent a few fleeting seconds hearing her son and daughter-in-law laugh and say,

"Hi! There you are! We're still here. You're doing okay!"

Her lips tried to move, she nodded weakly, her eyes blinked a few weary times, and a thin smile crossed her lips. The sleep returned, as her breathing became more labored.

She rallied one last time, bravely, in the traditional Judy Smith fashion, when the rest of her family arrived just after dark. They talked to her, and she nodded and responded to their greetings and questions with grunts, barely audible laughs, and sounds of recognition.

She had waited the entire day to see all of her family, from oldest to youngest, first generation to third generation, and was hanging-on when most would have already succumbed.

It was taking a toll on her, and all could see that she was intentionally clinging to life, struggling, successfully accomplishing her *pas de deux* with death, gracefully and courageously remaining conscious to enjoy her family again. For one last time, she was breathing the same air with them, feeling the same love with them, exchanging glances and words, recalling memories, laughing, sighing, and dying.

Within the hour, the nursing staff came into the room to change her bed linens and give her a bath. The family left, gave the staff their 30-minute window of personal care, and then checked on her again.

She was unresponsive. The sleep was deep. The goal had been reached. She had seen, and had touched, all of her family.

It was time to go now.

The family left, with un-answered farewells for the night and promises to 'see you tomorrow.'

Tom and Kathy stayed, in hopes of seeing the hospice physician when he made his late-night rounds.

They waited. Her breathing continued its laborious pace.

More morphine was administered, as the Saturday midnight crew returned to dispense their narcotic cocktails of pain killers and comfort enhancers. Judy returned to her stroll along the Memory-Gardens, where a railroad weaved around mounds of pink roses, lumbered across an ivy-covered trestle that forged a crystalline river sparkling with lights as if fairies were dancing along its banks and beneath its surface, and ambled along lazily beneath trees adorned with ripe, round oranges.

  A steam train, full of years, followed the rails through the Memory-Gardens, sounding its melancholy whistle as the clock approached midnight. She could see the passengers in each car, some looked familiar, all of them looked peacefully tucked into their seats, passing through the years … the laughter … the joys … the pleasures … the pains that weren't so bad. She felt a soft wind from the train as it moved slowly by her, the rhythmic engine delivering a smooth, soothing cloud of rich steam that enveloped her.

  She felt someone squeeze her hand, and heard him speak to her through the mist, the railroad steam, and the rhythm of the rails.

  "You're okay, Mom. We're still here."

  The train slowed, whistled again, and stopped.

  She felt herself being helped into the train, found a seat with her name on it, and a note clipped onto a clothespin. She quietly and proudly eased herself into the seat. The train whistled once more, the steam began pouring from the engine, and it returned to its journey through the years.

  She settled comfortably into her reserved seat on the Last Train to Heaven, the same seat on the same train that Red had taken almost two years ago. She reached for the note, released it from the clothespin, and saw 'Judy' written on it, in Red's sharp, pointed cursive. She easily opened the envelope, with graceful hands like a musician playing a piano, or a sculptor placing a poignant smile on a marble goddess. The note read:

*"I am waiting for you. I will see you at the East Gate, by the Tree of Life. I love you. Red"*

She could still smell his aftershave on the note.

*"He has been here,"* she thought to herself.

She looked at the note, turning it over and over with her nimble fingers, reading the cursive with the visual acuity of her youth.

*"I can read again! I can see!"* she exhaled.

The seat was soft. The ride was smooth.

The engine steam drifted through the partially open window, gingerly bathing her face with rich, soft wetness, and she heard someone in the distance, perhaps outside the train, say,

"You're doing okay, Mom. We're still here."

She nodded in agreement, a faint smile on her face, behind the oxygen mask.

She felt someone, the porter, *Yes, the porter,* holding her hand, brushing something aside on her face, speaking into her ear.

*Would you like to have a pillow, Ma'am?"*

*"Thank you",* she said to the porter on the train.

She took the pillow, fluffed it up nicely, and the porter helped her place it behind her head.

*"I'm comfortable. That will do just fine. Thank you."*

The rails sang their cadence of Peace on Earth, Good Will to Men; the engineer occasionally evoked a peaceful refrain from the whistle; and the Pullman car gently rocked from side to side, like a pendulum on a clock, somewhere in the distance, marking their dutiful reminders that the ride was nearing its end, the station was just ahead, in the mist.

She smiled.

*"Prepare for arrival,"* someone pronounced, from the front of the Pullman.

She smiled again.

"We'll see you later, Mom," she heard her son say, from somewhere outside the train, yet so clear and distinct that he could have been speaking directly into her ear.

Moments passed, perhaps a few seconds, maybe an hour. Maybe a few years. It didn't seem to matter. All was so right, so wonderful, *so perfectly perfect*, she thought.

*I am really going home!*

The soft, rich steam from the train drifted around her, muffling the sounds from afar, providing a calming ointment for her tired, sore limbs.

Her heart slowed, her breathing stopped. The tube and mask continued their steady stream of oxygen. For a few minutes, her weakened heart continued its eighty-six-year chore of irregular beating. The irregular rhythm that remained was slowly weakening, as the train coasted into the station. The sound of the oxygen mask, becoming more like train-steam now, accompanied her thoughts as they transitioned from flesh to spirit.

Her soul began picking up her few belongings, the recollections, the songs, the Bible verses she had memorized, and was beckoned by the Higher Power to proceed to the exit.

A gentle wind was blowing across the station, lifting her up, giving her the sensation of being carried across a vast ocean, taking her from her earthly home to a heavenly home, miles through the night, just over the dawn.

A team of dreamy dolphins was following her journey from the waves below, protecting her route, playfully jumping in and out of the water, their smooth, broad shadows appearing on the water's surface against a backdrop of total stillness. She, and the myriad of dolphins, were all being helped along by that gentle warm wind, the wind that had guided her and accompanied her all the moments of her life, finally bringing the exhausted pilgrim home.

The uncommonly warm, gentle December wind tenderly left the Earth and touched the Heavens, depositing its precious consignment at the East Gate, near the Tree of Life.

She could still feel the warm, gentle breeze delicately blowing against her slender, energized body, lightly brushing the brown, curly hair across her temples and brow, teasing her ears with a song of peace, comfort, and unimaginable tranquility.

She opened her eyes, and saw a landscape of color, clarity, and depth seen only in the most detailed of dreams. She looked down at her arm, flexed her tactile fingers, and touched the silky fabric of her clean, white dress, embroidered with a thick pattern of tiny, pink rosettes.

*"What a pretty dress!"* she thought, excitedly.

She looked up, and saw people standing around her. They were gazing with amazement and honor at the young woman who had just appeared before them. Some of the onlookers were waving, some had outstretched arms.

*I KNOW these people,* she thought.

A singularly magnificent man stood among them, clothed in the purest, cleanest, whitest robe she had ever seen, one arm resting at His side, the other reaching toward her, a deeply scarred hand extended in a welcoming gesture.

His lightly bearded face held an expression of acceptance and mercy, and His head was nodding in approval.

Her senses were keenly aware, her memories awakened, her eyes unexpectedly clear, her vision sharp as she viewed the gathering crowd in the foreground and the strikingly gorgeous towers along the distant horizon, all as lucid and unmistakable as the landscapes of her youth.

She heard a voice from behind her, an immediately familiar voice that seemed to fill the dreamscape around her, and she turned, as if floating, around to see the young man, wearing a yellow shirt and blue dungarees, the ringlets of his red, curly hair bouncing in the same warm, gentle breeze. He approached her, a broad, toothy grin on his face, the timeless smile of her love, her life-mate, now reunited for eternity.

She inhaled the immaculate air, with no shortness of breath nor pain of lung, and exhaled slowly. She raised her shoulders in a little girl giggly way, and then looked at him with her infinitely attentive blue eyes, and said,

"Oh, Red….."

The young man approached, his strong arms outstretched, each muscular hand reaching closer to her, wrapping around her waist, in an embrace as fresh as the love they had always shared, as timeless an embrace as the one they had once shared in a Texas cotton-field seven decades earlier.

Their foreheads touched, and she sighed. She was home, in a Place where Time was no longer pertinent.

He winked one playful, penetrating eye, and spoke, in a clear voice, with a thick East Texas accent.

"Welcome to Paradise, Judy."

# AFTERWARD

## A NOTE FROM THE AUTHOR

As the Texas sun rises and sets every day on the soft, green grass of Fort Sam Houston National Cemetery in San Antonio, Texas, Horace G. "Red" Smith and Clara Juliette "Judy" Smith lie in perfect union in Section 72, Plot 620.

Surrounded by the military heroes and comrades-in-arms of World War I, World War II, the Korean War, the Vietnam War, and the two wars in Iraq and Afghanistan, they await the Final Reveille of the coming of Christ and the beginning of the Eternal State.

Across this Field of Honored Veterans many flags wave and many flowers paint the spaces between the rows-upon-rows of white marble memorials, as families and friends pay tribute to what these veterans did to keep freedom free.

Red and Judy Smith welcome your visit to this hallowed ground of patriots.

# SOURCES OF INFORMATION

*United States Army in World War II, The War in the Pacific.* Washington, DC: Center of Military History, United States Army, 1996

*Field Manual 72-20.* Washington, DC: War Department, 1944.

Jan Valtin. *Children of Yesterday.* The Battery Press, 1946.

Mary H. Williams. *Unites States Army in World War II Chronology 1941-1945.* Whitman Publishing, 2012

Francis Heller. *Steel Helmet and Mortarboard, An Academic in Uncle Sam's Army.* University of Missouri Press, 2009.

Cleta Gresham Rokey and Robin Rokey. *Bark at the Moon.* 2012

Cindy Ely, *Dear Mrs. Gray.* CreateSpace Independent Publishing Platform, 2010.

Walt Rogers Memoirs. *Veterans History Project.* American Folklife Center of the Library of Congress, 2017

Nathan N. Prefer. *Leyte 1944 The Soldiers' Battle.* Casemate Publishers, 2012.

National Archives of Australia

The National Archives and Records Administration, Washington, DC

Rocky R. Miracle. *Mrs. Cordie's Soldier Son A World War II Saga.* Texas A&M University Press, College Station, Texas. 2008.

Author Unknown. *A Camera Trip Through Camp Wolters.* Boyce Ditto Public Library, The Portal to Texas History. Date Unknown.

Jesse M. Coker. *My Unforgettable Memories of World War II.* Prestige Press. 2003.

M. Hamlin Cannon. *Leyte: Return to the Philippines.* United States Army in World War II, The War in the Pacific, Volume V. Washington DC, US Government Printing. 1954.

War Department Records Branch. *Okayama Task Force After Action Report.* The Adjutant General's Office. Washington DC. 1945.

Red River County Historical Society. *Clarksville and Red River County.* Arcade Publishing. 2010.

War Department Records Branch. *History of the Hollandia Operation Reckless Task Force.* The Adjutant General's Office. Washington DC. 1945.

Waimea Nature Park. *Self-Guiding Booklet.* Project of Waimea Outdoor Circle. Hagadone Printing Company. 2015.

Peter Dunn. *Camp Caves Near Rockingham, Queensland.* Australia at War. www.ozatwar.com 2008.

State of Queensland Department of Environment and Heritage Protection. *Queensland WWII Historic Places.* Queensland Government. 2016.

Hawaiian Service, Louis and George T. Armitage. *Detailed Map and Guide of Honolulu and the Island of Oahu.* The Honolulu Star Bulletin. 1944.

G. Williford and T. McGovern. *Defenses of Pearl Harbor and Oahu 1907-1950.* Osprey Publishing, Limited. 2003.

Sixth Army. *Report of the Leyte Operation: 2 October 1944 – 25 December 1944, Sixth Army, Part 1.* BiblioGov Project. The Command and General Staff College Library, Fort Leavenworth Kansas, Publication Date Unknown.

Kevin C. Holzimmer. *General Walter Krueger Unsung Hero of the Pacific War.* University Press of Kansas. 2007.

Milan Vego. *The Battle for Leyte, 1944 Allied and Japanese Plans, Preparations, and Execution.* Naval Institute Press. 2006.

Samuel Elliot Morison. *History of United States Naval Operations in World War II New Guinea and the Mariana March 1944 – August 1944.* Castle Books. 1953.

Stephen R. Taaffe. *MacArthur's Jungle War The 1944 New Guinea Campaign.* University Press of Kansas. 1998.

Samuel Elliot Morison. *History of United States Naval Operations in World War II Leyte 1944 – January 1944.* Castle Books. 1958.

George W. Neill. *Infantry Soldier Holding the Line at the Battle of the Bulge.* University of Oklahoma Press, Norman Oklahoma. 2000.

British Pathe. *World War II Newreels*. 1943-1945. www.britishpath.com

Critical Past. *World War II Newsreel*. 1943-1945. www.criticalpast.com

Movietone News. *World War II Newsreels*. 1942-3-1945. www.aparchive.com

W. A. Mattice. *The Weather of 1941 in the United States*. Washington, DC: Weather Bureau, 1942

*Engineers of the Southwest Pacific, 1941-1945*

Newspapers.com. *Wellington Leader,* Wellington, TX, 1945

Portal to Texas History, *Collingsworth County Museum Photo Collections.* 2019

CPSIA information can be obtained
at www.ICGtesting.com
Printed in the USA
BVHW031725271019
562182BV00001B/1/P